THE

WORLD

OF

TIERS

Tor Books by Philip José Farmer

The Cache
Dayworld Breakup
Father to the Stars
More Than Fire
The Other Log of Phileas Fogg
Riders of the Purple Wage
Red Orc's Rage
Time's Last Gift
Traitor to the Living
The World of Tiers, Volume One
(comprising *The Maker of Universes, The Gates of Creation,*
and *A Private Cosmos*)

THE WORLD OF TIERS

VOLUME ONE

THE MAKER OF UNIVERSES
THE GATES OF CREATION
A PRIVATE COSMOS

PHILIP JOSÉ FARMER

TOR®

A TOM DOHERTY ASSOCIATES BOOK / NEW YORK

THE WORLD OF TIERS: VOLUME ONE

This is an omnibus edition, consisting of the novels: *The Maker of Universes,* copyright © 1965 by Ace Books, Inc.; *The Gates of Creation,* copyright © 1966 by Philip José Farmer; and *A Private Cosmos,* copyright © 1968 by Philip José Farmer.

This book is printed on acid-free paper.

A Tor Book
Published by Tom Doherty Associates, Inc.
175 Fifth Avenue
New York, NY 10010

Tor Books on the World Wide Web:
http://www.tor.com

Tor® is a registered trademark of Tom Doherty Associates, Inc.

Library of Congress Cataloging-in-Publication Data

Farmer, Philip José.
    The world of tiers / Philip José Farmer.
        p.   cm.
    "A Tom Doherty Associates book."
    Contents: The maker of universes—The gates of creation—A private cosmos.
        ISBN 0-312-85761-6 (pbk)
        ISBN 0-312-85762-4 (hc)
    1. Science fiction, American.   I. Title.
    PS3556.A72W6   1996
    813'.54—dc20   96-23840
                                                        CIP

Printed in the United States of America

0 9 8 7 6 5 4 3 2

CONTENTS

THE MAKER

OF

UNIVERSES

1

THE GHOST OF A TRUMPET CALL WAILED FROM THE OTHER SIDE of the doors. The seven notes were faint and far off, ectoplasmic issue of a phantom of silver, if sound could be the stuff from which shades are formed.

Robert Wolff knew that there could be no horn or man blowing upon it behind the sliding doors. A minute ago, he had looked inside the closet. Nothing except the cement floor, the white plasterboard walls, the clothes rod and hooks, a shelf and a lightbulb was there.

Yet he had heard the trumpet notes, feeble as if singing from the other wall of the world itself. He was alone, so that he had no one with whom to check the reality of what he knew could not be real. The room in which he stood entranced was an unlikely place in which to have such an experience. But he might not be an unlikely person to have it. Lately, weird dreams had been troubling his sleep. During the day, strange thoughts and flashes of images passed through his mind, fleeting but vivid and even startling. They were unwanted, unexpected, and unresistible.

He was worried. To be ready to retire and then to suffer a mental breakdown seemed unfair. However, it could happen to him as it had to others, so the thing to do was to be examined by a doctor. But he could not bring himself to act as reason demanded. He kept waiting, and he did not say anything to anybody, least of all to his wife.

Now he stood in the recreation room of a new house in the Hohokam Homes development and stared at the closet doors. If the horn bugled again, he would slide a door back and see for himself that nothing was there. Then, knowing that his own diseased mind was generating the notes, he would forget about buying this house. He would ignore his wife's hysterical protests, and he would see a medical doctor first and then a psychotherapist.

His wife called: "Robert! Haven't you been down there long enough? Come up here. I want to talk to you and Mr. Bresson!"

"Just a minute, dear," he said.

She called again, so close this time that he turned around. Brenda Wolff stood at the top of the steps that led down to the recreation room. She was his age, sixty-six. What beauty she had once had was now buried under fat, under heavily rouged and powdered wrinkles, thick spectacles, and steel-blue hair. He winced on seeing her, as he winced every time he looked into the mirror and saw his own bald head, deep lines from nose to mouth, and stars of grooved skin radiating from the reddened eyes. Was this his trouble? Was he unable to adjust to that which came to all men, like it or not? Or was what he disliked in his wife and himself not the physical deterioration but the knowledge that neither he nor Brenda had realized their youthful dreams? There was no way to avoid the rasps and files of time on the flesh, but time had been gracious to him in allowing him to live this long. He could not plead short duration as an excuse for not shaping his psyche into beauty. The world could not be blamed for what he was. He and he alone was responsible; at least he was strong enough to face that. He did not reproach the universe or that part of it that was his wife. He did not scream, snarl, and whine as Brenda did.

There had been times when it would have been easy to whine or weep. How many men could remember nothing before the age of twenty? He thought it was twenty, for the Wolffs, who had adopted him, had said that he'd looked that age. He had been discovered wandering in the hills of Kentucky, near the Indiana border, by old man Wolff. He had not known who he was or how he had come there. Kentucky or even the United States of America had been meaningless to him, as had all the English tongue.

The Wolffs had taken him in and notified the sheriff. An investigation by the authorities had failed to identify him. At another time, his story might have attracted nationwide attention; however, the nation had been at war with the Kaiser and had had more important things to think about. Robert, named after the Wolff's dead son, had helped work on the farm. He had also gone to school, for he had lost all memory of his education.

Worse than his lack of formal knowledge had been his ignorance of how to behave. Time and again he had embarrassed or offended others. He had suffered from the scornful or sometimes savage reaction of the hill-folk, but had learned swiftly—and his willingness to work hard, plus his great strength in defending himself, had gained respect.

In an amazingly quick time, as if he had been relearning, he had studied and passed through grade and high school. Although he had lacked by many years the full time of attendance required, he had taken and passed the entrance examinations to the university with no trouble. There he'd begun his lifelong love affair with the classical languages. Most of all he loved Greek, for it struck a chord within him; he felt at home with it.

After getting his Ph.D at the University of Chicago, he had taught at various Eastern and Midwestern universities. He had married Brenda, a beautiful girl with a lovely soul. Or so he had thought at first. Later, he had been disillusioned, but still he was fairly happy.

Always, however, the mystery of his amnesia and his origin had troubled him. For a long time it had not disturbed him, but then, on retiring . . .

"Robert," Brenda said loudly, "come up here right now! Mr. Bresson is a busy man."

"I'm certain that Mr. Bresson has had plenty of clients who like to make a leisurely surveillance," he replied mildly. "Or perhaps you've made up your mind that you don't want the house?"

Brenda glared at him, then waddled indignantly off. He sighed because he knew that, later, she would accuse him of deliberately making her look foolish before the real estate agent.

He turned to the closet doors again. Did he dare open them? It was absurd to freeze there, like someone in shock or in a psychotic state of indecision. But he could not move, except to give a start as the bugle again vented the seven notes, crying from behind a thick barricade but stronger in volume.

His heart thudded like an inward fist against his breast bone. He forced himself to step up to the doors and to place his hand within the brass-covered indentation at waist-level and shove the door to one side. The little rumble of the rollers drowned out the horn as the door moved to one side.

The white plaster boards of the wall had disappeared. They had become an entrance to a scene he could not possibly have imagined, although it must have originated in his mind.

Sunlight flooded in through the opening, which was large enough for him to walk through if he stooped. Vegetation that looked something like trees—but no trees of Earth—blocked part of his view. Through the branches and fronds he could see a bright green sky. He lowered his eyes to take in the scene on the ground beneath the trees. Six or seven nightmare creatures were gathered at the base of a giant boulder. It was of red, quartz-impregnated rock and shaped roughly like a toadstool. Most of the things had their black, furry, misshapen bodies turned away from him, but one presented its profile against the green sky. Its head was brutal, sub-human, and its expression was malevolent. There were knobs on its body and on its face and head, clots of flesh which gave it a half-formed appearance, as if its Maker had forgotten to smooth it out. The two short legs were like a dog's hind legs. It was stretching its long arms up toward the young man who stood on the flat top of the boulder.

This man was clothed only in a buckskin breechcloth and moccasins. He was tall, muscular, and broad-shouldered; his skin was sun-browned; his long thick hair was a reddish bronze; his face was strong and craggy with a long upper lip. He held the instrument which must have made the notes Wolff had heard.

The man kicked one of the misshapen things back down from its hold on the boulder as it crawled up toward him. He lifted the silver horn to his lips to blow again, then saw Wolff standing beyond the opening. He grinned widely, flashing white teeth. He called, "So you finally came!"

Wolff did not move or reply. He could only think, *Now I have gone crazy! Not just auditory hallucinations, but visual! What next? Should I run screaming, or just calmly walk away and tell Brenda that I have to see a doctor now? Now! No waiting, no explanations. Shut up, Brenda, I'm going.*

He stepped back. The opening was beginning to close, the white walls were reasserting their solidity. Or rather, he was beginning to get a fresh hold on reality.

"Here!" the youth on top of the boulder shouted. "Catch!"

He threw the horn. Turning over and over, bouncing sunlight off the silver as the light fell through the leaves, it flew straight toward the opening. Just before the walls closed in on themselves, the horn passed through the opening and struck Wolff on his knees.

He exclaimed in pain, for there was nothing ectoplasmic about the sharp impact. Through the narrow opening he could see the red-haired man holding up one hand, his thumb and index forming an O. The youth grinned and cried out, "Good luck! Hope I see you soon! I am Kickaha!"

Like an eye slowly closing in sleep, the opening in the wall contracted. The light dimmed, and the objects began to blur. But he could see well enough to get a final glimpse, and it was then that the girl stuck her head around the trunk of a tree.

She had unhumanly large eyes, as big in proportion to her face as those of a cat. Her lips were full and crimson, her skin golden-brown. The thick wavy hair hanging loose along the side of her face was tiger-striped: slightly zigzag bands of black almost touched the ground as she leaned around the tree.

Then the walls became white as the rolled-up eye of a corpse. All was as before except for the pain in his knees and the hardness of the horn lying against his ankle.

He picked it up and turned to look at it in the light from the recreation room. Although stunned, he no longer believed that he was insane. He had seen through into another universe and something from it had been delivered to him—why or how, he did not know.

The horn was a little less than two and a half feet long and weighed less than a quarter of a pound. It was shaped like an African buffalo's horn except at the mouth, where it flared out broadly. The tip was fitted with a mouthpiece of some soft golden material; the horn itself was of silver or silver-plated metal. There were no valves, but on turning it over he saw seven little buttons in a row. A half-inch inside the mouth was a web of silvery threads. When the horn was held at an angle to the light from the bulbs overhead, the web looked as if it went deep into the horn.

It was then the light also struck the body of the horn so that he saw what he had missed during his first examination: a hieroglyph was lightly inscribed halfway down the length. It looked like nothing he had seen before, and he was an expert on all types of alphabetic writing, ideographs, and pictographs.

"Robert!" his wife said.

"Be right up, dear!" He placed the horn in the right-hand front corner of the closet and closed the door. There was nothing else he could do except to run out of the house with the horn. If he appeared with it, he would be questioned by both his wife and Bresson. Since he had not come into the house with the horn, he could not claim it was his. Bresson would want to take the instrument into his custody, since it would have been discovered on property of his agency.

Wolff was in an agony of uncertainty. How could he get the horn out of the house? What was to prevent Bresson from bringing around other clients, perhaps today, who would see the horn as soon as they opened the closet door? A client might call it to Bresson's attention.

He walked up the steps and into the large living room. Brenda was still glaring. Bresson, a chubby, spectacled man of about thirty-five, looked uncomfortable, although he was smiling.

"Well, how do you like it?" he asked.

"Great," Wolff replied. "It reminds me of the type of house we have back home."

"I like it," Bresson said. "I'm from the Midwest myself. I can appreciate that you might not want to live in a ranchtype home. Not that I'm knocking them. I live in one myself."

Wolff walked to the window and looked out. The midafternoon May sun shone brightly from the blue Arizona skies. The lawn was covered with the fresh Bermuda grass, planted three weeks before, new as the houses in this just-built development of Hohokam Homes.

"Almost all the houses are ground level," Bresson was saying. "Excavating in this hard caliche costs a great deal, but these houses aren't expensive. Not for what you get."

Wolff thought, *If the caliche hadn't been dug away to make room for the recreation room, what would the man on the other side have seen when the opening appeared? Would he have seen only earth and thus been denied the chance to get rid of that horn? Undoubtedly.*

"You may have read why we had to delay opening this development," Bresson said. "While we were digging, we uncovered a former town of the Hohokam."

"Hohokam?" Mrs. Wolff said. "Who were they?"

"Lots of people who come into Arizona have never heard of them," Bresson replied. "But you can't live long in the Phoenix area without running across references to them. They were the Indians who lived a long time ago in the Valley of the Sun; they may have come here at least 1200 years ago. They dug irrigation canals, built towns here, had a swinging civilization. But something happened to them, no one knows what. They just up and disappeared several hundred years ago. Some archeologists claim the Papago and Pima Indians are their descendants."

Mrs. Wolff sniffed and said, "I've seen them. They don't look like they could build anything except those rundown adobe shacks on the reservation."

Wolff turned and said, almost savagely, "The modern Maya don't look as if they could ever have built their temples or invented the concept of zero, either. But they did."

Brenda gasped. Mr. Bresson smiled even more mechanically. "Anyway, we had to suspend digging until the archeologists were through. Held up operations about three months, but we couldn't do a thing because the state tied our hands.

"However, this may be a lucky thing for you. If we hadn't been held up, these homes might all be sold now. So everything turns out for the best, eh?"

He smiled brightly and looked from one to the other.

Wolff paused, took a deep breath, knowing what was coming from Brenda, and said, "We'll take it. We'll sign the papers right now."

"Robert!" Mrs. Wolff shrilled. "You didn't even ask me!"

"I'm sorry, my dear, but I've made up my mind."

"Well, I haven't!"

"Now, now, folks, no need to rush things," Bresson said. His smile was desperate. "Take your time, talk it over. Even if somebody should come along and buy this particular house—and it might happen before the day's over; they're selling like hot-cakes—well, there's plenty more just like this."

"I want *this* house."

"Robert, are you out of your mind?" Brenda wailed. "I've never seen you act like this before."

"I've given in to you on almost everything," he said. "I wanted you to be happy. So, now, give in to me on this. It's not much to ask. Besides, you said this morning that you wanted this type of house, and Hohokam Homes are the only ones like this that we can afford.

"Let's sign the preliminary papers now. I can make out a check as an earnest."

"I won't sign, Robert."

"Why don't you two go home and discuss this?" Bresson said. "I'll be available when you've reached a decision."

"Isn't my signature good enough?" Wolff replied.

Still holding his strained smile, Bresson said, "I'm sorry, Mrs. Wolff will have to sign, too."

Brenda smiled triumphantly.

"Promise me you won't show it to anybody else," Wolff said. "Not until tomorrow, anyway. If you're afraid of losing a sale, I'll make out an earnest."

"Oh, that won't be necessary." Bresson started toward the door with a haste that betrayed his wish to get out of an embarrassing situation. "I won't show it to anyone until I hear from you in the morning."

On the way back to their rooms in the Sands Motel in Tempe, neither spoke. Brenda sat rigidly and stared straight ahead through the windshield. Wolff glanced over at her now and then, noting that her nose seemed to be getting sharper and her lips thinner; if she continued, she would look exactly like a fat parrot.

And when she finally did burst loose, talking, she would sound like a fat parrot. The same old tired yet energetic torrent of reproaches and threats would issue. She would upbraid him because of his neglect of her all these years, remind him for the latest in God-knew-how-many-times that he kept his nose buried in his books or else was practicing archery or fencing, or climbing mountains, sports she could not share with him because of her arthritis. She would unreel the years of unhappiness, or claimed unhappiness, and end by weeping violently and bitterly.

Why had he stuck with her? He did not know except that he had loved her very much when they were young and also because her accusations were not entirely untrue. Moreover, he found the thought of separation painful, even more painful than the thought of staying with her.

Yet he was entitled to reap the harvests of his labors as a professor of English and classical languages. Now that he had enough money and leisure time, he could pursue studies that his duties had denied him. With this Arizona home as a base, he could even travel. Or could he? Brenda would not refuse to go with him—in fact, she would insist on accompanying him. But she would be so bored that his own life would be miserable. He could not blame her for that, for she did not have the same interests as he. But should he give up the things that made life rich for him just to make her happy? Especially since she was not going to be happy anyway?

As he expected, her tongue became quite active after supper. He listened, tried to remonstrate quietly with her and point out her lack of logic and the injustice and baselessness of her recriminations. It was no use. She ended as always, weeping and threatening to leave him or to kill herself.

This time, he did not give in.

"I want that house, and I want to enjoy life as I've planned to," he said firmly. "That's that."

He put on his coat and strode to the door. "I'll be back later. Maybe."

She screamed and threw an ashtray at him. He ducked; the tray bounced off the door, gouging out a piece of the wood. Fortunately, she did not follow him and make a scene outside, as she had on previous occasions.

It was night now, the moon was not yet up, and the only lights came from the windows of the motel, the lamps along the streets, and numerous headlights of the cars along Apache Boulevard. He drove his car out onto the boulevard and went east, then turned south. Within a few minutes he was on the road to the Hohokam Homes. The thought of what he meant to do made his heart beat fast and turned his skin cold. This was the first time in his life that he had seriously considered committing a criminal act.

The Hohokam Homes were ablaze with lights and noisy with music over a PA system and the voices of children playing out in the street while their parents looked at the houses.

He drove on, went through Mesa, turned around and came back through Tempe and down Van Buren and into the heart of Phoenix. He cut north, then east, until he was in the town of Scottsdale. Here he stopped off for an hour and a half at a small tavern. After the luxury of four shots of *Vat 69*, he quit. He wanted no more—rather, feared to take more, because he did not care to be fuddled when he began his project.

When he returned to Hohokam Homes, the lights were out and silence had returned to the desert. He parked his car behind the house in which he had been that afternoon. With his gloved right fist, he smashed the window which gave him access to the recreation room.

By the time he was within the room, he was panting and his heart beat as if he had run several blocks. Though frightened, he had to smile at himself. A man who lived much in his imagination, he had often conceived of himself as a burglar—not the ordinary kind, of course, but a Raffles. Now he knew that his respect for law was too much for him ever to become a great criminal or even a minor one. His conscience was hurting him because of this small act, one that he had thought he was fully justified in carrying out. Moreover, the idea of being caught almost made him give up the horn. After living a quiet, decent and respectable life, he would be ruined if he were to be detected. Was it worth it?

He decided it was. Should he retreat now, he would wonder the rest of his life what he had missed. The greatest of all adventures waited for him, one such as no other man had experienced. If he became a coward now, he might as well shoot himself, for he would not be able to endure the loss of the horn or the self-recriminations for his lack of courage.

It was so dark in the recreation room that he had to feel his way to the closet with his fingertips. Locating the sliding doors, he moved the left-hand one, which he had pushed aside that afternoon. He nudged it slowly to avoid noise, and he stopped to listen for sounds outside the house.

Once the door was fully opened, he retreated a few steps. He placed the mouthpiece of the horn to his lips and blew softly. The blast that issued from it startled him so much that he dropped it. Groping, he finally located it in the corner of the room.

The second time, he blew hard. There was another loud note, no louder than the first. Some device in the horn, perhaps the silvery web inside its mouth, regulated the decibel level. For several minutes he stood poised with the horn raised and almost to his mouth. He was trying to reconstruct in his mind the exact sequence of the seven notes he had heard. Obviously the seven little buttons on the underside determined the various harmonies. But he could not find out which was which without experimenting and drawing attention.

He shrugged and murmured, "What the hell."

Again he blew, but now he pressed the buttons, operating the one closest to him first. Seven loud notes soared forth. Their values were as he remembered them but not in the sequence he recalled.

As the final blast died out, a shout came from a distance. Wolff almost panicked. He swore, lifted the horn back to his lips, and pressed the buttons in an order which he hoped would reproduce the open sesame, the musical key, to the other world.

At the same time, a flashlight beam played across the broken window of the room, then passed by. Wolff blew again. The light returned to the window. More shouts arose. Desperate, Wolff tried different combinations of buttons. The third attempt seemed to be the duplicate of that which the youth on top of the toadstool-shaped boulder had produced.

The flashlight was thrust through the broken window. A deep voice growled, "Come on out, you in there! Come out, or I'll start shooting!"

Simultaneously, a greenish light appeared on the wall, broke through, and melted a hole. Moonlight shone through. The trees and the boulder were visible only as silhouettes against a green-silver radiating from a great globe of which the rim alone was visible.

He did not delay. He might have hesitated if he had been unnoticed, but now he knew he had to run. The other world offered uncertainty and danger, but this one had a definite, inescapable ignominy and shame. Even as the watchman repeated his demands, Wolff left him and his world behind. He had to stoop and to step high to get through the shrinking hole. When he had turned around on the other side to get a final glimpse, he saw through an opening no larger than a ship's porthole. In a few seconds, it was gone.

2

WOLFF SAT DOWN ON THE GRASS TO REST UNTIL HE QUIT breathing so hard. He thought of how ironic it would be if the excitement were to be too much for his sixty-six-year-old heart. Dead on arrival. DOA. They—whoever "they" were—would have to bury him and put above his grave: the unknown earthman.

He felt better then. He even chuckled while rising to his feet. With some courage and confidence, he looked around. The air was comfortable enough, about seventy degrees, he estimated. It bore strange and very pleasant, almost fruity, perfumes. Bird calls—he hoped they were only those—came from all around him. Somewhere far off, a low growl sounded, but he was not frightened. He was certain, with no rational ground for certainty, that it was the distance-muted crash of surf. The moon was full and enormous, two and a half times as large as Earth's.

The sky had lost the bright green it had had during the day and had become, except for the moon's radiance, as black as the night-time sky of the world he had left. A multitude of large stars moved with a speed and in directions that made him dizzy with fright and confusion. One of the stars fell toward him, became bigger and bigger, brighter and brighter, until it swooped a few feet overhead. By the orange-yellow glow from its rear, he could see four great elliptoid wings and dangling skinny legs and, briefly, the silhouette of an antennaed head.

It was a firefly of some sort with a wingspread of at least ten feet.

Wolff watched the shifting and expanding and contracting of the living constellations until he became used to them. He wondered which direction to take, and the sound of the surf finally decided him. A shoreline would give a definite point of departure, wherever he went after that. His progress was slow and cautious, with frequent stops to listen and to examine the shadows.

Something with a deep chest grunted nearby. He flattened himself on the grass under the shadow of a thick bush and tried to breathe slowly. There was a rustling noise. A twig crackled. Wolff lifted his head high enough to look out into the moonlit clearing before him. A great bulk, erect, biped, dark, and hairy, shambled by only a few yards from him.

It stopped suddenly, and Wolff's heart skipped a beat. Its head moved back and forth, permitting Wolff to get a full view of a gorrilloid profile. However, it was not a gorilla—not a Terrestrial one, anyway. Its fur was not a solid black. Alternate stripes of broad black and narrow white zigzagged across its body and legs. Its arms were much shorter than those of its counterpart on Earth, and its legs were not only longer but straighter. Moreover, the forehead, although shelved with bone above the eyes, was high.

It muttered something, not an animal cry or moan but a sequence of clearly modulated syllables. The gorilla was not alone. The greenish moon exposed a patch of bare skin on the side away from Wolff. It belonged to a woman who walked by the beast's side and whose shoulders were hidden by his huge right arm.

Wolff could not see her face, but he caught enough of long slim legs, curving buttocks, a shapely arm, and long black hair to wonder if she were as beautiful from the front.

She spoke to the gorilla in a voice like the sound of silver bells. The gorilla answered her. Then the two walked out of the green moon and into the darkness of the jungle.

Wolff did not get up at once, for he was too shaken.

Finally, he rose to his feet and pushed on through the undergrowth, which was not as thick as that of an Earth jungle. Indeed, the bushes were widely separated. If the environment had not been so exotic, he would not have thought of the flora as a jungle. It was more like a park, including the soft grass, which was so short it could have been freshly mown.

Only a few paces further on, he was startled when an animal snorted and then ran in front of him. He got a glimpse of reddish antlers, a whitish nose, huge pale eyes, and a polka-dot body. It crashed by him and disappeared, but a few seconds later he heard steps behind him. He turned to see the same cervine several feet away. When it saw that it was detected, it stepped forward slowly and thrust a wet nose into his outstretched hand. Thereafter, it purred and tried to rub its flank against him. Since it weighed perhaps a quarter of a ton, it tended to push him away from it.

He leaned into it, rubbed it behind its large cupshaped ears, scratched its nose, and lightly slapped its ribs. The cervine licked him several times with a long wet tongue that rasped as roughly as that of a lion. His hopes that it would tire of its affections were soon realized. It left him with a bound as sudden as that which had brought it within his ken.

After it was gone, he felt less endangered. Would an animal be so friendly to a complete stranger if it had carnivores or hunters to fear?

The roar of the surf became louder. Within ten minutes he was at the edge of the beach. There he crouched beneath a broad and towering frond and examined the moon-brushed scene. The beach itself was white and, as his outstretched hand verified, made of very fine sand. It ran on both sides for as far as he could see, and the breadth of it, between forest and sea, was about two hundred yards. On both sides, at a distance, were fires around which capered the silhouettes of men and women. Their shouts and laughter, though muted by the distance, reinforced his impression that they must be human.

Then his gaze swept back to the beach near him. At an angle, about three hundred yards away and almost in the water, were two beings. The sight of them snatched his breath away.

It was not what they were doing that shocked him but the construction of their bodies. From the waist up the man and woman were as human as he, but at the point where their legs should have begun the body of each tapered into fins.

He was unable to restrain his curiosity. After caching the horn in a bed of feathery grasses, he crept along the edge of the jungle; when he was opposite the two, he stopped to watch. Since the male and female were now lying side by side and talking, their position allowed him to study them in more detail. He became convinced they could not pursue him with any speed on land and had no weapons. He would approach them. They might even be friendly.

When he was about twenty yards from them, he stopped to examine them again. If they were mermen, they certainly were not half-piscine. The fins at the end of their long tails were on a horizontal plane, unlike those of fish, which are vertical. And the tail did not seem to have scales. Smooth brown skin covered their hybrid bodies from top to bottom.

He coughed. They looked up, and the male shouted and the female screamed. In a motion so swift he could not comprehend the particulars but saw it as a blur, they had risen on the ends of their tails and flipped themselves upward and out into the waves. The moon flashed on a dark head rising briefly from the waves and a tail darting upward.

The surf rolled and crashed upon the white sands. The moon shone hugely and greenly. A breeze from the sea patted his sweating face and passed on to cool the jungle. A few weird cries issued from the darkness behind him, and from down the beach came the sound of human revelry.

For awhile he was webbed in thought. The speech of the two merpeople had had something familiar about it, as had that of the zebrilla (his coinage for the gorilla) and the woman. He had not recognized any individual words, but the sounds and the associated pitches had stirred something in his memory. But what? They certainly spoke no language he had ever heard before. Was it similar to one of the living languages of Earth and had he heard it on a recording or perhaps in a movie?

A hand closed on his shoulder, lifted him and whirled him around. The Gothic snout and caverned eyes of a zebrilla were thrust in his face, and an alcoholic breath struck his own nostrils. It spoke, and the woman stepped out from the bushes. She walked slowly toward him, and at any other time he would have caught his breath at the magnificent body and beautiful face. Unfortunately, he was having a hard time breathing now for a different cause. The giant ape could hurl him into the sea with even more ease and speed than that which the merpeople had shown when they had dived away. Or the huge hand could close on him and meet on crushed flesh and shattered bone.

The woman said something, and the zebrilla replied. It was then that Wolff understood several words. Their language was akin to pre-Homeric Greek, to Mycenaean.

He did not immediately burst into speech to reassure them that he was harmless and his intentions good. For one thing, he was too stunned to think clearly enough. Also, his knowledge of the Greek of that period was necessarily limited, even if it was close to the Aeolic-Ionic of the blind bard.

Finally, he managed to utter a few inappropriate phrases, but he was not so concerned with the sense as to let them know he meant no harm. Hearing him, the zebrilla grunted, said something to the girl, and lowered Wolff to the sand. He sighed with relief, but he grimaced at the pain in his shoulder. The huge hand of the monster was enormously powerful. Aside from the magnitude and hairiness, the hand was quite human.

The woman tugged at his shirt. She had a mild distaste on her face; only later was he to discover that he repulsed her. She had never seen a fat old man before. Moreover, the clothes puzzled her. She continued pulling at his shirt. Rather than have her request the zebrilla to remove it from him, he pulled it off himself. She looked at it curiously, smelled it, said, "Ugh!" and then made some gesture.

Although he would have preferred not to understand her and was even more reluctant to obey, he decided he might as well. There was no reason to frustrate her and perhaps anger the zebrilla. He shed his clothes and waited for more orders. The woman laughed shrilly; the zebrilla barked and pounded his thigh with his huge hand so that it sounded as if an axe were chopping wood. He and the woman put their arms around each other and, laughing hysterically, staggered off down the beach.

Infuriated, humiliated, ashamed, but also thankful that he had escaped without injury, Wolff put his pants back on. Picking up his underwear, socks, and shoes, he trudged through the sand and back into the jungle. After taking the horn from its hiding place, he sat for a long while, wondering what to do. Finally, he fell asleep.

He awoke in the morning, muscle-sore, hungry, and thirsty.

The beach was alive. In addition to the merman and merwoman he had seen the night before, several large seals with bright orange coats flopped back and forth over the sand in pursuit of amber balls flung by the merpeople, and a man with ram's horns projecting from his forehead, furry legs and a short goatish tail chased by a woman who looked much like the one who had been with the zebrilla. She, however, had yellow hair. She ran until the horned man leaped upon her and bore her, laughing, to the sand. What happened thereafter showed him that these beings were as innocent of a sense of sin, and of inhibitions, as Adam and Eve must have been.

This was more than interesting, but the sight of a mermaid eating aroused him in other and more demanding directions. She held a large oval yellow fruit in one hand and a hemisphere that looked like a coconut shell in the other. The female counterpart of the man with ram's horns squatted by a fire only a few yards from him and fried a fish on the end of a stick. The odor made his mouth water and his belly rumble.

First he had to have a drink. Since the only water in sight was the ocean, he strode out upon the beach and toward the surf.

His reception was what he had expected: surprise, withdrawal, apprehension to some degree. All stopped their activities, no matter how absorbing, to stare at him. When he approached some of them he was greeted with wide eyes, open mouths, and retreat. Some of the males stood their ground, but they looked as if they were ready to run if he said boo. Not that he felt like challenging them, since the smallest had muscles that could easily overpower his tired old body.

He walked into the surf up to his waist and tasted the water. He had seen others drink from it, so he hoped that he would find it acceptable. It was pure and fresh and had a tang that he had never experienced before. After drinking his fill, he felt as if he had had a transfusion of young blood. He walked out of the ocean and back across the beach and into the jungle. The others had resumed their eating and recreations, and though they watched him with a bold direct stare they said nothing to him. He gave them a smile, but quit when it seemed to startle them. In the jungle, he searched for and found fruit and nuts such as the merwoman had been eating. The yellow fruit had a peach pie taste, and the meat inside the pseudo-coconut tasted like very tender beef mixed with small pieces of walnut.

Afterward he felt very satisfied, except for one thing: he craved his pipe. But tobacco was one thing that seemed to be missing in this paradise.

The next few days he haunted the jungle or else spent some time in or near the ocean. By then, the beach crowd had grown used to him and even began to laugh when he made his morning appearances. One day, some of the men and women jumped him and, laughing uproariously, removed his clothes. He ran after the woman with the pants, but she sped away into the jungle. When she reappeared she was emptyhanded. By now he could speak well enough to be understood if he uttered the phrases slowly. His years of teaching and study had given him a very large Greek vocabulary, and he had only to master the tones and a number of words that were not in his Autenreith.

"Why did you do that?" he asked the beautiful black-eyed nymph.

"I wanted to see what you were hiding beneath those ugly rags. Naked, you are ugly, but those things on you made you look even uglier."

"Obscene?" he said, but she did not understand the word.

He shrugged and thought, *When in Rome . . .* Only this was more like the Garden of Eden. The temperature by day or night was comfortable and varied about seven degrees. There was no problem getting a variety of food, no work demanded, no rent, no politics, no tension except an easily relieved sexual tension, no national or racial animosities. There were no bills to pay. Or were there? That you did not get something for nothing was the basic principle of the universe of Earth. Was it the same here? Somebody should have to foot the bill.

At night he slept on a pile of grass in a large hollow in a tree. This was only one of thousands of such hollows, for a particular type of tree offered this natural accommodation. Wolff did not stay in bed in the mornings, however. For some days he got up just before dawn and watched the sun arrive. Arrive was a better word than rise, for the sun certainly did not rise. On the other side of the sea was an enormous mountain range, so extensive that he could see neither end. The sun always came around the mountain and was high when it came. It proceeded straight across the green sky and did not sink but disappeared only when it went around the other end of the mountain range.

An hour later, the moon appeared. It, too, came around the mountain, sailed at the same level across the skies, and slipped around the other side of the mountain. Every other night it rained hard for an hour. Wolff usually woke then, for the air did get a little chillier. He would snuggle down in the leaves and shiver and try to get back to sleep.

He was finding it increasingly more difficult to do so with each succeeding night. He would think of his own world, the friends and the work and the fun he had there—and of his wife. What was Brenda doing now? Doubtlessly she was grieving for him. Bitter and nasty and whining though she had been too many times, she loved him. His disappearance would be a shock and a loss. However, she would be well taken care of. She had always insisted on his carrying more insurance than he could afford; this had been a quarrel between them more than once. Then it occurred to him that she would not get a cent of insurance for a long time, for proof of his death would have to be forthcoming. Still, if she had to wait until he was legally declared dead, she could survive on social security. It would mean a drastic lowering of her living standards, but it would be enough to support her.

Certainly he had no intention of going back. He was regaining his youth. Though he ate well, he was losing weight, and his muscles were getting stronger and harder. He had a spring in his legs and a sense of joy lost sometime during his early twenties. The seventh morning, he had rubbed his scalp and discovered that it was covered with little bristles. The tenth morning, he woke up with pain in his gums. He rubbed the swollen flesh and wondered if he were going to be sick. He had forgotten that there was such a thing as disease, for he had been extremely well and none of the beach crowd, as he called them, ever seemed ill.

His gums continued to hurt him for a week, after which he took to drinking the naturally fermented liquor in the "punchnut." This grew in great clusters high at the top of a slender tree with short, fragile, mauve branches and tobacco-pipe-shaped yellow leaves. When its leathery rind was cut open with a sharp stone, it exuded an odor as of fruity punch. It tasted like a gin tonic with a dash of cherry bitters and had a kick like a slug of tequila. It worked well in killing both the pain in his gums and the irritation the pain had generated in him.

Nine days after he first experienced the trouble with his gums, ten tiny, white, hard teeth began to shove through the flesh. Moreover, the gold fillings in the others were being pushed out by the return of the natural material. And a thick black growth covered his formerly bald pate.

This was not all. The swimming, running, and climbing had melted off the fat. The prominent veins of old age had sunk back into smooth firm flesh. He could run for long stretches without being winded or feel as if his heart would burst. All this he delighted in, but not without wondering why and how it had come about.

He asked several among the beach-crowd about their seemingly universal youth. They had one reply: "It's the Lord's will."

At first he thought they were speaking of the Creator, which seemed strange to him. As far as he could tell, they had no religion. Certainly they did not have one with any organized approach, rituals, or sacraments.

"Who is the Lord?" he asked. He thought that perhaps he had mistranslated their word *wanaks*, that it might have a slightly different meaning than that found in Homer.

Ipsewas, the zebrilla, the most intelligent of all he had so far met, answered, "He lives on top of the world, beyond Okeanos." Ipsewas pointed up and over the sea, toward the mountain range at its other side. "The Lord lives in a beautiful and impregnable palace on top of the world. He it was who made this world and who made us. He used to come down often to make merry with us. We do as the Lord says and play with him. But we are always frightened. If he becomes angry or is displeased, he is likely to kill us. Or worse."

Wolff smiled and nodded his head. So Ipsewas and the others had no more rational explanation of the origins or workings of their world than the people of his. But the beach-crowd did have one thing lacking on Earth. They had uniformity of opinion. Everyone he asked gave him the same answer as the zebrilla.

"It is the will of the Lord. He made the world, he made us."

"How do you know?" Wolff asked. He did not expect any more than he had gotten on Earth when he asked the question. But he was surprised.

"Oh," replied a mermaid, Paiawa, "the Lord told us so. Besides, my mother told me, too. She ought to know. The Lord made her body; she remembers when he did it, although that was so long, long ago."

"Indeed?" Wolff said, wondering whether or not she were pulling his leg, and thinking also that it would be difficult to retaliate by doing the same to her. "And where is your mother? I'd like to talk to her."

Paiawa waved a hand toward the west. "Somewhere along there."

"Somewhere" could be thousands of miles away, for he had no idea how far the beach extended.

"I haven't seen her for a long time," Paiawa added.

"How long?" Wolff said.

Paiawa wrinkled her lovely brow and pursed her lips. Very kissable, Wolff thought. And that body! The return of his youth was bringing back a strong awareness of sex.

Paiawa smiled at him and said, "You *are* showing some interest in me, aren't you?"

He flushed and would have walked away, but he wanted an answer to his question. "How many years since you saw your mother?" he asked again.

Paiawa could not answer. The word for "year" was not in her vocabulary.

He shrugged and walked swiftly away, to disappear behind the savagely colored foliage by the beach. She called after him, archly at first, then angrily when it became evident he was not going to turn back. She made a few disparaging remarks about him as compared to the other males. He did not argue with her—it would have been beneath his dignity, and besides, what she said was true. Even though his body was rapidly regaining its youth and strength, it still suffered in comparison with the near-perfect specimens all around him.

He dropped this line of thought, and considered Paiawa's story. If he could locate her mother or one of her mother's contemporaries in age, he might be able to find out more about the Lord. He did not discredit Paiawa's story, which would have been incredible on Earth. These people just did not lie. Fiction was a stranger to them. Such truthfulness had its advantages, but it also meant that they were decidedly limited in imagination and had little humor or wit. They laughed often enough, but it was over rather obvious and petty things. Slapstick was as high as their comedy went—and crude practical jokes.

He cursed because he was having difficulty in staying on his intended track of thought. His trouble with concentration seemed to get stronger every day. Now, what had he been thinking about when he'd strayed off to his unhappiness over his maladjustment with the local society? Oh, yes, Paiawa's mother! Some of the oldsters might be able to enlighten him—if he could locate any. How could he identify any when all adults looked the same age? There were only a very few youngsters, perhaps three in the several hundred beings he had encountered so far. Moreover, among the many animals and birds here (some rather weird ones, too), only a half-dozen had not been adults.

If there were few births, the scale was balanced by the absence of death. He had seen three dead animals, two killed by accident and the third during a battle with another over a female. Even that had been an accident, for the defeated male, a lemon-colored antelope with four horns curved into figure-eights, had turned to run away and broken his neck while jumping over a log.

The flesh of the dead animal had not had a chance to rot and stink. Several omnipresent creatures that looked like small bipedal foxes with white noses, floppy basset-hound ears, and monkey paws had eaten the corpse within a matter of an hour. The foxes scoured the jungle and scavenged everything—fruit, nuts, berries, corpses. They had a taste for the rotten; they would ignore fresh fruits for bruised. But they were not sour notes in the symphony of beauty and life. Even in the Garden of Eden, garbage collectors were necessary.

At times Wolff would look across the blue, white-capped Okeanos at the mountain range, called Thayaphayawoed. Perhaps the Lord did live up there. It might be worthwhile to cross the sea and climb up the formidable steps on the chance that some of the mystery of this universe would be revealed. But the more he tried to estimate the height of Thayaphayawoed, the less he thought of the idea. The black cliffs soared up and up and up until the eye wearied and the mind staggered. No man could live on its top, because there would be no air to breathe.

3

ONE DAY ROBERT WOLFF REMOVED THE SILVER HORN FROM ITS hiding place in the hollow of a tree. Setting off through the forest, he walked toward the boulder from which the man who called himself Kickaha had thrown the horn. Kickaha and the bumpy creatures had dropped out of sight as if they never existed and no one to whom he had talked had ever seen or heard of them. He would re-enter his native world and give it another chance. If he thought its advantages outweighed those of the Garden planet, he would remain there. Or, perhaps, he could travel back and forth and so get the best of both. When tired of one, he would vacation in the other.

On the way, he stopped for a moment at an invitation from Elikopis to have a drink and to talk. Elikopis, whose name meant "Bright-eyed," was a beautiful, magnificently rounded dryad. She was closer to being "normal" than anyone he had so far met. If her hair had not been a deep purple, she would, properly clothed, have attracted no more attention on Earth than was usually bestowed on a woman of surpassing fairness.

In addition, she was one of the very few who could carry on a worthwhile conversation. She did not think that conversation consisted of chattering away or laughing loudly without cause and ignoring the words of those who were supposed to be communicating with her. Wolff had been disgusted and depressed to find that most of the beach-crowd or the forest-crowd were monologists, however intensely they seemed to be speaking or however gregarious they were.

Elikopis was different, perhaps because she was not a member of any "crowd," although it was more likely that the reverse was the cause. In this world along the sea, the natives, lacking even the technology of the Australian aborigine (and not needing even that) had developed an extremely complex social relationship. Each group had definite beach and forest territories with internal prestige levels. Each was able to recite to detail (and loved to) his/her horizontal/vertical position in comparison with each person of the group, which usually numbered about thirty. They could and would recite the arguments, reconciliations, character faults and virtues, athletic prowess or lack thereof, skill in their many childish games, and evaluate the sexual ability of each.

Elikopis had a sense of humor as bright as her eyes, but she also had some sensitivity. Today, she had an extra attraction, a mirror of glass set in a golden circle encrusted with diamonds. It was one of the few artifacts he had seen.

"Where did you get that?" he asked.

"Oh, the Lord gave it to me," Elikopis replied. "Once, a long time ago, I was one of his favorites. Whenever he came down from the top of the world to visit here, he would spend much time with me. Chryseis and I were the ones he loved the most. Would you believe it, the others still hate us for that? That's why I'm so lonely—not that being with the others is much help."

"And what did the Lord look like?"

She laughed and said, "From the neck down, he looked much like any tall, well-built man such as you."

She put her arm around his neck and began kissing him on his cheek, her lips slowly traveling toward his ear.

"His face?" Wolff said.

"I do not know. I could feel it, but I could not see it. A radiance from it blinded me. When he got close to me, I had to close my eyes, it was so bright."

She shut his mouth with her kisses, and presently he forgot his questions. But when she was lying half-asleep on the soft grass by his side, he picked up the mirror and looked into it. His heart opened with delight. He looked like he had when he had been twenty-five. This he had known but had not been able to fully realize until now.

"And if I return to Earth, will I age as swiftly as I have regained my youth?"

He rose and stood for awhile in thought. Then he said, "Who do I think I'm kidding? I'm not going back."

"If you're leaving me now," Elikopis said drowsily, "look for Chryseis. Something has happened to her; she runs away every time anybody gets close. Even I, her only friend, can't approach her. Something dreadful has occurred, something she won't talk about. You'll love her. She's not like the others; she's like me."

"All right," Wolff replied absently. "I will."

He walked until he was alone. Even if he did not intend to use the gate through which he had come, he did want to experiment with the horn. Perhaps there were other gates. It was possible that at any place where the horn was blown, a gate would open.

The tree under which he had stopped was one of the numerous cornucopias. It was two hundred feet tall, thirty feet thick, had a smooth, almost oily, azure bark, and branches as thick as his thigh and about sixty feet long. The branches were twigless and leafless. At the end of each was a hard-shelled flower, eight feet long and shaped exactly like a cornucopia.

Out of the cornucopias intermittent trickles of chocolatey stuff fell to the ground. The product tasted like honey with a very slight flavor of tobacco—a curious mixture, yet one he liked. Every creature of the forest ate it.

Under the cornucopia tree, he blew the horn. No "gate" appeared. He tried again a hundred yards away but without success. So, he decided, the horn worked only in certain areas, perhaps only in that place by the toadstool-shaped boulder.

Then he glimpsed the head of the girl who had come from around the tree that first time the gate had opened. She had the same heart-shaped face, enormous eyes, full crimson lips, and long tiger-stripes of black and auburn hair.

He greeted her, but she fled. Her body was beautiful; her legs were the longest, in proportion to her body, that he had ever seen in a woman. Moreover, she was slimmer than the other too-curved and great-busted females of this world.

Wolff ran after her. The girl cast a look over her shoulder, gave a cry of despair, and continued to run. He almost stopped then, for he had not gotten such a reaction from any of the natives. An initial withdrawal, yes, but not sheer panic and utter fright.

The girl ran until she could go no more. Sobbing for breath, she leaned against a moss-covered boulder near a small cataract. Ankle-high yellow flowers in the form of question-marks surrounded her. An owl-eyed bird with corkscrew feathers and long forward-bending legs stood on top of the boulder and blinked down at them. It uttered soft *wee-wee-wee!* cries.

Approaching slowly and smiling, Wolff said, "Don't be afraid of me. I won't harm you. I just want to talk to you."

The girl pointed a shaking finger at the horn. In a quavery voice she said, "Where did you get that?"

"I got it from a man who called himself Kickaha. You saw him. Do you know him?"

The girl's huge eyes were dark green; he thought them the most beautiful he had ever seen. This despite, or maybe because of, the catlike pupils.

She shook her head. "No. I did not know him. I first saw him when those"—she swallowed and turned pale and looked as if she were going to vomit—"things chased him to the boulder. And I saw them drag him off the boulder and take him away."

"Then he wasn't ended?" Wolff asked. He did not say *killed* or *slain* or *dead,* for these were taboo words.

"No. Perhaps those things meant to do something even worse than . . . ending him?"

"Why run from me?" Wolff said. "I am not one of those things."

"I . . . I can't talk about it."

Wolff considered her reluctance to speak of unpleasantness. These people had so few repulsive or dangerous phenomena in their lives, yet they could not face even these. They were overly conditioned to the easy and the beautiful.

"I don't care whether or not you want to talk about it," he said. "You must. It's very important."

She turned her face away. "I won't."

"Which way did they go?"

"Who?"

"Those monsters. And Kickaha."

"I heard him call them *gworl*," she said. "I never heard that word before. They . . . the gworl . . . must come from somewhere else." She pointed seawards and up. "They must come from the mountain. Up there, somewhere."

Suddenly she turned to him and came close to him. Her huge eyes were raised to his, and even at this moment he could not help thinking how exquisite her features were and how smooth and creamy her skin was.

"Let's get away from here!" she cried. "Far away! Those things are still here. Some of them may have taken Kickaha away, but all of them didn't leave! I saw a couple a few days ago. They were hiding in the hollow of a tree. Their eyes shone like those of animals, and they have a horrible odor, like rotten fungus-covered fruit!"

She put her hand on the horn. "I think they want this!"

Wolff said, "And I blew the horn. If they're anywhere near, they must have heard it!"

He looked around through the trees. Something glittered behind a bush about a hundred yards away.

He kept his eyes on the bush, and presently he saw the bush tremble and the flash of sunlight again. He took the girl's slender hand in his and said, "Let's get going. But walk as if we'd seen nothing. Be nonchalant."

She pulled back on his hand and said, "What's wrong?"

"Don't get hysterical. I think I saw something behind a bush. It might be nothing, then again it could be the gworl. Don't look over there! You'll give us away!"

He spoke too late, for she had jerked her head around. She gasped and moved close to him. "They . . . they!"

He looked in the direction of her pointing finger and saw two dark, squat figures shamble from behind the bush. Each carried a long, wide, curved blade of steel in its hand. They waved the knives and shouted something in hoarse rasping voices. They wore no clothes over their dark furry bodies, but broad belts around their waists supported scabbards from which protruded knife-handles.

Wolff said, "Don't panic. I don't think they can run very fast on those short bent legs. Where's a good place to get away from them, someplace they can't follow us?"

"Across the sea," she said in a shaking voice. "I don't think they could find us if we got far enough ahead of them. We can go on a *histoikhthys.*"

She was referring to one of the huge molluscs that abounded in the sea. These had bodies covered with paper-thin but tough shells shaped like a racing yacht's hull. A slender but strong rod of cartilage projected vertically from the back of each, and a triangular sail of flesh, so thin it was transparent, grew from the cartilage mast. The angle of the sail was controlled by muscular movement, and the force of the wind on the sail, plus expulsion of a jet of water, enabled the creature to move slightly in a wind or a calm. The merpeople and the sentients who lived on the beach often hitched rides on these creatures, steering them by pressure on exposed nerve centers.

"You think the gworl will have to use a boat?" he said. "If so, they'll be out of luck unless they make one. I've never seen any kind of sea craft here."

Wolff looked behind him frequently. The gworl were coming at a faster pace, their bodies rolling like those of drunken sailors at every step. Wolff and the girl came to a stream which was about seventy feet broad and, at the deepest, rose to their waists. The water was cool but not chilling, clear, with silvery fish darting back and forth in it. When they reached the other side, they hid behind a large cornucopia tree. The girl urged him to continue, but he said, "They'll be at a disadvantage when they're in the middle of the stream."

"What do you mean?" she asked.

He did not reply. After placing the horn behind the tree, he looked around until he found a stone. It was half the size of his head, round, and rough enough to be held firmly in his hand. He hefted one of the fallen cornucopias. Though huge, it was hollow and weighed no more than twenty pounds. By then, the two gworl were on the bank of the opposite side of the stream. It was then that he discovered a weakness of the hideous creatures. They walked back and forth along the bank, shook their knives in fury, and growled so loudly in their throaty language that he could hear them from his hiding place. Finally, one of them stuck a broad splayed foot in the water. He withdrew it almost immediately, shook it as a cat shakes a wet paw, and said something to the other gworl. That one rasped back, then screamed at him.

The gworl with the wet foot shouted back, but he stepped into the water and reluctantly waded through it. Wolff watched him and also noted that the other was going to hang back until the creature had passed the middle of the stream; then he picked up the cornucopia in one hand, the stone in the other, and ran toward the stream. Behind him, the girl screamed. Wolff cursed because it gave the gworl notice that he was coming.

The gworl paused, the water up to its waist, yelled at Wolff and brandished the knife. Wolff reserved his breath, for he did not want to waste his wind. He sped toward the edge of the water, while the gworl resumed his progress to the same bank. The gworl on the opposite edge had frozen at Wolff's appearance; now he had plunged into the stream to help the other. This action fell in with Wolff's plans. He only hoped that he could deal with the first before the second reached the middle.

The nearest gworl flipped his knife; Wolff lifted the cornucopia before him. The knife thudded into its thin but tough shell with a force that almost tore it from his grasp. The gworl began to draw another knife from its scabbard. Wolff did not stop to pull the first knife from the cornucopia; he kept on running. Just as the gworl raised the knife to slash at Wolff, Wolff dropped the stone, lifted the great bell-shape high, and slammed it over the gworl.

A muffled squawk came from within the shell. The cornucopia tilted over, the gworl with it, and both began floating downstream. Wolff ran into the water, picked up the stone, and grabbed the gworl by one of its thrashing feet. He took a hurried glance at the other and saw it was raising its knife for a throw. Wolff grabbed the handle of the knife that was sticking in the shell, tore it out, and then threw himself down behind the shelter of the bell-shape. He was forced to release his hold on the gworl's hairy foot, but he escaped the knife. It flew over the rim of the shell and buried itself to the hilt in the mud of the bank.

At the same time, the gworl within the cornucopia slid out, sputtering. Wolff stabbed at its side; the knife slid off one of the cartilaginous bumps. The gworl screamed and turned toward him. Wolff rose and thrust with all his strength at its belly. The knife went in to the hilt. The gworl grabbed at it; Wolff stepped back; the gworl fell into the water. The cornucopia floated away, leaving Wolff exposed, the knife gone, and only the stone in his hand. The remaining gworl was advancing on him, holding its knife across its breast. Evidently it did not intend to try for a second throw. It meant to close in on Wolff.

Wolff forced himself to delay until the thing was only ten feet from him. Meanwhile, he crouched down so that the water came to his chest and hid the stone, which he had shifted from his left to his right hand. Now he could see the gworl's face clearly. It had a very low forehead, a double ridge of bone above the eyes, thick mossy eyebrows, close-set lemon-yellow eyes, a flat, single-nostriled nose, thin black animal lips, a prognathous jaw which curved far out and gave the mouth a froglike appearance, no chin, and the sharp, widely separated teeth of a carnivore. The head, face, and body were covered with long, thick, dark fur. The neck was very thick, and the shoulders were stooped. Its wet fur stank like rotten fungus-diseased fruit.

Wolff was scared at the thing's hideousness, but he held his ground. If he broke and ran, he would go down with a knife in his back.

When the gworl, alternately hissing and rasping in its ugly speech, had come within six feet, Wolff stood up. He raised his stone, and the gworl, seeing his intention, raised his knife to throw it. The stone flew straight and thudded into a bump on the forehead. The creature staggered backward, dropped the knife, and fell on its back in the water. Wolff waded toward it, groped in the water for the stone, found it, and came up from the water in time to face the gworl. Although it had a dazed expression and its eyes were slightly crossed, it was not out of the fight. And it held another knife.

Wolff raised the stone high and brought it down on top of the skull. There was a loud crack. The gworl fell back again, disappearing in the water, and appeared several yards away floating on its face.

Reaction took him. His heart was hammering so hard he thought it would rupture, he was shaking all over, and he was sick. But he remembered the knife stuck in the mud and retrieved it.

The girl was still behind the tree. She looked too horror-struck to speak. Wolff picked up the horn, took the girl's arm with one hand, and shook her roughly.

"Snap out of it! Think how lucky you are! You could be dead instead of them!"

She burst into a long wailing, then began weeping. He waited until she seemed to have no more grief in her before speaking. "I don't even know your name."

Her enormous eyes were reddened, and her face looked older. Even so, he thought, he had not seen an Earthwoman who could compare with her. Her beauty made the terror of the fight thin away.

"I'm Chryseis," she said. As if she were proud of it but at the same time shy of her proudness, she said, "I'm the only woman here who is allowed that name. The Lord forbade others to take it."

He growled, "The Lord again. Always the Lord. Who in hell is the Lord?"

"You really don't know?" she replied as if she could not believe him.

"No, I don't." He was silent for a moment, then said her name as if he were tasting it. "Chryseis, heh? It's not unknown on Earth, although I fear that the university at which I was teaching is full of illiterates who've never heard the name. They know that Homer composed the Iliad, and that's about it.

"Chryseis, the daughter of Chryses, a priest of Apollo. She was captured by the Greeks during the siege of Troy and given to Agamemnon. But Agamemnon was forced to restore her to her father because of the pestilence sent by Apollo."

Chryseis was silent for so long that Wolff became impatient. He decided that they should move away from this area, but he was not certain which direction to take or how far to go.

Chryseis, frowning, said, "That was a long time ago. I can barely remember it. It's all so vague now."

"What are you talking about?"

"Me. My father. Agamemnon. The war."

"Well, what about it?" He was thinking that he would like to go to the base of the mountains. There, he could get some idea of what a climb entailed.

"I am Chryseis," she said. "The one you were talking about. You sound as if you had just come from Earth. Oh, tell me, is it true?"

He sighed. These people did not lie, but there was nothing to keep them from believing that their stories were true. He had heard enough incredible things to know that they were not only badly misinformed but likely to reconstruct the past to suit themselves. They did so in all sincerity, of course.

"I don't want to shatter your little dream-world," he said, "but this Chryseis, if she even existed, died at least 3000 years ago. Moreover, she was a human being. She did not have tiger-striped hair and eyes with feline pupils."

"Nor did I . . . then. It was the Lord who abducted me, brought me to this universe, and changed my body. Just as it was he who abducted the others, changed them, or else inserted their brains in bodies he created."

She gestured seaward and upward. "He lives up there now, and we don't see him very often. Some say that he disappeared a long time ago, and a new Lord has taken his place."

"Let's get away from here," he said. "We can talk about this later."

They had gone only a quarter of a mile when Chryseis gestured at him to hide with her behind a thick purple-branched, gold-leaved bush. He crouched by her and, parting the branches a little, saw what had disturbed her. Several yards away was a hairy-legged man with heavy ram's horns on top of his head. Sitting on a low branch at a level with the man's eyes was a giant raven. It was as large as a golden eagle and had a high forehead. The skull looked as if it could house a brain the size of a fox terrier's.

Wolff was not surprised at the bulk of the raven, for he had seen some rather enormous creatures. But he was shocked to find the bird and the man carrying on a conversation.

"The Eye of the Lord," Chryseis whispered. She stabbed a finger at the raven in answer to his puzzled look. "That's one of the Lord's spies. They fly over the world and see what's going on and then carry the news back to the Lord."

Wolff thought of Chryseis' apparently sincere remark about the insertion of brains into bodies by the Lord. To his question, she replied, "Yes, but I do not know if he put human brains into the ravens' heads. He may have grown small brains with the larger human brains as models, then educated the ravens. Or he could have used just part of a human brain."

Unfortunately, though they strained their ears, they could only catch a few words here and there. Several minutes passed. The raven, loudly croaking a goodbye in distorted but understandable Greek, launched himself from the branch. He dropped heavily, but his great wings beat fast, and they carried him upward before he touched ground. In a minute he was lost behind the heavy foliage of the trees. A little later, Wolff caught a glimpse of him through a break in the vegetation. The giant black bird was gaining altitude slowly, his point of flight the mountain across the sea.

He noticed that Chryseis was trembling. He said, "What could the raven tell the Lord that would scare you so?"

"I am not frightened so much for myself as I am for you. If the Lord discovers you are here, he will want to kill you. He does not like uninvited guests in his world."

She placed her hand on the horn and shivered again. "I know that it was Kickaha who gave you this, and that you can't help it that you have it. But the Lord might not know it isn't your fault. Or, even if he did, he might not care. He would be terribly angry if he thought you'd had anything to do with stealing it. He would do awful things to you; you would be better off if you ended yourself now rather than have the Lord get his hands on you."

"Kickaha stole the horn? How do you know?"

"Oh, believe me, I know. It is the Lord's. And Kickaha must have stolen it, for the Lord would never give it to anyone."

"I'm confused," Wolff said. "But maybe we can straighten it all out someday. The thing that bothers me right now is, where's Kickaha?"

Chryseis pointed toward the mountain and said, "The gworl took him there. But before they did . . ."

She covered her face with her hands; tears seeped through the fingers.

"They did something to him?" Wolff said.

She shook her head. "No. They did something to . . . to . . ."

Wolff took her hands from her face. "If you can't talk about it, would you show it to me?"

"I can't. It's . . . too horrible. I get sick."

"Show me anyway."

"I'll take you near there. But don't ask me to look at . . . her . . . again."

She began walking, and he followed her. Every now and then she would stop, but he would gently urge her on. After a zigzag course of over half a mile, she stopped. Ahead of them was a small forest of bushes twice as high as Wolff's head. The leaves of the branches of one bush interlaced with those of its neighbors. The leaves were broad and elephant-ear-shaped, light green with broad red veins, and tipped with a rusty fleur-de-lys.

"She's in there," Chryseis said. "I saw the gworl . . . catch her and drag her into the bushes. I followed . . . I . . ." She could talk no more.

Wolff, knife in one hand, pushed the branches of the bushes aside. He found himself in a natural clearing. In the middle, on the short green grass, lay the scattered bones of a human female. The bones were gray and devoid of flesh, and bore little toothmarks, by which he knew that the bipedal vulpine scavengers had gotten to her.

He was not horrified, but he could imagine how Chryseis must have felt. She must have seen part of what had taken place, probably a rape, then murder in some gruesome fashion. She would have reacted like the other dwellers in the Garden. Death was something so horrible that the word for it had long ago become taboo and then dropped out of the language. Here, nothing but pleasant thoughts and acts were to be contemplated, and anything else was to be shut out.

He returned to Chryseis, who looked with her enormous eyes at him as if she wanted him to tell her that there was nothing within the clearing. He said, "She's only bones now, and far past any suffering."

"The gworl will pay for this!" she said savagely. "The Lord does not allow his creatures to be hurt! This Garden is his, and any intruders are punished!"

"Good for you," he said. "I was beginning to think that you may have become frozen by the shock. Hate the gworl all you want; they deserve it. And you need to break loose."

She screamed and leaped at him and beat on his chest with her fists. Then she began weeping, and presently he took her in his arms. He raised her face and kissed her. She kissed him back passionately, though the tears were still flowing.

Afterward, she said, "I ran to the beach to tell my people what I'd seen. But they wouldn't listen. They turned their backs on me and pretended they hadn't heard me. I kept trying to make them listen, but Owisandros"—the ram-horned man who had been talking with the raven—"Owisandros hit me with his fist and told me to go away. After that, none of them would have anything to do with me. And I . . . I needed friends and love."

"You don't get friends or love by telling people what they don't want to hear," he said. "Here or on Earth. But you have me, Chryseis, and I have you. I think I'm beginning to fall in love with you, although I may just be reacting to loneliness and to the most strange beauty I've ever seen. And to my new youth."

He sat up and gestured at the mountain. "If the gworl are intruders here, where did they come from? Why were they after the horn? Why did they take Kickaha with them? And who is Kickaha?"

"He comes from up there, too. But I think he's an Earthman."

"What do you mean, Earthman? You say you're from Earth."

"I mean he's a newcomer. I don't know. I just had a feeling he was."

He stood up and lifted her up by her hands. "Let's go after him."

Chryseis sucked in her breath and, one hand on her breast, backed away from him. "No!"

"Chryseis, I could stay here with you and be very happy. For awhile. But I'd always be wondering what all this is about the Lord and what happened to Kickaha. I only saw him for a few seconds, but I think I'd like him very much. Besides, he didn't throw the horn to me just because I happened to be there. I have a hunch that he did it for a good reason, and that I should find out why. And I can't rest while he's in the hands of those things, the gworl."

He took her hand from her breast and kissed the hand. "It's about time you left this Paradise that is no Paradise. You can't stay here forever, a child forever."

She shook her head. "I wouldn't be any help to you. I'd just get in your way. And . . . leaving . . . leaving I'd, well, I'd just end."

"You're going to have to learn a new vocabulary," he said. "Death will be just one of the many new words you'll be able to speak without a second thought or a shiver. You will be a better woman for it. Refusing to say it doesn't stop it from happening, you know. Your friend's bones are there whether or not you can talk about them."

"That's horrible!"

"The truth often is."

He turned away from her and started toward the beach. After a hundred yards, he stopped to look back. She had just started running after him. He waited for her, took her in his arms, kissed her, and said, "You may find it hard going, Chryseis, but you won't be bored, won't have to drink yourself into a stupor to endure life."

"I hope so," she said in a low voice. "But I'm scared."

"So am I, but we're going."

4

HE TOOK HER HAND IN HIS AS THEY WALKED SIDE BY SIDE TOWARD the roar of the surf. They had traveled not more than a hundred yards when Wolff saw the first gworl. It stepped out from behind a tree and seemed to be as surprised as they. It shouted, snatched its knife out, then turned to yell at others behind it. In a few seconds, a party of seven had formed, each gworl with a long curved knife.

Wolff and Chryseis had a fifty-yard headstart. Still holding Chryseis' hand, the horn in his other hand, Robert Wolff ran as fast as he could.

"I don't know!" she said despairingly. "We could hide in a tree hollow, but we'd be trapped if they found us."

They ran on. Now and then he looked back: the brush was thick hereabouts and hid some of the gworl, but there were always one or two in evidence.

"The boulder!" he said. "It's just ahead. We'll take that way out!"

Suddenly he knew how much he did not want to return to his native world. Even if it meant a route of escape and a temporary hiding place, he did not want to go back. The prospect of being trapped there and being unable to return here was so appalling that he almost decided not to blow the horn. But he had to do so. Where else could he go?

The decision was taken away from him a few seconds later. As he and Chryseis sped toward the boulder, he saw several dark figures hunched at its base. These rose and became gworl with flashing knives and long white canines.

Wolff and the girl angled away while the three at the boulder joined the chase. These were nearer than the others, only twenty yards behind the fugitives.

"Don't you know any place?" he panted.

"Over the edge," she said. "That's the only place they might not follow us. I've been down the face of the rim; there're caves there. But it's dangerous."

He did not reply, saving his breath for the run. His legs felt heavy and his lungs and throat burned. Chryseis seemed to be in better shape than he: she ran easily, her long legs pumping, breathing deeply but not agonizingly.

"Another two minutes, we'll be there," she said.

The two minutes seemed much longer, but every time he felt he had to stop, he took another look behind him and renewed his strength. The gworl, although even further behind, were in sight. They rolled along on their short, crooked legs, their bumpy faces set with determination.

"Maybe if you gave them the horn," Chryseis said, "they'd go away. I think they want the horn, not us."

"I'll do it if I have to," he gasped. "But only as a last resort."

Suddenly, they were going up a steep slope. Now his legs did feel burdened, but he had caught his second wind and thought that he could go awhile longer. Then they were on top of the hill and at the edge of a cliff.

Chryseis stopped him from walking on. She advanced ahead of him to the edge, halted, looked over, and beckoned him. When he was by her side, he, too, gazed down. His stomach clenched like a fist.

Composed of hard black shiny rock, the cliff went straight down for several miles. Then, nothing.

Nothing but the green sky.

"So . . . it is the edge . . . of the world!" he said.

Chryseis did not answer him. She trotted ahead of him, looking over the side of the cliff, halting briefly now and then to examine the rim.

"About sixty yards more," she said. "Beyond those trees that grow right up to the edge."

She started running swiftly with him close behind her. At the same time, a gworl burst out of the bushes growing on the inner edge of the hill. He turned once to yell, obviously notifying his fellows that he had found the quarry. Then he attacked without waiting for them.

Wolff ran toward the gworl. When he saw the creature lift its knife to throw, he hurled the horn at it. This took the gworl by surprise—or perhaps the turning horn reflected sunlight into his eyes. Whatever the cause, his hesitation was enough for Wolff to get the advantage. He sped in as the gworl both ducked and reached a hand out for the horn. The huge hairy fingers curled around the horn, a cry of grating delight came from the creature, and Wolff was on him. He thrust at the protruding belly; the gworl brought his own knife up; the two blades clanged.

Having missed the first stroke, Wolff wanted to run again. This thing was undoubtedly skilled at knife-fighting. Wolff knew fencing quite well and had never given up its practice. But there was a big difference between dueling with the rapier and dirty in-close knivery, and he knew it. Yet he could not leave. In the first place, the gworl would down him with a thrown blade in his back before he could take four steps. Also, there was the horn, clenched in the gnarled left fist of the gworl. Wolff could not leave that.

The gworl, realizing that Wolff was in a very bad situation, grinned. His upper canines shone long and wet and yellow and sharp. With those, thought Wolff, the thing did not need a knife.

Something goldenbrown, trailing long black-and-auburn-striped hair, flashed by Wolff. The gworl's eyes opened, and he started to turn to his left. The butt end of a pole, a long stick stripped of its leaves and part of its bark, drove into the gworl's chest. At the other end was Chryseis. She had run at top speed with the dead branch held like a vaulter's pole, but just before impact she had lowered it and it hit the creature with enough speed and weight behind it to bowl him over backward. The horn dropped from his fist, but the knife remained in the other.

Wolff jumped forward and thrust the end of his blade between two cartilaginous bosses and into the gworl's thick neck. The muscles were thick and tough there, but not enough to stop the blade. Only when the steel severed the windpipe did it halt.

Wolff handed Chryseis the gworl's knife. "Here, take it!"

She accepted it, but she seemed to be in shock. Wolff slapped her savagely until the glaze went from her eyes. "You did fine!" he said. "Which would you rather see dead, me or him?"

He removed the belt from the corpse and fastened it on himself. Now he had three knives. He scabbarded the bloody weapon, took the horn in one hand, Chryseis' hand in the other, and began running again. Behind them, a howl arose as the first of the gworl came over the edge of the hill. However, Wolff and Chryseis had about thirty yards' start, which they maintained until they reached the group of trees growing on the rim. Chryseis took the lead. She let herself face down on the rim and rolled over. Wolff looked over once before blindly following and saw a small ledge about six feet down from the rim. She had already let herself down the ledge and now was hanging by her hands. She dropped again, this time to a much more narrow ledge. But it did not end; it ran at a forty-five degree angle down the face of the cliff. They could use it if they faced inward against the stone cliff-wall and moved sideways, their hands spread to gain friction against the wall.

Wolff used both hands also; he had stuck the horn through the belt.

There was a howl from above. He looked up to see the first of the gworl dropping onto the ledge. Then he glanced back at Chryseis and almost fell off from shock. She was gone.

Slowly, he turned his head to see over his shoulder and down below. He fully expected to find her falling down the face of the cliff, if not already past it and plunging into the green abyss.

"Wolff!" she said. Her head was sticking out from the cliff itself. "There's a cave here. Hurry."

Trembling, sweating, he inched along the ledge to her and presently was inside an opening. The ceiling of the cave was several feet higher than his head; he could almost touch the walls on both sides when he stretched out his arms; the interior ran into the darkness.

"How far back does it go?"

"Not very far. But there's a natural shaft, a fault in the rock, that leads down. It opens on the bottom of the world; there's nothing below, nothing but air and sky."

"This can't be," he said slowly. "But it is. A universe founded on physical principles completely different than those of my universe. A flat planet with edges. But I don't understand how gravity works here. Where is its center?"

She shrugged and said, "The Lord may have told me a long time ago. But I've forgotten. I'd even forgotten he told me that Earth was round."

Wolff took the leather belt off, slid the scabbards off it, and picked up an oval black rock weighing about ten pounds. He slipped the belt through the buckle and then placed the stone within the loop. After piercing a hole near the buckle with the point of his knife, he tightened the loop. He had only to buckle the belt, and he was armed with a thong at the end of which was a heavy stone.

"You get behind and to one side of me," he said. "If I miss any, if one gets in past me, you push while he's off-balance. But don't go over yourself. Do you think you can do it?"

She nodded her head but evidently did not trust herself to speak.

"This is asking a lot of you. I'd understand if you cracked up completely. But, basically, you're made of sturdy ancient-Hellenic stock. They were a pretty tough lot in those days; you can't have lost your strength, even in this deadening pseudo-Paradise."

"I wasn't Achaean," she said. "I was Sminthean. But you are, in a way, right. I don't feel as badly as I thought I would. Only . . ."

"Only it takes getting used to," he said. He was encouraged, for he had expected a different reaction. If she could keep it up, the two of them might make it through this. But if she fell apart and he had a hysterical woman to control, both might fall under the attack of the gworl.

"Speaking of which," he muttered as he saw black, hairy, gnarled fingers slide around the corner of the cave. He swung the belt hard so that the stone at its end smashed the hand. There was a bellow of surprise and pain, then a long ululating scream as the gworl fell. Wolff did not wait for the next one to appear. He got as close to the lip of the cave ledge as he dared and swung the stone again. It whipped around the corner and thudded against something soft. Another scream came, and it, too, faded away into the nothingness of the green sky.

"Three down, seven to go! Provided that no more have joined them."

He said to Chryseis, "They may not be able to get in here. But they can starve us out."

"The horn?"

He laughed. "They wouldn't let us go now even if I did hand them the horn. And I don't intend for them to get it. I'll throw the horn into the sky rather than do that."

A figure was silhouetted against the mouth of the cave as it dropped from above. The gworl, swinging in, landed on his feet and teetered for a second. But he threw himself forward, rolled in a hairy ball, and was up on his feet again. Wolff was so surprised that he failed to react immediately. He had not expected them to be able to climb above the cave and let themselves down, for the rock above the cave had looked smooth. Somehow, one had done it, and now he was inside, on his feet, a knife in hand.

Wolff whirled the stone at the belt-end and loosed it at the gworl. The creature flipped its knife at him; Wolff dodged but spoiled his aim of the stone. It flew over the furry bumpy head; the thrown knife brushed him lightly on his shoulder. He jumped for his own knife on the floor of the cave, saw another dark shape drop into the cave from above, and a third come around the corner of the mouth.

Something hit his head. His vision blurred, his senses grew dim, his knees buckled.

When he awoke, a pain in the side of his head, he had a frightening sensation. He seemed to be upside down and floating above a vast polished black disc. A rope was tied around his neck, and his hands were tied behind his back. He was hanging with his feet up in the empty air, yet there was only a slight tension of rope around his neck.

Bending his head back, he could see that the rope led upward into a shaft in the disc and that at the far end of the shaft was a pale light.

He groaned and closed his eyes, but opened them again. The world seemed to spin. Suddenly he was reoriented. Now he knew that he was not suspended upside down against all the laws of gravity. He was hanging by a rope from the bottom underside of the planet. The green below him was the sky.

He thought, *I should have strangled before now. But there is no gravity pulling me downward.*

He kicked his feet, and the reaction drove him upward. The mouth of the shaft came closer. His head entered it, but something resisted him. His motion slowed, stopped, and, as if there were an invisible and compressed spring against his head, he began to move back down. Not until the rope tightened again did he stop his flight.

The gworl had done this to him. After knocking him out, they had let him down the shaft, or more probably, had carried him down. The shaft was narrow enough for a man to get down it with his back to one wall and his feet braced against the other. The descent would scrape the skin off a man, but the hairy hide of the gworl had looked tough enough to withstand descent and ascent without injury. Then a rope had been lowered, placed around his neck, and he had been dropped through the hole in the bottom of the world.

There was no way of getting himself back up. He would starve to death. His body would dangle in the winds of space until the rope rotted. He would not then fall, but would drift about in the shadow cast by the disc. The gworl he had knocked off the ledge had fallen, but their acceleration had kept them going.

Though despairing because of his situation, he could not help speculating about the gravitational configuration of the flat planet. The center must be at the very bottom; all attraction was upward through the mass of the planet. On this side, there was none.

What had the gworl done to Chryseis? Had they killed her as they had her friend?

He knew then that however they had dealt with her, they had purposely not hung her with him. They had planned that part of his agony would be that of not knowing her fate. As long as he could live at the end of this rope, he would wonder what had happened to her. He would conjure a multitude of possibilities, all horrible.

For a long time he hung suspended at a slight degree from the perpendicular, since the wind held him steady. Here, where there was no gravity, he could not swing like a pendulum.

Although he remained in the shadow of the black disc, he could see the progress of the sun. The sun itself was invisible, hidden by the disc, but the light from it fell on the rim of the great curve and slowly marched along it. The green sky beneath the sun glowed brightly, while the unlit portions before and after became dark. Then a paler lighting along the edge of the disc came into his sight, and he knew that the moon was following the sun.

It must be midnight, he thought. *If the gworl are taking her someplace, they could be some distance out on the sea. If they've been torturing her, she could be dead. If they've hurt her, I hope she's dead.*

Abruptly, while he hung in the gloom beneath the bottom of the world, he felt the rope at his neck jerk. The noose tightened, although not enough to choke him, and he was being drawn upward toward the shaft. He craned his neck to see who was hauling him up, but he could not penetrate the darkness of the mouth of the shaft. Then his head broke through the web of gravity—like surface tension on water, he thought—and he was hoisted clear of the abyss. Great strong hands and arms came around him to hug him against a hard, warm, furry chest. An alcoholic breath blew into his face. A leathery mouth scraped his cheek as the creature hugged him closer and began inching up the shaft with Wolff in its arms. Fur scraped on rock as the thing pushed with its legs. There was a jerk as the legs came up suddenly and took a new hold, followed by another scrape and lunge upward.

"Ipsewas?" Wolff said.

The zebrilla replied, "Ipsewas. Don't talk now. I have to save my wind. This isn't easy."

Wolff obeyed, although he had a difficult time in not asking about Chryseis. When they reached the top of the shaft, Ipsewas removed the rope from his neck and tossed him onto the floor of the cave.

Now at last he dared to speak. "Where is Chryseis?"

Ipsewas landed on the cave floor softly, turned Wolff over, and began to untie the knots around his wrists. He was breathing heavily from the trip up the shaft, but he said, "The gworl took her with them to a big dugout and began to sail across the sea toward the mountain. She shouted at me, begged me to help her. Then a gworl hit her, knocked her unconscious, I suppose. I was sitting there, drunk as the Lord, half-unconscious myself with nut juice, having a good time with Autonoe—you know, the *akowile* with the big mouth.

"Before Chryseis was knocked out, she screamed something about you hanging from the Hole in the Bottom of the World. I didn't know what she was talking about, because it's been a long time since I was here. How long ago I hate to say. Matter of fact, I don't really know. Everything's pretty much of a haze anymore, you know."

"No, I don't," Wolff said. He rose and rubbed his wrists. "But I'm afraid that if I stay here much longer, I might end up in an alcoholic fog, too."

"I was thinking about going after her," Ipsewas said. "But the gworl flashed those long knives at me and said they'd kill me. I watched them drag their boat out of the bushes, and about then I decided, what the hell, if they killed me, so what? I wasn't going to let them get away with threatening me or taking poor little Chryseis off to only the Lord knows what. Chryseis and I were friends in the old days, in the Troad, you know, although we haven't had too much to do with each other here for some time. I think it's been a long time. Anyway, I suddenly craved some real adventure, some genuine excitement—and I loathed those monstrous bumpy creatures.

"I ran after them, but by then they'd launched the boat, with Chryseis in it. I looked around for a *histoikhthys,* thinking I could ram their boat with it. Once I had them in the water, they'd be mine, knives or not. The way they acted in the boat showed me that they felt far from confident on the sea. I doubt they can even swim."

"I doubt it, too." Wolff said.

"But there wasn't a *histoikhthys* in reaching distance. And the wind was taking the boat away; it had a large lateen sail. I went back to Autonoe and took another drink. I might have forgotten about you, just as I was trying to forget about Chryseis. I was sure she was going to get hurt, and I couldn't bear to think about it, so I wanted to drink myself into oblivion. But Autonoe, bless her poor boozed-up brain, reminded me of what Chryseis had said about you."

"I took off fast, and looked around for awhile, because I couldn't remember just where the ledges were that led to the cave. I almost gave up and started drinking again. But something kept me going. Maybe I wanted to do just one good thing in this eternity of doing nothing, good or evil."

"If you hadn't come, I'd have hung there until I died of thirst. Now, Chryseis has a chance, if I can find her. I'm going after her. Do you want to come along?"

Wolff expected Ipsewas to say yes, but he did not think that Ipsewas would stick to his determination once the trip across the sea faced him. He was surprised, however.

The zebrilla swam out, seized a projection of shell as a *histoikhthys* sailed by, and swung himself upon the back of the creature. He guided it back to the beach by pressing upon the great nerve spots, dark purple blotches visible on the exposed skin just back of the cone-shaped shell that formed the prow of the creature.

Wolff, under Ipsewas' guidance, maintained pressure on a spot to hold the sailfish (for that was the literal translation of *histoikhthys*) on the beach. The zebrilla gathered several armloads of fruit and nuts and a large collection of the punchnuts.

"We have to eat and drink, especially drink," Ipsewas muttered. "It may be a long way across Okeanos to the foot of the mountain. I don't remember."

A few minutes after the supplies had been stored in one of the natural receptacles on the sailfish's shell, they left. The wind caught the thin cartilage sail, and the great mollusc gulped in water through its mouth and ejected it through a fleshy valve in its rear.

"The gworl have a headstart," Ipsewas said, "but they can't match our speed. They won't get to the other side long before we do." He broke open a punchnut and offered Wolff a drink. Wolff accepted. He was exhausted but nervestrung. He needed something to knock him out and let him sleep. A curve of the shell afforded a cavelike ledge for him to crawl within. He lay hugged against the bare skin of the sailfish, which was warm. In a short time he was asleep, but his last glimpse was of the shouldering bulk of Ipsewas, his stripes blurred in the moonlight, crouching by the nerve spots. Ipsewas was lifting another punchnut above his head and pouring the liquid contents into his outthrust gorilloid lips.

When Wolff awoke, he found the sun was just coming around the curve of the mountain. The full moon (it was always full, for the shadow of the planet never fell on it) was just slipping around the other side of the mountain.

Refreshed but hungry, he ate some of the fruit and the protein-rich nuts. Ipsewas showed him how he could vary his diet with the "bloodberries." These were shiny maroon balls that grew in clusters at the tips of fleshy stalks that sprouted out of the shell. Each was large as a baseball and had a thin, easily torn skin that exuded a liquid that looked and tasted like blood. The meat within tasted like raw beef with a soupçon of shrimp.

"They fall off when they're ripe, and the fish get most of them," Ipsewas said. "But some float in to the beach. They're best when you get them right off the stalk."

Wolff crouched down by Ipsewas. Between mouthfuls, he said, "The *histoikhthys* is handy. They seem almost too much of a good thing."

"The Lord designed and made them for our pleasure and his," Ipsewas replied.

"The Lord made this universe?" Wolff said, no longer sure that the story was a myth.

"You better believe it," Ipsewas replied, and took another drink. "Because if you don't, the Lord will end you. As it is, I doubt that he'll let you continue, anyway. He doesn't like uninvited guests."

Ipsewas lifted the nut and said, "Here's to your escaping his notice. And a sudden end and damnation to the Lord."

He dropped the nut and leaped at Wolff. Wolff was so taken by surprise he had no chance to defend himself. He went sprawling into the hollow of shell in which he had slept, with Ipsewas' bulk on him.

"Quiet!" Ipsewas said. "Stay curled up inside here until I tell you it's all right. It's an Eye of the Lord."

Wolff shrank back against the hard shell and tried to make himself one with the shadow of the interior. However, he did look out with one eye and thus he saw the ragged shadow of the raven scud across, followed by the creature itself. The dour bird flashed over once, wheeled, and began to glide in for a landing on the stern of the sailfish.

"Damn him! He can't help seeing me," Wolff muttered to himself.

"Don't panic," Ipsewas called. "Ahhh!"

There was a thud, a splash, and a scream that made Wolff start up and bump his head hard against the shell above him. Through the flashes of light and darkness, he saw the raven hanging limply within two giant claws. If the raven was eagle-sized, the killer that had dropped like a bolt from the green sky seemed, in that first second of shock, to be as huge as a roc. Wolff's vision straightened and cleared, and he saw an eagle with a light-green body, a pale red head, and a pale yellow beak. It was six times the bulk of the raven, and its wings, each at least thirty feet long, were flapping heavily as it strove to lift higher from the sea into which its missile thrust had carried both it and its prey. With each powerful downpush, it rose a few inches higher. Presently it began climbing higher, but before it got too far away, it turned its head and allowed Wolff to see its eyes. They were black shields mirroring the flames of death. Wolff shuddered; he had never seen such naked lust for killing.

"Well may you shudder," Ipsewas said. His grinning head was thrust into the cave of the shell. "That was one of Podarge's pets. Podarge hates the

Lord and would attack him herself if she got the chance, even if she knew it would be her end. Which it would. She knows she can't get near the Lord, but she can tell her pets to eat up the Eyes of the Lord. Which they do, as you have seen."

Wolff left the cavern of the shell and stood for awhile, watching the shrinking figure of the eagle and its kill.

"Who is Podarge?"

"She is, like me, one of the Lord's monsters. She, too, once lived on the shores of the Aegean; she was a beautiful young girl. That was when the great king Priamos and the godlike Akhilleus and crafty Odysseus lived. I knew them all; they would spit on the Kretan Ipsewas, the once-brave sailor and spear-fighter, if they could see me now. But I was talking of Podarge. The Lord took her to this world and fashioned a monstrous body and placed her brain within it.

"She lives up there someplace, in a cave on the very face of the mountain. She hates the Lord; she also hates every normal human being and will eat them, if her pets don't get them first. But most of all she hates the Lord."

That seemed to be all that Ipsewas knew about her, except that Podarge had not been her name before the Lord had taken her. Also, he remembered having been well acquainted with her. Wolff questioned him further, for he was interested in what Ipsewas could tell him about Agamemnon and Achilles and Odysseus and the other heroes of Homer's epic. He told the zebrilla that Agamemnon was supposed to be a historical character. But what about Achilles and Odysseus? Had they really existed?

"Of course they did," Ipsewas said. He grunted, then continued, "I suppose you're curious about those days. But there is little I can tell you. It's been too long ago. Too many idle days. Days?—centuries, millenia!—the Lord alone knows. Too much alcohol, too."

During the rest of the day and part of the night, Wolff tried to pump Ipsewas, but he got little for his trouble. Ipsewas, bored, drank half his supply of nuts and finally passed out snoring. Dawn came green and golden around the mountain. Wolff stared down into the waters, so clear that he could see the hundreds of thousands of fish, of fantastic configurations and splendors of colors. A bright-orange seal rose from the depths, a creature like a living diamond in its mouth. A purple-veined octopus, shooting backward, jetted by the seal. Far, far down, something enormous and white appeared for a second, then dived back toward the bottom.

Presently the roar of the surf came to him, and a thin white line frothed at the base of Thayaphayawoed. The mountain, so smooth at a distance, was now broken by fissures, by juts and spires, by rearing scarps and frozen fountains of stone. Thayaphayawoed went up and up and up; it seemed to hang over the world.

Wolff shook Ipsewas until, moaning and muttering, the zebrilla rose to his feet. He blinked reddened eyes, scratched, coughed, then reached for another punchnut. Finally, at Wolff's urging, he steered the sailfish so that its course paralleled the base of the mountain.

"I used to be familiar with this area," he said. "Once I thought about climbing the mountain, finding the Lord, and trying to . . ." He paused, scratched his head, winced, and said, "Kill him! There! I knew I could remember the word. But it was no use. I didn't have the guts to try it alone."

"You're with me now," Wolff said.

Ipsewas shook his head and took another drink. "Now isn't then. If you'd been with me then . . . Well, what's the use of talking? You weren't even born then. Your great-great-great-great-grandfather wasn't born then. No, it's too late."

He was silent while he busied himself with guiding the sailfish through an opening in the mountain. The great creature abruptly swerved; the cartilage sail folded up against the mast of stiff bone-braced cartilage; the body rose on a huge wave. And then they were within the calm waters of a narrow, steep, and dark fjord.

Ipsewas pointed at a series of rough ledges.

"Take that. You can get far. How far I don't know. I got tired and scared and I went back to the Garden. Never to return, I thought."

Wolff pleaded with Ipsewas. He said that he needed Ipsewas' strength very much and that Chryseis needed him. But the zebrilla shook his massive somber head.

"I'll give you my blessing, for what it's worth."

"And I thank you for what you've done," Wolff said. "If you hadn't cared enough to come after me, I'd still be swinging at the end of a rope. Maybe I'll see you again. With Chryseis."

"The Lord is too powerful," Ipsewas replied. "Do you think you have a chance against a being who can create his own private universe?"

"I have a chance," Wolff said. "As long as I fight and use my wits and have some luck, I have a chance."

He jumped off the decklike shell and almost slipped on the wet rock. Ipsewas called, "A bad omen, my friend!"

Wolff turned and smiled at him and shouted, "I don't believe in omens, my superstitious Greek friend! So long!"

5

HE BEGAN CLIMBING AND DID NOT STOP TO LOOK DOWN UNTIL about an hour had passed. The great white body of the *histoikhthys* was a slim, pale thread by then, and Ipsewas was only a black dot on its axis. Although he knew he could not be seen, he waved at Ipsewas and resumed climbing.

Another hour's scrambling and clinging on the rocks brought him out of the fjord and onto a broad ledge on the face of the cliff. Here it was bright sunshine again. The mountain seemed as high as ever, and the way was as hard. On the other hand, it seemed no more difficult, although that was nothing over which to exult. His hands and knees were bleeding and the ascent had made him tired. At first he was going to spend the night there, but he changed his mind. As long as the light lasted, he should take advantage of it.

Again he wondered if Ipsewas was correct about the gworl probably having taken just this route. Ipsewas claimed that there were other passages along the mountain where the sea rammed against it, but these were far away. He had looked for signs that the gworl had come this way and had found none. This did not mean that they had taken another path—if you could call this ragged verticality a path.

A few minutes later he came to one of the many trees that grew out of the rock itself. Beneath its twisted gray branches and mottled brown and green leaves were broken and empty nutshells and the cores of fruit. They were fresh. Somebody had paused for lunch not too long ago. The sight gave him new strength. Also, there was enough meat left in the nutshells for him to half-satisfy the pangs in his belly. The remnants of the fruits gave him moisture to put in his dry mouth.

Six days he climbed, and six nights rested. There was life on the face of the perpendicular, small trees and large bushes grew on the ledges, from the caves, and from the cracks. Birds of all sorts abounded, and many little animals. These fed off the berries and nuts or on each other. He killed birds with stones and ate their flesh raw. He discovered flint and chipped out a crude but sharp knife. With this, he made a short spear with a wooden shaft and another flint for the tip. He grew lean and hard with thick callouses on his hands and feet and knees. His beard lengthened.

One the morning of the seventh day, he looked out from a ledge and estimated that he must be at least twelve thousand feet above the sea. Yet the air was no thinner or colder than when he had begun climbing. The sea, which must have been at least two hundred miles across, looked like a broad river. Beyond was the rim of the world's edge, the Garden from which he had set out in pursuit of Chryseis and the gworl. It was as narrow as a cat's whisker. Beyond it, only the green sky.

At midnoon on the eighth day, he came across a snake feeding upon a dead gworl. Forty feet long, it was covered with black diamond spots and crimson seals of Solomon. The feet that arrayed both sides grew out of the body without the blessing of legs and were distressingly human-shaped. Its jaws were lined with three rows of sharkish teeth.

Wolff attacked it boldly, because he saw that a knife was sticking from its middle part and fresh blood was still oozing out. The snake hissed, uncoiled, and began to back away. Wolff stabbed at it a few times, and it lunged at him. Wolff drove the point of the flint into one of the large dull-green eyes. The snake hissed loudly and reared, its two-score of five-toed feet kicking. Wolff tore the spear loose from the bloodied eye and thrust it into the dead white area just below the snake's jaw. The flint went in deeply; the snake jerked so violently that it tore the shaft loose from Wolff's grip. But the creature fell over on its side, breathing deeply, and after awhile it died.

There was a scream above him, followed by a shadow. Wolff had heard that scream before, when he had been on the sailfish. He dived to one side and rolled across the ledge. Coming to a fissure, he crawled within it and turned to see what had threatened him. It was one of the enormous, wide-winged, green-bodied, red-headed, yellow-beaked eagles. It was crouched on the snake and tearing out gobbets with a beak as sharp as the teeth in the snake's jaws. Between gulps it glared at Wolff, who tried to shrink even further within the protection of the fissure.

Wolff had to stay within his crevice until the bird had filled its crop. Since this took all the rest of the day and the eagle did not leave the two corpses that night, Wolff became hungry, thirsty, and more than uncomfortable. By morning, he was also getting angry. The eagle was sitting by the two corpses, its wings folded around its body and its head drooping. Wolff thought that, if it were asleep, now would be the time to make a break. He stepped out of the crevice, wincing with the pain of stiff muscles. As he did so, the eagle jerked its head up, half-spread its wings, and screamed at him. Wolff retreated to the crevice.

By noon, the eagle still showed no intention of leaving. It ate little and seemed to be fighting drowsiness. Occasionally it belched. The sun beat down upon the bird and the two corpses. All three stank. Wolff began to despair. For all he knew, the eagle would remain until it had picked both reptile and gworl bare to the bone. By that time, he, Wolff, would be half-dead of starvation and thirst.

He left the fissure and picked up the spear. This had fallen out when the bird had ripped out the flesh around it. He jabbed threateningly at the eagle, which glared, hissed, and then screamed at him. Wolff shouted back and slowly backed away from the bird. It advanced with short slow steps, rolling slightly. Wolff stopped, yelled again, and jumped at the eagle. Startled, it leaped back and screamed again.

Wolff resumed his cautious retreat, but this time the eagle did not go after him. Only when the curve of the mountain took the predator out of view did Wolff resume climbing. He made sure that there was always a place to dodge into if the bird should come after him. However, no shadow fell on him. Apparently the eagle had wanted only to protect its food.

The middle of the next morning, he came across another gworl. This one had a smashed leg and was sitting with its back against the trunk of a small tree. It brandished a knife at a dozen red and rangy hoglike beasts with hooves like those of mountain goats. These paced back and forth before the crippled gworl and grunted in their throats. Now and then one made a short charge, but stopped a few feet away from the waving knife.

Wolff climbed a boulder and began throwing rocks at the hooved carnivores. A minute later, he wished he had not drawn attention to himself. The beasts clambered up the steep boulder as if stairs had been built for them. Only by rapid thrusting with the spear did he manage to push them back down on the ledge below. The flint tip dug into their tough hides a little but not enough to seriously hurt them.

Squealing, they landed on the rock below, only to scramble back up toward him. Their boar-tusks slashed close to him; a pair almost snipped one of his feet. He was busy trying to keep them from swarming over him when a moment came when all were on the ledge and none on the boulder. He dropped his spear, lifted a rock twice the size of his head, and hurled it down on the back of a boar. The beast screamed and tried to crawl away on its two undamaged front legs. The pack closed in on his paralyzed rear legs and began eating them. When the wounded beast turned to defend himself, he was seized by the throat. In a moment he was dead and being torn apart.

Wolff picked up his spear, climbed down the other side of the rock, and walked to the gworl. He kept an eye upon the feeders, but they did no more than raise their heads briefly to check on him before resuming their tearing at the carcass.

The gworl snarled at Wolff and held its knife ready. Wolff stopped far enough away so that he could dodge if the knife were thrown. A splinter of bone stuck out from the ravaged leg below the knee. The eyes of the gworl, sunk under the pads of cartilage on its low forehead, looked glassy.

Wolff had an unexpected reaction. He had thought that he would at once and savagely kill any gworl he came across. But now he wanted to talk to him. So lonely had he become during the days and nights of climbing that he was glad to speak even to this loathsome creature.

He said, in Greek, "Is there any way in which I can help you?"

The gworl spoke in the back-of-the-throat syllables of its kind and raised the knife. Wolff started walking toward it, then hurled himself to one side as the knife whished by his head. He retrieved the knife, then walked up to the gworl and spoke to him again. The thing grated back, but in a weaker voice. Wolff, bending over to repeat his question, was struck in the face with a mass of saliva.

That triggered off his hate and fear. He rammed the knife into the thick neck; the gworl kicked violently several times and died. Wolff wiped the knife on the dark fur and looked through the leather bag attached to the gworl's belt. It contained dried meat, dried fruit, some dark, hard bread, and a canteen with a fiery liquor. Wolff was not sure about where the meat came from, but he told himself that he was too hungry to be picky. Biting into the bread was an experience; it was almost as hard as stone but, when softened with saliva, tasted like graham crackers.

Wolff kept on climbing. The days and nights passed with no more signs of the gworl. The air was as thick and warm as at sea level, yet he estimated that he must be at least 30,000 feet up. The sea below was a thin silver girdle around the waist of the world.

That night he awakened to feel dozens of small furry hands on his body. He struggled, only to find that the many hands were too strong. They gripped him fast while others tied his hands and feet together with a rope that had a grassy texture. Presently he was lifted high and carried out onto the stone apron before the small cave in which he had slept. The moonlight showed several score bipeds, each about two and a half feet high. They were covered with sleek gray fur, mouselike, but had a white ruff around their necks. The faces were black and pushed in and resembled a bat's. Their ears were enormous and pointed.

Silently, they rushed him over the apron and into another fissure. This opened to reveal a large chamber about thirty feet wide and twenty high. Moonlight bored through a crack in the ceiling and revealed what his nose had already detected, a pile of bones with some rotting flesh. He was set down near the bones while his captors retreated to one corner of the cave. They began talking, or at least twittering, among themselves. One walked over to Wolff, looked at him a moment, and sank onto his knees by Wolff's throat. A second later, he was gnawing at the throat with tiny but very sharp teeth. Others followed him; teeth began chewing all over his body.

It was all done in a literally deadly silence. Even Wolff made no noise beyond his harsh breathing as he struggled. The sharp little pains of the teeth quickly passed, as if some mild anaesthetic were being released into his blood.

He began to feel drowsy. Despite himself, he quit fighting. A pleasant numbness spread through him. It did not seem worthwhile to battle for his life; why not go out pleasantly? At least his death would not be useless. There was something noble in giving his body so that these little beings could fill their bellies and be well-fed and happy for a few days.

A light burst into the cave. Through the warm haze, he saw the bat-faces leap away from him and run to the extreme end of the cave, where they cowered together. The light became stronger and was revealed as a torch of burning pine. An old man's face followed the light and bent over him. He had a long white beard, a sunken mouth, a curved sharp nose, and huge supraorbital ridges with bristling eyebrows. A dirty white robe covered his shrunken body. His big-veined hand held a staff on the end of which was a sapphire, large as Wolff's fist, carved in the image of a harpy.

Wolff tried to speak but could only mutter a tangled speech, as if he were coming up out of ether after an operation. The old man gestured with the staff, and several of the batfaces detached themselves from the mass of fur. They scurried sideways across the floor, their slanted eyes turned fearfully toward the old man. Quickly, they untied Wolff. He managed to rise to his feet, but he was so wobbly that the old man had to support him out of the cave.

The ancient spoke in Mycenaean Greek. "You'll feel better soon. The venom does not last long."

"Who are you? Where are you taking me?"

"Out of this danger," the old man said. Wolff pondered the enigmatic answer. By the time that his mind and body were functioning well again, they had come to another entrance to a cave. They went through a complex of chambers that gradually led them upward. When they had covered about two miles, the old man stopped before a cave with an iron door. He handed the torch to Wolff, pulled the door open, and waved him on in. Wolff entered into a large cavern bright with torches. The door clanged behind him, succeeded by the thud of a bolt shooting fast.

The first thing that struck him was the choking odor. The next, the two green red-headed eagles that closed in on him. One spoke in a voice like a giant parrot's and ordered him to march on ahead. He did so, noting at the same time that the batfaces must have removed his knife. The weapon would not have done him much good. The cave was thronged with the birds, each of which towered above him.

Against one wall were two cages made of thin iron bars. In one was a group of six gworl. In the other was a tall well-built youth wearing a deerskin breechcloth. He grinned at Wolff and said, "So you made it! How you've changed!"

Only then did the reddish-bronze hair, long upper lip, and craggy but merry face become familiar. Wolff recognized the man who had thrown the horn from the gworl-besieged boulder and who called himself Kickaha.

6

WOLFF DID NOT HAVE TIME TO REPLY, FOR THE CAGE DOOR WAS opened by one of the eagles, who used his foot as effectively as a hand. A powerful head and hard break shoved him into the cage; the door ground shut behind him.

"So, here you are," Kickaha said in a rich baritone voice. "The question is, what do we do now? Our stay here may be short and unpleasant."

Wolff, looking through the bars, saw a throne carved out of rock, and on it a woman. A half-woman, rather, for she had wings instead of arms and the lower part of her body was that of a bird. The legs, however, were much thicker in proportion than those of a normal-sized Earth eagle. They had to support more weight, Wolff thought, and he knew that here was another of the Lord's laboratory-produced monsters. She must be the Podarge of whom Ipsewas had spoken.

From the waist up she was such a woman as few men are privileged to see. Her skin was white as a milky opal, her breasts superb, the throat a column of beauty. The hair was long and black and straight and fell on both sides of a face that was even more beautiful than Chryseis', an admission that he had not thought it possible to evoke from him.

However, there was something horrible in the beauty: a madness. The eyes were fierce as those of a caged falcon teased beyond endurance.

Wolff tore his eyes from hers and looked about the cave. "Where is Chryseis?" he whispered.

"Who?" Kickaha whispered back.

With a few quick sentences, Wolff described her and what had happened to him.

Kickaha shook his head. "I've never seen her."

"But the gworl?"

"There were two bands of them. The other must have Chryseis and the horn. Don't worry about them. If we don't talk our way out of this, we're done for. And in a very hideous way."

Wolff asked about the old man. Kickaha replied that he had once been

Podarge's lover. He was an aborigine, one of those who had been brought into this universe shortly after the Lord had fashioned it. The harpy now kept him to do the menial work which required human hands. The old man had come at Podarge's order to rescue Wolff from the batfaces, undoubtedly because she had long ago heard from her pets of Wolff's presence in her domain.

Podarge stirred restlessly on her throne and unfolded her wings. They came together before her with a splitting noise like distant lightning.

"You two there!" she shouted. "Quit your whispering! Kickaha, what more do you have to say for yourself before I loose my pets?"

"I can only repeat, at the risk of seeming tiresome, what I said before!" Kickaha replied loudly. "I am as much the enemy of the Lord as you, and he hates me, he would kill me! He knows I stole his horn and that I'm a danger to him. His Eyes rove the four levels of the world and fly up and down the mountains to find me. And . . ."

"Where is this horn you said you stole from the Lord? Why don't you have it now? I think you are lying to save your worthless carcass!"

"I told you that I opened a gate to the next world and that I threw it to a man who appeared at the gate. He stands before you now."

Podarge turned her head as an eagle swivels hers, and she glared at Wolff. "I see no horn. I see only some tough stringy meat behind a black beard!"

"He says that another band of gworl stole it from him," Kickaha replied. "He was chasing after them to get it back when the batfaces captured him and you so magnanimously rescued him. Release us, gracious and beautiful Podarge, and we will get the horn back. With it, we will be in a position to fight the Lord. He can be beaten! He may be the powerful Lord, but he is not all-powerful! If he were, he would have found us and the horn long ago!"

Podarge stood up, preened her wings, and walked down the steps from the throne and across the floor to the cage. She did not bob as a bird does when walking, but strode stiff-legged.

"I wish that I could believe you," she said in a lower but just as intense voice. "If only I could! I have waited through the years and the centuries and the millenia, oh, so long that my heart aches to think of the time! If I thought that the weapons for striking back at him had finally come within my hands . . ."

She stared at them, held her wings out before her, and said, "See! 'My hands,' I said. But I do not have hands, nor the body that was once mine. That . . ." And she burst into a raging invective that made Wolff shrink. It was not the words but the fury, bordering on divinity or mindlessness, that made him grow cold.

"If the Lord can be overthrown—and I believe he can—you will be given back your human body," Kickaha said when she had finished.

She panted with a clench of her anger and stared at them with the lust of murder. Wolff felt that all was lost, but her next words showed that the passion was not for them.

"The old Lord has been gone for a long time, so the rumor says. I sent one of my pets to investigate, and she came back with a strange tale. She said that there is a new Lord there, but she did not know whether or not it was the same Lord in a new body. I sent her back to the Lord, who refused my pleas to be given my rightful body again. So it does not matter whether or not there is another Lord. He is just as evil and hateful as the old one, if he is indeed not the old one. But I must know!

"First, whoever now is the Lord must die. Then I will find out if he had a new body or not. If the old Lord has left this universe, I will track him through the worlds and find him!"

"You can't do that without the horn," Kickaha said. "It and it alone opens the gate without a counter-device in the other world."

"What have I to lose?" Podarge said. "If you are lying and betray me, I will have you in the end, and the hunt might be fun. If you mean what you say, then we will see what happens."

She spoke to the eagle beside her, and it opened the gate. Kickaha and Wolff followed the harpy across the cave to a great table with chairs around it. Only then did Wolff see that the chamber was a treasure house; the loot of a world was piled up in it. There were large open chests crammed with gleaming jewels, pearl necklaces, and golden and silver cups of exquisite shape. There were small figurines of ivory and of some shining hard-grained black wood. There were magnificent paintings. Armor and weapons of all kinds, except firearms, were piled carelessly at various places.

Podarge commanded them to sit down in ornately wrought chairs with carved lion's feet. She beckoned with a wing, and out of the shadows stepped a young man. He carried a heavy golden tray on which were three finely chiseled cups of crystal-quartz. These were fashioned as leaping fish with wide open mouths; the mouths were filled with a rich dark red wine.

"One of her lovers," Kickaha whispered in answer to Wolff's curious stare at the handsome blond youth. "Carried by her eagles from the level known as Dracheland or Teutonia. Poor fellow! But it's better than being eaten alive by her pets, and he always has the hope of escaping to make his life bearable."

Kickaha drank and breathed out satisfaction at the heavy but blood-brightening taste. Wolff felt the wine writhe as if alive. Podarge gripped the cup between the tips of her two wings and lifted it to her lips.

"To the death and damnation of the Lord. Therefore, to your success!"

The two drank again. Podarge put her cup down and flicked Wolff lightly across the face with the ends of the feathers of one wing. "Tell me your story."

Wolff talked for a long while. He ate from slices of a roast goat-pig, a light brown bread, and fruit, and he drank the wine. His head began reeling, but he talked on and on, stopping only when Podarge questioned him about something. Fresh torches replaced the old and still he talked.

Abruptly, he awoke. Sunshine was coming in from another cave, lighting the empty cup and the table on which his head had lain while he had slept. Kickaha, grinning, stood by him.

"Let's go," he said. "Podarge wants us to get started early. She's eager for revenge. And I want to get out before she changes her mind. You don't know how lucky we are. We're the only prisoners she's ever given freedom."

Wolff sat up and groaned with the ache in his shoulders and neck. His head felt fuzzy and a little heavy, but he had had worse hangovers.

"What did you do after I fell asleep?" he said.

Kickaha smiled broadly. "I paid the final price. But it wasn't bad, not bad at all. Rather peculiar at first, but I'm an adaptable fellow."

They walked out of the cave into the next one and from thence onto the wide lip of stone jutting from the cliff. Wolff turned for one last look and saw several eagles, green monoliths, standing by the entrance to the inner cave. There was a flash of white skin and black wings as Podarge crossed stiff-legged before the giant birds.

"Come on," Kickaha said. "Podarge and her pets are hungry. You didn't see her try to get the gworl to plead for mercy. I'll say one thing for them, they didn't whine or cry. They spat at her."

Wolff jumped as a ripsaw scream came from the cave mouth. Kickaha took Wolff's arm and urged him into a fast walk. More jagged cries tore from eagle beaks, mingled with the ululations from beings in fear and pain of death.

"That'd be us, too," Kickaha said, "if we hadn't had something to trade for our lives."

They began climbing and by nightfall were three thousand feet higher. Kickaha untied the knapsack of leather from his back and produced various articles. Among these was a box of matches, with one of which he started a fire. Meat and bread and a small bottle of the Rhadamanthean wine followed. The bag and the contents were gifts from Podarge.

"We've got about four days of climbing before we get to the next level," the youth said. "Then, the fabulous world of Amerindia."

Wolff started to ask questions, but Kickaha said the he ought to explain the physical structure of the planet. Wolff listened patiently, and when he had heard Kickaha out, he did not scoff. Moreover, Kickaha's explanation corresponded with what he had so far seen. Wolff's intentions to ask how Kickaha, obviously a native of Earth, had come here were frustrated. The youth, complaining that he had not slept for a long time and had had an especially exhausting night, fell asleep.

Wolff stared for awhile into the flames of the dying fire. He had seen and experienced much in a short time, but he had much more to go through. That is, he would if he lived. A whooping cry rose from the depths, and a great green eagle screamed somewhere in the air along the mountain-face.

He wondered where Chryseis was tonight. Was she alive and if so, how was she faring? And where was the horn? Kickaha had said that they had to find the horn if they were to have any success at all. Without it, they would inevitably lose.

So thinking, he too fell asleep.

Four days later, when the sun was in the midpoint of its course around the planet, they pulled themselves over the rim. Before them was a plain that rolled for at least 160 miles before the horizon dropped it out of sight. To both sides, perhaps a hundred miles away, were mountain ranges. These might be large enough to cause comparison with the Himalayas. But they were mice beside the monolith, Abharhploonta, that dominated this section of the multilevel planet. Abharhploonta was, so Kickaha claimed, fifteen hundred miles from the rim, yet it looked no more than fifty miles away. It towered fully as high as the mountain up which they had just climbed.

"Now you get the idea," Kickaha said. "This world is not pear-shaped. It's a planetary Tower of Babylon. A series of staggered columns, each smaller than the one beneath it. On the very apex of this Earth-sized tower is the palace of the Lord. As you can see, we have a long way to go.

"But it's a great life while it lasts! I've had a wild and wonderful time! If the Lord struck me at this moment, I couldn't complain. Although, of course, I would, being human and therefore bitter about being cut off in my prime! And believe me, my friend, I'm prime!"

Wolff could not help smiling at the youth. He looked so gay and buoyant, like a bronze statue suddenly touched into animation and overflowingly joyous because he was alive.

"Okay!" Kickaha cried. "The first thing we have to do is get some fitting clothes for you! Nakedness is chic in the level below, but not on this one. You have to wear at least a breechcloth and a feather in your hair; otherwise the natives will have contempt for you. And contempt here means slavery or death for the contemptible."

He began walking along the rim, Wolff with him.

"Observe how green and lush the grass is and how it is as high as our knees, Bob. It affords pasture for browsers and grazers. But it is also high enough to conceal the beasts that feed on the grass-eaters. So beware! The plains puma and the dire wolf and the striped hunting dog and the giant weasel prowl through the grasses. Then there is Felis Atrox, whom I call the atrocious lion. He once roamed the plains of the North American

Southwest, became extinct there about 10,000 years ago. He's very much alive here, one-third larger than the African lion and twice as nasty.

"Hey, look there! Mammoths!"

Wolff wanted to stop to watch the huge gray beasts, which were about a quarter of a mile away. But Kickaha urged him on. "There're plenty more around, and there'll be times when you wish there weren't. Spend your time watching the grass. If it moves contrary to the wind, tell me."

They walked swiftly for two miles. During this time, they came close to a band of wild horses. The stallions whickered and raced up to investigate them, then stood their ground, pawing and snorting, until the two had passed. They were magnificent animals, tall, sleek, and black or glossy red or spotted white and black.

"Nothing of your Indian pony there," Kickaha said. "I think the Lord imported nothing but the best stock."

Presently, Kickaha stopped by a pile of rocks. "My marker," he said. He walked straight inward across the plain from the cairn. After a mile they came to a tall tree. The youth leaped up, grabbed the lowest branch, and began climbing. Halfway up, he reached a hollow and brought out a large bag. On returning, Kickaha took out of the bag two bows, two quivers of arrows, a deerskin breechcloth, and a belt with a skin scabbard in which was a long steel knife.

Wolff put on the loincloth and belt and took the bow and quiver.

"You know how to use these?" Kickaha said.

"I've practised all my life."

"Good. You'll get more than one chance to put your skill to the test. Let's go. We've many a mile to cover."

They began wolf-trotting: run a hundred steps, walk a hundred steps. Kickaha pointed to the range of mountains to their right.

"There is where my tribe, the Hrowakas, the Bear People, live. Eighty miles away. Once we get there, we can take it easy for awhile, and make preparations for the long journey ahead of us."

"You don't look like an Indian," Wolff said.

"And you, my friend, don't look like a sixty-six-year-old man, either. But here we are. Okay. I've put off telling my story because I wanted to hear yours first. Tonight I'll talk."

They did not speak much more that day. Wolff exclaimed now and then at the animals he saw. There were great herds of bison, dark, shaggy, bearded, and far larger than their cousins of Earth. There were other herds of horses and a creature that looked like the prototype of the camel. More mammoths and then a family of steppe mastodons. A pack of six dire wolves raced alongside the two for awhile at a distance of a hundred yards. These stood almost as high as Wolff's shoulder.

Kickaha, seeing Wolff's alarm, laughed and said, "They won't attack us unless they're hungry. That isn't very likely with all the game around here. They're just curious."

Presently, the giant wolves curved away, their speed increasing as they flushed some striped antelopes out of a grove of trees.

"This is North America as it was a long time before the white man," Kickaha said, "Fresh, spacious, with a multitude of animals and a few tribes roaming around."

A flock of a hundred ducks flew overhead, honking. Out of the green sky, a hawk fell, struck with a thud, and the flock was minus one comrade. "The Happy Hunting Ground!" Kickaha cried. "Only it's not so happy sometimes."

Several hours before the sun went around the mountain, they stopped by a small lake. Kickaha found the tree in which he had built a platform.

"We'll sleep here tonight, taking turns on watch. About the only animal that might attack us in the tree is the giant weasel, but he's enough to worry about. Besides, and worse, there could be war parties."

Kickaha left with his bow in hand and returned in fifteen minutes with a large buck rabbit. Wolff had started a small fire with little smoke; over this they roasted the rabbit. While they ate, Kickaha explained the topography of the country.

"Whatever else you can say about the Lord, you can't deny he did a good job of designing this world. You take this level, Amerindia. It's not really flat. It has a series of slight curves each about 160 miles long. These allow the water to run off, creeks and rivers and lakes to form. There's no snow anywhere on the planet—can't be, with no seasons and a fairly uniform climate. But it rains every day—the clouds come in from space somewhere."

They finished eating the rabbit and covered the fire. Wolff took first watch. Kickaha talked all through Wolff's turn at guard. And Wolff stayed awake through Kickaha's watch to listen.

In the beginning, a long time ago, more than 20,000 years, the Lords had dwelt in a universe parallel to Earth's. They were not known as the Lords then. There were not very many of them at that time, for they were the survivors of a millenia-long struggle with another species. They numbered perhaps ten thousand in all.

"But what they lacked in quantity they more than possessed in quality," Kickaha said. "They had a science and technology that makes ours, Earth's, look like the wisdom of Tasmanian aborigines. They were able to construct these private universes. And they did.

"At first each universe was a sort of playground, a microcosmic country club for small groups. Then, as was inevitable, since these people were human beings no matter how godlike in their powers, they quarreled. The feeling of property was, is, as strong in them as in us. There was a struggle among them. I suppose there were also deaths from accident and suicide. Also, the isolation and loneliness of the Lords made them megalomaniacs, natural when you consider that each played the part of a little god and came to believe in his role.

"To compress an eons-long story into a few words, the Lord who built this particular universe eventually found himself alone. Jadawin was his name, and he did not even have a mate of his own kind. He did not want one. Why should he share this world with an equal, when he could be a Zeus with a million Europas, with the loveliest of Ledas?

"He had populated this world with beings abducted from other universes, mainly Earth's, or created in the laboratories in the palace on top of the highest tier. He had created divine beauties and exotic monsters as he wished.

"The only trouble was, the Lords were not content to rule over just one universe. They began to covet the worlds of the others. And so the struggle was continued. They erected nearly impregnable defenses and conceived almost invincible offenses. The battle became a deadly game. This fatal play was inevitable, when you consider that boredom and ennui were enemies the Lords could not keep away. When you are near-omnipotent, and your creatures are too lowly and weak to interest you forever, what thrill is there besides risking your immortality against another immortal?"

"But how did you come into this?" Wolff said.

"I? My name on Earth was Paul Janus Finnegan. My middle name was my mother's family name. As you know, it also happens to be that of the Latin god of gates and of the old and new year, the god with two faces, one looking ahead and one looking behind."

Kickaha grinned and said, "Janus is very appropriate, don't you think? I am a man of two worlds, and I came through the gate between. Not that I have ever returned to Earth or want to. I've had adventures and I've gained a stature here I never could have had on that grimy old globe. Kickaha isn't my only name, and I'm a chief on this tier and a big shot of sorts on other tiers. As you will find out."

Wolff was beginning to wonder about him. He had been so evasive that Wolff suspected Kickaha had another identity about which he did not intend to talk.

"I know what you're thinking, but don't you believe it," Kickaha said. "I'm a trickster, but I'm leveling with you. By the way, did you know how I came by my name among the Bear People? In their language, a *kickaha* is a mythological character, a semidivine trickster. Something like the Old Man Coyote of the Plains or Nanabozho of the Ojibway or Wakdjunkaga of the Winnebago. Some day I'll tell you how I earned that name and how I became a councilor of the Hrowakas. But I've more important things to tell you now."

7

IN 1941, AT THE AGE OF TWENTY-THREE PAUL FINNEGAN HAD volunteered for the U.S. Cavalry because he loved horses. A short time later, he found himself driving a tank. He was with the Eighth Army and so eventually crossed the Rhine. One day, after having helped take a small town, he discovered an extraordinary object in the ruins of the local museum. It was a crescent of silvery metal, so hard that hammer blows did not dent it nor an acetylene torch melt it.

"I asked some of the citizens about it. All they knew was that it had been in the museum a long time. A professor of chemistry, after making some tests on it, had tried to interest the University of Munich in it but had failed.

"I took it home with me after the war, along with other souvenirs. Then I went back to the University of Indiana. My father had left me enough money to see me through for a few years, so I had a nice little apartment, a sports car, and so on.

"A friend of mine was a newspaper reporter. I told him about the crescent and its peculiar properties and unknown composition. He wrote a story about it which was printed in Bloomington, and the story was picked up by a syndicate. It didn't create much interest among scientists—in fact, they wanted nothing to do with it.

"Three days later, a man calling himself Mr. Vannax appeared at my apartment. I thought he was Dutch because of his name and his foreign accent. He wanted to see the crescent. I obliged. He got very excited, although he tried to to appear calm. He said he'd like to buy it from me. I asked how much he'd pay, and he said he'd give ten thousand dollars, but no more.

" 'Sure you can go higher,' I said," Kickaha continued. " 'Because if you don't, you'll get nowhere.'

" 'Twenty thousand?' Vannax said.

" 'Let's pump it up a bit,' I said.

" 'Thirty thousand?' "

Finnegan decided to plunge. He asked Vannax if he would pay

$100,000. Vannax became even redder in the face and swelled up "like a hoppy toad," as Finnegan-Kickaha said. But he replied that he would have the sum in twenty-four hours.

"Then I knew I really had something," Kickaha said to Wolff. "The question was, what? Also, why did this Vannax character so desperately want it? And what kind of a nut was he? No one with good sense, no normal human being, would rise so fast to the bait. He'd be cagier."

"What did Vannax look like?" Wolff asked.

"Oh, he was a big guy, a well-preserved sixty-five. He had an eagle beak and eagle eyes. He was dressed in expensive conservative clothes. He had a powerful personality, but he was trying to restrain it, to be real nice. And having a hell of a time doing it. He seemed to be a man who wasn't used to being balked in any thing."

" 'Make it $300,000, and it's yours' I said. I never dreamed he'd say yes. I thought he'd get mad and take off. Because I wasn't going to sell the crescent, not if he offered me a million."

Vannax, although furious, said that he would pay $300,000 but Finnegan would have to give him an additional twenty-four hours.

" 'You have to tell me why you want the crescent and what good it is first,' I said.

" 'Nothing doing!' he shouted. 'It is enough for you to rob me, you pig of a merchant, you, you earth . . . worm!'

" 'Get out before I throw you out. Or before I call the police,' I said."

Vannax began shouting in a foreign tongue. Finnegan went into his bedroom and came out with a .45 automatic. Vannax did not know it was not loaded. He left, although he was cursing and talking to himself all the way to his 1940 Rolls-Royce.

That night Finnegan had trouble getting to sleep. It was after 2:00 A.M. before he succeeded, and even then he kept waking up. During one of his rousings he heard a noise in the front room. Quietly, he rolled out of bed and took the .45, now loaded, from under his pillow. On the way to the bedroom door he picked up his flashlight from the bureau.

Its beam caught Vannax stooping over in the middle of the living room. The silvery crescent was in his hand.

"Then I saw the second crescent on the floor. Vannax had brought another with him. I'd caught him in the act of placing the two together to form a complete circle. I didn't know why he was doing it, but I found out a moment later.

"I told him to put his hands up. He did so, but he lifted his foot to step into the circle. I told him not to move even a trifle, or I'd shoot. He put one foot inside the circle, anyway. So I fired. I shot over his head, and the slug went into a corner of the room. I just wanted to scare him, figuring if he got shaken up enough he might start talking. He was scared all right; he jumped back.

"I walked across the room while he backed up toward the door. He was babbling like a maniac, threatening me in one breath and offering me half a million in the next. I thought I'd back him up against the door and jam the .45 in his belly. He'd really talk then, spill his guts out about the crescent.

"But as I followed him across the room I stepped into the circle formed by the two crescents. He saw what I was doing and screamed at me not to. Too late then. He and the apartment disappeared, and I found myself still in the circle—only it wasn't quite the same—and in this world. In the palace of the Lord, on top of the world."

Kickaha said he might have gone into shock then. But he had avidly read fantasy and science-fiction since the fourth grade of grammar school. The idea of parallel universes and devices for transition between them was familiar. He had been conditioned to accept such concepts. In fact, he half-believed in them. Thus he was flexible-minded enough to bend without breaking and then bounce back. Although frightened, he was at the same time excited and curious.

"I figured out why Vannax hadn't followed me through the gate. The two crescents, placed together, formed a 'circuit'. But they weren't activated until a living being stepped within whatever sort of 'field' they radiated. Then one semicircle remained behind on Earth while the other was gated through to this universe, where it latched onto a semicircle waiting for it. In other words, it takes three crescents to make a circuit. One in the world to which you're going, and two in the one you're leaving. You step in; one crescent transfers over to the single one in the next universe, leaving only one crescent in the world you just left.

"Vannax must have come to Earth by means of these crescents. And he would not, could not, do so unless there had been a crescent already on Earth. Somehow, maybe we'll never know, he lost one of them on Earth. Maybe it was stolen by someone who didn't know its true value. Anyway, he must've been searching for it, and when that news story went out about the one I had found in Germany, he knew what it was. After talking to me, he concluded I might not sell it. So he got into my apartment with the crescent he did have. He was just about to complete the circle and pass on over when I stopped him.

"He must be stranded on Earth and unable to get here unless he finds another crescent. For all I know, there may be others on Earth. The one I got in Germany might not even be the one he lost."

Finnegan wandered about the "palace" for a long while. It was immense, staggeringly beautiful and exotic and filled with treasure, jewels and artifacts. There were also laboratories, or perhaps bioprocess chambers was a better title. In these, Finnegan saw strange creatures slowly forming within huge transparent cylinders. There were many consoles with many operating devices, but he had no idea what they did. The symbols beneath the buttons and levers were unfamiliar.

"I was lucky. The palace is filled with traps to snare or kill the uninvited. But they were not set—why, I don't know, any more than I knew then why the place was untenanted. But it was a break for me."

Finnegan left the palace for awhile to go through the exquisite garden that surrounded it. He came to the edge of the monolith on which the palace and garden were.

"You've seen enough to imagine how I felt when I looked over the edge. The monolith must be at least thirty thousand feet high. Below it is the tier that the Lord named Atlantis. I don't know whether the Earth myth of Atlantis was founded on this Atlantis or whether the Lord got the name from the myth.

"Below Atlantis is the tier called Dracheland. Then, Amerindia. One sweep of my eye took it in, just as you can see one side of the Earth from a rocket. No details, of course, just big clouds, large lakes, seas, and outlines of continents. And a good part of each successively lower tier was obscured by the one just above it.

"But I could make out the Tower of Babylon structure of this world, even though I didn't, at that time, understand what I was seeing. It was just too unexpected and alien for me to apprehend any sort of *gestalt*. It didn't mean anything."

Finnegan could, however, understand that he was in a desperate situation. He had no means of leaving the top of this world except by trying to return to Earth through the crescents. Unlike the sides of the other monoliths, the face of this one was smooth as a bearing ball. Nor was he going to use the crescents again, not with Vannax undoubtedly waiting for him.

Although he was in no danger of starving—there was food and water enough to last for years—he could not and did not want to stay there. He dreaded the return of the owner, for he might have a very nasty temper. There were some things in the palace which made Kickaha feel uneasy.

"But the gworl came," Kickaha said. "I suppose—I know—they came from another universe through a gate similar to that which had opened the way for me. At the time, I had no way of knowing how or why they were in the palace. But I was glad I'd gotten there first. If I'd fallen into their hands . . . ! Later, I figured out they were agents for another Lord. He's sent them to steal the horn. Now, I'd seen the horn during my wandering about the palace, and had even blown it. But I didn't know how to press the combinations of buttons on it to make it work. As a matter of fact, I didn't know its real purpose.

"The gworl came into the palace. A hundred or so of them. Fortunately, I saw them first. Right away, they let their lust for murder get them into trouble. They tried to kill some of the Eyes of the Lord, the eagle-sized ravens in the garden. These hadn't bothered me, perhaps because they thought I was a guest or didn't look dangerous.

"The gworl tried to slit a raven's throat, and the ravens attacked them. The gworl retreated into the palace, where the big birds followed them. There were blood and feathers and pieces of bumpy hairy hide and a few corpses of both sides all over that end of the palace. During the battle, I noticed a gworl coming out of a room with the horn. He went through the corridors as if looking for something."

Finnegan followed the gworl into another room, about the size of two dirigible hangars. This held a swimming pool and a number of interesting but enigmatic devices. On a marble pedestal was a large golden model of the planet. On each of its levels were several jewels. As Finnegan was to discover, the diamonds, rubies, and sapphires were arranged to form symbols. These indicated various points of resonance.

"Points of resonance?"

"Yes. The symbols were coded mnemonics of the combination of notes required to open gates at certain places. Some gates open to other universes, but others are simply gates between the tiers on this world. These enabled the Lord to travel instantaneously from one level to the next. Associated with the symbols were tiny models of outstanding characteristics of the resonant points on the various tiers."

The gworl with the horn must have been told by the Lord how to read the symbols. Apparently, he was testing for the Lord to make sure he had the correct horn. He blew seven notes toward the pool, and the waters parted to reveal a piece of dry land with scarlet trees around it and a green sky beyond.

"It was the conceit of the original Lord to enter into the Atlantean tier through the pool itself. I didn't know at that time where the gate led to. But I saw my only chance to escape from the trap of the palace, and I took it. Coming up from behind the gworl, I snatched the horn from his hand and pushed him sideways into the pool—not into the gate, but into the water.

"You never heard such squawks and screams and such thrashings around. All the fear they don't have for other things is packed into a dread of water. This gworl went down, came up sputtering and yelling, and then managed to grab hold of the side of the gate. A gate has definite edges, you know, tangible if changing.

"I heard roars and shouts behind me. A dozen gworl with big and bloody knives were entering the room. I dived into the hole, which had started shrinking. It was so small I scraped the skin off my knees going through. But I got through, and the hole closed. It took off both the arms of the gworl who was trying to get out of the water and follow me. I had the horn in my hand, and I was out of their reach for the time being."

Kickaha grinned as if relishing the memory. Wolff said, "The Lord who sent the gworl ahead is the present Lord, right? Who is he?"

"Arwoor. The Lord who's missing was known as Jadawin. He must be the man who called himself Vannax. Arwoor moved in, and ever since he's been trying to find me and the horn."

Kickaha outlined what had happened to him since he had found himself on the Atlantean tier. During the twenty years (of Earth time), he had been living on one tier or another, always in disguise. The gworl and the ravens, now serving the Lord Arwoor, had never stopped looking for him. But there were long periods of time, sometimes two or three years on end, when Kickaha had not been disturbed.

"Wait a minute," Wolff said. "If the gates between the tiers were closed, how did the gworl get down off the monolith to chase you?"

Kickaha had not been able to understand that either. However, when captured by the gworl in the Garden level, he had questioned them. Although surly, they had given him some answers. They had been lowered to the Atlantean tier by cords.

"Thirty thousand feet?" Wolff said.

"Sure, why not? The palace is a fabulous many-chambered storehouse. If I'd had a chance to look long enough, I'd have found the cords myself. Anyway, the gworl told me they were charged by the Lord Arwoor not to kill me. Even if it meant having to let me escape at the time. He wants me to enjoy a series of exquisite tortures. The gworl said that Arwoor had been working on new and subtle techniques, plus refining some of the well established methods. You can imagine how I was sweating it out on the journey back."

After his capture in the Garden, Kickaha was taken across Okeanos to the base of the monolith. While they were climbing up it, a raven Eye stopped them. He had carried the news of Kickaha's capture to the Lord, who sent him back with orders. The gworl were to split into two bands. One was to continue with Kickaha. The other was to return to the Garden rim. If the man who now had the horn were to return through the gate with it, he was to be captured. The horn would be brought back to the Lord.

Kickaha said, "I imagine Arwoor wanted you brought back, too. He probably forgot to relay such an order to the gworl through the raven. Or else he assumed you'd be taken to him, forgetting that the gworl are very literal-minded and unimaginative.

"I don't know why the gworl captured Chryseis. Perhaps they intend to use her as a peace-offering to the Lord. The gworl know he is displeased with them because I've led them such a long and sometimes merry chase. They may mean to placate him with the former Lord's most beautiful masterpiece."

Wolff said, "Then the present Lord can't travel between tiers via the resonance points?"

"Not without the horn. And I'll bet he's in a hot-and-cold running sweat right now. There's nothing to prevent the gworl from using the horn to go to another universe and present it to another Lord. Nothing except their ignorance of where the resonance points are. If they should find one . . . However, they didn't use it by the boulder, so I imagine they won't try it elsewhere. They're vicious but not bright."

Wolff said, "If the Lords are such masters of super-science, why doesn't Arwoor use aircraft to travel?"

Kickaha laughed for a long time. Then he said, "That's the joker. The Lords are heirs to a science and power far surpassing Earth's. But the scientists and technicians of their people are dead. The ones now living know how to operate their devices, but they are incapable of explaining the principles behind them or of repairing them.

"The millenia-long power struggle killed off all but a few. These few, despite their vast powers, are ignoramuses. They're sybarites, megalomaniacs, paranoiacs, you name it. Anything but scientists.

"It's possible that Arwoor may be a dispossessed Lord. He had to run for his life, and it was only because Jadawin was gone for some reason from this world that Arwoor was able to gain possession of it. He came empty-handed into the palace; he has no access to any powers except those in the palace, many of which he may not know how to control. He's one up in this Lordly game of musical universes, but he's still handicapped."

Kickaha fell asleep. Wolff stared into the night, for he was on first watch. He did not find the story incredible, but he did think that there were holes in it. Kickaha had much more explaining to do. Then there was Chryseis. He thought of an achingly beautiful face with delicate bone structure and great cat-pupiled eyes. Where was Chryseis, how was she faring, and would he ever see her again?

8

DURING WOLFF'S SECOND WATCH, SOMETHING BLACK AND LONG and swift slipped through the moonlight between two bushes. Wolff sent an arrow into the predator, which gave a whistling scream and reared up on its hind legs, towering twice as high as a horse. Wolff fitted another arrow to the string and fired it into the white belly. Still the animal did not die, but went whistling and crashing away through the brush.

By then Kickaha, knife in hand, was beside him. "You were lucky," he said. "You don't always see them, and then, pffft! They go for the throat."

"I could have used an elephant gun," Wolff said, "and I'm not sure that would have stopped it. By the way, why don't the gworl—or the Indians, from what you've told me—use firearms?"

"It's strictly forbidden by the Lord. You see, the Lord doesn't like some things. He wants to keep his people at a certain population level, at a certain technological level, and within certain social structures. The Lord runs a tight planet.

"For instance, he likes cleanliness. You may have noticed that the folk of Okeanos are a lazy, happy-go-lucky lot. Yet they always clean up their messes. No litter anywhere. The same goes on this level, on every level. The Amerindians are also personally clean, and so are the Drachelanders and Atlanteans. The Lord wants it that way, and the penalty for disobedience is death."

"How does he enforce his rules?" Wolff asked.

"Mostly by having implanted them in the mores of the inhabitants. Originally, he had a close contact with the priests and medicine men, and by using religion—with himself as the deity—he formed and hardened the ways of the populace. He liked neatness, disliked firearms or any form of advanced technology. Maybe he was a romantic; I don't know. But the various societies on this world are mainly conformist and static."

"So what? Is progress necessarily desirable or a static society undesirable? Personally, though I detest the Lord's arrogance, his cruelty and lack of humanity, I approve of some of the things he's done. With some exceptions, I like this world, far prefer it to Earth."

"You're a romantic, too!"

"Maybe. This world is real and grim enough, as you already know. But it's free of grit and grime, of diseases of any kind, of flies and mosquitoes and lice. Youth lasts as long as you live. All in all, it's not such a bad place to live in. Not for me, anyway."

Wolff was on the last watch when the sun rounded the corner of the world. The starflies paled, and the sky was green wine. The air passed cool fingers over the two men and washed their lungs with invigorating currents. They stretched and then went down from the platform to hunt for breakfast. Later, full of roast rabbit and juicy berries, they renewed their journey.

The evening of the third day after, while the sun was a hand's breadth from slipping around the monolith, they were out on the plain. Ahead of them was a tall hill beyond which, so Kickaha said, was a small woods. One of the high trees there would give them refuge for the night.

Suddenly a party of about forty men rode around the hill. They were dark-skinned and wore their hair in two long braids. Their faces were painted with white and red streaks and black X's. Their lower arms bore small round shields, and they held lances or bows in their hands. Some wore bear-heads as helmets; others had feathers stuck into caps or wore bonnets with sweeping bird feathers.

Seeing the two men on foot before them, the riders yelled and urged their horses into a gallop. Lances tipped with steel points were leveled. Bows were fitted with arrows, and heavy steel axes or blade-studded clubs were lifted.

"Stand firm!" Kickaha said. He was grinning. "They are the Hrowakas, the Bear People. My people."

He stepped forward and lifted his bow above him with both hands. He shouted at the charging men in their own tongue, a speech with many glottalized stops, nasalized vowels, and a swift-rising but slow-descending intonation.

Recognizing him, they shouted, *"AngKungawas TreKickaha!"* They galloped by, their spears stabbing as closely as possible without touching him, the clubs and axes whistling across his face or above his head, and arrows plunging near his feet or even between them.

Wolff was given the same treatment, which he bore without flinching. Like Kickaha, he showed a smile, but he did not think that it was relaxed.

The Hrowakas wheeled their horses and charged back. This time they pulled their beasts up short, rearing, kicking, and whinnying. Kickaha leaped up and dragged a feather-bonneted youth from his animal. Laughing and panting, the two wrestled on the ground until Kickaha had pinned the Hrowaka. Then Kickaha arose and introduced the loser to Wolff.

"NgashuTangis, one of my brothers-in-law."

Two Amerinds dismounted and greeted Kickaha with much embracing and excited speech. Kickaha waited until they were calmed down and then began to speak long and earnestly. He frequently jabbed his finger toward Wolff. After a fifteen-minute discourse, interrupted now and then by a brief question, he turned smiling to Wolff.

"We're in luck. They're on their way to raid the Tsenakwa, who live fairly close to the Trees of Many Shadows. I explained what we were doing here, though not all of it by any means. They don't know we're bucking the Lord himself, and I'm not about to tell them. But they do know we're on the trail of Chryseis and the gworl and that you're a friend of mine. They also know that Podarge is helping us. They've got a great respect for her and her eagles and would like to do her a favor if they could.

"They've got plenty of spare horses, so take your choice. Only thing I hate about this is that you won't get to visit the lodges of the Bear People and I'll miss seeing my two wives, Giushowei and Angwanat. But you can't have everything."

The war party rode hard that day and the next, changing horses every half-hour. Wolff became saddle-sore—blanket-sore, rather. By the third morning he was in as good a shape as any of the Bear People and could stay on a horse all day without feeling that he had lockjaw in every muscle of his body and even in some of the bones.

The fourth day, the party was held up for eight hours. A herd of the giant bearded bison marched across their path; the beasts formed a column two miles across and ten miles long, a barrier that no one, man or animal, could cross. Wolff chafed, but the others were not too unhappy, because riders and horses alike needed a rest. Then, at the end of the column, a hundred Shanikotsa hunters rode by, intent on driving their lances and arrows into the bison on the fringes. The Hrowakas wanted to swoop down upon them and slay the entire group and only an impassioned speech by Kickaha kept them back. Afterwards, Kickaha told Wolff that the Bear People thought one of them was equal to ten of any other tribe.

"They're great fighters, but a little bit overconfident and arrogant. If you know how many times I've had to talk them out of getting into situations where they would have been wiped out!"

They rode on, but were halted at the end of an hour by NgashuTangis, one of the scouts for that day. He charged in yelling and gesturing. Kickaha questioned him, then said to Wolff, "One of Podarge's pets is a couple of miles from here. She landed in a tree and requested NgashuTangis to bring me to her. She can't make it herself; she's been ripped up by a flock of ravens and is in a bad way. Hurry!"

The eagle was sitting on the lowest branch of a lone tree, her talons clutched about the narrow limb, which bent under her weight. Dried red-black blood covered her green feathers, and one eye had been torn out. With the other, she glared at the Bear People, who kept a respectful distance. She spoke in Mycenaean to Kickaha and Wolff.

"I am Aglaia. I know you of old, Kickaha—Kickaha the trickster. And I saw you, O Wolff, when you were a guest of great-winged Podarge, my sister and queen. She it was who sent many of us out to search for the dryad Chryseis and the gworl and the horn of the Lord. But I, I alone, saw them enter the Trees of Many Shadows on the other side of the plain.

"I swooped down on them, hoping to surprise them and seize the horn. But they saw me and formed a wall of knives against which I could only impale myself. So I flew back up, so high they could not see me. But I, far-sighted treader of the skies, could see them."

"They're arrogant even while dying," Kickaha said softly in English to Wolff. "Rightly so."

The eagle drank water offered by Kickaha, and continued. "When night fell, they camped at the edge of a copse of trees. I landed on the tree below which the dryad slept under a deerskin robe. It had dried blood on it, I suppose from the man who had been killed by the gworl. They were butchering him, getting ready to cook him over their fires.

"I came down to the ground on the opposite side of the tree. I had hoped to talk to the dryad, perhaps even enable her to escape. But a gworl sitting near her heard the flutter of my wings. He looked around the tree, and that was his mistake, for my claws took him in his eyes. He dropped his knife and tried to tear me loose from his face. And so he did, but much of his face and both eyes came along with my talons. I told the dryad to run then, but she stood up and the robe fell off. I could see then that her hands and her legs were bound.

"I went into the brush, leaving the gworl to wail for his eyes. For his death, too, because his fellows would not be burdened with a blind warrior. I escaped through the woods and back to the plains. There I was able to fly off again. I flew toward the nest of the Bear People to tell you, O Kickaha and O Wolff, beloved of the dryad. I flew all night and on into the day.

"But a hunting pack of the Eyes of the Lord saw me first. They were above and ahead of me, in the glare of the sun. They plummeted down, those play-hawks, and took me by surprise. I fell, driven by their impact and by the weight of a dozen with their talons clamped upon me. I fell, turning over and over and bleeding under the thrusts of flint-sharp beaks.

"Then, I, Aglaia, sister of Podarge, righted myself and also gathered my senses. I seized the shrieking ravens and bit their heads off or tore their wings or legs off. I killed the dozen on me, only to be attacked by the rest of the pack. These I fought, and the story was the same. They died, but in their dying they caused my death. Only because they were so many."

There was a silence. She glared at them with her remaining eye, but the life was swiftly unraveling from it to reveal the blank spool of death. The Bear People had fallen quiet; even the horses ceased snorting. The wind whispering in from the skies was the loudest noise.

Abruptly, Aglaia spoke in a weak but still arrogantly harsh voice.

"Tell Podarge she need not be ashamed of me. And promise me, O Kickaha—no trickster words to me—promise me that Podarge will be told."

"I promise, O Aglaia," Kickaha said. "Your sisters will come here and carry your body far out from the rims of the tiers, out in the green skies, and you will be launched to float through the abyss, free in death as in life, until you fall into the sun or find your resting place upon the moon."

"I hold you to it, manling," she said.

Her head drooped, and she fell forward. But the iron talons were locked in on the branch so that she swung back and forth, upside down. The wings sagged and spread out, the tips brushing the ends of the grass.

Kickaha exploded into orders. Two men were dispatched to look for eagles to be informed of Aglaia's report and of her death. He said nothing, of course, about the horn, and he had to spend some time in teaching the two a short speech in Mycenaean. After being satisfied that they had memorized it satisfactorily, he sent them on their way. Then the party was delayed further in getting Aglaia's body to a higher position in the tree, where she would be beyond the reach of any carnivore except the puma and the carrion birds.

It was necessary to chop off the limb to which she clung and to hoist the heavy body up to another limb. Here she was tied with rawhide to the trunk and in an upright position.

"There!" Kickaha said when the work was done. "No creature will come near her as long as she seems to be alive. All fear the eagles of Podarge."

The afternoon of the sixth day after Aglaia the party made a long stop at a waterhole. The horses were given a chance to rest and to fill their bellies with the long green grass. Kickaha and Wolff squatted side by side on top of a small hill and chewed on an antelope steak. Wolff was gazing interestedly at a small herd of mastodons only four hundred yards away. Near them, crouched in the grass, was a striped male lion, a 900-pound specimen of Felix Atrox. The lion had some slight hopes of getting a chance at one of the calves.

Kickaha said, "The gworl were damn lucky to make the forest in one piece, especially since they're on foot. Between here and the Trees of

Many Shadows are the Tsenakwa and other tribes. And the Khing-GatawriT."

"The Half-Horses?" Wolff said. In the few days with the Hrowakas, he had picked up an amazing amount of vocabulary items and was even beginning to grasp some of the complicated syntax.

"The Half-Horses. *Hoi Kentauroi*. Centaurs. The Lord made them, just as he's made the other monsters of this world. There are many tribes of them on the Amerindian plains. Some are Scythian or Sarmatian speakers, since the Lord snatched part of his centaur material from those ancient steppe-dwellers. But others have adopted the tongues of their human neighbors. All have adopted the Plains tribal culture—with some variations."

The war party came to the Great Trade Path. This was distinguisable from the rest of the plain only by posts driven into the ground at mile-intervals and topped by carved ebony images of the Tishquetmoac god of commerce, Ishquettlammu. Kickaha urged the party into a gallop as they came near it and it did not slow until the Path was far behind.

"If the Great Trade Path ran to the forest, instead of parallel with it," he told Wolff, "we'd have it made. As long as we stayed on it, we'd be undisturbed. The Path is sacrosanct; even the wild Half-Horses respect it. All the tribes get their steel weapons, cloth blankets, jewelry, chocolate, fine tobacco, and so on from the Tishquetmoac, the only civilized people on this tier. I hurried us across the Path because I wouldn't be able to stop the Hrowakas from tarrying for a few days' trade if we came across a merchant caravan. You'll notice our braves have more furs than they need on their horses. That's just in case. But we're okay now."

Six days went by with no sign of enemy tribes except the black-and-red striped tepees of the Irennussoik at a distance. No warriors rode out to challenge them, but Kickaha did not relax until many miles had fallen behind them. The next day the plain began to change: the knee-high and bright green grass was interspersed with a bluish grass only several inches high. Soon the party was riding over a rolling land of blue.

"The stamping ground of the Half-Horse," Kickaha said. He sent the scouts to a greater distance from the main party.

"Don't let yourself be taken alive," he reminded Wolff.

"Especially by the Half-Horse. A human plains tribe might decide to adopt you instead of killing you if you had guts enough to sing merrily and spit in their faces while they roasted you over a low fire. But the Half-Horses don't even have human slaves. They'd keep you alive and screaming for weeks."

On the fourth day after Kickaha's warning, they topped a rise and saw a black band ahead.

"Trees growing along the Winnkaknaw River," Kickaha said. "We're almost halfway to the Trees of Many Shadows. Let's push the horses until we get to the river. I've got a hunch we've eaten up most of our luck."

He fell silent as he and the others saw a flash of sun on white several miles to their right. Then the white horse of Wicked Knife, a scout, disappeared into a shallow between rises. A few seconds later, a dark mass appeared on the rise behind him.

"The Half-Horse!" Kickaha yelled. "Let's go! Make for the river! We can make a stand in the trees along it, if we can get there!"

9

WITH A SINGLE LURCH, THE ENTIRE WAR PARTY BROKE INTO A gallop. Wolff crouched over his horse, a magnificent roan stallion, urging it on although it needed no encouragement. The plain sped by as the roan stretched his heart to drive his legs. Despite his intensity on speed, Wolff kept glancing to his right. Wicked Knife's white mare was visible now and then as she came over a swell of the plain. The scout was directing her at an angle toward his people. Less than a quarter of a mile behind, and gaining, was the horde of Half-Horse. They numbered at least a hundred and fifty, maybe more.

Kickaha brought his stallion, a golden animal with a pale silvery mane and tail, alongside Wolff. "When they catch up with us—which they will— stay by my side! I'm organizing a column of twos, a classic maneuver, tried and true! That way, each man can guard the other's side!"

He dropped back to give orders to the rest. Wolff guided his roan to follow in line behind Wolverine Paws and Sleeps Standing Up. Behind him, White Nose Bear and Big Blanket were trying to maintain an even distance from him. The rest of the party was strung out in a disorder which Kickaha and a councillor, Spider Legs, were trying to break up.

Presently, the forty were arranged in a ragged column. Kickaha rode up beside Wolff and shouted above the pound of hooves and whistling of wind: "They're stupid as porcupines! They wanted to turn and charge the centaurs! But I talked some sense into them!"

Two more scouts, Drunken Bear and Too Many Wives, were riding in from the left to join them. Kickaha gestured at them to fall in at the rear. Instead, the two continued their 90-degree approach and rode on past the tail of the column.

"The fools are going to rescue Wicked Knife—they think!"

The two scouts and Wicked Knife approached toward a converging point. Wicked Knife was only four hundred yards away from the Hrowakas with the Half-Horses several hundred yards behind him. They were lessening the gap with every second, traveling at a speed no horse burdened with a rider could match. As they came closer, they could be seen in enough detail for Wolff to understand just what they were.

They were indeed centaurs, although not quite as the painters of Earth had depicted. This was not surprising. The Lord, when forming them in his biolabs, had had to make certain concessions to reality. The main adjustment had been regulated by the need for oxygen. The large animal part of a centaur had to breathe, a fact ignored by the conventional Terrestrial representations. Air had to be supplied not only to the upper and human torso but to the lower and theriomorphic body. The relatively small lungs of the upper part could not handle the air requirements.

Moreover, the belly of the human trunk would have stopped all supply of nourishment to the large body beneath it. Or, if the small belly was attached to the greater equine digestive organs to transmit the food, diet was still a problem. Human teeth would quickly wear out under the abrasion of grass.

Thus the hybrid beings coming so swiftly and threateningly toward the men did not quite match the mythical creatures that had served as their models. The mouths and necks were proportionately large to allow intake of enough oxygen. In place of the human lungs was a bellowslike organ which drove the air through a throatlike opening and thence into the great lungs of the hippoid body. These lungs were larger than a horse's, for the vertical part increased the oxygen demands. Space for the bigger lungs was made by removal of the larger herbivore digestive organs and substitution of a smaller carnivore stomach. The centaur ate meat, including the flesh of his Amerind victims.

The equine part was about the size of an Indian pony of Earth. The hides were red, black, white, palomino, and pinto. The horsehair covered all but the face. This was almost twice as large as a normal-sized man's and was broad, high-cheekboned, and big-nosed. They were, on a larger scale, the features of the Plains Indians of Earth, the faces of Roman Nose, Sitting Bull, and Crazy Horse. Warpaint streaked their features and feathered bonnets and helmets of buffalo hides with projecting horns were on their heads.

Their weapons were the same as those of the Hrowakas, except for one item. This was the bola: two round stones, each secured to the end of a strip of rawhide. Even as Wolff wondered what he would do if a bola were cast at him, he saw them put into action. Wicked Knife and Drunken Bear and Too Many Wives had met and were racing beside each other about twenty yards ahead of their pursuers. Drunken Bear turned and shot an arrow. The missile plunged into the swelling bellows-organ beneath the human-chest of a Half-Horse. The Half-Horse went down and turned over and over and then lay still. The upper torso was bent at an angle that could result only from a broken spine. This despite the fact that a universal joint of bone and cartilage at the juncture of the human and equine permitted extreme flexibility of the upper torso.

Drunken Bear shouted and waved his bow. He had made the first kill, and his exploit would be sung for many years in the Hrowakas Council House.

If there's anybody left to tell about it, Wolff thought.

A number of bolas, whirled around and around till the stones were barely visible, were released. Rotating like airplane propellers that had spun off from their shafts, the bolas flew through the air. The stone at the end of one struck Drunken Bear on the neck and hurled him from his horse, cutting off his victory chant in the middle. Another bola wrapped itself around the hind leg of his horse to send it crashing into the ground.

Wolff, at the same time as some of the Hrowakas, released an arrow. He could not tell if it went home, for it was difficult to get a good aim and release from a position on a galloping horse. But four arrows did strike, and four Half-Horses fell. Wolff at once drew another arrow from the quiver on his back, noting at the same time that Too Many Wives and his horse were on the ground. Too Many Wives had an arrow sticking from his back.

Now, Wicked Knife was overtaken. Instead of spearing him, the Half-Horses split up to come in on either side of him.

"No!" Wolff cried. "Don't let them do it!"

Wicked Knife, however, had not earned his public name for no good reason. If the Half-Horse passed up the chance to kill him so they could take him alive for torture, they would have to pay for their mistake. He flipped his long Tishquetmoac knife through the air into the equine body of the Half-Horse closest to him. The centaur cart-wheeled. Wicked Knife drew another blade from his scabbard and, even as a spear was driven into his horse, he launched himself onto the centaur who had thrust the spear.

Wolff caught a glimpse of him through the massed bodies. He had landed on the back of the centaur, which almost collapsed at the impact of his weight but managed to recover and bear him along. Wicked Knife drove his knife into the back of the human torso. Hooves flashed; the centaur's tail rose into the air above the mob, followed by the rump and the hindlegs.

Wolff thought that Wicked Knife was finished. But no, there he was, miraculously on his feet and then, suddenly, on the horse-barrel of another centaur. This time Wicked Knife held the edge of his blade against his enemy's throat. Apparently he was threatening to cut the jugular vein if the Half-Horse did not carry him out and away from the others.

But a lance, thrust from behind, plunged into Wicked Knife's back. Not, however, before he had carried out his threat and slashed open the neck of the Half-Horse he rode.

"I saw that!" Kickaha shouted. "What a man, that Wicked Knife! After what he did, not even the savage Half-Horse would dare mutilate his body!

They honor a foe who gives them a great fight, although they'll eat him, of course."

Now the KhingGatawriT came up closely behind the end of the Hrowakas train. They split up into parts and increased their speed to over-take them on both sides. Kickaha told Wolff that the Half-Horses would not, at first, close in on the Hrowakas in a mass charge. They would try to have some fun with their enemies and would also give their untried young warriors a chance to show their skill and courage.

A black-and-white-spotted Half-Horse, wearing a single hawk's feather in a band around his head, detached himself from the main group on the left. Whirling a bola in his right hand, holding a feathered lance in his left, he charged at an angle toward Kickaha. The stones at the rawhide ends cir-cled to become a blur, then darted from his hand. Their path of flight was downward, toward the legs of his enemy's horse.

Kickaha leaned out and deftly stuck the tip of his lance at the bola. The lancehead was so timed that it met the rawhide in the middle. Kickaha raised the lance, the bola whirled around and around it, and wrapped it-self shut. A good part of the energy of the bola was absorbed by the length of the lance. Also, the lance was brought over in an arc to Kickaha's right side nearly striking Wolff, who had to duck. Even so, Kickaha almost lost the lance, for it slid from his hand, carried by the inertia of the bola. But he kept his grip and shook the lance with the bola at its upper end.

The frustrated Half-Horse shook his fist in fury and would have charged Kickaha with his lance. A roar of acclamation and admiration arose from the two columns of centaurs. A chief raced out to forestall the youngster. He spoke a few words to send him in shame back to the main body. The chief was a large roan with a many-feathered bonnet and a number of black chevrons, crossed with a bar, painted on his equine ribs.

"Charging Lion!" Kickaha shouted in English. "He thinks I'm worthy of his attention!"

He yelled something in the chief's language and then whooped with laughter as the dark skin became even darker. Charging Lion shouted back and spurted forward to bring him even with his insulter. The lance in his right hand stabbed at Kickaha, who countered with his own. The two shafts bounced off each other. Kickaha immediately detached his small mammoth-hide shield from his left arm. He blocked another thrust from the centaur's lance with his lance, then spun the shield like a disc. It sailed out and struck Charging Lion's right foreleg.

The centaur slipped and fell on his front legs and skidded upright through the grass. When he attempted to rise, he found that his right front leg was lamed. A yell broke loose from his group; a dozen bonneted chiefs ran with leveled lances at Charging Lion. He bore himself bravely and waited for his death with folded arms as a great, but now defeated and crip-pled, Half-Horse should.

"Pass the word along to slow down!" Kickaha said. "The horses can't keep this pace up much longer; their lungs are foaming out now. Maybe we can spare them and gain some time if the Half-Horses want to blood some more of their untrieds. If they don't, well, what's the difference?"

"It's been fun," Wolff said. "If we don't make it, we can at least say we weren't bored."

Kickaha rode close enough to clap Wolff on the shoulder. "You're a man after my own heart! I'm happy to have known you. Oh oh! Here comes an unblooded now! But he's going to pick on Wolverine Paws!"

Wolverine Paws, one of Kickaha's fathers-in-law, was at the head of the Hrowakas column and just in front of Wolff. He screamed insults at the Half-Horse charging in with circling bola, and then threw his lance. The Half-Horse, seeing the weapon flying toward him, loosed the bola before he had intended. The lance pierced his shoulder; the bola went true anyway and wrapped itself around Wolverine Paws. Unconscious from a blow by one of the stones, he fell off his horse.

The horses of both Wolff and Kickaha leaped over his body, which was lying before them. Kickaha leaned down to his right and stabbed Wolverine Paws with his lance.

"They won't take delight in torturing you, Wolverine Paws!" Kickaha said. "And you have made them pay for a life with a life."

A period of individual combat followed. Again and again a young untried charged out of the main group to challenge one of the human beings. Sometimes the man won, sometimes the centaur. At the end of a nightmare thirty minutes, the forty Hrowakas had become twenty-eight. Wolff's turn was with a large warrior armed with a club tipped with steel points. He also carried a small round shield with which he tried to duplicate Kickaha's trick. It did not work, for Wolff deflected the shield with the point of his lance. However, his guard was open for a moment, during which the centaur took his advantage. He galloped in so close that Wolff could not turn to draw far back enough to use the lance.

The club was raised high; the sun glittered on the sharp tips of its spike. The huge broad painted face was split with a grin of triumph. Wolff had no time to dodge and if he tried to grab the club he would end with a smashed and mangled hand. Without thinking, he did a thing that surprised both himself and the centaur. Perhaps he was inspired by Wicked Knife's feat. He launched himself from his horse, came in under the club, and grappled the Half-Horse around the neck. His foe squawked with dismay. Then they went down to the ground with a shock that knocked the wind from both.

Wolff leaped up, hoping that Kickaha had grabbed his horse so he could remount. Kickaha was holding it, but he was making no move to bring it back. Indeed, both the Hrowakas and Half-Horse had stopped.

"Rules of war!" Kickaha shouted. "Whoever gets the club first should win!"

Wolff and the centaur, now on his hooves, made a dash for the club, which was about thirty feet behind them. Four-legged speed was too much for two-legged. The centaur reached the club ten feet ahead of him. Without checking his pace, the centaur leaned his human trunk down and scooped up the club. Then he slowed and whirled, so swiftly that he had to rear up on his hind legs.

Wolff had not stopped running. He came in and then up at the Half-Horse even as it reared. A hoof flashed out at him, but he was by it, though the leg brushed against him. He crashed into the upper part, carried it back a little with him, and both fell again.

Despite the impact, Wolff kept his right arm around the centaur's neck. He hung on while the creature struggled to his hooves. The centaur had lost the club and now strove to overcome the human with sheer strength. Again he grinned, for he outweighed Wolff by at least seven hundred pounds. His torso, chest, and arms were also far bulkier than Wolff's.

Wolff braced his feet against the shoving weight of the centaur and would not move back. The grip around the huge neck tightened, and suddenly the Half-Horse could not breathe.

Then the Half-Horse tried to get his knife out, but Wolff grabbed the wrist with his other hand and twisted. The centaur screamed with the pain and dropped the knife.

A roar of surprise came from the watching Half-Horses. They had never seen such power in a mere man before.

Wolff strained, jerked, and brought the struggling warrior to his foreknees. His left fist punched into the heaving bellows beneath the ribs and sank in. The Half-Horse gave a loud whoosh. Wolff released his hold, stepped back, and used his right fist against the thick jaw of the half-unconscious centaur. The head snapped back, and the centaur fell over. Before he could regain consciousness, his skull was smashed by his own club.

Wolff remounted, and the three columns rode on at a canter. For awhile, the Half-Horse made no move against their enemies. Their chiefs seemed to be discussing something. Whatever it was they intended to do, they lost their chance a moment later.

The cavalcades went over a slight rise and down into a broad hollow. This was just enough to conceal from them the pride of lions that had been lying there. Apparently the twenty or so of Felis Atrox had fed off a protocamel the night before and had been too drowsy to pay any attention to the noise of the approaching hooves. But now that the intruders were suddenly among them, the great cats sprang into action. Their fury was aggravated even more by their desire to protect the cubs among them.

Wolff and Kickaha were lucky. Although there were huge shapes bounding on every side, none came at them. But Wolff did get close enough to a male to view every awe-inspiring detail, and that was as close as he ever cared to be. The cat was almost as large as a horse and, though he lacked the mane of the African lion, he did not lack for majesty and ferocity. He bounded by Wolff and hurled himself upon the nearest centaur, which went down screaming. The jaws closed on the centaur's throat, and it was dead. Instead of worrying the corpse, as he might normally have done, the male sprang upon another Half-Horse, and this one went down as easily.

All was a chaos of roaring cats and screaming horses, men, and Half-Horse. It was everyone for himself; to hell with the battle that had been going on.

It took only thirty seconds for Wolff and Kickaha and those Hrowakas who had been fortunate enough not to be attacked to ride out of the hollow. They did not need to urge their horses to speed, but they did have trouble keeping them from running themselves to death.

Behind them, but at a distance now, the centaurs who had evaded the lions streamed out of the hollow. Instead of pursuing the Hrowakas at once, they rode to a safe distance from the lions and then paused to evaluate their losses. Actually, they had not suffered more than a dozen casualites, but they had been severely shaken up.

"A break for us!" Kickaha shouted. "However, unless we can get to the woods before they catch up again, we're done for! They aren't going to continue the individual combats anymore. They'll make a concerted charge!"

The woods that they longed for still looked as far off as ever. Wolff did not think that his horse, magnificent beast though it was, could make it. Its coat was dark with sweat, and it was breathing heavily. Yet it pounded on, an engine of finely tempered flesh and spirit that would run until its heart ruptured.

Now the Half-Horse were in full gallop and slowly catching up with them. In a few minutes they were within arrow range. A few shafts came flying by the pursued and plunged into the grass. Thereafter, the centaurs held their fire, for they saw that bows were too inaccurate with the speed and unevenness at which both archer and target were traveling.

Suddenly Kickaha gave a whoop of delight. "Keep going!" he shouted at them all. "May the Spirit of AkjawDimis favor you!"

Wolff did not understand him until he looked at where Kickaha's finger was pointing. Before them, half-hidden by the tall grass, were thousands of little mounds of earth. Before these sat creatures that looked like striped prairie dogs.

The next moment, the Hrowakas had ridden into the colony with the Half-Horse immediately behind them. Shouts and screams arose as horses and centaurs, stepping into holes, went crashing down. The beasts and the Half-Horses that had fallen down kicked and screamed with the pain of broken legs. The centaurs just behind the first wave reared to halt themselves, and those following rammed into them. For a minute, a pile of tangled and kicking four-legged bodies was spread across the border of the prairie-dog field. The Half-Horses lucky enough to be far enough behind halted and watched their stricken comrades. Then they trotted cautiously, intent on where they placed their hooves. They cut the throats of those with broken legs and arms.

The Hrowakas, though aware of what was taking place behind them, had not stayed to watch. They pushed on but at a reduced pace. Now, they had ten horses and twelve men; Hums Like A Bee and Tall Grass were riding double with two whose horses had not broken their legs.

Kickaha, looking at them, shook his head. Wolff knew what he was thinking. He would have to order Hums Like A Bee and Tall Grass to get off and go on foot. Otherwise, not only they but the men who had picked them up would inevitably be overtaken. Then Kickaha, saying, "To hell with it, I won't abandon them!" dropped back. He spoke briefly to the tandem riders and brought his horse back up alongside Wolff. "If they go, we all go," he said. "But you don't have to stay with us, Bob. Your loyalty lies elsewhere. No reason for you to sacrifice yourself for us and lose Chryseis and the horn."

"I'll stay," Wolff said.

Kickaha grinned and slapped him on the shoulder. "I'd hoped we could get to the woods, but we won't make it. Almost but not quite. By the time we get to that big hill just half a mile ahead, we'll be caught up with. Too bad. The woods are only another half-mile away."

The prairie-dog colony was as suddenly behind them as it had been before them. The Hrowakas urged their beasts to a gallop. A minute later, the centaurs had passed safely through the field, and they, too, were at full speed. Up the hill went the pursued and at the top they halted to form a circle.

Wolff pointed down the side of the hill and across the plain at a small river. There were woods along it, but it was not that which caused his excitement. At the river's edge, partially blocked by the trees, white tepees shone.

Kickaha looked long before saying, "The Tsenakwa. The mortal enemy of the Bear People, as who isn't?"

"Here they come," Wolff said. "They must have been notified by sentinels."

He gestured at a disorganized body of horsemen riding out of the woods, the sun striking off white horses, white shields, and white feathers and sparking the tips of lance.

One of the Hrowakas, seeing them, began a high-pitched wailing song. Kickaha shouted at him, and Wolff understood enough to know that Kickaha was telling him to shut up. Now was no time for a death-song; they would cheat the Half-Horse and the Tsenakwa yet.

"I was going to order our last stand here," Kickaha said. "But not now. We'll ride toward the Tsenakwa, then cut away from them and toward the woods along the river. How we come out depends on whether or not both our enemies decide to fight. If one refuses, the other will get us. If not . . . Let's go!"

Haiyeeing, they pounded their heels against the ribs of their beasts. Down the hill, straight toward the Tsenakwa, they rode. Wolff glanced back over his shoulder and saw that the Half-Horse were speeding down the side of the hill after them. Kickaha yelled, "I didn't think they'd pass this up. There'll be a lot of women wailing in the lodges tonight, but it won't be only among the Bear People!"

Now the Hrowakas were close enough to discern the devices on the shields of the Tsenakwa. These were black swastikas, a symbol Wolff was not surprised to see. The crooked cross was ancient and widespread on Earth; it was known by the Trojans, Cretans, Romans, Celts, Norse, Indian Buddhists and Brahmans, the Chinese, and throughout pre-Columbian North America. Nor was he surprised to see that the oncoming Indians were red-haired. Kickaha had told him that the Tsenakwa dyed their black locks.

Still in an unordered mass but now bunched more closely together, the Tsenakwa leveled their lances and gave their charge-cry, an imitation of the scream of a hawk. Kickaha, in the lead, raised his hand, held it for a moment, then chopped it downward. His horse veered to the left and away, the line of the Bear people following him, he the head and the others the body of the snake.

Kickaha had cut it close, but he had used correct and exact timing. As the Half-Horse and Tsenakwa plunged with a crash and flurry into each other and were embroiled in a melee, the Hrowakas pulled away. They gained the woods, slowed to go through the trees and underbrush, and then were crossing the river. Even so, Kickaha had to argue with several of the braves. These wanted to sneak back across the river and raid the tepees of the Tsenakwa while their warriors were occupied with the Half-Horse.

"Makes sense to me," Wolff said, "if we stay there only long enough to pick up horses. Hums Like A Bee and Tall Grass can't keep on riding double."

Kickaha shrugged and gave the order. The raid took five minutes. The Hrowakas recrossed the river and burst from the trees and among the tepees with wild shouts. The women and children screamed and took refuge in the trees or lodges. Some of the Hrowakas wanted not only the horses but loot. Kickaha said that he would kill the first man he caught stealing anything besides bows and arrows. But he did reach down off his horse and give a pretty but battling woman a long kiss.

"Tell your men I would have taken you to bed and made you forever after dissatisfied with the puny ones of your tribe!" Kickaha said to her. "But we have more important things to do!" Laughing, he released the woman, who ran into her lodge. He did pause long enough to make water into the big cooking pot in the middle of the camp, a deadly insult, and then he ordered the party to ride off.

10

THEY RODE ON FOR TWO WEEKS AND THEN WERE AT THE EDGE of the Trees of Many Shadows. Here Kickaha took a long farewell of the Hrowakas. These also each came to Wolff and, laying their hands upon his shoulders, made a farewell speech. He was one of them now. When he returned, he should take a house and wife among them and ride out on hunts and war with them. He was *KwashingDa*, the Strong One; he had made his kill side by side with them; he had outwrestled a Half-Horse; he would be given a bear cub to raise as his own; he would be blessed by the Lord and have sons and daughters, and so forth and so on.

Gravely, Wolff replied that he could think of no greater honor than to be accepted by the Bear People. He meant it.

Many days later, they had passed through the Many Shadows. They lost both horses one night to something that left footprints ten times as large as a man's, and four-toed. Wolff was both saddened and enraged, for he had a great affection for his animal. He wanted to pursue the WaGanassit and take vengeance. Kickaha threw his hands up in horror at the suggestion.

"Be happy you weren't carried off, too!" he said. "The WaGanassit is covered with scales that are half-silicon. Your arrows would bounce off. Forget about the horses. We can come back someday and hunt it down. They can be trapped and then roasted in a fire, which I'd like to do, but we have to be practical. Let's go."

On the other side of the Many Shadows, they built a canoe and went down a broad river that passed through many large and small lakes. The country was hilly here, with steep cliffs at many places. It reminded Wolff of the dells of Wisconsin.

"Beautiful land, but the Chacopewachi and the Enwaddit live here."

Thirteen days later, during which they had had to paddle furiously three times to escape pursuing canoes of warriors, they left the canoe. Having crossed a broad and high range of hills, mostly at night, they came to a great lake. Again they built a canoe and set out across the waters. Five days of paddling brought them to the base of the monolith, Abharhploonta. They began their slow ascent, as dangerous as that up the first monolith. By the time they reached the top, they had expended their supply of arrows and were suffering several nasty wounds.

"You can see why traffic between the tiers is limited," Kickaha said. "In the first place, the Lord has forbidden it. However, that doesn't keep the irreverent and adventurous, nor the trader, from attempting it.

"Between the rim and Dracheland is several thousand miles of jungle with large plateaus interspersed here and there. The Guzirit River is only a hundred miles away. We'll go there and look for passage on a riverboat."

They prepared flint tips and shafts for arrows. Wolff killed a tapirlike animal. Its flesh was a little rank, but it filled their bellies with strength. He wanted then to push on, finding Kickaha's reluctance aggravating.

Kickaha looked up into the green sky and said, "I was hoping one of Podarge's pets would find us and have news for us. After all, we don't know which direction the gworl are taking. They have to go toward the mountain, but they could take two paths. They could go all the way through the jungle, a route not recommended for safety. Or they could take a boat down the Guzirit. That has its dangers, too, especially for rather outstanding creatures like the gworl. And Chryseis would bring a high price in the slave market."

"We can't wait forever for an eagle," Wolff said.

"No, nor will we have to," Kickaha said. He pointed up, and Wolff, following the direction of his fingertip, saw a flash of yellow. It disappeared, only to come into view a moment later. The eagle was dropping swiftly, wings folded. Shortly, it checked its drop and glided in.

Phthie introduced herself and immediately thereafter said that she carried good news. She had spotted the gworl and the woman, Chryseis, only four hundred miles ahead of them. They had taken passage on a merchant boat and were traveling down the Guzirit toward the Land of Armored Men.

"Did you see the horn?" Kickaha said.

"No," Phthie replied. "But they doubtless have it concealed in one of the skin bags they were carrying. I snatched one of the bags away from a gworl on the chance it might contain the horn. For my troubles, I got a bag full of junk and almost received an arrow through my wing."

"The gworl have bows?" Wolff asked, surprised.

"No. The rivermen shot at me."

Wolff, asking about the ravens, was told that there were many. Apparently the Lord must have ordered a number to keep watch on the gworl.

"That's bad," Kickaha said. "If they spot us, we're in real trouble."

"They don't know what you look like," Phthie said. "I've eavesdropped on the ravens when they were talking, hiding when I longed to seize them and tear them apart. But I have orders from my mistress, and I obey. The gworl have tried to describe you to the Eyes of the Lord. The ravens are looking for two traveling together, both tall, one black-haired, the other bronze-haired. But that is all they know, and many men conform to that description. The ravens, however, will be watching for two men on the trail of the gworl."

"I'll dye my beard, and we'll get Khamshem clothes," Kickaha said.

Phthie said that she must be getting on. She had been on her way to report to Podarge, having left another sister to continue the surveillance of the gworl, when she had spied the two. Kickaha thanked her and made sure that she would carry his regards to Podarge. After the giant bird had launched herself from the rim of the monolith, the men went into the jungle.

"Walk softly, speak quietly," Kickaha said. "Here be tigers. In fact, the jungle's lousy with them. Here also be the great axebeak. It's a wingless bird so big and fierce even one of Podarge's pets would skedaddle away from it. I saw two tigers and an axebeak tangle once, and the tigers didn't hang around long before they caught on it'd be a good idea to take off fast."

Despite Kickaha's warnings, they saw very little life except for a vast number of many-colored birds, monkeys, and mouse-sized antlered beetles. For the beetles, Kickaha had one word: "poisonous." Thereafter, Wolff took care before bedding down that none were about.

Before reaching their immediate destination, Kickaha looked for a plant, the *ghubharash*. Locating a group after a half-day's search, he pounded the fibers, cooked them, and extracted a blackish liquid. With this he stained his hair, beard, and his skin from top to bottom.

"I'll explain my green eyes with a tale of having a slave-mother from Teutonia," he said. "Here. Use some yourself. You could stand being a little darker."

They came to a half-ruined city of stone and wide-mouthed squatting idols. The citizens were a short, thin, and dark people who dressed in maroon capes and black loincloths. Men and women wore their hair long and plastered with butter, which they derived from the milk of piebald goats that leaped from ruin to ruin and fed on the grasses between the cracks in the stone. These people, the Kaidushang, kept cobras in little cages and often took their pets out to fondle. They chewed dhiz, a plant which turned their teeth black and gave their eyes a smoldering look and their motions a slowness.

Kickaha, using H'vaizhum, the pidgin rivertalk, bartered with the elders. He traded a leg of a hippopotamuslike beast he and Wolff had killed for Khamshem garments. The two donned the red and green turbans adorned with *kigglibash* feathers, sleeveless white shirts, baggy pantaloons of purple, sashes that wound around and around their waists many times, and the black, curling-toed slippers.

Despite their dhiz-stupored minds, the elders were shrewd in their trading. Not until Kickaha brought a very small sapphire from his bag—one of the jewels given him by Podarge—would they sell the pearl-encrusted scabbards and the scimitars in their hidden stock.

"I hope a boat comes along soon," Kickaha said. "Now that they know I have stones, they might try to slit our throats. Sorry, Bob, but we're going to have to keep watch at night. They also like to send in their snakes to do their dirty work for them."

That very day, a merchantman sailed around the bend of the river. At sight of the two standing on the rotting pier and waving long white hand-kerchiefs, the captain ordered the anchor dropped and sails lowered.

Wolff and Kickaha got into the small boat lowered for them and were rowed out to the *Khrillquz*. This was about forty feet long, low amidships but with towering decks fore and aft, and one fore-and-aft sail and jib. The sailors were mainly of that branch of Khamshem folk called the Shibacub. They spoke a tongue the phonology and structure of which had been de-scribed by Kickaha to Wolff. He was sure that it was an archaic form of Se-mitic influenced by the aboriginal tongues.

The captain, Arkhyurel, greeted them politely on the poop deck. He sat cross-legged on a pile of cushions and rich rugs and sipped on a tiny cup of thick wine.

Kickaha, calling himself Ishnaqrubel, gave his carefully prepared story. He and his companion, a man under a vow not to speak again until he re-turned to his wife in the far off land of Shiashtu, had been in the jungle for several years. They had been searching for the fabled lost city of Ziqooant.

The captain's black and tangled eyebrows rose, and he stroked the dark-brown beard that fell to his waist. He asked them to sit down and to accept a cup of the Akhashtum wine while they told their tale. Kickaha's eyes shone and he grinned as he plunged into his narration. Wolff did not understand him, yet he was sure that his friend was in raptures with his long, richly detailed, and adventurous lies. He only hoped Kickaha would not get too carried away and arouse the captain's incredulity.

The hours passed while the caravel sailed down the river. A sailor clad only in a scarlet loincloth, bangs hanging down below his eyes, played softly on a flute on the foredeck. Food was carried to them on silver and gold platters: roasted monkey, stuffed bird, a black hard bread, and a tart jelly. Wolff found the meat too highly spiced, but he ate.

The sun neared its nightly turn around the mountain, and the captain arose. He led them to a little shrine behind the wheel; here was an idol of green jade, Tartartar. The captain chanted a prayer, the prime prayer to the Lord. Then Arkhyurel got down on his knees before the minor god of his own nation and made obeisance. A sailor sprinkled a little incense on the tiny fire glowing in the hollow in Tartartar's lap. While the fumes spread over the ship, those of the captain's faith prayed also. Later, the mariners of other gods made their private devotions.

That night, the two lay on the mid-deck on a pile of furs which the captain had furnished them.

"I don't know about this guy Arkhyurel," Kickaha said. "I told him we failed to locate the city of Ziqooant but that we did find a small treasure cache. Nothing to brag about but enough to let us live modestly without worry when we return to Shiashtu. He didn't ask to see the jewels, even though I said I'd give him a big ruby for our passage. These people take their time in their dealings; it's an insult to rush business. But his greed may overrule his sense of hospitality and business ethics if he thinks he can get a big haul just by cutting our throats and dumping our bodies into the river."

He stopped for a moment. Cries of many birds came from the branches along the river; now and then a great saurian bellowed from the bank or from the river itself.

"If he's going to do anything dishonorable, he'll do it in the next thousand miles. This is a lonely stretch of river; after that, the towns and cities begin to get more numerous."

The next afternoon, sitting under a canopy erected for their comfort, Kickaha presented the captain with the ruby, enormous and beautifully cut. With it, Kickaha could have purchased the boat itself and the crew from the captain. He hoped that Arkhyurel would be more than satisfied with it; the captain himself could retire on its sale if he wished. Kickaha then did what he had wanted to avoid but knew that he could not. He brought out the rest of the jewels: diamonds, sapphires, rubies, garnets, tourmalines and topazes. Arkhyurel smiled and licked his lips and fondled the stones for three hours. Finally he forced himself to give them back.

That night, while lying on their beds on the deck, Kickaha brought out a parchment map which he had borrowed from the captain. He indicated a great bend of the river and tapped a circle marked with the curlicue syllabary symbols of Khamshem writing.

"The city of Khotsiqsh. Abandoned by the people who built it, like the one from which we boarded this boat, and inhabited by a half-savage tribe, the Weezwart. We'll quietly leave the ship the night we drop anchor there and cut across the thin neck of land to the river. We may be able to pick up enough time to intercept the boat that's carrying the gworl. If we don't, we'll still be way ahead of this boat. We'll take another merchant. Or, if none is available, we'll hire a Weezwart dugout and crew."

Twelve days later the Khrillquz tied up alongside a massive but cracked pier. The Weezwart crowded the stone tongue and shouted at the sailors and showed them jars of dhiz, and of laburnum, singing birds in wooden cages, monkeys and servals on the end of leashes, artifacts from hidden and ruined cities in the jungle, bags and purses made from the pebbly hides of the river saurians, and cloaks from tigers and leopards. They even had a baby axeback, which they knew the captain would pay a price for and would sell to the Bashishub, the king, of Shibacub. Their main wares, however, were their women. These, clad from head to foot in cheap cotton robes of scarlet and green, paraded back and forth on the pier. They would flash open their robes and then quickly close them, all the while screaming the price of a night's rent to the women-starved sailors. The men, wearing only white turbans and fantastic codpieces, stood to one side, chewed dhiz, and grinned. All carried six-foot-long blow-guns and long, thin, crooked knives stuck into the tangled knots of hair on top of their heads.

During the trading between the captain and Weezwart, Kickaha and Wolff prowled through the cyclopean stands and falls of the city. Abruptly, Wolff said, "You have the jewels with you. Why don't we get a Weezwart guide and take off now? Why wait until nightfall?"

"I like your style, friend," Kickaha said. "Okay. Let's go."

They found a tall thin man, Wiwhin, who eagerly accepted their offer when Kickaha showed him a topaz. At their insistence, he did not tell his wife where he was going but straightway led them into the jungle. He knew the paths well and, as promised, delivered them to the city of Qirruqshak within two days. Here he demanded another jewel, saying that he would not tell anybody at all about them if he was given a bonus.

"I did not promise you a bonus," Kickaha said. "But I like the fine spirit of free enterprise you show, my friend. So here's another. But if you try for a third, I shall kill you."

Wiwhin smiled and bowed and took the second topaz and trotted off into the jungle. Kickaha, staring after him, said, "Maybe I should've killed him anyway. The Weezwart don't even have the word *honor* in their vocabulary."

They walked into the ruins. After a half-hour of climbing and threading their way between collapsed buildings and piles of dirt, they found themselves on the river-side of the city. Here were gathered the Dholinz, a folk of the same language family as the Weezwart. But the men had long, drooping moustaches and the women painted their upper lips black and wore nose-rings. With them was a group of merchants from the land which had given all the Khamshem-speakers their name. There was no river-caravel by the pier. Kickaha, seeing this, halted and started to turn back into the ruins. He was too late, for the Khamshem saw him and called out to them.

"Might as well brave it out," Kickaha muttered to Wolff. "If I holler, run like hell! Those birds are slave-dealers."

There were about thirty of the Khamshem, all armed with scimitars and daggers. In addition, they had about fifty soldiers, tall broad-shouldered men, lighter than the Khamshem, with swirling patterns tattooed on their faces and shoulders. These, Kickaha said, were the Sholkin mercenaries often used by the Khamshem. They were famous spearmen, mountain people, herders of goats, scorners of women as good for nothing but housework, fieldwork, and bearers of children.

"Don't let them take you alive," was Kickaha's final warning before he smiled and greeted the leader of the Khamshem. This was a very tall and thickly muscled man named Abiru. He had a face that would have been handsome if his nose had not been a little too large and curved like a scimitar. He answered Kickaha politely enough, but his large black eyes weighed them as if they were so many pounds of merchandisable flesh.

Kickaha gave him the story he had told Arkhyurel but shortened it considerably and left out the jewels. He said that they would wait until a merchant boat came along and would take it back to Shiashtu. And how was the great Abiru doing?

(By now, Wolff's quickness at picking up languages enabled him to understand the Khamshem tongue when it was on a simple conversational basis.)

Abiru replied that, thanks to the Lord and Tartartar, this business venture had been very rewarding. Besides the usual type of slave-material picked up, he had captured a group of very strange creatures. Also, a woman of surpassing beauty, the like of which had never been seen before. Not, at least, on this tier.

Wolff's heart began to beat hard. Was it possible?

Abiru asked if they would care to take a peek at his captives.

Kickaha flicked a look of warning at Wolff but replied that he would very much like to see both the curious beings and the fabulously beautiful woman. Abiru beckoned to the captain of the mercenaries and ordered him and ten of his men to come along. Then Wolff scented the danger of which Kickaha had been aware from the beginning. He knew that they should run, though this was not likely to be successful. The Sholkin seemed accustomed to bringing down fugitives with their spears. But he wanted desperately to see Chryseis again. Since Kickaha made no move, Wolff decided not to do so on his own. Kickaha, having more experience, presumably knew how best to act.

Abiru, chatting pleasantly of the attractions of the capital city of Khamshem, led them down the underbrush-grown street and to a great stepped building with broken statues on the levels. He halted before an entrance by which stood ten more Sholkin. Even before they went in, Wolff knew that the gworl were there. Riding over the stink of unwashed human bodies was the rotten-fruit odor of the bumpy people.

The chamber within was huge and cool and twilighty. Against the far wall, squatting on the dirt piled on the stone floor, was a line of about a hundred men and women and thirty gworl. All were connected by long, thin iron chains around iron collars about their necks.

Wolff looked for Chryseis. She was not there.

Abiru, answering the unspoken question, said, "I keep the cat-eyed one apart. She has a woman attendant and a special guard. She gets all the attention and care that a precious jewel should."

Wolff could not restrain himself. He said, "I would like to see her."

Abiru stared and said, "You have a strange accent. Didn't your companion say you were from the land of Shiashtu, also?"

He waved a hand at the soldiers, who moved forward, their spears leveled. "Never mind. If you see the woman, you will see her from the end of a chain."

Kickaha sputtered indignantly. "We are subjects of the king of Khamshem and free men! You cannot do this to us! It will cost you your head, after certain legal tortures, of course!"

Abiru smiled. "I do not intend to take you back to Khamshem, friend. We are going to Teutonia, where you will bring a good price, being a strong man, albeit too talkative. However, we can take care of that by slicing off your tongue."

The scimitars of the two men were removed along with the bag. Herded by the spears, they moved to the end of the line, immediately behind the gworl, and were secured with iron collars. Abiru, dumping the contents of the bag on the floor, swore as he saw the pile of jewels.

"So, you did find something in the lost cities? How fortunate for us. I'm almost—but not quite—tempted to release you for having enriched me so."

"How corny can you get?" Kickaha muttered in English. "He talks like a grade-B movie villain. Damn him! If I get the chance, I'll cut out more than his tongue."

Abiru, happy with his riches, left. Wolff examined the chain attached to the collar. It was made of small links. He might be able to break it if the iron was not too high a quality. On Earth, he had amused himself, secretly of course, by snapping just such chains. But he could not try until nightfall.

Behind Wolff, Kickaha whispered, "The gworl won't recognize us in this get-up, so let's leave it that way."

"What about the horn?" Wolff said.

Kickaha, speaking the early Middle High German form of Teutonic, tried to engage the gworl in conversation. After narrowly missing getting hit in the face with a gob of saliva, he quit. He did manage to talk to one of the Sholkin soldiers and some of the human slaves. From them he gleaned much information.

The gworl had been passengers on the *Qaqiirzhub,* captained by one Rakhhamen. Putting in at this city, the captain had met Abiru and invited him aboard for a cup of wine. That night—in fact, the night before Wolff had entered the city—Abiru and his men had seized the boat. During the struggle, the captain and several of his sailors had been slain. The rest were now in the chain-line. The boat had been sent on down the river and up a tributary with a crew to be sold to a river-pirate of whom Abiru had heard.

As for the horn, none of the crew of the *Qaqiirzhub* had heard of it. Nor would the soldiers supply any news. Kickaha told Wolff that he did not think that Abiru was likely to let anybody else learn about it. He must recognize it, for everybody had heard of the horn of the Lord. It was part of the universal religion and described in the various sacred literatures.

Night came. Soldiers entered with torches and food for the slaves. After meal time, two Sholkin remained within the chamber and an unknown number stood guard outside. The sanitary arrangements were abominable; the odor became stifling. Apparently Abiru did not care about observing the proprieties as laid down by the Lord. However, some of the more religious Sholkin must have complained, for several Dholinz entered and cleaned up. Water in buckets was dashed over each slave, and several buckets were left for drinking. The gworl howled when the water struck them and complained and cursed for a long time afterwards. Kickaha added to Wolff's store of information by telling him that the gworl, like the kangaroo rat and other desert animals of Earth, did not have to drink water. They had a biological device, similar to the arid-dwellers, which oxidized their fat into the hydrogen oxide required.

The moon came up. The slaves lay on the floor or leaned against the wall and slept. Kickaha and Wolff pretended to do likewise. When the moon had come around into position so that it could be seen through the doorway, Wolff said, "I'm going to try to break the chains. If I don't have time to break yours, we'll have to do a Siamese twin act."

"Let's go," Kickaha whispered back.

The length of the chain between each collar was about six feet. Wolff slowly inched his way toward the nearest gworl to give himself enough slack. Kickaha crept along with him. The journey took about fifteen minutes, for they did not want the two sentinels in the chamber to become aware of their progress. Then Wolff, his back turned to the guards, took the chain in his two hands. He pulled and felt the links hold fast. Slow tension would not do the job. So, a quick jerk. The links broke with a noise.

The two Sholkin, who had been talking loudly and laughing to keep each other awake, stopped. Wolff did not dare to turn over to look at them. He waited while the Sholkin discussed the possible origin of the sound. Apparently it did not occur to them that it could be the chain parting. They spent some time holding the torches high and peering up toward the ceiling. One made a joke, the other laughed, and they resumed their conversation.

"Want to try for two?" Kickaha said.

"I hate to, but we'll be handicapped if I don't," Wolff said.

He had to wait a awhile, for the gworl to whom he had been attached had been awakened by the breaking. He lifted his head and muttered something in his file-against-steel speech. Wolff began sweating even more heavily. If the gworl sat up or tried to stand up, his motion would reveal the damage.

After a heart-piercing minute, the gworl settled back down and soon was snoring again. Wolff relaxed a little. He even grinned tightly, for the gworl's actions had given him an idea.

"Crawl up toward me as if you wanted to warm yourself against me," Wolff said softly.

"You kidding?" Kickaha whispered back. "I feel as if I'm in a steam bath. But okay. Here goes."

He inched forward until his head was opposite Wolff's knees.

"When I snap the chain, don't go into action," Wolff said. "I have an idea for bringing the guards over here without alarming those outside."

"I hope they don't change guards just as we're starting to operate," Kickaha said.

"Pray to the Lord," Wolff replied. "Earth's."

"He helps him who helps himself," Kickaha said.

Wolff jerked with all his strength; the links parted with a noise. This time, the guards stopped talking and the gworl rose up abruptly. Wolff bit down hard on the toe of the gworl. The creature did not cry out but grunted and started to rise. One of the guards ordered him to remain seated, and both started toward him. The gworl did not understand the language. He did understand the tone of voice, and the spear waved at him. He lifted his foot and began to rub it, meanwhile grating curses at Wolff.

The torches became brighter as the feet of the guards scraped against the stone exposed beneath the loose dirt. Wolff said, "Now!"

He and Kickaha arose simultaneously, whirled, and were facing the surprised Sholkin. A spearhead was within Wolff's reach. His hand slid along it, grasped the shaft just behind the point, and jerked. The guard opened his mouth to yell, but it snapped shut as the lifted butt of the spear cracked against his jaw.

Kickaha had not been so fortunate. The Sholkin stepped back and raised his spear to throw it. Kickaha went at him as a tackler after the man with the ball; he came in low, rolled, and the spear clanged against the wall.

By then, the silence was gone. One guard started to yell. The gworl picked up the weapon that had fallen by his side and threw it. The head drove into the exposed neck of the guard, and the point came out through the back of the neck.

Kickaha jerked the spearhead loose, drew the dead guard's knife from his scabbard, and flipped it. The first Sholkin to enter from outside received it to the hilt in his solar plexus. Seeing him go down, others who had been so eager to follow him withdrew. Wolff took the knife from the other corpse, shoved it into his sash, and said, "Where do we go from here?"

Kickaha slid the knife from the solar plexus and wiped it on the corpse's hair. "Not through that door. Too many."

Wolff pointed at a doorway at the far end and started to run toward it. On the way, he scooped up the torch dropped by the guard. Kickaha did the same. The doorway was partly choked up by dirt, forcing them to get down on their hands and knees and crawl through. Presently they were at the place through which the dirt had dropped. The moon revealed an empty place in the stone slabs of the ceiling.

"They must know about this," Wolff said. "They can't be that careless. We'd better go further back in."

They had scarcely moved past the point below the break in the roof when torches flared above. The two scuttled ahead as fast as they could while Sholkin voices came excitedly through the opening. A second later, a spear slammed into the dirt, narrowly missing Wolff's leg.

"They'll be coming in after us, now that they know we've left the main chamber," Kickaha said.

They went on, taking branches which seemed to offer access to the rear. Suddenly the floor sank beneath Kickaha. He tried to scramble on across before the stone on which he was would drop, but he did not make it. One side of a large slab came up, and that side which had dropped propelled Kickaha into a hole. Kickaha yelled, at the same time releasing the hold on his torch. Both fell.

Wolff was left staring at the tipped slab and the gap beside it. No light came from the hole, so the torch had either gone out or the hole was so deep that the flare was out of sight. Moaning in his anxiety, he crawled forward and held the torch over the edge while he looked below. The shaft was at least ten feet wide and fifty deep. It had been dug out of the dirt. But there was no Kickaha nor even a depression to indicate where he had landed.

Wolff called his name, at the same time hearing the shouts of the Sholkin as they crawled through the corridors in pursuit.

Receiving no answer, he extended his body as far as he dared over the lip of the shaft and examined the depth more closely. All his waving about of the torch to illuminate the dark places showed nothing but the fallen extinguished torch.

Some of the edges of the bottom remained black as if there were holes in the sides. He could only conclude that Kickaha had gone into one of these.

Now the sound of voices became louder and the first flickerings of a torch came from around the corner at the end of the hall. He could do nothing but continue. He rose as far as possible, threw his torch ahead of him to the other side, and leaped with all the strength of his legs. He shot in an almost horizontal position, hit the lip, which was wet soft earth, and slid forward on his face. He was safe, although his legs were sticking out over the edge.

Picking up the torch, which was still burning, he crawled on. At the end of the corridor he found one branch completely blocked by fallen earth. The other was partially stopped up by a great slab of smoothly cut stone lying at a forty-five degree angle to horizontal. By the sacrifice of some skin on his chest and back, he squeezed through between the earth and the stone. Beyond was an enormous chamber, even larger than the one in which the slaves had been kept.

There was a series of rough terraces formed by slippage of stone at the opposite end. He made his way up these toward the corner of the ceiling and the wall. A patch of moonlight shone through this, his only means of exit. He put his torch out. If the Sholkin were roaming around the top of the building, they would see the light from it coming through the small hole. At the cavity, he crouched for awhile on the narrow ledge beneath it and listened carefully. If his torch had been seen, he would be caught as he slid out of the hole, helpless to defend himself. Finally, hearing only distant shouts, and knowing that he must use this only exit, he pulled himself through it.

He was near the top of the mound of dirt which covered the rear part of the building. Below him were torches. Abiru was standing in their light, shaking his fist at a soldier and yelling.

Wolff looked down at the earth beneath his feet, imagined the stone and the hollows they contained, and the shaft down which Kickaha had hurtled to his death.

He raised his spear and murmured, "Ave atque vale, Kickaha!"

He wished he could take some more Sholkin lives—especially that of Abiru—in payment for Kickaha's. But he had to be practical. There was Chryseis, and there was the horn. But he felt empty and weak, as if part of his soul had left him.

11

THAT NIGHT HE HID IN THE BRANCHES OF A TALL TREE SOME distance from the city. His plan was to follow the slavers and rescue Chryseis and the horn at the first chance. The slavers would have to take the trail near which he waited; it was the only one leading inward to Teutonia. Dawn came while he waited, hungry and thirsty. By noon he became impatient. Surely they would not still be looking for him. At evening, he decided that he had to have at least a drink of water. He climbed down and headed for a nearby stream. A growl sent him up another tree. Presently a family of leopards slipped through the bush and lapped at the water. By the time they were through and had slid back into the bush, the sun was close to the corner of the monolith.

He returned to the trail, confident that he had been too close to it for a large train of human beings to walk by unheard. Yet no one came. That night he sneaked into the ruins and close to the building from which he had escaped. No one was in evidence. Sure now that they had left, he prowled through the bush-grown lanes and streets until he came upon a man sitting against a tree. The man was half-unconscious from dhiz, but Wolff woke him by slapping him hard against his cheeks. Holding his knife against his throat, he questioned him. Despite his limited Khamshem and the Dholinz's even lesser mastery, they managed to communicate. Abiru and his party had left that morning on three large war-canoes with hired Dholinz paddlers.

Wolff knocked the man unconscious and went down to the pier. It was deserted, thus giving him a choice of any craft there he wanted. He took a narrow light boat with a sail and set off down the river.

Two thousand miles later, he was on the borders of Teutonia and the civilized Khamshem. The trail had led him down the Guzirit River for three hundred miles, then across country. Although he should have caught up with the slow-moving train long before, he had lost them three times and been detained at other times by tigers and axebeaks.

Gradually the land sloped upward. Suddenly a plateau rose from the jungle. A climb of a mere six thousand feet was nothing to a man who had twice scaled thirty thousand. Once over the rim, he found himself in a different country. Though the air was no cooler, it bred oak, sycamore, yew, box elder, walnut, cottonwood and linden. However, the animals differed. He had walked no more than two miles through the twilight of an oak forest before he was forced to hide.

A dragon slowly paced by him, looked at him once, hissed, and went on. It resembled the conventional Western representations, was about forty feet long, ten feet high, and was covered with large scaly plates. It did not breathe fire. In fact, it stopped a hundred feet from Wolff's tree-branch refuge and began to eat upon a tall patch of grass. So, Wolff thought, there was more than one type of dragon. Wondering how he would be able to tell the carnivous type from the herbivorous without first assuring a safe observation post, Wolff climbed down from the tree. The dragon continued to munch while its belly, or bellies, emitted a weak thunder of digestion.

More cautiously than before, Wolff passed beneath the giant limbs of the trees and the moss, cataracts of green that hung from the limbs. Dawn of the next day found him leaving the edge of the forest. Before him the land dipped gently. He could see for many miles. To his right, at the bottom of a valley, was a river. On the opposite side, topping a column of shaggy rock, was a tiny castle. At the foot of the rock was a minute village. Smoke rose from the chimneys to bring a lump in his throat. It seemed to him that he would like nothing better than to sit down at a breakfast table over a cup of coffee with friends, after a good night's sleep in a soft bed, and chatter away about nothing in particular. God! How he missed the faces and the voices of genuine human beings, of a place where every hand was not against him!

A few tears trickled down his cheek. He dried them and went on his way. He had made his choice and must take the bad with the good, just as he would have in the Earth he had renounced. And this world, at this moment, anyway, was not so bad. It was fresh and green with no telephone lines, billboards, paper and cans strewn along the countryside, no smog or threat of bomb. There was much to be said for it, no matter how bad his present situation might be. And he had that for which many men would have sold their souls: youth combined with the experience of age.

Only an hour later, he wondered if he would be able to retain the gift. He had come to a narrow dirt road and was striding along it when a knight rode around the bend in the road, followed by two men-at-arms. His horse was huge and black and accoutered partly in armor. The knight was clad in black plate-and-mail armor which, to Wolff, looked like the type worn in Germany of the thirteenth century. His visor was up, revealing a grim hawk's face with bright blue eyes.

The knight reined in his horse. He called to Wolff in the Middle High German speech with which Wolff had become acquainted through Kickaha and also through his studies on Earth. The language had, of course, changed somewhat and was loaded with Khamshem and aboriginal loanwords. But Wolff could make out most of what his accoster said.

"Stand still, oaf!" the man cried. "What are you doing with a bow?"

"May it please your august self," Wolff replied sarcastically, "I am a hunter and so bear the king's license to carry a bow."

"You are a liar! I know every lawful hunter for miles hereabouts. You look like a Saracen to me or even a Yidshe, you are so dark. Throw down your bow and surrender, or I will cut you down like the swine you are!"

"Come and take it," Wolff said, his rage swelling.

The knight couched his lance, and his steed broke into a gallop.

Wolff resisted the impulse to hurl himself to either side or back from the glittering tip of the lance. At what he hoped was the exact split-second, he threw himself forward. The lance dipped to run him through, slid less than an inch over him, and then drove into the ground. Like a pole-vaulter, the knight rose from the saddle and, still clutching the lance, described an arc. His helmet struck the ground first at the end of the arc, the impact of which must have knocked him out or broken his neck or back, for he did not move.

Wolff did not waste his time. He removed the scabbarded sword of the knight and placed the belt around his waist. The dead man's horse, a magnificent roan, had come back to stand by his ex-master. Wolff mounted him and rode off.

Teutonia was so named because of its conquest by a group of The Teutonic Order or Teutonic Knights of St. Mary's Hospital at Jerusalem. This order originated during the Third Crusade but later deviated from its original purpose. In 1229 *der Deutsche Orden* began the conquest of Prussia to convert the Baltic pagans and to prepare for colonization by Germans. A group had entered the Lord's planet on this tier, either through accident, which did not seem likely, or because the Lord had deliberately opened a gate for them or forcibly caused them to enter.

Whatever the cause, the Ritters of the Teutonic Knights had conquered the aborigines and established a society based on that which they had left on Earth. This, of course, had changed both because of natural evolution and the Lord's desire to model it to his own wishes. The original single kingdom or Grand Marshalry had degenerated into a number of independent kingdoms. These, in turn, consisted of loosely bound baronetcies and a host of outlaw or robber baronetcies.

Another aspect of the plateau was the state of Yidshe. The founders of this had entered through a gate coevally with the Teutonic Knights. Again, whether they had entered accidentally or through design of the Lord was unknown. But a number of Yiddish-speaking Germans had established themselves at the eastern end of the plateau. Though originally merchants, they had become masters of the native population. Also, they had adopted the feudal-chivalry setup of the Teutonic Order—probably had had to do so to survive. It was this state that the first knight had referred to when he had accused Wolff of being a Yidshe.

Thinking of this, Wolff had to chuckle. Again, it might have been accident that the Germans had entered into a level where the archaic-Semitic Khamshem already existed and where their contemporaries were the despised Jews. But Wolff thought he could see the ironic face of the Lord smiling behind the situation.

Actually, there were not any Christians or Jews in Dracheland. Although the two faiths still used their original titles, both had become perverted. The Lord had taken the place of Yahweh and Gott, but he was addressed by these names. Other changes in theology had followed: ceremonies, rituals, sacraments, and the literature had subtly become twisted. The parent faiths of both would have rejected their descendants in this world as heretics.

Wolff made his way toward von Elgers'. He could not do so as swiftly as he wished, because he had to avoid the roads and the villages along the way. After being forced to kill the knight, he did not even dare cut through the baronetcy of von Laurentius, as he had at first planned. The entire country would be searching for him; men and dogs would be everywhere. The rough hills marking the boundary were his most immediate form of passage, which he took.

Two days later, he came to a point where he could descend without being within the suzerainty of von Laurentius. As he was clambering down a steep but not especially difficult hill, he came around a corner. Below him was a broad meadow by a riverlet. Two camps were pitched at opposite ends. Around the brave flag-and-pennon draped pavilions in the center of each were a number of smaller tents, cooking fires, and horses. Most of the men were in two groups. They were watching their champion and his antagonist, who were charging each other with couched lances. Even as Wolff saw them, they met together in the middle of the field with a fearful clang. One knight went sailing backward with the lance of the other jammed into his shield. The other, however, lost his balance and fell with a clang several seconds later.

Wolff studied the tableau. It was no ordinary jousting tourney. The peasants and the townspeople who should have thronged the sides and the jerrybuilt stadium with its flowerbed of brilliantly dressed nobility and ladies were absent. This was a lonely place beside the road where champions had pitched their tents and were taking on all qualified passersby.

Wolff worked his way down the hill. Although exposed to the sight of those below, he did not think that they would take much interest in a lone traveler at this time. He was right. No one hastened from either camp to question him. He was able to walk up to the edge of the meadow and make a leisurely inspection.

The flag above the pavilion to his left bore a yellow field with a Solomon's seal. By this he knew that a Yidshe champion had pitched his tent here. Below the national flag was a green banner with a silver fish and hawk. The other camp had several state and personal pennons. One of them leaped out into Wolff's gaze and caused him to cry out with surprise. On a white field was a red ass's head with a hand below it, all fingers clenched but the middle. Kickaha had once told him of it, and Wolff had gotten a big laugh out of it. It was just like Kickaha to pick such a coat of arms.

Wolff sobered then, knowing that, more likely, it was borne by the man who took care of Kickaha's territory while he was gone.

He changed his decision to pass on by the field. He had to determine for himself that the man using that banner was not Kickaha, even though he knew that his friend's bones must be rotting under a pile of dirt at the bottom of a shaft in a ruined city of the jungle.

Unchallenged, he made his way across the field and into the camp at the western end. Men-at-arms and retainers stared, only to turn away from his glare. Somebody muttered, "Yidshe dog!" but none owned to the comment when he turned. He went on around a line of horses tethered to a post and up to the knight who was his goal. This one was clad in shining red armor, visor down, and held a huge lance upright while he waited his turn. The lance bore near its tip a pennon on which were the red ass's head and human hand.

Wolff placed himself near the prancing horse, making it even more nervous. He cried out in German, "Baron von Horstmann?"

There was a muffled exclamation, a pause, and the knight's hand raised his visor. Wolff almost wept with joy. The merry long-lipped face of Finnegan-Kickaha-von Horstmann was inside the helmet.

"Don't say anything," Kickaha cautioned. "I don't know how in hell you found me, but I'm sure happy about it. I'll see you in a moment. That is, if I come back alive. This funem Laksfalk is one tough hombre."

12

TRUMPETS FLARED. KICKAHA RODE OUT TO A SPOT INDICATED BY the marshals. A shaven-headed, long-robed priest blessed him while, at the other end of the field, a rabbi was saying something to Baron funem Laksfalk. The Yidshe champion was a large man in a silver armor, his helmet shaped like a fish's head. His steed was a huge powerful black. The trumpets blew again. The two contenders dipped their lances in salute. Kickaha briefly gripped his lance with his left hand while he crossed himself with his right. (He was a stickler for observing the religious rules of the people among whom he happened to be at the moment.)

Another blast of long-shafted, big-mouthed trumpets was followed by the thunder of the hooves of the knight's horses and the cheers of the onlookers. The two met exactly in the middle of the field, as did the lance of each in the middle of the other's shield. Both fell with a clangor that startled the birds from the nearby trees, as they had been startled many times that day. The horses rolled on the ground.

The men of each knight ran out onto the field to pick up their chief and to drag away the horses, both of which had broken their necks. For a moment, Wolff thought that the Yidshe and Kickaha were also dead, for neither stirred. After being carried back, however, Kickaha came to. He grinned feebly, and said, "You ought to see the other guy."

"He's okay," Wolff said after a glance at the other camp.

"Too bad," Kickaha replied. "I was hoping he wouldn't give us any more trouble. He's held me up too long as it is."

Kickaha ordered all but Wolff to leave the tent. His men seemed reluctant to leave him but they obeyed, though not without warning looks at Wolff. Kickaha said, "I was on my way from my castle to von Elgers' when I passed funem Laksfalk's pavilion. If I'd been alone, I would have thumbed my nose at his challenge and ridden on. But there were also Teutoniacs there, and I had my own men to consider. I couldn't afford to get a reputation of cowardice; my own men would've pelted me with rotten cabbage and I'd have had to fight every knight in the land to prove my courage. I figured that it wouldn't take me long to straighten out the Yidshe on who the best man was, and then I could take off.

"It didn't work out that way. The marshals had me listed in the Number Three position. That meant I had to joust with three men for three days before I'd get to the big time. I protested; no use. So I swore to myself and sweated it out. You saw my second encounter with funem Laksfalk. We both knocked each other off the saddle the first time, too. Even so, that's more than the others have done. They're burned up because a Yidshe has defeated every Teuton except me. Besides, he's killed two already and crippled another for life."

While listening to Kickaha, Wolff had been taking the armor off. Kickaha sat up suddenly, groaning and wincing, and said, "Hey, how in hell did you get here?"

"I walked mostly. But I thought you were dead."

"The report wasn't too grossly exaggerated. When I fell down that shaft I landed halfway up on a ledge of dirt. It broke off and started a little cave-in that buried me after I landed on the bottom. But I wasn't knocked out long, and the dirt only lightly covered my face, so I wasn't asphyxiated. I lay quiet for a while because the Sholkin were looking down the hole then. They even threw a spear down, but it missed me by a mole's hair.

"After a couple of hours, I dug myself out. I had a time getting out, I can tell you. The dirt kept breaking off, and I kept falling back. It must've taken me ten hours, but I was lucky at that. Now, how did *you* get here, you big lunk?"

Wolff told him. Kickaha frowned and said, "So I was right in figuring that Abiru would come to von Elgers' on his way. Listen, we got to get out of here and fast. How would you like to take a swing at the big Yid?"

Wolff protested that he knew nothing of the fine points of jousting, that it took a lifetime to learn. Kickaha said, "If you were going to break a lance with him, you'd be right. But we'll challenge him to a contest with swords, no shields. Broadswording isn't exactly duelling with a rapier or saber; it's main strength and that's what you've got!"

"I'm not a knight. The others saw me enter as a common vagrant."

"Nonsense! You think these chevaliers don't go around in disguise all the time? I'll tell them you're a Saracen, pagan Khamshem, but you're a real good friend of mine, I rescued you from a dragon or some cock-and-bull story like that. They'll eat it up. I got it! You're the Saracen Wolff—there's a famous knight by that name. You've been journeying in disguise, hoping to find me and pay me back for saving you from the dragon. I'm too hurt to break another lance with funem Laksfalk—that's no lie; I'm so stiff and sore I can hardly move—and you're taking up the gauntlet for me."

Wolff asked what excuse he would give for not using the lance.

Kickaha said, "I'll give them some story. Say a thieving knight stole your lance and you've sworn never to use one until you get the stolen one back.

They'll accept that. They're always making some goofy vow or other. They act just like a bunch of knights from King Arthur's Round Table. No such knights ever existed on Earth, but it must have pleased the Lord to make these act as if they just rode out of Camelot. He was a romantic, whatever else you can say about him."

Wolff said he was reluctant, but if it would help speed them to von Elgers', he would do anything. Kickaha's own armor was not large enough for Wolff, so the armor of a Yidshe knight Kickaha had killed the day before was brought in. The retainers clad him in blue plates and chain-mail and then led him out to his horse. This was a beautiful palomino mare that had also belonged to the knight Kickaha had slain, the Ritter oyf Roytfeldz. With only a little difficulty, Wolff mounted the charger. He had expected that the armor would be so heavy a crane would have to lift him upon the saddle. Kickaha told him that that might have once been true here, but the knights had long since gone back to lighter plates and more chain-mail.

The Yidshe go-between came to announce that funem Laksfalk had accepted the challenge despite the Saracen Wolf's lack of credentials. If the valiant and honorable robber Baron Horst von Horstmann vouched for the Wolf, that was good enough for funem Laksfalk. The speech was a formality. The Yidshe champion would not for one moment have thought of turning down a challenge.

"Face is the big thing here," Kickaha said to Wolff. Having managed to limp out of his tent, he was giving his friend last-minute instructions. "Man, am I glad you came along. I couldn't have taken one more fall, and I didn't dare back out."

Again, the trumpets flourished. The palomino and the black broke into a headlong gallop. They passed each other going at full speed, during which time both men swung their swords. They clanged together; a paralyzing shock ran down Wolff's hand and arm. However, when he turned his charger, he saw that his antagonist's sword was on the ground. The Yidshe was dismounting swiftly to get to the blade before Wolff. He was in such a hurry he slipped and fell headlong onto the ground.

Wolff rode his horse up slowly and took his time dismounting to allow the other to recover. At this chivalrous move, both camps broke into cheers. By the rules, Wolff could have stayed in the saddle and cut funem Laksfalk down without permitting him to pick up his weapon.

On the ground, they faced each other. The Yidshe knight raised his visor, revealing a handsome face. He had a thick moustache and pale blue eyes. He said, "I pray you let me see your face, noble one. You are a true knight for not striking me down while helpless."

Wolff lifted his visor for a few seconds. Both then advanced and brought their blades together again. Once more, Wolff's stroke was so powerful that it tore the blade of the other from his grip.

Funem Laksfalk raised his visor, this time with his left arm. He said, "I cannot use my right arm. If you will permit me to use my left?"

Wolff saluted and stepped back. His opponent gripped the long hilt of his sword and, stepping close, brought it around from the side with all his force. Once more, the shock of Wolff's stroke broke the Yidshe's grasp.

Funem Laksfalk lifted his visor for the third time. "You are such a champion as I have never met. I am loath to admit it, but you have defeated me. And that is something I have never said nor thought to say. You have the strength of the Lord himself."

"You may keep your life, your honor, and your armor and horse," Wolff replied. "I want only that my friend von Horstmann and I be allowed to go on without further challenges. We have an appointment."

The Yidshe answered that it would be so. Wolff returned to his camp, there to be greeted joyously, even by those who had thought of him as a Khamshem dog.

Chortling, Kickaha ordered camp struck. Wolff asked him if he did not think they could make far better time unencumbered with a train.

"Sure, but it's not done very often," Kickaha replied. "Oh, well, you're right. I'll send them on home. And we'll get these damn locomotive plates off."

They had not ridden far before they heard the drum of hooves. Coming up the road behind them was funem Laksfalk, also minus his armor. They halted until he had overtaken them.

"Noble knights," he said, smiling, "I know that you are on a quest. Would it be too much to ask for me to ask to join? I would feel honored. I also feel that only by assisting you can I redeem my defeat."

Kickaha looked at Wolff and said, "It's up to you. But I like his style."

"Would you bind yourself to aid us in whatever we do? As long as it is not dishonorable, of course. You may release yourself from your oath at any time, but you must swear by all that's holy that you will never aid our enemies."

"By God's blood and the beard of Moses, I swear."

That night, while they made camp in a brake alongside a brook, Kickaha said, "There's one problem that having funem Laksfalk along might complicate. We have to get the stain off your skin, and that beard has to go, too. Otherwise, if we run into Abiru, he might identify you."

"One lie always leads to another," Wolff said. "Well, tell him that I'm the younger son of a baron who kicked me out because my jealous brother falsely accused me. I've been traveling around since then, disguised as a Sàracen. But I intend to return to my father's castle—he's dead now—and challenge my brother to a duel."

"Fabulous! You're a second Kickaha! But what about when he learns of Chryseis and the horn?"

"We'll think of something. Maybe the truth. He can always back out when he finds he's bucking the Lord."

The next morning they rode until they came to the village of Etzelbrand. Here Kickaha purchased some chemicals from the local white-wizard and made a preparation to remove the stain. Once past the village, they stopped off at the brook. Funem Laksfalk watched with interest, then amazement, then suspicion as the beard came off, followed by the stain.

"God's eyes! You were a Khamshem, now you could be a Yidshe!"

Kickaha thereupon launched into a three-hour, much-detailed story in which Wolff was the bastard son of a Yidshe maiden lady and a Teutoniac knight on a quest. The knight, a Robert von Wolfram, had stayed at a Yidshe castle after covering himself with glory during a tournament. He and the maiden had fallen in love, too much so. When the knight had ridden out, vowing to return after completing his quest he had left Rivke pregnant. But von Wolfram had been killed and the girl had had to bear young Robert in shame. Her father had kicked her out and sent her to a little village in Khamshem to live there forever. The girl had died when giving birth to Robert, but a faithful old servant had revealed the secret of his birth to Robert. The young bastard had sworn that when he gained manhood, he would go to the castle of his father's people and claim his rightful inheritance. Rivke's father was dead now but his brother, a wicked old man, held the castle. Robert intended to wrest the baronetcy from him if he would not give it up.

Funem Laksfalk had tears in his eyes at the end of the story. He said, "I will ride with you, Robert, and help you against your wicked uncle. Thus may I redeem my defeat."

Later, Wolff reproached Kickaha for making up such a fantastic story, so detailed that he might easily be tripped up. Moreover, he did not like to deceive such a man as the Yidshe knight.

"Nonsense! You couldn't tell him the whole truth, and it's easier to make up a whole lie than a half-truth! Besides, look at how much he enjoyed his little cry! And, I am Kickaha, the *kickaha,* the tricky one, the maker of fantasies and of realities. I am the man whom boundaries cannot hold. I slip from one to another, in-again-out-again Finnegan. I seem to be killed, yet I pop up again, alive, grinning, and kicking! I am quicker than men who are stronger than me, and stronger than those who are quicker! I have few loyalties, but those are unshakable! I am the ladies' darling wherever I go, and many are the tears shed after I slip through the night like a red-headed ghost! But tears cannot hold me any more than chains! Off I go, and where I will appear or what my name will be, few know! I am the Lord's gadfly; he cannot sleep at nights because I elude his Eyes, the ravens, and his hunters, the gworl!"

Kickaha stopped and began laughing uproariously. Wolff had to grin back. Kickaha's manner made it plain that he was poking fun at himself.

However, he did half-believe it, and why should he not? What he said was not actually exaggeration.

This thought opened the way to a train of speculation that brought a frown to Wolff. Was it possible that Kickaha was the Lord himself in disguise? He could be amusing himself by running with hare and hound both. What better entertainment for a Lord, a man who has to look far and deep for something new with which to stave off ennui? There were many unexplained things about him.

Wolff, searching Kickaha's face for some clue to the mystery, felt his doubts evaporate. Surely that merry face was not the mask for a hideously cold being who toyed with lives. And then there was Kickaha's undeniably Hoosier accent and idioms. Could a Lord master these?

Well, why not? Kickaha had evidently mastered other languages and dialects as well.

So it went in Wolff's mind that long afternoon as they rode. But dinner and drink and good fellowship dispelled them so that, at bedtime, he had forgotten his doubts. The three had stopped at a tavern in the village of Gnazelschist and eaten heartily. Wolff and Kickaha devoured a roast suckling pig between them. Funem Laksfalk, although he shaved and had other liberal views of his religion, refused the taboo pork. He ate beef—although he knew it had not been slaughtered à la kosher. All three downed many steins of the excellent local dark beer, and during the drink-conversation Wolff told funem Laksfalk a somewhat edited story about their search for Chryseis—a noble quest indeed, they agreed, and then they all staggered off to bed.

In the morning, they took a shortcut through the hills which would save them three days' time—if they got through. The road was rarely traveled, and with good reason, for outlaws and dragons frequented the area. They made good speed, saw no men-of-the-woods and only one dragon. The scaly monster scrambled up from a ditch a hundred yards ahead of them. It snorted and disappeared into the trees on the other side of the road, as eager as they to avoid a fight.

Coming down out of the hills to the main highway, Wolff said, "A raven's following us."

"Yeah, I know it, but don't get your neck hot. They're all over the place. I doubt that it knows who we are. I sincerely hope it doesn't."

At noon of the following day, they entered the territory of the Komtur of Tregyln. More than twenty-four hours later, they arrived within sight of the castle of Tregyln, the Baron von Elgers' seat of power. This was the largest castle Wolff had so far seen. It was built of black stone and was situated on top of a high hill a mile from the town of Tregyln.

In full armor, pennoned lances held upright, the three rode boldly to the moat that surrounded the castle. A warder came out of a small blockhouse by the moat and politely inquired of them their business.

"Take word to the noble lord that three knights of good fame would be his guests," Kickaha said. "The Barons von Horstmann and von Wolfram and the far-famed Yidshe baron, funem Laksfalk. We look for a noble to hire us for fighting or to send us on a quest."

The sergeant shouted at a corporal, who ran off across the drawbridge. A few minutes afterwards, one of von Elgers' sons, a youth splendidly dressed, rode out to welcome them. Inside the huge courtyard, Wolff saw something that disturbed him. Several Khamshem and Sholkin were lounging around or playing dice.

"They won't recognize either one of us," Kickaha said. "Cheer up. If they're here, then so are Chryseis and the horn."

After making sure that their horses were well taken care of, the three went to the quarters given them. They bathed and put on the brilliantly colored new clothes sent up to them by von Elgers. Wolff observed that these differed little from the garments worn during the thirteenth century. The only innovations, Kickaha said, were traceable to aboriginal influence.

By the time they entered the vast dining-hall, the supper was in full blast. Blast was the right word, for the uproar was deafening. Half the guests were reeling, and the others did not move much because they had passed the reeling stage. Von Elgers managed to rise to greet his guests. Graciously, he apologized for being found in such a condition at such an early hour.

"We have been entertaining our Khamshem guest for several days. He has brought unexpected wealth to us, and we've been spending a little of it on a celebration."

He turned to introduce Abiru, did so too swiftly, and almost fell. Abiru rose to return their bow. His black eyes flickered like a sword point over them; his smile was broad but mechanical. Unlike the others, he appeared sober. The three took their seats, which were close to the Khamshem because the previous occupants had passed out under the table. Abiru seemed eager to talk to them.

"If you are looking for service, you have found your man. I am paying the baron to conduct me to the hinterland, but I can always use more swords. The road to my destination is long and hard and beset with many perils."

"And where is your destination?" Kickaha asked. No one looking at him would have thought him any more than idly interested in Abiru for he was hotly scanning the blonde beauty across the table from him.

"There is no secret about that," Abiru said. "The lord of Kranzelkracht is said to be a very strange man, but it is also said that he has more wealth even than the Grand Marshal of Teutonia."

"I know that for a fact," Kickaha replied. "I have been there, and I have seen his treasures. Many years ago, so it is said, he dared the displeasure of the Lord and climbed the great mountain to the tier of Atlantis. He robbed the treasure house of the Rhadamanthus himself and got away with a bagful of jewels. Since then, von Kranzelkracht has increased his wealth by conquering the states around his. It is said that the Grand Marshal is worried by this and is thinking of organizing a crusade against him. The Marshal claims that the man is a heretic. But if he were, would not the Lord have blasted him with lightning long ago?"

Abiru bowed his head and touched his forehead with his fingertips.

"The Lord works in mysterious ways. Besides, who but the Lord knows the truth? In any event, I am taking my slaves and certain possessions to Kranzelkracht. I expect to make an enormous profit from my venture, and those knights bold enough to share it will gain much gold—not to mention fame."

Abiru paused to drink from a glass of wine. Kickaha, aside to Wolff, said, "The man's as big a liar as I am. He intends to use us to get him as far as Kranzelkracht, which is near the foot of the monolith. Then he will take Chryseis and the horn up to Atlantis, where he should be paid with a houseful of jewels and gold for the two.

"That is, unless his game is even deeper than I think at this moment."

He lifted his stein and drank for a long time, or appeared to. Setting the stein down with a crash, he said, "I'll be damned if there isn't something familiar about Abiru! I had a funny feeling the first time I saw him, but I was too busy thereafter to think much about it. Now, I know I've seen him before."

Wolff replied that that was not amazing. How many faces had he seen during his twenty-year wanderings?

"Maybe you're right," Kickaha muttered. "But I don't think it was any slight acquaintance I had with him. I'd sure like to scrape off his beard."

Abiru arose and excused himself, saying that it was the hour of prayer to the Lord and his personal deity, Tartartar. He would be back after his devotions. At this, von Elgers beckoned to two men-at-arms and ordered them to accompany him to his quarters and make sure that he was safe. Abiru bowed and thanked him for his consideration. Wolff did not miss the intent behind the baron's polite words. He did not trust the Khamshem, and Abiru knew it. Von Elgers, despite his drunkenness, was aware of what was going on and would detect anything out of the way.

"Yeah, you're right about him," Kickaha said. "He didn't get to where he is by turning his back on his enemies. And try to conceal your impatience, Bob. We've got a long wait ahead of us. Act drunk, make a few passes at the ladies—they'll think you're queer if you don't. But don't go off with any. We got to keep each other in sight so we can take off together when the right time comes."

13

WOLFF DRANK ENOUGH TO LOOSEN THE WIRES THAT SEEMED TO be wound around him. He even began to talk with the Lady Alison, wife of the baron of the Wenzelbricht March. A dark-haired and blue-eyed woman of statuesque beauty, she wore a clinging white samite gown. It was so low cut that she should have been satisfied with its exhilarating effect on the men, but she kept dropping her fan and picking it up herself. At any time other than this, Wolff would have been happy to break his woman-fast with her. It was obvious he would have no trouble doing so, for she was flattered that the great von Wolfram was interested in her. She had heard of his victory over funem Laksfalk. But he could think only of Chryseis, who must be somewhere in the castle. Nobody had mentioned her, and he dared not. Yet he was aching to do so and several times found that he had to bite the question off the tip of his tongue.

Presently, and just at the right time for him—since he could not any longer refuse the Lady Alison's bold hints without offending her— Kickaha was at his side. Kickaha had brought Alison's husband along to give Wolff a reasonable excuse for leaving. Later, Kickaha revealed that he had dragged von Wenzelbricht away from another woman on the pretext that his wife demanded he come to her. Both Kickaha and Wolff walked away, leaving the beer-stupored baron to explain just what he wanted of her. Since neither he nor his wife knew, they must have had an interesting, if mysti-fying conversation.

Wolff gestured at funem Laksfalk to join them. Together, the three pre-tended to stagger off to the toilet. Once out of sight of those in the dining-hall, they hurried down a hall away from their supposed destination. Un-hindered, they climbed four flights of steps. They were armed only with daggers, for it would have been an insult to wear armor or swords to din-ner. Wolff, however, had managed to untie a long cord from the draperies in his apartment. He wore this coiled around his waist under his shirt.

The Yidshe knight said, "I overheard Abiru talk with his lieutenant, Rhamnish. They spoke in the trade language of H'vaizhum, little knowing that I have traveled on the Guzirit River in the jungle area. Abiru asked Rhamnish if he had found out yet where von Elgers had taken Chryseis. Rhamnish said that he had spent some gold and time in talking to servants and guards. All he could find out was that she is on the east side of the castle. The gworl, by the way, are in the dungeon."

"Why should von Elgers keep Chryseis from Abiru?" Wolff said. "Isn't she Abiru's property?"

"Maybe the baron has some designs on her," Kickaha said. "If she's as extraordinary and beautiful as you say . . ."

"We've got to find her!"

"Don't get your neck hot. We will. Oh, oh, there's a guard at the end of the hall. Keep walking toward him—stagger a little more."

The guard raised his spear as they reeled in front of him. In a polite but firm voice, he told them they must go back. The baron had forbidden anybody, under pain of death, to proceed further.

"All right," Wolff said, slurring the words. He started to turn, then suddenly leaped and grabbed the spear. Before the startled sentry could loose the yell from his open mouth, he was slammed against the door and the shaft of the spear was brought up hard against his throat. Wolff continued to press it. The sentry's eyes goggled, his face became red, then blue. A minute later, he slumped forward, dead.

The Yidshe dragged the body down the hall and into a side-room. When he returned, he reported that he had hidden the corpse behind a large chest.

"Too bad," Kickaha said cheerfully. "He may have been a nice kid. But if we have to fight our way out, we'll have one less in our way."

However, the dead man had had no key to unlock the door.

"Von Elgers is probably the only man who has one, and we'd play hell getting it off him," Kickaha said. "Okay. We'll go around."

He led them back down the hall to another room. They climbed through its tall pointed window. Beyond its ledge was a series of projections, stones carved in the shape of dragon heads, fiends, boars. The adornments had not been spaced to provide for easy climbing, but a brave or desperate man could ascend them. Fifty feet below them, the surface of the moat glittered dully in the light of torches on the drawbridge. Fortunately, thick black clouds covered the moon and would prevent those below from seeing the climbers.

Kickaha looked down at Wolff, who was clinging to a stone gargoyle, one foot on a snake-head. "Hey, did I forget to tell you that the baron keeps the moat stocked with water-dragons? They're not very big, only about twenty feet long, and they don't have any legs. But they're usually underfed."

"There are times when I find your humor in bad taste," Wolff said fiercely. "Get going."

Kickaha gave a low laugh and continued climbing. Wolff followed, after glancing down to make sure that the Yidshe was doing all right. Kickaha stopped and said, "There's a window here, but it's barred. I don't think there's anyone inside. It's dark."

Kickaha continued climbing. Wolff paused to look inside the window. It was black as the inside of a cave fish's eye. He reached through the bars and groped around until his fingers closed on a candle. Lifting it carefully so that it would come out of its holder, he passed it through the bars. With one arm hooked around a steel rod, he hung while he fished a match from the little bag on his belt with the other hand.

From above, Kickaha said, "What are you doing?"

Wolff told him, and Kickaha said, "I spoke Chryseis' name a couple of times. There's no one in there. Quit wasting time."

"I want to make sure."

"You're too thorough; you pay too much attention to detail. You got to take big cuts if you want to chop down a tree. Come on."

Not bothering to reply, Wolff struck the match. It flared up and almost went out in the breeze, but he managed to stick it inside the window quickly enough. The flare of light showed a bedroom with no occupant.

"You satisfied?" Kickaha's voice came, weaker because he was climbing upward. "We got one more chance, the bartizan. If there's no one . . . Anyway, I don't know how—*ugh!*"

Afterwards, Wolff was thankful that he had been so reluctant to give up his hopes that Chryseis would be in the room. He had let the match burn out until it threatened his fingers and only then let go of it. Immediately after that and Kickaha's muffled exclamation, he was struck by a falling body. The impact felt as if it had almost torn his arm loose from its socket. He gave a grunt that echoed the one from above and hung on with one arm. Kickaha clung to him for several seconds, shivered, then breathed deeply and resumed his climb. Neither said a word about it, but both knew that if it had not been for Wolff's stubbornness, Kickaha's fall would also have knocked Wolff from a precarious hold on a gargoyle. Possibly funem Laksfalk would have been dislodged also, for he was directly below Wolff.

The bartizan was a large one. It was about one third of the way up the wall, projected far outward from the wall, and a light fell from its cross-shaped window. The wall a little distance above it was bare of decoration.

An uproar broke loose below and a fainter one within the castle. Wolff stopped to look down toward the drawbridge, thinking that they must have been seen. However, although there were a number of men-at-arms and guests on the drawbridge and the grounds outside, many with torches, not a single one was looking up toward the climbers. They seemed to be searching for someone in the bushes and trees.

He thought that their absence and the body of the guard had been noted. They would have to fight their way out. But let them find Chryseis first and get her loose; then would be time to think of battle.

Kickaha, ahead of him, said, "Come on, Bob!" His voice was so excited that Wolff knew he must have located Chryseis. He climbed swiftly, more swiftly than good sense permitted. It was necessary to climb to one side of the projection, for its underside angled outward. Kickaha was lying on the flat top of the bartizan and just in the act of pulling himself back from its edge. "You have to hang upside down to look in the window, Bob. She's there, and she's alone. But the window's too narrow for either of you to go through."

Wolff slid out over the edge of the projection while Kickaha grabbed his legs. He went out and over, the black moat below, and bent down until he would have fallen if his legs had not been held. The slit in the stone showed him the face of Chryseis, inverted. She was smiling but tears were rolling down her cheeks.

Afterward, he did not exactly remember what they said to each other, for he was in a fever of exaltation, succeeded by a chill of frustration and despair, then followed by another fever. He felt as if he could talk forever, and he reached his hand out to touch hers. She strained against the opening in the rock in vain to reach him.

"Never mind, Chryseis," he said. "You know we're here. We're not going to leave until we take you away, I swear it."

"Ask her where the horn is!" Kickaha said.

Hearing him, Chryseis said, "I do not know, but I think that von Elgers has it."

"Has he bothered you?" Wolff asked savagely.

"Not so far, but I do not know how long it will be before he takes me to bed," she replied. "He's restrained himself only because he does not want to lower the price he'll get for me. He says he's never seen a woman like me."

Wolff swore, then laughed. It was like her to talk thus frankly, for in the Garden world self-admiration was an accepted attitude.

"Cut out the unnecessary chatter," Kickaha said. "There'll be time for that if we get her out."

Chryseis answered Wolff's questions as concisely and clearly as possible. She described the route to this room. She did not know how many guards were stationed outside her door or on the way up.

"I do know one thing that the baron does not," she said. "He thinks that Abiru is taking me to von Kranzelkracht. I know better. Abiru means to ascend the Doozvillnava to Atlantis. There he will sell me to the Rhadamanthus."

"He won't sell you to anybody, because I'm going to kill him," Wolff said. "I have to go now, Chryseis, but I'll be back as soon as possible. And I won't be coming this way. Until then, I love you."

Chryseis cried, "I have not heard a man tell me that for a thousand years! Oh, Robert Wolff, I love you! But I am afraid! I . . ."

"You don't have to be afraid of anything," he said. "Not while I am alive, and I don't intend to die."

He gave the word for Kickaha to drag him back onto the rooftop of the bartizan. He rose and almost fell over from dizziness, for his head was gorged with blood.

"The Yidshe has already started down," Kickaha said. "I sent him to find out if we can get back the way we came and also to see what's causing the uproar."

"Us?"

"I don't think so. The first thing they'd do, they'd check on Chryseis. Which they haven't done."

The descent was even slower and more dangerous than the climb up, but they made it without mishap. Funem Laksfalk was waiting for them by the window which had given them access to the outside.

"They've found the guard you killed," he said. "But they don't think we had anything to do with it. The gworl broke loose from the dungeon and killed a number of men. They also seized their own weapons. Some got outside but not all."

The three left the room and merged quickly with the searchers. They had no chance to go up the flight of steps at the end of which was the room where Chryseis was imprisoned. Without a doubt, von Elgers would have made sure that the guards were increased.

They wandered around the castle for several hours, acquainting themselves with its layout. They noted that, though the shock of the gworl's escape had sobered the Teutons somewhat, they were still very drunk. Wolff suggested that they go to their room, and talk about possible plans. Perhaps they could think of something reasonably workable.

Their room was on the fifth story and by a window at an angle below the window of Chryseis' bartizan. To get to it, they had to pass many men and women, all stinking of beer and wine, reeling, babbling away, and accomplishing very little. Their room could not have been entered and searched, for only they and the chief warder had the keys. He had been too busy elsewhere to get to their room. Besides, how could the gworl enter through a locked door?

The moment Wolff stepped into his room, he knew that they had somehow entered. The musty rotten-fruit stench hit him in the nostrils. He pulled the other two inside and swiftly shut and locked the door behind them. Then he turned with his dagger in his hand. Kickaha also, his nostrils dilating and his eyes stabbing, had his blade out. Only funem Laksfalk was unaware that anything was wrong except for an unpleasant odor.

Wolff whispered to him; the Yidshe walked toward the wall to get their swords, then stopped. The racks were empty.

Silently and slowly, Wolff went into the other room. Kickaha, behind him, held a torch. The flame flickered and cast humped shadows that made Wolff start. He had been sure that they were the gworl.

The light advanced; the shadows fled or changed into harmless shapes. "They're here," Wolff said softly. "Or they've just left. But where could they go?"

Kickaha pointed at the high drapes that were drawn over the window. Wolff strode up to them and began thrusting through the red-purple velvet cloth. His blade met only air and the stone of the wall. Kickaha pulled the drapes back to reveal what the dagger had told him. There were no gworl.

"They came in through the window," the Yidshe said. "But why?"

Wolff lifted his eyes at the moment, and he swore. He stepped back to warn his friends, but they were already looking upward. There, hanging upside down by their knees from the heavy iron drapery rod, were two gworl. Both had long, bloody knives in their hands. One, in addition, clutched the silver horn.

The two creatures stiffened their legs the second they realized they were discovered. Both managed to flip over and come down heads-up. The one to the right kicked out with his feet. Wolff rolled and then was up, but Kickaha had missed with his knife and the gworl had not. It slid from his palm through a short distance into Kickaha's arm.

The other threw his knife at funem Laksfalk. It struck the Yidshe in the solar plexus with a force that made him bend over and stagger back. A few seconds later, he straightened up to reveal why the knife had failed to enter his flesh. Through the tear in his shirt gleamed the steel of light chain-mail.

By then, the gworl with the horn had gone through the window. The others could not rush to the window because the gworl left behind was putting up a savage battle. He knocked down Wolff again, but with his fist this time. He threw himself like a whirlwind at Kickaha, his fists flailing, and drove him back. The Yidshe, his knife in hand, jumped at him and thrust for his belly, only to have his wrist seized and turned until he cried out with the pain and the knife fell from his fist.

Kickaha, lying on the floor, raised one leg and then drove the heel of his foot against the gworl's ankle. He fell, although he did not hit the floor because Wolff seized him. Around and around, their arms locked around each other, they circled. Each was trying to break the other's back and also trying to trip the other. Wolff succeeded in throwing him over. They toppled against the wall with the gworl receiving the most damage when the back of his head struck the wall.

For a flicker of an eyelid, he was stunned. This gave Wolff enough time to pull the stinking, hairy, bumpy creature hard against him and pull with all his strength against the gworl's spine. Too heavily muscled and too heavily boned, the gworl resisted the spine-snapping. By then, the other two men were upon him with their knives. They thrust several times and would have continued to try for a fatal spot in the tough cartilage-roughened hide had Wolff not told them to stop.

Stepping back, he released the gworl, who fell bleeding and glaze-eyed to the floor. Wolff ignored him for a moment to look out the window after the gworl who had escaped with the horn. A party of horsemen, holding torches, was thundering over the drawbridge and out into the country. The light showed only the smooth black waters of the moat; there was no gworl climbing down the wall. Wolff turned back to the gworl who had remained behind.

"His name is Diskibibol, and the other is Smeel," Kickaha said.

"Smeel must have drowned," Wolff said. "Even if he could swim, the water-dragons might have gotten him. But he can't swim."

Wolff thought of the horn lying in the muck at the bottom of the moat. "Apparently no one saw Smeel fall. So the horn's safe there, for the time being."

The gworl spoke. Although he used German, he could not master the sounds accurately. His words grated deep in the back of his throat. "You will die, humans. The Lord will win; Arwoor is the Lord; he cannot be defeated by filth such as you. But before you die, you will suffer the most . . . the . . . the most . . ."

He began coughing, threw up blood, and continued to do so until he was dead.

"We'd better get rid of his body," Wolff said. "We might have a hard time explaining what he was doing here. And von Elgers might connect the missing horn with their presence here."

A look out of the window showed him that the search party was far down the trail road leading to the town. For the moment, at least, no one was on the bridge. He lifted the heavy corpse up and shoved it out the window. After Kickaha's wound was bandaged, Wolff and the Yidshe wiped up the evidences of the struggle.

Only after they were through did funem Laksfalk speak. His face pale and grim. "That was the horn of the Lord. I insist that you tell me how it got here and what your part is in this . . . this seeming blasphemy."

"Now's the time for the whole truth," Kickaha said. "You tell him, Bob. For once, I don't feel like hogging the conversation."

Wolff was concerned for Kickaha, for his face, too, was pale, and the blood was oozing out through the thick bandages. Nevertheless, he told the Yidshe what he could as swiftly as possible.

The knight listened well, although he could not help interjecting questions frequently or swearing when Wolff told him something particularly amazing.

"By God," he said when Wolff seemed to be finished, "this tale of another world would make me call you a liar if the rabbis had not already told me that my ancestors, and those of the Teutons, had come from just such a place. Then there is the Book of the Second Exodus, which says the same thing and also claims that the Lord came from a different world.

"Still, I had always thought these tales the stuff that holy men, who are a trifle mad, dream up. I would never have dreamed of saying so aloud, of course, for I did not want to be stoned for heresy. Also, there's always the doubt that these could be true. And the Lord punishes those who deny him; there's no doubt of that.

"Now, you put me in a situation no man could envy. I know you two for the most redoubtable knights it has ever been my fortune to encounter. You are such men as would not lie; I would stake my life on that. And your story rings true as the armor of the great dragon-slayer, fun Zilberbergl. Yet, I do not know."

He shook his head. "To seek to enter the citadel of the Lord himself, to strike against the Lord! That frightens me. For the first time in my life, I, Leyb funem Lakfalk, admit that I am afraid."

Wolff said, "You gave your oath to us. We release you but ask that you do as you swore. That is, you tell no one of us or our quest."

Angrily, the Yidshe said, "I did not say I would quit you! I will not, at least not yet. There is this that makes me think you might be telling the truth. The Lord is omnipotent, yet his holy horn has been in your hands and those of the gworl, and the Lord has done nothing. Perhaps . . ."

Wolff replied that he did not have time to wait for him to make up his mind. The horn must be recovered now, while there was the opportunity. And Chryseis must be freed at the first chance. He led them from the room and into another, unoccupied at the moment. There they took three swords to replace theirs, which the gworl must have cast out of the window into the moat. Within a few minutes, they were outside the castle and pretending to search through the woods for the gworl.

By then most of the Teutons outside had returned to the castle. The three waited until the stragglers decided that no gworl were around. When the last of these had gone across the drawbridge, Wolff and his friends put out their torches. Two sentries remained at the guardhouse by the end of the bridge. These, however, were a hundred yards distant and could not see into the shadows where the three crouched. Moreover, they were too busy discussing the events of the night and looking into the darkness of the woods. They were not the original sentries, for these had been killed by the gworl when they had made their dash for freedom across the bridge.

"The point just below our window should be where the horn is," Wolff said. "Only . . ."

"The water-dragons," Kickaha said. "They'll have dragged off Smeel and

Diskibibol's bodies to their lairs, wherever those are. But there might be some others cruising around. I'd go, but this wound of mine would draw them at once."

"I was just talking to myself," Wolff said. He began to take off his clothes. "How deep's the moat?"

"You'll find out," Kickaha said.

Wolff saw something gleam redly in the reflected light from the distant bridge torches. An animal's eyes, he thought. The next moment, he and the others were caught within something sticky and binding. The stuff, whatever it was, covered his eyes and blinded him.

He fought savagely but silently. Though he did not know who his assailants were, he did not intend to arouse the castle people. However the struggle came out, the issue did not concern them; he knew that.

The more he thrashed, the tighter the webs clung to him and bound him. Eventually, raging, breathing hard, he was helpless. Only then did a voice speak, low and rasping. A knife cut the web to leave his face exposed. In the dim light of the distant torches, he could see two other figures wrapped in the stuff and a dozen crooked shapes. The rotten-fruit stench was powerful.

"I am Ghaghrill, the Zdrrikh'agh of Abbkmung. You are Robert Wolff and our great enemy Kickaha, and the third one I do not know."

"The Baron funem Laksfalk!" the Yidshe said. "Release me, and you will soon find out whether I am a good man to know or not, you stinking swine!"

"Quiet! We know you have somehow slain two of my best killers, Smeel and Diskibibol, though they could not have been so fierce if they allowed themselves to be defeated by such as you. We saw Diskibibol fall from where we hid in the woods. And we saw Smeel jump with the horn."

Ghaghril paused, then said, "You, Wolff, will go after the horn into the waters and bring it back to us. If you do, I swear by the honor of the Lord that we will release all three of you. The Lord wants Kickaha, too, but not as badly as the horn, and he said that we were not to kill him, even if we had to let him go to keep from killing him. We obey the Lord, for he is the greatest killer of all."

"And if I refuse?" Wolff said. "It is almost certain death for me with the water-dragons in the moat."

"It will be certain death for you if you don't."

Wolff considered. He was the logical choice, he had to admit. The quality and relationship of the Yidshe was unknown to the gworl, so they could not let him go after the horn; he might fail to return. Kickaha was a prize second only to the horn. Besides, he was wounded, and the blood from the wound would attract the water-monsters. Wolff, if he cared for Kickaha, would return. They could not, of course, be sure of the depth of his feelings for Kickaha. That was a chance they would have to take.

One thing was certain. No gworl was about to venture into such deep water if he had someone else to do it for him.

"Very well," Wolff said. "Let me loose, and I will go after the horn. But at least give me a knife to defend myself against the dragons."

"No," Ghaghrill said.

Wolff shrugged. After he was cut loose of the web-net, he removed all of his clothes except his shirt. This covered the cord wound around his waist.

"Don't do it, Bob," Kickaha said. "You can't trust a gworl any more than his master. They will take the horn from you and then do to us what they wish. And laugh at us for being their tools."

"I don't have any choice," Wolff said. "If I find the horn, I'll be back. If I don't return, you'll know I died trying."

"You'll die anyway," Kickaha replied. There was a smack of a fist against flesh. Kickaha cursed but did so softly.

"Speak any more, Kickaha," Ghaghrill said, "and I will cut out your tongue. The Lord did not forbid that."

14

WOLFF LOOKED UP AT THE WINDOW, FROM WHICH A TORCH light still shone. He walked into the water, which was chilly but not cold. His feet sank into thick gluey mud which evoked images of the many corpses whose rotting flesh must form part of this mud. And he could not keep from thinking of the saurians swimming out there. If he was lucky, they would not be in the immediate neighborhood. If they had dragged off the bodies of Smeel and Diskibibol . . . Better quit dwelling on them and start swimming.

The moat was at least two hundred yards wide at this point. He even stopped at the midway point to tread water and turn around to look at the shore. From this distance he could see nothing of the group.

On the other hand, they could not see him either. And Ghaghrill had given him no time limit to return. However, he knew that if he were not back before dawn, he would not find them there.

At a spot immediately below the light from the window, he dived. Down he went, the water becoming colder almost with every stroke. His ears began to ache, then to hurt intensely. He blew some bubbles of air out to relieve the pressure, but he was not helped much by this. Just as it seemed that he could go no deeper without his ears bursting, his hand plunged into soft mud. Restraining the desire to turn at once and swim upwards for the blessed relief from pressure and the absolutely needed air, he groped around on the floor of the moat. He found nothing but mud and, once, a bone. He drove himself until he knew he had to have air.

Twice he rose to the surface and then dived again. By now, he knew that even if the horn were lying on the bottom, he might not ever find it. Blind in the murky waters, he could pass within an inch of the horn and never know it. Moreover, it was possible that Smeel had thrown the horn far away from him when he had fallen. Or a water-dragon could have carried it off with Smeel's corpse, even swallowed the horn.

The third time, he swam a few strokes to the right from his previous dives before plunging under. He dived down at what he hoped was a ninety-degree angle from the bottom. In the blackness, he had no way of determining direction. His hand plowed into the mud; he settled close to it to feel around, and his fingers closed upon cold metal. A quick slide of them along the object passed over seven little buttons.

When he reached the surface, he trod water and gasped for wind. Now to make the trip back, which he hoped he could do. The water-dragons could still show up.

Then he forgot the dragons, for he could see nothing. The torchlight from the drawbridge, the feeble moonglow through the clouds, the light from the window overhead, all these were gone.

Wolff forced himself to keep on treading water while he thought his situation through. For one thing, there was no breeze. The air was stale. Thus, he could only be in one place, and it was his fortune that such a place happened to be just where he had dived. Also, it was his luck that he had come up from the bottom at an oblique angle.

Still, he could not see which way was shoreward and which way was castleward. To find out took only a few strokes. His hand contacted stone— stone bricks. He groped along it until it began to curve inward. Following the curve, he finally came to that which he had hoped for. It was a flight of stone steps that rose out of the water and led upward.

He climbed up it, slowly, his hand out for a sudden obstacle. His feet slid over each step, ready to pause if an opening appeared or a step seemed loose. After twenty steps upward, he came to their end. He was in a corridor cut out of stone.

Von Elgers, or whoever had built the castle, had constructed a means for secret entrance and exit. An opening below water level in the walls led to a chamber, a little port, and from thence into the castle. Now, Wolff had the horn and a way to get unnoticed into the castle. But he did not know what to do. Should he return the horn to the gworl first? Afterward, he and the two others could return this way and search for Chryseis.

He doubted that Ghaghrill would keep his word. However, even if the gworl were to release their captives, if they swam to this place, Kickaha's wound would draw the saurians and all three would be lost. Chryseis would have no chance of getting free. Kickaha could not be left behind while the other two went back to the castle. He would be exposed as soon as dawn came. He could hide in the woods, but the chances were that another hunting party would be searching that area then. Especially after it was discovered that the three stranger knights were gone.

He decided to go on down the hall. This was too good a chance to pass up. He would do his best before daylight. If he failed, then he would go back with the horn.

The horn! No use taking that with him. Should he be captured without it, his knowledge of its location might help him.

He returned to where the steps came to an end below the water. He dived down to a depth of about ten feet and left the horn on the mud.

Back in the corridor, he shuffled until he came to more steps at its end. The flight led upward on a tight spiraling course. A count of steps led him to think that he had ascended at least five stories. At every estimated story he felt around the narrow walls for doors or releases to open doors. He found none.

At what could have been the seventh story, he saw a tiny beam of light from a hole in the wall. Bending down, he peered through it. By the far end of the room, seated at a table, a bottle of wine before him, was Baron von Elgers. The man seated across the table from the baron was Abiru.

The baron's face was flushed by more than drink. He snarled at Abiru, "That's all I intend to say, Khamshem! You will get the horn back from the gworl, or I'll have your head! Only first you'll be taken to the dungeon! I have some curious iron devices there that you will be interested in!"

Abiru rose. His face was as pale beneath its dark pigment as the baron's was crimson.

"Believe me, sire, if the horn has been taken by the gworl, it will be recovered. They can't have gone far with it—if they have it—and they can easily be tracked down. They can't pass themselves off as human beings, you know. Besides, they're stupid."

The baron roared, stood up, and crashed his fist against the top of the table.

"Stupid! They were clever enough to break out of my dungeon, and I would would have sworn that no one could do that! And they found my room and took the horn! You call that stupid!"

"At least," Abiru said, "they didn't steal the girl, too. I'll get something out of this. She should fetch a fabulous price."

"She'll fetch nothing for you! She is mine!"

Abiru glared and said, "She is my property. I obtained her at great peril and brought her all this way at much expense. I am entitled to her. What are you, a man of honor or a thief?"

Von Elgers struck him and knocked him down. Abiru, rubbing his cheek, got to his feet at once. Looking steadily at the baron, his voice tight, he said, "And what about my jewels?"

"They are in my castle!" the baron shouted. "And what is in my castle is the von Elgers'!"

He strode away out of Wolff's sight but apparently opened a door. He bellowed for the guard, and when they had come they took Abiru away between them.

"You are fortunate I do not kill you!" the baron raged. "I am allowing you to keep your life, you miserable dog! You should get down on your knees and thank me for that! Now get out of the castle at once. If I hear that you are not making all possible speed to another state, I will have you hung on the nearest tree!"

Abiru did not reply. The door closed. The baron paced back and forth for awhile, then abruptly came toward the wall behind which Wolff was crouched. Wolff left the peephole and retreated far down the steps. He hoped he had chosen the right direction in which to go. If the baron came down the staircase, he could force Wolff into the water and perhaps back out into the moat. But he did not think the baron intended to come that way.

For a second the light was cut off. A section of wall swung out with the baron's finger thrust through the hole. The torch held by von Elgers lit the well. Wolff crouched down behind the shadow cast by a turn of the corkscrew case. Presently, the light became weaker as the baron carried it up the steps. Wolff followed.

He could not keep his eyes on von Elgers all the time, for he had to dodge down behind various turns to keep from being detected if the baron should look downward. So it was that he did not see von Elgers leave the stairs nor know it until the light suddenly went out.

He went swiftly after the baron, although he did pause by the peephole. He stuck his finger in it and lifted upward. A small section gave way, a click sounded, and a door swung open for him. The inner side of the door formed part of the wall of the baron's quarters. Wolff stepped into the room, chose a thin eight-inch dagger from a rack in the wall, and went back out to the stairs. After shutting the door, he climbed upward.

This time he had no light from a hole to guide him. Nor was he even sure that he had stopped at the same place as the baron. He had made a rough estimate of the height from himself to the baron when the baron had disappeared. There was nothing else to do but feel around for the device which the baron must have used to open another door. When he placed his ear against the wall to listen for voices, he heard nothing.

His fingers slid over bricks and moisture-crumbled mortar until they met wood. That was all he could find: stone and a wooden frame in which a broad and high panel of wood was smoothly inset. There was nothing to indicate an open-sesame.

He climbed a few steps more and continued to probe. The bricks were innocent of any trigger or catch. He returned to the spot opposite the door and felt the wall there. Nothing.

Now he was frantic. He was sure that von Elgers had gone to Chryseis' room, and not just to talk. He went back down the steps and fingered the walls. Still nothing.

Again he tried the area around the door with no success. He pushed on one side of the door, only to find it would not budge. For a moment he thought of hammering on the wood and attracting von Elgers. If the baron were to come through to investigate, he would be helpless for a moment to an attack from above.

He rejected the idea. The baron was too canny to fall for such a trick.

While he was unlikely to go for help, because he would not want to reveal the passageway to others, he could leave Chryseis' room through the regular door. The guard posted outside might wonder where he came from, although he would probably think that the baron had been inside before the watch had been changed. In any case, the baron could permanently shut the mouth of a suspicious guard. Wolff pushed in on the other side of the door, and it swung inward. It had not been locked; all it needed was pressure on the correct side.

He groaned softly at missing the obvious so long and stepped through. It was dark beyond the door; he was in a small room, almost a closet. This was composed of mortared bricks, except at one side. Here a metal rod poked from the wooden wall. Before working it, Wolff placed his ear against the wall. Muffled voices came through, too faint for him to recognize.

The metal rod had to be pulled out to activate the release on the door. Dagger in hand, Wolff stepped through it. He was in a large chamber of great stone blocks. There was a large bed with four ornately carved posters of glossy black wood and a bright-pink tassled canopy. Beyond it was the narrow cross-shaped window through which he had looked earlier that night.

Von Elgers' back was to him. The baron had Chryseis in his arms and was forcing her toward the bed. Her eyes were closed, and her head was turned away to avoid von Elgers' kisses. Both of them were still fully clothed.

Wolff bounded across the room, seized the baron by the shoulder, and pulled him backward. The baron let loose of Chryseis to reach for the dagger in his scabbard, then remembered that he had brought none. Apparently he had not intended to give Chryseis a chance to stab him.

His face, so flaming before, was gray now. His mouth worked, the cry for help to the guards outside the door frozen by surprise and fear.

Wolff gave him no chance to summon help. He dropped the dagger to strike the baron on the chin with his fist. Von Elgers, unconscious, slumped. Wolff did not want to waste any time, so he brushed by Chryseis, huge-eyed and pale. He cut off two strips of cloth from the bedsheets. The smaller he placed inside the baron's mouth, the larger he used as a gag. Then he removed a piece of the cord around his waist and tied von Elgers' hands in front of him. Hoisting the limp body over his shoulder, he said to Chryseis, "Come on. We can talk later."

He did pause to give instructions to Chryseis to close the wall-door behind them. There was no sense in letting others find the passageway when they finally came to investigate the baron's long absence. Chryseis held the torch behind him as they went down the steps. When they had come to the water, Wolff told her what they must do to escape. First, he had to retrieve the horn. Having done so, he scooped up water with his hands and threw it on the baron's face. When he saw his eyes open, he informed him of what he must do.

Von Elgers shook his head no. Wolff said, "Either you go with us as hostage and take your chances with the water-dragons or you die right now. So which is it?"

The baron nodded. Wolff cut his bonds but attached the end of the cord to his ankle. All three went into the water. Immediately, von Elgers swam out to the wall and dived. The others followed under the wall, which only went about four feet below the surface. Coming up on the other side, Wolff saw that the clouds were beginning to break. The moon would soon be bearing down in all her green brightness.

As directed, the baron and Chryseis swam at an angle toward the other side of the moat. Wolff followed with the end of the cord in one hand. With its burden, they could not go swiftly. In fifteen minutes the moon would be rounding the monolith, with the sun not far behind at the other corner. There was not much time for Wolff to carry out his plan, but it was impossible to keep control of the baron unless they took their time.

Their point of arrival at the bank of the moat was a hundred yards beyond where the gworl and their captives waited. Within a few minutes they were around the curve of the castle and out of sight of the gworl and the guards on the bridge even if the moon became unclouded. This path was a necessary evil—evil because every second in the water meant more chance for the dragons to discover them.

When they were within twenty yards of their goal, Wolff felt rather than saw the roil of water. He turned to see the surface lift a little and a small wave coming toward him. He drew up his feet and kicked. They struck something hard and solid enough to allow him to spring away. He shot backward, dropping the end of the cord at the same time. The bulk passed between him and Chryseis, struck von Elgers, and was gone.

So was Wolff's hostage.

They abandoned any attempt to keep from making splashing noises. They swam as hard as they could. Only when they reached the bank and scrambled up onto it and ran to a tree did they stop. Sobbing for breath, they clung to the trunk.

Wolff did not wait until he had fully regained his breath. The sun would be around Doozvillnavava within a few minutes. He told Chryseis to wait for him. If he did not return shortly after sunaround, he would not be coming for a long time—if ever. She would have to leave and hide in the woods and then do whatever she could.

She begged him not to go, for she could not stand the idea of being all alone there.

"I have to," he said, handing her an extra dagger which he had stuck through his shirt and secured by knotting the shirttail about it.

"I will use it on myself if you are killed," she said.

He was in agony at the thought of her being so helpless, but there was nothing he could do about it.

"Kill me now before you leave me," she said. "I've gone through too much; I can't stand any more."

He kissed her lightly on the lips and said, "Sure you can. You're tougher than you used to be and always were tougher than you thought. Look at you now. You can say *kill* and *death* without so much as flinching."

He was gone, running crouched over toward the spot where he had left his friends and the gworl. When he estimated he was about twenty yards from them, he stopped to listen. He heard nothing except the cry of a night-bird and a muffled shout from somewhere in the castle. On his hands and knees, the dagger in his teeth, he crawled toward the place opposite the light from the window of his quarters. At any moment he expected to smell the musty odor and to see a clump of blackness against the lesser dark.

But there was nobody there. Only the glimmer-gray remnants of the web-nets remained to show that the gworl had actually been there.

He prowled around the area. When it became evident that there was no clue and that the sun would shortly expose him to the bridge guards, he returned to Chryseis. She clung to him and cried a little.

"See! I'm here after all," he said. "But we have to get out of here now."

"We're going back to Okeanos?"

"No, we're going after my friends."

They trotted away, past the castle and toward the monolith. The absence of the baron would soon be noticed. For miles around, no ordinary hiding place would be safe. And the gworl, knowing this, must also be making speed toward Doozvillnavava. No matter how badly they wanted the horn, they could not hang around now. Moreover, they must think that Wolff had drowned or been taken by a dragon. To them, the horn might be out of reach just now, but they could return when it was safe to do so.

Wolff pushed hard. Except for brief rests, they did not stop until they had reached the thick forest of the Rauhwald. There they crawled beneath the tangled thorns and through the intertwined bushes until their knees bled and their joints ached. Chryseis collapsed. Wolff gathered many of the plentiful berries for them to feed upon. They slept all night, and in the morning resumed their all-fours progress. By the time they had reached the other side of the Rauhwald, they were covered with thorn-wounds. There was no one waiting for them on the other side, as he had feared there would be.

This and another thing made him happy. He had come across evidence that the gworl had also passed his way. There were bits of coarse gworl hair on thorns and pieces of cloth. No doubt Kickaha had managed to drop these to mark the way if Wolff should be following.

15

AFTER A MONTH, THEY FINALLY ARRIVED AT THE FOOT OF THE monolith, Doozvillnavava. They knew they were on the right trail, since they had heard rumors of the gworl and even talked with those who had sighted them from a distance.

"I don't know why they've gone so far from the horn," he said. "Perhaps they mean to hole up in a cave in the face of the mountain and will come back down after the cry for them has died out."

"Or it could be," Chryseis said, "that they have orders from the Lord to bring Kickaha back first. He has been like an insect on the Lord's eardrum so long that the Lord must be crazed even by the thought of him. Maybe he wants to make sure that Kickaha is out of the way before he sends the gworl again for the horn."

Wolff agreed that she could be right. It was even possible that the Lord was going to come down from the palace via the same cords by which he had lowered the gworl. That did not seem likely, however, for the Lord would not want to be stranded. Could he trust the gworl to hoist him back up?

Wolff looked at the eye-staggering heights of the continent-broad tower of Doozvillnavava. It was, according to Kickaha, at least twice as high as the monolith of Abharhploonta, which supported the tier of Dracheland. It soared 60,000 feet or more, and the creatures that lived on the ledges and recesses and in the caves were fully as dreadful and hungry as those on the other monoliths. Doozvillnavava was gnarled and scoured and slashed and bristly; its ravaged face had an enormous recession that gave it a dark and gaping mouth; the giant seemed ready to eat all who dared to annoy it.

Chryseis, also examining the savage cliffs and their incredible height, shivered. But she said nothing; she had quit voicing her fears some time ago.

It could be that she was no longer concerned with herself, Wolff thought, but was intent upon the life within her. She was sure that she was pregnant.

He put his arm around her, kissed her, and said, "I'd like to start at once, but we'll have to make preparations for several days. We can't attack that monster without resting or without enough food."

Three days later, dressed in tough buckskin garments and carrying ropes, weapons, climbing tools, and bags of food and water, they began the ascent. Wolff bore the horn in a soft leather bag tied to his back.

Ninety-one days later, they were at an estimated half-way point. And at least every other step had been a battle against smooth verticality, rotten and treacherous rock, or against the predators. These included the many-footed snake he had encountered on Thayaphayawoed, wolves with great rock-gripping paws, the boulder ape, ostrich-sized axebeaks, and the small but deadly downdropper.

When the two climbed over the edge of the top of Doozvillnavava, they had been 186 days on the journey. Neither was the same, physically or mentally, as at the start. Wolff weighed less but he had far more endurance and wiriness to his strength. He bore the scars of downdroppers, boulder apes, and axebeaks on his face and body. His hatred for the Lord was even more intense, for Chryseis had lost the foetus before they had gotten 10,000 feet up. Such was to be expected, but he could not forget that they would not have had to make the climb if it had not been for the Lord.

Chryseis had been toughened in body and spirit by her experiences before she had started up Doozvillnavava. Yet the things and situations on this monolith had been far worse than anything previously, and she might have broken. That she did not vindicated Wolff's original feeling that she was basically of strong fiber. The effect of the millenia of sapping life in the Garden had been sloughed off. The Chryseis who conquered this monolith was much like the woman who had been abducted from the savage and demanding life of the ancient Aegean. Only she was far wiser.

Wolff waited for several days to rest and hunt and repair the bows and make new arrows. He also kept a watch for an eagle. He had not been in contact with any since he had talked to Phthie in the ruined city by the river of Guzirit. No green-bodied yellow-headed bird appeared, so he reluctantly decided to enter the jungle. As on Dracheland, a thousand-mile thick belt of jungle circled the entire rim. Within the belt was the land of Atlantis. This, exclusive of the monolith in its center, covered an area the size of France and Germany combined.

Wolff had looked for the pillar on top of which was the Lord's palace, since Kickaha had said that it could be seen from the rim even though it was much more slender than any of the other monoliths. He could see only a vast and dark continent of clouds, jagged and coiled with lightning. Idaquizzoorhruz was hidden. Nor, whenever Wolff ascended a high hill or climbed a tall tree, could he see it. A week later, the stormclouds continued to shroud the pillar of stone. This worried him, for he had not seen such a storm in the three and a half years he had been on this planet.

Fifteen days passed. On the sixteenth, they found on the narrow green-fraught path a headless corpse. A yard away in the bush was the turbaned head of a Khamshem.

"Abiru could be trailing the gworl, too," he said. "Maybe the gworl took his jewels when they left von Elgers' castle. Or, more likely, he thinks they have the horn."

A mile and a half further on, they came across another Khamshem, his stomach ripped open and his entrails hanging out. Wolff tried to get information out of him until he found that the man was too far gone. Wolff put him out of his pain, noting that Chryseis did not even look away while he did so. Afterward, he put his knife in his belt and held the Khamshem's scimitar in his right hand. He felt that he would soon need it.

A half-hour later, he heard shouts and whoops down the trail. He and Chryseis concealed themselves in the foilage beside the path. Abiru and two Khamshem came running with death loping after them in the form of three squat Negroids with painted faces and long kinky scarlet-dyed beards. One threw his spear; it sailed through the air to end in the back of a Khamshem. He plunged forward without a sound and slid on the soft damp earth like a sailboat launched into eternity, the spear as the mast. The other two Khamshem turned to make a stand.

Wolff had to admire Abiru, who fought with great skill and courage. Although his companion went down with a spear in his solar plexus, Abiru continued to slash with his scimitar. Presently two of the savages were dead, and the third turned tail. After the Negroid had disappeared, Wolff came up silently behind Abiru. He struck with the edge of his palm to paralyze the man's arm and cause the scimitar to drop.

Abiru was so startled and scared he could not talk. On seeing Chryseis step out from the bushes, his eyes bulged even more. Wolff asked him what the situation was. After a struggle, Abiru regained his tongue and began to talk. As Wolff had guessed, he had pursued the gworl with his men and a number of Sholkin. Some miles from here, he had caught up with them. Rather, they had caught him. The ambush had been half-successful, for it had slain or incapacitated a good third of the Khamshem. All this had been done without loss to the gworl, who had cast knives from trees or from the bushes.

The Khamshem had broken away and fled, hoping to make a stand in a better place down the trail—if they could find one. Then both hunted and hunter had run into a horde of black savages.

"And there'll be more of them soon looking for you," Wolff said. "What about Kickaha and funem Laksfalk?"

"I do not know about Kickaha. He was not with the gworl. But the Yid-she knight was."

For a moment, Wolff thought of killing Abiru. However, he disliked doing it in cold blood and he also wanted to ask him more questions. He believed that there was more to him than he pretended to be. Shoving Abiru on ahead with the point of the scimitar, he went down the trail. Abiru protested that they would be killed; Wolff told him to shut up. In a few minutes they heard the shouts and screams of men in battle. They crossed a shallow stream and were at the bottom of a steep, high hill.

This was so rocky that comparatively little vegetation covered it. Along a line up the hill was the wake of the fight—dead and wounded gworl, Khamshem, Sholkin, and savages. Near the top of the hill, their backs against a V-shaped wall and under an overhang formed by two huge boulders, three held off the blacks. These were a gworl, a Khamshem, and the Yidshe baron. Even as Wolff and Chryseis started to go up, the Khamshem fell, pierced by several of the shovel-sized spearheads. Wolff told Chryseis to go back. For answer, she fitted an arrow to her bow and shot. A savage in the rear of the mob fell backward, the shaft sticking from his back.

Wolff smiled grimly and began to work his own bow. He and Chryseis chose only those at the extreme rear, hoping to shoot down a number before those at the front noticed. They were successful until the twelfth fell. A savage happened to glance back and see the man behind him crumple. He yelled and pulled at the arms of those nearest him. These immediately brandished their spears and began running down the hill toward the two, leaving most of their party to attack the gworl and the Yidshe. Before they had reached the bottom half of the hill, four more were down.

Three more tumbled headlong and rolled down with shafts in them. The remaining six lost their zeal to come at close quarters. Halting, they threw their spears, which were launched at such a distance that the archers had no trouble dodging them. Wolff and Chryseis, operating coolly and skillfully from much practice and experience, then shot four more. The two survivors, screaming, ran back up to their fellows. Neither made it, although one was only wounded in the leg.

By then, the gworl had fallen. Funem Laksfalk was left alone against forty. He did have a slight advantage, which was that they could get to him only two at a time. The walls of the boulders and the barricade of corpses prevented the others from swarming over him. Funem Laksfalk, his scimitar bloody and swinging, sang loudly some Yiddish fighting song.

Wolff and Chryseis took partial cover behind two boulders and renewed their rear attack. Five more fell, but the quivers of both were empty. Wolff said, "Pull some from the corpses and use them again. I'm going to help him."

He picked up a spear and ran at an angle across and up the hill, hoping that the savages would be too occupied to see him. When he had come around the hill, he saw two savages crouched on top of the boulder. These were kept from jumping down upon the Yidshe's rear by the overhang of the roughly shaped boulders. But they were waiting for a moment when he would venture too far out from its protection.

Wolff hurled his spear and caught one in the buttocks. The savage cried out and pitched forward from the rock and, presumably, on his fellows below. The other stood up and whirled around in time to get Wolff's knife in his belly. He fell backwards off the rock.

Wolff lifted a small boulder and heaved it on top of one of the great boulders and climbed up after it. Then he lifted the small boulder again, raised it above his head, and walked to the front of the great boulder. He yelled and threw it down into the crowd. They looked up in time to see the rock descending on them. It smashed at least three and rolled down the hill. At that, the survivors fled in a panic. Perhaps they thought that there must be others than Wolff. Or because they were undisciplined savages, they had been unnerved by too many losses already. The sight of so many of their dead shot down behind them must also have added to their panic.

Wolff hoped they would not return. To add fuel to their fright, he leaped down and picked up the boulder again and sent it crashing down the hill after them. It leaped and bounded as if it were a wolf after a rabbit and actually struck one more before it reached bottom.

Chryseis, from behind her boulder, put two more arrows into the savages.

He turned to the baron and found him lying on the ground. His face was gray, and blood was welling from around the spearhead driven into his chest.

"You!" he said faintly. "The man from the other world. You saw me fight?"

Wolff stepped down by him to examine the wound. "I saw. You fought like one of Joshua's warriors, my friend. You fought as I have never seen a man fight. You must have slain at least twenty."

Funem Laksfalk managed to smile a trifle. "It was twenty-five. I counted them."

Then he smiled broadly and said, "We are both stretching the truth a trifle, as our friend Kickaha would say. But not too much. It was a great fight. I only regret that I had to fight unfriended and unarmored and in a lonely place where none will ever know that a funem Laksfalk added honor to the name. Even if it was against a bunch of howling and naked savages."

"They will know," Wolff said. "I will tell them some day."

He did not give false words of comfort. He and the Yidshe both knew that death was around the corner, sniffing eagerly at the end of the track.

"Do you know what happened to Kickaha?" he said.

"Ah, that trickster? He slipped his chains one night. He tried to loosen mine, too, but he could not. Then he left, with the promise that he would return to free me. And so he will, but he will be too late."

Wolff looked down the hill. Chryseis was climbing toward him with several arrows which she had recovered from corpses. The blacks had regrouped at the foot and were talking animatedly among themselves. Others came out of the jungle to join them. The fresh ones swelled the number to forty. These were led by a man garbed in feathers and wearing a hideous wooden mask. He whirled a bull-roarer, leaped up and down, and seemed to be haranguing them.

The Yidshe asked Wolff what was happening. Wolff told him. The Yidshe spoke so weakly that Wolff had to put his ear close to the knight's mouth.

"It was my fondest dream, Baron Wolff, that I would some day fight by your side. Ah, what a noble pair of knights we would have made, in armor and swinging our . . . *S'iz kalt.*"

The lips became silent and blue. Wolff rose to look down the hill again. The savages were moving up and also spreading out to prevent flight. Wolff set to work dragging bodies and piling them to form a rampart. The only hope, a weak one, was to permit passage for only one or two to attack at a time. If they lost enough men, they might get discouraged and leave. He did not really think so, for these savages showed a remarkable persistence despite what must be to them staggering losses. Also, they could always retreat just far enough to wait for Wolff and Chryseis to be driven from their refuge by thirst and hunger.

The savages stopped halfway up to give those who had gone around the hill time to establish their stations. Then, at a cry from the man in the wooden mask, they climbed up as swiftly as possible. The two defenders made no move until the thrown spears rattled against the sides of the boulders or plunged into the barricade of dead. Wolff shot twice, Chryseis three times. Not one arrow missed.

Wolff loosed his final shaft. It struck the mask of the leader and knocked him back down the hill. A moment later he threw off the mask. Although his face was bleeding, he led the second charge.

A weird ululation arose from the jungle. The savages stopped, spun, and became silent as they stared at the green around the hill. Again, the swelling-falling cry came from somewhere in the trees.

Abruptly, a bronze-haired man clad only in a leopard loincloth raced from the jungle. He carried a spear in one hand and a long knife in the other. Coiled around his shoulder was a lariat, and a quiver and bow were hung from a belt over the other shoulder. Behind him, a mass of hulking, long-armed, mound-chested, and long-fanged apes poured from the trees.

At sight of these, the savages cried out aloud and tried to run around the hill. Other apes appeared from the other side; like hairy jaws, the two columns closed on the blacks.

There was a brief fight. Some apes fell with spears in their bellies, but most of the blacks threw down their weapons and tried to run or else crouched, trembling and paralyzed. Only twelve escaped.

Wolff, smiling and laughing in his relief, said to the man in the leopard-skin, "And how are you named on this tier?"

Kickaha grinned back. "I'll give you one guess."

His smile died when he saw the baron. "Damn it! It took me too much time to find the apes and then to find you! He was a good man, the Yidshe; I liked his style. Damn it! Anyway, I promised him that if he died I'd take his bones back to his ancestral castle, and that's one promise I'll keep. Not just now, though. We have some business to attend to."

Kickaha called some of the apes to be introduced. "As you'll notice," he said to Wolff, "they're built more like your friend Ipsewas than true apes. Their legs are too long and their arms too short. Like Ipsewas and unlike the great apes of my favorite childhood author, they have the brains of men. They hate the Lord for what he has done to them; they not only want revenge, they want a chance to walk around in human bodies again."

Not until then did Wolff remember Abiru. He was nowhere to be seen. Apparently he had slipped off when Wolff had gone to funem Laksfalk's aid.

That night, around a fire and eating roast deer, Wolff and Chryseis heard about the cataclysm taking place in Atlantis. It had started with the new temple that the Rhadamanthus of Atlantis had started to build. Ostensibly the tower was for the greater glory of the Lord. It was to reach higher than any building ever known on the planet. The Rhadamanthus recruited his entire state to erect the temple. He kept on adding story to story until it looked as if he wanted to reach the sky itself.

Men asked each other when there would be an end to the work. All were slaves with but one purpose in mind: build. Yet they dared not speak openly, for the soldiers of the Rhadamanthus killed all who objected or who failed to labor. Then it became obvious that the Rhadamanthus had something else besides a temple in his crazed mind. The Rhadamanthus intended to erect a means to storm the heavens themselves, the palace of the Lord.

"A thirty-thousand-foot building?" said Wolff.

"Yeah. It couldn't be done, of course, not with the technology available in Atlantis. But the Rhadamanthus was mad; he really thought he could do it. Maybe he was encouraged because the Lord hadn't appeared for so many years, and he thought that maybe the rumors were true that the Lord was gone. Of course, the ravens must have told him different, but he could have figured they were lying to protect themselves."

Kickaha said that the devastating phenomena now destroying Atlantis were proof of more than that the Lord was revenging himself against the hubris of Rhadamanthus. The Lord must have finally unlocked the secrets of how to operate some of the devices in the palace.

"The Lord who disappeared would have taken precautions against a new occupant manipulating his powers. But the new Lord has at last succeeded in learning where the controls of the storm-makers are."

Proof: the gigantic hurricanes, tornados, and continual rain sweeping the land. The Lord must be out to rid this tier of all life.

Before reaching the edge of the jungle, they met the tidal wave of refugees. These had stories of horses and great buildings blown down, of men picked up and carried off and smashed by the winds, of the floods that were stripping the earth of trees and all life and even washing away the hills.

By then, Kickaha's party had to lean to walk against the wind. The clouds closed around them; rain struck them; lightning blinded and crashed on all sides.

Even so, there were periods when the rain and lightning ceased. The energies loosed by Arwoor had to spend themselves, and new forces had to be built up before being released again. In these comparative lulls, the party made progress, although slowly. They crossed swollen rivers bearing the wreck of a civilization: houses, trees, furniture, chariots, the corpses of men, women, children, dogs, horses, birds and wild animals. The forests were uprooted or smashed by the strokes of electrical bolts. Every valley was running with water; every depression was filled. And a choking stench filled the air.

When their journey was little more than half-completed; the clouds began to thin away. They were in the sunshine again, but in a land silent with death. Only the roar of water or the cry of a bird that had somehow survived broke the stone of quiet. Sometimes the howl of a demented human being sent chills through them, but these were few.

The last cloud was carried off. And the white monolith of Idaquiz-zoorhruz shone before them, three hundred miles away on the horizonless plain. The city of Atlantis—or what was left of it—was a hundred miles distant. It took them twenty days to reach its outskirts through flood and debris.

"Can the Lord see us now?" Wolff asked.

Kickaha said, "I suppose he could with some sort of telescope. I'm glad you asked, though, because we'd better start traveling by night. Even so, we'll be spotted by them."

He pointed at a raven flying over.

Passing through the ruins of the capital city, they came near the imperial zoo of Rhadamanthus. There were some strong cages left standing, and one of these contained an eagle. On the muddy bottom were a number of bones, feathers, and beaks. The caged eagles had evaded starvation by eating each other. The lone survivor sat emaciated, weak and miserable on the highest perch.

Wolff opened the cage, and he and Kickaha talked to the eagle, Armonide. At first, Armonide wanted nothing but to attack them, enfeebled though she was. Wolff threw her several pieces of meat, then the two men continued their story. Armonide said that they were liars and had some human, and therefore evil, purpose in mind. When she had heard Wolff's story through and his pointing out that they did not have to release her, she began to believe. When Wolff explained that he had a plan in mind to gain revenge upon the Lord, the dullness in her eyes was replaced by a sharp light. The idea of actually assaulting the Lord, perhaps successfully, was more food than meat itself. She stayed with them for three days, eating, gaining strength, and memorizing exactly what she was to tell Podarge.

"You will see the Lord's death yet, and new and youthful and lovely maiden bodies will be yours," Wolff said. "But only if Podarge does as I ask her."

Armonide launched herself from a cliff, swooped down, flapped her spreading wings, and began to climb. Presently the green feathers of her body were absorbed by the green sky. Her red head became a black dot, and then it too was gone.

Wolff and his party remained in the tangle of fallen trees until night before going on. By now, through some subtle process, Wolff had become the nominal leader. Before, Kickaha had had the reins in his hands with the approval of all. Something had happened to give Wolff the power of decision-making. He did not know what, for Kickaha was as boisterous and vigorous as before. And the passing of captainship had not been caused by a deliberate effort on Wolff's part. It was as if Kickaha had been waiting until Wolff had learned all he could from him. Then Kickaha had handed over the baton.

They traveled strictly within the night-hours, during which time they saw very few ravens. Apparently there was no need for them in this area since it was under the close surveillance of the Lord himself. Besides, who would dare intrude here after the anger of the Lord had been so catastrophically wrought?

On arriving at the great tumbled mass of Rhadamanthus' tower, they took refuge within the ruins. There was more than enough metal for Wolff's plan. Their only two problems were getting enough food and trying to conceal the noise of their sawing and hammering and the glare of their little smithies. The first was solved when they discovered a storehouse of grain and dried meat. Much of the supplies had been destroyed by fire and then by water, but there was enough left to see them through several weeks. The second was dealt with by working deep within the underground chambers. The tunneling took five days, a period which did not concern Wolff because he knew that it would be some time before Armonide would reach Podarge—if she got to her destination at all. Many things could happen to her on the way, especially an attack by the ravens.

"What if she doesn't make it?" Chryseis asked.

"Then we'll have to think of something else," Wolff replied. He fondled the horn and pressed its seven buttons. "Kickaha knows the gate through which he came when he left the palace. We could go back through it. But it would be folly. The present Lord would not be so stupid as not to leave a heavy guard there."

Three weeks passed. The supply of food was so low that hunters would have to be sent out. This was dangerous even at night, for there was no telling when a raven might be around. Moreover, for all Wolff knew the Lord could have devices for seeing as easily at night as at day.

At the end of the fourth week, Wolff had to give up his dependence on Podarge. Either Armonide had not reached her or Podarge had refused to listen.

That very night, as he sat under cover of a huge plate of bent steel and stared at the moon, he heard the rustle of wings. He peered into the darkness. Suddenly, moonlight shone on something black and pale, and Podarge was before him. Behind her were many winged shapes and the gleam of moon on yellow beaks and redly shining eyes.

Wolff led them down through the tunnels and into a large chamber. By the small fires, he looked again into the tragically beautiful face of the harpy. But now that she thought she could strike back at the Lord, she actually looked happy. Her flock had carried food along, so, while all ate, Wolff explained his plan to her. Even as they were discussing the details, one of the apes, a guard, brought in a man he had caught skulking about the ruins. He was Abiru the Khamshem.

"This is unfortunate for you and a sorry thing for me," Wolff said. "I can't just tie you up and leave you here. If you escaped and contacted a raven, the Lord would be forewarned. So, you must die. Unless you can convince me otherwise."

Abiru looked about him and saw only death.

"Very well," he said. "I had not wanted to speak nor will I speak before everyone, if I can avoid it. Believe me, I must talk to you alone. It is as much for your life as for mine."

"There is nothing you can say that could not be said before all," Wolff replied. "Speak up."

Kickaha placed his mouth close to Wolff's ear and whispered, "Better do as he says."

Wolff was astonished. The doubts about Kickaha's true identity came back to him. Both requests were so strange and unexpected that he had a momentary feeling of disassociation. He seemed to be floating away from them all.

"If no one objects, I will hear him alone," he said. Podarge frowned and opened her mouth, but before she could say anything she was interrupted by Kickaha. "Great One, now is the time for trust. You must believe in us, have confidence. Would you lose your only chance for revenge and for getting your human body back? You must go along with us on this. If you interfere, all is lost."

Podarge said, "I do not know what this is all about, and I feel that I am somehow being betrayed. But I will do as you say, Kickaha, for I know of you and know that you are a bitter enemy of the Lord. But do not try my patience too far."

Then Kickaha whispered an even stranger thing to Wolff. "Now I recognize Abiru. The beard and the stain on his skin fooled me, plus not having heard his voice for twenty years."

Wolff's heart beat fast with an undefined apprehension. He took his scimitar and conducted Abiru, whose hands were bound behind him, into a small room. And here he listened.

16

AN HOUR LATER, HE RETURNED TO THE OTHERS. HE LOOKED stunned.

"Abiru will go with us," he said. "He could be very valuable. We need every hand we can get and every man with knowledge."

"Would you care to explain that?" Podarge said. She was narrow-eyed, the mask of madness forming over her face.

"No, I will not and cannot," he replied. "But I feel more strongly than ever that we have a good chance for victory. Now, Podarge how strong are your eagles? Have they flown so far tonight that we must wait until to-morrow night for them to rest?"

Podarge answered that they were ready for the task ahead of them. She wanted to delay no longer.

Wolff gave his orders, which were relayed by Kickaha to the apes, since they obeyed only him. They carried out the large crossbars and the ropes to the outside, and the others followed them.

In the bright light of the moon, they lifted the thin but strong cross-bars. The human beings and the fifty apes then fitted themselves into the weblike cradles beneath the crossbars and tied straps to secure themselves. Eagles gripped the ropes attached to each of the four ends of the bars and another gripped the rope tied to the center of the cross. Wolff gave the sig-nal. Though there had been no chance to train, each bird jumped simul-taneously into the air, flapped her wings, and slowly rose upward. The ropes were paid out to over fifty feet to give the eagles a chance to gain altitude before the cross-bars and the human attached to each had to be lifted.

Wolff felt a sudden jerk, and he uncoiled his bent legs to give an extra push upward. The bar tilted to one side, almost swinging him over against one of the bars. Podarge, flying over the others, gave an order. The eagles pulled up more rope or released more length to adjust for balance. In a few seconds, the cross-bars were at the correct level.

On Earth this plan would not have been workable. A bird the size of the eagle probably could not have gotten into the air without launching herself from a high cliff. Even then, her flight would have been very slow, maybe too slow to keep from stalling or sinking back to Earth. However, the Lord had given the eagles muscles with strength to match their weight.

They rose up and up. The pale sides of the monolith, a mile away, glimmered in the moonlight. Wolff clutched the straps of his cradle and looked at the others. Chryseis and Kickaha waved back. Abiru was motionless. The shattered and prone wreck of Rhadamanthus' tower became smaller. No ravens flew by to be startled and to wing upward to warn the Lord. Those eagles not serving as carriers spread wide to forestall such a possibility. The air was filled with an armada; the beat of their wings drummed loudly in Wolff's ears, so loudly that he could not imagine the noise not traveling for miles.

The time came when this side of ravaged Atlantis was spread out in the moonlight for him to scan in one sweep of the eye. Then the rim appeared, and part of the tier below it. Dracheland became visible as a great half-disc of darkness. The hours crept by. The mass of Amerindia appeared, grew and was suddenly chopped off at the rim. The garden of Okeanos, so far below Amerindia and so narrow, could not be seen.

Both the moon and the sun were visible now because of the comparative slenderness of this monolith. Nevertheless, the eagles and their burdens were still in darkness, in the shadow of Idaquizzoorhruz. It would not last for long. Soon this side would be under the full glare of the daytime luminary. Any ravens would be able to see them from miles away. The party had, however, drifted close to the monolith, so that anyone on top would have to be on the edge to detect them.

At last, after over four hours, just as the sun touched them, they were level with the top. Beside them was the garden of the Lord, a place of flaming beauty. Beyond rose the towers and minarets and flying buttresses and spiderweb architectures of the palace of the Lord. It soared up for two hundred feet and covered, according to Kickaha, more than three hundred acres.

They did not have time to appreciate its wonder, for the ravens in the garden were screaming. Already the hundreds of Podarge's pets had swooped down upon them and were killing them. Others were winging toward the many windows to enter and seek out the Lord.

Wolff saw a number get inside before the traps of the Lord could be activated. Shortly thereafter, those attempting to climb in through the openings disappeared in a clap of thunder and a flash of lighting. Charred to the bone, they fell off the ledges and onto the ground below or on the rooftops or buttresses.

The human beings and the apes settled to the ground just outside a diamond-shaped door of rose stone set with rubies. The eagles released the ropes and gathered by Podarge to wait for her orders.

Wolff untied the ropes from the metal rings on the cross-bars. Then he lifted the bars above his head. After running to a point just a few feet from the diamond-shaped doorway, he cast the steel cross into it. One bar went through the entrance; the two at right angles to it jammed against the sides of the door.

Flame exploded again and again. Thunder deafened him. Tongues of searing voltage leaped out at him. Suddenly, smoke poured from within the palace, and the lightning ceased. The ravaging device had either burned out from the load or was temporarily discharged.

Wolff took one glance around him. Other entrances were also spurting blasts of flame or else their defenses had burned out. Eagles had taken many of the cross-bars and were dropping them at an angle into the windows above. He leaped over the white-hot liquid of his cross-bar and through the door. Chryseis and Kickaha joined him from another entrance. Behind Kickaha came the horde of giant apes. Each carried a sword or battle-axe in his hand.

Kickaha asked, "Is it coming back to you?"

Wolff nodded. "Not all, but enough, I hope. Where's Abiru?"

"Podarge and a couple of the apes are keeping an eye on him. He could try something for his own purposes."

Wolff in the lead, they walked down a hall the walls of which were painted with murals that would have delighted and awed the most critical of Terrestrials. At the far end was a low gate of delicate and intricate tracery and of a shimmering bluish metal. They proceeded toward it but stopped as a raven, fleeing for its life, sped over them. Behind it came an eagle.

The raven passed over the gate, and as it did so it flew headlong into an invisible screen. Abruptly, the raven was a scatter of thin slices of flesh, bones and feathers. The pursuing eagle screamed as it saw this and tried to check her flight, but too late. She too was cut into strips.

Wolff pulled the left section of the gate toward him instead of pushing in on it as he would naturally have done. He said, "It should be okay now. But I'm glad the raven triggered the screen first. I hadn't remembered it."

Still, he stuck his sword forward to test, then it came back to him that only living matter activated the trap. There was nothing to do but to trust that he could remember correctly. He walked forward without feeling anything but the air, and the others followed.

"The Lord will be holed up in the center of the palace, where the defense control room is," he said. "Some of the defenses are automatic, but there are others he can operate himself. That is, if he's found out how to operate them, and he's certainly had enough time to learn."

They padded through a mile of corridors and rooms, each one of which could have detained anyone with a sense of beauty for days. Every now and then a boom or a scream announced a trap set off somewhere in the palace.

A dozen times, they were halted by Wolff. He stood frowning for awhile until he suddenly smiled. Then he would move a picture at an angle or touch a spot on the murals: the eye of a painted man, the horn of a buffalo in a scene of the Amerindian plains, the hilt of a sword in the scabbard of a knight in a Teutoniac tableau. Then he would walk forward.

Finally, he summoned an eagle. "Go bring Podarge and the others," he said. "There is no use their sacrificing themselves any more. I will show the way."

He said to Kickaha, "The sense of *déjà vu* is getting stronger every minute. But I don't remember all. Just certain details."

"As long as they're the significant details, that's all that matters at this moment," Kickaha said. His grin was broad, and his face was lit with the delight of conflict. "Now you can see why I didn't dare to try re-entry by myself. I got the guts but I lack the knowledge."

Chryseis said, "I don't understand."

Wolff pulled her to him and squeezed her. "You will soon. That is, if we make it. I've much to tell you, and you have much to forgive."

A door ahead of them slid into the wall, and a man in armor clanked toward them. He held a huge axe in one hand, swinging it as if it were a feather.

"It's no man," Wolff said. "It's one of the Lord's taloses."

"A robot!" Kickaha said.

Wolff thought, *Not quite in the sense Kickaha means.* It was not all steel and plastic and electrical wires. Half of it was protein, formed in the biobanks of the Lord. It had a will for survival that no machine of all-inanimate parts could have. This was a strength and also a weakness.

He spoke to Kickaha, who ordered the apes behind him to obey Wolff. A dozen stepped forward, side by side, and hurled their axes simultaneously. The talos dodged but could not evade all. It was struck with a force and precision that would have chopped it apart if it had not been armor-plated. It fell backward and rolled, then rose to its feet. While it was down, Wolff ran at it. He struck at it with his scimitar at the juncture of shoulder and neck. The blade broke without cutting into the metal. However, the force of the blow did knock the talos down again.

Wolff dropped his weapons, seized the talos around its waist, and lifted it. Silently, for it had no voice-chords, the armored thing kicked and reached down to grip Wolff. He hurled it against the wall, and it crashed down on the floor. As it began to get to its feet once more, Wolff drew his dagger and drove it into one of the eye-holes. There was a crack as the plastic over the eye gave way and was dislodged. The tip of the knife broke off, and Wolff was hurled back by a blow from the mailed fist. He came back quickly, grabbed the extended fist again, turned, and flopped it over his back. Before it could arise, it found itself gripped and hoisted high again. Wolff ran to the window and threw it headlong out.

It turned over and over and smashed against the ground four stories below. For a moment it lay as if broken, then it began to rise again. Wolff shouted at some eagles outside on a buttress. They launched themselves, soared down, and a pair grabbed the talos' arms. Up they rose, found it too heavy, and sank back. But they were able to keep it aloft a few inches from the ground. Over the surface, between buttresses and curiously carved columns, they flew. Their destination was the edge of the monolith, from which they would drop the talos. Not even its armor could withstand the force at the end of the 30,000-foot fall.

Wherever the Lord was hidden, he must have seen the fate of the single talos he had released. Now, a panel in the wall slid back, and twenty taloses came out, each with an axe in his hand. Wolff spoke to the apes. These hurled their axes again, knocking down many of the things. The gorilla-sized anthropoids charged in and several seized each talos. Although the mechanical strength of each android was more than that of a single ape, the talos was outmatched by two. While one ape wrestled with an android, the other gripped the helmet-head and twisted. Metal creaked under the strain; suddenly, neck-mechanisms broke with a snap. Helmets rolled on the floor with an ichorish liquid flowing out. Other taloses were lifted up and passed from hand to hand and dumped out of the window. Eagles carried each one off to the rim.

Even so, seven apes died, cut down by axes or with their own heads twisted off. The quick-to-learn protein brains of the semiautomatons imitated the actions of their antagonists, if it was to their advantage.

A little further on in the hall, thick sheets of metal slid down before and behind them to block off advance or retreat. Wolff had forgotten this until just a second before the plates were lowered. They descended swiftly but not so swiftly that he did not have time to topple a marble stone pedestal with a statue on it. The end of the fallen column lay under the plate and prevented its complete closure. The forces driving the plate were, however, so strong that the edge of the plate began to drive into the stone. The party slid on their backs through the decreasing space. At the same time, water flooded into the area. If it had not been for the delay in closing the plate, they would have been drowned.

Sloshing ankle deep in water, they went down the hall and up another flight of steps. Wolff stopped them by a window, through which he cast an axe. No thunder and lightning resulted, so he leaned out and called Podarge and her eagles in to him. Having been blocked off by the plates, they had gone outside to find another route.

"We are close to the heart of the palace, to the room in which the Lord must be," he said. "Every corridor from here on in has walls which hold dozens of laser beam-projectors. The beams can form a network through which no one could penetrate alive."

He paused, then said, "The Lord could sit in there forever. The fuel for his projectors will not give out, and he has food and drink enough to last for any siege. But there's an old military axiom which states that any defense, no matter how formidable, can be broken if the right offense is found."

He said to Kickaha, "When you took the gate through the Atlantean tier, you left the crescent behind you. Do you remember where?"

Kickaha grinned and said, "Yeah! I stuck it behind a statue in a room near the swimming pool. But what if it was found by the gworl?"

"Then I'll have to think of something else. Let's see if we can find the crescent."

"What's the idea?" Kickaha said in a low voice.

Wolff explained that Arwoor must have an escape route from the control room. As Wolff remembered it, there was a crescent set in the floor and several loose ones available. Each of these, when placed in contact with the immobile crescent, would open a gate to the universe for which the loose one had a resonance. None of them gave access to other levels of the planet in this universe. Only the horn could effect a gate between tiers.

"Sure," Kickaha said. "But what good will the crescent do us even if we find it? It has to be matched up against another, and where's the other? Anyway, anyone using it would only be taken through to Earth."

Wolff pointed over his back to indicate the long leather box slung there by a strap. "I have the horn."

They started down a corridor. Podarge strode after them. "What are you up to?" she asked fiercely.

Wolff answered that they were looking for means to get within the control room. Podarge should stay behind to handle any emergency. She refused, saying that she wanted them in her sight now that they were so close to the Lord. Besides, if they could get through to the Lord, they would have to take her along. She reminded Wolff of his promise that the Lord would be hers to do with as she wished. He shrugged and walked on.

They located the room in which was the statue behind which Kickaha had concealed the crescent. But it had been overturned in the struggle between apes and gworl. Their bodies lay sprawled around the room. Wolff stopped in surprise. He had seen no gworl since entering the palace and had taken it for granted that all had perished during the fight with the savages. The Lord had not sent all of them after Kickaha.

Kickaha cried, "The crescent's gone!"

"Either it was found some time ago or someone just found it after the statue was knocked over," Wolff said. "I have an idea of who did take it. Have you seen Abiru?"

Neither of the others had seen him since shortly after the invasion of the palace had started. The harpy, who was supposed to keep an eye on him, had lost him.

Wolff ran toward the labs with Kickaha and Podarge, wings half-opened, behind him. By the time he had covered the 3000 feet to it, Wolff was winded. Breathing hard, he stopped at the entrance.

"Vannax may be gone already and within the control room," he said. "But if he's still in there working on the crescent, we'd better enter quietly and hope to surprise him."

"Vannax?" Podarge said.

Wolff swore mentally. He and Kickaha had not wanted to reveal the identity of Abiru until later, Podarge hated the Lord so much that she would have killed him at once. Wolff wanted to keep him alive because Vannax, if he did not try to betray them, could be valuable in the taking of the palace. Wolff had promised Vannax that he could go into another world to try his luck there if he helped them against Arwoor. And Vannax had explained how he had managed to get back to this universe. After Kickaha (born Finnegan) had accidentally come here, taking a crescent with him, Vannax had continued his search for another. He had been successful in, of all places, a pawn shop in Peoria, Illinois. How it had gotten there and what Lord had lost it on Earth would never be known. Doubtless there were other crescents in obscure places on Earth. However, the crescent he had found had passed him through a gate located on the Amerindian tier. Vannax had climbed Thayaphayawoed to Khamshem, where he had been lucky enough to capture the gworl, Chryseis, and the horn. Thereafter, he had made his way toward the palace hoping to get within.

Wolff muttered, "The old saying goes that you can't trust a Lord."

"What did you say?" Podarge asked. "And I repeat, who is Vannax?"

Wolff was relieved that she did not know the name. He answered that Abiru had sometimes disguised himself under that name. Not wanting to reply to any more questions, and feeling that time was vital, he entered the laboratory. It was a room broad enough and high-ceilinged enough to house a dozen jet airliners. Cabinets and consoles and various apparatuses, however, gave it a crowded appearance. A hundred yards away, Vannax was bent over a huge console, working with the buttons and levers.

Silently, the three advanced on him. They were soon close enough to see that two crescents were locked down on the console. On the broad screen above Vannax was the ghostly image of a third semicircle. Wavy lines of light ran across it.

Vannax suddenly gave an *ah!* of delight as another crescent appeared by the first on the screen. He manipulated several dials to make the two images move toward each other and then merge into a single one again.

Wolff knew that the machine was sending out a frequency-tracer and had located that of the crescent set into the floor of the control room. Next, Vannax would subject the crescents clamped to the console to a treatment which would change their resonance to match that of the control room. Where Vannax had gotten the two semicircles was a mystery until Wolff thought of that crescent which must have accompanied him when he passed through the gate to the Amerindian tier. Somehow, during the time between his capture and the flight, he had gotten hold of this crescent. He must have hidden it in the ruins before the ape had captured him.

Vannax looked up from his work, saw the three, glanced at the screen, and snatched the two crescents from the spring-type clamps on the console. The three ran toward him as he placed one crescent on the floor and then the other. He laughed, made an obscene gesture, and stepped into the circle, a dagger in his hand.

Wolff gave a cry of despair, for they were too far away to stop him. Then he stopped and threw a hand over his eyes, but too late to shut out the blinding flash. He heard Kickaha and Podarge, also blinded, shouting. He heard Vannax's scream and smelled the burned flesh and clothes.

Sightlessly, he advanced until his feet touched the hot corpse.

"What the hell happened?" Kickaha said. "God, I hope we're not permanently blinded!"

"Vannax thought he was slipping in through Arwoor's gate in the control room," Wolff said. "But Arwoor had set a trap. He could have been satisfied with wrecking the matcher, but it must have amused him to kill the man who would try it."

He stood and waited, knowing that time was getting short and that he was not serving his cause or anyone else's by his patience with his blindness. But there was nothing else he could do. And, after what seemed like an unbearably long time, sight began to come back.

Vannax was lying on his back, charred and unrecognizable. The two crescents were still on the floor and undamaged. These were separated a moment later by Wolff with a scribe from a console.

"He was a traitor," Wolff said in a low voice to Kickaha. "But he did us a service. I meant to try the same trick, only I was going to use the horn to activate the crescent you hid after I'd changed its resonance."

Pretending to inspect other consoles for boobytraps, he managed to get Kickaha and himself out of ear-range of Podarge.

"I didn't want to do it," he whispered. "But I'm going to have to. The horn must be used if we're to drive Arwoor out of the control room or get him before he can use his crescents to escape."

"I don't get you," Kickaha said.

"When I had the palace built, I incorporated a thermitic substance in the plastic shell of the control room. It can be triggered only by a certain sequence of notes from the horn, combined with another little trick. I don't want to set the stuff off because the control room will then also be lost. And this place will be indefensible later against any other Lords."

"You better do it," Kickaha said. "Only thing is, what's to keep Arwoor from getting away through the crescents?"

Wolff smiled and pointed at the console. "Arwoor should have destroyed that instead of indulging his sadistic imagination. Like all weapons, it's two-edged."

He activated the control, and, again, an image of the crescent shone on the screen. Curving lines of light ran across the plate. Wolff went to another console and opened a little door on the top to reveal a panel with unmarked controls. After flipping two, he pressed a button. The screen went blank.

"The resonance of his crescent has been changed," Wolff said. "When he goes to use it with any of the others he has, he'll get a hell of a shock. Not the kind Vannax got. He just won't have a gate through which to escape."

"You Lords are a mean, crafty, sneaky bunch," Kickaha said. "But I like your style, anyway."

He left the room. A moment later, his shouts came down the corridor. Podarge started to leave the room, then stopped to glare suspiciously at Wolff. He broke into a run. Podarge, satisfied he was coming, raced ahead. Wolff stopped and removed the horn from the case. He reached a finger into its mouth, hooked it through the only opening in the weblike structure therein large enough to accept his finger. A pull drew the web out. He turned it around and inserted it with its front now toward the inside of the horn. Then he put the horn back into the case and ran after the harpy.

She was with Kickaha, who was explaining that he thought he had seen a gworl but it was just a prowling eagle. Wolff said they must go back to the others. He did not explain that it was necessary that the horn be within a certain distance of the control room walls. When they had returned to the hall outside the control room, Wolff opened the case. Kickaha stood behind Podarge, ready to knock her unconscious if she started any trouble. What they could do with the eagles, besides sicking the apes on them, was another matter.

Podarge exclaimed when she saw the horn but made no hostile move. Wolff lifted the horn to his lips and hoped he could remember the correct sequence of notes. Much had come back to him since he had talked with Vannax; much was yet lost.

He had just placed the mouthpiece to his lips when a voice roared out. It seemed to come from ceiling and walls and floor, from everywhere. It spoke in the language of the Lords, for which Wolff was glad. Podarge would not know the tongue.

"Jadawin! I did not recognize you until I saw you with the horn! I thought you looked familiar—I should have known. But it's been such a long time! How long?"

"It's been many centuries, or millenia, depending upon the time scale. So, we two old enemies face each other again. But this time you have no way out. You will die as Vannax died."

"How so?" roared Arwoor's voice.

"I will cause the walls of your seemingly impregnable fortress to melt. You will either stay inside and roast or come out and die another way. I don't think you'll stay in."

Suddenly he was seized with a concern and a sense of injustice. If Podarge should kill Arwoor, she would not be killing the man who was responsible for her present state. It did not matter that Arwoor would have done the same thing if he had been the Lord of this world at that time.

On the other hand, he, Wolff, was not to blame, either. He was not the Lord Jadawin who had constructed this universe and then manipulated it so foully for so many of its creatures and abducted Terrestrials. The attack of amnesia had been complete; it had wiped all of Jadawin from him and made him a blank page. Out of the blankness had emerged a new man, Wolff, one incapable of acting like Jadawin or any of the other Lords.

And he was still Wolff, except that he remembered what he had been. The thought made him sick and contrite and eager to make amends as best he could. Was this the way to start, by allowing Arwoor to die horribly for a crime he had not commited?

"Jadawin!" boomed Arwoor. "You may think you have won this move! But I have topped you again! I have one more coin to put on the table, and its value is far more than what your horn will do to me!"

"And what is that?" Wolff asked. He had a black feeling that Arwoor was not bluffing.

"I've planted one of the bombs I brought with me when I was dispossessed of Chiffaenir. It's under the palace, and when I so desire, it will go off and blow the whole top of this monolith off. It's true I'll die, too, but I'll take my old enemy with me! And your woman and friends will die, too! Think of them!"

Wolff was thinking of them. He was in agony.

"What are your terms?" he asked. "I know that you don't want to die. You're so miserable you *should* want to die, but you've clung to your worthless life for ten thousand years."

"Enough of your insults! Will you or won't you? My finger is an inch above the button." Arwoor chuckled and continued, "Even if I'm bluffing, which I'm not, you can't afford to take the chance."

Wolff spoke to the others, who had been listening without understanding but knew something drastic had happened. He explained as much as he dared, omitting any connection of himself with the Lords.

Podarge, her face a study in combined frustration and madness, said, "Ask him what his terms are."

She added, "After this is all over, you have much to explain to me, O Wolff."

Arwoor replied, "You must give me the silver horn, the all-precious and unique work of the master, Ilmarwolkin. I will use it to open the gate in the pool and pass through to the Atlantian tier. That is all I want, except your promise that none will come after me until the gate is closed."

Wolff considered for a few seconds. Then he said, "Very well. You may come out now. I swear to you on my honor as Wolff and by the Hand of Detiuw that I will give you the horn and I will send no one after you until the gate is closed."

Arwoor laughed and said, "I'm coming out."

Wolff waited until the door at the end of the hall was swinging out. Knowing that he could not be overheard by Arwoor then, he said to Podarge, "Arwoor thinks he has us, and he may well be confident. He will emerge through the gate at a place forty miles from here, near Ikwekwa, a suburb of the city of Atlantis. He would still be at the mercy of you and your eagles if there were not another resonant point only ten miles from there. This point will open when the horn is blown and admit him to another universe. I will show you where it is after Arwoor goes through the pool."

Arwoor advanced confidently. He was a tall, broad-shouldered and good-looking man with wavy blond hair and blue eyes. He took the horn from Wolff, bowed ironically, and walked on down the hall. Podarge stared at him so madly that Wolff was afraid that she would leap upon him. But he had told her that he must keep his promises: the one to her and the one to Arwoor.

Arwoor strode past the silent and menacing files as if they were no more than statues of marble. Wolff did not wait for him to get to the pool, but went at once into the control room. A quick examination showed him that Arwoor had left a device which would depress the button to set off the bomb. Doubtless he had given himself plenty of time to get away. Nevertheless, Wolff sweated until he had removed the device. By then, Kickaha had returned from watching Arwoor go through the gate in the pool.

"He got away, all right," he said, "but it wasn't as easy as he had thought. The place of emergence was under water, caused by the flood he himself had created. He had to drop into the water and swim for it. He was still swimming when the gate closed."

Wolff took Podarge into a huge map room, and indicated the town near which the gate was. Then, in the visual-room, he showed her the gate at close range on a screen. Podarge studied the map and the screen for a minute. She gave an order to her eagles, and they trooped out after her. Even the apes were awed by the glare of death in their eyes.

Arwoor was forty miles from the monolith, but he had ten miles to travel. Moreover, Podarge and her pets were launching themselves from a point 30,000 feet up. They would descend at such an angle and for such a distance that they could build up great speed. It would be a close race between Podarge and her quarry.

While he waited before the screen, Wolff had time to do much thinking. Eventually, he would tell Chryseis who he was and how he had come to be Wolff. She would know that he had been to another universe to visit one of the rare friendly Lords. The Vaernirn became lonely, despite their great powers, and wanted to socialize now and then with their peers. On his return to this universe, he had fallen into a trap set by Vannax, another dispossessed Lord. Jadawin had been hurled into the universe of Earth, but he had taken the surprised Vannax with him. Vannax had escaped with a crescent after the savage tussle on the hill slope. What had happened to the other crescent, Wolff did not know. But Vannax had not had it, that was sure.

Amnesia had struck then, and Jadawin had lost all memory—had become, in effect, a baby, a *tabula rasa*. Then the Wolffs had taken him in, and his education as an Earthman had begun.

Wolff did not know the reason for the amnesia. It might have been caused by a blow on the head during his struggle with Vannax. Or it might have resulted from the terror of being marooned and helpless on an alien planet. Lords had depended upon their inherited sciences so long that, stripped of them, they became less than men.

Or his loss of memory might have come from the long struggle with his conscience. For years before being thrust willynilly into another world, he had been dissatisfied with himself, disgusted with his ways and saddened by his loneliness and insecurity. No being was more powerful than a Lord, yet none was lonelier or more conscious that any minute might be his last. Other Lords were plotting against him; all had to be on guard every minute.

Whatever the reason, he had become Wolff. But, as Kickaha pointed out, there was an affinity between him and the horn and the points of resonance. It had been no accident that he had happened to be in the basement of that house in Arizona when Kickaha had blown the horn. Kickaha had had his suspicions that Wolff was a dispossessed Lord deprived of his memory.

Wolff knew now why he had learned the languages here so extraordinarily quickly. He was remembering them. And he had had such a swift and powerful attraction to Chryseis because she had been his favorite of all the women of his domain. He had even been thinking of bringing her to the palace and making her his Lady.

She did not know who he was on meeting him as Wolff because she had never seen his face. That cheap trick of the dazzling radiance had concealed his features. As for his voice, he had used a device to magnify and distort it, merely to further awe his worshippers. Nor was his great strength natural, for he had used the bioprocesses to equip himself with superior muscles.

He would make such amends as he could for the cruelty and arrogance of Jadawin, a being now so little a part of him. He would make new human bodies in the biocylinders and insert in them the brains of Podarge and her sisters, Kickaha's apes, Ipsewas, and any others who so desired. He would allow the people of Atlantis to rebuild, and he would not be a tyrant. He was not going to interfere in the affairs of the world of tiers unless it was absolutely necessary.

Kickaha called him to the screen. Arwoor had somehow found a horse in that land of the dead and was riding him furiously.

"The luck of the devil!" Kickaha said, and he groaned.

"I think the devil's after him," Wolff said. Arwoor had looked behind and above him and then begun to beat his horse with a stick.

"He's going to make it!" Kickaha said. "There's a Temple of the Lord only a half-mile ahead!"

Wolff looked at the great white stone structure on top of a high hill. Within it was the secret chamber which he himself had used when he had been Jadawin.

He shook his head and said, "No!"

Podarge swooped within the field of vision. She was coming at great speed, her wings flapping, her face thrust forward, white against the green sky. Behind her came her eagles.

Arwoor rode the horse as far up the hill as he could. Then the mare's legs gave out, and she collapsed. Arwoor hit the ground running. Podarge dived at him. Arwoor dodged like a rabbit fleeing from a hawk. The harpy followed him in his zigzags, guessed which way he would go during one of his sideleaps, and was on him. Her claws struck his back. He threw his hands in the air and his mouth became an O through which soared a scream, voiceless to the watchers of the screen.

Arwoor fell with Podarge upon him. The other eagles landed and gathered to watch.

THE GATES

OF

CREATION

1

THOUSANDS OF YEARS AGO, THE LORDS HAD USED DRUGS, ELEC-
tronics, hypnotism, and psychotechniques to do without sleep. Their bodies stayed fresh and vigorous, their eyes unclouded, for days and nights,
for months. But their minds eventually crumbled. Hallucinations, un-
bounded anger, and an unreasonable sense of doom gripped them. Some
went mad forever and had to be killed or imprisoned.

It was then that the Lords found that even they, makers of universes,
owners of a science that put them only one step below the gods, must
dream. The unconscious mind, denied communication with the sleeping
conscious, revolted. Its weapon was madness, with which it toppled the pillars of reason.

So, all Lords now slept and dreamed.

Robert Wolff, once called Jadawin, Lord of the Planet of Many Levels,
of a world that was constructed like a Tower of Babylon, dreamed.

He dreamed that a six-pointed star had drifted through a window into
his bedroom. Whirling, it hung in the air above the foot of his bed. It was
a *pandoogaluz*, one of the ancient symbols of the religion in which the
Lords no longer believed. Wolff, who tended to think mostly in English,
thought of it as a hexaculum. It was a six-sided star, its center glowing white,
each of its facets flashing a ray, a scarlet, an orange, an azure, a purple, a
black, and a yellow. The hexaculum pulsed like the heart of the sun, and
the rays javelined out, raking his eyelids lightly. The beams scratched the
skin as a house cat might extend a claw to wake its sleeping master with
the tiniest sting.

"What do you want?" Wolff said, and knew he was dreaming. The hexaculum was a danger; even the shadows that formed between its beams were
thick with evil. And he knew that the hexaculum had been sent by his father, Urizen, whom he had not seen for two thousand years.

"Jadawin!"

The voice was silent, the words formed by the six rays, which now bent
and coiled and writhed like snakes of fire. The letters into which they

shaped themselves were of the ancient alphabet, the original writing of the Lords. He saw them glowing before him, yet he understood them not so much through the eye as through a voice that spoke deep within him. It was as if the colors reached into the center of his mind and evoked a long-dead voice. The voice was deep, so deep it vibrated his innermost being, whirled it, and threatened to bend it into nightmare figures that would forever keep their shape.

"Wake up, Jadawin!" his father's voice said. By these words, Wolff knew that the flashing-rayed hexaculum was not only in his mind but existed in reality. His eyes opened, and he stared up at the concave ceiling, self-luminous with a soft and shifting light, veined with red, black, yellow, and green. He put out his left hand to touch Chryseis, his wife, and found that her side of the bed was empty.

At this, he sat upright and looked to left and right and saw that she was not in the room. He called, "Chryseis!" Then he saw the glittering pulsing six-rayed object that hung six feet above the edge of his bed. Out of it came, in sound, not fire, his father's voice.

"Jadawin, my son, my enemy! Do not look for the lesser being you have honored by making your mate. She is gone and will not be back."

Wolff stood up and then sprang out of bed. How had this thing gotten into his supposedly impregnable castle? Long before it had reached the bedroom in the center of the castle, alarms should have wakened him, massive doors should have slid shut throughout the enormous building, laser beams should have been triggered in the many halls, ready to cut down intruders, the hundred different traps should have been set. The hexaculum should have been shattered, slashed, burned, exploded, crushed, drowned.

But not a single light shone on the great wall across the room, the wall that seemed only an arabesqued decoration but was the alarm and control diagram-panel of the castle. It glimmered quietly as if an uninvited guest were not within a million miles.

Urizen laughed, and said, "You did not think you could keep the Lord of Lords out with your puny weapons, did you? Jadawin, I could kill you now where you stand gaping so foolishly, so pale and quivering and filmed in sweat."

"Chryseis!" Wolff cried out again.

"Chryseis is gone. She is no longer safe in your bed and in your universe. She has been taken as quickly and as silently as a thief steals a jewel."

"What do you want, Father?" Wolff asked.

"I want you to come after her. Try to get her back."

Wolff bellowed, leaped up onto the bed, and launched himself over its edge at the hexaculum. For that moment, he forgot all reason and caution, which had told him that the object could be fatal. His hands gripped the many-colored glowing thing. They closed on air and came together and he was standing on the floor, looking up above him at the space where the hexaculum had been. Even as his hands touched the area filled by the starred polyhedron, it had vanished.

So, perhaps, it had not been physical. Perhaps it had after all been a projection stirred in him by some means.

He did not believe so. It was a configuration of energies, of fields momentarily held together and transmitted from some remote place. The projector might be in the universe next door or it might be a million universes away. The distance did not matter. What did matter was that Urizen had penetrated the walls of Wolff's personal world. And he had spirited Chryseis away.

Wolff did not expect any more word from his father. Urizen had not indicated where he had taken Chryseis, how Wolff was to find her, or what would be done to Chryseis. Yet Wolff knew what he had to do. Somehow, he would have to locate the hidden self-enclosed cosmos of his father. Then he would have to find the gate that would give entrance to the pocket universe. At the same time that he got access, he would have to detect and avoid the traps set for him by Urizen. If he succeeded in doing this—and the probabilities were very low—he would have to get to Urizen and kill him. Only thus could he rescue Chryseis.

This was the multimillennia-old pattern of the game played among the Lords. Wolff himself, as Jadawin, the seventh son of Urizen, had survived 10,000 years of the deadly amusement. But he had managed to do so largely by being content with staying in his own universe. Unlike many of the Lords, he had not grown tired of the world he had created. He had enjoyed it—although it had been a cruel enjoyment, he had to admit now. Not only had he exploited the natives of his world for his own purposes, he had set up defenses that had snared more than one Lord—male and female, some his own brothers and sisters—and the trapped ones had died slowly and horribly. Wolff felt contrition for what he had done to the inhabitants of his planet. For the Lords he had killed and tortured, he suffered no guilt. They knew what they were doing when they came into his world, and if they had beaten his defenses, they would have given him a painful time before he died.

Then Lord Vannax had succeeded in hurling him into the universe of Earth, although at the cost of being taken along with Jadawin. A third Lord, Arwoor, had moved in to possess Jadawin's world.

Jadawin's memory of his former life had been repressed by the shock of dispossession, of being cast weaponless into an alien universe and without the means to return to his own world; Jadawin had become a blank, a *tabula rasa*. Adopted by a Kentuckian named Wolff, the amnesiac Jadawin had taken the name of Robert Wolff. Not until he was sixty-years old did he discover what had happened before the time that he had stumbled down a Kentucky mountain. He had retired from a lifetime of teaching Latin, Greek, and Hebrew to the Phoenix area of Arizona. And there, while looking through a newly built house for sale, he had begun the series of adventures that took him through a "gate" back into the universe he had created and had ruled as Lord for 10,000 years.

There he had fought his way up from the lowest level of the monoplanet, an Earth-sized Tower of Babylon, to the palace-castle of Lord Arwoor. There he had met and fallen in love with Chryseis, one of his own semicreations. And he had become the Lord again, but not the same Lord as the one who had left it. He had become human.

His tears, loosed by his anguish at the loss of Chryseis and the terror of what could happen to her, were proof of his humanity. No Lord shed tears over another living being, although it was said that Urizen had cried with joy when he had trapped two of his sons some thousands of years ago.

No time-waster, Wolff set about doing what had to be done. First, he must make sure that someone occupied the castle while he was gone. He did not want to repeat what had happened the last time he had left this world. On returning, he had found another Lord in his place. Now there was only one man who was capable of filling his shoes and whom he could trust. That was Kickaha (born Paul Janus Finnegan in Terre Haute, Indiana, Earth). It was Kickaha who had given him the horn that had enabled him to get back into this world. Kickaha had given him the indispensable help that had permitted him to regain his Lordship.

The horn!

With that, he would be able to track down Urizen's world and gain entrance to it! He strode across the chrysoprase floor to the wall and swung down a section of the wall, carved in the semblance of a giant eagles of this planet. He stopped and gasped with shock. The hiding place no longer had a horn to hide. The hollowed out part in which the horn had lain was empty.

So, Urizen had not only taken Chryseis but he had stolen the ancient Horn of Shambarimen.

So be it. Wolff would weep over Chryseis but he would spend no time in useless mourning for an artifact, no matter how treasured.

He walked swiftly through the halls, noting that none of the alarms were triggered. All slept as if this were just another day in the quiet but happy times since Wolff had regained possession of the palace on top of the world. He could not help shivering. He had always feared his father. Now that he had such evidence of his father's vast powers, he dreaded him even more. But he did not fear to go after him. He would track him down and kill him or die trying.

In one of the colossal control rooms, he seated himself before a pagoda-shaped console. He set a control which would automatically bring him, in sequence, views of all the places on this planet where he had set videos. There were ten thousand of these on each of the four lower levels, disguised as rocks or trees. They had been placed to allow him to see what was happening in various key areas. For two hours he sat while the screen flashed views. Then, knowing that he could be there for several days, he plugged in the eidolon of Kickaha and left the viewer. Now, if Kickaha were seen, the screen would lock on the scene and an alarm would notify Wolff.

He placed ten more consoles in operation. These automatically began to scan throughout the cosmos of the "parallel" universes to detect and identify them. The records were seventy years old, so it was to be presumed that universes created since then would swell the known number of one thousand and eight. It was these that Wolff was interested in. Urizen no longer lived in the original one of Gardazrintah, where Wolff had been raised with many of his brothers, sisters, and cousins. In fact, Urizen, who grew tired of entire worlds as swiftly as a spoiled child became weary with new toys, had moved three times since leaving Gardazrintah. And the chances were that he was now in a fourth and this last one had to be identified and penetrated.

Even when all had been recorded, he could not be sure that his father's universe was located. If a universe were entirely sealed off, it was undetectable. A universe could be found only through the "gates," each of which gave off a unique frequency. If Urizen wanted to make it really difficult for Wolff to find him, he could set up an on-off-on gate. This would open at regular intervals or at random times, depending upon Urizen's choice. And if it happened not to open at the time that Wolff's scanner was searching that "parallel corridor," it would not be detected. As far as the scanners were concerned, that area would be an "empty" one.

However, Urizen wanted him to come after him and so should not make it too difficult or impossible for him to do so.

Lords must eat. Wolff had a light breakfast served by a *talos*, one of the half-protein robots, looking like knights in armor, of which he had over a thousand. Then he shaved and showered in a room carved out of a single emerald. Afterwards, he clothed himself. He wore corduroy shoes, tight-fitting corduroy trousers, a corduroy short-sleeved shirt, open at the neck but with a collar that curved up in back, a broad belt of mammoth leather, and a golden chain around his neck. From the chain hung a red jade image of Shambarimen, given to him by the great artist and artificer of the Lords, when he, Wolff, had been a boy of ten. The red of the jade was the only bright color of his garments, the rest being a thrush-brown. When in the castle, he dressed simply or not at all. Only during the rare occasions when he went down to the lower levels for state ceremonies did he dress in the magnificent robes and complex hat of a Lord. In most of his descents, he went incognito, clad in the garments or nongarments of the local natives.

He left the walls of the castle to go out onto one of the hundreds of great balcony-gardens. There was an Eye sitting in a tree, a raven large as a bald eagle. He was one of the few survivors of the onslaught of the castle when Wolff had taken this world back from Arwoor. Now that Arwoor was dead, the ravens had transferred their loyalty to Wolff.

Wolff told the raven that he was to fly out and look for Kickaha. He would inform other Eyes of the Lord of his mission and also tell the eagles of Podarge. They must inform Kickaha that he was wanted at once. If Kickaha did get their message and came to the castle, only to find Wolff gone, he was to remain there as Lord *pro tem*. If, after a reasonable interval, Wolff did not return, Kickaha could then do whatever he wanted.

He knew that Kickaha would come after him and that it was no use forbidding him to do so.

The raven flew off, happy to have a mission. Wolff went back into the castle. The viewers were still searching, without success, for Kickaha. But the gate-finders, needing only microseconds to scan and identify, had gone through all the universes and were already on their sixth sweep. He allowed them to continue on the chance that some gates might be intermittent and the search scan and gate on-state had not coincided. The results of the first five searches were on paper, printed in the classical ideographs of the ancient language.

There were thirty-five new universes. Of these, only one had a single gate.

Wolff had the spectral image of this placed upon a screen. It was a six-pointed star with the center red instead of white as he had seen it. Red for danger.

As plainly as if Urizen had told him, he knew that this was the gate to Urizen's world. Here I am. Come and get me—if you dare.

He visualized his father's face, the handsome falcon features with large eyes like wet black diamonds. Lords were ageless, their bodies held in the physiological grip of the first twenty-five years of life. But emotions were stronger even than the science of the Lords—working with their ally, time, they slashed away at the rocks of flesh. And the last time he had seen his father, he had seen the lines of hate. God alone knew how deep they were now, since it was evident that Urizen had not ceased to hate.

As Jadawin, Wolff had returned his father's enmity. But he had not been like so many of his brothers and sisters in trying to kill him. Wolff had just not wanted to have anything at all to do with him. Now, he loathed him because of what he had done to innocent Chryseis. Now, he meant to slay him.

The fabrication of a gate which would match the frequency-image of the hexaculum-entrance to Urizen's world was automatic. Even so, it took twenty-two hours for the machines to finish the device. By then, the planetary viewers had all reported in. Kickaha was not in their line of sight. This did not mean that the elusive fellow was not on the planet. He could be just outside the scope of the viewers or he could be a hundred thousand places elsewhere. The planet had even more land area than Earth, and the viewers covered only a tiny part of it. Thus, it might be a long long time before Kickaha was apprehended.

Wolff decided not to waste any time. The second the matching hexaculum was finished, he went into action. He ate a light meal and drank water, since he did not know how long he might have to do without either once he stepped through the gate. He armed himself with a beamer, a knife, a bow, and a quiverful of arrows. The primitive weapons might seem curious arms to take along in view of the highly technological death-dispensers he would have to face. But it was one of the ironies of the Lords' technology that the set-ups in which they operated sometimes permitted such weapons to be effective.

Actually, he did not expect to be able to use any of his arms. He knew too well the many types of traps the Lords had used.

"And now," Wolff said, "it must be done. There is no use waiting any longer."

He walked into the narrow space inside the matching hexaculum.

Wind whistled and tore at him. Blackness. A sense as of great hands gripping him. All in a dizzying flash.

He was standing upon grass, giant fronds at a distance from him, a blue sea close by, a red sky above, hugging the island and the rim of the sea. There was light from every quarter of the heavens and no sun. His clothes were still upon his body, although he had felt as if they were being ripped off when he had gone through the gate. Moreover, his weapons were still with him.

Certainly, this was not the interior of Urizen's stronghold. Or, if it were, it was the most unconventional dwelling-place of a Lord that he had ever seen.

He turned to see the hexaculum which had received him. It was not there. Instead, a tall wide hexagon of purplish metal rose from a broad flat boulder. He remembered now that something had pushed him out through it and that he had had to take several steps to keep from falling. The energy that had shoved him had caused him to pass out of it and a few paces from the boulder.

Urizen had set another gate within his hexaculum and had shunted him off to this place, wherever it was. Why Urizen had done so would become apparent quickly enough.

Wolff knew what would happen if he tried to walk back through the gate. Nevertheless, not being one to take things for granted, he did attempt it. With ease, he stepped out on the other side upon the boulder.

It was a one-way gate, just as he had expected.

Somebody coughed behind him, and he whirled, his beamer ready.

2

THE LAND ENDED ABRUPTLY AGAINST THE SEA WITH NO INTER-vening beach. The animal had just emerged from the sea and was only a few feet from him. It squatted like a toad on huge webbed feet, its colum-nar legs folded as if they were boneless. The torso was humanoid and sheathed in fat, with a belly that protruded like that of a Thanksgiving goose. The neck was long and supple. At its end was a human head, but the nose was flat and had long narrow nostrils. Tendrils of red flesh sprouted out around the mouth. The eyes were very large and moss-green. There were no ears. The pate was covered, like the face and body, with a dark-blue oily fur.

"Jadawin!" the creature said. It spoke in the ancient language of the Lords. "Jadawin! Don't kill me! Don't you know me?"

Wolff was shocked but not so much that he forgot to look behind him. This creature could be trying to distract him.

"Jadawin! Don't you recognize your own brother!"

Wolff did not know him. The frog-seal body, lack of ears, blue fur, and squashed long-slitted nose made identification too difficult. And there was Time. If he had really called this thing brother, it must have been millen-nia ago.

That voice. It dug away at the layers of dusty memory, like a dog after an old bone. It scraped away level after level, it . . .

He shook his head and glanced behind him and at the feathery vege-tation. "Who are you?" he asked.

The creature whined, and by this he knew that his brother—if it were his brother—must have been imprisoned in that body for a long long time. No Lord whined.

"Are you going to deny me? Are you like the others? They'd have noth-ing to do with me. They mocked at me, they spat upon me. They drove me away with kicks and laughs. They said . . ."

It clapped its flippers together and twisted its face and large tears ran from the moss-green eyes and down the blue cheeks. "Oh, Jadawin, don't be like the rest! You were always my favorite, my beloved! Don't be cruel like them!"

The others, Wolff thought. There had been others. How long ago?

Impatiently, he said, "Let's not play games—whoever you are. Your name!"

The creature rose on its boneless legs, muscles raising the fat that coated them, and took a step forward. Wolff did not back away, but he held the beamer steady. "That's far enough. Your name."

The creature stopped, but its tears kept on flowing. "You are as bad as the others. You think of nobody but yourself; you don't care what's happened to me. Doesn't my suffering and loneliness and agonies all this time—oh, this immeasurable time—touch you at all?"

"It might if I knew who you were," Wolff said. "And what's happened to you."

"Oh, Lord of the Lords! My own brother!"

It advanced another giant splayfoot, the wetness squishing from out under the webs. It held out a flipper as if beseeching a tender hand. Then it stopped, and the eyes flicked at a spot just to one side of Wolff. He jumped to his left and whirled, the beamer pointing to cover both the creature and whoever might have been behind him. There was no one.

And, as the thing had planned, it leaped for Wolff at the same time that Wolff jumped and turned. Its legs uncoiled like a catapult released and shot him forward. If Wolff had only turned, he would have been knocked down. Standing to one side, he escaped all but the tip of the thing's right flipper. Even that, striking his left shoulder and arm, was enough to send him staggering numbly to one side, making him drop the beamer. Wolff was enormously solid and powerful himself, with muscles and nerve impulses raised to twice their natural strength and speed by the Lords' science. If he had been a normal Earthman, he would have been crippled forever in his arm, and he would not have been able to escape the second leap of the creature.

Squalling with fury and disappointment, it landed on the spot where Wolff had been, sank on its legs as it they were springs, spun, and launched itself at Wolff again. All this was done with such swiftness that the creature looked as if it were an actor in a speeded-up film.

Wolff had succeeded in regaining his balance. He jumped out for the beamer. The shadow of the creature passed over him; its shrieking was so loud it seemed as if its lips were pressed against his ear. Then he had the beamer in his hands, had rolled over and over, and was up on his feet. By then the thing had propelled itself again towards him. Wolff reversed the beamer, and using his right hand, brought the light but practically indestructible metal stock down on top of the creature's head. The impact of the huge body hurled him backward; he rolled away. The sea-thing was lying motionless on its face, blood welling from its seal-like scalp.

Hands clapped, and he turned to see two human beings thirty yards away inland, under the shadow of a frond. They were male and female, dressed in the magnificent clothes of Lords. They walked towards him, their hands empty of weapons. Their only arms were swords in crude leather, or fish-skin, scabbards. Despite this seeming powerlessness, Wolff did not relax his guard. When they had approached within twenty yards of him, he told them to stop. The creature groaned and moved its head but made no effort to sit up. Wolff moved away from it to be outside its range of leap.

"Jadawin!" the woman called. She had a lovely contralto voice which stirred his heart and his memory. Although he had not seen her in five hundred or more years, he knew her then.

"Vala!" he said. "What are you doing here?" The question was rhetorical; he knew she must have also been trapped by their father. And now he recognized the man. He was Rintrah, one of his brothers. Vala, his sister, and Rintrah, his brother, had fallen into the same snare.

Vala smiled at him, and his heart sprang again. She was of all women he had known the most beautiful, with two exceptions. His lovely Chryseis and his other sister, Anana the Bright, surpassed her. But he had never loved Anana as he had Vala. Just as he had never hated Anana as he had Vala.

Vala applauded again, and said, "Well done, Jadawin! You have lost none of your skill or wits. That thing is dangerous, even if detestable. It cringes and whines and tries to gain your trust, and then, bang! It's at your throat! It almost killed Rintrah when he first came here and would have if I had not struck it unconscious with a rock. So, you see, I, too, have dealt with it."

"And why did you not kill it then?" Wolff said.

Rintrah smiled and said, "Don't you know your own little brother, Jadawin? That creature is your beloved, your cute little Theotormon."

Wolff said, "God! Theotormon! Who did this to him?"

Neither of the two answered, nor was an answer needed. This was Urizen's world; only he could have refashioned their brother thus.

Theotormon groaned and sat up. One flipper placed over the bloody spot on his head, he rocked back and forth and moaned. His lichen-green eyes glared at Wolff, and he silently mouthed vituperation he did not dare voice.

Wolff said, "You're not trying to tell me you spared his life because of fraternal sentiment? I know you better than that."

Vala laughed and said, "Of course not! I thought he could be used later on. He knows this little planet well, since he has been here such a long long time. He is a coward, brother Jadawin. He did not have the courage to test his life in the maze of Urizen; he stayed upon this island and became as one of the degenerate natives. Our father tired of waiting for him to summon up a nonexistent manhood. To punish him for his lack of bravery, he caught him and took him off to his stronghold, Appirmatzum. There he re-shaped him, made him into this disgusting sea-thing. Even then, Theotor-mon did not dare to go through the gates into Urizen's palace. He stayed here and lived as a hermit, hating and despising himself, hating all other living beings, especially Lords.

"He lives upon the fruit of the islands, the birds and fish and other sea-things he can catch. He eats them raw, and he kills the natives and eats them when he gets a chance. Not that they don't deserve their fate. They are the sons and daughters of other Lords who, like Theotormon, were craven. They lived out their miserable lives upon this planet, had babies, raised these, and then died.

"Urizen did to them as he did to Theotormon. He took them to Ap-pirmatzum, made them into loathsome shapes, and brought them back here. Our father thought that surely the monstering of them would make them hate him so much they would then test the trapdoor planets, try to get into Appirmatzum, and revenge themselves. But they were cowards all. They preferred to live on, even in their stomach-turning metamorphosis, rather than die as true Lords."

Wolff said, "I have much to learn about this little arrangement of our father. But how do I know that I can trust you?"

Again Vala laughed. "All of us who have fallen into Urizen's traps are upon this island. Most of us have been here only a few weeks, although Luvah has been here for half a year."

"Who are the others?"

"Some of your brothers and cousins. Besides Rintrah and Luvah, there are two other brothers, Enion and Ariston. And your cousins Tharmas and Palamabron."

She laughed merrily and pointed at the red sky and said, "All, all snared by our father! All gathered together again after a heartrending absence of millennia. A happy family reunion such as mortals could not imagine."

"I can imagine," Wolff said. "You still have not answered my question about trust."

"We have all sworn to a common-front truce," Rintrah said. "We need each other, so we must put aside our natural enmity and work together. Only thus will it be possible to defeat Urizen."

"There hasn't been a common-front truce for as long as I can remem-ber," Wolff said. "I remember Mother telling me that there had been one once, four thousand years before I was born, when the Black Bellers threat-ened the Lords. Urizen has performed two miracles. He has trapped eight Lords all at once, and he has forced a truce. May this be his downfall."

Wolff then said that he would swear to the truce. By the name of the Father of all Lords, the great Eponym Los, he swore to observe all the rules of the peace-agreement until such time as all agreed to abandon it or all were dead but one. He knew even as he took the oath that the others could not be relied upon not to betray him. He knew that Rintrah and Vala were aware of this and trusted him no more than he did them. But at least they would all be working together for a while. And it was not likely that any would lightly break truce. Only when a great opportunity and strong like-lihood of escaping punishment coincided would any do so.

Theotormon whined, "Jadawin. My own brother. My favorite brother, he who said he would always love me and protect me. You are like the oth-ers. You want to hurt me, to kill me. Your own little brother."

Vala spat at him and said, "You filthy craven beast! You are no Lord nor brother of ours. Why do you not dive to the deeps and there drown your-self, take your fearfulness and treachery out of our sight and the sight of all beings that breathe air? Let the fish feed upon your fat carcass, though even they may vomit you forth."

Crouching, extending a flipper, Theotormon shuffled towards Wolff. "Jadawin. You don't know how I've suffered. Is there no pity in you for me? I always thought you, at least, had what these others lacked. You had a warm heart, a compassion, that these soulless monsters lacked."

"You tried to kill me," Wolff said. "And you would try again if you thought you had a good chance of doing it."

"No, no," Theotormon said, attempting to smile. "You misunderstood me entirely. I thought you would hate me because I loved even a base life more than I did a death as a Lord. I wanted to take your weapons away so you couldn't hurt me. Then I would have explained what had happened to me, how I came to be this way. You would have understood then. You would have pitied me and loved me as you did when you were a boy in the palace of our father and I was your infant brother. That is all I wanted to do, ex-plain to you and be loved again, not hated. I meant you no harm. By the name of Los, I swear it."

"I will see you later," Wolff said. "Now, for the present, be gone."

Theotormon walked away spraddle-legged. When he had reached the edge of the island, he turned and shouted obscenities and abuse at Wolff. Wolff raised his beamer, although he meant only to scare Theotormon. The thing squawked and leaped like a giant frog out over the water, his rubbery legs and webbed toes trailing behind him. He went into the water and did not come up again. Wolff asked Vala how long he could stay under the sur-face.

"I do not know. Perhaps half an hour. But I doubt that he is holding his breath. He is probably in one of the caverns that exist in the roots and bladders that form the base of this island."

She said that they must go to meet the others. While they walked through the frond-forest, she explained the physical facts of this world, as far as she knew them.

"You must have noticed how close the horizon is. This planet has a diameter of about 2170 miles." (About the size of earth's moon, Wolff thought.) "Yet the gravity is only a little less than that of our home-planet." (Not much stronger than Earth's, Wolff thought.)

"The gravity fades off abruptly above the atmosphere," she said, "and extends weakly through this universe. All the other planets have similar fields."

Wolff did not wonder at this. The Lords could do things with fields and gravitons that the terrestrials had never dreamed of as yet.

"This planet is entirely covered with water."

"What about this island?" he said.

"It floats. Its origin is a plant which grows on the bottom of the sea. When it's half-grown, it's bladder starts to fill with gas, produced by a bacteria. It unroots itself and floats to the surface. There it extends roots or filaments, which meet with the filaments of others of its kind. Eventually, there's a solid mass of such plants. The upper part of the plant dies off, while the lower part continues to grow. The decaying upper forms a soil. Birds add their excrement to it. They come to new islands from old islands, and bring seeds in their droppings. These produce the fronds you see and the other vegetation." She pointed at a clump of bamboo-like plants.

He asked, "Where did those rocks come from?"

There were several whitish boulders, with a diameter of about twelve feet, beyond the bamboos.

"The gas bladder plants that form islands are only one of perhaps several thousand species. There's a type that attaches itself to sea-bottom rocks and that carries the rock to the surface when they're buoyant enough. The natives bring them in and place them on the islands if they're not too big. The white ones attract the *garzhoo* bird for some reason, and the natives kill the *garzhoo* or domesticate it."

"What about the drinking water?"

"It's a fresh-water ocean."

Wolff, glancing through a break in the wilderness of purplish, yellow-streaked fronds and waist-high berry-burdened bushes, saw a tremendous black arc appear on the horizon. In sixty seconds, it had become a sphere and was climbing above the horizon.

"Our moon," she said. "Here, things are reversed. There is no sun; the light comes from the sky. So the moon provides night or absence of light. It is a pale sort of night, but better than none.

"Later, you will see the planet of Appirmatzum. It is in the center of this universe, and around it the five secondary planets revolve. You will see them, too, all black and sky-filling like our moon."

Wolff asked how she knew so much about the structure of Urizen's world. She answered that Theotormon had given the information, though not willingly. He had learned much while a prisoner of Urizen. He had not wanted to part with the information, since he was a surly and selfish beast.

But when his brothers, cousins, and sister had caught him, they had forced him to talk.

"Most of the scars are healed up," she said. She laughed.

Wolff wondered if Theotormon did not have good reasons after all for wanting to kill them. And he wondered how much of her story of their dealings with him was true. He would have to have a talk with Theotormon some time, at a safe distance from him, of course.

Vala stopped talking and seized Wolff's arm. He started to jerk away, thinking that she meant to try some trick. But she was looking upwards with alarm and so was Rintrah.

3

THE FRONDS, SIXTY FEET HIGH, HAD HIDDEN THE OBJECT IN
the sky. Now he saw a mass at least a quarter-mile wide, fifty feet thick,
and almost a mile long floating fifty feet in the air. It was drifting with the
wind, which came from an unknown quarter of the compass. In this world
without sun, north, south, east, and west meant nothing.

"What is that?" he said.

"An island that floats in the air. Hurry. We have to get to the village before the attack starts."

Wolff set off after the others. From time to time, he looked up through
the fronds at the *aeronesus*. It was descending rather swiftly at the opposite end of the island. He caught up with Vala and asked her how the
floater could be navigated. She replied that its inhabitants used valves in
the giant bladders to release their hydrogen. This procedure required almost all the natives, since each bladder-valve was operated by hand. During a descent, they would all be occupied with the navigation.

"How do they steer it?"

"The bladders have vents. When the *abutal* want the island to go in one
direction, they release gas from banks of bladders on the side opposite to
that in which they want to go. They don't get much power thrust, but
they're very skillful. Even so, they have to contend with the winds and don't
always maneuver effectively. We've been attacked twice before by the *abutal,* and both times they missed our island. They'll drop sea-anchors—big
stones on the ends of cables—to slow them down. The first attackers settled down close to our island instead of just above it and had to content
themselves with an attack by sea. They failed."

She stopped, then said, "Oh, no! These must be the Ilmawir. Los help
us."

At first, Wolff thought that the fifty craft that had launched from the
floater were small airplanes. Then, as they circled to land against the wind,
he saw that they were gliders. The wings, fifty feet long, were of some pale
shimmering stuff and scalloped on the edges. A painted image of an eye

with crossed swords above it was on the underside of each wing. The fuselage was an uncovered framework, and its structure and the rudder and ailerons were painted scarlet. The pilot sat in a wickerwork basket just forward of the monowings. The nose of the craft was rounded and had a long horn projecting to a length of about twenty feet in front of it. Like the horn of a narwhal, Wolff thought. As he later found out, the horns were taken from a giant fish.

A glider passed above them on a path which would make it land ahead of them. Wolff got a glimpse of the pilot. His red hair stood at least a foot high; the hair shone with some fixative oil. His face was painted like a red Indian's with red and green circles, and black chevrons ran down his neck and across his shoulders.

"The village is about a half-mile from here," Vala said. "On the extreme end of the island."

Wolff wondered why she was so concerned. What did a Lord care what happened to others? She explained that if the Ilmawir made a successful landing, they would kill every human being on the island. They would then plant some of their surplus people as a colony.

The island was not entirely flat. There were rises here and there, formed by the uneven growth of the bladders. Wolff climbed to the top of one and looked over the fronds. The *abuta* was down to fifty feet now, settling slowly and headed directly for the village. This was a group of about one hundred beehive-shaped huts, built of fronds. A wall twenty feet high surrounded the village. It looked as if it were constructed of stones, bamboo, fronds, and some dull gray poles that could be the bones of colossal sea-creatures.

Men and women were stationed behind the walls and several groups were out in the open. They were armed with spears and bows and arrows.

Beyond the village were docks built of bamboo. Along them and on the shore were boats of various builds and sizes. Its bottom was a dense tangle of thick roots. There were, however, openings in it, and from several of these large stones at the ends of cables of vegetable matter were dropped. The stones were white, gypsum-like, and carved into flat discs. They trailed in the sea as they were dragged along by the island, then struck the land. The cables of some caught under the docks.

Other anchors fell and struck against the walls of the village. They were snagged in the tangle of stuff forming the high-piled walls. They bumped along the grassless ground and slammed into the sides of the huts. These collapsed under the impact of the stones. At the same time, arrows were shot, spears and rocks dropped, and flaming objects cast from the hatches onto the people below. Some islanders were struck down; huts started to burn. The flaming objects exploded, and a dense black smoke rose from them.

The defenders, however, were not helpless. From a large central building came men and women with curious devices. They lit and released them, and they rose swiftly towards the underpart of the floater. They caught in the tangle of roots and burned there. Then they exploded, and fire spread among the roots.

The roof of a hut lifted up and fell over to one side, like the roof of a trapdoor spider. The walls collapsed in orderly fashion outwards, falling to the ground and forming a petal-figure. In the center of the hut was a catapult, a giant bow with an arrow made from the horns of the creature that had provided the booms on the noses of the gliders. To it were attached a number of flaming bladders. The bow was released, and the burning arrow shot upwards and buried itself deep within the under part of the floater.

The catapult crew began to wind the string back. A man fell from an opening in the floater and was followed by ten more. They came down as if parachuting. Their descent was checked by a cluster of bladders attached to a harness around the shoulders and chest. An arrow caught the first *abutal* just before he struck the ground, and then three more of the ten behind him were transfixed.

The survivors landed untouched a few feet from the catapult. They unstrapped their harness, and the bladders rose away from them. By then, they were surrounded. They fought so fiercely—one got to the catapult, only to be run through with two spears.

The island-floater, driven by the wind, began to pass over the village. Other stones on cables had been dropped, and a few had caught in the tangle of the walls without breaking. Then ropes fell onto the fronds and the huge loops tightened around them.

Caught at the forward end, the floater swung around so that its bulk hung over this part of the surface island. By then, the gliders had made their landing, not all successfully. Because of the density of the vegetation, the crafts had to come down upon fronds. Some were flipped over; some crashed through several fronds before being caught and held. Some slipped down between the fronds and smashed into the tough thick bushes.

But from where he stood, Wolff could see at least twenty pilots, unhurt, who were now slipping through the jungle. And there had to be others.

He heard his name called. Vala had come back and was standing at the foot of the hill.

"What do you intend to do?" she said angrily. "You have to take sides, Jadawin, whether you want to or not. The *abutal* will kill you."

"You may be right," he said as he came down the hill. "I wanted to get some idea of what was going on. I didn't want to rush blindly into this without knowing where everybody was, how the fight was going on. . . ."

"Always the cautious and crafty Jadawin," she said. "Well, that's all right; it shows you are no fool, which I already know. Believe me, you need me as much as I need you. You can't go this thing alone."

He followed her, and presently they came upon Rintrah, crouching under a frond. He gestured at them for silence. When they were beside him, Wolff looked at where Rintrah was pointing. Five *abutal* warriors were standing not twenty yards from them. The tail of a wrecked glider rose from behind a crushed bush to their left. They carried small round shields of bone, javelins of bone tipped with bamboo, and several had bows and arrows. The bows were made of some hornlike substance, were short and recurved, and formed of two parts that were joined in a central socket of horn. The warriors were too far away for him to overhear their conference.

"What's the range of your beamer?" Vala said.

"It kills up to fifty feet," he said. "Third-degree burns for the next twenty feet, and after that, second-degree burns up through a light singe to no effect."

"Now's your chance. Rush them. You can kill all five with one sweep before they know what's going on."

Wolff sighed. There would have been a time when he would not even have waited for Vala's urgings. He would have killed them all by now and been tempted to continue the work with Vala and Rintrah. But he was no longer Jadawin; he was Robert Wolff. Vala would not understand this, or if she did, she would see his hesitation as a weakness. He did not want to kill, but he doubted that there was any way of forcing the *abutal* to call off their attack. Vala knew these people, and she was probably telling him the truth about them. So, like it or not, he had to take sides.

There was a yell behind them. Wolff rolled over and sat up to see three more *abutal* warriors about forty feet from them. They had burst out from behind a frond and were charging towards them, their javelins raised.

Wolff twisted around to face the three *abutal,* and he pressed on a plate on the underside of the three-foot long barrel. A dazzling white ray, pencil-thick, traced across the bellies of all three. The vegetation between and in back of them smoked. The three fell forward, the javelins dropping from their hands, and they slid on the grass, face down.

Wolff rose to one knee, turned, and faced the five. The two archers stopped and took aim. Wolff dropped them first, then the other three. He continued to crouch and looked about him for others who might have been attracted by the cries. Only the wind through the fronds and the hushed cries and muffled explosions of the battle at the village could be heard.

The odor of burned flesh sickened him. He rose and turned over the three corpses, then the five. He did not think that any were still alive, but he wanted to make sure. Each was almost cut in half by the beam. The skin along the gashes was crisped under the blood. There was not much blood, since the energy of the beam, absorbed by the bodies, had cooked their lungs and intestines. Their bowels, contracting, had ejected their contents.

Vala looked at the beamer. She was very curious but knew better than to ask Wolff if she could handle it. "You have two settings," she said. "What can it do on full power?"

"It can cut through a ten-foot slab of steel," he replied. "But the charge won't last more than sixty seconds. On half-power, it can project for ten minutes before needing recharging."

She looked at his pockets, and he smiled. He had no intention of telling her many fresh charges were in his pockets.

"What happened to your weapons?" he said.

Vala cursed and said, "They were stolen while we slept. I don't know whether Urizen or that slimy Theotormon did it."

He started to walk towards the battle; the two followed close behind. The island above threw them into a pale shadow which would be deepened soon when the night-bringing moon covered this side of the planet. Ilmawir, men and women both, were still dropping out of the openings in the bottom. Others, buoyed up by larger clusters of bladders, were working on the bottom as fire-fighters. They used many-faceted objects that, when squeezed, spurted out water.

"Those are living sea-creatures," she said. "Amphibians. They travel on land by spurting out jets of water and rolling with the thrusts."

Wolff set the beamer at full power. Whenever they came near a rope tangled in a tree or a stone anchor, he cut the cable loose. Three times he came across *abutal* and set the beamer on half-power. By the time he was a few yards from the village, he had severed forty cables and killed twenty-two men and women.

"A lucky thing for us you came when you did," Vala said. "I don't think we could have driven them off if you hadn't arrived."

Wolff shrugged. He ejected a power-pack and slipped another of the little cylinders into the breach. He had six left, and if this continued he would soon be out. But there was nothing he could do to conserve them.

The village was surrounded on the land side by about ninety *abutal*. Apparently, those who had dropped into the village had been wiped out, but the villagers were busy putting out fires. However, they no longer had to worry about attack from directly overhead. The Ilmawir island had been affected by the cutting of so many cables. It had slipped on downwind by a quarter-mile and only because a hundred other ropes and anchors had been used had it managed to keep from losing the surface-island altogether.

Wolff beamed the group of officers who were standing on top of the only hill near the village. Presently, the other *abutal* became aware of what was happening. Half left the siege to surround the hill. The area bristled with spears and arrows. The Lords would have been open to a concentrated fire of arrows, but they were protected behind a group of four white stone idols on the hill.

Vala said, "They're on the defensive now. If they don't know it now, they soon will. And that will be good for us. Perhaps . . ."

She was silent for a while. Wolff shot three men as they ran towards a hollow in the hill. He said, "Perhaps what?"

"Our beloved father left a message for us on this island. He told us some of what we have to do if we hope to get within his castle. Apparently, we have to find the gates which lead to him. There are none on this island. He says there is a pair on another island, but he did not say just where. We have to find them by ourselves, so I was thinking . . ."

A roar arose from the *abutals,* and the front lines rushed the hill. The archers sent a covering fire of at least thirty arrows per volley. Vala and Rintrah cowered behind an idol, as Wolff had told them to do. Much as he hated to expend his power, he was forced to do so. He put the beamer on full and shot over the heads of the front lines. Smoke arose from vegetation and flesh alike as he described a circle with the white ray. The archers had had to expose themselves to get good shots, and so most fell.

Arrows rattled around Wolff, leaping off the stone idols. One creased his shoulder; another ricocheted off stone and flew between his legs. Then, there were no more arrows. The *abutal* in the second ranks, seeing those crumple before them, smelling the fried flesh, wavered. Wolff began on them, and they fled back into the jungle.

"You were thinking?" he said to Vala.

"We could search a thousand years, using this island as our ship, and not find one island that has the gates. Perhaps that is Father's idea. He would enjoy seeing us in a futile search, enjoy our despair. And the friction and murder that such long association would make inevitable among us. But if we were on an *abuta,* which would enable us not only to travel faster but to see far more from its altitude . . ."

"It's a fine idea," he said. "How do we talk the *abutal* into letting us accompany them? And what guarantee is there that they would not turn on us the first chance they got?"

"You have forgotten much about your younger sister. How could you, of all who have loved me, not remember how persuasive I can be?"

She stood up and shouted at the seemingly uninhabited jungle. For a while there was no response. She repeated her demands. Presently, an officer walked out from behind a frond. He was a tall well-built man in his early thirties, handsome behind the garish circles on his face. Besides the black chevrons down neck and shoulders, he was decorated with a painted seabird on his chest. This was an *iiphtarz,* and it indicated a commander of the glider force. Behind him came his wife, clad in a short skirt of red and blue seabird feathers, her red hair coiled on top of her head, her face painted with green and white lozenges, a necklace of fingerbones around her neck, an *iiphtarz* painted across her breasts, and three concentric circles of crimson, black, and yellow painted around her navel. As was the custom among the *abutal,* she accompanied her husband in battle. If he died, it was her duty to attack his killers until she slew them or died herself.

The two advanced up the hill until Wolff told them to come no further. Vala began talking, and the man began to smile. His wife, however, watched Vala closely and scowled throughout the conversation.

4

DUGARNN, THE OFFICER, CAPITULATED ONLY WHEN CERTAIN terms had been agreed upon. He refused to leave the island until he had gotten at least part of what the Ilmawir had intended to take when they attacked. Vala did not hesitate to promise him that the defenders' domestic fowl and animals (sea-rats and small seals) would be his prize of war. Moreover, the *abutal* could mutilate the corpses of their enemies and scalp them.

The surface-islanders, who called themselves Friiqan, objected when they heard these terms. Wolff told their leaders that if they did not accept, they would find the war continued. And he, Wolff, would take no sides this time. Surlily, they said they would do as he wished. The *abutal* stripped the villagers of everything they considered valuable.

The other Lords—Luvah, Enion, Ariston, Tharmas, and Palamabron—had been in the village when the attack started. They were very surprised to see him, and they could not hide their envy of his beamer. Only Luvah seemed glad to see him. Luvah, the runt of the lot, was sandy-haired and fine-featured except for a broad and full mouth. His eyes were a deep blue, and he had a faint milky way of freckles across the bridge of his nose and cheeks. He threw his arms around Wolff and hugged him and even wept a little. Wolff permitted the embrace because he did not believe that Luvah would take the chance to stab him. As children, the two had always been close, and had much in common, both being imaginative and inclined to let others do and think as they wished. In fact, Luvah had never indulged in the Lords' deadly game of trying to dispossess or slay the others.

"How did our father manage to entice you out from your world, where you were safe and happy?" Wolff said.

Luvah grinned crookedly and said, "I might ask you the same thing. Perhaps he played the same trick on you as on me. He sent a messenger, a glowing hexaculum, and it said that it was sent by you. You wanted me to come visit you; you were lonely and wished to talk again to the one member of your family who did not want to kill you. So, after taking what I thought were good precautions, I left my universe. I entered what I thought was your gate, only to find myself on this island."

Wolff shook his head and said, "You were always too impetuous, brother, too rash. Yet, I feel honored that you would forsake your safety to visit me. Only . . ."

"Only I should have been much more careful, more sure that the messenger was from you. At another time, I might have been. But at the moment the hexaculum arrived, I was thinking of you and longing for you. Even we Lords have our weaknessess, you know."

Wolff was silent for a while, watching the exultant Ilmawir carry away fowl, animals, necklaces, and rings of sea-jade. Then he said, "We are in the most desperate situation we have ever faced, Luvah. The greatest peril, of course, is our father. But almost as deadly are those on whom we have to depend most. Despite their word of honor, they will always need watching. Now I propose that we support each other. When I sleep, you watch. When you sleep, I stand guard."

Luvah smiled one-sidedly again and said, "And when you sleep, you will keep one eye open to watch me, heh, brother?"

Wolff frowned, and Luvah said hastily, "Do not be angry, Jadawin. You and I have managed to survive so long because we never fully gave our trust. With the best of reasons. How sad it is that all of us, our sisters, brothers, and cousins, once lived and studied and played together in innocence and even love. Yet, today, we are as hungry wolves at each others' throats. And why, I ask you? Why? I will tell you. It is because the Lords are mad. They think they are gods, when all the time they are only human beings, really no better than these savages here. Only they happen to be heir to a great power, a science and technology which they use without understanding the principles behind it. They are as evil children with toys that create whole worlds and destroy whole worlds. The great and wise men who devised the toys have long since died; knowledge and science have died out; and the good inherent in the cosmic powers is twisted for their benefit and theirs only."

"I know that well, brother," Wolff said. "Better than you, perhaps, since I was once as selfish and vicious as those others. Yet I underwent an experience which I will tell you about sometime. It changed me into a human being—I hope—into a being only you have the ability to appreciate."

The Ilmawir had dropped great balloon-like ladders with weights on them from the *abuta*. The loot was tied to these and floated back up along guide-ropes into the hatches in the bottom of the island. Those gliders worth repairing were also returned to the floater. When the stripping of the Friiqan was done, the *abutal* ascended. Wolff rode up in a harness attached to a pair of bladders. He held his beamer ready, since now the *abutal* had him in a position where they could attempt murder and have some hope of success. However, no moves were made. He rose through the opening and was seized by two grinning women. They dragged him to one side and unharnessed him. The bladders were taken into the dim interior of a large chamber, where other bladders were stored.

When all the Lords were landed, they were led by Dugarnn and his woman, Sythaz, up a winding flight of steps to the upper part of the island. The stairs were made of very light, paper-thin but strong material. This was the hardened shell of gas-bladders. On the *abuta,* where weight was critical, everything was as light as possible. This consideration had even affected the language as he was to discover. Although the speech differed little in basic vocabulary from the parent, it had undergone some sound changes. And new words relating to weight, shape, flexibility, size, and vertical and horizontal direction had arisen. These were used as classifiers in a sense unknown to the pristine speakers. Indeed, no noun and few adjectives could be used without accompanying classifiers. In addition, a detailed nautical and aeronavigational terminology had arisen.

The stairwell was a shaft cut through a hard tangle of roots. On coming out at its top, he found himself on the floor of a sort of amphitheater. The floor was made of broad strips of bladder-covering, and the sloping walls were composed of huge bladders tied together with roots. There was only one building on the great deck, a thatch-roofed opensided longhouse. This was the social and recreational building. It had flat stones on which each family cooked the meals. Domestic fowl and sea-rats ran loose, and meat-seals played in an inch-deep pool of water near the center.

Sythaz, the commander's wife, showed them where they would live. These quarters consisted of cubicles cut out of the roots and floored and walled with bladder-shells. Openings were cut in the floor and descent was made by a portable ladder. The only light came from through the hatch or from small fish-oil lamps. There was just enough room to take two steps one way and two another. The beds were coffin-shaped holes in the wall in which were mattresses of feathers stuffed into sealskin. Most of the daily and nightly activity took place on the "main-deck." There was absolutely no privacy except in the chief's bridge.

Wolff had expected the *abutal* to hoist anchor and sail off at once. Dugarnn said that they must wait a while. For one thing, the island needed more altitude before it could start out over the open seas. The bacteria that generated gas in the bladders worked very fast when fed nutrient, but it still would take two days before the bladders were filled enough for Dugarnn to consider it safe to cast loose.

Secondly, the invasion had cost the *abutal* a relatively staggering number of casualties. There were just not enough people to work the island efficiently. So, Dugarnn proposed something that the *abutal* had not had to do for a long time. The shortage of population would be made up by recruiting from the Friiqan. After making sure his "guests" knew where they were to be quartered, Dugarnn went back to the surface. Wolff, curious,

accompanied him. Vala insisted on going with him. Whether this was to satisfy her curiosity or just to keep an eye on him, Wolff did not know. Probably, she had both motives.

Dugarnn explained to the chief of the Friiqan what he wanted. The
chief, dispirited, waved a hand to indicate that he did not care what happened. Dugarnn gathered the survivors together and made his offer. To
Wolff's surprise, many volunteered. Vala told him that the two peoples were
thorough enemies, but that the Friiqan had lost face. Moreover, many of
the young considered an aerial life as romantic.

Dugarnn looked the volunteers over and picked out those who had dis-
tinguished themselves during the fighting. He chose more women than
men, especially those with children. There was an initial ceremony of ritual torture, which consisted of lightly burning the candidate on his or her
groin. Normally, a captured enemy was tortured to death unless he exhib-
ited exceptional stoicism and bravery. Then he could be initiated into the
tribe.

In emergencies, such as now, the torture was only token.

Later, after the island had set sail, the initiates would go through a ceremony in which each would mingle his blood with that of an Ilmawir. This
prevented revenge from the surface-people, since blood-brotherhood was
sacred.

"There's another reason besides needing more crew," Vala said. "The
abutal—in fact both surface and air islanders—have a tendency to inbreed.
To avoid this, prisoners are sometimes adopted into the tribe."

She was very friendly with Wolff now and insisted on being with him
every moment. She had even resumed calling him *wivkrath*, the Lords'
term for "darling." She leaned against him every time she had a chance and
once even gave him a light kiss on the cheek. Wolff did not respond. He
had not forgotten, even after 500 years, that they had been lovers and yet
she had tried to kill him.

Wolff set out for the area of the gate through which he had entered.
Vala went with him. To her questions, he answered that he wanted to talk
to Theotormon once more.

"That sea-slug! What can he have that you would want?"

"Information, perhaps."

They came to the gate. Theotormon was not in sight. Wolff walked along
the edge of the island, noting that here and there the land sank slightly
under his weight. Apparently, the bladders were not so thick in these
places.

"How many of these islands are there on this planet and what is the maximum size?" he said.

"I do not know. We have sighted two since we've been here, and the
Friiqan say that there are many more. They speak of the Mother of Islands,
a relatively huge island that they claim to have heard of. There are many

aerial islands, too, but none larger than the Ilmawirs'. Why do you want to talk of boring things like that, when we have ourselves to discuss?"

"Like what?" he said.

She faced him, so close that her upraised lips almost touched his chin. "Why can't we forget what happened to us? After all, that was a long time ago, when we were much younger and therefore not so wise."

"I doubt that you've changed," he said.

She smiled and said, "How would you know? Let me prove that I am different now."

She put her arms around him and placed her head on his chest.

"Different in everything but one. I loved you once, and now that I see you again, I realize I've never really stopped loving you."

"Even when you tried to murder me in my bed?" he said.

"Oh, that! Darling, I thought you were with that loathsome and conniving Alagraada. I thought you were betraying me. Can you blame me because I was crazed with jealousy? You know how terribly possessive I am."

"I know only too well." He pushed her away and said, "Even as a child, you were selfish. All Lords are selfish, but few to the degree to which you were. I cannot see now why I ever loved you."

"You toad!" she cried. "You loved me because I am Vala. That's all, just that I am Vala."

He shook his head and said, "That may have been true once. But it is not true any longer. Nor will it ever be true again."

"You love another! Do I know her? It's not Anana, not my stupid murderous sister."

"No," he said. "Anana is murderous, but she's not stupid. She didn't fall into Urizen's trap. I don't see her here. Or has something happened to her? Is she dead?"

Vala shrugged, turned away, and said, "I haven't heard of her for three hundred years. But your concern shows that you do care for her. Anana! Who would have thought it?"

Wolff did not try to change her mind. He did not think that it was wise to mention Chryseis, even though Vala might never have contact with her. There was no use taking a chance.

Vala spun around and said, "What happened to that Earth girl?"

"What Earth girl?" he said, taken aback at her viciousness.

"What Earth girl?" she mimicked. "I mean that Chryseis, the mortal you abducted from Earth some two and a half millennia ago. From a region the Earthlings call Troy or something like that. You made her immortal, and she became your mistress."

"Along with quite a few thousand others," he said. "Why pick on her?"

"Oh, I know, I know. You have really become degenerate, my brother Wolff-Jadawin."

"So you know my Earth name, the name by which I prefer to be called? And how much else do you know about me? And why?"

"I've always made it my business to have as much information about the Lords as it is possible to get," she said. "That is why I have stayed alive so long."

"And why so many others have died."

Her voice became soft again, and she smiled at him. "There's no reason for you to pick a quarrel with me. Why can't we let bygones be bygones?"

"Who picked a quarrel? No, there's no reason why bygones can't be just that, provided they are bygones. But the Lords never remember a good turn or forget an injury. And until you've convinced me otherwise, I will regard you as the same old Vala. As beautiful, maybe even more beautiful, but still with a black and rotten soul."

She tried to smile. "You always were too blunt. Maybe that was one reason why I loved you so much. And you were more of a man than the others. You were the greatest of all my lovers."

She waited for him to return the compliment. Instead, he said, "Love is what makes a lover. I did love you. *Did.*"

He walked away from her along the edge of the shore. He looked back from time to time. She was following him at a distance of twenty feet. Now and then, the earth sank beneath his feet. He stopped for her to catch up with him and said, "There must be many caves on the bottom. How can Theotormon be called out?"

"He can't. There are many caves, yes. Sometimes a whole group of bladders die, either from disease, old age, or from being eaten by a fish which finds them tasty. Then caverns exist for a while, although they're eventually filled up by new growths."

Wolff filed this information away for possible use. If things went too badly, a man could always take refuge under the island. Vala must have guessed what he was thinking—a gift he had found irritating when they had been mates—and she said, "I wouldn't go under there. The water swarms with man-eaters."

"How does Theotormon survive?"

"I don't know. Maybe he's too fast and strong for the fish. After all, he's adapted for that kind of life—if you want to call it a life."

Wolff decided that he would have to give up on Theotormon. He walked back into the jungle with Vala close behind. By now he permitted her to be at his back. She needed him too much to kill him.

He had gone only a few yards when he was knocked down from behind. At first, he thought that she had leaped upon him. He rolled away from her, trying to draw his beamer from its holster at the same time. He saw then that she had been propelled into him by another. The huge glistening wet body of Theotormon was flying at him. The bulk came flat down on him, and his breath was knocked out by the impact of 400 pounds. Then Theotormon was sitting on top of him and striking savagely at his face with the flippers. The first blow knocked him half-unconscious; the second drove him into darkness.

5

ALTHOUGH HE HAD NO RECOLLECTION OF THE FEW SECONDS after his senses had dissolved, he must not have been entirely unconscious. He had gotten his two arms out from under the pinning mass and seized the flippers. Slippery as they were, he managed to keep a grip on them. He regained full consciousness just as he yanked savagely on them, so strongly that Theotormon shrieked with pain and half-rose. That was enough for Wolff. He shoved against the bulging paunch and thrust himself partly free. He bent his free right leg and kicked. Now it was Theotormon's turn to gasp for breath.

Wolff rose to his feet and kicked hard again, his shoe driving into the weakest part of the monster, his head. Theotormon, caught on the forehead, slumped back. Wolff kicked him in the jaw and then half-buried another kick in the paunch. Theotormon, the moss-green eyes glazed, fell back, his legs doubled under him.

Yet he was not out, and when Wolff advanced on him to finish his work, Theotormon kicked with a huge foot. Wolff caught the foot and so denied its full impact, but he was shoved backwards. Theotormon arose, crouched, and leaped again. Wolff also leaped forward, his right knee driving upward. It caught Theotormon on his chin, and both fell to the ground again. Wolff scrambled up, felt for his beamer, and found it was not in his holster. His brother also rose. They faced each other at a distance of six feet, both breathing heavily and just becoming aware of the pain of the blows they had taken.

Wolff's natural strength had been increased twofold by artificial means, and his bones had been toughened, without being made brittle, to match the muscular strength. However, all Lords had undergone the same treatment, so that when they engaged in physical combat among themselves, the original strength was, relatively, the same. Theotormon's body had been reshaped by Urizen, and he outweighed his brother by at least one hundred and sixty pounds. Apparently, Urizen had not increased Theotormon's power by much, since Wolff had been able to match him so far.

Weight meant much in a fight, though, and it was this that Wolff had to watch for. He must not give Theotormon another chance to use it.

Theotormon, his wind having returned, growled, "I will batter you into unconsciousness again, Jadawin. And then I will carry you into the sea, dive into a cavern, and hold you while my pets eat you alive."

Wolff looked around. Vala was standing to one side and smiling very curiously. He did not waste his breath or time asking for her aid. He charged Theotormon, leaped high into the air, and kicked out with both feet. His brother had frozen for a second at the unexpected attack, then he ducked. Wolff had hoped that he would. He kicked low, but Theotormon was very fast. Wolff's shoes came down hard on his back, the shoes slipped on the wet back, and Wolff skidded down the back. He whirled even as he shot off Theotormon. The monster turned and leaped, expecting, or hoping to find Wolff flat on his back. Instead, he was caught by another kick in the jaw.

This time, Theotormon did not get up. His dark seal fur red with blood from a torn lip and gashed jaw and mashed nose, he lay breathing noisily. Wolff kicked him several times in the ribs to make sure he stayed down.

Vala applauded Wolff and said, "Well done. You are the man I once loved—still love."

"And why didn't you help me?" he said.

"You didn't need it. I knew you'd knock that bag of blubber out of his pinhead-mind."

Wolff looked through the grass for his beamer but could not find it.

Vala did not move from where she stood. She said, "Why didn't you use your knife?"

"I would have if it had been necessary. But I want him alive. We're taking him along with us."

Her eyes widened. "In the name of Los, why?"

"Because he has certain abilities we may be able to use."

Theotormon groaned and sat up. Wolff kept an eye on him but continued his search. Finally, he said, "All right, Vala. Hand it over."

She reached within her robe and brought out the beamer. "I could kill you now."

"Do it then, but don't waste my time with idle threats. You don't scare me."

"All right. Have it then," she said fiercely. She raised the beamer and for a moment Wolff thought he had goaded her too far. After all, the Lords were proud, far too proud, and overly swift to react to insult.

But she pointed the beamer carefully at Theotormon, and a white rod of light touched the end of one flipper. Smoke curled up; burnt flesh stank. Theotormon fell backwards, his mouth open, his eyes staring.

Vala, smiling, reversed the weapon and handed it to Wolff.

He swore and said, "There was no reason but viciousness for that, Vala.

Viciousness and stupidity. I tell you, he might have been the difference between death and life for us."

She walked—strolled—over to the huge wetness and bent over to
look at him. She raised the flipper, the end of which was charred.

"He's not dead—yet. You can save him, if you want to. But you'll have
to cut off the flipper. It'll be cooked halfway to his shoulder."

Wolff walked away without further comment. He recruited a number
of Ilmawir to help him get Theotormon on the island. Hoisted by four bladders, Theotormon rose up through a hatch. There he was pulled to one side
and stretched out on the floor of a "brig." This was a cage with very light
but steel-strong bars of laminated bladder-shells. Wolff did the surgery himself. After forcing a drugged drink, provided by the Ilmawir wizard, down
Theotormon's throat, he examined a number of saws and other surgical
tools. These were the property of the wizard, who took care of both the
spiritual and physical welfare of his people.

With several saws fitted with the teeth of a sharklike fish, Wolff cut off
the flipper just below the shoulder. The flesh went quickly; the bones offered enough resistance to dull two saws. The wizard thrust the red-hot
end of a torch against the huge wound to seal off the blood vessels. Moreover, the wizard applied a salve to the burn, assuring Wolff that it had saved
the lives of men who had been burned over half their bodies.

Vala watched the entire operation with a slight sneer. Once, her gaze
met Wolff's as he looked up from his work, and she laughed. He shuddered,
although she had a beautiful and striking laugh. It reminded him of a gong
he had once heard while voyaging down the Guzirit river in the land of
Khamshem on the third level of the planet of his own universe. It had
golden notes to it, that was the only way to describe the laughter. The gong
had probably been of bronze, hanging in the dark adytum of an ancient and
crumbling temple of jade and chalcedony, muffled by stone and the green
density of the jungle. It was bronze, but it gave forth golden vibrations. And
this was how the laughter of Vala sounded, bronze and golden and also with
something dark and smoldering in it.

She said, "He'll never be able to grow a new flipper unless you keep
peeling off the scab. You know regeneration won't take place if there's scar
tissue."

"You let me worry about those things," he said. "You've interfered
enough."

She sniffed and went up the narrow corkscrewing staircase to the maindeck. Wolff waited a while. After it seemed reasonable that Theotormon
was not going to die of shock, he also went up onto the deck. The Friiqan
adoptees were being trained for their new duties, and he watched them
for a while. He asked Dugarnn how the great gas-plants were fed, since it
seemed to him that the nutrient would weigh much. There were at least
four thousand of the bladders, each as large as the cell in a zeppelin.

Dugarnn explained. A growing bladder did not have to be fed. But when it matured, it died. The skin would become dry and hard but was specially treated to preserve flexibility and expandability. New colonies of gas-generating bacteria were placed therein. These had to be fed, but the amount of gas they produced was very high in proportion to the amount of food they needed. This was mainly the heart-stuff of growing plants, although the bacteria could work on fish, meat, or decaying vegetable matter.

Dugarnn left him, saying there was much work to be done. The shadow of the moon passed, and full daylight returned. The island began to tug harder against the ropes. Finally, Dugarnn decided that it was buoyant enough to cast loose. The stone anchors were drawn up, and the ropes around the fronds cut. The island drifted past the fronds and slowly rose. It settled at a hundred and fifty feet for a while. Then, as the gas continued to fill the bladders, it rose to five hundred feet. Dugarnn ordered the bacteria food to be reduced. He inspected the entire island, a trip which took several hours, and returned to the bridge. Wolff went down to see how Theotormon was coming along. The wizard reported that his patient was doing even better than could be expected.

Wolff climbed up a flight of steps to the top of the walls. Here he found Luvah and one of his cousins, Palamabron. The latter was a well-built and handsome man, darkest of the family. He wore a conical hat with hexagonal rim, both decorated with emerald-green owls. His cloak had a turned-up collar in back and epaulets in the shape of lions couchant. The fabric was a green shimmering stuff with a pattern of trefoils pierced with a bleeding lance. His shirt was electric-blue and piped with white skulls. A great belt of leather was bossed with gold and set with diamonds, emeralds, and topazes. His baggy pants were white-and-black striped and calf-length. The boots were of some pale soft red leather.

He made a striking and handsome figure, of which he was well aware. He nodded at Wolff's greeting, then left. Wolff, watching him, chuckled. He said, "Palamabron never did care too much for me. I would worry if he did."

"They won't do anything as long as we're on this aerial island," Luvah said. "At least, they won't unless this search takes too long. I wonder how long it will take? We could float forever over these seas and never happen across the gates."

Wolff looked at the red skies and the green-blue oceans and at the island they had left, a piece of unattached land seemingly no larger than a penny now. White birds with enormous wings and yellow curved beaks and orange-ringed eyes flew over them and gave forth shrill ululations. One settled down not far from where they stood and cocked its head and fastened an unblinking green eye upon them. Wolff remembered the ravens of his own world. Did some of these great birds have a slice of human brain within their unbird-like-sized craniums? Were they watching and listening for Urizen? Their father had some means of observing them, otherwise he would not be getting full enjoyment from this game.

"Dugarnn told me that the *abuta* is pushed always by the same wind. It takes it around and around this world of water in a spiraling path. Eventually, it covers every area."

"But the island that has the gates may always be on a different course. Always out of sight."

Wolff shrugged and said, "Then we won't find it."

"Perhaps that is the way Urizen wants it. He would like us to go mad from frustration and boredom and slit each others' throats."

"Perhaps. However, the *abuta* can change course when its people so wish. It's a slow process, but it can be done. Also . . ."

He was silent for so long that Luvah became uneasy. "Also what?"

"Our good father has placed other creatures here besides man, birds, a few animals, and fish. I understand that some of the islands, water and air alike, are populated by rather vicious flying creatures."

Vala called from below, saying that their meals were prepared. They went down to eat at one end of the chief's table. Here they heard what Dugarnn was planning. He was ready to thrust the *abuta* off course. Somewhere to the southwest was another floating island, that of their most bitter enemies, the Waerish. Now that the Ilmawir had Wolff and his beamer, they could join battle for the last time with the Waerish. It would be a glorious victory for the Ilmawir; the Waerish would be swallowed up by the ocean forever.

Wolff agreed, since there was little else he could do at that moment. He hoped that the Waerish would not be found, since he wanted to conserve the power packs of the beamer for more important matters.

The bright red days and pale red nights that followed were many and unvaried. They were, at first, however, busy for Wolff. He learned all he could about the management of the *abuta*. He studied the mores of the tribe and the idiosyncrasies of each member. The other Lords, with the exception of Vala, showed little interest in any of these. They spent their time at the bow, looking for the island that was supposed to contain the gates of Urizen. Or they complained to the *abutal* or to each other. And always one Lord was insulting another, although in a way that barely avoided an outright challenge from the insulted.

Wolff became more disgusted with them as each day passed. Except for Luvah, none was worth saving. They had an arrogance that displeased the *abutal*. Wolff warned the Lords against this many times, saying that their lives were dependent upon the natives. Should these be too antagonized, they were likely to dump the Lords overboard. His advice was taken for a while, and then the lifelong belief in their near-divinity would take hold of the Lords again.

Wolff spent much time on the bridge with Dugarnn. It was necessary to do this to smooth out the ridges of ill-feeling his brothers and cousins raised. He also went into the glider-training school, since the *abutal* could not fully give a man admiration and respect unless he had won his wings. Wolff asked Dugarnn why this was so. To Wolff, the gliders seemed more of a hindrance and unnecessary expense and trouble than anything else.

Dugarnn was astonished at the question. He groped for words, then said, "Why, it's just because . . . it is. That's all. No man is a man until he makes his first solo landing. As for your implications that gliders aren't worth the trouble, I deny those. When the day comes that we find an enemy, you will eat your words."

The next day, Wolff went up in a glider. He got into a tandem seat instruction ship, which was hauled aloft at the end of a cable borne by two great bladders. The craft rose upward until the *abuta* was a small brown oval below. Here the swifter upper winds carried them along until they were several miles ahead of the island. Then the instructor, Dugarnn, unlocked the lift mechanism. The bladders were then hauled down back to the *abuta* with a slim but strong cord, to be used again.

As Jadawin, Wolff had flown many types of craft. On Earth, he had gotten a private pilot's license qualifying him to fly single-motor craft. He had not flown for many years now, but he had not forgotten all his old skills, either. Dugarnn let him handle the controls for a while as they spiraled downwards. He tapped Wolff's shoulders and nodded approvingly, then took the controls over. The glider came in upwind, sideslipping at the last moment and landing on one side of the broad deck.

Wolff took five more lessons, during the last two of which he made the landings. On the fourth day, he soloed. Dugarnn was very impressed, saying that most students required twice that time. Wolff asked what happened if a soloing student missed the *abuta*. How could the islanders pick him up?

Dugarnn smiled and lifted his hands, palms up, and said that the unfortunate was left behind. No more was said about that, although Wolff noted that Dugarnn had insisted that the beamer be left on the island when Wolff had gone up. Wolff had placed it in the care of Luvah, whom he did not think would misuse it. Not to the extent the others would, anyway.

Thereafter, Wolff went bare-chested, as befitted a man who wore a painted *iiphtarz* upon his chest. Dugarnn insisted that Wolff also become a blood-brother. On hearing this, the other Lords scoffed.

"What, Jadawin, son of the great Lord Urizen, direct descendant of the Los himself, be brother to these painted ignorant savages? Have you no pride, brother?"

"Brother me no brother, brothers," he replied. "These people have at least not tried to slay me. That is more than I can say for any of you except Luvah. And they are not to be despised by the likes of you. They are masters of their own little worlds. You are homeless and trapped like dull-witted fat geese. So do not be so ready to scorn me or them. You would be far better off if you would condescend to make friends with them. The time may come when you will need them very much."

Theotormon, his flipper pink and half-grown out now, was squatting in the inch-deep pool. He said, "The whole accursed lot of you are doomed; long may you scream when Urizen finally closes the trap on you. But this I will say for Jadawin. He is twice the man any of you are. And I wish him luck. I wish he may get to our beloved father and exact vengeance from him, while the rest of you die horribly."

"Shut your ugly mouth, you toad!" Ariston cried. "It is bad enough to have to look at you. My stomach wrings itself out when I see you. To have to hear you, you abomination, is too much. I wish that I were in my own lovely world again and had you at my feet and in chains. Then I would make you talk, monsterling, so fast your words would be a gabble for mercy. And then I would feed you inch by inch to some special pets of my own, oh, beautiful little pets."

"And I," Theotormon said, "will pitch you over the side of this floating island some night and will laugh as I watch you flailing at the air and hear your last scream."

"Enough of this childish bickering," Vala said. "Don't you know now that when you quarrel among yourselves, you delight the heart of our father? He would love to see you tear each other apart."

"Vala is right," Wolff said. "You call yourselves Lords, makers and rulers of entire universes. Yet you behave like spoiled, and evil, brats. If you hate each other, remember that the one who taught you this horrible hatred, and who now has set the stage for your death, still lives. He must die. If we have to die ourselves in making sure of his death, so be it. But at least try to live with dignity and so dignify your deaths."

Suddenly, Ariston strode towards Wolff. His face was red, and his mouth was twisted. He towered over Wolff, though he was not as broad. He waved his arms, and the saffron robes, set with scarlet and green imbrications, flapped.

"I have put up with enough from you, detested brother!" he howled. "Your insults and your insinuations that you are better than us now because you have become less than us—one of those animals—have enraged me. I hate you as I have always hated you, hated you far more than the others. You are nothing—a . . . a . . . foundling!"

With this insult, the worst the Lords could conceive, for they could think of nothing worse than not to be of the true lineage of Lords, he began to draw his knife. Wolff bent his knees, ready to fight if he had to but hoping he would not. It would look very bad for the Lords if they brawled in front of the *abutal.*

At that moment, a cry arose from the gondola on the prow of the island. Drums began to beat, and the *abutal* dropped what they were doing. Wolff caught hold of a man running by and asked what the alarm was about.

The man pointed to the left, indicating something in the sky. Wolff turned to see an object, dark and fuzzy against the red dome of the sky.

6

EVEN AS WOLFF RAN TOWARDS THE BRIDGE, ANOTHER OBJECT appeared. Before he had reached the gondola, he saw two more. They made him prickle with uneasiness and a sense of strangeness. He could not identify the reason for this at first. But before he reached the gondola, he knew. The objects were not drifting with the wind but were coming in at right angles to it. Something was propelling them.

On the bridge, Dugarnn told Wolff what he wanted of him. He was to stay by his side until ordered otherwise. As for the other Lords, now was the time for them to earn their keep. Dugarnn had heard them boasting of their prowess. Let them put their swords where their mouths were— or words to that effect.

Communication on the island-surface during a battle was by drum. Orders to those inside the island, stationed on the ports on the sides or the hatches at the bottom, were transmitted by another means. Throughout the *abuta* was a network of thin narrow pipes. These were fashioned from the bones of the *girrel* fish, and had the property of transmitting sound quite well. The *abutal* could use voice over the girrel-bones up to seventy-five feet. Past this distance, a code was rapped out by a tiny hammer.

Wolff watched Dugarnn issue orders, which were performed swiftly by the well-trained people. Even children were carrying out duties within their capabilities, and so relieving adults for more difficult and dangerous posts. To Vala, who had come up to the bridge, Wolff said, "We so-called divine Lords could learn much about cooperation from these so-called savages."

"No doubt," Vala replied. She looked out across the oceans and said, "There are six now. What are they?"

"Dugarnn mentioned the Nichiddor, but he had no time to tell me what they are. Be patient. We'll know soon enough. Too soon, I suspect."

The gliders had been fastened to the lift-bladders. The pilots got into the cockpits while the "ground" crews fitted the explosive bladder-bombs to the wings. Then the wizard, clad in robes and a mask, passed along the gliders. He carried a double-ankh with which he blessed the pilots and their craft. Between each glider, he stopped to shake the double-ankh at the *ufo* and hurl maledictions. Dugarnn became impatient but dared not hurry the wizard. As soon as the last of the twenty airmen had been touched by the ankh and prayed over, Dugarnn gave the signal. The bladders with their white-winged cargoes were released. They soared up and up until they had attained a height of a thousand feet above the island.

Dugarnn said, "They'll release themselves as soon as the Nichiddor nests get within range. Los guard them, since few will get through. But if the nests can be destroyed . . ."

"There are eight now," Wolff said. The nearest was a half-mile away. Ball-shaped, it had a diameter of about three hundred yards. The fuzzy appearance had been caused by the many uneven projections of plants. These grew out to conceal the gas-bladders that formed irregular concentric rings. On the surface of the spheroid nest were hundreds of tiny figures. An aerial dung-ball, Wolff thought.

Dugarnn pointed above him, and Wolff saw a number of small dark objects. "Scouts," Dugarnn said. "The Nichiddor won't attack until the scouts report to them."

"Who are the Nichiddor?"

"There's one now, coming down to take a close look."

The wings were black-feathered and had a spread of at least fifty feet. They sprouted out from the five-foot wide shoulders, below which was a hairless human torso. The breast-bone projected several feet and under it was the abdomen with a human navel. The legs were thin and ended in huge feet that were mainly clawlike toes. A long black feathered tail spread out behind it. The face was human except for the nose. This extended like an elephant's proboscis for several feet and was as flexible. As the Nichiddor swept over them, it raised the proboscis and trumpeted shrilly.

Dugarnn glanced at Wolff's beamer. Wolff shook his head and said, "I'd rather they didn't know yet what they're up against. My supply of charges is limited. I want to wait until I can get a number with a single shot."

He watched the Nichiddor flap heavily away towards the nearest nest. The creatures were undoubtedly the work of Urizen, who had placed them here for his own amusement. They must be human beings—although not necessarily Lords—he had transmuted in the laboratory. They could have been abducted from other worlds than his; some might even be descended from Earthmen. Now they lived a strange life beneath red skies and a dark moon, born and raised on an aerial nest that drifted with the winds of this landless world. They lived largely on fish, which they caught as an osprey catches fish, with their talons. But when they came across a surface or air-island, they killed to eat raw human flesh.

By now Wolff could see why the nests were going against the wind. The hundreds of Nichiddors on it had gripped the plants in their talons and were flapping their wings in unison. The foul chariot of the skies was drawn by as strange birds as ever existed.

When the nest had come within a quarter-mile, the wings stopped beating. Now the other nests drew up slowly. Two settled downwards; from these the Nichiddor would attack the bottom of the island. Two others veered around behind the island and then came on the other side. Dugarnn waited calmly until the Nichiddor had set their attack pattern.

Wolff asked him why he did not order the gliders to attack.

"If they were released before the main body of Nichiddor came at us," Dugarnn said, "every Nichiddor would rise to bar the way. The gliders could not possibly get through them. But with only a small number of Nichiddor attacking the gliders, we have a chance of getting through to the nests. At least, that has been my experience so far."

"Wouldn't it be wisest, from the Nichiddors' viewpoint, to eliminate the gliders first?" Wolff asked.

Dugarnn shrugged and said, "You'd think so. But they never do what seems to me the most strategic thing. It's my theory that, being deprived of hands, the Nichiddor have suffered a lessening of intelligence. It's true they can manipulate objects to some extent with their feet and their trunks, but they're far less manual than we.

"Then again, I could be wrong. Perhaps the Nichiddor derive a certain pleasure from giving the gliders a fighting chance. Or perhaps they are as arrogant as sea-eagles, which will attack a shark that outweighs them by a thousand pounds, a vicious creature that an eagle cannot possibly kill or, if it could, would not be able to carry off to some surface island."

The wind carried to the *abuta* the gabble of hundreds of voices and the trumpeting of hundreds of proboscises. Suddenly, there was a silence. Dugarnn froze, but his eyes were busy. Slowly, he raised his hand. A warrior standing near him held a bladder in his hand. By him was a bowl-shaped stone with some hot coals. He held his gaze upon his chief.

The silence was broken with the united scream of Nichiddor through their snaky noses. There was a clap as of thunder as they launched themselves from the nests and brought their wings together in the first beat. Dugarnn dropped his hand. The warrior dipped the short fuse of the bladder into the fire and then released it. It soared upwards to fifty feet and exploded.

The gliders dropped from their lifts, each towards the nest appointed to it. Wolff looked at the dark hordes advancing and lost some of his confidence in his beamer. Yet, the Ilmawir had beaten off attacks by the Nichiddor before—although with great loss. But never before had eight nests ringed the *abuta*.

A great-winged white bird passed overhead. Its cry came down to him, and he wondered if this could be an eye of Urizen. Was his father watching through the eyes and brains of these birds? If so, he was going to see a spectacle that would delight his bloody heart.

The Nichiddor, so thick they were a brown and black cloud, surrounded the island. Just out of bow-range, they stopped advancing and began to fly around the island. Around and around they flew, in an ever-diminishing circle. The Ilmawir archers, all males, waited for their chief to signal to fire. The women were armed with slings and stones, and they also waited.

Dugarnn, knowing that it would weaken them to spread out his people along the top of the walls, had concentrated them at the prow. There was nothing to prevent the Nichiddor from landing at the far end. However, they did not settle down there. They hated to walk on their weak legs.

Wolff looked out at the gliders. Some had dropped below his line of vision to attack the two nests below the underside. The others were coming down swiftly in a steep glide. A number of Nichiddor rose from the nest to meet them.

Two fliers passed over the nearest nest. Small objects, trailing smoke, dropped from them and fell on the nests. Females, flapping their wings, scrambled towards them. Then, there was an explosion. Smoke and fire billowed out. Another explosion followed.

The two gliders pulled up sharply. Carried upward by the momentum of their steep dives, they turned and came back for another and final pass. Again, their bombs hit. Fire spread through the dry plants and caught and enfolded some of the giant gas-cells. The females screamed so loudly they could be heard even above the wing-beatings and trumpetings of the circling horde. They rose from the burning nest, their infants clutched in their toes. The entire nest blew apart, catching some of the females, burning them in flight or hurling them head over heels. Infants dropped towards the sea below, their short wings ineffectively flapping.

Wolff saw one mother fold her wings and drop like a fish-hawk towards her infant. She caught it, beat her wings, and lifted slowly towards an untouched nest.

Two nest, burning and exploding, spun towards the ocean. By then several hundreds of males had detached themselves from the ring around the island. They flew after the gliders, which by now were far down, headed towards a landing on the waves.

The nests on a level with the island were out of range of his beamer. It was possible the two below might not be. Wolff told Dugarnn what he meant to do and went down a fifty-foot winding staircase to a hatch at its bottom. The nests there had risen close, and he caught both of them with a sweep of the full power of the beamer. They blew up with such violence that he was lifted and almost knocked off the platform. Smoke poured up through the hatch. Then, as it cleared away, he saw the flaming pieces of vegetation falling. The bodies of the children and females plummeted into the sea.

The male warriors from the nests were trying to get through the bottom hatches. Wolff put the beamer on half-power and cleared the area. Then he ran along the gangplank, stopping at every hatch to fire again. He accounted for at least a hundred attackers. Some had gotten through the defending *abutal* at the hatches at the far end. It took him a while to kill these, since he had to be careful not to touch the many great bladders. Even though he slew thirty, he could not get them all. The island was too large for him to cover all the bottom area.

By the time he climbed back up to the hatch, he found that the Nichiddor had launched their mass attack. This end of the island was a swirling, screeching, shouting, screaming mob. There were bodies everywhere.

The archers and slingers had taken a heavy toll of the first wave and a lighter toll of the second. Then the Nichiddor were upon them, and the battle became a melee. Although the winged men had no weapons other than their wings and feet, these were powerful. With a sweep of a wing, a Nichiddor could knock down an Ilmawir. He could then leap upon his stunned and bruised foe and tear at him with the heavy hooked clawlike toenails. The *abutal* defended themselves with spears, swords which were flat blades lined with shark's teeth, and knives formed from a bamboolike surface plant.

Wolff methodically set about to kill all those in the neighborhood of the maindeck. The Lords had made a compact group, all facing outwards and slashing with their swords. Wolff took careful aim and slew the Nichiddor pressing them. A shadow fell on him, and he fell on his back and fired upwards. Two Nichiddor struck the deck on each side of him, the wing of one buffeting him. It covered him like a banner and stank of fish. He crawled out from under just in time to shoot two that had forced Dugarnn back against the wall. Dugarnn's wife lay near him, her spear stuck in a winged man's belly. Her face and breasts were ripped into shreds, and the Nichiddor who had done it was tearing out her belly. He fell backwards, his claws caught in her entrails, as Wolff shot him from behind.

For the next minute, it was near-death for him. At least two dozen Nichiddor came at him from all sides and from above. He spun like a top, using the beam as a spray, around him and in the air. The corpses, half-severed, smoking, stinking, piled up around him. Then he was over them, out in the open, on the fringes of the eddying battle. He shot everywhere and usually hit his target, though twice an *abutal* was borne by the thrust of the fight into the beam. This could not be helped; he was lucky that he had not hit more.

The Ilmawir, despite a fierce resistance, had lost half their numbers. Even with Wolff's help, they were being defeated. The Nichiddor, despite casualties that should have made them retreat, refused to stop. They were intent on extermination of their foe, even if it meant near-extermination for them.

Wolff cleared the attackers around the Lords again. They were all on their feet and swinging their swords, although covered with blood. Wolff called to them to form around him. While they kept off the winged men, he would shoot over them. He stood upon a pile of Nichiddor, his feet braced on the slippery corpses, and coolly resumed firing. Suddenly, he realized that he was down to his last two power packs. He had hoped to save some for Urizen's stronghold, but there was nothing he could do to conserve them now. If he did not use the beamer, he and all that fought with him would die.

Vala, standing just in front of him, yelled. He looked upward where she was pointing. A dark object spanned the skies: a black comet. It had appeared while all were intent upon the fight.

The *abutal* near them also looked up. They gave a cry of despair and threw down their weapons. Ignoring the winged men, they ran towards the nearest hatches. The Nichiddor, after searching the skies for the cause of the panic, also reacted with terror. They launched themselves into the air to get to the nests or to escape to the protecting underside of the island.

Wolff did not throw down his beamer, but he was as frenzied as the others in their attempt to get to the closest cover. Dugarnn had told him of the black comets that occasionally visited the space above this planet. He had warned of that which always accompanied the comet.

As Wolff raced towards a hatch, there were small whistling noises around him. Holes appeared in the foliage of the walls; little curls of smoke rose from the sheathing of the maindeck. A Nichiddor, ten feet up, flapping his fifty-foot wings frantically, screamed. He fell to the deck, his skin pierced in several places, smoke coming from one wing. Another and another winged man dropped, and with them some *abutal*. The corpses jerked with the impact of the tiny drops.

Wolff's beamer was knocked out of his hand by the blow of a drop of quicksilver. He stooped and picked it up and resumed his run. For a moment, he could not get into the hatchway because of the Lords jammed before it. They fought each other, cursed, and cried to Los. Some even cried out for their father, Urizen, or their long-dead mother.

For one wild second, Wolff thought of clearing the way for him with the beamer. It was exactly what any of them, with the possible exception of Luvah, would have done. To stay out here was to be dead. Every bit of time counted.

Then whoever was the cause of the pile-up got through, and the others clawed and bit and scratched their way in.

Wolff went through the hatch in a dive, headfirst. Something touched his pants. His calf burned. There was a splashing noise, and hot mercury clung to the back of his head. He fell past the shallow ladder and hit the floor with his two hands, dropping the beamer before the hit. He absorbed most of the shock with his bent arms and then rolled over. He brought up against Palamabron, who was just starting down the second ladder. Palamabron yelled and pitched forward. Wolff, looking down the well, saw Palamabron on top of a pile of Lords. All were shouting and cursing. None, however, seemed to be hurt badly.

At another time Wolff would have laughed. Now he was too concerned with scraping the globules of hot mercury from his hair. He examined his leg to make sure that the hit there had only been glancing. Then he went on down the steps. It was best to get as far below as possible. If this were a heavy and steady mercury-drop shower, the entire upper decks could be destroyed. If the big gas-bladders were penetrated, good-bye forever to all.

7

VALA GREETED HIM IN THE TWILIGHT OF A GANGPLANK BY A spheroid cell. She was laughing. Her laughter was not hysteria but genuine amusement. He was sure that if there were enough light, he would be able to see her eyes shining with mirth.

"I'm glad that you find this funny," he said. He was covered with Nichiddor blood, which was rapidly being carried off by his heavy sweating, and he was shaking. "You were always a strange one, Vala. Even as a child, you loved teasing the rest of us and playing cruel jokes upon us. And as a woman, you loved blood and suffering—in others—more than you loved love."

"So I am a true Lord," she said. "My father's daughter. And, I might add, my brother's sister. You were just like me, dear Jadawin, before you became the namby-pamby human Wolff, the degenerate half-Earthling."

She came closer, and, lowering her voice, said, "It has been a long time since I have had a man, Jadawin. And you have not touched a woman since you came through the gate. Yet I know that you are like a he-goat, brother, and that you begin to suffer when a day passes without taking a woman to bed. Can you put aside your so-evident loathing of me—which I do not understand—and go with me now? There are a hundred hiding places in this island, dark and warm and private places where no one will disturb us. I ask you, though my pride is great."

She spoke truly. He was an exceedingly strong and vigorous man. Now he felt longing come upon him, a longing that he had put aside every day by constant activity. When night came and he went to bed, he had bent his mind to plots against his father, trying to foresee a thousand contingencies and the best way to dispose of them.

"First the blood-feast and then the lust-dessert," he said. "It's not I who rouses you but the thrust of the blade and the spurt of blood."

"Both do," she said. She held out her hand to him. "Come with me."

He shook his head. "No. And I want to hear no more of this. The subject is forever dead."

She snarled, "As you will soon be. No one can . . ."

Vala turned and walked away, and when he next saw her, she was talking earnestly to Palamabron. After a while, the two walked off into the dimness of a corridor.

He thought for a moment of ordering them back. They were in effect deserting their posts. The danger from the Nichiddor seemed to be over, but if the mercury shower became heavier, the island could be badly crippled or destroyed.

He shrugged and turned away. After all, he had no delegated authority. The cooperation among the Lords was only a spoken agreement; there was no formal agreement of organization with a system of punishments. Also, if he tried to interfere, he would be accused of doing so because of jealousy. The charge would not be entirely baseless. He did feel a pang at seeing Vala go off with another man. And this was a measure of what he had once felt for her, that after five hundred years and what she had tried to do to him, he should care even the fraction of a bit.

He said to Dugarnn, "How long does a shower last?"

"About a half-hour," the chief replied. "The drops are carried along with the black comets. The laughter of Urizen, we call them, since he must have created them. Urizen is a cruel and bloody god who rejoices in the sufferings of his people."

Dugarnn did not have exactly the same attitude towards Urizen that the Lords did. In the course of the many thousands of years since the descendants of the trapped Lords had been here, the name of Urizen had become that of the evil god in the *abutal* pantheon. Dugarnn had no true idea of the universe in which he was born. To him, this world was *the* world, the only one. The Lords were demigods, sons and daughters of Urizen by mortal women. The Lords were mortal, too, though extraordinarily powerful.

There was an explosion, and Wolff feared for a moment that one of the gas-bladders at the far end of the island had been penetrated. One of the *abutal* said that a Nichiddor nest had gone up. Less protected then the island, it had received a concentration of drops, one bladder had blown up another, and in the chain reaction the whole nest was hurled apart.

Wolff went over to where Theotormon crouched in a corner. His brother looked up at him with hate and misery. He turned his head away when Wolff spoke to him. After a while, as Wolff squatted quietly by him, Theotormon began to fidget. He finally looked at Wolff and said, "Father told me that there are four planets that revolve in orbit about a central fifth. This is Appirmatzum, the planet on which is his stronghold. Each planet is about the size of this one, and all are separated from Appirmatzum by only twenty thousand miles. This universe is not a recent one. It was created as one of a series by our father at least fifteen thousand years ago. They were kept hidden, their gates only being activated when Father wished to enter or leave one. Thus, the scanners failed to detect them."

"Then that is why I've seen only three of the planets," Wolff said. "The outer ones are at the corners of an equilateral quadrangle. The planet opposite is always hidden by Appirmatzum."

He did not wonder at the forces which enabled such large bodies to be so relatively close and yet stay in undeviating paths. The science of the Lords was beyond his comprehension—as a matter of fact, it was beyond the understanding of any of the Lords. They had inherited and used a power the principles of which they no longer understood. They did not care to understand. It was enough that they could use the powers.

This very lack of knowledge of principles made the Lords so vulnerable at times. Each only had so many weapons and machines. If any were destroyed, lost, or stolen, a Lord could only replace them by stealing them from other Lords—if there were any still in existence. And the defenses they set up against other Lords always had holes in them, no matter how impregnable the defenses seemed. The vital thing was to live long enough while attacking to find these holes. So, no matter how powerless the group seemed at the moment, Wolff had hopes that he could win.

While waiting for the mercury shower to cease, he had time to think. From some corner of his mind came an irrelevancy that had been bothering him for a long long time. It had nothing to do with the present situation. It might have been sent by the unconscious to keep him from worrying about Chryseis, for whom he could do nothing at all at this moment.

The names of his father, brothers, sisters, and cousins had made him wonder ever since he had regained his memory of his life as Jadawin, Lord of the World of Tiers. Urizen, Vala, Luvah, Anana, Theotormon, Palamabron, Enion, Ariston, Tharmas, Rintrah, these were the names of the vast and dark cosmogens found in William Blake's Didactic and Symbolical Works. It was no coincidence that they were the same. Of that Wolff was convinced. But how had the mystical English poet come across them? Had he known a dispossessed Lord, wandering on Earth, who had told him of the Lords for some reason? It was possible. And Blake must have used some of the Lord's story as a basis for his apocalyptic poetry. But the story had been very much distorted by Blake.

Some day, if Wolff got out of this trap, he would do some research on Earth and also among those Lords who would let him get close enough to them to talk.

The pounding of the quicksilver stopped. After waiting for half an hour to make sure that the storm was all over, the islanders went back upon the maindeck. The floor was broken up, pitted, and scorched. The walls had been pierced so many times that the roots and leaves were rags of vegetation. The gondola had been hit by an especially heavy concentration and was a wreck. Tiny globules of mercury lay all over the deck.

Theotormon said, "The mercury shower can't be compared to a meteor shower. The drops are only traveling about a hundred miles an hour when they hit the atmosphere, and they are considerably slowed up and broken up before they reach the surface. Yet . . ."

He waved a flipper to indicate the damage.

Wolff looked out over the sea. The surviving nests were drifting slowly away. The winged men had enough problems of their own without resuming the attack. One nest was so overburdened with refugees from others that it was losing altitude.

Dugarnn was sad. He had lost so many people that it would be very difficult to maneuver the island and impossible to defend it against another attack. Now they would drift helplessly around and around the world. Not until the children had grown up would they become powerful again. It was unlikely that the island would be left alone long enough for the children to become adults.

"My people are doomed," he said.

"Not as long as you keep fighting," Wolff said. "After all, you can avoid battle with other *abutal* islands and with the surface islands. You told me that the only reason two *abuta* get together for a conflict is that both maneuver to approach each other. You can quit doing that. And the Nichiddor are rare. This is the first time in fifteen years that you have met a cluster of nests."

"What! Run away from a fight!" Dugarnn said. His mouth hung open. "That . . . that's unthinkable. We would be cowards. Our names would be a scornword in the mouths of our enemies."

"That's a lot of nonsense," Wolff said. "The other *abutal* can't even get close enough to identify you unless you let them. But that's up to you. Die because you can't change your ways, if that's what you want."

Wolff was busy helping to clean up the island. The dead and wounded Nichiddor were dumped overboard. The dead *abutal* were given a long burial ceremony, officiated over by Dugarnn, since the wizard had had his head twisted off during the battle. Then the bodies were slipped over the side and received by the sea.

Days and nights drifted by as slowly as the wind-driven island. Wolff spent much time observing the great brown spheres of the other planets. Appirmatzum was only twenty thousand miles away. So near and yet so far. It might as well be a million miles. Or was it truly so impossible to get there? A plan began to form, a plan so fantastic that he almost abandoned it. But, if he could get the materials, he might, just might, carry it out.

The *abuta* passed over the polar area, the surface of which looked just like the others. Twice, they saw enemy islands at a distance. When these began to work their way towards Dugarnn's island, Dugarnn sadly ordered his island to flee. The banks of gas-bladders on one side were operated to give the island a slow lateral thrust, and the distance between the two was kept equal. After a while, the enemy gave up, having used up as much gas in his bladders as he dared.

Dugarnn explained that the maneuvers which brought two *abuta* into battle-conflict sometimes took as much as five days.

"I've never seen people so anxious to die," was Wolff's only comment.

One day, when it seemed to all the Lords that they would drift above the featureless waters forever, a lookout gave a cry that brought them running.

"The Mother of All Islands!" he shouted. "Dead ahead! The Mother of Islands!"

If this was the mother of islands, then her babies must be small indeed. From three thousand feet, Wolff could span the floating mass from shore to shore with one sweep of the eye. It was not more than thirty miles wide at the broadest and twelve miles long. But most things are relative, and on this world it was a continent.

There were bays and inlets and even broken spaces that formed lakes of sea-water. At various times, some force, perhaps collision with other islands, had crumpled up parts of the island. These formed hills. And it was on top of one of the hills that Wolff saw the gates.

There were two, hexagons of some self-illuminated metal, each huge as the open end of a zeppelin hangar.

Wolff hurried to notify Dugarnn. The commander was aware of the gates and was barking out orders. A long time ago, he had promised Wolff that when the gates were found, he would terminate the agreement. Wolff and the beamer and the Lords could leave the *abuta*.

There was not near enough time to valve off gas to lower the island. Before the desired altitude could be reached, the *abuta* would have drifted far past the Mitza, the mother. So the Lords hastened to the lowest deck, where jump-bladder harnesses were ready for them. They strapped the belts around their shoulders, chests, and legs and then were towed to the hatch. Dugarnn and the *abutal* crowded around them to say farewell. They said no words of good-bye to any of the Lords but Wolff and Luvah. These two they kissed, and they pressed the flower of the young gas-plant in their hands. Wolff said farewell and stepped through the hatch. He fell as swiftly as a man below an open parachute. The other Lords followed him. There was an open space among the fronds in which he tried to land, but he miscalculated the wind. He crashed into the top of a frond, which bent beneath him and so broke his fall. The others also made good landings, though some were bruised. Theotormon had an extra large jump-harness because of his four hundred and fifty pounds, but he came down faster than the others anyway. His rubbery legs bent under him; he rolled; and he was up on his feet, squawking because he had banged his head.

Wolff waited until they were recovered. He waved at the Ilmawir, who were peering down at him from the hatches. Then the island passed on and presently was out of their sight. The Lords made their way through the jungle towards the hill. They were alert, since they had seen many native villages from the *abuta*. But they came to the hill-gates without seeing the aborigines and presently were standing before the towering hexagons.

"Why two?" Palamabron said.

Vala said, "That is another of our father's riddles, I'm sure. One gate must lead to his palace on Appirmatzum. The other, who knows where?"

"But how will we know?" Palamabron said.

"Stupid!" Vala said. "We won't know until we go through one or the other."

Wolff smiled slightly. Ever since she had gone off with Palamabron, she had treated him with even more contempt and scorn than the others. Palamabron was bewildered by this. Evidently, he had been expecting some sort of gratitude.

Wolff said, "We should all go through the same one. It won't be wise to split up our forces. Wrong one or right one, we must be united."

Palamabron said, "You are right, brother. Besides, if we split, and one group were to get into Urizen's stronghold and kill him, then that group would have control. And they would betray the second group."

"That is not why I think we should stay together," Wolff said. "But you have a good point."

"On top of his head," Vala said. "Palamabron is no more of a thinker than he is a lover."

Palamabron reddened, and he put his hand upon the hilt of his sword. "I am through swallowing your insults, you vixen in heat," he said. "One more, and your head will roll off your shoulders."

"We have enough fighting ahead of us," Wolff said. "Save your fury for that which lies on the other side of one of those gates."

He saw a movement in the bushes a hundred yards away. Presently, a face showed. A native was watching them. Wolff wondered if any of the natives had tried to go through the gates. If one had, his disappearance would have terrified the others. Possibly, this area was tabu.

He was interested in the natives' reactions, because he considered that they might be of some help, someday. Just now, he did not have time or did not wish to take time. Chryseis was in Urizen's stronghold, and every minute there must be agony. It might not be agony only of spirit; she could be tormented physically by his father.

He shuddered and tried to put out of his mind the pictures that this thought painted. One thing at a time.

He looked at the others. They were watching him intently. Although they would have strongly denied it, they regarded him as a leader. He was not the oldest brother and one of his cousins was older. But he had taken immediate and forceful measures whenever any crisis had come up on this world. And he had the beamer. Moreover, they seemed to detect something different in him, a dimension that they lacked—although they would have denied this, too. His experience as Robert Wolff, the Earthman, had given him a grip upon matters that they had always considered too mundane to bother with. Insulated from hard labor, from having to deal with things at a primitive level, they felt lost. Once they had been makers and semidivine rulers of their own private universes. Now they were no better—perhaps not as good—as the savages they so despised. Jadawin—or Wolff, as they were beginning to call him—was a man who knew his way around in a world of savages.

Wolff said, "It's one fate or the other. A case of eenie meenie minie moe."

"And what barbaric language is that?" Vala said.

"Earth type. I'll tell you what. Vala is the only woman here . . ."

"But more of a man than most of you," Vala said.

". . . so why don't we let her pick out which one we enter? It's as good a method as any for choosing."

"That bitch never did anything right in her life," Palamabron said. "But I say, let her designate the gate. Then we won't go wrong if we enter the one she doesn't choose."

"Do what you like," Vala said. "But I say—that one."

She pointed at the right-hand hexagon.

"Very well," Wolff said. "Since I have the beamer, I'll go first. I don't know what's on the other side. Rather, I know what is there—death—but I don't know what form it'll take. Before I go, I'd like to say this. There was a time, brothers, cousins, sister, when we loved each other. Our mother lived then, and we were happy with her. We were in awe of our father, the gloomy, remote, forbidding Urizen. But we did not hate him. Then our mother died. How she died, we still don't know. I think, as some of you do, that Urizen killed our mother. It was only three days after she died that he took to wife Araga, the Lord of her own world, and so united his domain with hers.

"Whoever murdered our mother, we know what happened after that. We found out that Urizen was beginning to be sorry that he had children. He was one of the very few Lords to have children being raised as Lords. The Lords are dying out; they are paying for their immortality, so-called, and for their power, with gradual extinction. They have also paid with the loss of that one thing that makes life worthwhile: love."

"Love!" said Vala. She laughed, and the others joined her. Luvah half-smiled, but he did not laugh.

"You sound like a pack of hyenas," Wolff said. "Hyenas are carrion-eaters, powerful, nasty, vicious brutes, whose stench and habits make them despised and hated everywhere. However, they do serve a useful function, which is more than I can say for you.

" 'Love,' I said. And I repeat it again. The word means nothing to you; it has been too many thousands of years since you felt it. And I doubt that any of you felt it very strongly then. Anyway, as I was saying, we found out that Urizen was considering doing away with us. Or at least disowning us and driving us out to live with the aborigines on a planet in one of his universes, a world which he intended to make gateless so we could never strike back at him. We fled. He came after us and tried to kill us. We got away, and we killed other Lords and took over their worlds.

"Then we forgot we were brothers and sisters and cousins and became true Lords. Hateful, scheming, jealous, possessive. Murderers, cruel alike to each other and to the miserable beings who populated our worlds."

"Enough of this, brother," Vala said. "What are you getting at?"

Wolff sighed. He was wasting his breath.

"I was going to say that perhaps Urizen has done us a favor without meaning to. Perhaps we could somehow find it in ourselves to resurrect the childhood love, to act as brothers should. We . . ."

He stopped. Their faces were like those of stone idols. Time could break them, but love would never soften them.

He turned and stepped through the right-hand gate.

His feet slid out from under him, and he fell on his side. He caught a glimpse of smooth glassy surfaces as he slid down the hill on top of which the gate was set. The stuff on which he raced downhill was dry and slippery, although it gave an impression of oiliness. No matter how he tried to dig his heels in, how strongly he placed the flats of his hands against the stuff to brake himself, he sped on down. It was like being on ice.

He shot on, gaining speed. Throwing himself over with a convulsive twist, he managed to face the direction in which, willynilly, he was going. Ahead was a gentling of the slope, and when he reached it his velocity slowed somewhat. Still, he was going at least sixty miles an hour with no way of stopping himself. His head was raised to keep his face from being burned and his hands were upheld. By then his clothes should have been burned off him, and his flesh should have been crisped and unraveling from the friction, but he sped on with only a slight feeling of warmth.

The skies were purple, and just above the edge of the horizon, the arc of a moon—he thought it was a moon—was showing. The arc was a deeper purple than the skies. He was not inside any Lord's palace; he was on another planet. Judging from the distance of the horizon, this planet was about the size of the one he had just left. In fact, he was sure that it was one of the bodies that he had seen in the skies from the surface of the waterworld.

Urizen had tricked them. He had set up the gate through which they had gone to jump them to one of the bodies circling about Appirmatzum. The other gate back on the waterworld might have led to Urizen's world. Or, it might have led to here also. There was no way of knowing now.

Whichever way the other entrance presented, it was too late to do anything about it. He was caught helplessly in one of his father's jokes. A practical joke, if you could consider death as practical.

He had traveled perhaps two miles when the incline began to turn upwards. Within a half-mile, he was slowed down to what seemed a thirty-mile an hour velocity, although it was difficult to tell with the few references he had. Off to his right, at a long distance, were a number of peculiar-looking trees. Not knowing how tall they were or how far away, he could not determine just how fast he was traveling.

And then, just as he slowed down to about ten miles an hour, and the incline sloped sharply upwards, he rose over its edge. He was in the air, out over the lip of the rise, beyond the edge of a precipice. He fell, unable to hold back a scream. Below him, forty or fifty feet, was a one hundred foot wide stream of water. The other side was blocked off by a wall of the same vitreous substance on which he had slid.

He dropped into the canyon, kicking to maintain an upright position so he could hit the water feet-first. The water was not as far away as he had thought, however, being only thirty-five feet down. He struck with his feet and plunged into tepid waters. He went on down, down, then began to swim upwards. The current carried him on swiftly between the canyon walls and took him around a bend. Just before he was carried around it, he saw a Lord hit the surface and another halfway down the wall.

Then the canyon opened out, and the river broadened. He was sliding and bumping over rapids. Fortunately, the rocks were smooth and slick, vitreous also. He escaped cuts but did suffer some bruises. Once past the rapids, he found that the current had slowed. He swam to the shore, which led up gently from the water. But he could not keep a handhold on the land and slid back into the river.

There was nothing to do but swim along the shoreline and hope that eventually he would find a place which would enable him to scramble onto the land. His clothes and the bow and arrows and knife and beamer weighed him down. As long as he could, he resisted the need to abandon them. When he began to tire, he slipped off the bow and quiver. Later, he unstrapped his belt and holster and scabbard. These he dropped into the water, but slipped the beamer and his knife inside his pants. After a while, he rid himself of the knife.

Now and then, he looked back. Eight heads were bobbing up and down. All had survived so far, but if the banks continued to resist grasping, they would all soon be drowned. All except Theotormon. He could outswim and outfloat them all, even with one flipper only half-grown out.

It was then that Wolff got an idea. He swam against the current, although the effort took more strength than he could afford. He swam until Luvah and Vala and Tharmas were close to him. Then he yelled at them to also swim against the current, if they wished to be saved.

Presently Theotormon's huge, oily, blue-black bulk was beside him. Behind him came Ariston, Enion, and Rintrah. Last of all, the most boastful but the most fearful to enter the gate, was Palamabron. His face was white, and he was breathing even more heavily than the rest.

"Save me, brother!" he cried. "I can't go on much longer. I will die."

"Save your breath," Wolff said. To Theotormon, he said, "We have need of you, brother. Now you, the once-despised, can help us. Without you, we shall all drown."

Theotormon, swimming easily against the current, chuckled. He said, "Why should I? You all spit on me; you say I make you sick."

"I have never spit upon you," Wolff said. "Nor have I said you sicken me. And it was I who insisted that you come with us. I did so because I knew that we would need you. There are things you can do with that body that we cannot. It is ironic that Urizen, who set this trap, and who also transformed you into a sea-thing, prepared you to survive in his trap. He unwittingly gave you the means to escape and so to help us escape."

It was a long speech under the circumstances and left him winded. Nevertheless, he had to praise Theotormon; otherwise, he would leave them to die and laugh while doing so.

Theotormon said, "You mean Urizen outwitted himself?"

Wolff nodded.

"And how can I escape from this?" Theotormon said.

"You are swift and strong as a seal in the water. You can propel yourself so swiftly that you can shoot through the water and on up onto the bank. You can also shove us, one by one, onto the bank. I know that you can do this."

Theotormon grinned slyly. "And why should I push you to safety?"

"If you don't, you'll be left alone on this strange world," Wolff said. "You can live for a while. But you'll be lonely. I doubt that there's anyone here you can talk to. Moreover, if we're to get off this world, we have to find the gates which will lead us off. Can you do this alone? Once on land, you'll need us."

"To hell with you!" Theotormon screamed. He upended and disappeared beneath the surface.

"Theotormon!" Wolff called.

The others echoed his call. They treaded water and looked despairingly at each other. There was nothing of the haughty Lord in their faces now.

Suddenly, Vala screamed. She threw her hands up into the air and went under. So swiftly she went, she must have been pulled under.

A few seconds passed. Then Theotormon's oily blue-black head appeared and a moment later Vala's red hair. Her brother's long toes were entangled in her hair, her head held by the foot.

"Say you're sorry!" Theotormon shouted. "Apologize! Tell me I'm not a loathsome mass of blubber! Tell me I'm beautiful! Promise to love me as you did Palamabron on the island!"

She tore her hair loose, leaving some dark red strands between his toes. She screamed, "I'll kill you, you blotch! I'm a long way from dying yet! And if I were, I'd go gladly to my death rather than make up to you!"

His eyes wide, Theotormon paddled away from her with his feet. He turned to Wolff and said, "See! Why should I save her or any of you? You would still hate me, just as I would hate you."

Palamabron began to yell and to splash violently. "Save me, Theotormon! I can't stay up any longer! I'm too tired! I'll die!"

"Remember what I said about your being alone," Wolff gasped.

Theotormon grinned and dived, and presently he was pushing Palamabron ahead of him. With his head on his brother's buttocks, he pushed, driving with his flippers and his great webbed feet. Palamabron slid from the water and two body lengths onto the glassy shore. There he lay, breathing like a sick horse, the water running from his nose and saliva from his mouth.

One by one, Theotormon propelled the others onto the bank, where they lay like dead men. Only Vala refused his offer. She swam as hard as she could, summoning strength that Wolff would not have believed possible she had left. She skidded up a body's length and soon was nudging herself, very slowly, on up the gentle slope. When she had reached a level spot, she carefully got to a sitting position. She looked down at the others and said with scorn, "So these are my brothers? The all-mighty Lords of the universes! A pack of half-drowned rats. Sycophants of a sea-slug, begging for their lives."

Theotormon slid upon the bank and past the men. He walked on his bent legs past Vala and did not look at her. And when the others had regained some of their strength and breath, they too crawled to the level land. They were sorry looking, since most of them had slipped off their clothes and their swords in the water. Only Wolff and Vala had retained their clothes. He had lost all his weapons but his beamer. She still had her sword. Except for her hair, she looked as if she had never been in the water. Her garments had the property of repelling liquids.

Luvah had scooted over to Wolff after trying twice to walk to him and ending on his buttocks both times. His color had come back to his face, so that the freckles across his cheeks and nose did not stand out so sharply. He said, "We were caught by our father as easily as children playing hide-and-seek are caught. Now, from children we have become infants. We cannot even walk, but must crawl like babies. Do you suppose that our father is trying to tell us something?"

"I do not know about that," Wolff said. "But this I do know. Urizen has been planning this for a long long time. I am beginning to believe that he made the planets that revolve around Appirmatzum for one reason only. This world and the others are designed to torment and to test us."

Luvah laughed without much merriment. "And if we survive the torment and pass the tests, what is our reward?"

"We get a chance to be killed by our father or to kill him."

"Do you really believe he will play fair? Won't he make the stronghold absolutely impregnable? I cannot believe that our father will be fair."

"Fair? What is fair? There is supposed to be an unspoken agreement that every Lord will leave some slight loophole in his defense. Some defect whereby an extremely skillful and clever attacker can get through. Whether this is true in all cases, I do not know. But Lords have been killed or dispossessed, and these Lords thought they were safe from the most powerful and clever. I do not think that the successful ones were successful because of built-in weaknesses by the defender. The chinks in the armor were there for another reason.

"That reason is that the Lords have inherited their weapons. What they haven't inherited or taken from others, they cannot get. The race has lost its ancient wisdom and skill; it has become users, consumers, not creators. So, a Lord must use what he has. And if these weapons do not cover every contingency, if they leave holes in the armor, then they can be penetrated.

"There is another aspect to this. The Lords fight for their lives and fight to kill each other. But most have lived too long. They weary of everything. They want to die. Deep in the abyss of their minds, below the thousands of strata of the years of too much power and too little love, they want to die. And so, there are cracks in the walls."

Luvah was astonished. "You do not really believe this wild theory, brother? I know I am not tired of living. I love life now as much as when I was a hundred. And the others, they fight to live as much as they ever did."

Wolff shrugged and said, "It's only a theory of mine. I have evolved it since I became Robert Wolff. I can see things that I could not see before and that none of you can see."

He crawled to Vala and said, "Lend me your sword for a moment. I want to try an experiment."

"Like cutting my head off?" she said.

"If I wanted to kill you, I have the beamer," he replied.

She took the short blade from its scabbard and handed it to him. He tapped the sharp edge gently on the glassy surface. When the first blow left the stuff unmarked, he struck harder.

Vala said, "What are you doing? You'll ruin the edge."

He pointed at the scratch left by the second blow. "Looks like a scratch made in ice. This stuff is far slipperier, more frictionless than ice, but in other respects it seems to resemble frozen water."

He handed the weapon to her and drew his beamer. After putting it on half-power, he aimed it at a spot on the surface. The stuff grew red, then bubbled. Liquid flowed from it. He turned the beamer off and blew the liquid from the hole. The others crawled over to watch him.

"You're a strange man," Vala said. "Whoever would have thought of doing this?"

"Why is he doing it?" Palamabron said. "Is he crazy, cutting holes in the ground?"

Palamabron had recovered his haughtiness and his measured way of speaking.

Vala said, "No, he's not crazy. He's curious, that's all. Have you forgotten what it is to be curious, Palamabron? Are you as dead as you look . . . and act. You were certainly lively enough a little while ago."

Palamabron flushed, but he said nothing. He was watching the growth of tiny crystals on the walls of the hole and along the edges of the scratch.

"Self-regeneration," Wolff said. "Now, I have read as much as possible on the old science of our ancestors, but I have never read or heard of anything like this. Urizen must have knowledge lost to others."

"Perhaps," Vala said, "he has gotten it from Red Orc. It is said that Orc knows more than all of the other Lords put together. He is the last of the old ones; it is said that he was born over a half a million years ago."

"It is said. It is said," Wolff mimicked. "The truth is that nobody has seen Red Orc for a hundred millennia. I think he is a dead man but his legend lives on. Enough of this. We have to find the next set of gates, though where those will lead us, I don't know."

He rose carefully and shuffled slowly a few steps forward. The surface of this world was not entirely barren vitreosity. There were widely spaced trees several hundred yards away and between them mushroom-shaped bushes. The trees had thin spiraling trunks that were striped with red and white, like barber poles. The trunks rose straight for twenty feet, then curved to left or right. Where the curve began, branches grew. These were shaped like horizontal 9's and covered with a thin gray fuzz, the strands of which were about two feet long.

Rintrah, naked, shivered and said, "It is not cold, but something makes me uneasy and quivers through me. Perhaps it is the silence. Listen, and you hear nothing."

They fell silent. There was only a distant soughing, the wind rippling through the bushes and the stiff projections on the end-curled branches, and the slursh-slursh of the river. Aside from that, nothing. No bird calls. No animal cries. No human voices. Only the sound of wind and river and even that hushed as if pressed down by the purple of the skies.

Around them the pale white land rolled away to the four horizons. There were some high rounded hills, the tallest of which was that which had sent them speeding down the hill. From where they stood, they could see its mound and the gate, a tiny dark object, on its top. The rest was low hills and level spaces.

Where do we go from here? Wolff thought. *Without some clue, we could wander forever. We could wander to the end of our lives, provided we find something to eat on the way.*

He spoke aloud. "I believe we should follow along the river. It leads downward, perhaps to some large body of water. Urizen cast us into the river; this may mean that the river is to be our guide to the next gate . . . or gates."

"That may be true," Enion said. "But your father and my uncle has a crooked brain. In his perverse way, he may be using the river as an indication that we should go up it, not down it."

"You may be right, cousin," Wolff replied. "However there is only one way to find out. I suggest we go downriver, if only because it will be easier traveling." He said to Vala, "What do you think?"

She shrugged and said, "I don't know. I picked the wrong gate the last time. Why ask me?"

"Because you were always the closest to father. You know better than the rest of us how he thinks."

She smiled slightly. "I do not think you mean to compliment me by that. But I will take it as such. Much as I hate Urizen, I also admire and respect his abilities. He has survived where most of his contemporaries have not. Since you ask, I say we go downriver."

"How about the rest of you?" Wolff said. He had already made up his mind which direction he was going, but he did not want the others complaining if they went the wrong way. Let them share the responsibility.

Palamabron started to speak. "I say, no, I insist, that . . ."

A **WAIL CAME DOWN AGAINST THE WIND, AND THEY TURNED TO** stare upriver. Several hundred yards away, an animal tall as an elephant had appeared from around a hill. Now it stood between two large boulders, the head on the end of its long neck much like that of a camel's with antlers. Its eyes were enormous and its teeth long and sharp, a carnivore's. Its body was red-brown and furry and sloped sharply back from the shoulders. The legs were thin as a giraffe's, despite the heavy body. They ended in great spreading dark-blue cups.

On seeing the cup-feet, Wolff guessed their function. They looked too much like suckers or vacuum pads, which would be one of the few means to enable an animal to walk across this smooth surface.

"Stand still," he said to the others. "We can't run; if we could, there'd be no place to go."

The beast snorted and slowly advanced towards them. It swiveled its neck back and forth, turning its head now and then to look behind it. The right front foot and left rear foot raised in unison, the cups giving a plopping noise. These came down to give it a hold in its forward progress. Then the left front foot and the right rear one raised, and so it came towards them. When it was fifty yards from them, it stopped and raised its head. It gave a cry that was half-bray and half-banshee wail. It lowered its neck until the jaw was on the ground and then scraped the jaw against the ground. The head slid back and forth on the pale surface.

Wolff thought that this motion could be the equivalent of the pawing of dirt of a Terrestrial bull before it charged. He put his beamer on half-power and waited. Suddenly, the creature raised its head as high as it would go, screamed—much like a wounded rabbit—and galloped at them. It was necessarily a slow gallop, since the suction cups did not come off easily. To the humans, it seemed too swift.

Wolff could afford to wait to determine if the beast were bluffing. At twenty yards, he placed the end of the beam at the juncture of neck and chest. Smoke curled up from the red-brown fur, which blackened. The animal screamed again but did not stop its charge. Wolff continued to hold the beam as steadily as he could. Then, seeing that its impetus might carry it to the point where its fanged head could seize them, he switched to full-power.

The beast gave a last scream; its long thin legs crumpled; its body came down on them. The cups stuck to the ground, the legs cracking beneath the weight, the body settling slowly. The neck went limp and the head lolled, the red-purple tongue sticking out, the hazel eyes glassy.

There was silence, broken by Vala's laugh. "There's our dinner and breakfast and dinner again, already cooked for us."

"If it's edible," Wolff said. He watched while Vala and Theotormon, knife handled by one foot, stripped off the hide and cut out half-burnt steaks. Theotormon refused to test the meat. Wolff shuffled forward very carefully, but even so his feet went out from under him. Vala and Theotormon, who had gotten to the beast without slipping, laughed. Wolff arose and continued his journey. He said, "If no one else dares, I'll try the meat. We can't stand around debating whether it's safe or not."

Vala said, "I'm not afraid of it, just disgusted. It has such a rank odor." She bit into it, chewed with distaste, and swallowed. Wolff decided that there was no use his testing it now. With the others, he waited. When a half-hour passed, and Vala showed no ill effects, he started to eat it. The others shuffled or crawled to the carcass and also ate. There was not too much they could stomach, since most of the meat was charred, leaving only a narrow area where the heat had cooked or half-cooked the flesh.

Wolff borrowed Theotormon's knife and cut out other steaks. Reluctantly, because he wished to conserve the power of the beamer, he cooked the steaks. Then they each took an armful and began to march down the river. Wolff lingered for a while, considering the possibility of severing the suction-pads and using them for his locomotion. He gave up the idea after feeling the thickness of the bones of the legs and the toughness of bone and cartilage at juncture of pad and leg. Vala's sword might do the job, but its edge would be too blunted for use afterward.

At the end of a two-mile crawl, they came to a group of bushes near the riverbank. These were three feet high and mushroom in shape, the upper part spreading out far from the slender base. The branches were thick and corkscrew and, like the trees, grew fuzz. At close range, the fuzz looked more like slender needles. There were also large dark-red berries in clusters at the ends of the branches.

Wolff picked one and smelled it. The odor reminded him of pecan nuts. The skin was smooth and slightly moist.

He hesitated about biting into the berry. Again, it was Vala who dared the strange food. She ate one, exclaiming all the while over its deliciousness. A half-hour went by, during which she ate six more. Wolff then ate several. The others picked them off. Palamabron, the last to try them, complained that there were not many left for him.

Vala said, "It is not our fault that you are such a coward."

Palamabron glared at her but did not answer. Theotormon, thinking that here he had found someone who would not dare to answer him back, took up the insults where Vala left off. Palamabron slapped Theotormon in the face. Theotormon bellowed with rage and leaped at Palamabron. His feet slipped out and he skidded on his face into Palamabron's legs. Palamabron went down like a bowling pin. He slid sidewise, out of reach of Theotormon's flailing flipper. Both made a frenzied but vain effort to get at each other's throat.

Finally, Wolff, who had not shared the scornful laughter of the others, called a halt. He said, "If these time-wasting displays of childishness continue, I'll put a stop to them. Not with the beamer, since I don't care to use up power on the likes of you. We'll just go on without you or send you away. We have to have unity and a minimum of discord. Otherwise, Urizen will have the pleasure of seeing us destroy ourselves."

Theotormon and Palamabron spat at each other but quit their struggles. Silently, in the pale purple shade of the moon overhead, they continued to slide their feet forward. The night had brought an end to the silence. They heard bleatings as of sheep and bellowings as of cattle from a distance. Something roared like a lion. They passed another clump of bushes and saw small bipedal animals feeding off the berries. These were about two and a half feet tall, brown-furred, and lemur-faced. They had big rabbit ears and slit eyes. Their upper legs ended in paws; their lower, in suction discs. They had short scarlet tails, like a rabbit's. On seeing the human beings, they stopped eating and faced them, their noses wiggling. After being convinced that the newcomers were no danger, they resumed eating. But one fellow kept his eyes on them and barked like a dog at them.

Presently, a four-legged animal the size of a Norwegian elkhound came around a low hill. It was shaggy as a sheep-dog, yellowish, and built like a fox. At the ends of its feet were thin skates of bone on which it raced towards the bipeds. These barked in alarm and all took off in a body. They made swift progress, despite the pads, but the skate-wolf was far faster. The leader of the bipeds, seeing that they had no chance, dropped behind until he was even with the slowest of his charges. He shoved against the laggard, knocking him over, then he ran on. The sacrifice screamed and tried to get back up on its suckers, only to be knocked down again by the snarling skate-wolf. There was a brief struggle, ending when the wolf's jaws closed on the biped's throat.

Wolff said, "There's your explanation for the scratches we've seen now and then on the surface. Some of these creatures are skaters."

He was silent for a while, thinking that skates would enable them to make much better progress. The problem was getting them down.

They passed another long-necked, hyena-bodied, deer-antlered beast. This one did not offer to bother them. It bit into a rock of the vitreous substance, ripped out a chunk, and chewed upon it. It kept its eye upon them, groaning with delight at the taste of the rock, its stomach rumbling like defective plumbing in an old house.

They went on and soon came within three hundred yards of a herd of the creatures, all grazing upon the rocks. There were young among them, awkwardly chasing each other in play or nursing from the mothers. Some of the bulls bray-wailed at the intruders, and one kept pace with them for a while. They passed antelope-like animals, marked with red diamond-shapes on white and with two horns that intertwined. Bone skates grew at the end of their legs.

Wolff began to look for a place to sleep. He led them into a semi-amphitheater, a level between four hills. "I'll stand first watch," he said. He designated Luvah as next and Enion after him. Enion protested, asking by what authority Wolff could pick him.

"You can refuse to take your share of responsibility, if you wish," Wolff said. "But if you sleep when your turn comes, you may wake up in the jaws of that."

He pointed past Enion's shoulder, and Enion whirled so swiftly he lost his footing. The others looked in the direction in which Wolff's finger was pointing. On top of one of the hills, a huge maned animal was glaring down at them. Its head was that of a short-snouted crocodile and its body was cat-shaped, the feet ending in broad cups.

Wolff put the beamer on half-power and shot. He flicked the actuation plate briefly and aimed towards the hairs of the mane. The hairs crisped and smoked, and the beast roared, turned, and disappeared beyond the hill.

Wolff said, "Now, somebody has to be officially given authority. So far, we've avoided, that is, you've avoided, a decision. You've more or less let me run things. Mostly because you're too lazy or too occupied with your own petty problems to face this issue. All right, now's the time to settle this. Without a leader whose orders will be immediately obeyed in emergencies, we're all lost. So what do you say?"

"Beloved brother," Vala said, "I think that you have shown that you're the man to follow. I vote for you. Besides, you have the beamer, and that makes you the most powerful of all. Unless, of course, some of us have hidden weapons we've not displayed as yet."

"You're the only one who has enough clothes to conceal weapons," he said. "As for the beamer, whoever is on guard will have it."

They all raised their eyebrows at this. He said, "It's not because I trust your loyalty. It's just that I don't think any of you would be quite stupid enough to try to keep it for yourself or try to take off on your own. When we resume the march, I expect to get the beamer back."

All then voted, except for Palamabron. He said that he did not have to vote, since it was obvious that he would be overruled by the majority, anyway.

"Surely brother, you were not going to nominate yourself," Vala said. "Even you, with all your hideous egotism, could not think of that."

Palamabron ignored her. To Wolff he said, "Why am I not one of the sentinels? Don't you trust me?"

"You can stand first watch tomorrow night," Wolff replied. "Now, let's all get some sleep."

Wolff sat guard while the others slept on their hard beds of white rock. He listened to the distant animal cries: the bray-wails, roars, and some new sounds, a shrill fluting, a plaintive sobbing, a whistling. Once, something beat out a gonging, and there was the flutter of wings overhead. He rose to his feet now and then and slowly pivoted around to cover all points of the compass. At the end of a half-hour, he woke up Enion and gave him the beamer. He had no watch to determine the time, any more than the others did, but, like them, he knew the measured passage of time. As a child, he had gone through a species of hypnosis which enabled him to clock the seconds as accurately as the most precise of chronometers.

For a while, he did not sleep. He was worried about the first watch of the next night, when Palamabron would be entrusted with the beamer. Of all the Lords, he was the most unstable. He hated Vala even more than the others. Could he withstand the temptation to kill her while she slept? Wolff decided he would have a talk with Palamabron in the morning. His brother must understand that if he killed her, he would have to kill them all. This he could do with the beamer, but he would be alone from then on. This was a curious thing. Though the Lords could not stand to be with each other, they could stand the idea of being alone even less. In other circumstances, they would want no one but themselves, of course. In these, they shared a dread of their father and some comfort in having companions in misery and peril.

Just before he went to sleep, he had an idea. He swore. Why had he not thought of it? Why had not the others? It was so obvious. There was no need to creep and slip along on the ground. With boats, they could travel swiftly and much more surely. They would be safe from the predators. He would see what they could do about this in the morning.

He was propelled from sleep at dawn by shouting. He sat up to see Tharmas shooting at a maned beast, one just like the liongator he had scared off by singeing its hair. The beast came down the hill swiftly, plop-plopping as its suction pads pulled free. Behind it lay three dead mates. The survivor came within ten feet and then dropped, its snout cut half off.

Tharmas held the beamer while he stared at the carcass. Wolff shouted at him to turn the power off. The ray was drilling into the side of the hill.

Tharmas suddenly realized what he was doing and deactivated the weapon. By then, most of the charge was gone. Groaning, Wolff took the beamer back. Now he was down to his final power pack.

The others went to work swiftly. They took turns with the knives of Theotormon and Vala and stripped the tough hides off the dead beasts. This was slow work, both because of their ineptness and because they kept sliding on the glassy surface. And they could not refrain from arguing with him, saying that all the hard work was for nothing. Where would he get the framework for the boats he planned? Even if he could use these hides as coverings for the boats, there were not enough to go around.

He told them to shut up and keep on working. He knew what he was doing. With Luvah, Vala, and Theotormon, he shuffled off to the nearest bushes. Here it was necessary to use more power to kill an animal that was eating the berries and refused to give up its claim. It was like a Chinese dragon. It hissed and struck threateningly at them before they got within its range. Its skin was as thick and ridged as armor plate and could be penetrated only by a beam at full-power. Even its eyes were protected. When Wolff shot at these, the ray struck transparent coverings. The creature began waving its head wildly so that Wolff could not keep the beam on one spot. Eventually, he cut through the armor back of the head, and it turned over and died, exposing the serrated plates and tiny suction discs on which it made progress.

"If this keeps up, we'll be out of power," he said to the others. "Pray that that time does not come."

Wolff tested the toughness of the bark of the bushes and found it to be strong indeed. Chopping down the bushes and slicing off lengths to make a framework for the rough coracles he had in mind would be long hard work and ruin the sword. It was then, glancing at the caterdragon—as he called it—that he saw a ready-made vessel. Well, not quite finished, but it should need less work to complete than the original boat he had in mind.

The sword, driven by his powerful arm, was equal to the task of separating the caterdragon's locomotion plates from the body armor. Thereafter, the sword and the knife cut up the internal organs. By then the other Lords were with them, and they took turns at the work. All were soon covered with blood, which also ran over the area and made the surface even more frictionless. Several of the liongators, attracted by the odor of blood, and then driven frantic by it, attacked. Wolff had to expend more power in killing them.

The only possible sources for paddles were the 9-shaped branches on the trees. The bark of these resisted the edge of the sword. Again, Wolff had to use his beamer. He cut enough branches to make ten paddles, three extra, since Theotormon could not handle one with his flippers. The needles came off easily when cut with a knife.

They had a rather flexible canoe, sixty feet long. The only openings to worry about were the mouth and nostrils. These were disposed of by bending the hollow front part back and up and tying a small boulder to it with Vala's cloak. The weight of the boulder stopped the forward part from straightening out and thus kept it above the water level—they hoped. Again, Wolff had to use some more power to burn off the pieces of gristle and the blood that adhered to the inside walls of the armor-plate. Then, walking on their knees, the Lords shoved their makeshift boat towards the river.

Near the edge of the river, they rose to their feet and got into the dragonboat by falling over the sides and into the bottom. They did so by teams of twos, one on each side, to keep the craft from falling to one side. When all but Wolff and Vala had gotten in, the two urged the boat down. Fortunately, there was a very gentle incline. As the craft picked up a little speed, Wolff and Vala clung to the sides and the others pulled them aboard.

The night-bringing moon crossed the horizon, and the dragoncraft floated with the current. Two Lords stayed on paddle-duty to keep the boat straight while the others tried to sleep. The moon passed, and after it came the bright purple of the naked skies. The river was smooth, disturbed only by tiny waves and ripples. They passed through canyons and came out again between rolling ground. The day passed without incident. They complained about the stench from the meat and blood they had not been able to clear away. They made jokes as each had to rid himself of food and drink. They spoke grouchily of their lack of sleep the previous night. They talked about what might face them when—or if—they ever found the gate that would lead them into the palace of their father.

A day and a night floated by. Several hours after the second dawn, they came around a wide bend of the river. Ahead was a rock that split the river, a dome of white about thirty feet high. On top of it, side by side, was a pair of towering and golden hexagonal frames.

10

FROM THE EDGE OF THE RIVER, WHERE THE DRAGONBOAT
was beached, Wolff studied the problem. It was useless to try to climb
the near-perpendicular and near-frictionless rock without some aids. A
rope had to be thrown up to catch on something. The hexagons were too
wide to try to settle a noose around them.

A grappling hook might do the job. It could be presumed that the
other side of the gate—that which opened onto another planet, he
hoped—would hold a grapple.

The hides of animals could be cut and and tied or sewn together to
make a rope, although the strips would have to be tanned to give them flexibility. The metal for the hooks was a big problem.

There might be metal somewhere in this world, perhaps not too far
away. But getting to it across the land would be a slow process. So, there
was only one thing to do, and he did not expect that the two most vital in
this particular project would be cooperative.

Nor were they. Vala did not want to give up her sword and Theotormon refused to part with his knife.

Wolff argued with them for several hours, pointing out that if they did
not give up their weapons, they would be dead in time anyway.

Wolff said, after Theotormon's violent refusal, "Very well. Be pig-
headed. But if the rest of us find a way to get through the gate, we will not
take you with us. I swear it! You will be pushed back into this pale world
of icestone, and you will stay here until an animal devours you or you die
of old age."

Vala looked around at the Lords who sat in a circle about her. She smiled
and said, "Very well. You may have my sword."

"You won't get my knife, I promise you that," Theotormon said.

The others began to scoot on their buttocks towards him. He stood up
and tried to run past them. His huge feet gave him a better grip on the white
stuff than the others could manage, but Wolff reached out and clutched
his ankle, and he went down. He fought as best he could, submerged

under the pile of bodies. Eventually, weeping, he gave up. Then, muttering, scowling, he went off to sit down on the river's edge by himself.

With some chalky stone he found, Wolff traced lines on Vala's sword.
He set the beamer at full power and quickly cut out triangles. He then
arranged the three pieces and set several round pieces of the sword on top
of them. With the beamer at half-power he fused the three prongs and
round pieces into a single unit. After plunging these into cold water, he
heated the prongs in their middles and hammered them into slightly
hooked shapes. He curved another strip of sword with heat and hammered
and fused this onto the top of the prong so that a rope could be tied around
it.

Since he did not have to use Theotormon's knife, he gave it back to him.
He cut the end of Vala's sword into a point and thus provided her with a
somewhat short sword. As he pointed out, it was better than nothing.

Making the rope took several days. It was not difficult to kill and flay
the animals and then cut out strips for rope lengths. Tanning presented dif-
ficulties. He searched for materials but could find nothing. Finally, he decided to grease the plaited rawhide with animal fat and hope for the best.

One dawn, as the empurpling shadow of the moon withdrew, the
dragonboat was launched well above the gaterock. With the Lords behind
him paddling backwards, Wolff stood up in the prow, and he cast the grapple upwards in an arc and released the rope after it.

The three-pronged device went through the gate and disappeared. He
pulled in on it as the boat rammed into the base of the rock. For a second,
he thought he had a hold. Then the grapple came flying out of the gate,
and he fell back. He caught himself, but the uneasy equilibrium of the boat
was upset. It turned over, and all went into the water. They clung to the
upturned bottom, and Wolff managed to keep hold of the rope and grapple.

A half-hour later, they tried again.

"Try and try again," Wolff told them. "That's an old Earth saying."

"Spare me your proverbs," Rintrah said. "I'm soaked as a drowning rat
and as miserable. Do you think there's any use trying again?"

"What else is there to do? Let's get at it. Give it the old college try."

They looked at him uncomprehendingly and then reluctantly launched
the boat again. Now Wolff made a more difficult cast. He threw for the very
top of the hexagon. It was at least twelve feet high, which made the top of
the frame forty-two feet above water. Nevertheless, he threw well, the
prongs gripping the other side of the frame.

"I got it!" he said grinning. He pulled in on the rope to take up the slack.
The boat slid on by the right side of the rock, rubbing against it. He or-
dered the men to continue backwatering, which they tried without success.
The boat began to bend as the current wrapped it around the rock. Wolff,

in the bow, knew that if he continued to be carried with the boat, he would slide the prongs sidewise off the top of the frame.

He clung to the rawhide rope and allowed the boat to be taken off from under him. Then Wolff was hanging onto the rope, his feet in the water. He lifted his feet to brace himself against the rock, only to have them slide away. He quit this method of climbing and hauled himself up, hand-over-hand, on the greasy rope. This was not easy to do, since the rock curved just gently enough to make the rope follow it closely, the tension being greatest just above his handhold. Without slack, he had to force his hands to slide between rope and rock.

He rose slowly. Halfway up, he felt the tension go. There was a crack, barely audible above the swirl of water at the rock-base. Yelling with disappointment, he fell back into the river.

When he was hauled out by Vala and Enion, he discovered that two of the prongs had broken across where they joined the top part. The pieces were now somewhere at the bottom of the river.

"What do we do now?" Palamabron snarled at him. "You have used up all our weapons and drained your beamer of much of its power. And we are no closer to getting through the gate than before. Less, I say. Look at us. Look at me. Spouting water like an old fish brought up from the abyss and weary, oh, Los, how weary!"

"Go fly a kite," Wolff said. "Another old Earth saying."

He stopped, eyes widening, and said, "I wonder . . ."

Palamabron threw his hands up into the air and said, "Oh, no, not another of your wonderful ideas!"

"Wonderful or not, they're ideas," Wolff said. "So far, I'm the only one who's had anything to offer . . . besides whinings, complaints, and backbitings."

He lay on his back for a while, staring up at the purple skies and chewing on a piece of meat Luvah had handed him. Was a kite a fantastic thought? Even if it could be built, would it work?

He discarded the kite. If one were made big enough to carry a heavy prong, it would not go through the hexagon. Wait a minute. What if the kite, dangling a hook on the end of a rope, were flown above the hexagon? He groaned and gave up the kite again. It just would not work.

Suddenly, he sat up and shouted. "It might do it! Two!"

"Two what?" Luvah said, startled out of his drowse.

"Not kites!"

"Who said anything about kites?" Luvah replied.

"Two boats and two good men to throw," Wolff cried. "It might work. It better. I've about exhausted my ideas, and it's evident I'm not going to get any from the rest of you. You've used your brains these many thousands of years for only one purpose: to kill each other. You're good for nothing else. But, by Los, I'm going to make you good for something else!"

"You're tired," Vala said. "Lie down and rest." She was grinning at him. That surprised him. Now, what would she be amused about? She was wet and muscle-aching and as frustrated as the others.

Could it be that she still had some love for him beneath that hate? Perhaps she was proud of him that he continued to improvise and to fight while the others only nursed their resentments.

Or was she trying to make him think that she still loved him and was proud of him? Did she have a secret reason for this display of amiability?

He did not know. To be a Lord was to mistrust every motive of another Lord, and with good reason.

By the time the first two coracles were half-made, Wolff changed his plan. Originally, he had wanted to have two of the little round boats approach the gaterock on each side. But then he decided that three would be better.

Using wood of the bushes and tree branches and strips of hide for ties, he made a high scaffolding. Each of its four legs was placed on a boat, one on the dragoncraft and each one of the other three on a coracle. Then, after rehearsing the Lords many times in what they must do, Wolff began the operation. Slowly, the boats at the base of the rectangular scaffolding were pushed into the water. The current near the shore was not as swift as out in the river's center, so the Lords could keep it from being carried off at once. While they swam and shoved against the boats, Wolff climbed up the narrow ladder built on one leg of the scaffolding. This was supported by the larger dragon boats, and thus the leg with Wolff on it did not tip over too far. Even so, for a moment, he feared a turnover. Then, as he hitched himself on his belly along the planking of the scaffolding, the structure righted.

The other Lords, working in teams, climbed into the big boat and the three small ones. They went in simultaneously, to distribute the weight equally. Vala, Theotormon, and Luvah were each already in a coracle, and they helped Palamabron, Enion, and Ariston. Tharmas was very agile; he got into the dragonboat with a quick heave and twist of his body.

The Lords began paddling to direct the scaffolding. They had some trouble at first, since the coracles, built more like tubs than boats, were difficult to navigate. But they had launched the structure well above their goal so that they could get the feel of their awkward craft before they reached the rock. Wolff clung to the forward part of the structure, the bridge, which projected out above the water. The bridge pitched and rolled, and twice he thought sure that it would go over with him. Then the white dome of the rock with the twin golden hexagons was dead ahead. He shouted down to the Lords, and they began backpaddling. It was vital that the scaffolding not crash into the rock with much speed. Fragile, it could not resist a strong impact.

Wolff had decided that he would enter the left gate, since the last time they had taken the right. But as the end of the bridge neared, the scaffolding veered. The bridge drove in at a slant towards the left hexagon. Wolff rose to a crouch, and, as the structure rammed with a loud noise into the rock, he leaped forward. He shot through the hexagon with his beamer in his belt and a rope coiled around his shoulders.

11

HE DID NOT HAVE THE SLIGHTEST IDEA OF WHAT HE WOULD find on the other side. He expected either another planet or Urizen's stronghold. He suspected that Urizen was not through playing with them, and that he would find himself on the third of the planets that revolved around Appirmatzum. He might have a comfortable landing or be dropping into a pit of wild beasts or down a precipice.

As he landed, he realized that he had come in against an incline. He bent his knees and put out his hands and so stopped himself from banging into the stone. It was smooth but not frictionless, and it leaned away from him at a forty-five degree angle. Turning, he saw why the grapples had slid back out of the gate at his first experiment. The base of the hexagon on this side was set flush with the stone. There was no purchase for any hold.

He smiled, knowing that his father had foreseen hooks and had set up the trap against them. But his son had gotten through.

Wolff pushed against the seemingly empty area within the hexagon. Unlike the gate through which they had entered the waterworld, this was not oneway. Urizen did not care, for some reason or another, whether they went back into the planet of purple skies. Or he knew that they would never want to return to it.

Wolff climbed up the stone incline, which was set on the side of a hill. He tied one end of his rope around a small tree and then went back to the gate. He flipped the free end of the rope through the gate. It jerked, and presently Vala's face appeared. He helped her through, and the two of them grabbed hold of the other Lords as they climbed through.

When Rintrah, the last, was safe, Wolff stuck his head through the gate for a final look. He made it quick, because it gave him a frightening feeling to know that his body was on a planet twenty thousand miles distant from his head. And it would be a grim joke, exactly to his father's tastes, if Urizen should deactivate the gate at that moment.

The end of the bridge was only three feet from the hexagon. The scaffolding was still holding straight, although in time the currents would swing one of the boats supporting a leg and carry off the whole structure.

He withdrew his head, his neck feeling as if it had just escaped a guillotine.

The Lords should have been exultant, but they were too tired from their labors, and they were burdened with the future. By now, they knew that they were on another of the satellites of Appirmatzum. The sky was a deep yellow. The land around them was, apart from this hill, flat. The ground was covered with a six-inch high grass, and there were many bushes. These were much like the Terrestrial plants Wolff knew. There were at least a dozen species which bore berries of different sizes, colors, and shapes.

The berries had one thing in common, however. They all had a very disagreeable odor.

Near the hill of the gate was the shore of a sea. Along the sea ran a broad yellow sandbeach that extended as far as they could see. Wolff looked inland and saw mountains. The side of one had some curious formations that resembled a face. The longer he looked at it, the more sure he was that it was a face.

He said to the other Lords, "Our father has given us a sign, I think. A marker on the road to the next gate. I also think that he is not directing us just for our benefit."

They started across the plain towards the distant ranges. Presently, they came to a broad river and followed its course. They found its water to be pure and sweet, and they ate the meat and berries they had brought with them from the white-and-purple world. Then the night-bringing moon swung around the horizon. This was mauve and, like the other satellites, swept the surface of the primary with a pale dusk.

They slept and marched all the next day. They were a silent troop now, tired and footsore and nervous because of their lack of weapons. Their silence was also a reflection of the hush of this world. Not an animal or bird cried, nor did they see any life besides themselves and the vegetation. Several times they thought they saw a small creature in the distance, but when they neared the place, they could find nothing.

The mountains were three days away. As they got closer, the features became more distinct. The evening of the second day, the face became that of Urizen. It was smiling at them, the eyes looking down. Then the Lords became even more silent and startful, since they could not escape the gigantic stone face of their father. Always, he seemed to be mocking them.

Halfway through the fourth day, they stood at the foot of the mountain and below the brobdingnagian chin of Urizen. The mountain was of solid stone, flesh-pink and very hard. Near where they stood was an opening, a narrow canyon that rose to the top of the mountain, at least ten thousand feet above.

Wolff said, "There doesn't seem any other way to go than through there. Unless we go around the mountains. And I think we'd be wasting our time if we did that."

Palamabron said, "Why should we do what our father wants?"

"We have no choice," Wolff said.

"Yes, we'll dance to his tune, and then he'll catch us and spit us on a roast, like fowl," Palamabron said. "I have a notion to quit this trudging, this weary weary road."

"And where will you settle down?" Vala said. "Here? In this paradise? You may be too stupid to have noticed it, brother, but we are almost out of food. The meat is almost gone, and we ate the last of the berries this morning. We have seen nothing on this world that seems edible. You may try the berries, if you wish. But I think they're poisonous."

"Oh, Los! Do you think Urizen means to starve us to death?" Palamabron said.

Wolff said, "I think we'll starve unless we find some food. And we won't find any standing here."

He led the way into the canyon. Their path took them on smooth bare rock that had once been the bed of the stream. The river had shifted to the other side of the canyon and was now several feet below the stone banks. Bushes grew sparsely on the lip of the stone.

The Lords followed a meandering course all day. That night, they ate the last of their food. When dawn came, they rose with empty bellies and a feeling that this time their fortune had deserted them. Wolff led them as swiftly as he dared, thinking that the sooner they got out of the gloomy canyon, the better. Moreover, this place offered no food. There were no fish in the river; there were not even insects.

The second day of their starvation, they saw their first living creature. They came around a bend, all silent and walking slowly. Their noiselessness, plus their approach from downwind, enabled them to be close to the animal before it detected them. Two feet high, it was standing on its kangaroo-like hind legs and holding a branch with two lemur-like front paws. On seeing them, it quit eating the berries, glanced wildly around, and then launched itself away with great leaps. Its long thin tail projected stiffly behind it.

Wolff started to run after it, but quit as soon as he realized its speed. The animal stopped when it was a hundred yards away and turned to face them. Its head was much like a purebred Persian cat's except that the ears were a jackrabbit's. The body was khaki; the head, chocolate; the ears, magenta.

Wolff advanced steadily towards it, and it fled until it was out of sight. He decided that it would be a good thing if the Lords had clubs in case they came within close range of the hopper again. He cut the bushes to make sticks that would be heavy enough to do the job.

Palamabron asked him why he did not kill the beast with his beamer.

Wolff answered that he was trying to waste as little power as possible. The thing took off so swiftly that he was not sure he could hit it. The next time, power conservation or not, he would shoot. They had to have something to eat. They continued on their way and began seeing more of the hoppers. These must have been warned by the first, since they all kept well out of range.

Two hours later, they came to a wide fissure in the canyon walls. Wolff went down it and found that it led to a box canyon. This was about thirty feet lower than the main one, about three hundred yards wide and four hundred deep. The floor was thick with bushes, among which he saw one hopper.

He went back to the others and told them what they were to do. Luvah and Theotormon stayed within the narrow passage while the rest walked out into the canyon. They spread out in a wide circle to close in on the lone animal.

The hopper stood in a large clearing, its nose twitching, its head turning quickly from side to side. Wolff told the others to stop, and he walked slowly towards it, the club held behind his back. The animal waited until Wolff was within ten feet of it. Then it disappeared.

Wolff whirled around, thinking that it had jumped with such swiftness that he had not been able to see it. There was no animal behind him. There were only the Lords, gaping and asking what had happened.

Approximately three seconds later, the beast reappeared. It was now thirty feet from him. Wolff took a step towards it, and it was gone again.

Three seconds later, there were two animals in the clearing. One was ten feet away from Vala. The other was to Wolff's left and fifteen feet away.

"What the hell?" Wolff said. It took much to startle him. Now he was far more than startled. He was bewildered.

The animal near Vala disappeared. Now there was one left. Wolff ran towards it, his club raised and shouting, hoping to freeze the animal long enough to get a chance to strike it.

It vanished. A little later, it reappeared to his right. A second hopper was with it.

The Lords closed in on them. The two beasts suddenly became five.

After that, there was much yelling, screaming, and confusion. Some of the animals had popped up behind the Lords, and several Lords turned to give chase.

Then there were two of the creatures that Wolff was to call tempus-fudgers.

These two became three as the wild chase continued for another three seconds.

Then there was one.

The Lords pursued that one and suddenly had two before them.

Three animals were being chased three seconds later.

Then there was one.

The Lords came in on it from all directions at full speed. Two animals reappeared, one directly in front of Palamabron. He was so startled, he tried to stop, stumbled, and fell on his face. The creature hopped over him and then vanished as Rintrah swung at it with his stick.

There were two now.

Three.

All of a sudden, none.

The Lords stopped running and stared at each other. Only the wind and their heavy breathing sounded in the box canyon.

Abruptly three of the beasts were in their midst.

The chase started again.

There was one.

Five.

Three.

Six.

For six seconds, three.

Six again.

Wolff called a halt to the milling chase. He led the Lords back to the entrance, where they sat down to recover their breath. Having done that, they began chattering away to each other, all asking the same questions and no one with an answer.

Wolff studied the six animals a hundred yards away. They had forgotten their panic, though not the cause of it, and were nibbling away at the berries.

A silence fell upon the Lords again. They looked at their pensive brother, and Vala said, "What do you make of it, Jadawin?"

"I've been thinking back to the time that the first animal we saw vanished," he said. "I've been trying to calculate the lengths of their disappearances and the correlation between the number at one time and at succeeding times."

He shook his head. "I don't know. Maybe. It doesn't seem possible. But how else to explain it. Or, if not explain, describe, anyway."

"Tell me, have any of you ever heard of a Lord having success with time-travel experiments?"

Palamabron laughed.

Vala said, "Jackass!" She spoke to Wolff. "I have heard that Blind Orc tried for many years to discover the principles of time. But it is said that he gave up. He claimed that trying to dissect time was a problem as insolvable as explaining the origin of the universe."

"Why do you ask?" Ariston said.

"There is a tiny subatomic particle which Earth scientists call the neutrino," Wolff answered. "It's an uncharged particle with zero rest mass. Do you know what I'm talking about?"

All shook their heads. Luvah said, "You know we were all exceedingly well educated at one time, Jadawin. But it has been thousands of years since we took any interest in science except to use the devices we had at hand for our purposes."

"You are indeed a bunch of ignorant gods," Wolff said. "The most powerful beings of the cosmos, yet barbaric, illiterate divinities."

"What has that got to do with our present situation?" Enion said. "And why do you insult us? You yourself said we must quit these insults if we are to survive."

"Forgive me," Wolff said. "It's just that I am sometimes overwhelmed at the discrepancy . . . never mind. Anyway, the neutrino behaves rather peculiarly. In such a manner, in fact, that it might be said to go backward in time."

"It really does?" Palamabron said.

"I doubt it. But it's behavior can be described in time-travel terms, whether the neutrino actually does go into reverse chronological gear or not.

"I believe the same applies to those beasts out there. Maybe they can go forward or backwards in time. Perhaps Urizen had the power to create such animals. I doubt it. He may have found them in some universe we don't know about and imported them.

"Whatever their origin, they do have an ability which makes them *seem* to hop around in time. Within a three-second limit, I'd say."

He drew a circle in the dirt with the end of his stick. "This represents the single animal we first saw."

He drew a line from it and described another circle at its end. "This represents the disappearance of it, its nonexistence in our time. It was going forward in time, or seemed to."

"I'll swear it was not gone for three seconds when it first disappeared," Vala said.

Wolff extended a line from the second circle and made a third circle at its end. Then he scratched a line at right angles to it, and bent it back to a position opposite the second circle.

"It leaped forward into time, or can be described as doing so. Then it went back to the time-slot it did not occupy when it made the first jump. Thus, we saw a beast for six seconds but did not know that it had gone forward and backward.

"Then the animal—let's call it a tempusfudger—jumped forward again to the time at which its first—avatar—had come out of the first jump.

"Now we have two. The same animal, fissioned by time-travel.

"One jumped the three seconds forward again, and we did not see it during that time. The other did not jump but ran about. It jumped when tempusfudger No. 2 reappeared.

"Only No. 1 also jumped back just as No. 2 came out of the time-hop. So we have two again."

"But all of a sudden there were five?" Rintrah said.

"Let's see. We had two. Now No. 1 had made a jump, and he was one of the five. He jumped back to be one of the previous two. Then he jumped forward again to become No. 3 of the five.

"No. 2 had jumped, when there was only one tempusfudger, to become No. 2 of the five. No. 1 and No. 2 jumped forward and then back to also become No. 4 and 5 of the five.

"No. 4 and 5 then jumped ahead to the period when there were only two. Meanwhile, No. 1 had leaped over three seconds, No. 4 didn't leap, and No. 5 did. So there were only two at that instant."

He grinned at their lax faces. "Now do you understand?"

"That's impossible," Tharamas said. "Time-travel! You know it's impossible!"

"Sure, I know. But if these animals aren't time-traveling, what are they doing? You don't know any more than I do. So, if I can describe their behavior as chronosaltation, and the description helps us catch them, why object?"

"Why don't you use your beamer?" Rintrah said. "We're all very hungry. I'm weak after chasing those flickering on-again-off-again things."

Wolff shrugged and arose and walked towards the fudgers. They continued eating but kept watching him. When he was within thirty yards, they hopped away. He followed them until they were getting close to the blind wall of the canyon. They scattered. He put the beamer on half-power and aimed at one.

Perhaps the tempusfudger was startled by the raising of the weapon. It disappeared just as he fired, and the beam's energy was absorbed by a boulder beyond it.

He cursed, flicked off the power, and aimed at another. This leaped to one side and avoided the first shot. He kept the power on and swung the beam to catch it. The animal jumped again, narrowly escaping the ray. Wolff twisted his wrist to bring the fudger within touch of the beam. The animal disappeared.

Quickly, he swung the weapon back towards the others. A fudger sprang across his field of vision, and he brought the white ray upon it.

It disappeared at the same time. There was a shout behind him. He turned to see the Lords pointing at a dead animal a few yards to his left. It lay in a heap, its fur scorched.

He blinked. Vala came running and said, "It dropped out of the air; it was dead and cooked when it hit the ground."

"But I didn't hit anything except just now," he said. "And the animal I hit hasn't reappeared yet."

"That fudger was dead on arrival three seconds ago, maybe a little more," she said. "Three seconds before you hit the other."

She stopped, grinned, and said, "What do I mean . . . other? It's the same one you hit. Killed before you hit it. Or just as you hit it. Only it jumped back."

Wolff said, slowly, "You're telling me I killed it first, then shot it."

"No, not really. But it looked that way. Oh, I don't know. I'm confused."

"Anyway, we have something to eat," he said. "But not much. There's not enough meat there to satisfy us."

He whirled and brought the beam around to describe a horizontal arc. It struck some rocks, then came to a fudger. And the beam went out.

He continued to aim the beamer steadily at the fudger, which stood poised upon its hind legs, its big eyes blinking.

"The power's gone," he said. He ejected the power pack and stuck the beamer into his belt. It was useless now, but he had no intention of throwing it away. The time might come when he would get his hands on some fresh packs.

He wanted to continue the hunt with sticks. The others vetoed him. Weak and hungry, they needed food at once. Although the meat was half-charred, they devoured it greedily. Their bellies quit rumbling a little. They rested a moment, then got to their feet and went after the tempus-fudgers again.

Their plan was to spread out in a wide circle which would contract to bring all the animals within reach of the clubs. The fudgers began hopping wildly and flickering in and out of existence . . . or time. At one moment, there were none, when all must have simultaneously decided to jump forward or to jump backward. It was difficult to tell what was going on during the hunt.

Wolff made no effort at the beginning to keep count. There were six, then zero, and then six, then three, then six, then one, then seven.

Back and forth, in and out, while the Lords ran around and howled like wolves and swung their sticks, hoping to connect with a fudger just as it came out of the chronoleap. Suddenly, Tharmas' club thudded against the side of the head of one of the animals as it materialized. It collapsed, jerked several times, and died.

Eight had dropped out of the air. One had stayed behind as a carcass while the others became invisible. There should have been seven the next time, but there were eight again. Three seconds later, there were three. Another three seconds, nine. Zero. Nine. Two. Eleven. Seven. Two.

Eleven, and Wolff threw his stick and caught one in the back. It pitched forward on its face. Vala was on it with her stick and beat it to death before it could recover from its stunned condition.

There were fifteen, quickly cut to thirteen when Rintrah and Theotormon each killed one. Then, zero.

Within a minute, the tempusfudgers seemed to go riot. Terrified, they hurled themselves back and forth and became twenty-eight, zero, twenty-eight, zero, and fifty-six, or so Wolff roughly estimated it. It was, of course, impossible to make an accurate count. A little later, he was sure, only because his arithmetic assured him it should be so, that the doubling had resulted in one thousand seven hundred and ninety-two.

There had been no more casualties among the fudgers to reduce the number. The Lords had been unable to kill any. They were being buffeted by the ever-increasing horde, knocked down by hoppers appearing in front of them, behind them, and beside them, stepped upon, scratched, kicked, and hammered.

Suddenly, the little animals stampeded towards the exit of the canyon. They hurtled over the floor and should have jammed into the narrow pass, but somehow formed an orderly arrangement and were gone.

Slowly, sore and shaken, the Lords arose. They looked at the four dead animals and shook their heads. Out of almost eighteen hundred that had been at hand, easy prey—in theory—these pitiful four were left.

"Half a fudger will make one good meal for each of us," Vala said. "That's better than none. But what will we do tomorrow?"

The others did not answer. They began collecting wood for the cooking fires. Wolff borrowed Theotormon's knife and started the skinning.

In the morning, they ate the scraps left over from the evening's feast. Wolff led them on up. The canyon remained as silent as before, except for the river's murmuring. The walls kept on pressing in. The sky burned yellow far above. Fudgers appeared at a distance. Wolff tried throwing rocks at them. He almost struck one, only to see it disappear as if it had slipped around a corner of air. It came into sight again, three seconds later, twenty feet away and hopping as if it had an important engagement it had suddenly recalled.

Two days after they had last eaten, the Lords were almost ready to try the berries. Palamabron argued that the repulsive odor of the berries did not necessarily mean that they had a disagreeable taste. Even if they did, they were not necessarily poisonous. They were going to die, anyway, so why not test the berries?

"Go ahead," Vala said. "It's your theory and your desire. Eat some!"

She was smiling peculiarly at him, as if she were enjoying the conflict between his hunger and fear.

"No," Palamabron said. "I will not be your guinea pig. Why should I sacrifice myself for all of you? I will eat the berries only if all eat at the same time."

"So you can die in good company," Wolff said. "Come on, Palamabron. Put up or shut up—old Earth proverb. You're wasting our time arguing. Either do it yourself or forget about it."

Palamabron sniffed at the berry he was holding, made a face, and let the berry fall on the rocky floor. Wolff started to walk away, and the Lords followed. About an hour later, he saw another side-canyon. On the way into it, he picked up a round stone which was just the right size and weight for throwing. If only he could sneak up close enough to a fudger and throw the rock while it was looking the other way.

The canyon was a little smaller than that in which the Lords had made their first hunt. At its far end was a single tempusfudger, eating the berries. Wolff got down on his hands and knees and began the slow crawl towards it. He took advantage of every rock for covering and managed to get halfway across the canyon before the animal noticed anything. It suddenly quit moving its jaws, sat up, and looked around, its nose wiggling, its ears vibrating like a TV antenna in a strong wind.

Wolff hugged the ground and did not move at all. He was sweating with the effort and tension, since the starvation diet had weakened him considerably. He wanted to jump up and run at the fudger and hurl himself upon it, tear it apart, eat it raw. He could have devoured the entire animal from the tips of its ears down to the tip of its tail and then broken the bones open to suck out the marrow.

He forced himself to stay motionless. The animal must get over its suspiciousness soon, after which Wolff could resume his turtle-like approach.

Then, from behind a rock near the fudger, another beast appeared. It was gray except for red wolflike ears, had a long pointed face, a bushy tail, and was about midway in size between a fox and a coyote. It sprang at the tempusfudger, coming up from behind it just as it was looking the other way.

Its teeth closed on air. The fudger had disappeared, escaping the jaws by a fraction of an inch.

The predator also disappeared, vanishing before it struck the ground.

Three animals appeared, two fudgers and one predator. Wolff, who liked to tag unknown things, at once called it a chronowolf. For the first time, he was seeing the creature that nature—or Urizen—had placed here to keep the fudger from overpopulating this world.

Wolff now had time to figure out what was happening with the leapers. There had been two. Then there were none. Then, three. So the original fudger and the chronowolf had jumped ahead. But the fudger had stayed only a microsecond, and leaped back also. So that he had reproduced himself and now there were two for the wolf to chase.

Again, the animals vanished. They reappeared, four in number. Two fudgers, two chronowolves. The chase was on, not only in space but in the strange gray corridors of backwards-forwards time.

Another simultaneous jump into the tempolimbo. Wolff ran towards a boulder around which grew a number of bushes. He hurled himself down and then peered between the bushes.

Seven again. This time a wolf had come out of wherever he had been just behind his quarry. He hurled himself forward, and his jaws closed around the neck of the fudger. There was a loud crack; the fudger dropped dead.

Seven living, and one dead. A fudger had gone back and then forward again.

The living vanished. Evidently the wolf did not intend to stay behind and eat his kill.

Then six were jumping around the plain. Savagely, a wolf bit another wolf on the neck, and the attacked crumpled in death.

Nothing for three seconds. Wolff ran out and threw himself down on the ground. Although not hidden behind anything this time, he hoped that his motionlessness, combined with the terror of the fudgers and the blood-lust of the wolves, would make them not notice him.

Another wolf had been born out of time's womb. Parthenogenesis of chronoviators.

Two wolves launched themselves at each other, while the third watched them, and the fudgers hopped around in apparent confusion.

The observer predator became participant, not in the struggle between his fellows, but in the hunt. He caught a fudger by the throat as it hurtled by him in its blind panic.

A fudger and a wolf died.

The living flickered out again. When they came back into his sight, a wolf gripped a fudger's neck and cracked it.

Wolff slowly rose to his feet. At the exact moment that one of the wolves died, he hurled his stone at the winner. It must have caught the motion out of the corner of its eyes, since it vanished just before the stone would have struck. And when it shot out of the chute of time, it was going as swiftly as its four legs would take it towards the exit.

"I'm sorry to deprive you of the spoils of victory," Wolff called out after it. "But you can resume the hunt elsewhere."

He went to call the other Lords and to tell them that their luck had changed. Six animals would fill their bellies and furnish a little over for the next day.

There came the time again when the Lords had been without food for three days. They were gaunt, their cheeks hollow, their eyes crouched within dark and deep caves, their bellies advancing towards their spines. That day Wolff sent them out in pairs to hunt. He had intended to go alone but Vala insisted that he take Luvah with him. She would hunt by herself. Wolff asked her why she wanted it that way, and she replied that she did not care to be accompanied by only one man.

"You think you might become the victim of a cannibal?" Wolff said.

"Exactly," she said. "You know that if we continue to go hungry, it's inevitable that we'll start eating one another. It may even have been planned

234 PHILIP JOSÉ FARMER

by Urizen. He would very much enjoy seeing us kill one another and stuff our bellies with our own flesh and blood."

"Have it your own way," Wolff said. He left with Luvah to explore a series of side-canyons. The two sighted a number of fudgers eating from bushes and began the patient, hours-long creeping upon them. They came within an inch of success. The stone, thrown by Wolff, went past the head of his intended victim. After that, all was lost. The fudgers did not even bother to take refuge in time but leaped away and were lost in another canyon.

Wolff and Luvah continued to look until near the time for the moon to bring another night of hunger-torn sleeplessness. When they got back to the meeting-place, they found the others, looking very perturbed. Palamabron and his hunting-companion, Enion, were missing.

"I don't know about the rest of you," Tharmas said, "but I'm too exhausted to go looking for the damn fools."

"Maybe we should," Vala said. "They might have had some luck and even now be stuffing themselves with good meat, instead of sharing it with us."

Tharmas cursed. However, he refused to search for them. If they had had luck, he said, he would know it when he next saw their faces. They would not be able to hide their satisfaction from him. And he would kill them for their selfishness and greed.

"They wouldn't be doing anything you wouldn't if you had their chance," Wolff said. "What's all the uproar about? We don't know that they've caught anything. After all, it was only a suggestion by Vala. There's no proof, not the slightest."

They grumbled and cursed but soon were asleep with utter weariness.

Wolff slept, too, but awoke in the middle of the night. He thought he had heard a cry in the distance. He sat up and looked at the others. They were all there, except for Palamabron and Enion.

Vala sat up also. She said, "Did you hear something, brother? Or was it the wailing of our bellies?"

"It came from upriver," he said. He rose to his feet. "I think I shall go look."

She said, "I'll go with you. I cannot sleep any longer. The thought that they might be feasting keeps me angry and awake."

"I do not think the feasting will be on the little hoppers," he said.

She said, "You think . . ."

"I do not know. You spoke of the possibility. It becomes stronger every day, as we become weaker and hungrier."

He picked up his stick, and they walked along the edge of the river. They had little difficulty seeing where they were going. The moon brought only a half-darkness. Even though the walls of the canyon deepened the twilight, there was still enough light for them to proceed with confidence.

So it was that they saw Palamabron before he saw them. His head appeared for a moment above a boulder near the wall of the canyon. His profile was presented to them, then he disappeared. On bare feet, they crept towards him. The wind carried to them the noise he was making. It sounded as if he were striking one stone against another.

"Is he trying to make a fire?" Vala whispered.

Wolff did not answer. He was sick, since he could think of only one reason why Palamabron would want to build a fire. When he came to the huge rock behind which Palamabron was, he hesitated. He did not want to see what he thought he must when he came around the boulder.

Palamabron had his back to them. He was on his knees before a pile of branches and leaves and was knocking a piece of flint against a rock that was heavy in iron.

Wolff breathed a sigh of relief. The body beside Palamabron was that of a fudger.

Where was Enion?

Wolff came up silently behind Palamabron, his stick raised high. He spoke loudly. "Well, Palamabron?"

The Lord gave a short scream and dived forward over the firepile. He rolled and came up on his feet, facing them. He held a very crude flint knife.

"It's mine," he snarled. "I killed it, and I want it. I have to have it. I'll die if I don't get to eat!"

"So will we all," Wolff said. "Where is your brother?"

Palamabron spit and said, "The beast! He's no brother of mine. How should I know where he is? Why should I care?"

"You went out with him," Wolff said.

"I don't know where he is. We got separated while we were hunting."

"We thought we heard a cry," Vala said.

"It was a fudger, I think," Palamabron said. "Yes, it was. The one I killed a little while ago. I found it sleeping and killed it and it cried out as it died."

"Maybe," Wolff said. He backed away from Palamabron until he was at a safe distance. He continued on up the rivershore. Before he had gone a hundred yards, he saw the hand lying beside a boulder. He went around it and found Enion. The back of his head was crushed in; beside him lay the bloody rock that had killed him.

He returned to Palamabron and Vala. She was still there; the Lord and the fudger were gone.

"Why didn't you stop him?" Wolff said.

She shrugged and smiled. "I'm only a woman. How could I stop him?"

"You could have," he replied. "I think you wanted to enjoy the chase after him. Well, let me tell you, there won't be any. None of us have the strength to waste it climbing around here. And when he eats, he'll have enough strength to outclimb or outrun us."

"Very well," she said. "So what do we do now?"

"Keep on going and hope for the best."

"And starve!" she said. She pointed at the boulder which hid Enion's body. "There's enough food for all of us."

Wolff did not reply for a moment. He had not wanted to think about this, but, since he was faced with it, he would do what had to be done. Vala was right. Without this food, however horrible it was to think about it, they might well die. In a way, Palamabron had done them a favor. He had taken the guilt upon himself of killing for them. They could eat without considering themselves murderers. Not that killing would bother the rest of them. He, however, would have suffered agonies if he had been forced into a position where he had to slay a human being to survive.

As for the actual eating, he was now feeling only a slight repulsion. Hunger had deadened his normal horror against cannibalism.

He returned to wake the others while Vala picked up the rocks dropped by Palamabron. By the time they returned, she had not only started a fire but was intent on the butchering. Wolff held back for a moment. Then, thinking that if he was to share in the food, he should also share in the work, he took Theotormon's knife. The others offered a hand, but he turned them down. It was as if he wanted to punish himself by making himself do most of the grisly work.

When the meal was cooked, half-cooked, rather, he took his share and went around the boulder to eat. He was not sure that he could keep the meat down, and he was sure that if he watched the others eat, he would not be able to keep from vomiting. Somehow, it did not seem so bad if he were alone.

Dawn had found them still cooking. Not until the middle of the morning did they start traveling again. The meat that had not been eaten was wrapped in leaves.

"If Urizen was watching us," Wolff said, "he must really be laughing."

"Let him laugh," Vala said. "My turn will come."

"*Your* turn? You mean, *our* turn."

"You may do what you like. All I'm interested in is what I do."

"Typical of the Lords," said Wolff without elaborating. He watched her for a while after that. She had amazing vitality. Perhaps it was the food that had given her such a swift walk and had filled out her cheeks and arms. He did not think so. Even during the starvation, she had not seemed to suffer as much as the rest or to waste away as swiftly.

If anybody could survive to get at her father's throat, it would be Vala, he thought.

May I not be far behind her, he prayed. *Not so much for vengeance on Urizen, though I want that, as to rescue Chryseis.*

12

THEY HAD BEEN WITHOUT FOOD FOR A DAY WHEN THEY emerged from the canyon. Before them, at the foot of a long gentle hill, was a plain that stretched to the horizon. A quarter of a mile away was a small hill, and on this were two giant hexagons.

They stopped to look dully at their goal. Wolff said, "I suggest we take one or the other gate immediately. Perhaps there may be food on the other side."

"If not?" Tharmas said.

"I'd rather die quickly trying to get through Urizen's defenses than starve slowly. Which, at the moment, looks as if it might . . ."

He let his voice trail off, thinking that the Lords felt low enough.

They followed him sluggishly up to the foot of the golden, gem-studded frames. He said to Vala, "Sister, you have the honor of choosing the right or the left entrance for us. Continue. Only be quick about it. I can hear my strength ebbing away."

She picked up a stone, turned her back to the gates, and cast the stone over her head. It sailed through the right gate, almost striking the frame.

"So be it," Wolff said. He looked at them and laughed. "What a crew! Brave Lords! Tramps rather! Sticks, a broken sword, a knife, and muscles shaking with weakness and bellies groaning for meat. Was ever a Lord attacked in his own stronghold by such a contemptible bunch?"

Vala laughed and said, "At least you have some spirit left, Jadawin. That may mean something."

"I hope so," he said, and he ran forward and jumped through the right gate. He came out under a deep-blue sky and onto ground that gave under his feet a little. The topography was flat except for a few steep hills, so rough and dark that they looked more like excrescences than mounds of dirt. He doubted they were dirt, since the surface on which he stood was not earth. It was brownish but smooth and with small holes in it. A foot-high stalk, thin as a pipestem cleaner, grew out of each hole.

Almost like the skin of a giant, he thought.

The only vegetation, if it could be called that, was a number of widely separated trees. These were about forty feet high, were thinly trunked, and had smooth, sharply pointed branches that projected at a forty-five degree angle upwards from the trunk. The branches were darker than the saffron of the main shaft and sparsely covered with blade-like leaves about two feet long.

The other Lords came through the gate a minute later. He turned and said, "I'm glad I didn't find anything I couldn't have handled without your help."

Vala said, "They all were sure that this time the gate would lead into Urizen's stronghold."

"And perhaps I'd trip a few traps before I went down," he said. "And so give the rest of you a chance to live a few minutes longer."

They did not reply. Wolff gazed reproachfully at Luvah, whose cheeks reddened.

Wolff tested the gate. It had either been deactivated or else was unipolar. He saw a long black line that could be the shore of a lake or sea. This world, unlike the one they had just left, gave no indications of the direction they must take. On the side, where he had first stepped, however, he had seen two rough dark hills very close together. These might or not be some sort of sign from Urizen. There was only one way to find out, which Wolff took without hesitation.

He set out on the slightly springy ground, the others trailing. The shadow of a bird passed before them, and they looked up. It was white with red legs, about the size of a bald eagle, and had a monkey face with a curving bird's beak instead of a nose. It swooped so low that Luvah threw his stick at it. The stick passed behind its flaring tail. It squawked indignantly and climbed away swiftly.

Wolff said, "That looks like a nest on that tree. Let's see if it could have eggs."

Luvah ran forward to recover his stick, then stopped. Wolff stared where Luvah was pointing.

The earth was rippling. It rose in inch-high waves and advanced towards the stick. Luvah turned to run, thought better of it, turned again, and ran to pick up the stick. Behind him, the earth swelled, rose up and up, and raced forward, like a surfer's wave.

Wolff yelled. Luvah whirled, saw the danger, and ran away from it. He ran at an angle, towards the end of the wave. Wolff came along behind it, not knowing what he could do to help Luvah but hoping to do something.

Then the wave collapsed. Wolff and Luvah stopped. Abruptly, Wolff felt the earth rising below his feet and saw that another swelling had started some ten feet from Luvah. Both turned and raced away, the earth—or whatever it was—chasing after them.

They made it back to the area around the gate, which had been stable and would continue to be so—they hoped.

They got to the safety zone just in time to escape the sudden sinking of the land behind them. A hole, broad and shallow at first, appeared. Then it narrowed and deepened. The sides closed in on themselves, there was a smacking sound, and the hole reversed its original process. It widened out until all was smooth as before, except that the foot-high, thin growths sprouting from each depression kept on vibrating.

"What in Los' name!" Luvah said over and over. He was pale, and the freckles stood out like a galaxy of fear.

Wolff was a little sick himself. Feeling the earth tremble under him had been like being caught in an earthquake. In fact, that was what he had thought when it first happened.

Somebody yelled behind him. He spun to see Palamabron trying to get back through the gate through which he had just stepped only to go flying vainly through the frame. He must have been following them and waited until he thought they had gone some distance from the gate. Now, he was trapped as much as they.

More so, since Wolff had use for him. Wolff shoved the others away from Palamabron's throat and shouted at them to leave him alone. They drew back while Palamabron shook and his teeth chattered.

"Palamabron," Wolff said, "you have been sentenced to death because you broke truce with us and murdered your brother."

Palamabron, seeing that he was not to be killed out of hand, took courage. Perhaps he thought he had a chance. He cried, "At least I did not eat my own brother! And I had to kill him! He attacked me first!"

"Enion was struck in the back of the head," Wolff said.

"I knocked him down!" Palamabron shouted. "He started to rise when I seized a rock and hit him with it. It was not my fault he had his back turned. Would you ask me to wait until he had turned around?"

"There's no use talking about this," Wolff said. "But you can go free. Your blood will not be on our hands. Only, you can't stay with us. None of us would feel safe to sleep at night or turn our backs on you."

"You are letting me go?" Palamabron said. "Why?"

"Don't waste time talking," Wolff said. "If you don't get out of our sight within ten minutes, I'll let the others at you. You'd better leave. Now!"

"Wait a minute," Palamabron said. "There's something very suspicious about this. No, I won't go."

Wolff gestured at the others. "Go ahead. Kill him."

Palamabron screamed, turned, and ran away as swiftly as he could. He seemed weak, and his legs began to move slowly after the first thirty yards. He looked back several times, then, seeing that they were not coming after him, he quit running.

The earth swelled behind him and built up until it was twice as high as his head. At the moment it gained its peak, Palamabron looked over his shoulder again. He saw the giant wave racing towards him, and he screamed and began to run again. The wave collapsed, the tremors following the collapse upsetting Palamabron and knocking him off his feet. He scrambled up and continued to go on, although he was staggering by now.

A hole opened up ahead of him. He screamed and darted off at right angles to it, seeming to gain new strength from terror. The hole disappeared, but a second gaped ahead of him. Again, he raced away, this time diagonally to the hole.

Another wave began to build up before him. He whirled, slipped, fell hard, rolled over, and stumbled away. Presently, the swelling, which had risen directly between Palamabron and the Lords, grew so high that it walled him off from their sight. After that, the wave froze for a moment, rigid except for a slight trembling. Gradually, it subsided, and the plain was flat again, with the exception of a six-foot long mound.

"Swallowed up," Vala said. She seemed thrilled. Her eyes were wide open, her mouth parted, the lower lip wet. Her tongue flicked out to trace with its tip the oval of both lips.

Wolff said, "Our father has indeed created a monster for us. Perhaps, this entire planet is covered with the skin of . . . of this *Weltthier.*"

"What?" said Theotormon. His eyes were still glazed with terror. And though he had been shrinking during the starvation on the last world, he now seemed to have dwindled off fifty pounds in the past two minutes. His skin hung in loops.

"*Weltthier.* World-animal. From German, a Terrestrial language."

A planet covered with skin, he thought. Or maybe it was not so much a skin as a continent-sized amoeba spread out over the globe. The idea made him boggle.

The skin existed; there was no denying that. But how did it keep from starving to death? The millions and millions of tons of protoplasm had to be fed. Certainly, although it ate animals, it could not get nearly enough of these to maintain itself.

Wolff decided to investigate the subject, if he ever got the chance. He was as curious as a monkey or a Siamese cat, always probing, pondering, speculating, and analyzing. He could not rest until he knew the why and how.

He sat down to rest while he considered what to do. The others, Vala excepted, also sat or lay down. She walked from the "safety zone," placing her feet carefully with each step. Watching her, he understood what she was doing. Why had he not thought of that? She was avoiding contact with the plants (hairs?) that grew from the holes (pores?). After traveling on a circle with a radius of about twenty-five yards, she returned to the gate area. Not once had the skin trembled or begun to form threatening shapes.

Wolff stood up and said, "Very good, Vala. You beat me to it. The beast, or whatever it is, detects life by touch through the feelers or hairs. If we navigate as cautiously as ships going through openings in reefs, we can cross over this thing. Only trouble is, how do we get past those?"

He pointed outwards to the horny buttes, the excrescentoid hills. The hairs began to crowd together at their bases, and beyond the buttes they cartpeted the ground.

She shrugged and said, "I don't know."

"We'll worry about it when we get to it," he said. He began walking, looking downwards to guide himself among the feelers. The Lords followed him in Indian file, with Vala again being the only exception. She paralleled his course at a distance of five or six yards to his right.

"It's going to be very difficult to hunt animals for food under these conditions," he said. "We'll have to keep one eye on the hairs and one on the animal. A terrible handicap."

"I wouldn't worry," she said. "There may be no animals."

"There is one I'm sure exists," Wolff said. He did not say anything more on the subject although it was evident that Vala was wondering what he meant. He headed towards the "tree" in a branch of which he saw the nest. A circular pile of sticks and leaves, it was lodged at the junction of the trunk and a branch and was about three feet across. The sticks and leaves seemed to be held together with a gluey substance.

He stepped between two feelers, propped his club against the tree, and shinnied up the trunk. Halfway up, he saw the tops of two hexagons on one of the buttes. When he got to the nest, he clung to the trunk with his legs, one arm around the trunk, while with the other hand he poked through leaves on top of the nest. He uncovered two eggs, speckled green and black and about twice the size of turkey eggs. Removing them one by one, he dropped them to Vala.

Immediately thereafter, the mother returned. Larger than a bald eagle, she was white with bluish chevrons, furry, monkey-faced, falcon-beaked, saber-toothed, wolf-eared, bat-winged, archeopteryx-tailed, and vulture-footed.

She shot down on him with wings folded until just before she struck. The wings opened with a whoosh of air, and she screamed like iron being ripped apart. Perhaps the scream was intended to freeze the prey. If so, it failed. Wolff just let loose of the trunk and dropped. Above him came a crash and another scream, this time of frustration and panic, as the beast rammed partly into the nest and partly into the trunk. Evidently, it had expected to have its momentum absorbed by Wolff's body. And it may have underestimated its speed in its fury.

Wolff hit the ground and rolled, knowing that he was disturbing the feelers but unable to prevent it. He came up on his feet, clumps of glued-together sticks and leaves raining around him from the shattered nest. He got to one side just in time to escape being hit by the body of the half-stunned flier. However, the blow would not have been a full one, since the creature had slowed its fall with an instinctive outspreading of wings.

By then, the earth-skin was reacting to the messages transmitted by the feelers. Not only Wolff had contacted them. The other Lords had scattered when Wolff fell, and they had brushed against hairs all around the tree.

"Back to the tree," Wolff yelled at them. Vala had anticipated his advice; she was already halfway up the trunk. He began shinnying after Vala, only to feel talons sharp and hot as glowing-white hooks fasten into his back. The flying beast had recovered and was at him again. Once more, he let loose and fell backward. He kicked his feet against the trunk and shoved out to throw himself into a horizontal attitude. And so he came down hard but with the beast below him.

Two breaths whooshed out, his and that of the beast crushed beneath him. Less hurt, Wolff rolled off, stood up, and kicked the thing in the ribs. Its mouth gaped beneath the brownish beak, its two saber teeth covered with saliva and blood. Wolff kicked again and turned back to the tree. He was bowled over by two Lords frantic to get to the safety of the tree. Tharmas stepped on his head and used it as a springboard to leap for the trunk. Rintrah pulled him down, shoved him away, and started to climb. Staggering back from the push, Tharmas fell over Wolff, who was just getting to his hands and knees.

From her perch near the top of the tree, Vala was laughing hysterically. She laughed and pounded her thigh and then, suddenly, shrieked. Her hold lost, she fell hard, broke off a branch, turned over, and came down on her shoulder. She lay stunned at the base of the tree.

Theotormon was perhaps the most terrified. Still huge despite the many pounds of fat that had thawed off him, and handicapped by having flippers, he had a hard time scaling the tree. He kept slipping back down, the while he could not refrain from looking over his shoulder and gibbering.

Wolff managed to get to his feet. Around him, around the tree, rather, the skin was going mad. It rose in great waves that chased after Luvah and Ariston. These two were going around in circles with great speed, their fright giving their weary and hungry bodies fresh strength. Behind them, the earthflesh rose up, moved swiftly after them, then began to curl over. Other waves appeared ahead of them, and pits yawned beneath their feet.

Suddenly, Luvah and Ariston passed each other, and the various moving tumors and depressions hot on their heels collided. Wolff was confused by the chaos of tossing, bumping, smacking, gulping shapes of protoplasm. More than anything, the scene resembled a collection of maelstroms.

Before the skin could get its signals straight and reorganize, it had lost Ariston and Luvah. They gained the trunk of the tree, but they impeded each other's ascent. While they were clawing at each other, Wolff picked up the body of the flier and hurled it from him as far as he could. It landed on an advancing swell, which stopped the moment it detected the carcass. A depression appeared around and beneath the body. Slowly, it sank until it was below the surface. Then the lips of the hole closed over it, and there was only a mound and a seam to show what was beneath.

The flier had been a sacrifice, since Wolff had wanted to keep the body for food. The area around the tree smoothed out, made a few ripples, and became as inert as if it were truly made of earth. Wolff went around the tree to examine Vala. She was sitting up, breathing hard, her face twisted with pain. Since the skin was springy, the impact had not been as hard as if it had occurred on hard dirt. She was bruised on her shoulder and the side of her face, and for a while she could not move her arm.

Her worst injury seemed to be her dignity. She cursed them for a pack of cowardly fools and males fit only to be slaves—if that. The Lords were abashed by her insults or sullen. They felt that she was right; they were ashamed. But they were certainly not going to admit the truth.

Wolff began to think the whole affair had been funny. He started laughing, then straightened up with a groan. He had forgotten the gashes inflicted by the flier's talons. Luvah looked at his back and clucked. The blood was still oozing out, although he expected that it would soon stop flowing. He certainly hoped that Wolff would not become infected, since there was no medicine to be had.

"You're very cheerful," Wolff growled. He looked around for the eggs. One was smashed and spread over the base of the tree. The other was nowhere in sight and presumably had been swallowed by the skin.

"Oh, Los!" moaned Ariston. "What do we do now? We're about to die of hunger; we're lost; we can't leave this tree without being swallowed alive by that monster. Our father has killed us, and we have not even gotten close to his stronghold."

"You Lords and Makers of Universes are pitiful creatures indeed when stripped of your fortress walls and your weapons," Wolff said. "I'll tell you another old Earth proverb. There's more than one way to skin a cat."

"What cat? Where?" Theotormon said. "I could eat a dozen cats right now."

Wolff rolled his eyes upwards but did not answer. He told the others either to get on the other side of the tree or go up it. Then he took Theotormon's knife and went out a few feet from the tree. Squatting, he jammed the knife with all his strength into the skin. If it was flexible enough to shape itself into rough pseudopods or holes, it had to be vulnerable.

He snatched the knife out of the wound and rose and retreated a few steps. The skin shrank away, became a hole, then a cone formed around the wound, and the cone thrust up, like a crater slowly building itself.

Wolff stood patiently. Soon the crater flattened out, and the wound was revealed. Instead of the blood he had been half-expecting, a thin pale liquid oozed out.

He approached the wound, taking care to avoid the hairs near it. Quickly he slashed at the skin again, dug out a quivering mass of flesh, and ran back to the tree. There was a storm of protoplasmic shapes once more: waves, craters, ridges, and brief swirlings in which the flesh formed corkscrew pillars. Then it subsided.

Wolff said, "The skin immediately around the tree seems to be tougher and less flexible than that further away. I think we're safe as long as we stand on it, although the skin might be capable of a . . . a tidal wave that could sweep us off. Anyway, we can eat."

The other Lords took turns cutting out chunks. The raw flesh was tough, slimy with ichor, and ill-smelling, but it could be chewed and swallowed. With something in their bellies, they felt stronger and more optimistic. Some lay down to sleep; Wolff walked to the shore. Vala and Theotormon followed him, and Luvah, seeing them, decided to go along. The land area ended abruptly with no beach for transition. Along the edge there were so few feelers they could relax a little. Wolff stood on the very edge and looked into the water. Despite the fact that there was no sun to cast its beams, the clear water allowed him to see quite deep into it.

There were many fish of various sizes, shapes, and colors swimming close to the shore. Even as he watched, he saw a long slender pale tentacle shoot out from under the edge and seize a large fish. The fish struggled but was drawn quickly back under the edge. Wolff got down on all fours and leaned out over the edge to see what kind of creature it was that had caught the prey. The rim on which he stood extended out quite far. In fact, he could not see the base of the land. Instead, he saw a mass of writhing tentacles, many of which gripped fish. And farther back were tentacles that hung deep into the abyss. Presently, one coiled upon itself and brought up a gigantic fish from the deeps.

He withdrew his head hastily, since one of the nearby tentacles was snaking out and up in his general direction. He said, "I wondered how such a monster could get enough to eat. It must feed mainly on the sea life. And I'll bet that this animal on which we stand is a vast floater. Like the islands of the waterworld, this thing is free, unattached to any base."

"That's nice to know," Luvah said. "But how does that help us?"

"We need more to eat," Wolff replied. "Theotormon, you're the swimmer among us. Would you jump in and swim around a bit? Stay close to shore and be ready to shoot back in. Come out fast, like a seal."

Theotormon said, "Why should I? You saw how those tentacles grabbed those fish."

"I think they're grabbing blindly. Maybe they can detect vibrations in

the water, I don't know. But you're fast enough to evade them. And the tentacles immediately under this edge are small."

Theotormon shook his head. "No, I won't risk my life for you."

"You'll starve if you don't," Wolff said. "We can't keep on cutting out
chunks of skin. It gets too violent."

He pointed at a fish that was just skimming by below the surface. It
was fat and sluggish with a head shaped like a sphinx. "Wouldn't you like
to sink your teeth in that?"

Theotormon drooled, and his belly thundered, but he would not go
after it.

"Give me your knife, then," Wolff said. He removed the weapon from
its scabbard before Theotormon, standing on one leg, could lift the other
to clutch the hilt with his toes. He turned and ran and dived out as far as
he could. The fish wheeled away from him and scooted away. It was slow
but not so slow that he could catch it. Nor had he thought he could. He
was interested in finding out if a tentacle, feeling the vibrations of the splash
and his strokes, would come probing for him.

One did. It undulated down from the fleshy base to which it was attached and then out towards him. He swam back towards the shore, dipping his head below the water to watch it. When he saw it suddenly gain
speed as it neared him, he reached out one hand and grabbed its tip. Until
then, he had not been certain that the tentacle was not poisonous, like a
jellyfish's. However, the fish that had been seized had fought vigorously with
no indication of being envenomed.

The tentacle doubled up on itself, looped, and went around him. He
released the tip, turned, and grabbed the tentacle about twelve inches back
from its tip. He began to saw at the skin with the knife, which went through
fairly easy. The tentacle abandoned its efforts to wrap itself around him and
began to pull back. He kept hold with one hand and continued to cut. The
water became darker as he was carried back under the edge. Then, the
knife was through, and he was swimming back up with the severed part in
his teeth.

He heaved the tentacle up on shore and was beginning to pull himself
out when he felt something enfold his right foot. He looked down at a
mouth on the end of another tentacle. The mouth was toothless but strong
enough to keep its grip on his foot. He clung with his arms on the edge
and gasped, "Help me!"

Theotormon took a few steps towards him on his rubbery legs and then
halted. Vala looked down at the thing and smiled. Luvah snatched the broken sword from her scabbard and went into the water. At that, Vala laughed,
and she followed Luvah in. She came back up, took Wolff's dagger, and
dived back down. She and Luvah went to work on the tentacle a few feet
from the mouth. The shaft parted; Wolff pulled himself on out with the
amputated mouth-part still ensocked on his foot.

The two pieces of flesh could be eaten only after being pounded against the treetrunk to tenderize them. Even then, eating them was almost like chewing on rubber. But it was more food in the stomach.

Afterwards, they advanced gingerly over the plain. At the point by the first butte, where the hairs began to cluster thickly, they halted. Now they could see their goal. A half-mile away, on top of a tall butte, was the pair of golden hexagons.

Wolff had picked up the branch that Vala's fall had broken off. He threw this hard as he could and watched it come down in the hairs. The whole area reacted at once and far more violently than the less haired area. The skin stormed.

"Oh, Los!" Ariston said. "We're done for! We could never get across that." He shook his fist at the sky and shouted, "You, our father! I hate you! I loathe you, and abominate the day that you jetted me from your foul loins! You may think you have us where you want us! But, by Los and crooked Enitharmon, I swear that we'll get to you yet!"

"That's the spirit," Wolff said. "For a moment, I thought you were going to whine like a sick dog. Tell the old bastard off! He can probably hear you."

Ariston, breathing hard, fists still clenched, said, "Brave enough talk. But I still would like to know what to do."

Wolff said to the others, "Any ideas?"

They shook their heads. He said, "Where is all the diabolical cleverness and weasel agility of mind that the children of Urizen are supposed to have? I've heard tales of each one of you, of how you have assailed the stronghold of many a Lord and by your wits and powers have taken his universe from him. What is the matter now?"

Vala said, "They were brave enough and clever enough when they had their weapons. But I think they're still recovering from the shock of being taken so easily by our father. And of being deprived of their devices. Without those, they lose that which made them Lords. Now, they're only men, and pretty sorry men at that."

"We're so tired," Rintrah said. "My muscles ache and burn. They sag as if I were on a heavy planet."

"Muscles!" Wolff said. "Muscles!"

He led them back to the tree. Despite the flame in his back every time he pulled on a branch—agony from the talon-wounds—he worked with a will. The other Lords helped him, and each soon had a bundle of branches in his arms. They returned to the rim of the overgrown area and here began to cast the sticks as far out into the feelers as they could. They did not do it all at once but spaced their throws. The skin reared up like a sea in a hurricane. Waves, craters, wavelets coursed back and forth.

But as the skin continued to be activated, its ragings became less. Near the end of the supply of branches, it began to react feebly. The last stick got no more than a shallow hole and a weak and quickly subsiding wave.

Wolff said, "It's tired now. Its rate of recovery may be very swift, however. So I suggest we get going now."

He led the way, walking swiftly. The skin quivered and humped up in response to the warnings from the feelers and broad three-or-four-inch deep holes appeared. Wolff skirted them, then decided he should trot. He did not stop until he had reached the foot of the butte. This, like the first they had passed, seemed to be an excrescence, a huge wart on the skin. Though its sides rose perpendicularly, it was wrinkled enough to give hand and footholds. The ascent was not easy but was not impossible. They all got to the top without mishap.

Wolff said, "Yours is the honor again, Vala. Which gate?"

Ariston said, "She hasn't done very well so far. Why let her pick it?"

Vala turned on him like a tigress. "Brother, if you think you can do any better, you choose! But you should show your confidence in yourself by being the first to go through the gate!"

Ariston stepped back and said, "Very well. No use breaking with the custom."

Vala said, "So it's a custom now! Well, I choose the left one."

Wolff did not hesitate. Although he felt that this time he might find himself, weak and weaponless, in Urizen's fortress, he stepped through.

For a moment, he could not understand where he was or what was happening, he was so dizzy and the objects that hurtled above him were so strange.

13

HE WAS ON A HUGE GRAY METALLIC CYLINDER THAT WAS RO-
tating swiftly. Above him, on both sides, and also coming into view as the
cylinder whirled, were other gray cylinders. The sky behind them was a pale
pink.

Between each of the cylinders were three glowing beams of mauve
light. These began about ten feet from the ends of the cylinders and from
the middle. Every now and then, colored lights burst along the lengths of
the beams and ran up and down them. Red, orange, black, white, purple,
they burst like Very lights and then bobbed along the beams as if jerked
along by an invisible cord. When they came to a point about twelve feet
from the cylinders, they flared brightly and quickly died out.

Wolff closed his eyes to fight off the dizziness and the sickness. When
he opened them again, he saw that the others had come through the gates.
Ariston and Tharmas fell to the surface and clung as tightly as they could.
Theotormon sat down as if he feared the spinning would send him scoot-
ing across the metal or perhaps might hurl him out into the space between
the cylinders. Only Vala seemed not to be affected. She was smiling, although it could have been a mere show of courage.

If so, she was to be admired for achieving even this.

Wolff studied the environment as best he could. The cylinders were all
about the size of skyscrapers.

Wolff did not understand why they were not all spun off immediately
by centrifugal force. Surely, these bodies could not have much gravity.

Yet, they did.

Perhaps—no perhaps—Urizen had set up a balance of forces which
enabled objects with such strong gravities to keep from falling on each
other. Perhaps the colored lights that ran along the beams were manifes-
tations of the continual rebalancing of whatever statics and dynamics were
being used to maintain the small but Earth-heavy bodies.

Wolff did not know anything except that the science that the Lords had
inherited was far beyond that which Terrestrials knew.

There must be thousands, perhaps hundreds of thousands, of these cylinders. They were about a mile apart from each other, spinning on their own axes and also shifting slowly about each other in an intricate dance.

From a distance, Wolff thought, the separate bodies would look like one solid bulk. This must be one of the planets he had observed from the waterworld.

There was one advantage to their predicament. On a world as tiny as this one, they would not have to go far to find the next set of gates. But it did not seem likely that Urizen would make things so easy for them.

Wolff stepped back to the gate and tried to reenter it. As he had expected, it only permitted him to step through the frame and back onto the cylinder. He turned and tested its other side, only to find that equally unfruitful. Then he set out to look for the gates by walking around the circumference. And when he had gotten less than halfway around, he saw the two hexagons.

These were at one end and hung a few inches above the surface, the pale sky gleaming pinkly between the lower frame and the cylinder surface. With the others, he set out to walk towards it. He kept his eyes on the gates and tried not to see the whirling shifting objects around him.

Wolff was in the lead and so was the first to notice the unexpected behavior of the twin hexagons. As he came within fifty feet of them, they began to move away. He increased his pace; the gates did not maintain quite the same distance. When he broke into a run, they went more swiftly but still he gained a little. He stopped; the gates stopped. He made a dash at them, only to see them start off just as quickly. As he stepped up his speed, he gained on them.

The other Lords were behind him. Their feet slapped on the metallic surface, and their gaspings whistled through the atmosphere. Wolff stopped again. The gates halted. The other Lords, except Vala, gathered around him and babbled.

"Los! First he starves us to death . . . then runs us to death."

Wolff waited until he had recovered his breath, then said, "I think they can be caught. They began to slow down in their speed as I went faster. It's a proportional decrease. But I don't think I can go quickly enough and long enough to catch them. Who's the fastest here?"

Luvah said, "I could always beat the rest of you in a foot race. But now I am so tired and weak . . ."

"Try," Wolff said.

Luvah grinned uncertainly at him and inched towards the gates. Hovering, they moved away. He broke into a dash and presently was gone around the curve of the cylinder out of their sight. Wolff turned and ran in the opposite direction. After him came Vala. The dizzyingly close horizon jumped at him; he sped on and then he saw Luvah and the gates. Luvah was now within ten feet of them, but he was slowing down. And as his legs refused to move as he wished and his breath burned out of his lungs, the gates drew away.

Wolff came up behind the gates. When he was as close to them as Luvah, the gates slipped sideways, like wet soap between two hands. Vala came in at an angle towards them, but they veered off. The panting Lords stopped, forming three corners of a square with the gates at the remaining corner.

"Where are the others?" Wolff said.

Luvah jerked a thumb. Wolff looked around to see them straggling around the curve of this minute world. He called to them, his voice sounding eerie in the strangely propertied atmosphere. Luvah started to go forward but stopped at Wolff's order.

Ariston, Tharmas, Rintrah, and Theotormon spread out. Under Wolff's directions, they formed a pentagon with the gates at the ends of two legs of the figure. Then all began to close in on their quarry. They kept the same distance between them and advanced at the same pace. The gates oscillated back and forth but made no break.

With two minutes of slow and patient closing in, the Lords were able to seize half of the frames. This time, Wolff did not bother to ask Vala which exit they should take. He went through the left.

The others came through on his heels and their look of dismay reflected his. They were on another cylinder, and down at the end was another pair of hexagons.

Again, they went through the tiring chase and the boxing in. Again, they stepped through a frame, the one to the right this time. Again, they were on another cylinder.

This occurred five times. The Lords looked at each other with fatigue-reddened and exhaustion-circled eyes. Their legs trembled, and their chests ached. They were covered with sweat and were as dry within as a Saharan wind. They could hardly keep their grips on the hexagons.

"We can't go on much longer," Rintrah said.

"Don't be so obvious," Vala said. "Try to say something original once in a while."

"Very well. I'm thirsty enough to drink your blood. And I may if I don't get a drink of water soon."

Vala laughed. "If you come close enough, I'll broach you with this sword. Your blood may be thin and ill-smelling, but at least it should be wet enough."

Wolff said, "Somehow, we always seem to take the gate that leads us everywhere but to Urizen. Perhaps we should split up this time. At least some might get to our father."

The others argued about this, Vala and Luvah only abstaining. Finally, Wolff said, "I'm going through one gate with Vala and Luvah. The rest of you will go through the other. That's that."

"Why Vala and Luvah?" Theotormon said. He was squinting suspiciously, and his voice had a faint whine. "Why them? Do you three know something we don't? Are you planning on deserting us?"

"I'm taking Luvah because he's the only one I can trust—I think," Wolff said. "And Vala is, as she's pointed out more than enough times, the best man among you."

He left them squabbling and, with his sister and Luvah, went through the left gate. A few minutes later, the others came through. They looked bewildered on seeing Wolff, Luvah, and Vala.

"But we went through the right-hand gate," Rintrah said.

Vala laughed and said, "Our father has played us another grim jest. Both gates of a pair lead to the same cylinder. I suspect that they all will."

"He's not playing fair!" Ariston said. At this, Wolff and Luvah laughed, and presently the others, Ariston excepted, had joined him in his mirth.

When the howling—which had a note of despair in it—had died, Wolff said, "I may be wrong. But I think that every one of these thousands of cylinders in this—this *birling* world—has a set of gates. And if we continue the same behavior, we'll go through every one of them. Only we'll die before we get a fraction of the way. We must think of something new."

There was a silence. They sat or lay on the hard gray shiny metal while they whirled around, the cylinders above them rotated about each other in a soundless and intricate saraband, and the twin hexagons at the end hovered and seemed to mock.

Finally, Vala said, "I do not think that we have been left without a way out. It would not be like our father to stop the game while we still have an atom of breath and of fight in us. He would want to drag out the agony until we broke. And I'm sure that he plans on allowing us eventually to find the gate that will conduct us into his stronghold. He must be planning some choice receptions for us, and he would be disappointed if he could not use them.

"So, I think that we have not been using our wits. Obviously, these gates lead only to other sets on other cylinders. That is, they do if we go through the regular way, through the side which is set with jewels. But what if the gates are bipolar? What if the other side would take us where we want to go?"

Wolff said, "I tested the other side when we first came through."

"Yes, you tested the initial gate. But have you tested any of the double gates?"

Wolff shook his head and said, "Exhaustion and thirst are robbing me of my wits. I should have thought of that. After all, it's the only thing left to try."

"Then let's up and at them," Vala said. "Summon your strength; this may be our exit from this cursed birling world."

Once more, they corraled the twin hexagons and seized them. Vala was the first to go through the side opposite the gem-set side. She disappeared, and Wolff followed her. On coming through and seeing another cylinder, he felt his spirits dissipate like wine in a vacuum then he saw the gate at the end and knew that they had taken the correct route.

There was only one golden hexagon. It, too, hovered a few inches above the surface. But it spun on its axis, around and around, completing a cycle every second and a half.

The others came through and cursed when they realized that they were still on a birling. But when they saw the single rotating gate, some brightened up; others sagged at the thought of facing a new peril.

"Why does it whirl?" Ariston said weakly.

"I really can't say, brother," Vala said. "But, knowing Father, I would suspect that the gate has only one safe side. That is, if we choose the right side, we'll go through unharmed. But if we take the wrong side . . . You'll observe that neither side has jewels; both are bare. So there's no way of distinguishing one side from another."

"I am so weary I do not care," Ariston said. "I would welcome death. To sleep forever, free of this agony of body and mind, that is all I desire."

"If you really feel that way," Vala said, "then you should be the first to test the gate."

Wolff said nothing, but the others added their voices to Vala's urgings. Ariston did not seem so eager to die now; he objected, saying that he was not fool enough to sacrifice himself for them.

"You are not only a weakling but a coward, brother," Vala said. "Very well, I will be the first."

Stung, Ariston started towards the spinning hexagon but stopped when a few feet from it. He stared at it and continued to stand motionless while Vala jeered him. She shoved him to one side so hard he staggered and fell on the gray surface. Then she crouched before the golden cycler and studied it intently for several minutes. Suddenly, she launched herself forward and went through the opening headfirst. The gate whirled on around.

Ariston arose without looking at the others or replying to their taunts. He walked up to the gate, bent his knees, and dived through.

And he came out on the other side and fell on the gray surface.

Wolff, the first to him, turned him over.

Ariston's mouth hung open; his eyes were glazing; his skin was turning gray.

Wolff stood up and said, "He went through the wrong side. Now we know what kind of gate this is."

"That bitch Vala has all the luck!" Tharmas said. "Did you notice which side she went through?"

Wolff shook his head. He studied the frame in the pink dusk. There were no markings of any kind on either side to distinguish one from the other. He spoke to Luvah, and they picked up Ariston's body by the feet and shoulders. They swung it back and forth until, at Wolff's shout, they released the corpse at the height of its forward swing. It shot through the frame and came out on the other side and fell on the surface.

Wolff and Luvah went to the other side and once more swung his body and then cast it through the frame. This time it did not reappear. Wolff said to Rintrah, "Are you counting?"

Rintrah nodded his head. Wolff said, "Lift your finger, and when the right side comes around, point it. Do it swiftly!"

Rintrah waited until two more turns had been made, then stabbed his finger. Wolff hurled himself through the frame, hoping that Rintrah had not made a mistake. He landed on Ariston's body. There was the sound of sea and a red sky above. Vala was standing nearby and laughing softly as if she were actually enjoying their father's joke.

They were back on an island of the waterworld.

14

THE OTHER LORDS CAME THROUGH THE GATE ONE BY ONE, RIN-
trah last. They did not look downcast as might have been expected. At least,
they were on familiar grounds, almost home, one might say. And, as
Theotormon did say, they could eat all they wanted.

The gate through which they had entered was the right one of an enormous pair. Both stood on a low hill. The immediate terrain looked familiar. After the Lords had gone to the shore to quench their thirst, they
cooked and ate the fish that Theotormon caught. They set up a guard-
rotation system and slept. The next day, they explored.

There was no doubt that they were back on the great island the natives
called the "Mother of Islands."

"Those gates are the same ones that started us off on the not-so-merry-
go-round," Wolff said. "We went through the right-hand one. So, the left
one may lead to Urizen's world."

Tharmas said, "Perhaps . . . well, this is not the most desirable of worlds.
But it is better to enjoy life here than to die or live in pain in one of Urizen's cells. Why not forget that gate? There is food and water here and native women. Let Urizen sit in his seat of power forever and rot waiting for
us to come to him."

"You forget that, without your drugs, you will get old and will die," Wolff
said. "Do you want that? Moreover, there is no guarantee that Urizen will
not come to us if we don't go to him. No, you may sit here in a lotus-eater's
dream if you want, but I intend to keep fighting."

"You see, Tharmas," Vala said, smiling crookedly. "Jadawin has stronger
reasons than we do. His woman—who is not a Lord, by the way, but an in-
ferior breed from Earth—is a prisoner of Urizen's. He cannot rest while
he knows she is in our father's hands."

"It's up to you to do what you want," Wolff said. "But I am my own
master."

He studied the red heavens, the two huge-seeming planets that were
in sight at this time, and a tiny streak that could have been a black comet.

He said, "Why go through the front door, where Urizen expects us? Why not sneak through the back door? Or, a better metaphor, through a window?"

In answer to their questions, he explained the idea that had come to him when he looked at the other planets and the comet. They replied that he was crazy. His concepts were too fantastic.

"Why not?" he said. "As I've said, everything we need can be gotten, even if we have to go through the gates again. And Appirmatzum is only twenty-five thousand miles away. Why can't we get there with the ship I proposed?"

"A balloon spacecraft?" Rintrah said. "Jadawin, your life on Earth has addled your wits!"

"I need the help of every one of you," Wolff said. "It's an undertaking of large magnitude and complexity. It'll take tremendous labors and a long time. But it can be done."

Vala said, "Even if it can be accomplished, what's to prevent our father from detecting our craft as it comes through the space between this world and his?"

"We'll have to take the chance that he's not set up detectors for spacecraft. Why should he? The only entrance to this universe is through the gate that he made himself."

"But what if one of us is a traitor?" she said. "Have you thought that one of us may be in Urizen's service and so spying for him?"

"Of course I've considered that. So has every one else. However, I can't see a traitor putting himself through the extreme dangers that we just went through."

"And how do we know that Urizen is not seeing and hearing everything right now?" Theotormon said.

"We don't. That's another chance we'll have to take."

"It's better than doing nothing," Vala said.

There was much argument after that with all the Lords finally agreeing to help him in his plan. Even the objectors knew that if Wolff succeeded, those who refused to aid him would be marooned on this island. The thought that their brothers might be true Lords again while the objectors would be no better than the natives was too much for them.

The first thing Wolff did was to find out the temper of the neighboring natives. To his surprise, he found that they were not hostile. They had seen the Lords disappear into the gate and then come out again. Only the gods or demigods could do this; therefore, the Lords must be special—and dangerous—creatures. The natives were more than happy to cooperate with Wolff. Their religion, a debased form of the Lords' original religion, determined this decision. They believed in Los as the good God and in Urizen as the evil one, their version of Satan. Their prophets and medicine men maintained that some day the evil one, Urizen, would be overthrown. When that happened, they would all go to Alulos, their heaven.

Wolff did not try to set them straight on the facts. Let them believe what they wished as long as they helped him. He set everybody to work on the things that could be done immediately and with materials available on this world. Then, he went through the gate that led to the other planets. Luvah went with him. Both were buoyed up by gas-bladders strapped to their backs and armed with short spears and bows and arrows. Through gate after gate they traveled, searching for the things that Wolff needed. They knew what to expect and what dangers to avoid. Even so, the adventures they met on this trip and the many trips thereafter were enough to have filled several books. But there were no more casualties.

Later, Vala and Rintrah accompanied Wolff and Luvah. They brought back chunks of the vitreous stuff from the world of the skating and suction-pad animals. From the Weltthier, they brought back piles of bird-droppings. These, added to the store of their own and the natives' excrement, were to provide the sodium nitrate crystals in Wolff's plan.

The mercury was gotten from the natives, who had large supplies picked up from the island after the showers that came with the black comets. The mercury droplets were religious objects and were given to Wolff only after he argued that they were to be used against Urizen. He discovered that one of the plants on the island was a source of wood alcohol. Other plants could be burned to give the charcoal he needed. And the planet of the tempusfudgers furnished sulphur.

Wolff had to have a platinum catalyst in the making of nitric acid. While on the cylinders of the birling world, he had thought that the cylinders might be composed of platinum or of a platinum alloy. This metal had a melting point of 1773.5 Centigrade and was resistant to cutting. Wolff had no means to melt it in the birling world or any tools sharp enough to cut out chunks from a cylinder. Luvah pointed this out, to which Wolff replied that they would use Urizen's own devices for the job.

He took all the Lords with him, even though Theotormon and Tharmas strongly objected. They cornered the mobile twin gates and then pulled them to the edge of the cylinder. Here Theotormon found out why it was necessary for him to make the trip. His weight was needed to force the gates halfway down over the arc of the edge of the cylinder. The forces that kept the gates upright were strong but could not resist the combined weight and muscles of the Lords.

A portion of the arc went through one of the gates. Had the gate been held motionless, the piece of the cylinder would merely have projected through its matching gate on another cylinder. But when the gate was pulled sidewise along the edge, something had to give. The gate acted like a shears and cut off the part which went through the frame.

After setting the gate upright, the Lords went through it to the next cylinder, where they found a chunk of the platinum. And they used the next gate to cut the chunk into smaller pieces.

On the cylinder of the whirling death-gate, Wolff tested it with several stones. As soon as a stone disappeared, he marked the safe side with a dab of yellow paint brought from the waterworld. Thereafter, they had no trouble distinguishing the death-side from the safe side.

Wolff had the gates that could be moved in the various worlds transported to a more advantageous location.

The island on the waterworld became one vast forge of smoke and stink. The Lords and the natives complained mightily. Wolff listened, scoffed, laughed, or threatened, as the occasion demanded. He drove them on. Three hundred and sixty dark moons passed. The work was slow, disappointing many times, and often dangerous. Wolff and Luvah kept on making trips through the gates, bringing back from the still perilous circuit the materials they needed.

By this time the balloon spacecraft was half-built. When finished, it would ascend with the Lords until it rose above the atmosphere. Here the pseudogravity field weakened rapidly—if Theotormon was to be believed—and the craft would use the drag of the dark moon to pick up more speed. Then blackpowder rockets would give it more velocity. And steering would be done through small explosions of power or through release of gas-jets from bladders.

The gondola would be airtight. Wolff had not yet worked out the problem of air-renewal and circulation or the other problems brought on by nongravity. Actually, they should have a certain amount of gravity. They would not be getting into space as a rocket does, which attains escape velocity. Levitated by the expanding gas in the lift-bladders, they would rise until the atmosphere gave out. Once past the atmosphere, the craft would lose its buoyancy, and would have to depend upon the pull of the moon and the weak reaction of wooden-cased rockets to give them thrust enough to escape the waterworld's grip.

Moreover, if they did pull lose from the waterworld, they would be in danger of being seized by the field of the moon.

"There's no way of determining the proper escape path and necessary vectors by mathematics," Wolff said to Luvah. "We'll just have to play it by ear."

"Let's hope we're not tone-deaf," Luvah said. "Do you think we really have a chance?"

"With what I have in mind, I think there is," Wolff replied. "Just now, today, I want to think of other things. There are the spacesuits to work on for instance. We'll have to wear them while in the gondola, since we can't rely on the gondola being too airtight."

The fulminate of mercury for the explosive caps was made. This was a dark-brown powder formed by reaction of mercury, alcohol, and concentrated nitric acid.

The nitric acid, which oxidized sulfur to sulfuric acid, was obtained through a series of steps. The sodium nitrate, gotten by crystallization from the bird droppings and human excrement, was heated with sulfuric acid. (The sulfuric acid was derived by burning sulfur with saltpeter, that is, potassium or sodium nitrate.)

Free nitrogen of the air was "fixed" by combining it with hydrogen (from the gas bladders) to form ammonia. The ammonia was mixed with oxygen (from an oxygen-producing bladder) at the correct temperature. The mixture was passed over a fine wire gauge made from smooth compact platinum to catalyze for catalysis.

The resulting nitrogen oxides were absorbed in water; the dilute acid was gotten by concentration through distillation.

The materials for the furnaces and containers and pipes were furnished by the vitreous stuff from the planet of skaters.

Black gunpowder was made from charcoal, sulfur, and the saltpeter.

Wolff also succeeded in making ammonium nitrate, a blasting power of considerable power.

One day Vala said, "Don't you think that you're making far too many explosives? We can't take more than a fraction on the ship. Otherwise, the ship'll never get off the ground."

"That's true," he replied. "Maybe you were also wondering why I've stocked the explosives at widely separated locations. That's because gunpowder is unstable. If one pile goes up, the others won't be affected."

Some of the Lords paled. Rintrah said, "You mean the explosives we'll be taking on the ship could go off at any time?"

"Yes. That's one more chance we'll be taking. None of this is easy or safe, you know. But I'd like to add a possibly cheering note. It is ironic and laughable, if we succeed, that Urizen himself has supplied the materials for his own undoing. He has furnished us with the basic weapons which might overthrow his supertechnology."

"If we live, we'll laugh," Rintrah said. "I think, however, that Urizen will be the laughter."

"Old Earth proverb: We'll at least give him a run for his money. Another proverb: He who laughs last laughs best."

That night Wolff went to Luvah's hut. Luvah woke up swiftly on feeling Wolff's hand on his shoulder. He started to draw the knife made of flint from the tempusfudger planet. Wolff said, "I'm here to talk, not kill. Luvah, you are the only one I can trust to help me. And I need help."

"I am honored, brother. You are by far the best man among us. And I know that you are not about to propose treachery."

"Part of what I plan may seem at first to be treachery. But it is necessary. Listen carefully, young brother."

Within the hour, they left the hut. Carrying digging and hacking tools, they went to the hill on which stood the twin gates. Here they were met by twenty natives, all of whom Wolff was sure he could trust. They began cutting and digging through the tangle of decayed vegetation and bladder roots that formed the island. All worked swiftly and hard, so that by the time the moon had passed and taken night with it, they had completed a trench around the hill. They kept on working until there was only a few inches of roots to go before coming to the water level. Then the natives placed ammonium nitrate and fulminate caps in the trench. When this was done, they threw in the chopped up roots and dirt and made an attempt to cover the signs of excavation.

"Anybody can see at a glance that digging has been done here," Wolff said. "I'm banking on nobody coming here, however. I told all of you that today would be a rest day so that you wouldn't rise until late."

He looked at the gates. "Now you and I must travel the circuit again. And we must do it swiftly."

When they came to the planet of the tempusfudgers, Wolff gave Luvah one of his blowguns. This was made of the hollow bamboo-like plants that grew on the mother-island. The natives used them to shoot darts tipped with a stupefacient made from a certain species of fish. They hunted the birds and the rats on the island with these.

Wolff and Luvah went into a canyon and there knocked out five of the fudgers. Wolff searched until he found the entrance to a burrow in which chronowolves lived. He placed the end of the blowgun inside the burrow and expelled the dart. After waiting a minute, he reached in and dragged out a sleeping wolf.

The animals, still unconscious, were cast into the gate that would open into Urizen's world. Or it should lead there. It was possible that both gates merely led to the next secondary planet, as the gates on the birling world had.

"I hope the little animals will trigger off Urizen's alarms," Wolff said. "The alarms will keep him busy for a while. There's also the possibility that the fudgers' and wolf's time-leaping and duplicating abilities will enable them to survive for a while. They may even multiply and spread through the palace and set off any number of traps and alarms. Urizen won't know what the hell's going on. And he'll be diverted from the gate through which he expected us to come."

"You don't know that," Luvah said. "Both these gates here, and both those on the waterworld, may just lead to another secondary."

"Nothing's certain in any of the multitudinous universes," Wolff said. "And even for the immortal Lords, Death waits around every corner. So let's go around the corner."

They passed through the gate into the Weltthier. There was no sign of the chronobeasts. Wolff took heart at this, thinking that the chances were very good that the animals had gone into Urizen's stronghold.

Back upon the waterworld, Luvah went off to accomplish his mission. Wolff watched him go. Perhaps he had been wrong in suspecting Vala of alliance with her father. But she had been too lucky in getting to a safe place whenever danger threatened. She had acted too quickly. Moreover, when they were in the river of the icerock planet, she had been too buoyant and just a little too assured. He suspected that the girdle around her waist contained devices to enable her to float. And there was the choosing of the gates by her. Every time, these had led to a secondary. They should have gone through one of Urizen's gates at least once. She had been too self-assured, even for her. It was as if she were playing a game.

Although she hated her father, she could have joined him to bring her brothers and cousins to death. She hated them as much as she hated her father. She could have transceivers implanted in her body. Thus, Urizen would be able to hear, and probably to see, all that she did. She would enjoy the game as a participant, perversely enjoy it even more if she were in some danger herself.

Urizen could take pleasure in the deadly games as if he were watching a TV set. It would be a genuine spectator sport for him.

Wolff returned to the hill to start the next-to-last phase. The natives were just about finished loading the ship with black powder, ammonium nitrate, and mercury fulminate. The half-built craft consisted of two skeletons of hollow bamboo in which the gas cells had been installed. One was the lower decks of the planned ship; the upper part was supposed to be attached at a later date.

From the beginning, he had known that using the ship as a space traveler was impossible. He doubted very much that it would work, or, if it would, that the voyage between this world and Appirmatzum could be made. The odds were far too high against success.

But he had pretended confidence in it, and so the work had gone on. Moreover, any spy among the Lords, or any other monitor for Urizen, would have been fooled.

Perhaps Urizen was watching him now and wondering what he meant to do. If so, by the time he found out, it would be too late.

The natives released the two halves of the ship from its moorings. They rose several feet and then stopped, weighed down by the several tons of explosives. This altitude was all that Wolff desired. He gave the signal and the natives pushed the crafts up the hill until their prows were almost inside the frame. There was just enough room for the ship to slide through the frames. Wolff had ordered it built in two sections because the fully built ship could not have negotiated the space. Even the partial frames had only an inch on either side on top and bottom to spare.

Wolff lit the fuses on each side of the two floating frameworks and signaled his men. Chanting, they pushed the crafts on in. Wolff, standing to one side, could see the landscape of the island on the other side of the gate. The first ship seemed to be chewed up, or lopped off, as if floated through the gate-frame. Presently, all but the aft of the second was gone, and then that, too, had disappeared.

Luvah appeared from the jungle with Vala's unconscious body over his shoulder. Behind him were the other Lords, alarmed, puzzled, and angry or frightened. Wolff explained to them what he meant to do. He said, "I could tell no one except Luvah because I could trust no one else. I suspect Vala of spying for our father, but she may be innocent. However, I could not take a chance on her. So I had Luvah knock her out while she slept. We'll take her along in case she is not guilty. By the time she wakes up, she'll be in the midst of it. Too late for her to do anything then.

"Now, get into the suits. As I've explained, they'll operate under water as well as in space. Better, since they were designed for diving."

Luvah looked at the gate. "Do you think the explosives went off?"

Wolff shrugged and said, "There's no way of telling. It's a one-way gate, of course, so there'll be no indication from the other side. But I hope that by now Urizen's initial traps have been destroyed. And I hope he's very upset, wondering what we've done."

Luvah put a suit on Vala and then donned one himself. Wolff supervised the touching off of the fuses to the explosives planted at the bottom of the ditch around the hill. The fuses led through hollow bamboo pipes to the gunpowder, ammonium nitrate, and fulminate of mercury.

15

THERE WAS A RUMBLE AND A SHAKING OF THE EARTH. UP ROSE the decayed vegetation and the roots in a great cloud of black smoke. When the debris had settled and the smoke had blown away, Wolff led the Lords towards the hill. It was sinking swiftly; its anchorage to the rest of the island severed and the lower part ripped apart. Under the weight of the heavy golden hexagons, it went down.

Wolff threw several fuse-lit bombs at the base of the gates to hasten the descent to the sea. The gates began to topple. Wolff held his men steady until the upper part struck the sides of the pit formed by the explosion. As the gates slid into the water below, he gave the order to jump. His mask over his face, the air tanks turned on, a flint-tipped spear in one hand, and a flint knife and flint axe in his belt, he leaped into the water.

The top of the gates disappeared just as he came up to the surface for a better look. The water was so foul with bits of roots and humus that he could not see anything. He grabbed the top of the frame and let its weight pull him down. It was on its way to the bottom of the sea, but he could go only a little way with it.

He felt Luvah, who was holding Vala in one arm, grab his ankle with the other. Another Lord should be getting hold of Luvah's ankle. Theotormon would be the only free swimmer until they got through the gate.

Wolff made sure, by feeling, that he was at the left gate. Then he began swimming. He had no trouble entering the gate. The inrush of sea-water carried him on in.

The current carried him down a long hall. The walls were self-luminous and radiated enough light for him to make out details. Some of the wall-plates were partially ripped off or bent. Down at the end of the hall, two thick white metal doors were twisted grotesquely. The explosion had done its work well. It was conceivable that the doors could have sealed off the rest of the palace from the flood of water. Eventually, the pressure of water from the sea bottom would have burst them open. By that time, the Lords would also have been dead from pressure.

Wolff went through the crumpled doors and on down another corridor. Seeing it come to an end, he twisted around until his feet were ahead of him. The water boiled at its end, striking the wall and then going off down a slightly sloping corridor. Wolff took the impact with his feet, shoved, and was off with the current down the hall. The light showed him a series of long metal spikes below him. Undoubtedly, they were prepared for the invading Lords, who were now passing above them.

The corridor suddenly dipped, and the water was racing down a fifty-degree angle. Wolff barely had time to see that it branched into two other corridors before he was carried helplessly out the great window at the end.

He fell, whirling over and over, seeing the palace walls rush by and a garden below. He was being hurled down by a cascade formed by the sea spouting out the window.

The crash into the pool at the bottom of the falls stunned him. Half-conscious, he swam up and away and was at the edge of the pool. Originally, the pool had been a sunken garden. Lucky for him, he thought, otherwise, he would have been smashed to death. He dragged himself up over the lip of stone, still clutching his spear.

The other Lords came bobbing up one by one. Theotormon was first. Luvah was next, with a conscious, and frightened, Vala behind him. Rintrah, swam in a few seconds later. Tharmas floated into the edge of the pool. He was face down, his arms, outspread. Wolff pulled him up and turned him over. He must have smashed into the side of the window before being carried out. His leg was snapped at the knee and the side of his face was crushed in.

Vala stormed at Wolff. He told her to shut up; they did not have time for talking. In a few words he explained what he had done and why.

Vala recovered quickly. She smiled, though still pale, and said, "You have done it again, Jadawin! Turned Urizen's own devices against him!"

"I do not know if you are guilty of allying yourself with our father or not," Wolff said. "Perhaps I am overly suspicious, though it may be impossible to be that when dealing with a Lord. If you are innocent, I will apologize. If not, well, our father must by now be convinced that you have betrayed him and are with us. So he will kill you before you can explain, unless you kill him first. You have no choice."

"Jadawin, you were always a fox! So be it! I will kill our father the first chance I get! Who knows, I may have the chance! I would have sworn up to a few hours ago that we would be trapped as soon as we entered his domain! But here we are, and he has a deadly problem on his hands!"

She pointed up at the great window through which the sea was cataracting. "Obviously the gate is on the highest level of the palace. And water flows downward. If he doesn't do something soon, he will be drowned like a rat caught in its own hole."

She turned to indicate the land outside the palace. "As you can see, the palace is in a valley surrounded entirely by high mountains. It will take some time, but the entire sea of the waterworld will come through the gates, unless the matching gates on the waterworld settle on a shallow bottom. This valley will be flooded, and then the water will spill over the mountains and inundate the rest of the planet."

Rintrah said, "Why don't we just climb the mountains and watch our father drown?"

Wolff shook his head. "No, Chryseis is in there."

Rintrah said, "What is that to the rest of us?"

"Urizen will have flying craft," Wolff said. "If he escapes the palace in one, he will pick us off. Even if we should hide from him, we would be doomed. He has merely to leave us here. Eventually, this world will be flooded. We will be trapped, perhaps to starve again. No, if you want to get away from here and back to your own universe, you will have to help me kill Urizen."

He said to Theotormon, "You were allowed a little freedom while you were his prisoner. If we could find the area you know, we could better avoid traps."

"There is an entrance at the bottom of the sunken garden, which is now a pool," Theotormon said. "That would be the best way to enter. We can swim up to the levels that are not yet flooded. If we avoid contact with the floor and walls, we can prevent setting off the traps."

They plunged into the water and, hugging the sides of the pool to avoid the impact of the falling waters, swam around behind the cataract. It was easy to locate the door, since a current was roaring through it. They let it sweep them through until they came to a staircase. This was broad and built of sculptured red and black stone. They swam up it and after many turnings, came to another level. This, too, was flooded, so they continued their ascent. The next floor was inches deep in water and filling swiftly. The Lords climbed on up the stairs until they were on the fourth story.

Urizen's palace was like every Lord's, magnificent in every respect. At another time, Wolff might have lingered to look at the paintings, drapes, sculptures, and treasures, loot of many worlds. Now he had but two thoughts. Kill Urizen and save his great-eyed wife, Chryseis.

Wolff looked around before giving the word to advance. He said, "Where's Vala?"

"She was behind me a moment ago," Rintrah said.

"Then she's in no trouble," Wolff replied. "But *we* may be. If she's sneaked off to join Urizen . . ."

"We'd better get to him before she does," Luvah said.

Wolff led the way, expecting at every second a trap. There was, however, a chance that Urizen had not set any here. Undoubtedly, there would be defenses at every entrance. But Urizen may have thought himself safe here. Moreover, the water pouring through from above and below might have deactivated the power supplies. Whatever contingency Urizen had prepared himself for, he had never thought of another planet's seas emptying themselves into his domain.

Theotormon said, "The floor above is the one where I was kept prisoner. Urizen's private apartments are also there."

Wolff took the first staircase they came to. He walked up slowly, looking intently for signs of traps. They came without mishap to the next floor and then stood for a moment. The closer they got to Urizen, the more nervous they became. Their hate was beginning to be tinged with some of the old awe they had felt for him when they were children.

They were in a huge chamber, the walls of which were white marble. There were many bas-reliefs carved on them, scenes from many planets. One showed Urizen seated on a throne. Below him, a new universe was forming out of chaos. Another scene showed him standing in a meadow with children at play around him. Wolff recognized himself, his brothers, sisters, and cousins. Those had been happy times, even though there were shadows now and then to forecast the days of hate and anxiety.

Theotormon said, "You can hear the rumble of the water above. It won't be long until this floor, too, is flooded."

"Chryseis is probably held in the same area in which you were prisoner," Wolff said. "You lead the way there."

Theotormon, his rubbery legs acting as springs, went swiftly. He traced his way without hesitation through a series of rooms and halls that would have been a bewildering labyrinth to a stranger.

Theotormon stopped before a tall oval entrance of scarlet stone with purplish masses that formed ragged silhouettes of winged creatures. Beyond was a great chamber that glowed a dull red.

"That is the room in which I spent most of my time," he said. "But I fear to go through the doorway."

Wolff extended his spear through the archway. Theotormon said, "Wait a minute. It may have a delayed reaction to catch whoever goes on it."

Wolff continued to hold the spear. He counted the seconds, estimating how far within the chamber he would have gone if he walked on in. There was a flare of light that blinded him and sent him reeling back.

When he regained his sight, he saw that his spear was shorn off. Heat billowed out from the expanding air in the chamber, and there was the odor of charred wood.

"Lucky for you that most of the heat was localized and went upward," Theotormon said.

The trap covered about twenty yards. Beyond that the room might be safe. But how to get past the death that waited?

He stepped back some paces, cast the butt of the spear through the archway, and turned his back. Again, light burst forth, driving the shadows of the Lords down along the corridor and then sending a wave of heat out after them. Wolff turned and threw an arrow into the room and gave the archway his back again while he counted. Three seconds passed before the trap was sprung again.

He gave an order and they returned to the level staircase, which was half below the rising waters. They put on their oxygen masks and dipped themselves into the water. Then they ran down the hall as swiftly as they could, hoping that the water would not dry off them. At the archway, Wolff tossed another arrow through. As soon as the light died, but before the heat had thoroughly dissipated, he dashed into the chamber. Behind him came Theotormon and Luvah. They had three seconds to cover twenty yards and a few feet. They made it. With the heat drying off the film of water on their suits and warming their backs. But they were through.

Rintrah cast an arrow into the room, and he and Tharmas ran into the heat. Wolff had turned around to watch him as soon as the light disappeared. He cried out because Tharmas had hesitated. Tharmas did not heed his warning to wait and try again, perhaps because he did not hear it. He was racing desperately, his eyes wide behind the goggles. Wolff shouted to the others to turn away as Rintrah sped past him. There was another nova of light, a scream, and a thud. Heat billowed over the Lords; they smelled the charred fish skin of the suit and burned human flesh.

Tharmas was a dark mass on the floor, his fingers and toes almost burned off.

Without a word, the others turned away and went on through the room. Near its other archway, Theotormon led them through a very narrow doorway, although he did not do so until after it had been tested. They came into a hemispherical room at least one hundred yards across. Within the room were many large cages, all empty except for one.

Wolff saw the occupant of the cage first.

He cried out, "Urizen!"

16

THE CAGE WAS TEN FEET BY TEN. IT WAS FURNISHED ONLY WITH a thin blanket on the floor, a pipe for drinking water, a hole for excretion, and an automatic food dispenser. The man within it was very tall and very thin. He had the face of a bearded and starved falcon. His hair fell down his back to his calves, and his beard hung below his knees. The black hairs were threaded with gray, by which Wolff knew that his father had been a long time in the cage. Even after the so-called immortality drugs were cut off, their effect lasted for years.

Urizen advanced towards the bars but he was careful not to touch them. Wolff warned the others back in a low voice. He walked up to the bars as if he meant to grip them. Urizen watched him with deep-sunken and feverish eyes but did not open his mouth. A few inches from the bars, Wolff stopped and said, "Do you still hate us so much, Father, that you would let us die?"

He raked the bars with the tip of an arrow; veins of light ran over the metal.

Urizen smiled grimly and spoke in a hollow, painshot voice, "Touching the bars is only painful, not fatal. Ah, Jadawin, you were always a fox! No one but you could have gotten this far. No one but you and your sister, Vala, and perhaps Red Orc."

"So she did evade all your traps and snared the snarer," Wolff said. "She is indeed a remarkable woman, my sister."

"Where is she?" Urizen asked. "Did she die this time? I know that she was with you because she told me what she intended to do."

"She is in the palace and still to be reckoned with," Wolff said. "All this time, she had us convinced that you were in the Seat of Power. She was playing with us, sharing our dangers, pretending to be our ally. I suspected her of working with you, but this . . . I never dreamed of."

"I am doomed," Urizen said. "I cannot get out; you cannot open this cage to release me. Even if you wanted to, you could not. And I must die soon unless I can get help. Vala has implanted a slowly acting and painful cancerous growth within me. In fact, she has done this three times, only to remove it each time before I died and then nurse me back to health."

"I would be lying if I said I was sorry, and you know it," Wolff said. "You are getting what you deserve."

"Moral lectures from you, Jadawin!" Urizen said. His eyes blazed with the old fire, and Wolff felt something within him quail. The dread of his father had not died yet.

"I heard that you had changed much since your life on Earth, but I could not believe it. Now I know it is true."

"I did not come here to argue with you," Wolff said. "There is little time for talk left, anyway. Tell me, Father, how we can get to the control room safely. If you want vengeance, you must tell us. Vala is loose again and probably in the control room right now."

Urizen said, "Why should I tell you anything? I am going to die, but I will at least have the pleasure of knowing that you, Luvah, and Theotormon will die with me."

"Does it give you pleasure to know that Vala will triumph? That she will live on? That your body, too, will be stuffed and mounted in the trophy hall?"

Urizen smiled bitterly. "If I tell you what you want, then Vala might die, but you would live. It is a loathsome choice to make. Either way, I lose."

"You may hate us," Wolff said, "but we have never done anything to you. Yet Vala . . ."

Theotormon said, "The seas will soon be flooding this level. Then we all die. And Vala, safe in her control room, will laugh. And she will take whatever vengeance she has been planning against Chryseis."

Wolff felt helpless. He could not threaten Urizen to make him talk. What more could he do to him than had been done?

He said, "Let's go. We can't waste any more time." To Urizen, he said, "Good-bye forever, Father. You must die and soon. You hold revenge against Vala in your heart, and if you would unlock your lips, you would get it. But hatred blinds you and makes you rob yourself."

Urizen called after them, "Wait!"

Eagerly, Wolff returned to the cage. Urizen licked his lips and said, "If I tell you, will you do me one favor?"

"I can't free you, Father," Wolff said. "You know we have no time to figure out how to do it. Moreover, even if I could, I wouldn't. I would kill you before I would loose you upon the world."

"The favor I trade is exactly that," Urizen said. "Death. I am suffering agonies, my son. My pride forbade me to say so until now. But one more minute of this life seems like a thousand years to me. If it were not for my pride, I would have gone down on my knees before you long ago, would have begged you to put me out of my torture. That I would never do. Urizen does not beg. But a trade, that is another thing."

"I agree," Wolff said. "An arrow between the bars will do it."

Urizen whispered and in a few words told them what they needed to know. He had just finished when there was laughter at the far end of the room. Wolff whirled to see Vala walking towards them. He fitted an arrow to a bow-string, knowing as he did so that Vala would not have shown herself unless she felt sufficiently protected.

Then he saw through Vala to the wall behind her and knew that it was a projection. He hoped that she had not also overheard Urizen. If she had, she would be able to do what she wished with them.

"I could not have done better if I had planned it this way," her image said. "It is fitting, and my greatest desire, to have all of you die together. A happy family reunion! You may witness each other's death struggles. How nice!

"And I will be leaving this planet and this universe and may then trap the surviving brother, and my beloved sister, Anana. Only I will rest for a while and amuse myself with your Chryseis."

"You have failed so far, and you will continue to fail!" Wolff shouted. "Even if you kill us, you will not live long to enjoy your triumph! You know about the *etsfagwo* poison of the natives of the waterworld, don't you? How it can be served in food and leaves no taste? How it goes through the veins and stays there for a long time with no ill effect? And then it suddenly reacts and doubles the victim up in terrible pain that lasts for hours? And how there is no antidote?

"Well, Vala, I suspected you of treachery. So I had the *etsfagwo* put in your supper last night. It will soon take hold of you, Vala, and then you will not be able to laugh about us."

Wolff had not done this and until this moment had not even thought of doing so. But he was determined that if he died, Vala would pay for it with some hours of mental anguish.

The image screamed with fury and desperation. It said, "You are lying, Jadawin! You would not do this; you could not! You are just trying to scare me!"

"You will know whether I tell the truth or not in a very short time!" Wolff shouted. He turned to shoot the arrow through the bars of the cage to fulfill his promise to Urizen. As he shifted, he saw Vala's image flicker out of existence. Immediately thereafter, a green foam spurted out of hidden pipes in the ceiling. It shot down with great force, spread out, rose to the knees of the Lords, and set them to coughing with its acrid fumes. Wolff's eyes watered, and he bent over. He leaned down to pick up the bow and arrow which he had dropped. The fumes made him cough even more violently.

Suddenly, the foam was to his neck. He struggled to get through it and to the door at the far end, although there might be another trap waiting there. The foam rose above his head. He held his breath while he put his air-mask on. Then he lifted it a little from his face and blew out the foam it had collected. He hoped the others had enough presence of mind to think of their masks.

Within a few steps of the exit, he felt the foam begin to harden. He strove against it, pushing as hard as he could. It continued to resist him, to reduce his progress to a very slow motion. Abruptly, the foam became a jelly and the green opacity cleared away. He was caught like a fly in amber.

Wolff could not see the others, who were behind him. He was facing the archway towards which he had struggled. He tried to move his arms and legs and found that he could make a little progress. With a vast effort, he could shove himself forward less than an inch. Then the jelly, like a tide, moved him back again and settled around him. There was nothing he could do except wait for his air supply to run out. The breathing system was a closed system, one that re-used air and did not dissipate the carbon dioxide. If it had been an open system, he would have been dead already. The jelly closed in around so tightly that there would have been no place for the breathed-out carbon dioxide to go.

He had perhaps a half-hour of life remaining. Vala would be laughing now. And Chryseis, great-eyed beautiful Chryseis, what was she doing? Was she being forced to watch this scene? Or was she listening to Vala's descriptions of what Vala intended for her?

Fifteen minutes passed by with his every thought seeking a way out. There was none. This was the end of over 25,000 years of life and the powers of a god. He had lived for nothing; he might as well never have been born. He would die, and Chryseis would die, and both would be stuffed and mounted and placed on exhibit in the trophy hall.

No, that was not true, at least. Vala would have to abandon this place. The waters roaring through the permanent gate at the top level of the palace would ensure that. She would be denied this pleasure. His body, and Chryseis', would lie beneath a sea, in darkness and cold, until the flesh rotted and the bones were tossed back and forth by the currents and strewn about.

The waters! He had forgotten that they were racing through the halls of the levels above and down the staircases. If only . . .

The first rush half-filled the corridor beyond the archway and ripped out a chunk of jelly. The corridor was quickly filled, and the jelly began to dissolve. The process took time, however. The waters crept towards him, eating their way and turning the jelly into a green foam that was absorbed by the liquid. More than half an hour had passed since he had estimated that he had about thirty minutes of air left. He felt that every breath would be his last.

The jelly became green foam and obscured his vision. The thick stuff melted away, and he was free. But now he was in as much danger as before. Submerged in water, he would drown as soon as the air ran out.

He swam towards the others, whom he could see through a green veil. He yanked them loose from the jelly that still held them, only to find that Rintrah was dead. He had gotten his mask on in time but something had gone wrong. Wolff gestured at Theotormon and Luvah and swam towards the other exit. It opened to their only hope. To try to go through the door through which the seas were pushing was impossible because of the current. They were carried, like it or not, towards the other archway.

Wolff dug at the jelly which clogged the doorway until it broke loose, and he was carried headlong into the next room. His brothers came at his heels and slid on their faces across the room and piled into him against the opposite wall. They rolled out of the stream and were on their feet. Wolff turned the air off and lifted his mask. He not only had to speak to them, but there would be a minute or two before the room filled in which they could conserve what little supply remained in the tanks.

"Urizen told me that there is a secret door to a duplicate control room! He had it prepared in case somebody ever did get into the main control room! It has controls which will deactivate those of the main room! But to get to it, we have to go through the doorway with the heat-ray trap. He didn't have time to tell me how to turn off the heat-rays! We'll put our masks back on when the water gets too high and then go through. The water should knock the projectors out! I hope!"

They placed the masks over their faces and crouched in a corner near the archway to gain protection from the full force of the current. The sea struck the wall opposite the archway and then raced off down the floor and through the door. Seeing that the water was not activating the rays, Wolff hurled his stone axe towards the door. Even through his closed lids, he saw the dazzle. When he opened his eyes, the water was boiling. The axe had been swept on through the arch.

The waters rose swiftly, carrying the treading Lords up towards the ceiling. When there was only a foot of air between the sea and the ceiling, they put on their masks. Wolff dived as close towards the floor as he could get and began swimming. Suddenly, the air shut off. He held his breath and continued swimming. There was a glare of light that blinded him, and the water seemed to burn his exposed hands and back of neck. He bumped against the side of the arch and was borne out into the next room. Here he shoved his feet against the floor and propelled himself upward. He held his hands out to soften the impact against the ceiling, which he could not yet see.

His head bumping against stone, he removed his mask and breathed in. His lungs filled with air, then water slapped him in the mouth and he coughed. His vision returned; Theotormon and Luvah were beside him. Wolff lifted his hand and pointed downward. "Follow me!"

He dived, his eyes open, his hands sliding along the wall. There was a green jade statue, a foot high, once an idol of some people in some universe, squatting in a niche. Wolff rotated its head, and a section of the wall opened inwards. The three Lords were carried into the large room. They scrambled to their feet, and Wolff ran to a console and pulled on a red-handled lever. The door closed slowly against the pressure of the water, leaving a foot of water in the room.

Identifying the console Urizen had told him about (there were at least thirty), Wolff pressed down a rectangular plate on which was an ideogram of the ancient writing once used by the Lords. He stepped back with the first smile he had had for a long time.

"Vala not only won't be able to use her controls any more," he said, "she's trapped in her control room as well. And all gates of escape in the room are deactivated. Only the permanent gates in the palace, like the gate to the waterworld, are still on."

Wolff reached towards the button that would activate the viewscreen in the other control room. He withdrew his hand and stood in thought for a moment.

"The less our sister knows of the true situation, the better for us," he said. "Theotormon, come here and listen carefully."

Wolff and Luvah hid behind a console and peered through a narrow opening between the console and its screen. Theotormon pushed the button with the end of his flipper. Vala was staring at him, her long hair dark-red with damp and her face twisted with fury.

"You!" she said.

"Greetings, sister," Theotormon answered. "Are you surprised to see me still living? And how do you feel knowing that I have sealed off your escape and rendered you powerless?"

"Where are your brothers, your betters?" Vala said, trying to see past him into the room.

"They're dead. Their airtanks gave out and so did mine. But this body that our father gave me enabled me to hold my breath until the water washed away your jelly."

"So Jadawin is finally dead? I don't believe it. You are trying to play a trick on me, you stupid slug!"

"You're in no position to call names."

"Let me see his body," she said.

Theotormon shrugged. "That's impossible. He's floating somewhere in the palace. I barely made it to this room myself. I can't go out to get him without flooding this room."

Vala looked at the water on the floor and then she smiled. "So you're trapped, too. You fish-stinking idiot, you don't even have the brains of a fish! You just told me what your situation is!"

Theotormon gaped. He said, "But . . . but . . ."

"You may think you have me in your power," Vala said. "And so you do, in a manner of speaking. But you are just as much in mine. I know where the spacecraft is. It can get us off this planet and to another, which has a gate through which we can leave this universe. Now, what do you propose to do about this impasse?"

Theotormon scratched the fur on his head with the tip of a flipper. "I don't know."

"Oh, yes, you do! You're stupid, but not that stupid! You'll make a trade with me. You let me out, and I'll let you leave with me in the ship. There's no other way out for either of us."

Wolff could not see Theotormon's expression, but he could deduce from his tone the cunningness and suspicion on his face.

"How do I know I can trust you?"

"You don't, any more than I can trust you. We'll have to arrange this so neither of us can possibly trip the other up. Do you agree?"

"Well, I don't know . . ."

"This control room won't be harmed if the seas get a mile high and sit forever on the palace. I have food and water enough for a year. I can just sit here and let you die. And then I'll figure some way to get out, believe me. I'll discover a way."

"In that case," Theotormon said, "why don't you do it?"

"Because I don't want to stay in this room for a year. I have too many things to do."

"All right. But what about Chryseis?"

"She comes with me. I have plans for her," Vala said.

Her voice became even more suspicious. "Why should you care about her?"

"I don't. I just wondered. Maybe . . . maybe you could give her to me. From what Jadawin said, she must be very beautiful."

Vala laughed and said, "That would be one form of torture for her. But it isn't enough. No, you can't have her."

"Then it's not a deal," Theotormon said. "You keep her. See how you like being cooped up with her for a year. Besides, I don't really think you can swim to the spacecraft. The water pressure will be too much."

Vala said, "You stupid selfish slimegut! You'd die yourself rather than let me have anything! Very well, take her then!"

Wolff smiled. He had told Theotormon to bring up Chryseis and so take her mind off him. This business about Chryseis was just irrelevant enough and so Theotormonically selfish that she might be convinced that he was not hiding the truth.

Theotormon clapped his flippers together with glee. Wolff hoped that his joy was all act, since he was not sure that Theotormon might not betray him at the last moment. Theotormon said, "All right. Now, how can we get to the spacecraft?"

"You'll have to release me first. I'm not going to tell you and then have you take off without me."

"But if I open the door to your room, you'll be able to get out ahead of me."

"Can't you set the controls so they'll open the doors by the time you get here?"

Theotormon grunted as if the thought were a new one. "All right. Only, you'll have to come out of the room with absolutely no clothes on. You must be both nude and emptyhanded. I'll come out of my room weaponless. We'll both leave at exactly the same time and meet in the corridor that links the two rooms."

Vala gasped and said, "I thought . . . ! You mean you knew all the time how to get here . . . so that's where the other controls are! And I thought the other end of the corridor was a wall."

"It won't do you any good to know," Theotormon said. "You can't get out until I let you. Oh, yes, strip Chryseis, too. I don't want you to hide any weapons on her."

Vala said, "You're not taking any chances, are you? Perhaps you're more intelligent than I thought."

What was she planning? If she did meet him in the middle of the corridor, she would be helpless against Theotormon's far greater strength. He would attack her the moment she revealed the location of the spacecraft, and she must know that.

The truth was that Wolff, Luvah, and Theotormon knew where the ship was. Theotormon had pretended ignorance only to seem to give her an advantage. She had to be lured out of the room, otherwise she would never come out. Wolff knew his sister. She would die and take Chryseis with her rather than surrender. To her it was inconceivable that a Lord would keep a promise not to harm her. She had good reason. In fact, Wolff himself, though he never thought of himself as a genuine Lord anymore, was not sure he would have kept his word to her. Certainly, he did not intend that Theotormon adhere to his assurances.

Then what did she have in mind?

Theotormon went over the method of conduct with Vala again, pretending that he was not quite sure. Then he deactivated the screen and turned to Wolff and Luvah. Wolff opened the door into the corridor so that he and Luvah could go out ahead of time. As Theotormon had said, the corridor linked the two control rooms. Both control rooms and the hall between were in an enclosed unit of fourteen feet-thick metal alloy. The unit could hold any pressure of water and was resistant even to a direct hit by a hydrogen bomb. The interior wall was coated with a substance which would repel the neutrons of a neutron bomb. Urizen had placed the secret control room in this unit, near the main control room for just such situations as this. Anyone who managed to get into the main room would not know that there was an exit to the corridor until part of the seemingly solid wall of the main control room opened.

The corridor itself, though an emergency convenience, had been furnished as if a reception for Lords were to be held in it. It contained paintings, sculptures, and furniture that a Terrestrial billionaire could not have purchased with all his fortune. A chandelier made from a single carved diamond, weighing half a ton, hung from a huge gold alloy chain. And this was not the most valuable object in the corridor.

Wolff hid behind a davenport covered with the silky chocolate-and-azure hide of an animal. Luvah concealed himself behind the base of a statue. Theotormon made sure that they were ready and returned to the control room to inform Vala that they could now proceed to meet each other as planned. He then pressed the button that operated the door to Vala's room.

The wall at the other end of the corridor slid upwards. Light poured out of the opening, and Vala stuck her head cautiously around the frame. Theotormon did the same from his door. He stepped out quickly, ready to hurl himself back if she had a weapon. She gave a low laugh and came out of the doorway, her hands held out to show their emptiness. She was naked and magnificent.

Wolff gave her a glance. He had eyes only for the woman who followed her. It was his Chryseis, the beautiful huge-eyed nymph with tiger-striped hair. She, too, was unclothed.

"The Horn of Shambarimen," Theotormon said. "I almost forgot! Where is it?"

"It is in the control room," Vala replied. "I did not bring it because you told me to be empty-handed."

"Go get it, Chryseis," Theotormon said. "But when you return with it, hold it up above your head at arm's length and do not point it at me. If you make a sudden motion with it, I will kill you."

Vala's laughter filled the corridor. "Are you so suspicious that you suspect even her? She would not hurt you! She is definitely not going to do anything for me!"

Theotormon did not reply. Instructed by Wolff, he was playing the role of the overly alert Lord to keep Vala from suspecting any treachery. If Theotormon had been too trusting, she would have scented something foul at once.

Vala and Theotormon then advanced towards each other, taking a step forward slowly and in unison. It was as if they were partners in a formal dance, they moved so stately and in such matching rhythm.

Wolff crouched and waited. He had taken his suit off so that it would not hinder his movements. The sweat of tension covered his body. Neither he nor Luvah were armed. They had lost all their own weapons before they reached the secret room. And the room, to his dismay, had contained no arms. Apparently, Urizen had not thought it necessary. Or, much more likely, there were weapons hidden behind the walls, accessible only to one who knew how to find them. Urizen had not had time to give that information—if he had ever intended to do so.

The plan was to wait until Vala had passed Luvah, hidden on the other side of the hall. When he rushed out behind her, Theotormon would jump her. Wolff would hurl himself from his hiding palace and help the other two.

Vala stopped several feet away from the diamond chandelier. Theotormon also stopped. She said, "Well, my ugly brother, it seems that you have kept your side of the bargain."

He nodded and said, "So where is the spaceship?"

He went forward one step in the hope that she, too, would take one and so place herself nearer. Vala stood still, however. Mockingly, she said, "The entrance to it is just on the other side of that rose-shaped mirror. You could have gone to it and left me to die—if you had known about it! You witless filth!"

Theotormon snarled and leaped at her. Luvah came out from behind the statue but bumped into Chryseis. Wolff rose and sped straight at Vala.

She screamed and held up her right hand, the palm at right angles to her arm, fingers stiffly pointing toward the ceiling. Out of the palm shot an intensely white beam no thicker than a needle. She moved her hand to her left in a horizontal arc. The beam slashed across Theotormon's neck, and his head fell off. For a moment, the body stood upright, blood fountaining upward from his neck. Then he fell forward.

Wolff whirled like a broken-field runner. He threw himself down on the floor behind Theotormon's feet. Vala, hearing Luvah curse as he recovered from his bump into Chryseis, spun around. Evidently she thought that this was the nearest danger and that she had enough time to deal with Wolff.

Chryseis had reacted quickly. On seeing the head of the seal-man fall off and roll back behind Theotormon, she had dived for the protection of a statue. Vala's ray took off a chunk of the base of the statue but missed Chryseis. Then Luvah was coming in, head down. Vala leaped adroitly aside and chopped down with the edge of the palm of her left hand. Luvah fell forward on his face, unconscious.

Why she had not killed him with the tiny beamer implanted in the flesh of her palm was a mystery. Perhaps she wanted someone to save as a torture victim, in keeping with the psychology of the Lords.

Wolff was helpless, or so Vala thought. She advanced towards him.

"You I shall kill now," she said. "You're too dangerous to leave alive for a second longer than necessary."

"I'm not dead yet," Wolff said. His fingers closed on Theotormon's head, and he hurled it at her. He was up on his feet at once and running towards her, knowing that he did not have a chance but hoping that something would happen to deflect her aim long enough.

She raised her hand to ward off the grisly projectile. The beam split the head in half, but one section continued to fly towards her.

The ray, directed towards the ceiling momentarily, cut the gold alloy chain. And the half-ton diamond chandelier came down upon her.

Wolff was still charging while all this occurred. He dived on the floor to be below her line of fire in case she was still living and could use the hand. She glared up at him, the light not yet gone from her eyes. Her arms and her body were pinned beneath the diamond, from beneath which blood ran.

"You . . . did it, brother," she gasped.

Chryseis came out from behind the statue to throw herself in his arms. She clung to him and sobbed. He could not blame her for this, but there were still things to do.

He kissed her a few times, hugged her, and pushed her away from him.

"We have to get out while we can," he said. "Push in on the third gargoyle to the left on the upper decoration on that mirror."

She did so; the mirror swung in. Wolff put his unconscious brother on his shoulders and started towards the entrance. Chryseis said, "Robert! What about her?"

He stopped. "What about her?"

"Are you going to let her suffer like this? It may take a long time before she dies."

"I don't think so," he said. "Besides, she has it coming."

"Robert!"

Wolff sighed. For a moment, he had been a complete Lord again, had become the old Jadawin.

He put Luvah on the floor and walked over to Vala. She twisted, and her hand came loose, a section of the shorn diamond falling over onto the floor. Wolff leaped at her and caught her hand just as the ray shot forth from the palm. He twisted her hand so violently that the bones cracked. She cried out once with pain before she died.

Directed by Wolff, the laser beam had half-guillotined her.

Wolff, Chryseis, and Luvah entered the spaceship. It rose straight up the launching shaft to the very top of the palace. Wolff headed the ship for the exit-gate, hidden in the mountains of the tempusfudger planet. Only then did he have time to find out how Vala had managed to get Chryseis from her bed and out of their world.

"The hexaculum awoke me," she said, "while you were still sleeping. It—Vala's voice—warned me that if I tried to wake you, you would be killed in a horrible way. Vala told me that only by following her instructions would I prevent your death."

"You should have known better," he said. "If she had been able to hurt me, she would have done it. But then, I suppose that you were too concerned for me. You did not dare to take the chance that she might be bluffing."

"Yes. I wanted to cry out, but I was afraid that she might be able to carry out her threats. I was so terrified for you that I was not thinking straight. So I went through the gate she designated, one of those gates that take you to a lower level of our planet. I deactivated the alarms before entering it, as she ordered. Vala was waiting in the cave where our gate took me. She had already set up a gate to take us to this universe. The rest you know."

Wolff turned the controls over to Luvah so that he could embrace and kiss her. She began to weep, and soon he was weeping, too. His tears were not only from relief for having gotten her back unharmed and relief from the unrelenting strain of the experiences in this world. He wept for his dead brothers and sister. He did not mourn those who had just died, the adults. He mourned for his brothers and sister as the children they had once been and for the love they had had for each other as children. He grieved for the loss of what they might have been.

A

PRIVATE COSMOS

INTRODUCTION

IT ALL GOES BACK TO MY CHILDHOOD OF ABOUT A YEAR AGO, WHEN I read *The Maker of Universes*. I recall it to have been a sunny Saturday in Baltimore and its morning, when I picked up Philip José Farmer's book with the green Gaughan sky and the gray Gaughan harpy (Podarge) on the front, to read a page or two before beginning work on a story of my own. I didn't do any writing that day.

I finished reading the book and immediately dashed off to my local purveyor of paperbacks, to locate the sequel which I knew existed, *The Gates of Creation*. When I'd finished reading it, the sunny morning in Saturday and its Baltimore had gone away and night filled the day all the way up to the top of the sky. The next thing that I wrote was not my story, but a fan letter to Philip José Farmer.

My intention was not to tell the man who had written *The Lovers* and *Fire and the Night* and *A Woman A Day* that I thought these two new ones were the best things he had ever done. If he'd done a painting, composed a piece of music, I couldn't compare them to his stories or even to each other. The two books I had just then finished reading were of the adventure-romance sort, and I felt they were exceedingly good examples of the type. They are different from his other stories, styles, themes, different even from each other, and hence, as always, incomparable. I had hoped there would be a third one, and I was very pleased to learn that he was working on it.

In other words, I looked forward for over a year to the book you are presently holding in your hands.

In considering my own feelings, to determine precisely what it was that caused me to be so taken by the first two books, I found that there are several reasons for the appeal they hold for me:

1) I am fascinated by the concept of physical immortality and the ills and benefits attendant thereto. This theme runs through the books like an highly polished strand of copper wire. 2) The concept of pocket universes— a thing quite distinct, as I see it, from various parallel worlds notions—the

idea of such universes, specifically created to serve the ends of powerful and intelligent beings, is a neat one. Here it allows for, among other things, the fascinating structure of the World of Tiers.

To go along with these concepts, Philip Farmer assembled a cast of characters of the sort I enjoy. Kickaha is a roguish fellow; heroic, tricky and very engaging. Also, he almost steals the first book from Wolff. The second book is packed with miserable, scheming, wretched, base, lowdown, mean and nasty individuals who would cut one another's throats for the fun of it, but unfortunately have their lots cast together for a time. Being devilish fond of the Elizabethan theater, I was very happy to learn early in the story that they were all of them close relatives.

> A sacred being may be attractive or repulsive—a swan or an octopus—beautiful or ugly—a toothless hag or a fair young child—good or evil—a Beatrice or a Belle Dame Sans Merci—historical fact or fiction—a person met on the road or an image encountered in a story or a dream—it may be noble or something unmentionable in a drawing room, it may be anything it likes on condition, but this condition is absolute, that it arouse awe.
>
> *Making, Knowing and Understanding*
> W. H. Auden

Philip José Farmer lives West of the Sun at the other end of the world from me in a place called California. We have never met, save in the pages of his stories. I admire his sense of humor and his facility for selecting the perfect final sentence for everything he writes. He can be stark, dark, smoky, bright, and any color of the emotional spectrum. He has a fascinating sense of the Sacred and the Profane. Put quite simply, he arouses awe. He has the talent and the skill to handle the sacred objects every writer must touch in order to convert the reader, in that timeless, spaceless place called Imagination.

Since I've invoked Auden, I must go on to agree with his observation that a writer cannot read another author's things without comparing them to his own. I do this constantly. I almost always come out feeling weak as well as awed whenever I read the works of three people who write science fiction: Sturgeon, Farmer and Bradbury. They know what's sacred, in that very special transsubjective way where personal specifics suddenly give way and become universals and light up the human condition like a neon-lined Christmas tree. And Philip José Farmer is special in a very unusual way . . .

Everything he says is something *I* would like to say, but for some reason or other, cannot. He exercises that thing Henry James called an "angle of vision" which, while different from my own a.v., invariably jibes with the way I feel about things. But I can't do it his way. This means that somebody can do what I love most better than I can, which makes me chew my beard and think of George London as Mephistopheles, back at the old Metropolitan Opera, in Gounoud's *Faust,* when Marguerita ascended to heaven: he reached out and an iron gate descended before him; he grasped a bar, looked On High for a moment, averted his face, sank slowly to his knees, his hand sliding down the bar: curtain then: that's how I feel. *I* can't do it, but *it* can be done.

Beyond this, what can I say about a particular Philip José Farmer story? Shakespeare said it better, in *Antony and Cleopatra:*

> *Lepidus.* What manner o' thing is your crocodile?
> *Antony.* It is shaped, sir, like itself; and it is as broad as it hath breadth. It is just so high as it is, and moves with its own organs. It lives by that which nourisheth it; and the elements once out of it, it transmigrates.
> *Lepidus.* What color is it of?
> *Antony.* Of its own color, too.
> *Lepidus.* 'Tis a strange serpent.
> *Antony.* 'Tis so. And the tears of it are wet.
> (Act II, Scene VII.)

Indeed, Sir, they are. It is the skill that goes with the talent that makes them so. Each of its products are different, complete, unique, and this one is no exception. I rejoice that such a man as Philip José Farmer walks among us, writes there, too. There aren't many like him. None, I'd say.

But read his story and see what I mean.

Now it is a cold, gray day in February and its Baltimore. But it doesn't matter. Philip José Farmer, out there somewhere West of the Sun, if by your writing you ever intended to give joy to another human being, know by this that you have succeeded and brightened many a cold, gray day in the seasons of my world, as well as having enhanced the lighter ones with something I'll just call splendor and let go at that.

The colors of this one are its own and the tears of it are wet. Philip José Farmer wrote it. There is nothing more to say.

ROGER ZELAZNY
Baltimore, Md.

1

UNDER A GREEN SKY AND A YELLOW SUN, ON A BLACK STALLION
with a crimson-dyed mane and blue-dyed tail, Kickaha rode for his life.

One hundred days ago, a thousand miles ago, he had left the village of
the Hrowakas, the Bear People. Weary of hunting and of the simple life,
Kickaha suddenly longed for a taste—more than a taste—of civilization.
Moreover, his intellectual knife needed sharpening, and there was much
about the Tisquetmoac, the only civilized people on this level, that he did
not know.

So he put saddles and equipment on two horses, said goodbye to the
chiefs and warriors, and kissed his two wives farewell. He gave them permission to take new husbands if he didn't return in six months. They said
they would wait forever, at which Kickaha smiled, because they had said
the same thing to their former husbands before these rode out on the
warpath and never came back.

Some of the warriors wanted to escort him through the mountains to
the Great Plains. He said no and rode out alone. He took five days to get
out of the mountains. One day he was lost because two young warriors of
the Wakangishush tribe stalked him. They may have been waiting for
months in the Black Weasel Pass, knowing that some day Kickaha would
ride through it. Of all the greatly desired scalps of the hundred great warriors of the fifty Nations of the Great Plains and bordering mountain ranges,
the scalp of Kickaha was the most valued. At least two hundred braves had
made individual efforts to waylay him, and none had returned alive. Many
war parties had come up into the mountains to attack the Hrowakas' stockaded fort on the high hill, hoping to catch the Bear People unawares and
lift Kickaha's scalp—or head—during the fighting. Of these, only the great
raid of the Oshangstawa tribe of the Half-Horses had come near to succeeding. The story of the raid and of the destruction of the terrible Half-
Horses spread through the 129 Plains tribes and was sung in their council
halls and chiefs' tepees during the Blood Festivals.

The two Wakangishush kept a respectable distance behind their quarry.

They were waiting for Kickaha to camp when night came. They may have succeeded where so many others had failed, so careful and quiet were they, but a red raven, eagle-sized, flew down over Kickaha at dusk and cawed loudly twice.

Then it flew above one hidden brave, circled twice, flew above the tree behind which the other crouched, and circled twice. Kickaha, glad that he had taken the trouble to train the intelligent bird, smiled while he watched it. That night, he put an arrow into the first to approach his camp and a knife into the other three minutes later.

He was tempted to go fifty miles out of his way to hurl a spear, to which the braves' scalps would be attached, into the middle of the Wakangishush encampment. Feats such as this had given him the name of Kickaha, that is, Trickster, and he liked to keep up his reputation. This time, however, it did not seem worthwhile. The image of Talanac, The City That Is A Mountain, glowed in his mind like a jewel above a fire.

And so Kickaha contented himself with hanging the two scalpless corpses upside down from a branch. He turned his stallion's head eastward and thereby saved some Wakangishush lives and, possibly, his own. Kickaha bragged a lot about his cunning and speed and strength, but he admitted to himself that he was not invincible or immortal.

Kickaha had been born Paul Janus Finnegan in Terre Haute, Indiana, U. S. A., Earth, in a universe next door to this one. (All universes were next door to each other.) He was a muscular broad-shouldered youth six feet one inch tall and weighing 190 pounds. His skin was deeply tanned with slightly copper spots, freckles, here and there, and more than three dozen scars, varying from light to deep, on parts of his body and face. His reddish-bronze hair was thick, wavy, and shoulder-length, braided into two pigtails at this time. His face was usually merry with its bright green eyes, snub nose, long upper lip, and cleft chin.

The lionskin band around his head was edged with bear teeth pointing upward, and a long black-and-red feather from the tail of a hawk stuck up from the right side of the headband. He was unclothed from the waist up; around his neck was a string of bear teeth. A belt of turquoise-beaded bearskin supported dappled fawnskin trousers, and his moccasins were lionskin. The belt held a sheath on each side. One held a large steel knife; the other, a smaller knife perfectly balanced for throwing.

The saddle was the light type which the Plains tribes had recently adopted in place of blankets. Kickaha held a spear in one hand and the reins in the other, and his feet were in stirrups. Quivers and sheaths of leather hanging from the saddle held various weapons. A small round shield on which was painted a snarling bear's head was suspended from a wooden hook attached to the saddle. Behind the saddle was a bearskin robe rolled to contain some light cooking equipment. A bottle of water in a clay wicker basket hung from another saddle hook.

The second horse, which trotted along behind, carried a saddle, some weapons, and light equipment.

Kickaha took his time getting down out of the mountains. Though he softly whistled tunes of this world, and of his native Earth, he was not care-free. His eyes scanned everything before him, and he frequently looked backward.

Overhead, the yellow sun arced slowly in the cloudless light green sky. The air was sweet with the odors of white flowers blooming, with pine needles, and an occasional whiff of a purpleberry bush. A hawk screamed once, and twice he heard bears grunting in the woods.

The horses pricked up their ears at this but they did not become nervous. They had grown up with the tame bears that the Hrowakas kept within the village walls.

And so, alertly but pleasantly, Kickaha came down off the mountains onto the Great Plains. At this point, he could see far over the country because this was the zenith of a 160 mile gentle curve of a section. His way would be so subtly downhill for eighty miles that he would be almost unaware of it. Then there would be a river or lake to cross, and he would go almost imperceptibly up. To his left, seeming only fifty miles away, but actually a thousand, was the monolith of Abharhploonta. It towered a hundred thousand feet upward, and on its top was another land and another monolith. Up there was Dracheland, where Kickaha was known as Baron Horst von Horstmann. He had not been there for two years, and if he were to return, he would be a baron without a castle. His wife on that level had decided not to put up with his long absences and so had divorced him and married his best friend there, the Baron Siegfried von Listbat. Kickaha had given his castle to the two and had left for the Amerind level, which, of all levels, he loved the most.

His horses pulling the ground along at a canter, Kickaha watched for signs of enemies. He also watched the animal life, comprised of those still known on Earth, of those that had died off there, and of animals from other universes. All of these had been brought into this universe by the Lord, Wolff, when he was known as Jadawin. A few had been created in the biolabs of the palace on top of the highest monolith.

There were vast herds of buffalo, the small kind still known in North America, and the giants that had perished some ten thousand years ago on the American plains. The great gray bulks of curving-tusked mammoths and mastodons bulked in the distance. Some gigantic creatures, their big heads weighted down with many knobby horns and down-curving teeth projecting from horny lips, browsed on the grass. Dire wolves, tall as Kickaha's chest, trotted along the edge of a buffalo herd and waited for a calf to stray away from its mother. Further on, Kickaha saw a tan-and-black striped body slinking along behind a clump of tall grass and knew that Felis

Atrox, the great maneless nine hundred pound lion that had once roamed the grassy plains of Arizona, was hoping to catch a mammoth calf away from its mother. Or perhaps it had some faint hopes of killing one of the multitude of antelope that was grazing nearby.

Above, hawks and buzzards circled. Once, a faint V of ducks passed overhead and a honking floated down. They were on their way to the rice swamps up in the mountains.

A herd of gawky long-necked creatures, looking like distant cousins of the camel, which they were, lurched by him. There were several skinny-legged foals with them, and these were what a pack of dire wolves hoped to pull down if the elders became careless.

Life and the promise of death was everywhere. The air was sweet; not a human being was in sight. A herd of wild horses galloped off in the distance, led by a magnificent roan stallion. Everywhere were the beasts of the plains. Kickaha loved it. It was dangerous, but it was exciting, and he thought of it as his world—his despite the fact that it had been created and was still owned by Wolff, the Lord, and he, Kickaha, had been an intruder. But this world was, in a sense, more his than Wolff's, since he certainly took more advantage of it than Wolff, who usually kept to the palace on top of the highest monolith.

The fiftieth day, Kickaha came to the Tishquetmoac Great Trade Path. There was no trail in the customary sense, since the grass was no less dense than the surrounding grass. But every mile of it was marked by two wooden posts the upper part of which had been carved in the likeness of Ishquet-tlammu, the Tishquetmoac god of commerce and of boundaries. The trail ran for a thousand miles from the border of the empire of Tishquetmoac, curving over the Great Plains to touch various semipermanent trading places of the Plains and mountain tribes. Over the trail went huge wagons of Tishquetmoac goods to exchange for furs, skins, herbs, ivory, bones, captured animals, and human captives. The trail was treaty-immune from attack; anyone on it was safe in theory, at least, but if he went outside the narrow path marked off by the carved poles, he was fair prey for anybody.

Kickaha rode on the trail for several days because he wanted to find a trade-caravan and get news of Talanac. He did not come across any and so left the trail because it was taking him away from the direct route to Talanac. A hundred days after he had left the Hworakas village, he encountered the trail again. Since it led straight to Talanac, he decided to stay on it.

An hour after dawn, the Half-Horses appeared.

Kickaha did not know what they were doing so close to the Tishquetmoac border. Perhaps they had been making a raid, because, although they did not attack anybody on The Great Trade Path, they did attack Tishquetmoac outside it.

Whatever the reason for their presence, they did not have to give Kickaha an excuse. And they would certainly do their best to catch him, since he was their greatest enemy.

Kickaha urged his two horses into a gallop. The Half-Horses, a mile away to his left, broke into a gallop the moment they saw him racing. They could run faster than a horse burdened with a man, but he had a good lead on them. Kickaha knew that an outpost was four miles ahead and that if he could get within its walls, he would be safe.

The first two miles he ran the stallion beneath him as swiftly as it would go. It gave its rider everything it had; foam blew from its mouth and wet his chest. Kickaha felt bad about this, but he certainly wasn't going to spare the animal if foundering it meant saving his own life. Besides, the Half-Horses would kill the stallion for food.

At the end of the two miles, the Half-Horses were close enough for him to determine their tribe. They were Shoyshatel, and their usual roving grounds were three hundred miles away, near the Trees of Many Shadows. They looked like the centaurs of Earth myth, except that they were larger and their faces and trappings certainly were not Grecian. Their heads were huge, twice as large as a human being's, and the faces were dark, high-cheekboned, and broad, the faces of Plains Indians. They wore feathered bonnets on their heads or bands with feathers; their hair was long and black and plaited into one or two pigtails.

The upright human body of the centaur contained a large bellows-like organ to pump air into the pneumatic system of the horse part. This swelled and shrank below the human breastbone and added to their weird and sinister appearance.

Originally, the Half-Horses were the creations of Jadawin, Lord of this universe. He had fashioned and grown the centaur bodies in his biolabs. The first centaurs had been provided with human brains from Scythian and Sarmatian nomads of Earth and from some Achaean and Pelasgian tribesmen. So it was that some Half-Horses still spoke these tongues, though most had long ago adopted the language of some Amerindian tribe of the Plains.

Now the Shoyshatel galloped hard after him, almost confident that they had their archenemy in their power. *Almost* because experience had disillusioned many of the Plains people of the belief that Kickaha could be easily caught. Or, if caught, kept.

The Shoyshatel, although they lusted to capture him alive so they could torture him, probably intended to kill him as soon as possible. Trying to take him alive would require restraint and delicacy on their part, and if they restrained themselves, they might find that he was gone.

Kickaha transferred to the other horse, a black mare with silver mane and tail, and urged it to its top speed. The stallion dropped off, its chest white with foam, shaking and blowing, and then fell when a Half-Horse speared it.

Arrows shot past him; spears fell behind him. Kickaha did not bother returning the fire. He crouched over the neck of his mare and shouted encouragement. Presently, as the Half-Horses drew closer, and the arrows and spears came nearer, Kickaha saw the outpost on top of a low hill. It was square and built of sharpened logs set upright in the ground, and had overhanging blockhouses on each side. The Tishquetmoac flag, green with a scarlet eagle swallowing a black snake, flew from a pole in the middle of the post.

Kickaha saw a sentry stare at them for a few seconds and then lift the end of a long slim bugle to his lips. Kickaha could not hear the alarm because the wind was against him and also because the pound of hooves was too loud.

Foam was pouring from the mare's mouth, but she raced on. Even so, the Half-Horses were drawing closer, and the arrows and spears were flying dangerously near. A bola, its three stones forming a triangle of death, almost struck him. And then, just as the gates to the fort opened and the Tishquetmoac cavalry rode out, the mare stumbled. She tried to recover and succeeded. Kickaha knew that the mishap was not caused by fatigue but by an arrow, which had plunged slantingly into her rump, piercing at such a shallow angle that the head of the arrow was out in the air again. She could not go much longer.

Another arrow plunged into the flesh just behind the saddle. She fell, and Kickaha threw himself out and away as she went down and then over. He tried to land running but could not because of the speed and rolled over and over. The shadow of the rolling horse passed over him; she crashed and lay still. Kickaha was up and running toward the Tishquetmoac.

Behind him, a Half-Horse shouted in triumph, and Kickaha turned his head to see a feather-bonneted chief, a spear held high, thundering in toward him. Kickaha snatched his throwing knife out, whirled, took a stance, and, as the centaur began the cast of spear at him, threw his knife. He jumped to one side immediately after the blade had left his hand. The spear passed over his shoulder, near his neck. The Half-Horse, the knife sticking out of the bellows organ below his chest, cartwheeled past Kickaha, bones of equine legs and backbone of the human upright part cracking with the impact. Then spears flew over Kickaha into the Half-Horses. One intercepted a brave who thought that he had succeeded where the chief had failed. His spear was in his hand; he was trusting to no skill in casting but meant to drive it through Kickaha with the weight of his nine hundred pound body.

The brave went down. Kickaha picked up the spear and hurled it into the horse-breast of the nearest centaur. Then the cavalry, which outnumbered the Half-Horses, was past him, and there was a melee. The Half-

Horses were driven off at great cost to the human beings. Kickaha got onto a horse which had lost its master to a Half-Horse tomahawk and galloped with the cavalry back to the post.

The commander of the outpost said to Kickaha, "You always bring much trouble with you. Always."

Kickaha grinned and said, "Confess now. You were glad for the excitement. You've been bored to death, right?"

The captain grinned back.

That evening, a Half-Horse, carrying a shaft of wood with a long white heron's feather at its tip, approached the fort. Honoring the symbol of the herald, the captain gave orders to withhold fire. The Half-Horse stopped outside the gates and shouted at Kickaha, "You have escaped us once again, Trickster! But you will never be able to leave Tishquetmoac, because we will be waiting for you! Don't think you can use the Great Trade Path to be safe from us! We will honor the Path; everyone on it will be untouched by the Half-Horses! Everyone except you, Kickaha! We will kill you! We have sworn not to return to our lodges, our women and children, until we have killed you!"

Kickaha shouted down to him, "Your women will have taken other husbands and your children will grow up without remembering you! You will never catch or kill me, you half-heehaws!"

The next day a relief party rode up, and the Tishquetmoac cavalry on leave rode out with Kickaha to the city of Talanac. The Half-Horses did not appear, and after Kickaha had been in the city for a while, he forgot about the threats of the Shoyshatel. But he was to remember.

2

THE WATCETCOL RIVER ORIGINATES IN A RIVER WHICH branches off from the Guzirit in Khamshemland, or Dracheland, on the monolith Abharhploonta. It flows through dense jungle to the edge of the monolith and then plunges through a channel which the river has cut out of hard rock. The river falls for a long distance as solid sheets of water, then, before reaching the bottom of the hundred thousand foot monolith, it becomes spray. Clouds roll out halfway down the monolith and hide the spray and foam from the eyes of men. The bottom is also hidden; those who have tried to walk into the fog have reported that it is like blackest night and, after a while, the wetness becomes solid.

A mile or two from the base the fog extends, and somewhere in there the fog becomes water again and then a river. The stream flows through a narrow channel in limestone and then broadens out later. It zigzags for about five hundred miles, straightens out for twenty miles and then splits to flow around a solid rock mountain. The river reunites on the other side of the mountain, turns sharply, and flows westward for sixty miles. There it disappears into a vast cavern, and it may be presumed that it drops through a network of caverns inside the monolith on top of which is the Amerindian level. Where it comes out, only the eagles of Podarge, Wolff, and Kickaha know.

The mountain which the river has islanded was a solid block of jade.

When Jadawin formed this universe, he poured out a three thousand foot high, roughly pyramid-shaped piece of mingled jadeite and nephrite, striated in apple-green, emerald-green, brown, mauve, yellow, blue, gray, red, and black and various shades thereof. Jadawin deposited it to cool on the edge of the Great Plains and later directed the river to flow around its base.

For thousands of years, the jade mountain was untouched except by birds that landed on it and fish that flicked against the cool greasy roots. When the Amerindians were gated through to his world, they came across the jade mountain. Some tribes made it their god, but the nomadic peoples did not settle down near it.

Then a group of civilized people from ancient Mexico were taken into this world near the jade mountain. This happened, as nearly as Jadawin (who later became Wolff) could recall, about 1,500 Earth-years ago. The involuntary immigrants may have been of that civilization which the later Mexicans called Olmec. They called themselves Tishquetmoac. They built wooden houses and wooden walls on the bank to the west and east of the mountain, and they called the mountain Talanac. Talanac was their name for the Jaguar God.

The *kotchulti* (literally, god-house) or temple of Toshkouni, deity, of writing, mathematics, and music, is halfway up the stepped-pyramid city of Talanac. It faces the Street of Mixed Blessings, and, from the outside, does not look impressively large. The front of the temple is a slight bulging of the mountainside, a representation of the bird-jaguar face of Toshkouni. Like the rest of the interior of this mountain, all hollowing out, all cleaving away, all bas- and alto-relief, have been done by rubbing or drilling. Jade cannot be chipped or flaked; it can be drilled, but most of the labor in making beauty out of the stone comes from rubbing. Friction begets loveliness and utility.

Thus, the white-and-black striated jade in this area had been worn away by a generation of slaves using crushed corundum for abrasives and steel and wooden tools. The slaves had performed the crude basic labor; then the artisans and artists had taken over. The Tishquetmoac claim that form is buried in the stone and that it is revealed seems to be true—in the case of Talanac.

"The gods hide; men discover," the Tishquetmoac say.

When a visitor to the temple enters through the doorway, which seems to press down on him with Toshkouni's cat-teeth, he steps into a great cavern. It is illuminated by sunlight pouring through holes in the ceiling and by a hundred smokeless torches. A choir of black-robed monks with shaven, scarlet-painted heads stands behind a waist-high white-and-red jade screen. The choir chants praises to the Lord of The World, Ollimaml, and to Toshkouni.

At each of the six corners of the chamber stands an altar in the shape of a beast or bird or a young woman on all fours. Cartographs bulge from the surfaces of each, and little animals and abstract symbols, all the result of years of dedicated labor and long-enduring passion. An emerald, as large as a big man's head, lies on one altar, and there is a story about this which also concerns Kickaha. Indeed, the emerald was one of the reasons Kickaha was so welcome in Talanac. The jewel had once been stolen and Kickaha had recovered it from the Khamshem thieves of the next level and returned it—though not gratis. But that is another story.

Kickaha was in the library of the temple. This was a vast room deep in the mountain, reached only by going through the public altar room and a long wide corridor. It, too, was lit by sunlight shooting through shafts in the ceiling and by torches and oil lamps. The walls had been rubbed until thousands of shallow niches were made, each of which now held a Tishquetmoac book. The books were rolls of lambskin sewn together, with the roll secured at each end to an ebony-wood cylinder. The cylinder at the beginning of the book was hung on a tall jade frame, and the roll was slowly unwound by the reader, who stood before it.

Kickaha was in one well-lit corner, just below a hole in the ceiling. A black-robed priest, Takoacol, was explaining to Kickaha the meaning of some cartographs. During his last visit, Kickaha had studied the writing, but he had memorized only five hundred of the picture-symbols, and fluency required knowing at least two thousand.

Takoacol was indicating with a long-nailed yellow-painted finger the location of the palace of the emperor, the *miklosiml.*

"Just as the palace of the Lord of this world stands on top of the highest level of the world, so the palace of the *miklosiml* stands on the uppermost level of Talanac, the greatest city in the world."

Kickaha did not contradict him. At one time, the capital city of Atlantis, the country occupying the inner part of the next-to-highest level, had been four times as large and populous as Talanac. But it had been destroyed by the Lord then in power, and now the ruins housed only bats, birds, and lizards, great and small.

"But," the priest said, "where the world has five levels, Talanac has thrice three times three levels, or streets."

The priest put the tips of the excessively long fingernails of his hands together, and, half-closing his slightly slanted eyes, intoned a sermon on the magical and theological properties of the numbers three, seven, nine, and twelve. Kickaha did not interrupt him, even though he did not understand some of the technical terms.

He had heard, just once, a strange clinking in the next room. Just once was enough for him, who had survived because he did not have to be warned twice. Moreover, the price he paid for still living was a certain uncomfortable amount of anxiety. Always, he maintained a minimum amount of tension even in moments of recreation and lovemaking. Thus, he never entered a place, not even in the supposedly safe palace of the Lord, without first finding the possible hiding places for ambushers, avenues of escape, and hiding places for himself.

He had no reason to think that there was any danger for him in this city and especially in the sacrosanct temple-library. But there had been many times when he had had no reason to fear danger and yet the danger was there.

The clinking was weakly repeated. Kickaha, without an "Excuse me!" ran to the archway through which the unidentified, hence sinister, noise had come. Many of the black-robed priests looked up from their slant-topped desks where they were painting cartographs on skin or looked aside from the books hanging before them. Kickaha was dressed like a well-to-do Tishquetmoac, since his custom was to look as much like a native as possible wherever he was, but his skin was two shades paler than the lightest of theirs. Besides, he wore two knives, and that alone marked him off. He was the first, aside from the emperor, to enter this room armed.

Takoacol called out to him, asking if anything was wrong. Kickaha turned and put a finger to his lips, but the priest continued to call. Kickaha shrugged. The chances were that he would end up by seeming foolish or overly apprehensive to the onlookers, as had happened many times in other places. He did not care.

As he neared the archway, he heard more clinkings and then some slight creakings. These sounded to him as if men in armor were slowly—perhaps cautiously—coming down the hallway. The men could not be Tishquetmoac because their soldiers wore quilted-cloth armor. They had steel weapons, but these would not make the sounds he had heard.

Kickaha thought of retreating across the library and disappearing into one of the exits he had chosen; in the shadows of an archway, he could observe the newcomers as they entered the library.

But he could not resist the desire to know immediately who the intruders were. He risked one fast peek around the corner.

Twenty feet away walked a man in a complete suit of steel armor. Close behind him, by twos, came four knights, then at least thirty soldiers, swordsmen and archers. There might be more because the line continued on around the curve of the hall. Kickaha had been surprised, startled, and shocked many times before. This time, he reacted more slowly than ever in his life. For several seconds, he stood motionless while the ice-armor of shock thawed.

The knight in the lead, a tall man whose face was visible because of the opened visor of his helmet, was the king of Eggesheim, Erich von Turbat.

He and his men had no business being on this level! They were Drachelanders of the level above this, all natives of the inland plateau on top of the monolith which soared up from this level. Kickaha, who was known as Baron Horst von Horstmann in Dracheland, had visited the king, von Turbat, several times and once had knocked him off a horse in a joust.

To see him and his men on this level was startling enough, since they would have had to climb down a hundred thousand feet of monolith cliff to get to it. But their presence within the city was incomprehensible. Nobody had ever penetrated the peculiar defences of the city, except for Kickaha on one occasion, and he had been alone.

Unfreezing, Kickaha turned and ran. He was thinking that the Teutoniacs must have used one of the "gates" which permitted instantaneous transportation from one place to another. However, the Tishquetmoac did not know where the three "gates" were or even guessed that they existed. Only Wolff, who was the Lord of this universe, his mate Chryseis, and Kickaha had ever used them; or, theoretically, they were the only ones who knew how to use them.

Despite this, the Teutoniacs were here. How they had found the gates and why they had come through them to this palace were questions to be answered later—if ever.

Kickaha felt a surge of panic which he rammed back down. This could only mean that an alien Lord had successfully invaded this universe. That he could send men after Kickaha meant that Wolff and Chryseis were unable to prevent him. And that might mean they were dead. It did mean that, if they were alive, they were powerless and therefore needed his help. Ha! His help! He was running for his life again!

There were three hidden gates. Two were in the Temple of Ollimaml on top of the city, next to the emperor's palace. One gate was a large one and must have been used by von Turbat's men if they had entered in any force. And they must have great force, otherwise they would never have been able to overcome the large and fanatical bodyguard of the emperor and the garrison.

Unless, Kickaha thought, unless the invaders had somehow been able to capture the emperor immediately. The Tishquetmoac would obey the commands of their ruler, even if they knew they originated from his captors. This would last for a time, anyway. The people of Talanac were, after all, human beings, not ants, and they would eventually revolt. They regarded their emperor as a god incarnate, second only to the all-powerful creator Ollimaml, but they loved their jade city, too, and they had a history of twice committing deicide.

In the meantime . . . in the meantime, Kickaha was running toward the archway opposite the one through which the invaders must be stepping just now. A shout spurred him on, then many were yelling. Some of the priests were crying out, but several of the cries were in the debased Middle High German of the Drachelanders. A clash of armors and of swords formed a base beneath the vocal uproar.

Kickaha hoped that the hallway was the only one the Drachelanders were using. If they had been able to get to all the entrances to this room— no, they couldn't. The arch ahead led to a hall which only went deeper into the mountain, as far as he knew. It could be entered by other halls, but none of these had openings to the outside. That is, he had been told so. Perhaps his informants were lying for some reason, or perhaps they hadn't understood his imperfect Tishquetmoac speech.

Lied to or not, he had to take this avenue. The only trouble with it, even if it were free of invaders, was that it would end up in the mountain.

3

THE LIBRARY WAS AN IMMENSE ROOM. IT HAD TAKEN FIVE HUN-
dred slaves, rubbing and drilling twenty-four hours a day, twenty years to
complete the basic work. The distance from the archway he had just left
to the one he desired was about 180 yards. Some of the invaders had time
to enter the library and take one shot at him.

Knowing this, Kickaha began to zigzag. When he neared the arch, he
threw himself down and rolled through the exit. Arrows slissed above him
and kukked into the stone wall or bunged off the floor near him. Kickaha
uncoiled to his feet and raced on down the hallway; he came to the inevitable curve, and then stopped. Two priests trotted past him. They looked
at him but said nothing. They forgot about him when shrill cries stung their
ears, and they ran toward the source of noise. He thought they would be
acting more intelligently if they ran the other way, since it sounded as if
the Drachelanders might be massacring the priests in the library.

However, the two would now run into the pursuers, and might delay
them for a few seconds. Too bad about the priests, but it wasn't his fault if
they were killed. Well, perhaps it was. But he did not intend to warn them
if silence would help him keep ahead of the hunters.

He ran on. Just before he came to another forty-five degree bend, he
heard screams behind him. He stopped and removed a burning torch from
its fixture on the wall. Holding it high, he looked upward. Twenty feet from
the top of his head was a round hole in the ceiling. It was dark, so Kickaha
supposed that the shaft bent somewhere before it joined another.

The entire mountain was pierced with thousands of these shafts. All
were at least three feet in diameter, since the slaves who had made the
shafts and tunnels could not work in an area less than this.

Kickaha considered this shaft but gave up on it. There was nothing available to help him get up to it.

Hearing the scrape of metal against stone, he ran around the curve and
then stopped. The first archer received a blazing torch in his face,

screamed, staggered back, and knocked down the archer behind him. The conical steel helmets of both fell off and clanged on the floor.

Stooping, Kickaha ran forward, using the archer with the burned face, who had sat up, as a shield. He pulled the archer's long sword from his sheath. The man was holding his face with both hands and screaming that he was blind. The soldier he had knocked down stood up, thus preventing the bowmen who did see Kickaha from shooting at him. Kickaha rose and brought the sword down on the unprotected head of the soldier. Then he whirled and ran, stooping again.

Too late, some of the bowmen fired. The arrows struck the walls. He entered a large storage room. There were many artifacts here, but those catching his attention were long extendible ladders for use in the library. He set one upright, its end propped against the lip of a shaft in the ceiling. He placed the sword at the foot of the ladder, then picked up another ladder and ran with it down the hall, went through a doorway into a branching hall, and stopped below another shaft.

Here he propped the ladder against the edge of the hole in the ceiling and climbed up. By bracing his back against one side of the shaft and his feet against the other, he could thrust-slide his body up the hollow.

He hoped that the first ladder and the sword by it would fool his pursuers, so they would waste time shooting arrows up its dark hole. When they realized he was not to be brought down like a bear in a hollow tree, they would think that he had managed to get to a branching shaft in time. Then some of them would go up the shaft after him. If they were smart, they would delay long enough to take off their heavy chain-mail shirts, skirts, leggings, and steel helmets.

If they were smart enough, though, they would also realize that he might be playing a trick. They would explore the halls deeper in. And they might soon be under this shaft and send an arrow through his body.

Inspired by this thought, he climbed more swiftly. He would back upward several inches, feet planted firmly, legs straining. Then he'd slide the feet up, then the back up, then the feet up—at least the walls were smooth and greasy-feeling jade, not rough steel, stone, or wood. After he had gone perhaps twenty feet upward—which meant a drop of forty feet to the floor—he came to a shaft which ran at right angles to his.

He had to twist around then so that he faced downward. He could see that the ladder still lay propped against the bright end of the shaft. There was no sound coming up the well. He pulled himself up and onto the horizontal floor.

At that moment, he heard a faint voice. The soldiers must have fallen for his ruse. They were either coming up that first tube after him or had already done so and were, possibly, in the same horizontal shaft in which he was.

Kickaha decided to discourage them. If he did find a way out, he might also find that they were right behind him—or worse, just below him. They could have passed bows and arrows from one to another up the shaft; if they had, they could shoot him down without danger to themselves.

Trying to figure out the direction of the shaft where he had left the first ladder, he came to a junction where three horizontal tunnels met above a vertical one. There the twilight of the place became a little brighter. He leaped across the hole in the floor and approached the brightening. On coming around a bend, he saw a Teutoniac bending over with his back to him. He was holding a torch, which a man in the vertical shaft had just handed to him. The man in the hole was muttering that the torch had scorched him. The man above was whispering fiercely that they should all be quiet.

The climbers had shed their armor and all arms except the daggers in the sheaths on their belts. However, a bow and a quiver of arrows was passed up to the soldier in the tunnel. The men in the vertical shaft were forming a chain to transport weapons. Kickaha noted that they would have been wiser to place six or seven in the tunnel first to prevent attack by their quarry.

Kickaha had thought of jumping the lone soldier at once, but he decided to wait until they had transported all the weapons they intended to use. And so bow after bow, quiver after quiver, swords, and finally even the armor was passed up and given to the man in the tunnel, who piled them neatly to one side. Kickaha was disgusted: didn't they understand that armor would only weigh them down and give their quarry an advantage? Moreover, the heavy thick mail and the heavy clothing underneath it would make them hot and sweaty. The only reason he could think of for this move was the rigidity of the military mind. If the regulations prescribed armor in every combat situation, then the armor would be worn, appropriate or not.

The soldier handling the material and those braced in the shafts bitched, though not loudly, about the heat and the strain. Kickaha could hear them plainly, but he supposed that the officers below could not.

At last, there were thirty-five bows, thirty-five quivers, and thirty-five swords, helmets, and chain mail suits piled on the floor. There were more soldiers than that in the hall when Kickaha had first seen the invaders, so it seemed that a number was going to stay below. Among them would be all the officers, who did not want to take the time and trouble to remove their steel plates and chain. From the shouted conversation between the man in the tunnel above and an officer below—which could have been done quietly if the men in the shaft had relayed the messages—the man in the tunnel was a noncom, a *shlikrum,* an aboriginal word borrowed by the medieval German conquerors from Earth to indicate a master sergeant.

Kickaha listened carefully, hoping to find out if any men were climbing up other shafts—he did not want to be trapped or jumped on from the rear. Nothing was said about other climbers, but this did not mean that there were none. Kickaha kept looking behind him, like a bird watching for cats, but he saw and heard nothing. The *shlikrum* should have been as nervously vigilant as he, but apparently he felt that he was safe.

That feeling evaporated like a glass of water in a vacuum. The *shlikrum* had bent over to help the top man out of the shaft when Kickaha plunged his knife several inches into the man's right buttock. The man screamed and then went headfirst into the hole, propelled by Kickaha's foot. He fell on the man he was trying to hoist out; the two fell on the man below; and so on until ten men, shrieking, dropped out of the hole in the ceiling. They spludded on top of each other, the sounds of impact weakening as the layer of bodies increased. The *shlikrum,* who had fallen further than the others, landed sprawling on the uppermost body. Although he was hurt, he was not knocked out. He leaped up, lost his footing, and fell down the pile of bodies onto the floor. There he lay moaning.

An officer in a full suit of armor strode clanking to him and bent over a little to speak to him. Kickaha could not hear the words because of the uproar in the hallway, so he aimed an arrow at the officer. The angle was awkward, but he had trained himself to shoot from many angles, and he sent the arrow true. It penetrated the juncture of shoulder and neck plates and drove deep into the flesh. The knight fell forward and on the noncom. Kickaha was curious about the silvery casket strapped to the knight's back, because he had never seen anything like it before. Now was not the time to indulge his curiosity, however.

The soldiers who had been unpiling the bodies dropped their work and ran out of Kickaha's sight. There was a babble of voices and then silence after an officer roared for it. Kickaha recognized von Turbat's voice. It was only then that he began to realize the implications of this invasion and savage hunt for him.

Von Turbat was the king of the independent nation of Eggesheim, a mountainous country with perhaps sixty thousand citizens. At one time, as Baron Horst von Horstmann, Kickaha had had fairly amicable relations with him. After he had been defeated by Kickaha in a lancing joust and had then caught Kickaha making love to his daughter, von Turbat had been hostile. Not actively so, although he had made it plain that he would not be responsible for avenging Horstmann's death, if someone should kill Horstmann while he was under von Turbat's roof. Kickaha had taken off immediately after hearing this, and later, playing his role of robber baron, he had plundered a trade caravan on its way to Eggesheim. But circumstances had forced Kickaha to abandon his castle and identity and run for his life to this level. That had been a few years ago.

There was no reason why von Turbat should take such a terrible risk now to get revenge on Kickaha. In the first place, how had the king ever found out that Kickaha was here? How could he even know that Kickaha was von Horstmann? Why, if he had actually discovered the gates and their use, would he invade the dangerous city of Talanac? There were too many questions.

Meanwhile, from the low voices and following sounds of leather boots running, and the sight of the end of a ladder being swung out and moved away, it was evident that the Teutoniacs would be coming up other shafts. Kickaha doubted that many of them would be armored or heavily armed, since he now had the armor and weapons of the majority. Of course, they would be sending off for reinforcements. He had better get moving.

Then one of the men in the pile crawled out, and Kickaha sent an arrow through him. He quickly shot five more bodies on the theory that if any of them were able to revive, he was eliminating a potential killer. He was busy for about five minutes, running up and down and across and back and forth through the various tunnels. Three times he was able to catch the soldiers coming up shafts and to shoot the top man. Twice he fired down through shafts at men walking in the hallway.

But he could not hope to run swiftly enough to cover all the shafts. And apparently the king was not counting casualties. The shafts originally entered were reentered, and lights and noises indicated that others were being climbed. Kickaha had to abandon all the weapons except for his knives in order to climb another vertical shaft. He intended to find a route to the openings of the shafts on the outside. There, high on the face of the mountain, above the Street of Mixed Blessings, he might be able to escape.

Von Turbat must surely know this, however; he would have archers on the streets above and below.

If he could only keep away from the soldiers in the networks of tunnels here until dark, he might be able to slip out across the jade cliffside. That is, he would if there were ornamental projections for him to use.

He became very thirsty. He had had no water all morning because he had been seized with the thirst for learning. Now the shock, the fighting and the running had dried him out. The roof of his mouth dripped a thick stalactitish saliva; his throat felt as if filled with desert pebbles dislodged from the hoof of a camel.

He might be able to go the rest of the day and the night without water if he had to, but he would be weakened. Therefore, he would get water. And since there was only one way to get it, he took that way.

He crept back toward the shaft up which he had just climbed but stopped a few feet from it. He smiled. What was the matter with him? He had been too shocked, his usual wiliness and unconventional thinking had been squeezed out of him for a while. He had passed up a chance to escape. It was a mad route to take, but its very insanity recommended it to him and, in fact, made it likely that he could succeed. If only he were not too late . . . !

The descent was easy. He came to the pile of armor. The soldiers had not yet approached this hole; they must still be coming up through shafts distant from this one. Kickaha removed his Tishquetmoac clothes and stuffed them in a mail shirt on the bottom of the pile. Hastily he put on a suit of armor, though he had to search to find a shirt and helmet big enough for him. Then he leaned over the hole and called down. He was a perfect mimic and, though it had been some years since he had heard the Eggesheimer dialect of German, he evoked it without difficulty.

The soldiers stationed below suspected a trick. They were not so dumb after all. They did not, however, imagine what had actually happened. They thought that Kickaha might be trying to lure them into range of his bow.

"Ikh'n d'untershlikrum Hayns Gimbat," he said. "I am the corporal Henry Gimbat."

Hayns was a common first name throughout Dracheland. Gimbat was an aboriginal name, as were most of the names ending in -bat. Gimbat was especially common in that area of Dracheland and among the lower classes, who were a mixture of aborigine and German. There were bound to be several men of that name among the invaders.

A sergeant strode out and then stopped to peer up the shaft.

"Vo iss de trickmensh?"

"E n'iss hir, nettrlikh. Ikh hap durss." Or, "He isn't here, of course. I'm thirsty."

"Frakk zu fyer de vass?" the sergeant bellowed. "You ask for water? At a time like this! Shaysskopp!"

The request was genuine, but it was also just the thing to take suspicion away from Kickaha. While the sergeant was raving, torches from both sides of the tunnel heralded the approach of soldiers who had climbed up. Kickaha left the shaft opening to speak to the officer of the newcomers. This knight had taken off his armor, after all, apparently because von Turbat thought that an officer should be in charge of the hunt.

Kickaha recognized him; he was Baron von Diebrs, ruler of a small principality on the border of Eggesheim. He had been at court briefly while Kickaha was visiting.

Kickaha kept his head bent so the helmet would put part of his face in shadow, and he made his voice less deep. Von Diebrs listened to him but paid no attention to his features. To the baron, Kickaha was just another faceless low-class soldier. Kickaha reported that the Trickster was gone without a trace. He also hastened to say that he had asked for water, but that the sergeant seemed to think it was an unreasonable request.

The baron, licking his lips, did not think it was unreasonable. And so bottles of water were lifted on the ends of poles by men standing on the ladders, and Kickaha got to drink. He then tried to drop back out of sight, so that he could get down to the hallway and, hopefully, out of the temple.

Von Diebrs frustrated him by ordering him to lead the way up the shaft to the next horizontal level. Von Diebrs also swore at him for putting the armor on, and Kickaha had to remove the mail. He was ready to strike or to run at the first sign of recognition from the baron, but von Diebrs was only interested in searching for the barbarian killer.

Kickaha wanted to ask questions. He could not, however, without making the others suspicious, so he kept quiet. He crawled up the shaft and then took the bows and quivers and long swords passed up. After that, the party split into two. One was to go one way; the other, down the opposite direction. When the party of which Kickaha was a member met another search party, they were to go upward again.

The levels they had just left became bright and noisy. More men were coming in, reinforcements to press the hunt. Von Turbat, or whoever was in charge of the entire invasion, must have affairs under excellent control, to spare so many soldiers.

Kickaha kept with the original group, since none of them knew him. And when they encountered other groups, Kickaha said nothing. He still wore the helmet, since he had not been ordered to take it off. A few others also had helmets.

The walking became more difficult, because the shafts were now so narrow that a man had to duckwalk to get through and a party must travel single file. The soldiers had thought they were in top condition, but this type of progress made their legs ache and quiver and their lower backs hurt. Although he was not suffering, Kickaha complained too, so that he did not appear different.

After what seemed like many hours but was probably no more than eighty minutes, the party of six crawled from a shaft into a little round chamber. The wall opposite had large round openings to the outside. The men leaned over the edge and looked down, where they could see troops on foot and mounted knights in the Street of Mixed Blessings. Though they were small figures, their markings were distinguishable. Kickaha recognized not only the flags and pennants and uniforms of Eggesheim but those of at least a dozen kingdoms and a few baronies.

There were some bodies—predominantly those of Tishquetmoac whose heads were stacked in a pyramid. The major fighting between the Teutoniacs and the Talanac garrisons must have taken place elsewhere, probably on top of the city.

Far below the streets was the river. The two bridges that Kickaha could see were jammed with refugees, all going outward and into the old city.

Presently, a Tishquetmoac rode down the long curving ramp from the street above and halted before von Turbat, who had just come out of the temple. The king got onto a horse before he would allow the Tishquetmoac to speak to him. This man was splendid in a headdress of long white curly feathers and a scarlet robe and green leggings. Probably, he was some functionary of the emperor. He was reporting to von Turbat, which must mean that the emperor had been captured.

There would be few hiding places for Kickaha even if he could get away. The people left in the city would obey their ruler's command, and if this was to report Kickaha's presence as soon as he was discovered, this they would do.

One of the soldiers with Kickaha spoke then of the reward offered for the capture of Kickaha or for information leading to the capture. Ten thousand *drachener* and the title, castle, lands, and citizens of the barony of Horstmann. If a commoner earned the reward, he and his family would automatically become nobles. The money was more than the king of Eggesheim got in taxes in two years.

Kickaha wanted to ask what had happened to Lisa von Horstmann, his wife, and von Listbat, his good friend who ran the barony in his absence. He dared not, but he sickened at the thought of what must have been their fate.

He leaned out of the window again to get fresh air, and he saw something that he had forgotten. Earlier, he had seen a knight just behind von Turbat, carrying a sword in one hand and a large steel casket under one arm. Now, this same knight accompanied von Turbat on the street, and when the king went back into the temple, he was followed closely by the knight with the casket.

Very strange, Kickaha thought. But this whole affair was very strange. He could explain nothing. One thing was certain, however: Wolff couldn't be operating effectively as Lord of this world, otherwise this would not be happening. Either Wolff was dead or captive in his own palace, or he was hiding in this world or in another.

The corporal presently ordered the party to go back down. Again, all the shafts in their sector were explored. When they reached the hallway, they were tired, hot, hungry, and cross. Their ill-feelings were made worse by the verbal assaults from their officers. The knights could not believe that Kickaha had escaped them. Neither could von Turbat. He talked with his officers, made more detailed plans, and then ordered the search renewed. There was a delay while bottles of water, hard biscuits, and dried sticks of meat were passed around to the men. Kickaha hunched down against the wall with the others and spoke only when spoken to. The others of his group had served together but did not ask him what his platoon was—they were too tired and disgruntled to talk much of anything.

It was an hour after dusk before the search was called off. An officer commented that the Trickster would not get away. For one thing, the flow of refugees at all the bridges had been cut off. Every bridge was heavily guarded, and the banks of the river opposite the city were being patrolled. Moreover, a house-to-house search was being started even now.

This meant that the search parties would not get the sleep they longed for. They would stay up all night looking for Kickaha. They would stay up all the next day, and the following night, if Kickaha was not found.

The soldiers did not protest; they did not want a whipping, ended by castration and then hanging. But among themselves, they muttered, and Kickaha paid attention to them to pick up information. They were tough, hardy men who griped but who would obey any order within reason and most senseless orders.

They marched along smartly enough though their thighs cried silently with pain. Kickaha had managed to get in the rear row of the platoon, and when they turned down onto a street with no natives and no other invaders, he disappeared into a doorway.

4

THE DOOR HE STOOD BY COULD NOT BE OPENED FROM THE
outside, of course. It was barred on the inside with the big bolt that all Talanac citizens used to protect themselves from the criminals that prowled
at night.

Where there is civilization, there are thieves. Kickaha was, at this moment, grateful for that fact. During the previous extended visit to Talanac,
he had deliberately become intimate with some of the criminal class. These
people knew many hidden routes in and out of the city, and Kickaha wanted
knowledge of these in case he needed them. Moreover, he found the criminals he knew, mainly smugglers, to be interesting. One of them, Clatatol,
was more than interesting. She was beautiful. She had long, straight, glossy
black hair, big brown eyes, very long and thick eyelashes, a smooth bronzish
skin, and a full figure, although, like most of the Tishquetmoac women, she
was just a little too wide in the hips and a little too thick-calved. Kickaha
seldom required perfection in others; he agreed that a little asymmetry was
the foundation of genuine beauty.

So he had become Clatatol's lover at the same time he was courting the
emperor's daughter. This double life had eventually tripped him up, and
he was asked politely to leave Talanac by the emperor's brother and the
chief of police. He could return whenever the emperor's daughter got
married and so would be shut up in purdah, as was the custom among the
nobility. Kickaha had left without even saying goodbye to Clatatol. He had
visited one of the little dependent kingdoms to the east, a nation of civilized peoples called the Quatsl-slet. These had been conquered long ago
and now paid tribute to Talanac but still spoke their own language and adhered to their own somewhat peculiar customs. While with them, Kickaha
heard that the emperor's daughter had married her uncle, as was the custom. He could return, but instead he had gone back to the Hrowakas, the
Bear People, in the mountains by the Great Plains.

So he would now get to Clatatol's house and find out if she could smug-
gle him out of the city . . . if she would have him, he thought. She had tried

to kill him the last time he had seen her. And if she had forgiven him since, she would be angry again because he had returned to Talanac and had not tried to see her.

"Ah, Kickaha!" he murmured to himself. "You think you're so smart, and you're always fouling up! Fortunately, I'm the only one who knows that. And, big-mouthed as I am, I'll never tell!"

The moon rose. It was not silver, like Earth's moon, but as green as the cheese which the humorist-folklorists had said constituted lunar material. It was two and a half times as large as Earth's moon. It swelled across the starless black sky and cast a silver-green light on the white-and-brown streaked jade avenue.

Slowly, the giant orb moved across the heavens, and its light, like a team of mice pulling it along, strained ahead and presently was swarming over the lintel of the doorway in which Kickaha stood.

Kickaha looked up at the moon and wished that he were on it. He had been on its surface many times, and, if he could get to one of the small hidden gates in Talanac, he could be on it again. However, the chances were that von Turbat knew of their location, since he knew of the large gates. Even so, it would be worth finding out for sure, but one of the small gates was in the fane of a temple three streets above the lowest and the other was in the temple. The invaders were closing off all avenues out, and they had begun the house-to-house search on the lowest level. They would work upward on the theory that, if Kickaha were hiding, he would be driven upward until he would run into the soldiers stationed in the two levels just below the palace. Meanwhile, the other streets between would be patrolled, but infrequently, and by small bodies of soldiers: Von Turbat did not have enough men to spare.

Kickaha left the doorway and drifted out across the street and over the rampart and climbed down on the gods, beasts, men, abstract symbols, and cartographs which projected from the mountain face between the two streets. He went slowly because the hand and footholds were not always secure on the smooth stone and because there were troops stationed at the foot of the ramp leading from the street above to that below. They were holding torches, and several were on horseback.

Halfway down, he clung to the wall, motionless as a fly that detects a vast shadowy hand, threatening, somewhere in the distance. A patrol of four soldiers on horseback clattered along below. They stopped to speak briefly to the guards stationed on the ramp, then moved on. Kickaha moved also, came to the street, and slid along the wall, along the fronts of houses and into and out of shadowy doorways. He still carried his bow and quiver, although he could move more smoothly and quietly while climbing without them. But he might need them desperately, and he chanced their rattling and their clumsy weight.

It took him until the moon was ready to sail around the monolith in the northwest before he reached Clatatol's street. This was the area of the poor, of slaves who had recently purchased their freedom, of lodgings and taverns for the sailors and smugglers of the riverboat trading-fleets and for the hired guards and drivers of the wagon trading-caravans of the Great Plains. There were also many thieves and murderers on whom the police had nothing tangible, and other thieves and murderers who were hiding from justice.

Normally, the Street of Suspicious Odors would have been crowded and noisy even at this late hour. But the curfew imposed by the invaders was effective. Not a person was to be seen except for several patrols, and every window and door was barred.

This level was like many of the lowest streets, rubbed into existence when the Tishquetmoac had begun their labor of making a mountain into a metropolis. There were houses and shops on the street itself. There was a secondary street on top of these houses, with other houses on that street, and a tertiary street on top of those houses, and still another street on top of these. In other words, the stepped-pyramid existed on a smaller scale within the larger.

These housetop streets were reached by narrow stairways which had been rubbed out of the jade between every fifth and sixth house on the main street. Small animals such as pigs and sheep could be driven up the steps, but a horse would go up at peril of slipping on the stone.

Kickaha scuttled across the Street of Green Birds, which was immediately above the fourth level of houses of the Street of Suspicious Odors. Clatatol's house—if she still lived there—fronted the third level. He intended to let himself over the fence, hang by his hands, and then drop to the rooftops of the fourth level and similarly to the third level street. There were no projections on which to climb down.

But as he went across the Street of Green Birds, he heard the *kulup-kulik* of iron horseshoes. Out of the darkness cast by a temple-front porch, came three men on black horses. One was a knight in full armor; two were men-at-arms. The horses cracked into a gallop; the horsemen bent low over the necks of their mounts; behind them their black capes billowed, sinister smoke from fire of evil intents.

They were far enough away so that Kickaha could have escaped them by going over the fence and dropping. But they probably had bows and arrows, though he could see none, and if they got down off the horses quickly enough, they might be able to shoot him. The light from the moon was about twice as powerful as that from Earth's full moon. Moreover, even if their shafts missed him, they would call in others and start a house-to-house probing.

Well, he thought, the search would start now whatever happened, but . . . no, if he could kill them before the others heard . . . perhaps . . . it was worth trying. . . .

Under other circumstances, Kickaha would have tried for the riders. He loved horses. But when it came to saving his life, sentimentality evaporated. All creatures had to die, but Kickaha intended that his death should come as late as possible.

He aimed for the horses and in rapid succession brought two down. They both fell heavily on their right sides, and neither rider got up. The third, the knight, came unswervingly on, his lance aimed for Kickaha's belly or chest. The arrow went through the horse's neck; the animal fell front quarters first and went hooves over tail. The rider flew up and out; he held his lance most of the flight but dropped it and pulled up his legs and struck in a fetal position. His conical helmet, torn off, hit the stone, bounced, and went freewheeling down the street. The man slid on his side, his cloak ripping off and lying behind him as if his shadow had become dislodged.

Then, despite his armor, the knight was up and pulling his sword from its sheath. He opened his mouth to shout for whoever would hear and come running to his aid. An arrow drove past the teeth and through the spinal cord and he fell backward, sword *keluntking* on the jade.

A silver casket was tied to the saddle of the dead horse of the dead knight. Kickaha tried to open the casket but the key must have been on the knight someplace. He did not have time to look for it.

There were three dead horses, one dead man, possibly two other dead men. And no shouts in the distance to indicate that somebody had heard the uproar.

Carcass and corpse would not long remain unnoticed, however. Kickaha dropped his bow and quiver below and followed them. In less than sixty seconds, he was on the third level street and knocking on the thick wooden shutter over Clatatol's window. He rapped three times, counted to five, rapped twice, counted to four, and rapped once. He held a knife in his other hand.

There was no response which he could detect. He waited for sixty counts, per the code as he remembered it, and then rapped as prescribed again. Immediately thereafter, the sound of horseshoes came down to him and then an uproar. There were shouts and a bugle call. Lights began to gather on the street above and the main street below. Drums beat.

Suddenly, the shutter swung open. Kickaha had to dodge to avoid being hit in the face by it. The room within was dark, but the phantom of a woman's face and naked torso shone palely. An odor of garlic, fish, pork, and the rotten worm-infested cheese the Tishquetmoac loved puffed out past the woman. Kickaha associated the beauty of worked jade with these smells. His first visit had ruined him; he could not help it that he was a man of associations, not always desirable.

At this moment, the odor meant Clatatol, who was as beautiful as her cheese was dreadful. Or as beautiful as her language was foul and her temper hot as an Icelandic geyser.

"Shh!" Kickaha said. "The neighbors!"

Clatatol vomited another scatological and blasphemous spurt.

Kickaha clamped a hand over her mouth, twisted her head to remind her that he could easily break her neck, pushed her back so she went staggering, and climbed in through the window. He closed and locked the shutters and then turned to Clatatol. She had gotten up and found an oil lamp and lit it. By its flickering light, she advanced, swaying, to Kickaha and then embraced him and kissed him on his face, neck and chest while tears ran over these and she sobbed endearments.

Kickaha ignored her breath, thick with the resin-like wine and rotted cheese and garlic and sleep-clots, and he kissed her back. Then he said, "Are you alone?"

"Didn't I swear I would remain faithful to you?" she said.

"Yes, but I didn't ask for that. It was your idea. Besides," he said, "you couldn't be without a man for more than a week, as we both well know."

They laughed, and she took him into the back room, which was square except for the upper parts, which curved to form a dome. This was her bedroom and also her workroom since she planned smuggling operations here and dispensed various goods. Only the furniture was in evidence. This consisted mainly of the bed, a low broad wooden frame with leather straps stretched across it and mountain-lion furs and deerhides piled on the straps. Kickaha lay down on this. Clatatol exclaimed that he looked tired and hungry. She left him for the kitchen, and he called out after her to bring him only water, bread, and sticks of dried beef or some fresh fruit if she had it. Hungry as he was, he couldn't stand the cheese.

After he had eaten, he asked her what she knew of the invasion. Clatatol sat by him on the bed and handed him his food. She seemed ready to pick up their lovemaking where they had left off several years ago, but Kickaha discouraged her. The situation was too enwombed with fatality to think of love now.

Clatatol, who was practical, whatever other faults she had, agreed. She got up and put on a skirt of green, black, and white feathers and a rose-colored cotton cloak. She washed out her mouth with wine diluted with ten parts of water and dropped a bead of powerful perfume on her tongue. Then she sat down by him again and began to talk.

Even though plugged into the underworld grapevine, she could not tell him everything he wanted to know. The invaders had appeared as if out of nowhere from a back room in the great temple of Ollimaml. They had swept out and into the palace and seized the emperor and his entire family after overwhelming the bodyguard and then the garrison.

The taking of Talanac had been well planned and almost perfectly executed. While the co-leader, von Swindebarn, held the palace and began

to reorganize the Talanac police and the military to aid him, von Turbat
had led the ever-increasing numbers of invaders from the palace into the
city itself.

"Everybody was paralyzed," Clatatol said. "It was so absolutely unexpected. These white people in armor, pouring out of the temple of Ollimaml . . . it was as if Ollimaml Himself had sent them, and this increased
the paralysis."

The civilians and police who got in the way were cut down. The rest of
the population either fled into buildings or, when word reached the lowest levels, tried to get out across the river bridges. But these had been sealed
off.

"The strange thing is," Clatatol said, hesitating, then continuing
strongly, "the strange thing is that all this does not seem to be because of
a desire to conquer Talanac. No, the seizure of our city is a, what do you
call it, a byproduct? The invaders seem to be determined to take the city
only because they regard it as a pond which holds a very desirable fish."

"Meaning me," Kickaha said.

Clatatol nodded. "I do not know why these people should want you so
greatly. Do you?"

Kickaha said, "No. I could guess. But I won't. My speculations would
only confuse you and take much time. The first thing for me is to get out
and away. And that, my love, is where you come in."

"Now you love me," she said.

"If there were time . . ." he replied.

"I can hide you where we will have all the time we need," she said. "Of
course, there are the others . . ."

Kickaha had been wondering if she was holding back. He wasn't in a
position to get rough with her, but he did. He gripped her wrist and
squeezed. She grimaced and tried to pull away.

"What others?"

"Quit hurting me, and I'll tell. Maybe. Give me a kiss, and I'll tell for
sure."

It was worthwhile to spend a few seconds, so he kissed her. The perfume from her mouth filled his nostrils and seemingly filtered down to the
ends of his toes. He felt heady and began wondering if perhaps she didn't
deserve a reward after all this time.

He laughed then and gently released himself. "You are indeed the most
beautiful and desirable woman I have ever seen and I have seen a thousand times a thousand," he said. "But death walks the streets, and he is looking for me."

"When you see this other woman . . ." she said.

She became coy again, and then he had to impress upon her that coy-
ness automatically meant pain for her. She did not resent this, liked it, in
fact, since, to her, erotic love meant a certain amount of roughness and pain.

5

IT SEEMED THAT THREE STRANGERS HAD FLED FROM THE IN most parts of the temple of Ollimaml a few minutes ahead of von Turbat. They were white-skinned, also. One was the black haired woman whom Clatatol, a very jealous and deprecating woman, nevertheless said was the most beautiful she had ever seen. Her companions were a huge, very fat man and a short skinny man. All three were dressed strangely and none spoke Tishquetmoac. They did speak Wishpawaml, the liturgical language of the priests. Unfortunately, the thieves who had hidden the three knew only a few words of Wishpawaml; these were from the responses of the laity during services.

Kickaha knew then that the three were Lords. The liturgical language everywhere on this world was theirs.

Their flight from von Turbat indicated that they had been dispossessed of their own universes and had taken refuge in this. But what was the minor king, von Turbat, doing in an affair that involved Lords?

Kickaha said, "Is there a reward for these three?"

"Yes. Ten thousand *kwatluml*. Apiece! For you, thirty thousand, and a high official post in the palace of the emperor. Perhaps, though this is only hinted at, marriage into the royal family."

Kickaha was silent. Clatatol's stomach rumbled, as if ruminating the reward offers. Voices fluttered weakly through the air shafts in the ceiling. The room, which had been cool, was hot. Sweat seeped from his armpits; the woman's dark-brass skin hatched brass tadpoles. From the middle chamber, the kitchen-washroom-toilet, came gurgles of running water and little watery voices.

"You must have fainted at the thought of all that money," Kickaha said finally. "What's keeping you and your gang from collecting?"

"We are thieves and smugglers, killers even, but we are not traitors! The pinkfaces offered these . . ."

She stopped when she saw Kickaha grinning. She grinned back. "What I said is true. However, the sums *are* enormous! What made us hesitate, if you must know, you wise coyote, was what would happen after the pink-faces left. Or if there is a revolt. We don't want to be torn to pieces by a mob or tortured because some people might think we were traitors."

"Also . . . ?"

She smiled and said, "Also, the three refugees have offered to pay us many times over what the pinkfaces offer if we get them out of the city."

"And how will they do that?" Kickaha said. "They haven't got a universe to their name."

"What?"

"Can they offer you anything tangible—right now?"

"All *were* wearing jewels worth more than the rewards," she said. "Some—I've never seen anything like them. They're out of this world!"

Kickaha did not tell her that the cliché was literally true.

He was going to ask her if they had weapons but realized that she would not have recognized them as such if the three did have them. Certainly, the three wouldn't offer the information to their captors.

"And what of me?" he said, not asking her what the three had offered beyond their jewels.

"You, Kickaha, are beloved of the Lord, or so it is said. Besides, everybody says that you know where the treasures of the earth are hidden. Would a man who is poor have brought back the great emerald of Osh-quatsmu?"

Kickaha said, "The pinkfaces will be banging on your doors soon enough. This whole area is going to be unraveled. Where do we go from here?"

Clatatol insisted that he let her blindfold him and then cover him with a hood. In no position to argue, he agreed. She made sure he could not see and then turned him swiftly around a dozen times. After that, he got down on all fours at her order.

There was a creaking sound, stone turning on stone, and she guided him through a passageway so narrow he scraped against both sides. Then he stood and, his hand in hers, stumbled up 150 steps, walked 280 paces down a slight decline, went down a ramp three hundred paces, and walked forty more on a straightway. Clatatol stopped him and removed the hood and blindfold.

He blinked. He was in a round green-and-black striated chamber with a forty foot diameter and a three foot wide air shaft above. Flames writhed at the ends of torches in wall fixtures. There were chairs of jade and wood, some chests, piles of cloth bolts and furs, barrels of spices, a barrel of water, a table with dishes, biscuits, meat, stinking cheese, and some sanitation furniture.

Six Tishquetmoac men squatted against the wall. Their glossy black bangs fell over their eyes. Some smoked little cigars. They were armed with daggers, swords, and hatchets.

Three fair-skinned people sat in chairs. One was short, gritty-skinned, large-nosed, and shark-mouthed. The second was a manatee of a man, spilling over the chair in cataracts of fat.

On seeing the third, Kickaha gasped. He said, "Podarge!"

The woman was the most beautiful he had ever seen. But he had seen her before. That is, the face was in his past. But the body did not belong to that face.

"Podarge!" he said again, speaking the debased Mycenaean she and her eagles used. "I didn't know that Wolff had taken you from your harpy's body and put you—your brain—in a woman's body. I . . ."

He stopped. She was looking at him with an unreadable expression. Perhaps she did not want him to let the others know what had happened. And he, usually silent when the situation asked for it, had been so overcome that . . .

But Podarge had discovered that Wolff was in reality the Jadawin who had originally kidnapped her from the Peloponnese of 3200 years ago and put her brain into the body of a Harpy created in his biolab. She had refused to let him rectify the wrong; she hated him so much that she had stayed in her winged bird-legged body and had sworn to get revenge upon him.

What had made her change her mind?

Her voice, however, was not Podarge's. That, of course, would be the result of the soma transfer.

"What are you gibbering about, *leblabbiy?*" she said in the speech of the Lords.

Kickaha felt like hitting her in the face. *Leblabbiy* was the Lords' perjorative for the human beings who inhabited their universes and over whom they godded it. *Leblabbiy* had been a small pet animal of the universe in which the Lords had originated. It ate the delicacies which its master offered, but it would also eat excrement at the first chance. And it often went mad.

"All right, Podarge, pretend you don't understand Mycenaean," he said. "But watch your tongue. I have no love for you."

She seemed surprised. She said, "Ah, you are a priest?"

Wolff, he had to admit, had certainly done a perfect job on her. Her body was magnificent; the skin as white and flawless as he remembered it; the hair as long, black, straight, and shining. The features, of course, were not perfectly regular; there was a slight asymmetry which resulted in a beauty that under other circumstances would have made him ache.

She was dressed in silky-looking light green robes and sandals, almost as if she had been getting ready for bed when interrupted. How in hell had Podarge come to be mixed up with these Lords? And then the answer tapped his mind's shoulder. Of course, she was in Wolff's palace when it was invaded. But what had happened then?

He said, "Where is Wolff?"

"Who, *leblabbiy?*" she said.

"Jadawin, he used to be called," he said.

She shrugged and said, "He wasn't there. Or if he was, he was killed by the Black Bellers."

Kickaha was more confused. "Black Bellers?"

Wolff had spoken of them at one time. But briefly, because their conversation had been interrupted by a subject introduced by Chryseis. Later, after Kickaha had helped Wolff recover his palace from Vannax, Kickaha had intended to ask him about the Black Bellers. He had never done so.

One of the Tishquetmoac spoke harshly to Clatatol. Kickaha understood him; she was to tell Kickaha that he must talk to these people. The Tishquetmoac could not understand the speech.

The fair-skinned woman, replying to his questions, said, "I am Anana, Jadawin's sister. This thin one is Nimstowl, called the Nooser by the Lords. This other is Fat Judubra."

Kickaha understood now. Anana, called the Bright, was one of Wolff's sisters. And he had used her face as a model when he created Podarge's face in the biolab. Rather, his memory had supplied the features, since Wolff had not then seen his sister Anana for over a thousand years. Which meant that, as of now, he had not seen her for over four thousand.

Kickaha remembered now that Wolff had said that the Black Bellers were to have been used, partly, as receptacles for memory. The Lords, knowing that even the complex human brain could not hold thousands of years of knowledge, had experimented with the transfer of memory. This could, theoretically, be transferred back to the human brain when needed or otherwise displayed exteriorly.

A rapping sounded. A round door in the wall at the other end swung out, and another smuggler entered. He beckoned to the others, and they gathered around him to whisper. Finally, Clatatol left the group to speak to Kickaha.

"The rewards have been tripled," she whispered. "Moreover, this pink-face king, von Turbat, has proclaimed that, once you're caught, he'll withdraw from Talanac. Everything will be as it was before."

"If you'd planned on turning us in, you wouldn't be telling me this," he said. But it was possible that she was being overly subtle, trying to make him at ease, before they struck. Eight against one. He did not know what the Lords could do, so he would not count on them. He still had his two knives, but in this small room . . . ah, well, when the time came, he would see.

Clatatol added, "Von Turbat has also said that if you are not delivered to him within twenty-four hours, he will kill the emperor and his family and then he will kill every human being in this city. He said this in private to his officers, but a slave overheard him. Now the entire city knows."

"If von Turbat was talking German, how could a Tishquetmoac understand him?" Kickaha said.

"Von Turbat was talking to von Swindebarn and several others in the holy speech of the Lords," she said. "The slave had served in the temple and knew the holy speech."

The Black Bellers must be the as-yet unhooded lantern to illumine the mystery. He knew the two Teutoniac kings could follow the priest in the services, but they did not know the sacred language well enough to speak it. Thus, the two were not what they seemed.

He was given no time to ask questions. Clatatol said, "The pinkfaces have found the chamber behind the wall of my bedroom, and they will soon be breaking through it. We can't stay here."

Two men left the room but quickly returned with telescoping ladders. These were extended full-length up the air shaft. On seeing this, Kickaha felt less apprehensive. He said, "Now your patriotism demands that you hand us over to von Turbat. So . . . ?"

Two men had climbed up the ladder. The others were urging the Lords and Kickaha to go next. Clatatol said, "We have heard that the emperor is possessed by a demon. His soul had been driven out into the cold past the moon; a demon resides in his body, though not comfortably as yet. The priests have secretly transmitted this story throughout the city. They say for us to fight this most evil of evils. And we are not to surrender you, Kickaha, who is the beloved of the Lord, Ollimaml, nor should we give up the others."

Kickaha said, "Possessed? How do you know?"

Clatatol did not answer until after they had climbed the length of the shaft and were in a horizontal tunnel. One of the smugglers lit a dark lantern, and the ladder was pulled up, joint by joint, bent, folded, and carried along.

Clatatol said, "Suddenly, the emperor spoke only in the holy speech, so it was evident he did not understand Tishquetmoac. And the priests reported that von Turbat and von Swindebarn speak Wishpawaml only, and they have their priests to translate orders for them."

Kickaha did not see why a demon was thought to possess Quotshaml, the emperor. The liturgical language was supposed to scorch the lips of demons when they tried to speak it. But he was not going to point out the illogic when it favored him.

The party hurried down a tunnel with Fat Judubra wheezing loudly and complaining. He had had to be pulled through the shaft; his robes had torn and his skin had been scraped.

Kickaha asked Clatatol if the temple of Ollimaml was well guarded. He was hoping that the smaller secret gate had not been discovered. She replied that she did not know. Kickaha asked her how they were going to get out of the city. She answered that it would be better if he did not know;

if he was captured, then he could not betray the others. Kickaha did not argue with her. Although he had no idea of how they would leave the city, he could imagine what would happen after that. During his last visit, he had found out just how she and her friends got the contraband past the customs. She did not suspect that he knew.

He spoke to Anana, who was a glimmer of neck, arms, and legs ahead. "The woman Clatatol says that her emperor, and at least two of the invaders, are possessed. She means that they suddenly seem unable, or unwilling, to talk anything but the language of the Lords."

"The Black Bellers," Anana said after a pause.

At that moment, shouts cannoned down the tunnel. The party stopped; the lantern was put out. Lights appeared at both ends of the tunnel; voices flew down from the rigid mouths of shafts above and ballooned from mouths below.

Kickaha spoke to the Lords. "If you have weapons, get ready to use them."

They did not answer. The party formed into a single file, linked by holding hands, and a man led them into a cross-tunnel. They duckwalked for perhaps fifty yards, with the voices of the hunters getting louder, before they heard a distant roar of water. The lamp was lit again. Soon they were in a small chamber, exitless except for the four-foot-wide hole in the floor against the opposite wall. The roar, a wetness, and a stink funneled up from it.

"The shaft angles steeply, and the sewage tunnel to which it connects is fifty feet down. The slide, however, won't hurt," Clatatol said. "We use this way only if all others around here fail. If you went all the way down this shaft, you'd fall into the tunnel, which is full of sewage and drops almost vertically down into the river at an underwater point. If you lived to come up in the river, you would be caught by the pinkface patrol boats stationed there."

Clatatol told them what they must do. They sat down and coasted down the tube with their hands and feet braking. Two-thirds of the way down, or so it seemed, they stopped. Here they were pulled into a hole and a shaft unknown to the authorities, rubbed into existence by several generations of criminals. This led back up to a network above the level from which they had just fled.

Clatatol explained that it was necessary to get to a place where they could enter another great sewage pipe. This one, however, was dry, because it had been blocked off with great labor and some loss of life thirty years before by a large gang of criminals. The flow from above was diverted to two other sewage tunnels. The dry tunnel led directly downward to below the water level. Near its mouth was a shaft which went horizontally to an underwater port distant from the outlets being watched by the pinkfaces.

It was near the wharf where the river-trade boats were. To reach the boats, they would have to swim across the mile wide river.

Three streets up, within the face of the mountain, the party came to the horizontal shaft which opened to their avenue of escape, the dry tunnel slanting at fifty-five degrees to the horizontal.

Kickaha never found out what went amiss. He did not think that the Teutoniacs could have known where they were. There must have been some search parties sent at random to various areas. And this one was in the right place and saw their quarry before the quarry saw them.

Suddenly there were lights, yells, screams, and something thudding into bodies. Several Tishquetmoac men fell, and then Clatatol was sprawled out before him. In the dim light of the lantern lying on its side before him, Kickaha saw the skin, bluish-black in the light, the hanging jaw, eyes skewered on eternity, and the crossbow bolt sticking out of her skull an inch above the right ear. Blood gushed over the blue-black hair, the ear, the neck.

He crawled over the body, his flesh numb with the shock of the attack and with the shock of the bolt to come. He scuttled down the tunnel and into one that seemed to be free of the enemy. Behind him, in the dark, was heavy breathing; Anana identified herself. She did not know what had happened to the others.

They crawled and duckwalked until their legs and backs felt pain in the center of their bones, or so it seemed. They took left and right turns as they pleased, no pattern, and twice went up vertical shafts. The time came when they were in total darkness and quiet except for the blood punching little bags in their ears. They seemed to have outrun the hounds.

Thereafter, they went upward. It was vital to wait until night could veil their movements outside. This proved difficult to do. Though they were tired and tried to sleep, they kept awakening as if springing off the trampoline of unconsciousness into the upper air of open eyes. Their legs kicked, their hands twitched; they were aware of this but could not fully sleep to forget it nor be fully awake except when they soared out of nightmares.

Night appeared at the porthole of the shaft-end in the face of the mountain. They climbed out and up, seeing patrols below and hearing them above. After waiting until things were quiet above, they climbed over the ramparts and up the next wall and so to the next level of street. When they could not travel outside, they crawled into an air shaft.

The lower parts of the city were ablaze with torches. The soldiers and police were thoroughly probing the bottom levels. Then, as they went upward, the ring of men tightened because the area lessened. And there were spot-check search parties everywhere.

"If you're supposed to be taken alive, why did they shoot at us?" Anana said. "They couldn't see well enough to distinguish their targets."

"They got excited," Kickaha said. He was tired, hungry, thirsty, and feeling rage at the killers of Clatatol. Sorrow would come later. There would be no guilt. He never suffered guilt unless he had a realistic reason. Kickaha had some neurotic failings, and neurotic virtues—no way to escape those, being human—but inappropriate guilt was not among them. He was not responsible in any way for her death. She had entered this business of her own will and knowing that she might die.

There was even a little gladness reaped from her death. He could have been killed instead of her.

Kickaha went down a series of shafts after food and drink. Anana did not want to be left behind, since she feared that he might not be able to find her again. She went with him as far as the tube which led into the ceiling of a home, where the family snored loudly and smelled loudly of wine and beer. He came back with a rope, bread, cheese, fruit, beef, and two bottles of water.

They waited again until night sailed around the monolith and grappled the city. Then they went on up again, outside when they could, inside when they could. Anana asked him why they were going up; he replied that they had to, since the city below was swarming inside and outside.

IN THE MIDDLE OF THE NIGHT, THEY CAME OUT OF ANOTHER house, having entered by the air shaft, and stepped past the sleepers. This house was on the street just below the emperor's palace. From here on, there would be no internal shaft connections. Since all stairways and causeways were guarded, they could reach their goal only by climbing up on the outside for some distance. This would not be easy. For forty feet, the mountain face was purposely left smooth.

And then, while they were skulking in the shadows at the base of the wall, they came across two booted feet sticking out of a dark alcove. The feet belonged to a dead sentry; another man lay dead by him. One had been stabbed in the throat; the other, strangled with wire.

"Nimstowl has been here!" Anana whispered. "He is called the Nooser, you know."

The torches of an approaching patrol flared three hundred yards down the street. Kickaha cursed Nimstowl because he had left the bodies there. Actually, however, it would make little difference to the patrols if the sentries were dead or missing from their posts. There would be alarms.

The small gate set in the wall was unlocked. It could be locked from the outside only; Kickaha and Anana, after taking the sentries' weapons, went through it, and ran up the steep stairway between towering smooth walls. They were wheezing and sobbing when they reached the top.

From below, shouts rose. Torches appeared in the tiny gateway, and soldiers began to climb the steps. Drums thoomed; a bugle bararared.

The two ran, not toward the palace to their right but toward a steep flight of steps to their left. At the top of the steps, silver roofs and gray iron bars gleamed, and the odor of animals, straw, old meat and fresh dung reached them.

"The royal zoo," Kickaha said. "I've been here."

At the far end of a long flagstone walk, something gleamed like a thread in the hem of night. It shot across the moonlight and was in shadows, out again, in again. Then it faded into the huge doorway of a colossal white building.

"Nimstowl!" Anana said. She started after him, but Kickaha pulled her back roughly. Face twisted, white as silver poured out by the moon in a hideous mold, eyes wide as an enraged owl's, she snapped herself away from him.

"You dare to touch me, *leblabbiy*?"

"Any time," he said harshly. "For one thing, don't call me *leblabbiy* again. I won't just hit you. I'll kill you. I don't have to take that arrogance, that contempt. It's totally based on empty, poisonous, sick egotism. Call me that again, and I'll kill you. You aren't superior to me in any way, you know. You *are* dependent on me."

"I? Dependent? On you?"

"Sure," he said. "Do you have a plan for escape? One that might work, even if it is wild?"

Her effort to control herself made her shudder. Then she forced a smile. And if he had not known the concealed fury, he would have thought it the most beautiful, charming, seductive, etc., smile he had seen in two universes.

"No! I have no plan. You are right. I am dependent on you."

"You're realistic, anyway," he said. "Most Lords, I've heard, are so arrogant, they'd rather die than confess dependency or weakness of any kind."

This flexibility made her more dangerous, however. He must not forget that she was Wolff's sister. Wolff had told him that his sisters Vala and Anana were probably the two most dangerous human females alive. Even allowing for pardonable family pride, and a certain exaggeration, they probably were exceedingly dangerous.

"Stay here!" he said, and he went silently and swiftly after Nimstowl. He could not understand how the two Lords had managed to go straight here. How had they learned of the small secret gate in the temple? There could be only one way: during their brief stay in Wolff's palace, they had seen the map with its location. Anana had not been with them when that had happened, or if she had, she was keeping quiet for some reason of her own.

But if the two Lords could find out about it, why hadn't the Black Bellers also located it, since they would have had more time? Within a minute, he had his answer. The Bellers had known of the gate and had stationed two guards outside it. But these two were dead, one knifed, one strangled, and the corner of the building was swung open and light streamed out from it. Kickaha cautiously slipped through the narrow opening and into the small chamber. There were four silver crescents set into the stone of the floor; the four that had been hanging on the wall-pegs were gone. The two Lords had used a gate to escape and had taken the other crescents with them to make sure that no one used the others.

Furious, Kickaha returned to Anana and told her the bad news. "That way is out, but we're not licked yet," he said.

Kickaha walked on a curving path of diorite stones set at the edges with small jewels. He stopped before a huge cage. The two birds within stood side by side and glared at Kickaha. They were ten feet high. Their heads were pale red; their beaks, pale yellow; their wings and bodies were green as the noon sky; their legs were yellow. And their eyes were scarlet shields with black bosses.

One spoke in a giant parrot's voice. "Kickaha! What do you do here, vile trickster?"

Inside that great head was the brain of a woman abducted by Jadawin 3,200 years ago from the shores of the Aegean. That brain had been transplanted for Jadawin's amusement and use in the body created in his biolab. This eagle was one of the few human-brained left. The great green eagles, all females, reproduced parthenogenetically. Perhaps forty of the original five thousand still survived; the others, the millions now living, were their descendants.

Kickaha answered in Mycenaean Greek. "Dewiwanira! And what are you doing in this cage? I thought you were Podarge's pet, not the emperor's."

Dewiwanira screamed and bit at the bars. Kickaha, who was standing too close, jumped back, but he laughed.

"That's right, you dumb bird! Bring them running so they can keep you from escaping!"

The other eagle said, "Escape?"

Kickaha answered quickly. "Yes. Escape. Agree to help us get out of Talanac, and we will get you out of the cage. But say yea or nay now! We have little time!"

"Podarge ordered us to kill you and Jadawin-Wolff!" Dewiwanira said.

"You can try later," he said. "But if you don't give me your word to help us, you'll die in the cage. Do you want to fly again, to see your friends again?"

Torches were on the steps to the palace and the zoological gardens. Kickaha said, "Yes? No?"

"Yes!" Dewiwanira said. "By the breasts of Podarge, yes!"

Anana stepped out from the shadows to assist him. Not until then did the eagles see her face clearly. They jumped and flapped their wings and croaked, "Podarge!"

Kickaha did not tell them that she was Jadawin-Wolff's sister. He said, "Podarge's face had a model."

He ran to the storehouse, thankful that he had taken the trouble to inspect it during his tour with the emperor, and he returned with several lengths of rope. He then jumped into a pit set in stone and leaned heavily upon an iron level. Steel skreaked and the door to the cage swung open.

Anana stood guard with bow and arrow ready. Dewiwanira hunched through the door first and stood still while Kickaha tied each end of a rope to a leg. Antiope, the other eagle, left the cage and submitted to a rope being tied to her legs.

Kickaha told the others what he hoped they could do. Then, as soldiers ran into the gardens, the two huge birds hopped to the edge of the low rampart which enclosed the zoo. This was not their normal method of progress when on the ground; usually they strode. Now, only by spreading their wings to make their descent easier, could they avoid injury to their legs.

Kickaha got in between the legs of Dewiwanira, sat down with the rope under his buttocks, gripped each leg above the huge talons, and shouted, "Ready, Anana? All right, Dewiwanira! Fly!"

Both eagles bounded into the air several feet, even though weighted by the humans. Their wings beat ponderously. Kickaha felt the rope dig into his flesh. He was jerked up and forward; the rampart dropped from under him. The green-silver-spattered, torchflame-sparked, angling walls and streets of the city of Talanac were below him but rushing up frighteningly.

Far below, at least three thousand feet, the river at the foot of the mountain ran with black and tossed silver.

Then the mountain was sliding by perilously close. The eagles could support a relatively large weight, since their muscles were far stronger than those of an eagle of Earth, but they could not flap their wings swiftly enough to lift a human adult. The best they could do was to slow the rate of descent.

And so they paralleled the walls, pounding their wings frantically when they came to an outthrust of street, moved agonizingly slowly outward, or so it seemed to Kickaha, shot over the street and seemed to hurtle down again, the white or brown or red or gray or black or striped jade face of the mountain too too close, then they were rowing furiously to go outward once more.

The two humans had to draw their legs up during most of the whistling, booming, full-of-heart-stopping-crashes-just-ahead ride.

Twice they were scratched, raked, and beaten by the branches of trees as they were hauled through the upper parts. Once the eagles had to bank sharply to avoid slamming into a high framework of wood, built on top of a house for some reason. Then the eagles lost some distance between them and the mountain wall, and the two were bumped with loss of skin and some blood along brown and black jade which, fortunately, was smooth. Ornamental projections would have broken their bones or gashed them deeply.

Then the lowest level, the Street of Rejected Sacrifices, so named for some reason Kickaha had never found out, was behind them. They missed the jade fence on the outer edge of the street by a little more than an inch. Kickaha was so sure that he would be caught and torn on the points that he actually felt the pain.

They dropped toward the river at a steep angle.

The river was a mile wide at this place. On the shore opposite were docks and ships, and outside them, other ships at anchor. Most of these were long two-decked galleys with high poop decks and one or two square-rigged masts.

Kickaha saw this in two flashes, and then, as the eagles sank toward the gray and black dappled surface, he did that which he had arranged with Anana. Confident that the eagles would try to kill them as soon as they were out of danger of being caught inside the city, he had told Anana to release her hold and drop into the river at the first chance.

The river was still fifty feet below when Dewiwanira made her first attempt with her beak. Fortunately for her intended prey, she couldn't bend enough to seize or tear him. The huge yellow beak slashed eight inches above his head.

"Let go!" she screamed then. "You'll pull me into the water! I'll drown!"

Kickaha was tempted to do just that. He was afraid, however, that the obvious would occur to her. If she could sustain altitude enough while Antiope dropped so that her head was even with Kickaha, Antiope could then use her beak on him. And then the two birds could reverse position and get to Anana.

He threw himself backward, turned over, twice straightened out, and entered the water cleanly, head-down. He came up just in time to see the end of Anana's dive. They were about 250 yards from the nearest of five anchored galleys. A mile and a half down the river, torches moved toward them; beneath them, helmets threw off splinters of fire and oars rose and dipped.

The eagles were across the river now and climbing, black against the moonlight.

Kickaha called to Anana, and they swam toward the nearest boat. His clothes and the knives pulled at him, so he shed the clothes and dropped the larger knife into the depths. Anana did the same. Kickaha did not like losing the garments or the knife, but the experiences of the last forty-eight hours and the shortage of food had drained his energy.

They reached the boat finally and clung to the anchor chain while they sucked in air, unable to control the loud sobbing. No one appeared to investigate on the decks of the ship. If there was a watchman, he was sleeping.

The patrol boat was coming swiftly in their direction. Kickaha did not think, however, that he and Anana could be seen yet. He told her what they must do. Having caught up with his breathing, he dived down and under the hull. He turned when he thought he was halfway across and swam along the longitudinal axis toward the rear. Every few strokes, he felt upward. He came up under the overhanging poop with no success. Anana, who had explored the bottom of the front half, met him at the anchor chain. She reported failure, too.

He panted as he talked. "There's a good chance none of these five boats have secret chambers for the smugglers. In fact, we could go through a hundred and perhaps find nothing. Meanwhile, that patrol is getting closer."

"Perhaps we should try the land route," she said.

"Only if we can't find the hidden chambers," he said. "On land, we haven't much chance."

He swam around the boat to the next one and there repeated his search along the keel. This boat and a third proved to have solid bottoms. By then, though he could not see it, Kickaha knew that the patrol boat was getting close.

Suddenly, from the other side of the boat, something like an elephant gun seemed to explode. There was a second boom, and then the screams of eagles and men.

Though he could see nothing, he knew what had happened: the green eagles had returned to kill Kickaha. Not seeing, they had decided to take revenge on the nearest humans for their long captivity. So they had plunged out of the night sky onto the men in the boat. The booms had been their wings suddenly opening to check their fall. Now, they must be in the boat and tearing with beak and talon.

There were splashes. More screams. Then silence.

A sound of triumph, like an elephant's bugling, then a flapping of giant wings. Kickaha and Anana dived under the fourth boat, and they combined hiding from the eagles with their search.

Kickaha, coming up under the poop, heard the wings but could not see the birds. He waited in the shadow of the poop until he saw them rising out and away from the next boat. They could be giving up their hunt for him or they could be intending to plunge down out of the skies again. Anana was not in sight. She was gone so long that Kickaha knew she had either found what they were looking for or had drowned. Or had taken off by herself.

He swam along under the forepart of the boat, and presently his hand went past the lip of a well cut from the keel. He rose, opening his eyes, and saw a glimmer of darkest gray above. Then he was through the surface and in a square chamber lit by a small lamp. He blinked and saw Anana on all fours, knife in hand, staring down at him from a shelf. The shelf was two feet above the water and ran entirely around the chamber.

Beside her knife hand was the black hair of a man. Kickaha came up onto the shelf. The man was a Tishquetmoac, and he was sleeping soundly.

Anana smiled and said, "He was sleeping when I came out of the water.

A good thing, too, because he could have speared me before I knew what was going on. So I hit him in the neck to make sure he continued sleeping."

The shelf went in about four feet and was bare except for some furs, blankets, a barrel with the cartograph for gin on it, and some wooden metal-bound caskets that contained food—he hoped. The bareness meant that the smuggled goods had been removed, so there wouldn't be any influx of swimmers to take the contraband.

The smoke from the lamp rose toward a number of small holes in the ceiling and upper wall. Kickaha, placing his cheek near some of them, felt a slight movement of air. He was sure that the light could not be seen, by anyone on the deck immediately above, but he would have to make sure.

He said to Anana, "There are any number of boats equipped with these chambers. Sometimes the captains know about them; sometimes they don't."

He pointed at the man. "We'll question him later." He tied the man's ankles and turned him over to bind his hands behind him. Then, though he wanted to lie down and sleep, he went back into the water. He came up near the anchor chain, which he climbed. His prowlings on the galley revealed no watchmen, and he got a good idea of the construction of the ship. Moreover, he found some sticks of dried meat and biscuits wrapped in waterproof intestines. There were no eagles in sight, and the patrol boat had drifted so far away that he could not see bodies—if there were any—in it.

When he returned to the chamber, he found the man conscious.

Petotoc said that he was hiding there because he was wanted by the police—he would not say what the charge was. He did not know about the invasion. It was evident that he did not believe Kickaha's story.

Kickaha spoke to the woman. "We must have been seen by enough people so that the search for us in the city will be off. They'll be looking for us in the old city, the farms, the countryside, and they'll be searching every boat, too. Then, when they can't find us, they may let normal life resume. And this boat may set out for wherever it's going."

Kickaha asked Petotoc where he could get enough food to last the three of them for a month. Anana's eyes opened, and she said, "Live a month in this damp, stinking hole?"

"If you want to live at all," Kickaha said. "I sincerely hope we won't be here that long, but I like to have reserves for an emergency."

"I'll go mad," she said.

"How old are you?" he said. "About ten thousand, at least, right? And you haven't learned the proper mental attitudes to get through situations like this in all that time?"

"I never expected to be in such a situation," she snarled.

Kickaha smiled. "Something new after ten millennia, huh? You should be happy to be free of boredom."

Unexpectedly, she laughed. She said, "I am tired and edgy. But you are right. It is better to be scared to death than to be bored to death. And what has happened . . ."

She spread her palms out to indicate speechlessness.

Kickaha, acting on Petotoc's information, went topside again. He lowered a small boat, rowed ashore, and broke into a small warehouse. He filled the boat with food and rowed back to the ship. Here he tied the rowboat to the anchor and then swam under to get Anana. The many dives and swims, hampered by carrying food in nets, wore them out even more. By the end of their labors, they were so tired they could barely pull themselves up onto the shelf in the chamber. Kickaha let the rowboat loose so it could drift away, and then he made his final dive.

Shaking with cold and exhaustion, he wanted desperately to sleep, but he did not dare leave the smuggler unguarded. Anana suggested that they solve that problem by killing Petotoc. The prisoner was listening, but he did not understand, since they were talking in the speech of the Lords. He did see her draw her finger across her throat though, and then he knew what they were discussing. He turned pale under his dark pigment.

"I won't do that unless it's necessary," Kickaha said. "Besides, even if he's dead, we still have to keep a guard. What if other smugglers come in? We can't be caught sleeping. Clatatol and her bunch were able to resist the temptation of the reward—although I'm not sure they could have held out much longer—but others may not be so noble."

He took first watch and only kept awake by dipping water and throwing it in his face, by talking to Petotoc, by pacing savagely back and forth on the shelf. When he thought two hours had passed, he roused her with slaps and water. After getting her promise that she would not succumb to sleep, he closed his eyes. This happened twice more, and then he was awakened the third time. But now he was not to stand guard.

She had placed her hand over his mouth and was whispering into his ear. "Be quiet! You were snoring! There are men aboard."

He lay for a long while listening to the thumps of feet, the shouts and talking, the banging and knocking as cargo was moved about and bulkheads and decks were knocked on to check for hollow compartments.

After 1,200 seconds, each of which Kickaha had silently counted off, the search party moved on. Again, he and Anana tried to overtake their lost sleep in turns.

7

WHEN THE TIME CAME THAT THEY BOTH FELT REFRESHED enough to stay awake at the same time, he asked her how she had gotten into this situation.

"The Black Bellers," she said. She held up her right hand. A ring with a deep black metal band and a large dark-green jewel was on the middle finger.

"I gave the smugglers all my jewels except this," she said. "I refused to part with that; I said I'd have to be killed first. For a moment, I thought they *would* kill me for it.

"Let me see, how to begin? The Black Bellers were originally an artificial form of life created by the Lord scientists about ten thousand years ago. The scientists created the Bellers during their quest for a true immortality.

"A Beller is bell-shaped, black, of indestructible material. Even if one were attached to a hydrogen bomb, the Beller would survive the fission. Or a Beller could be shot into the heart of a star, and it would go unscathed for a billion years.

"Now, the scientists had originally constructed the Beller so that it was purely automatic. It had no mind of its own; it was a device only. When placed on a man's head, it detected the man's skin potential and automatically extruded two extremely thin but rigid needles. These bored through the skull and into the brain.

"Through the needles, the Beller could discharge the contents of a man's mind, that is, it could uncoil the chains of giant protein molecules composing memory. And it could dissociate the complex neural patterns of the conscious and unconscious mind."

"What could be the purpose of that?" Kickaha said. "Why would a Lord want his brain unscrambled, that is, discharged? Wouldn't he be a blank, a *tabula rasa*, then?"

"Yes, but you don't understand. The discharged and uncoiled mind belonged to a human subject of the Lords. A slave."

Kickaha wasn't easily shocked, but he was startled and sickened now. "What? But . . ."

Anana said earnestly, "This was necessary. The slave would die someday anyway, so what's the difference? But a Lord could live even if his body was mortally hurt."

She did not explain that the scientific techniques of the Lords enabled them to live for millennia, perhaps millions of years, if no accidents, homicide, or suicide occurred. Kickaha, of course, knew this. The agelessness was, to a slighter degree, prevalent for human beings throughout this, Wolff's universe. The waters of this world contained substances provided by Wolff which kept human beings from aging for approximately a thousand years. It also cut down on fertility, so that there was no increase in the birth rate.

"The Bellers were to provide a means whereby the mental contents of a Lord could be transferred to the brain of a host. Thus, the Lord could live on in a new body while the old one died of its wounds.

"The Beller was constructed so that the mental contents of the Lord could be stored for a very long time indeed if an emergency demanded this. The Beller contained a power-pack for operation of the stored mind if this was desired. Moreover, the Beller automatically drew on the neural energy of the host to charge the power-pack. The uncoiling and dematricising were actually the Beller's methods of scanning the mind and then recording it within the bell structure. Duplicating the mind, as it were. The duplication resulted in stripping the original brain, in leaving it blank.

"I'm repeating," she said, "but only to make sure you understand me."

"I follow you," he said. "But this stripping, dematricising, scanning, and duplication doesn't seem to me to be a true immortality. It's not like pouring the mental contents of one head into another. It's not a genuine brain transference. It consists, in reality, of recording cerebral complexes, forebrain and, I suppose, hindbrain, too, to get the entire mind—or don't Bellers have unconsciousnesses?—while destroying them. And then running off the records—tapes, if you will—to build an identical brain in a different container.

"The brain of the second party, however, is not the brain of the first party. In reality, the first party is dead. And though the second party thinks that it is the first party, because it has the brain complex of the first party, it is only a duplication."

"A baby speaks the wisdom of the ages," she said. "That would be true if there were no such thing as the psyche, or the soul, as you humans call it. But the Lords had indubitable proof that an extra-spatial, extra-temporal entity, coeval with every sentient being, exists. Even you humans have them. These duplicate the mental content of the body or soma. Rather, they reflect the psyche-soma, or perhaps it's vice versa.

"Anyway, the psyche is the other half of the 'real' person. And when the duplicate soma-brain is built up in the Beller, the psyche, or soul, transfers to the Beller. And when the Beller retransfers the mental contents to the new host, the psyche then goes to the new host."

Kickaha said, "You have proof of this psyche? Photographs? Sensual indications? And so on?"

"I've never seen any," she said. "Or known anyone who had seen the proofs. But we have been assured that the proofs existed at one time."

"Fine," he said with a sarcasm that she may or may not have detected. "So then?"

"The experiment took over fifty years, I believe, before the Bellers were one hundred percent safe and perfectly operational. Most of the research was done on human slaves, who often died or became idiots."

"In the name of science!"

"In the name of the Lords," she said. "In the name of immortality for the Lords. But the human subjects, and later the Lords who became subjects, reported an almost unendurable feeling of detachment from reality, an agony of separation, while their brains were housed in the Bellers. You see, the brains did have some perception of the world outside if the needle-antennae were extruded. But this perception was very limited.

"To overcome the isolation and panic, the perceptive powers of the antennae were improved. Sound, odor, and a limited sense of vision were made available through the antennae."

Kickaha said, "These Black Bellers are former Lords?"

"No! The scientists accidentally discovered that an unused bell had the potentialities for developing into an entity. That is, an unused bell was a baby Beller. And if it were talked to, played with, taught to speak, to identify, to develop its embryonic personality—well, it became, not a thing, a mechanical device, but a person. A rather alien, peculiar person, but still a person."

"In other words," he said, "The framework for housing a human brain could become a brain in its own right?"

"Yes. The scientists became fascinated. They made a separate project out of raising Bellers. They found that a Beller could become as complex and as intelligent as an adult Lord. Meanwhile, the original project was abandoned, although undeveloped Bellers were to be used as receptacles for storing excess memories of Lords."

Kickaha said, "I think I know what happened."

She continued, "No one knows what really happened. There were ten thousand fully adult Bellers in the project and a number of baby Bellers. Somehow, a Beller managed to get its needle-antennae into the skull of a Lord. It uncoiled and dematricised the Lord's brain and then transferred itself into the host's brain. Thereafter, one by one, the other Lords in the project were taken over."

Kickaha had guessed correctly. The Lords had created their own Frankensteins.

"At that time, my ancestors were creating their private custom-made universes," she said. "They were indeed Lords—gods if there ever were any. The home universe, of course, continued to be the base for the stock population.

"Many of the Bellers in the hosts' bodies managed to get out of the home universe and into the private universes. By the time that the truth was discovered, it was impossible to know who had or had not been taken over, there had been so many transfers. Almost ten thousand Lords had been, as it was termed, 'belled.'

"The War of the Black Bellers lasted two hundred years. I was born during this time. By then, most of the Lord scientists and technicians had been killed. Over half the laymen population was also dead. The home universe was ravaged. This was the beginning of the end of science and progress and the beginning of the solipsism of the Lords. The survivors had much power and the devices and machines in their control. But the understanding of the principles behind the power and the machines was lost.

"Of the ten thousand Bellers, all but fifty were accounted for. The 9,950 were placed inside a universe specially created for them. This was triple-walled so that nobody could ever get in or out."

"And the missing fifty?"

"Never found. From then on, the Lords lived in suspicion, on the verge of panic. Yet, there was no evidence that any Lords were belled. In time, though the panic faded, the missing fifty were not forgotten."

She held up her right hand. "See this ring? It can detect the bell-housing of a Black Beller when it comes within twenty feet. It can't detect a Beller who's housed in a host-body, of course. But the Bellers don't like to be too far from the bells. If anything should happen to the host-body, a Beller wants to be able to transfer his mind back into the bell before the body dies.

"The ring, detecting the bell, triggers an alarm device implanted in the brain of the Lord. This alarm stimulates certain areas of the neural system so that the Lord hears the tolling of a bell. Now, to my knowledge, the tolling of the alarm bell has not sounded for a little less than ten thousand years. But it sounded for three of us not two weeks ago. And we knew that the ancient horror was loose."

"The fifty are now accounted for?" he said.

"Not all fifty. At least, I've seen only a few," she replied. "I think what happened is that all fifty must have been cached together in some universe. They lay in suspended animation for ten millennia. Then some human, some *leb*—" She stopped on seeing his expression and then continued, "Some human stumbled across the cache. He was curious and put one of the bell shapes on his head. And the Beller automatically extruded the needle-antennae. At the same time, the Beller awoke from his ten thousand year sleep. It anesthetized the human through his skin so that he wouldn't struggle, bored into the skull and brain, discharged the human neural configuration and memories, and then transferred itself into the brain. After that, the human-Beller found hosts for the remaining forty-nine. Then the fifty set out on their swift and silent campaign."

There was no telling how many universes the Bellers had taken nor how many Lords they had slain or possessed. They had been unlucky with three: Nimstowl, Judubra, and Anana. She and Nimstowl had managed to inform Judubra of the situation, and he had permitted them to take refuge in his universe. Only the Black Bellers could have made a Lord forget his perpetual war against every other Lord. Judubra was resetting his defenses when the enemy burst through. All three Lords had been forced to gate through to Wolff's palace in this universe.

They had chosen his palace because they had heard that he was now soft and weak; he would not try to kill them if they were friendly. But the palace seemed to be vacant except for the taloses, the half-metal, half-protein machines that were servants and guards for Wolff and Chryseis.

"Wolff gone?" Kickaha said. "Chryseis, too? Where?"

"I do not know," Anana said. "We had little time to investigate. We were forced to gate out of the control room without knowing where we were going. We came out in the Temple of Ollimaml, from which we fled into the city of Talanac. We were fortunate to run into Clatatol and her gang. Not four days later, the Drachelanders invaded Talanac. I don't know how the Black Bellers managed to possess von Turbat, von Swindebarn, and the others."

"They gated through to Dracheland," he said, "and they took over the two kings without the kings' subjects knowing it, of course. They probably didn't know that I was in Talanac, but they must have known about me, I suppose, from films and recordings in the palace. They came here after you Lords, but heard that I was here also and so came after me."

"Why would they want you?"

"Because I know a lot about the secret gates and traps in the palace. For one thing, they won't be able to get into the armory unless they know the pattern of code-breaking. That's why they wanted me alive. For the information I had."

She asked, "Are there any aircraft in the palace?"

"Wolff never had any."

"I think the Bellers will be bringing in some from my world. But they'll have to dismantle them to get them through the narrow gates in the palace. Then they'll have to put them together again. But when the humans see the aircraft, the Bellers will have to do some explaining."

"They can tell the people they're magical vessels," Kickaha said.

Kickaha wished he had the Horn of Shambarimen, or of Ilmarwolkin, as it was sometimes called. When the proper sequence of notes was blown from it at a resonant point in any universe, that point became a gate between two universes. The Horn could also be used to gate between various points on this planet. All that business of matching crescents of gates could be bypassed. But she had not seen the Horn. Probably Wolff had taken it with him, wherever he had gone.

The days and nights that followed were uncomfortable. They paced back and forth to exercise and also let Petotoc stretch his muscles while Kickaha held a rope tied around Petotoc's neck. They slept jerkily. Though they had agreed not to burn the lamp much, because they wanted to save fuel, they kept it lit a good part of the time.

The third day, many men came aboard. The anchor was hauled and the boat was, apparently, rowed into dock. Sounds of cargo being loaded filtered through the wooden bulkheads and decks. These lasted forty-eight hours without ceasing. Then the boat left the dock, and the oarsmen went to work. The hammer of the pacer, the creak of locks, the dip and whish of oars went on for a long time.

8

THE JOURNEY TOOK ABOUT SIX DAYS. THEN THE BOAT STOPPED, the anchor was run out, and sounds of unloading beat at the walls of the chamber. Kickaha was sure that they had traveled westward to the edge of the Great Plains.

When all seemed quiet, he swam out. Coming up on the landward side, he saw docks, other boats, a fire in front of a large log building, and a low, heavily wooded hill to the east.

It was the terminus frontier town for the river boats. Here the trade goods were transferred to the giant wagons, which would then set out in caravans toward the Great Trade Path.

Kickaha had no intention of letting Petotoc go, but he asked him if he wished to stay with them or would he rather take his chances on joining the Tishquetmoac. Petotoc replied that he was wanted for the murder of a policeman—he would take his chances with them.

They sneaked onto a farm near the edge of town and stole clothes, three horses, and weapons. To do this, it was necessary to knock out the farmer, his wife, and the two sons while they slept. Then the three rode out past the stockaded town and the fort. They came to the edge of the Great Plains an hour before dawn. They decided to follow the trade path for a while. Kickaha's goal was the village of the Hrowakas in the mountains a thousand miles away. There they could plan a campaign which involved some secret gates on this level.

Kickaha had tried to keep up Anana's morale during their imprisonment in the hidden chamber in the boat, joking and laughing, though softly so that he would not be heard by the sailors. But now he seemed to explode, he talked and laughed so much. Anana commented on this, saying that he was now the happiest man she had ever seen; he shone with joy.

"Why not?" he said, waving his hand to indicate the Great Plains. "The air is drunk with sun and green and life. There are vast rolling prairies before us, much like the plains of North America before the white man came. But far more exotic or romantic or colorful, or whatever adjective you choose. There are buffalo by the millions, wild horses, deer, antelope, and the great beasts of prey, the striped Plains lion or Felis Atrox, the running lion, which is a cheetah-like evolution of the puma, the dire wolf and the Plains wolf, the coyote, the prairie dog! The Plains teem with life! Not only pre-Columbian animals but many which Wolff gated through from Earth and which have become extinct there. Such as the mastodon, the mammoth, the uintathere, the plains camel, and many others.

"And there are the nomadic tribes of Amerinds; a fusion of American Indian and Scythian and Sarmatian white nomads of ancient Russia and Siberia. And the Half-Horses, the centaurs created by Jadawin, whose speech and customs are those of the Plains tribes.

"Oh, there is much to talk about here! And much which I do not know yet but will some day! Do you realize that this level has a land area larger than that of the North and South Americas of my native Earth combined?

"This fabulous world! My world! I believe that I was born for it and that it was more than a coincidence that I happened to find the means to get to it! It's a dangerous world, but then what world, including Earth, isn't? I have been the luckiest of men to be able to come here, and I would not go back to Earth for any price. This is my world!"

Anana smiled slightly and said, "You can be enthusiastic because you are young. Wait until you are ten thousand years old. Then you will find little to enjoy."

"I'll wait," he said. "I am fifty years old, I think, but I look and feel a vibrant twenty-five, if you will pardon the slick-prose adjective."

Anana did not know what slick-prose meant, and so Kickaha explained as best he could. He found out that Anana knew something about Earth, since she had been there several times, the latest visit being in the Earth year A.D. 1888. She had gone there on "vacation" as she put it.

They came to a woods, and Kickaha said they should camp here for the night. He went hunting and came back with a pygmy deer. He butchered it and then chopped branches and made a platform in the fork of two large branches of a tree. They agreed to take one-hour watches. Anana was doubtful about sleeping while Petotoc remained awake, but Kickaha said that they did not have to worry. The fellow was too frightened at the idea of being alone in this wild area to think of killing them or trying to escape on his own. It was then that Anana confessed that she was glad Kickaha was with her.

He was surprised, but agreeably. He said, "You're human after all. Maybe there's some hope for you."

She became angry and turned her back on him and pretended to go to sleep. He grinned and took his watch. The moon bulged greenly in the sky. There were many sounds but all faraway, an occasional trumpet from a mammoth or mastodon, the thunder of a lion, once the whicker of a wild horse, and once the whistle of a giant weasel. This made him freeze, and it caused his horses to whinny. The beast he feared most on the Plains, aside from man and Half-Horse, was the giant weasel. But an hour passed without sound or sight of one, and the horses seemed to relax. He told Petotoc about the animal, warned him to strain all shadows for the great long slippery bulk of the weasel, and not to hesitate to shoot with his bow if he thought he saw one. He wanted to make sure that Petotoc would not fall asleep on guard-duty.

Kickaha was on watch at dawn. He saw the flash of light on something white in the sky. Then he could see nothing, but a minute later the sun gleamed on an object in the sky again. It was far away but it was dropping down swiftly, and it was long and needle-shaped. When it came closer, he could see a bulge on its back, something like an enclosed cockpit; briefly, he saw silhouettes of four men.

Then the craft was dwindling across the prairie.

Kickaha woke Anna and told her what he'd seen. She said, "The Bellers must have brought in aircraft from my palace. That is bad. Not only can the craft cover a lot of territory swiftly, it is armed with two long-range beamers. And the Bellers must have hand-beamers, too."

"We could travel at night," Kickaha said. "But even so, we'd sometimes have to sleep in the open during the day. There are plenty of small wooded areas on the Great Plains, but they are not always available on our route."

"They could have more than one craft," she said. "And one could be out at night. They have means for seeing at night and also for detecting bodies at some distance by radiated heat."

There was nothing to do but ride on out into the open and hope that chance would not bring the Bellers near them. The following day, as Kickaha topped the crest of a slight hill, he saw men on horseback far off. These were not Plains nomads as he would have expected, nor Tishquetmoac. Their armory gleamed in the sun: helmets and cuirasses. He turned to warn the others.

"They must be Teutoniacs from Dracheland," he said. "I don't know how they got out here so fast . . . wait a minute! Yes! They must have come through a gate about ten miles from here. Its crescents are embedded in the tops of two buried boulders near a waterhole. I was thinking about swinging over that way to investigate, though there wasn't much sense in that. It's a one-way gate."

The Teutoniacs must have been sent to search for and cut off Kickaha if he were trying for the mountains of the Hrowakas.

"They'd need a million men to look for me on the Great Plains, and even then I could give them the slip," Kickaha said. "But that aircraft. That's something else."

Three days passed without incident except once, when they came upon a family of Felis Atrox in a little hollow. The adult male and female sprang up and rumbled warnings. The male weighed at least nine hundred pounds and had pale stripes on a tawny body. He had a very small mane; the hairs were thick but not more than an inch long. The female was smaller, weighing probably only seven hundred pounds. The two cubs were about the size of half-grown ocelots.

Kickaha softly told the others to rein in behind him and then he turned his trembling stallion away from the lions, slowly, slowly, and made him walk away. The lions surged forward a few steps but stopped to glare and to roar. They made no move to attack, however; behind them the half-eaten body of a wild striped ass told why they were not so eager to jump the intruders.

The fourth day, they saw the wagon caravan of Tishquetmoac traders. Kickaha rode to within a half mile of it. He could not be recognized at that distance, and he wanted to learn as much as he could about the caravan. He could not answer Anana's questions about the exact goal of his curiosity—he just liked to know things so he would not be ignorant if the situation should change. That was all.

Anana was afraid that Petotoc would take advantage of this to run for the caravan. But Kickaha had his bow ready, and Petotoc had seen enough of his ability to handle the bow to respect it.

There were forty great wagons in the caravan. They were the double-decked, ten wheeled type favored by the Tishquetmoac for heavy-duty Plains transportation. A team of forty mules, larger than Percherons, drew each wagon. There were also a number of smaller wagons which furnished sleeping quarters and food for the cavalry protecting the caravan. The guards numbered about fifty. And there were strings of extra horses for the cavalry and mules for the wagons. There were about three hundred and fifty men, women, and children.

Kickaha rode along to one side and studied the caravan. Finally, Anana said, "What are you thinking?"

He grinned and said, "That caravan will go within two hundred miles of the mountains of the Hrowakas. It'll take a hell of a long time to get there, so what I have to mind wouldn't be very practical. It's too daring. Besides, Petotoc has to be considered."

After he had listened to her plead for some time, he told her what he'd been thinking. She thought he was crazy. Yet, after some consideration, she admitted that the very unconventionality and riskiness of it, its unexpectedness, might actually make it work . . . if they were lucky. But, as he had said, there was Petotoc to consider.

For some time, whenever the Tishquetmoac had not been close enough to hear, she had been urging that they kill him. She argued that he would stab them in the back if he felt he would be safe afterward. Kickaha agreed with her, but he could not kill him without more justification. He thought of abandoning him on the prairie, but he was afraid that Petotoc would be picked up by the searchers.

They swung away from the caravan but rode parallel with it for several days at a distance of a few miles. At night, they retreated even further, since Kickaha did not want to be surprised by them. The third day he was thinking about leaving the caravan entirely and traveling in a southerly direction. Then he saw the flash of white on an object in the sky, and he rode toward a group of widely separated trees, which provided some cover. After tying the horses to bushes, the three crawled up a hill through the tall grass and spied on the caravan.

They were far enough so that they could just distinguish the figures of men. The craft dropped down ahead of the lead wagon and hovered about a foot off the ground. The caravan stopped.

For a long time, a group of men stood by the craft. Even at this distance, Kickaha could see the violent arm-wavings. The traders were protesting, but after a while, they turned and walked back to the lead wagon. And there a process began which took all day, even though the Tishquetmoac worked furiously. Every wagon was unloaded, and the wagons were then searched.

Kickaha said to Anana, "It's a good thing we didn't put my plan into action. We'd have been found for sure! Those guys"—meaning the Bellers—"are thorough!"

That night, the three went deeper into the woods and built no fire. In the morning, Kickaha, after sneaking close, saw that the aircraft was gone. The Tishquetmoac, who must have gotten up very early, were almost finished reloading. He went back to the camping place and spoke to Anana.

"Now that the Bellers have inspected that caravan, they're not very likely to do so again. Now we could do what I proposed—if it weren't for Petotoc."

He did, however, revise his original plan to cut to the south. Instead, he decided to keep close to the caravan. It seemed to him that the Bellers would not be coming back this way again for some time.

The fifth day, he went out hunting alone. He returned with a small deer over his saddle. He had left Anana and Petotoc beneath two trees on the south slope of a hill. They were still there, but Petotoc was sprawled on his back, mouth open, eyes rigid. A knife was stuck in his solar plexus.

"He tried to attack me, the *leblabbiy!*" Anana said. "He wanted me to lie down for him! I refused, and he tried to force me!"

It was true that Petotoc had often stared with obvious lust at Anana, but this was something any man would do. He had never tried to put his hand on her or made any suggestive remarks. This did not mean that he hadn't been planning to do so at the first chance, but Kickaha did not believe that Petotoc would dare make an advance to her. He was, in fact, in awe of Anana, and much too scared of being left alone.

On the other hand, Kickaha could not prove any accusation of murder or of lying. The deed was done, and it could not be undone, so he merely said, "Pull your knife out and clean it. I've wondered what you'd do if I said I wanted to lie with you. Now I know."

She surprised him by saying, "You aren't that one. But you'll never know unless you try, will you?"

"No," he said harshly. He looked at her curiously. The Lords were, according to Wolff, thoroughly amoral. That is, most of them were. Anana was an exceedingly beautiful woman who might or might not be frigid. But ten thousand years seemed like a long time for a woman to remain frigid. Surely techniques or devices existed in the great science of the Lords to overcome frigidity. On the other hand, would a thoroughly passionate woman be able to remain passionate after ten thousand years?

But Wolff had said that even the long-lived Lords lived from day to day. Like mortals, they were caught in the stream of time. And their memories were far from perfect, fortunately for them. So that, though they were subject to much greater boredom and ennui than the so-called mortals, they still weren't overwhelmed. Their rate of suicide was, actually, lower than a comparable group of humans, but this could be attributed to the fact that those with suicidal tendencies had long ago done away with themselves.

Whatever her feelings, she was not revealing them to him. If she was suffering from sexual frustration, as he was at this time, she was not showing any signs. Perhaps the idea of lying with him, a lowly, even repulsive, mortal, was unthinkable to her. Yet he had heard stories of the sexual interest Lords took in their more attractive human subjects. Wolff himself had said that, when he was Jadawin, he had rioted among the lovely females of this world, had used his irresistible powers to get what he wanted.

Kickaha shrugged. There were more important matters to think about at this moment. Survival outweighed everything.

9

FOR THE NEXT TWO DAYS THEY HAD TO RIDE FAR AWAY FROM THE caravan because the hunting parties from it foraged wide in their quest for buffalo, deer, and antelope meat. And then, while dodging the Tishquetmoac, the two almost ran into a small band of Satwikilap hunters. These Amerinds, painted in white and black stripes from head to foot, their long black hair coiled on top of their heads, bones stuck through their septums, strings of lion teeth around their necks, wearing lionskin pantaloons and deer moccasins, rode within a hundred yards of Anana and Kickaha. But they were intent on shooting the buffalo in the rear of a running herd and did not see them.

Moreover, the Tishquetmoac hunters were after the same bison, but they were on the other side of the herd, separated from the Satwikilap by a mile of almost solid flesh.

Kickaha suddenly made up his mind. He told Anana that tonight was the time. She hesitated, then said they might as well try. Certainly, anything that would take them out of the sight of the Bellers should be tried.

They waited until the eating of roast meat and the drinking of gin and vodka was finished and the caravaneers had staggered off to bed. There were non-drinking sentries posted at intervals along the sides of the wagon train, but the caravan was within the borders of the Great Trade Path marked by the carved wooden images of the god of trade and business so the Tishquetmoac did not really worry about attack from men or Half-Horses. Some animal might blunder into the camp or a giant weasel or lion try for a horse or even for a Tishquetmoac, but this wasn't likely, so the atmosphere was relaxed.

Kickaha removed all harness from the horses and slapped them on the rumps so they would take off. He felt a little sorry for them, since they were domesticated beasts and not likely to flourish on the wild Great Plains. But they would have to take their chances, as he was taking his.

Then he and Anana, a pack of bottled water and dried meat and vegetables tied to their backs, knives in their teeth, crawled in the moonspattered darkness toward the caravan. They got by two guards, stationed forty yards apart, without being seen. They headed for a huge ten-wheeler wagon that was twentieth in line. They crept past small wagons holding snoring men, women, and children. Fortunately, there were no dogs with the caravan and for a good reason. The cheetah-like puma and the weasel were especially fond of dogs, so much so that the Tishquetmoac had long ago given up taking these pets along on the Plains voyage.

Arranging living quarters inside the tightly packed cargo in the lower deck of a wagon was not easy. They had to pull out a number of wooden boxes and bolts of cloth and rugs and then remass them over the hole in which they would spend their daylight hours. The dislodged cargo was jammed in with some effort wherever it would go. Kickaha hoped that nobody would notice that the arrangements were not what they were when the wagon left the terminus.

They had two empty bottles for sanitary purposes; blankets provided a fairly comfortable bed for them—until the wagon started rolling in the morning. The wagon had no springs; and though the prairie seemed smooth enough to a man walking, the roughnesses became exaggerated in the wagon.

Anana complained that she had felt shut-in in the boat chamber, but now she felt as if she were buried in a landslide. The temperature outside seldom got above seventy-five degrees Fahrenheit at noon, but the lack of ventilation and the closeness of their bodies threatened to stifle them. They had to sit up and stick their noses into the openings to get enough oxygen.

Kickaha widened the openings. He hated to do so because it made discovery by the caravaneers more likely; while the wagon was traveling however, no one was going to peep into the lower deck.

They got little sleep the first day. At night, while the Tishquetmoac slept, they crept out and crawled past the sentries into the open. Here they bathed in a waterhole, refilled their bottles, and discharged natural functions which had been impossible, or highly inconvenient, inside the wagon. They exercised to take the stiffness out of muscles caused by cramped conditions and the jostling and bouncing. Kickaha wondered if he was so clever after all. It had seemed the most impudent thing in the world, hiding out literally under the noses, not to mention the buttocks, of the Tishquetmoac. Alone, he might have been more comfortable, more at ease. But though Anana did not really complain much, her not-quite-suppressed groans and moans and invectives irked him. It was impossible in those closely walled quarters not to touch each other frequently, but she reacted overviolently every time. She told him to stay to his own half of the "coffin," not to make his body so evident, and so on.

Kickaha began to think seriously about telling her to take off on her own. Or, if she refused, knocking her out and dragging her away some place and leaving her behind. Or, at times, he fantasized about slitting her throat or tying her to a tree so the lions or wolves could get her.

It was, he told himself, a hell of a way for a love affair to start.

And then he caught himself. Yes, he had said that: *love affair.* Now, how could he be in love with such a vicious, arrogant, murderous bitch?

He was. Much as he hated, loathed, and despised her, he was beginning to love her.

Love was nothing new to Kickaha in this or that other world . . . but never under these circumstances.

Undoubtedly, except for Podarge, who looked just like Anana as far as the face was concerned, and the strange, really unearthly Chryseis, Anana was the most beautiful woman he had ever seen.

To Kickaha, this would not automatically bring love. He appreciated beauty in a woman, of course, but he was more liable to fall in love with a woman with an agreeable personality and a quick brain and humor than with a disagreeable and/or dumb woman. If the woman was only reasonably attractive or perhaps even plain, he could fall in love with her if he found certain affinities in her.

And Anana was certainly disagreeable.

So why this feeling of love side by side with the hostility he felt toward her?

Who knows? Kickaha thought. *Evidently, I don't. And that in itself is pleasing, since I would not like to become bored and predictable about myself.*

The bad thing about this affair was that it would probably be one-sided. She might take a sensual interest in him, but it would be ephemeral and there would be contempt accompanying it. Certainly, she could never love a *leblabbiy.* For that matter, he doubted that she could love anyone. The Lords were beyond love. Or at least that was what Wolff had told him.

The second day passed more quickly than the first; both were able to sleep more. That night, they were treed by a pride of lions that had come down to drink at a stream shortly after the two humans arrived. Finally, as the hours had gone by and the lions showed no desire to wander on, Kickaha became desperate. Dawn would soon lighten this area. It would be impossible to sneak back into the wagon. He told Anana that they would have to climb down and try to bluff the big cats.

Kickaha, as usual, had another motive than the obvious. He hoped that, if she had any weapons concealed or implanted in her body, she would reveal them now. But either she had none or she did not think the situation desperate enough to use them. She said that he could attempt to scare the monsters, if he wished, but she intended to stay in the tree until they went away.

"Under ordinary circumstances, I'd agree with you," he said. "But we have to get back inside the wagon within the next half hour."

"I don't have to," she said. "Besides, you didn't kill anything for us to eat before we went back. I don't want to spend another hungry day inside that coffin."

"You had plenty of dried meat and vegetables to eat," he said.

"I was hungry all day," she replied.

Kickaha started to climb down. Most of the lions seemed to be paying no attention to him. But a male sprang into the air and a long-clawed paw came within six inches of his foot. He went back up the tree.

"They don't seem to be in a mood to be bluffed," he said. "Some days they are. Today, well . . ."

From his height in the tree he could see part of the wagon train, even in the moonlight. Presently the moon went around the monolith and the sun followed it from the east. The caravaneers began to wake. Campfires were built, and the bustle of getting ready for breakfast and then breaking camp began. Presently, a number of soldiers, colorful in long-feathered wooden casques, scarlet quilt-cuirasses, green feathered kilts, and yellow-dyed leggings, mounted their horses. They formed a crescent within which men and women, carrying pots, kettles, jugs, and other utensils, marched. They headed toward the waterhole.

Kickaha groaned. Occasionally he outfoxed himself, and this could be one of the occasions.

There was not the slightest doubt about his choice. It would be far better to face the lions than to be captured by the Tishquetmoac. While he might be able to talk them out of turning him over to the Teutoniacs, he doubted it very much. Anyway, he could not afford to risk their mercy.

He said, "Anana, I'm going north, and I'm going fast. Coming along?"

She looked down at the big male lion, crouched at the foot of the tree and staring up with huge green eyes. His mouth also stared. Four canines, two up, two down, seemed as long as daggers.

"You must be crazy," she said.

"You stay here if you want to. So long, if ever!"

He began to climb down but on the other side of the tree, away from the lion. The great beast arose and roared, and then the others were on their feet and pointing toward the approaching humans. The wind had brought their scent.

For a moment, the cats did not seem to know what to do. Then the male under the tree roared and slunk off and the others followed him. Kickaha dropped the rest of the way and ran in the same direction as the lions. He did not look back, but he hoped that Anana would have enough presence of mind to follow him. If the soldiers caught her, or even saw her, they would search the area on the premise that other fugitives might be nearby.

He heard her feet thudding on the earth, and then she was close behind him. He looked back then, not at her but for signs of the cavalry. He saw the head of one soldier appear over a slight rise, and he grabbed Anana and pulled her down into the high grass.

There was a shout—the rider had seen them. It was to be expected. And now . . . ?

Kickaha stood up and looked. The first rider was in full view. He was standing up in the stirrups and pointing in their direction. Others were coming up behind him. Then the lead man was riding toward them, his lance couched.

Kickaha looked behind him. Plains and tall grass and a few trees here and there. Far off, a gray many-humped mass that was a herd of mammoths. The lions were somewhere in the grass.

The big cats would have to be his joker. If he could spring them at the right time, and not get caught himself, then he might get away.

He said, "Follow me!" and began to run as swiftly as he had ever run in his life. Behind him, the soldiers yelled and the horses' hooves krok-krok-krokked.

The lions failed him. They scattered away, bounding easily, not panicked but just not wanting to turn to fight at this moment. They did not give him the opportunity he sought to flee while horse and rider were being clawed down by lions at bay.

Some of the cavalry passed him and then they had turned and were facing him, their lances forming a crescent. Behind him, other lances made a half ring. He and Anana were between the crescents with no place to go unless they hurled themselves on the lance-points.

"This is what I get for being too smart," he said to Anana.

She did not laugh. He did not feel much like laughing himself.

He felt even less like it when they were brought back, bound and helpless, to the caravan. The chief, Clishquat, informed them that the rewards had been tripled. And though he had heard of Kickaha, and of course admired and respected him as the beloved of the Lord, well, things had changed, hadn't they?

Kickaha had to admit that they had. He asked Clishquat if the emperor was still alive. Clishquat was surprised at the question. Of course the *miklosiml* was alive. He was the one offering the rewards. He was the one who had proclaimed the alliance with the pinkface sorcerers who flew in a wheelless wagon. And so on.

Kickaha's intention to talk the caravaneers out of keeping him captive by telling them the true situation in Talanac did not work. The empire-wide system of signal drums and of pony express had acquainted the frontier towns with conditions in the capital city. It was true that some of the news was false, but Clishquat would not believe Kickaha concerning it. Kickaha could not blame him.

The two captives were given a full meal; and women bathed them, oiled their bodies and hair, combed their hair and put fresh clothes on them. During this, the chiefs, the underchiefs, and the soldiers who had captured the two, argued. The chief thought that the soldiers should split the reward with him. The underchiefs believed they should get in on the money. And then some representatives of the rest of the caravaneers marched up. They demanded that the reward be split evenly throughout the caravan.

At this, the chiefs and the soldiers began screaming at the newcomers. Finally, the chief quieted them down. He said that there was only one way to settle the matter. That would be to submit the case to the emperor. In effect, this meant the high court of judges of Talanac.

The soldiers objected. The case would limp along for years before being settled. By then, the legal fees would have devoured much of the reward money.

Clishquat, having scared everybody with this threat, then offered a compromise which he hoped would be satisfactory. One-third should go to the soldiers; one-third to the civilian leaders of the caravan, the chief and chieflings; one-third to be divided equally among the remaining men.

There was a dispute that lasted through lunch and supper. The train did not move during this.

Then, when everybody had agreed, more or less amicably, on the splitting of the reward, a new argument started. Should the caravan move on, taking the prisoners with them, in the hope that the magic airboat would come by again, as the pinkface sorcerers had promised? The prisoners could then be turned over to the sorcerers. Or should a number of soldiers take the prisoners back to Talanac while the caravan moved on to its business?

Some objectors said that the sorcerers might not return. Even if they did, they would not have room in the boat for the fugitives.

Others said that those picked to escort the prisoners home might claim the entire reward for themselves. By the time the caravan returned to civilization, it might find that the escort had spent the money. And suit in court would be useless.

And so on and so on.

Kickaha asked a woman how the pinkfaces had communicated with the caravan chief.

"There were four pinkfaces and each had a seat in the magic car," she replied. "But a priest talked for them. He sat by the feet of the one who was in a chair in front and to the right. The pinkfaces talked in the language of the Lords—I know it at least when I hear it, though I do not speak it as the priests do—and the priests listened and then spoke to the chief in our language."

Late at night, when the moon was halfway across the bridge of sky, the argument was still going on. Kickaha and Anana went to sleep in their beds of furs and blankets in the upper deck of a wagon. They awoke in the morning to find camp being broken. It had been decided to take the prisoners along with the hope that the magic flying car would return as its occupants had promised.

The two captives were permitted to walk behind the wagon during the day. Six soldiers kept guard throughout the day, and another six stood watch over the wagon at night.

THE THIRD NIGHT, EVENTS DEVELOPED AS KICKAHA HAD BEEN hoping they would. The six guards had been very critical of the decision to split the reward throughout the caravan. They spent a good part of the night muttering among themselves, and Kickaha, awake part of the time, testing his bonds, overheard much of what they said.

He had warned Anana to make no outcry or struggle if she should be awakened by the sentries. The two were rousted out with warnings to keep silent or die with slit throats. They were marched off between two unconscious sentries and into a small group of trees. Here were horses, saddled, packed, ready to be mounted by the six soldiers and two prisoners, and extra pack horses. The party rode out slowly for several miles, then began to canter. Their flight lasted the night and half the next day. They did not stop to make camp until they were sure that they were not pursued. Since they had left the trade trail and swung far north, they did not expect to be followed.

The next day, they continued parallel with the trade trail. On the third day, they began to angle back toward it. Being so long outside the safety of the trade path made them nervous.

Kickaha and Anana rode in the center of the party. Their hands were tied with ropes but loosely, so they could handle the reins. They stopped at noon. They were just finishing their cooked rabbit and greens boiled in little pots, when a lookout on a hill nearby called out. He came galloping toward them, and, when he was closer, he could be heard.

"Half-Horses!"

The pots were emptied on top of the fire, and dirt was kicked over the wet ashes. In a panic, the soldiers packed away most of their utensils. The two captives were made to remount, and the party started off southward, toward the trade trail, many miles away.

It was then that the soldiers saw the wave of buffalo moving across the plains. It was a tremendous herd several miles across and of a seemingly interminable length. The right flank was three miles from them, but the earth quivered under the impact of perhaps a quarter of a million hooves.

For some reason known only to the buffalo, they were in flight. They were stampeding westward, and they were going so swiftly that the Tishquetmoac party might not be able to get across the trade path in time. They had a chance, but they would not know how good it was until they got much closer to the herd.

The Half-Horses had seen the humans, and they had bent into full gallop. There were about thirty of them: a chief with a full-feathered and long-tailed bonnet, a number of blooded warriors with feathered headbands, and three or four unblooded juveniles.

Kickaha groaned; it seemed to him that they were of the Shoyshatel tribe. They were so far away that the markings were not quite distinct. But he thought that the bearing of the chief was that of the Half-Horse who had shouted threats at him when Kickaha had taken refuge at the Tishquetmoac fort.

Then he laughed, because it did not matter which tribe it was. All Half-Horse tribes hated Kickaha and all would treat him as cruelly as possible if they caught him.

He yelled at the leader of the soldiers, Takwoc, "Cut the ropes from our wrists! They're handicapping us! We can't get away from you, don't worry!"

Takwoc looked for a moment as if he might actually cut the ropes. The danger involved in riding so close to Kickaha, the danger of the horses knocking each other down or Kickaha knocking him off the saddle, probably made him change his mind. He shook his head.

Kickaha cursed and then crouched over the neck of the stallion and tried to evoke from him every muscle-stretching-contracting quota of energy in his magnificent body. The stallion did not respond because he was already running as swiftly as he could.

Kickaha's horse, though fleet, was half a body-length behind the stallion which Anana rode. Perhaps they were about equal in running ability, but Anana's lighter weight made the difference. The others were not too far behind and were spread out in a rough crescent, with horns curving away from him, three on each side. The Half-Horses were just coming over the rise; they slowed down a moment, probably in amazement at the sight of the tremendous herd. Then they waved their weapons and charged on down the hill.

The herd was rumbling westward. The Tishquetmoac and prisoners were coming on the buffalos' right at an angle of forty-five degrees. The Half-Horses had swung a little to the west before coming over the hill and their greater speed had enabled them to squeeze the distance down between them and their intended victims.

Kickaha, watching the corner formed by the flank of the great column of beasts and the front part—almost square—saw that the party could get across in front of the herd. From then on, speed and luck meant safety to the other side or being overwhelmed by the racing buffalo. The party could not directly cut across the advance; it would have to run ahead of the beasts and at an angle at the time time.

Whether or not the horses could keep up their present thrust of speed, whether or not a horse or all horses might slip, that would be known in a very short time.

He shouted encouragement at Anana as she looked briefly behind, but the rumble of the hooves, shaking the earth and sounding like a volcano ready to blow its crust, tore his voice to shreds.

The roar, the odor of the beasts, the dust, frightened Kickaha. At the same time, he was exhilarated. This wasn't the first time that he had been raised by his fright out of fright and into near-ecstasy. Events seemed to be on such a grand scale all of a sudden, and the race was such a fine one, with the prize sudden safety or sudden death, that he felt as if he were kin to the gods, if not a god. That moment when mortality was so near, and so probable, was the moment he felt immortal.

It was quickly gone, but while it lasted he knew that he was experiencing a mystical state.

Then he was seemingly heading for a collision with the angle formed by the flank and front of the herd.

Now he could see the towering shaggy brown sides of the giant buffalo, the humps heaving up and down like the bodies of porpoises soaring from wave to wave, the dark brown foreheads, massive and lowering, the dripping black snouts, the red eyes, the black eyes, the red-shot white eyes, the legs working so swiftly they were almost a blur, foam curving from the open foam-toothed mouths onto thick shaggy chests and the upper parts of the legs.

He could hear nothing at first but that rumbling as of the earth splitting open, so powerful that he expected, for a second, to see the plain open beneath the hooves and fire and smoke spurt out.

He could smell a million buffalo, beasts extinct for ten thousand years on Earth, monsters with horns ten feet across, sweating with panic and the heart-shredding labor of their flight, excrement of fear befouling them and their companions, and something that smelled to him like a mixture of foam from mouth and blood from lungs, but that, of course, was his imagination.

There was also the stink of his horse, sweat of panic and labor of flight and of foam from its mouth.

"Haiyeeee!" Kickaha shouted, turning to scream at the Half-Horses, wishing his hands were not tied and he had a weapon to shake at them. He could not hear his own defiance, but he hoped that the Half-Horses would see his open mouth and his grin and know that he was mocking them.

By now, the centaurs were within a hundred and fifty yards of their quarry. They were frenzied in their efforts to catch up; their great dark broad-cheekboned faces were twisted in agony.

They could not close swiftly enough, and they knew it. By the time their quarry had shot across the right shoulder of the herd at an angle, they would still be fifty or so yards behind. And by the time they reached the front of the herd, their quarry would be too far ahead. And after that, they would slowly lose ground before the buffalo, and before they could get to the other side, they would go down under the shelving brows and curving horns and cutting hooves.

Despite this, the Half-Horses galloped on. An unblooded, a juvenile whose headband was innocent of scalp or feather, had managed to get ahead of the others. He left the others behind at such a rate that Kickaha's eyes widened. He had never seen so swift a Half-Horse before, and he had seen many. The unblooded came on and on, his face twisted with an effort so intense that Kickaha would not have been surprised to see the muscles of the face tear loose.

The Half-Horse's arm came back, and then forward, and the lance flew ahead of him, arcing down, and suddenly Kickaha saw that what he had thought would be impossible was happening.

The lance was going to strike the hind quarters or the legs of his stallion. It was coming down in a curve that would fly over the Tishquetmoac riders behind him and would plunge into some part of his horse.

He pulled the reins to direct the stallion to the left, but the stallion pulled its head to one side and slowed down just a trifle. Then he felt a slight shock, and he knew that the lance had sunk into its flesh.

Then the horse was going over, its front legs crumpling, the back still driving and sending the rump into the air. The neck shot away from before him, and he was soaring through the air.

Kickaha did not know how he did it. Something took over in him as it had done before, and he did not fall or slide into the ground. He landed running on his feet with the black-and-brown wall of the herd to his left. Behind him, so close that he could hear it even above the rumble-roar of the herd, was the thunk of horses' hooves. Then the sound was all around him, and he could no longer stay upright because of his momentum, and he went into the grass on his face and slid.

A shadow swooped over him; it was that of a horse and rider as the horse jumped him. Then all seven were past him; he saw Anana looking back over her shoulder just before the advancing herd cut her—cut all the Tishquetmoac, too—from his sight.

There was nothing they could do for him. To delay even a second meant death for them under the hooves of the buffalo or the spears of the Half-Horses. He would have done the same if he had been on his horse and she had fallen off hers.

Surely the Half-Horses must have been yelling in triumph now. The stallion of Kickaha was dead, a lance projecting from its rump and its neck broken. Their greatest enemy, the trickster who had so often given them the slip when they knew they had him, even he could not now escape. Not unless he were to throw himself under the hooves of the titans thundering not ten feet away!

This thought may have struck them, because they swept toward him with the unblooded who had thrown the lance trying to cut him off. The others had thrown their lances and tomahawks and clubs and knives away and were charging with bare hands. They wanted to take him alive.

Kickaha did not hesitate. He had gotten up as soon as he was able and now he ran toward the herd. The flanks of the beasts swelled before him; they were six feet high at the shoulder and running as if time itself were behind them and threatening to make them extinct like their brothers on Earth.

Kickaha ran toward them, seeing out of the corner of his eyes the young unblooded galloping in. Kickaha gave a savage yell and leaped upward, his hands held before him. His foot struck a massive shoulder and he grabbed a shag of fur. He kicked upward and slipped and fell forward and was on his stomach on the back of a bull!

He was looking down the steep valley formed by the right and left sides of two buffalo. He was going up and down swiftly, was getting sick, and also was slowly sliding backward.

After loosing his hold on the tuft of hair, he grabbed another one to his right and managed to work himself around so that his legs straddled the back of the beast. The hump was in front of him; he was hanging onto the hair of it.

If Kickaha believed only a little in what had happened, the Half-Horse youth who had thought he had Kickaha in his hands believed it not at all.

He raced alongside the bull on which Kickaha was seated, and his eyes were wide and his mouth worked. His arms were extended in front of him as if he still thought he would scoop Kickaha up in them.

Kickaha did not want to let loose of his hold, insecure though it was, but he knew that the Half-Horse would recover in a moment. Then he would pull a knife or tomahawk from the belt around the lower part of his human torso, and he would throw it at Kickaha. If he missed, he had weapons in reserve.

Kickaha brought his legs up so that he was squatting on top of the spine of the great bull, his feet together, one hand clenching buffalo hair. He turned slowly, managing to balance himself despite the up-and-down jarring movement. Then he launched himself outward and onto the back of the next buffalo, which was running shoulder to shoulder with the animal he had just left.

Something dark rotated over his right shoulder. It struck the hump of a buffalo nearby and bounced up and fell between two animals. It was a tomahawk.

Kickaha pulled himself up again, this time more swiftly, and he got his feet under him and jumped. One foot slipped as he left the back, but he was so close to the other that he grabbed fur with both hands. He hung there while his toes just touched the ground whenever the beast came down in its galloping motion. Then he let himself slide down a little, pushed against the ground, and swung himself upward. He got one leg over the back and came up and was astride it.

The young Half-Horse was still keeping pace with him. The others had dropped back a little; perhaps they thought he had fallen down between the buffalo and so was ground into shreds. If so, they must have been shocked to see him rise from the supposed dead, the Trickster, slippery, cunning, many-turning, the enemy who mocked them from within death's mouth.

The unblooded must have been driven a little crazy when he saw Kickaha. Suddenly, his great body, four hooves flying, soared up and he was momentarily standing on the back of a buffalo at the edge of the herd. He sprang forward to the next one, onto its hump, like a mountain goat skipping on moving mountains.

Now it was Kickaha's turn to be amazed and dismayed. The Half-Horse held a knife in his hand, and he grinned at Kickaha as if to say, "At last, you are going to die, Kickaha! And I, I will be sung of throughout the halls and tepees of the Nations of the prairies and the mountains, by men and Half-Horses everywhere!"

Some such thoughts must have been in that huge head. And he would have become the most famous of all dwellers on and about the Plains, if he had succeeded. Trickster-killer he would have been named.

He Who Skipped Over Mad Buffalo To Cut Kickaha's Throat.

But on the third hump, a hoof slipped and he plunged on over the hump and fell down between two buffalo, his back legs flying and tail straight up. And that was the end of him, though Kickaha could not see what the buffalo hooves were doing.

Still, the attempt had been magnificent and had almost succeeded, and Kickaha honored him even if he was a Half-Horse. Then he began to think again about surviving.

11

SOME OF THE CENTAURS HAD DRAWN UP EVEN WITH HIM AND
began loosing arrows at him.

Before the first shaft was released, he had slipped over to one side of
the buffalo on which he was mounted, hanging on with both hands to fur,
one leg bent as a hook over the back. His position was insecure, because
the rough gallop loosened his grip a little with every jolt, and the beast next
to him was so close that he was in danger of being smashed.

Shafts passed over him; something touched the foot sticking up in the
air. A tomahawk bounced off the top of the buffalo's head. Suddenly, the
bull began coughing, and Kickaha wondered if his lungs had been penetrated by an arrow. The bull began to slow down, stumbled a little, recovered, and went on again.

Kickaha reached out for the next beast, grabbed a fistful of fur, released
the other hand, clutched more fur, let loose with the right leg, and his body
swung down. Like a trick horse rider, he struck the ground with both feet;
his legs and body swung up, and he hooked his left leg over the back just
behind the hump.

Behind him, the buffalo he had just left fell, slid, stopped, on its side,
kicking, two arrows sticking from it. Then the beasts behind it jumped, but
the third one tripped, and there was a pile-up of at least ten mammoth bodies kicking, struggling, goring, and then dying as even more crashed into
them and over them and on them.

Something was happening ahead. He could not see what it was because
he was hanging on the side of the buffalo, his view blocked by tails, rumps,
and legs. But the beasts were slowing down and were also turning to the
left.

The buffalo on the right bellowed as if mortally hurt. And so it was. It
staggered off, fortunately away from Kickaha, otherwise it would have
smashed him if it had fallen against him. It collapsed, blood running from
a large hole in its hump.

Kickaha became aware of two things: one, the thunder of the stampede had lessened so much that he could hear individual animals nearby as they cried out or bellowed; two, in addition to the other odors, there was now that of burned flesh and hair.

The beast on the other side fell away, and then that carrying Kickaha was alone. It charged on, passing the carcasses of just-killed buffalo. It bounded over a cow with its great head half cut off. And when it came down, the shock tore Kickaha's grip loose. He fell off and rolled over and over and came up on his feet, ready for he knew not what.

The world seesawed about him, then straightened out. He was gasping for breath, shaking, sweaty, bloody, filthy with buffalo dung and foam and dirt. But he was ready to jump this way or that, depending upon the situation.

There were dead buffalo everywhere. There were also dead Half-Horses here and there. The living in the herd were racing off to the left now; the torrent of millions of tons of flesh and hooves roared by and away.

A crash sounded, so unexpectedly and loudly that he jumped. It was as if a thousand large ships had simultaneously smashed into a reef. Something had killed all of the beasts in a line a mile across, killed them one after the other within six or seven seconds. And those behind the line stumbled over these, and those behind rammed them and went hoof-over-hoof.

Abruptly, the stampede had stopped. Those animals fortunate enough to stop in time stood stupidly about, wheezing for air. Those buried in the huge mounds of carcasses, but still living, bellowed; they were the only ones with enough motive to voice any emotion. The others were laboring to run their breaths down.

Kickaha saw the cause of the dead and of the halted stampede. To his left, a quarter of a mile away and about twenty feet up, was an aircraft. It was needle-shaped, wingless; its lower part was white with black arabesques, its upper part was transparent coaming. Five silhouettes were within the covering.

It was chasing after a Tishquetmoac who was trying to escape on his horse. Chasing was the wrong word. The craft moved swiftly enough but leisurely and made no effort to get immediately behind the horse. A bright white beam shot out from the cylinder mounted on the nose of the craft. Its end touched the rump of the horse which fell. The Tishquetmoac man threw himself out and, though he rolled heavily, he came up and onto his feet.

Kickaha looked around on all sides. Anana was a quarter of a mile away in the other direction. Several Tishquetmoac stood near her. A couple lay on the ground as if dead; one was caught beneath his horse. All the horses were dead, apparently rayed down by the craft.

Also dead were all the Half-Horses.

The Bellers had killed the horses to keep the party from escaping. They might not even know that the man and woman they were looking for were in this group. They might have spotted the chase and swung over for a look and decided to save the chased b̶ ̶ause they might have some information. On the other hand, both Anana and Kickaha were lighter skinned than the Tishquetmoac in the party. The Tishquetmoac did, however, vary somewhat in darkness; a small minority were not so heavily pigmented. So the Bellers would have decided to check them out. Or . . . there were many possibilities. None mattered now. The important thing was that he and Anana were, seemingly, helpless. They could not get away. And the weapons of the Bellers were overwhelming.

Kickaha did not just give up, although he was so tired that he almost felt like it. He thought, and while he was thinking, he heard a pound of hooves and a harsh rasping breathing. He launched himself forward and at an angle on the theory that he might evade whatever was attacking him—if he were being attacked.

A lance shot by him and then slid along the ground. A bellow sounded behind him; he whirled to see a Half-Horse advancing on him. The centaur was badly wounded; his hindquarters were burned, his tail was half charred off, and his back legs could scarcely move. But he was determined to get Kickaha before he died. He held a long heavy knife in his left hand.

Kickaha ran to the lance, picked it up, and threw it. The Half-Horse yelled with frustration and despair and tried to evade the spear. Handicapped by his crippled legs, he did not move fast enough. He took the lance in his human chest—Kickaha had aimed for the protruding bellows organ below the chest—and fell down. Up he came, struggling to his front legs while the rear refused to move again. He tore the lance out with his right hand, turned it, and, ignoring the spurt of blood from the wound, again cast it. This surprised Kickaha, who was running to push in on the lance and so finish him off.

The arm of the dying centaur was weak. The lance left his hand to fly a few feet and then plunged into the earth before Kickaha's feet. The Half-Horse gave a cry of deep desolation—perhaps he had hoped for glory in song here and a high place in the councils of the dead. But now he knew that if a Half-Horse ever slew Kickaha, he would not be the one.

He fell on his side, dropping the knife as he went down. His front legs kicked several times, his huge fierce face became slack, and the black eyes stared at his enemy.

Kickaha glanced quickly around him, saw that the aircraft was flying a foot above the ground about a quarter of a mile away. Apparently it was corraling several Tishquetmoac who were fleeing on foot. Anana was down. He did not know what had happened to her. Perhaps she was playing possum, which was what he intended to do.

He rubbed some of the centaur's blood over him, lay down in front of him, placed the knife so it was partly hidden under his hip, and then placed the lance point between his chest and arm. Its shaft rose straight up, looking from a distance as if the lance were in his chest, he hoped.

It was a trick born out of desperation and not likely to succeed. But it was the only one he had now, and there was the chance that the Bellers, being nonhuman, might not be on to certain human ruses. In any event, he would try it, and if it didn't work, well, he didn't really expect to live forever. And he had managed to survive so far because he had fought more energetically and cunningly than most.

For what seemed a long time afterward, nothing happened. The wind blew coolly on the blood and sweat. The sweat dried off and the blood dried up. The sun was sinking in the last quarter of the green sky. Kickaha wished that it were dusk, which would increase his chances, but if wishes were horses, he would ride out of here.

A shadow flitted over his eyes. He tensed, thinking it might be that of the aircraft. A harsh cry told him that it was a crow or raven, coming to feed. Soon the carrion eaters would be flying in thicker than pepper on a pot roast: crows, ravens, buzzards, giant vultures, even larger condors, hawks, and eagles, some of which would be the mammoth green eagles, Podarge's pets.

And the coyote, the Plains fox, the common wolf, and the dire wolf would be following their noses and running in to the toothsome feast.

And the greater predators, not too proud to eat meat which they had not brought down, would pad in from the tall grass and then roar to frighten away the lesser beasts. The nine hundred pound palely striped Plains lions would attend with much roaring and snarling and scrapping among themselves and slashes and dashes at the smaller beasts and birds.

Kickaha thought of this and began to sweat again. He shooed a crow away by hissing and cursing out of the corner of his mouth. Far away, a wolf howled. A condor sailed overhead and banked slowly as it glided in for a landing, probably on some fallen buffalo.

Then another shadow passed. Through his half-closed eyelids, he saw the aircraft slide silently over him. It dipped its nose and began to sink, but he could not follow it without turning his head. It had been about fifty feet up, which he hoped would be far enough away so that they might still believe the lance had gone into his chest or armpit.

Somebody shouted in the language of the Lords. The voice was downwind, so he could not distinguish many words.

After a silence, several voices came to him, this time from upwind. If the Bellers were still in the craft, then it had moved between him and Anana. He hoped that a Beller would get out and walk over to examine him; he hoped that the craft would not first fly to a point just above him, where the occupants could lean out and look at him. He knew that the Bellers probably had hand-beamers and that these would be in readiness. In addition, the Bellers left in the craft would be using the larger projectors to cover those outside.

He did not hear the footsteps of the approaching Beller. The fellow had undoubtedly had his beamer on Kickaha, ready to shoot if he thought Kickaha was pretending to be dead or unconscious. Kickaha would not have had a chance.

But luck was with him again. This time it was a bull buffalo. It rose behind the Beller and, bellowing, tried to charge him. The Beller whirled. Kickaha rolled over, using the dead Half-Horse as a shield, and looked over it. The buffalo was badly hurt and fell on its side again before it had taken three steps. The Beller did not even use his beamer. But his back was momentarily turned to Kickaha, and the attention of those in the craft seemed to be on the other Beller on the ground. He was walking toward Anana's pile of buffalo.

At the bellow, one of the men in the craft turned. He swung the projector on its pivot. The Beller on the ground waved reassuringly at him and pointed to the carcass. The fellow in the craft resumed watching the other Beller. Kickaha rose and rushed the man, knife in hand. The Beller turned slowly and he was completely taken by surprise. He swung his beamer up, and Kickaha hurled the knife even if it was unfamiliar and probably unsuited for such work.

He had spent literally thousands of hours in practicing knife-throwing. He had cast knives of many kinds at many distances from many angles, even while standing on his head. He had forced himself to engage in severe discipline; he had thrown knives until he began to think he was breathing knives and the sight of one made him lose his appetite.

The unending hours, the sweat, frustration, and discipline paid off. The knife went into the Beller's throat, and the Beller fell over backward. The beamer lay on the ground.

Kickaha threw himself at the weapon, picked it up, saw that, though not of a familiar make, it was operated like the others. A little catch on the side of the butt had to be depressed to activate the weapon. The trigger could then be pulled; this was a slightly protruding plate on the inner side of the butt.

The Beller in the rear of the craft was swinging the big projector around toward Kickaha. Its ray sprang out whitely and dug a smoking swath in the ground; it struck a mound of buffalo, which burst into flames. The projector was not yet on full-power.

Kickaha did not have to shoot the Beller. A ray struck the Beller from the side, and he slumped over. Then the ray rose and fell, and the craft was cut in half. The others in the cockpit had already been struck down.

Kickaha rose cautiously and shouted, "Anana! It's me! Kickaha! Don't shoot!"

Presently Anana's white face came around the hillock of shaggy, horned carcasses. She smiled at him and shouted back, "It's all right! I got all of them!"

He could see the outflung hand of the Beller who had been approaching her. Kickaha walked toward her, but he felt apprehensive.

Now that she had a beamer and a craft—part of a craft, anyway—would she need him?

Before he had taken four more steps, he knew that she still needed him. He increased his pace and smiled. She did not know this world as he did, and the forces against her were extremely powerful. She wasn't going to turn on such a valuable ally.

Anana said, "How in Shambarimen's name did you manage to live through all that? I would have sworn that you had been cut off by the herd and that the Half-Horses would get you."

"The Half-Horses were even more confident," he said, and he grinned. He told her what had happened. She was silent for a moment, then she asked, "Are you sure you're not a Lord?"

"No, I'm human and a mere Hoosier, though not so mere at that, come to think of it."

"You're shaking," she said.

"I'm naturally high-strung," he said, still grinning. "You look like you're related to an aspen leaf, yourself."

She glanced at the beamer, quivering in her hand, and smiled grimly. "We've both been through a lot."

"There's nothing to apologize for, for chrissakes," he said. "Okay, let's see what we have here."

The Tishquetmoac men were small figures in the distance. They had begun running when Anana had started beaming, and they evidently did not plan on returning. Kickaha was glad. He had no plans for them and did not want to be appealed to for help.

Anana said, "I played dead, and I threw a spear at him and killed him. The Bellers in the craft were so surprised that they froze. I picked up the beamer and killed them."

It was a nice, clean, simple story. Kickaha did not believe it. She had not been helped by a disturbance, as he had, and he could not see how she could have gotten up and thrown a spear before the beamer went into action. The Beller was pierced in the hollow of the throat with the spear, but there was little blood from the wound, and there was no wound that could have been made by a beamer. Kickaha was certain that a close investigation would find a small hole bored through the corpse somewhere. Probably through the armor too, because the Beller wore chain mail shirt and skirt and a conical helmet.

It wouldn't do to poke around the body and let her know his suspicions, though. He followed her to the craft, the two sections of which still hung two feet from the ground. A dead Beller sprawled in each part, and in the front section, huddled in a charred mass, was a Tishquetmoac priest, the Bellers' interpreter. Kickaha pulled the bodies out and examined the aircraft. There were four rows of two seats each with a narrow aisle running down between them. The front row was where the pilot and copilot or navigator sat. There were many instruments and indicators of various sorts on a panel. These were marked with hieroglyphs, which Anana told him were from the Lords' classic writing and used rarely.

"This craft is from my palace," she said. "I had four. I suppose the Bellers dismantled all four and brought them through."

She told him that the two parts did not fall because the keel-plate had been charged with gravitons in stasis when the craft halted. The operating equipment was in the front section, which could still be flown as if it were a whole craft. The rear part would continue to hover above the ground for some time. Then, as the graviton field decayed, it would slowly sink.

"It'd be a shame to waste the rear projector or let it fall into the hands of somebody else," Kickaha said. "And we've only got two good handbeamers; the others were ruined when you rayed the ship. Let's take it with us."

"And where are we going?" she said.

"To Podarge, the Harpy-queen of the green eagles," he said. "She's the only useful ally I can think of at this moment. If I can stop her from trying to kill us long enough to talk to us, she may agree to help."

He climbed into the rear section and took some tools out of the storage compartment. He began to disconnect the big projector from the pivot, but suddenly stopped. He grinned and said to Anana, "I can't wait to see the expressions on your face and Podarge's! You will be looking at yourselves!"

She did not answer. She was using the beamer and the knife to cut off parts of a buffalo calf. Later, they would fly the meat to a spring and cook it. Both were so hungry, they felt as if their bellies were ravening animals eating up their own bodies. They had to feed them swiftly or lose their flesh to their flesh.

Though they were so tired they had trouble moving their arms and legs, Kickaha insisted that they fly on after eating. He wanted to get to the nearest mountain range. There they could hide the craft in a cave or ledge and sleep. It was too dangerous to remain on the prairie. If the Bellers had other craft around, they might detect them and investigate. Or try to communicate with them.

Anana agreed that he was right, and she fell asleep. Kickaha had learned from her how to operate the craft, so he took it toward the mountains as swiftly as it would go. The wind did not strike him directly, since the cowling protected him, but it did curve in through the open rear part, and it howled and beat at him—at least it kept him awake.

THEY GOT TO THE MOUNTAINS JUST AS THE SUN WENT AROUND the monolith, and he flew around for fifteen minutes before finding exactly what he wanted. This was a shallow cave with an opening about twenty feet high; it was located two thousand feet up on the face of a sheer cliff. Kickaha backed the craft into the cave, turned off the controls, lay down on the floor of the aisle, and passed out.

Even in his exhaustion and in the safety of the cave, he did not sleep deeply; he swam just below the surface of unconsciousness. He dreamed much and awoke with a start at least a dozen times. Nevertheless, he slept better than he had thought, because the sun was quartering the sky before he fully awoke.

He breakfasted on buffalo steak and some round biscuits he had found in a compartment under one of the seats. Since this was the only food in the craft, he deduced that the fliers had been operating out of a camp not too far away from the scene of the stampede. Or else the craft had been out for a long time and rations were short. Or there might be another explanation.

If there was one thing certain in both worlds, it was uncertainty.

By the time Anana awoke, she found that her companion had eaten, exercised vigorously to remove the stiffness from his muscles, and had dabbed water on his face and hands. He had bathed in the spring the evening before and so was presentable enough. He did not worry about shaving, since he had applied a chemical which retarded beard growth for months, just before he left the Hrowakas' village. It was a gift from Wolff. It could be neutralized at any time by another chemical if he wished to have a beard, but this chemical was not available; it was in a cabin in the Hrowakas' village.

Anana had the ability to wake up looking as if she were getting ready to go to a party. She did complain, however, about a bad taste in her mouth. She also voiced dislike for the lack of privacy in excretion.

Kickaha shrugged and said that a ten thousand year old woman ought to be above such human inhibitions. She did not respond angrily, but merely said, "Do we take off now? Or could we rest today?"

He was surprised that she seemed to give him authority. It was not what he would have expected from a Lord. But apparently she had a certain resiliency and flexibility, a realistic attitude. She recognized that this was his world and that he knew it far better than she did. Also, it must be evident that he had a tremendous capacity for survival. Her true feelings about him were not apparent. She was probably going along with him for her own sake and would drop him if he became a liability rather than an asset—which was an attitude he approved, in some respects. At least, they were operating together smoothly enough. Not too smoothly, since she had made it obvious that she would never think of letting him make love to her.

"I'm all for resting," he said. "But I think we'll be better off if we rest among the Hrowakas. We can hide this boat in a cave near their village. And while we're living there, we can talk to my people. I'm planning on using them against the Bellers, if they're willing. And they will be. They love a fight."

Shortly afterward, Anana noticed a light flashing on the instrument panel. She said, "Another craft is trying to call this one or perhaps the headquarters in Jadawin's palace. They must be alarmed because it hasn't reported in."

"I'd bluff by talking to them, but I'm not fluent enough in Lord-speech to fool them," Kickaha said. "And you could try, but I don't think they'd accept a woman's voice either. Let it flash. But one thing does bother me: do the Bellers have any means for tracking down this craft?"

"Only if we transmit a message for several minutes," she said. "Or if the craft is in a line-of-sight position. These are my machines and I had them equipped with some protection devices. But not many."

"Yes, but they have the devices of four palaces to draw on," he said. "Wolff's, yours, Nimstowl's, and Judubra's. They may have removed devices from these to equip their crafts."

She pointed out that, if they had, they had not equipped this one. She yawned and got ready to take a catnap. Kickaha shouted that she had slept over twelve hours already, and she should get up off her beautiful rump. If they were to survive, they had better get in gear, stir their stumps, and so on with a number of earthier and more personal clichés.

She admitted he was right. This surprised him but did not put him off guard. She got into the pilot's seat, put on the stasis harness, and said that she was ready.

The machine slid parallel to the face of the mountain and then headed for the edge of the level, keeping a few feet above the surface of the jagged terrain. It took two hours to get out of the range, by which time they were on the lip of the monolith on which rested the Amerind level. The stone cliff dropped vertically—more or less—for over a hundred thousand feet.

At its base was Okeanos, which was not an ocean but a sea shaped like a ring, girdling the monolith and never more than three hundred miles wide.

On the other side of Okeanos, entirely visible from this height, was the strip of land which ran around the bottom of this planet. The strip was actually fifty miles across, but from the edge of the monolith, it looked thread-thin. On its comparatively smooth, well-treed surface lived human beings and half-human creatures and fabulous beasts. Many of them were the products of Jadawin's biolab; all owed their longevity and unfading youth to him. There were mermen and mermaids, goat-hoofed and goat-horned satyrs, hairy-legged and horned fauns, small centaurs, and other creatures which Jadawin had made to resemble the beings of Greek mythology. The strip was a type of Paradeisos and Garden of Eden with, in addition, a number of extra-terrestrial, extra-universal touches.

On the other side of the Garden strip was the edge of the bottom of the world. Kickaha had been down there several times on what he called "vacations" and once when he had been pursued by the horrible *gworl,* who wanted to kill him for the Horn of Shambarimen.

He had looked over the edge and been thrilled and scared. The green abyss below—nothing beneath the planet—nothing but green sky and a sense that he would fall forever if he lost his hold.

Kickaha told her of this and said, "We could hide down there for a long time. It's a great place—no wars, no bloodshed beyond an occasional bloody nose or two. It's strictly for sensual pleasure, no intellectualism, and it gets wearisome after a few weeks, unless you want to be an alcoholic or drug addict. But the Bellers'll be down there eventually. And by that time, they may be much stronger."

"You can be sure of that," she said. "They have started making new Bellers. I suppose that one of the palaces has facilities for doing this. Mine hasn't, but . . ."

"Wolff's has," he replied. "Even so, it'll take ten years for a Beller to mature and be educated enough to take its place in Beller society, right? Meantime, the Bellers are restricted to the original fifty. Forty-four, I mean."

"Forty-four or four, they won't stop until we three Lords, and you, are captured or killed. I doubt they'll invade any more universes until then. They've got all of us cornered in this world, and they'll keep hunting until they've got us."

"Or we've got them," Kickaha said.

She smiled and said, "That's what I like about you. I wish that you were a Lord. Then . . ."

He did not ask her to elaborate. He directed her to fly the machine down the monolith. As they descended, they saw that its seemingly smooth surface was broken, gnarled, and flattened in many places. There were ledges and projections which furnished roads for many familiar and many strange creatures. There were fissures which sometimes widened to become comparatively large valleys. There were streams in the valleys and cataracts hurled out of holes in the steep side and there was a half mile wide river which roared out of a large cave at the end of a valley-fissure and then fell over the edge and onto the sea seventy-five thousand feet below.

Kickaha explained that the surface area on all the levels of this planet, that is, the horizontal area on the tops of the monoliths, equaled the surface area of the watery bodies of Earth. This made the land area more than that of Earth's. In addition, the habitable areas on the verticalities of the monoliths were considerable. These alone probably equaled the land area of Earth's Africa. Moreover, there were immense subterranean territories, great caverns in vast networks that ran under the earth everywhere. And in these were various peoples and beasts and plants adapted to underground life.

"And when you consider all this, plus the fact that there are no arid deserts or ice- and snow-covered areas, you can see that the inhabitable land of this planet is about four times that of Earth."

Anana said that she had been on Earth briefly only and that she didn't remember its exact size. The planet in her own universe, however, was, if she remembered correctly, about the size of Earth.

Kickaha said, "Take my word for it, this is a hell of a big place. I've traveled a lot in the twenty-three years I've been here, but I've seen only a small part. I have a lot ahead of me to see. If I live, of course."

The machine had descended swiftly and now hovered about ten feet above the rolling waves of Okeanos. The surf shattered with a white bellow against the reefs or directly against the butt of the monolith. Kickaha wanted to make sure that the water was deep enough. He had Anana fly the craft two miles further out. Here he dumped the four caskets and bell-shaped contents into the sea. The water was pure and the angle of sunlight just right. He could see the caskets a long way before the darkness swallowed them. They fell through schools of fish that glowed all hues of all colors and by a Brobdingnagian octopus, striped purple and white, that reached out a tentacle to touch a casket as it went by.

Dumping the bells here was not really necessary, since they were empty. But Anana would not feel easy until they were sunk out of reach of any sentients.

"Six down. Forty-four to go," Kickaha said. "Now to the village of the Hrowakas, the Bear People. My people."

The craft followed the curve of the monolith base for about seven hundred miles. Then Kickaha took over the controls. He flew the craft up and in ten minutes had climbed a little over twelve miles of precipitousness to the edge of the Amerind level. Another hour of cautious threading through the valleys and passes of the mountain ranges and half an hour of reconnoitering brought them to the little hill on top of which was the village of the Hrowakas.

Kickaha felt as if a warlance had driven into his skull. The tall sharp-pointed logs that formed the wall around the village were gone. Here and there, a blackened stump poked through the ashes.

The great V-roofed council hall, the lodge for bachelor warriors, the bear pens, the horse barns, the granary storage, the smokehouses, and the log-cabin family dwellings—all were gone. Burned into gray mounds.

It had rained the night before, but smoke rose weakly from a few piles.

On the hillside were a dozen widely scattered charred corpses of women and children and the burned carcasses of a few bears and dogs. These had been fleeing when rayed down.

He had no doubt that the Black Bellers had done this. But how had they connected him with the Hrowakas?

His thoughts, wounded, moved slowly. Finally, he remembered that the Tishquetmoac knew that he came from the Hrowakas. However, they did not know even the approximate location of the village. The Hrowaka men always traveled at least two hundred miles from the village before stopping along the Great Trade Path. Here they waited for the Tishquetmoac caravan. And though the Bear People were talkers, they would not reveal the place of their village.

Of course, there were old enemies of the Bear People, and perhaps the Bellers had been informed by these. And there were also films of the village and of Kickaha, taken by Wolff and stored in his palace. The Bellers could have run these off and so found the Hrowakas, since the location was shown on a map in the film.

Why had they burned down the village and all in it? What could serve the Bellers by this act?

With a heavy halting voice, he asked Anana the same question. She replied in a sympathetic tone, and if he had not been so stunned, he would have been agreeably surprised at her reaction.

"The Bellers did not do this out of vindictiveness," she said. "They are cold and alien to our way of thinking. You must remember that while they are products of human beings"—Kickaha was not so stunned that he did not notice her identification of Lords with human beings at this time—"and were raised and educated by human beings, they are, in essence, mechanical life. They have self-consciousness, to be sure, which makes them *not* mere machines. But they were born of metal and in metal. They are as cruel as any human. But the cruelty is cold and mechanical. Cruelty is used only when they can get something desired through it. They can know passion, that is, sexual desire, when they are in the brain of a man or woman, just as they get hungry because their host-body is hungry.

"But they don't take illogical vengeance as a human would. That is, they wouldn't destroy a tribe just because it happened to be loved by you. No, they must have had a good reason—to them, anyway—for doing this."

"Perhaps they wanted to make sure I didn't take refuge here," he said. "They would have been smarter to have waited until I did and then move in."

They could be hiding someplace up on the mountains where they could observe everything. However, Kickaha insisted on scouting the area before he approached the village. If Bellers were spying on them, they were well concealed indeed. In fact, since the heat-and-mass detector on the craft indicated nothing except some small animals and birds, the Bellers would have to be behind something large. In which case, they couldn't see their quarry either.

It was more probably that the Beller machine, after destroying the village, had searched this area. Failing to find him, it had gone elsewhere.

"I'll take over the controls," Anana said softly. "You tell me how to get to Podarge."

He was still too sluggish to react to her unusual solicitude. Later, he would think about it.

Now he told her to go to the edge of the level again and to descend about fifty thousand feet. Then she was to take the craft westward at 150 MPH until he told her to stop.

The trip was silent except for the howling of the wind at the open rear end. Not until the machine stopped below an enormous overhang of shiny black rock did he speak.

"I could have buried the bodies," he said, "but it would have taken too long. The Bellers might have checked back."

"You're still thinking about them," she said with a trace of incredulity. "I mean, you're worrying because you couldn't keep the carrion eaters off them? Don't! They're dead; you can do nothing for them."

"You don't understand," he said. "When I called them my people, I meant it. I loved them, and they loved me. They were a strange people when I first met them, strange to me. I was a young, mid-twentieth century, Midwestern American citizen, from another universe, in fact. And they were descendants of Amerinds who had been brought to this universe some twenty thousand years ago. Even the ways of an Indian of America are alien and near-incomprehensible to a white American. But I'm very adaptable and flexible. I learned their ways and came to think something like them. I was at ease with them and they with me. And I was Kickaha, the Trickster, the man of many turns. Their Kickaha, the scourge of the enemy of the Bear People.

"This village was my home, and they were my friends, the best I've ever had, and I also had two beautiful and loving wives. No children, though Awiwisha thought she might be pregnant. It's true that I'd established other identities on two other levels, especially that of the outlaw Baron

Horst von Horstmann. But that was fading away. I'd been gone so long from Dracheland.

"The Hrowakas were my people, dammit! I loved them, and they loved me!"

And then he began to sob loudly. The cries tore the flesh as they mounted upward with spurs toward his throat. And even after he had quit crying, he hurt from deep within him. He did not want to move for fear he would hurt even more. But Anana finally cleared her throat and moved uneasily.

Then he said, "All right. I'm better. Set her down on that ledge there. The entrance to Podarge's cave is about ten miles westward. It'll be dangerous to get near it any time, but especially at night. The only time I was there was two or three years ago when Wolff and I talked Podarge into letting us out of her cage."

He grinned and said, "The price was that I should make love to her. Other captives had been required to do this, too, but a lot of them couldn't because they were too frightened, or too repulsed or both. When this happened, she'd shred them as if they were paper with her great sharp talons.

"And so, Anana," he continued, "in a way I've already made love to you. At least to a woman—a thing with a woman's face—with your face."

"You must be feeling better," she said, "if you can talk like that."

"I have to joke a little, to talk about things far removed from death," he said. "Can't you understand that?"

She nodded but did not say anything. He was silent, too, for a long while. They ate cold meat and biscuits—it would be wise not to make a fire. Lights might attract the Bellers or the green eagles. Or other things that would be crawling around the cliffs.

13

THE NIGHT PASSED WITHOUT INCIDENT, ALTHOUGH THEY WERE awakened from time to time by roars, screams, whoops, bellows, trumpetings, and whistlings, all at a distance.

After breakfast, they set out slowly in the craft along the cliffside. Kickaha saw an eagle out above the sea. He piloted the craft toward her, hoping she would not try to escape or attack. Her curiosity won over whatever other emotions she had. She circled the machine, which remained motionless. Suddenly, she swept past them, crying, "Kickaha-a-a!" and plunged down. He expected her to wing full speed toward Podarge's cave. Instead, behaving unexpectedly, as might be expected from a female—so he said to Anana—she climbed back up. Kickaha indicated that he was going to land on a ledge, where he would like to talk to her.

Perhaps she thought that this would give her a chance to attack him. She settled down beside the machine with a small blast of closing wings. She towered over him, her yellow hooked beak and glaring black red-rimmed eyes above his head. The cowling was open, but he held the beamer, and on seeing it, she stepped back. She squawked, "Podarge?" but said nothing more about Anana's face.

One eagle looked like another to Kickaha. She, however, remembered when he had been in the cage with Wolff and when the eagles had stormed the palace on top of the highest monolith, the pinnacle of the planet.

"I am Thyweste," she said in the great parrot's voice of the green eagle. "What are you doing here, Trickster? Don't you know that Podarge sentenced you to death? And torture before death, if possible?"

"If that's so, why don't you try to kill me," he said.

"Because Podarge has learned from Dewiwanira that you released her and Antiope from the Tishquetmoac cage. And she knows that something is gravely amiss in Talanac, but she hasn't been able to find out what yet. She has temporarily suspended the sentence on you—though not on Jadawin-Wolff—until she discovers the truth. The orders are that you shall be escorted to her if you show up begging for an audience. Although I will be fair, Kickaha, and warn you that you may never leave the cave, once you've entered it."

"I'm not *begging* for an audience," he said. "And if I go in, I go inside this craft and fully armed. Will you tell Podarge that? But also tell her that if she wants revenge on the Tishquetmoac for having killed and imprisoned many of her pets, then I will be able to help her. Also, tell her there is a great evil abroad. The evil does not threaten her—yet. But it will. It will close its cold fingers upon her and her eagles and their nestlings. I will tell her of this when—or if—I get to see her."

Thyweste promised to repeat what he had told her, and she flapped off. Several hours passed. Kickaha got increasingly nervous. He told Anana that Podarge was so insane that she was liable to act against her own interests. He wouldn't be surprised to see a horde of the giant eagles plunging down out of the camouflaging green sky.

But it was a single eagle who appeared. Thyweste said that he should come in the flying machine and bring the human female with him. He could bring all the weapons he wished; much good they would do him if he tried to lie or trick Podarge. Kickaha translated for Anana, since they spoke the degenerate descendant of Mycenaean Greek, the speech used by Odysseus and Agamemnon and Helen of Troy.

Anana was startled and then scornful. *"Human* female! Doesn't this stinking bird know a Lord when she sees one?"

"Evidently not," he replied. "After all, you look exactly like a human. In fact, you can breed with humans, so I would say that you are human, even if you do have a different origin. Or do you? Wolff has some interesting theories about that."

She muttered some invective or pejorative in Lord-speech. Kickaha sent the craft up and followed Thyweste to the entrance of the cave, where Podarge had kept house and court for five hundred years or so. She had chosen the site well. The cliff above the entrance slanted gently outward for several thousand feet and was almost as smooth as a mirror. There was a broad ledge in front of the cave, and the cave could be approached on the ledge from only one side. But this path was always guarded by forty giant eagles. Below the ledge, the cliff slanted inward. No creature could climb up to or down from the cave. An army of determined men could have dropped ropes from above to let themselves down to the cave, but they would have been open to attack.

The entrance was a round hole about ten feet in diameter. It opened to a long curving corridor of rock polished from five centuries of rubbing by feathered bodies.

The craft had to be driven through the tunnel with much grating and squealing. After fifty yards of such progress, it came out into an immense cavern. This was lit by torches and by huge plants resembling feathers, which glowed whitely. There were thousands of them hanging down from the ceiling and sticking out from the walls, their roots driven into the rock.

From somewhere, air brushed Kickaha's cheek softly.

The great chamber was much as he remembered it except that there was more order. Apparently, Podarge had done some housecleaning. The garbage on the floor had been removed, and the hundreds of large chests and caskets containing jewels, *objets d'art,* and gold and silver coins and other treasures had been stacked alongside the walls or carried elsewhere.

Two columns of eagles formed an aisle for the craft, the aisle crossed fifty yards of smooth granite floor to end at a platform of stone. This was ten feet high and attained by a flight of steps made from blocks of quartz. The old rock-carved chair was gone. In its place was a great chair of gold set with diamonds, formed in the shape of a phoenix with outstretched wings that was placed in the middle of the platform. The chair had been that of the Rhadamanthus of Atlantis, ruler of the next-to-highest level of this planet. Podarge had taken the chair in a raid on the capital city some four hundred years ago. Now there was no Rhadamanthus, almost no Atlanteans left alive, and the great city was shattered. And the plans of Wolff for recolonizing the land were interrupted by the appearance of the Black Bellers and by his disappearance.

Podarge sat upon the edge of the throne. Her body was that of a Harpy's as conceived by Wolff-as-Jadawin 3,200 years ago. The legs were long and avian, thicker than an ostrich's, so they could bear the weight of her body. The lower part of the body was also avian, green-feathered and long-tailed. The upper part was that of a woman with magnificent white breasts, long white neck, and the achingly beautiful face. Her hair was long and black; her eyes were mad. She had no arms—she had wings, very long and broad wings with green and crimson feathers.

Podarge called to Kickaha in a rich husky voice, "Stop your aerial car there! It may approach no closer!"

Kickaha asked for permission to get out of the machine and come to the foot of the steps. She said that would be granted. He told Anana to follow him and then walked with just a hint of a swagger to the steps. Podarge's eyes were wide on seeing Anana's face. She said, "Two-legged female, are you a creation of Jadawin's? He has given you a face that is modeled on mine!"

Anana knew that the situation was just the reverse, and her pride must have been pierced deeply. But she was not stupid in her arrogance. She replied, "I believe so. I do not know my origin. I have just been, that's all. For some fifty years, I think."

"Poor infant! Then you were the plaything of that monster Jadawin! How did you get away from him! Did he tire of you and let you loose on this evil world, to live or die as events determined?"

"I do not know," Anana said. "It may be. Kickaha thinks that Jadawin was merciful in that he removed part of my memory, so that I do not remember him or my life in his palace, if indeed I had one."

Kickaha approved of her story. She was as adept at lying as he. And then he thought, *Oh! Oh! She tripped up!* Fifty years ago, Jadawin wasn't even in the palace or in this universe. He was living in America as a young amnesiac who had been adopted by a man named Wolff. The Lord in the palace was Arwoor then.

But, he reassured himself, this made no difference. If Anana pretended to have no memory of her origin or palace, then she wouldn't know who had been Lord.

Podarge apparently wasn't thinking about this. She said to Kickaha, "Dewiwanira has told me of how you freed her and Antiope from the cage in Talanac."

"Did she also tell you that she tried to kill me in payment for having given her her freedom?" he said.

She raised her wings a little and glared. "She had her orders! Gratitude had nothing to do with it! You were the right-hand man of Jadawin, who now calls himself Wolff!"

She folded her wings and seemed to relax, but Kickaha was not deceived. "By the way, where is Jadawin? What is happening in Talanac? Who are these Drachelanders?" she asked.

Kickaha told her. He left out the two Lords, Nimstowl and Judubra, and made it appear that Anana had been gated through a long time ago to the Amerind level and had been a slave in Talanac. Podarge was insanely hostile to the Lords. If she found out that Anana was one, and especially if she suspected that Anana might be Wolff's sister, she would have ordered her killed. This would have put Kickaha into a predicament which he would have to settle within one or two seconds. He would either chose to live and so be able to fight the Bellers but have to let Anana die, or he could back Anana and so die himself. That the two of them could slaughter many eagles before they were overwhelmed was no consolation.

Or perhaps, he thought, *just perhaps, we might be able to escape. If I were to shoot Podarge quickly enough and so create confusion among the eagles and then get into the craft quickly enough and bring the big projectors to bear, maybe we could fight our way out.*

Kickaha knew in that moment that he had chosen for Anana.

Podarge said, "Then Jadawin may be dead? I would not like that, because I have planned for a long time on capturing him. I want him to live for a long long time while he suffers! While he pays! And pays! And pays!"

Podarge was standing up on her bird legs, her talons outspread, and she was screeching at Kickaha. He spoke from the corner of his mouth to Anana. "Oh, oh! I think she's cracked! Get ready to start shooting!"

But Podarge stopped yelling and began striding back and forth, like a great nightmare bird in a cage. Finally, she stopped and said, "Trickster! Why should I help you in your war against the enemies of Jadawin! Aside from the fact that they may have cheated me of my revenge?"

"Because they are your enemies, too," he said. "It is true that, so far, they have used only human bodies as hosts. But do you think that the Bellers won't be thinking of eagles as hosts? Men are earthbound creatures. What could compare with being housed in the body of a green eagle, of flying far above the planet, into the house of the sun, of hovering godlike above all beasts of earth and the houses and cities of man, of being un-reachable, yet seeing and knowing all, taking in a thousand miles with one sweep of the eye?

"Do you think that the Black Bellers won't realize this? And that when they do, they won't capture your eagles, perhaps you, Podarge, and will place the bell shape over your heads, and empty your brains of your thoughts and memory, uncoil you into death, and then possess your brains and bodies for their use?

"The Black Bellers use the bodies of flesh and blood creatures as we humans wear garments. When the garments are worn out, they are dis-carded. And so will you be discarded, thrown onto the trash heap, though of course it won't matter to you, since *you* will have died long before your body dies."

He stopped speaking for a moment. The eagles, ten foot high green towers, shifted uneasily and made tearing sounds in their throats. Podarge's expression was undecipherable, but Kickaha was sure she was thinking hard.

"There are only forty-four Black Bellers now in existence," he said. "They have great power, yes, but they are few. Now is the time to make sure they do not become a far greater threat. Because they will be making more infant Bellers in the laboratories of the Lords' palaces—you may be sure of that. The time will come when the Black Bellers will number thou-sands, millions perhaps, because they will want to ensure survival of their kind. And in numbers is survival of kind.

"The time will come when the Bellers will be so numerous and pow-erful that they will be irresistible. They can then do as they please. And if they want to enjoy the bodies of the green eagles, they will do so without a by-your-leave."

After a long silence, Podarge said, "You have spoken well, Trickster. I know a little about what is happening in Talanac because some of my pets have seized Tishquetmoacs and forced them to talk. They did not reveal much. For instance, they have never heard of the Black Bellers. But they say that the Talanac priests claim that their ruler is possessed by a demon. And the presence of this flying machine and of others which my pets have seen substantiates your story. It is too bad that you did not bring the captured bells here so that we could see them, instead of dumping them into the sea as you did."

"I am not always as clever as I think I am," Kickaha said.

"There is another thing to consider, even if your story is only half true or entirely a lie," Podarge said. "That is, I have long been planning revenge against the Tishquetmoac because they have killed some of my pets and caged others as if they were common beasts. They began to do that when the present ruler, Quotshaml, inherited the throne. That was only three years ago, and since then he has ignored the ancient understanding between his people and mine. In his crazed zeal to add specimens to that zoo of his and to mount stuffed creatures in that museum, he has waged war against us. I sent word that he should stop immediately, and he imprisoned my messengers. He is mad, and he is doomed!"

Podarge talked on. Apparently she tired of the eagles' conversation and longed for strangers with interesting news. Now that Kickaha had brought probably the most exciting news she had ever heard, aside from the call to storm the palaces of the Lords three years before, she wanted to talk and talk. And she did so with a disregard for the feelings of her guests which only an absolute monarch could display. She had food and drink brought in and joined them at a great table. They were glad for the nourishment, but after a while Anana became sleepy. Kickaha just became more exhilarated. He suggested to Anana that it would be wise if she did sleep. She guessed what he meant but did not comment. She rose and went to the craft and stretched out on the floor on a rug provided by Podarge.

WHEN SHE AWOKE, SHE SAW KICKAHA SLEEPING BESIDE HER.
His short-nosed, long-upper-lipped face looked like a baby's, but his breath
stank of wine and he smelled of some exotic perfume. Suddenly, he stopped
snoring and opened one eye. Its leafgreen iris shot out fine red lightning
veins. He grinned and said, "Good morning! Although I think it's closer to
afternoon!"

Then he sat up and patted her shoulder. She jerked herself away from
his touch. He smiled more broadly. "Could it be that the arrogant super-
woman Lord, Anana the Bright, could be a trifle jealous? Unthinkable!"

"Unthinkable is correct," she said. "How could I possibly care? How?
Why?"

He stretched and yawned. "That's up to you to figure out. After all, you
are a woman, even if you deny being human, and we've been in close, almost too-intimate, contact, if I do say so myself. I'm a handsome fellow and
a daredevil and a mighty warrior—if I do say so myself and I do, though
I'm just repeating what thousands have said. You couldn't help being attracted, even if you had some self-contempt for thinking of a *leblabbiy* as
attractive in any way."

"Have any women ever tried to kill you?" she snarled.

"At least a dozen. In fact, I've come closer to death from wounds inflicted by women than by all the great warriors put together."

He fingered two scars over his ribs. "Twice, they came very close to
doing what my most determined enemies could not do. And both claimed
they loved me. Give me your honest, open hate anytime!"

"I neither hate nor love you, of course," she said loftily. "I am a Lord,
and . . ."

She was interrupted by an eagle, who said that Podarge wanted to talk
to them while they breakfasted. The eagle was upset when Anana said that
she wanted to bathe first and were any cosmetics, perfumes, etc., available
in all these treasures? Kickaha smiled slightly and said he would go ahead
to Podarge and would take the responsibility for her not showing up im-

mediately. The eagle strode stiff-legged ahead of Anana to a corner of the cave where an ornately filigreed dresser held what she wanted.

Podarge was not displeased at Anana's coming late because she had other things to consider. She greeted Kickaha as if she held him in high regard and then said that she had some interesting news. An eagle had flown in at dawn with a tale of a great fleet of warriors on the river which the Tishquetmoac called Petchotakl. It was the broad and winding stream that ran along the edge of the Trees of Many Shadows.

There were one hundred longboats with about fifty men each. So the fleet would total about five thousand of the Red Beards, who called themselves the Thyuda, that is, People. Kickaha said that he had heard of them from the Tishquetmoac, who complained of increasing raids by the Red Beards on the frontier posts and towns. But what was a fleet this size intending to do? Surely, it must mean a raid on, perhaps a siege of, Talanac itself?

She said that the Thyuda came from a great sea to the west, beyond the Glittering Mountains. Kickaha said that he had not yet crossed the Glittering Mountains, though he had long intended to. But he did know that the sea was about a thousand miles long and three hundred wide. He had always thought that Amerinds, people like those on the Plains, lived on its shore.

No, Podarge said, self-satisfied because of the extent of her knowledge and power. No, her eagles reported that a long, long time ago there were feather-caps (Amerinds) there. But then Jadawin let in from Earth a tribe of tall light-skinned people with long beards. These settled down on the eastern shore and built fort-towns and ships. In time, they conquered and absorbed the dark-skins into the population. The dark-skins were slaves at first but eventually they became equals and they blended with the Thyuda, became Thyuda, in fact. The language became a simplified one, basically Thyuda but pidiginized and with many aboriginal loan-words.

The eastern end of the sea had been a federation under the joint kingship of Brakya, which meant Strife, and of Saurga, which meant Sorrow. But there had been a long hard civil war, and Brakya had been forced to flee with a loyal band of warriors and women. They had come over the Glittering Mountains and settled along the upper river. During the years they had increased in numbers and strength and begun their raiding of Tishquetmoac posts and riverboats and sometimes even caravans. They often encountered the Half-Horses and did not always win against them, as they did against all other enemies, but, for the most part, they thrived.

The Tishquetmoac had sent out several punitive expeditions, one of which had destroyed a rivertown; the others had been cut to pieces. And now it looked as if the Red Beards were making a big move against the people of Talanac. They were a well-disciplined body of tall, fierce warriors, but they apparently did not realize the size or the defenses of the nation against which they were marching.

"Perhaps," Kickaha said, "but by the time they get to Talanac, they will find the defenses greatly weakened. We will have attacked and perhaps conquered the City of Jade by then."

Podarge lost her good humor. "We will attack the Red Beards first and scatter them like sparrows before a hawk! I will not make their way easy for them!"

"Why not make them our allies?" Kickaha said. "The battle against Bellers, Tishquetmoac, and Drachelanders will not be easy, especially when you consider the aircraft and the beamers they have. We need all the help we can get. I suggest we get them on our side. There will be plenty of killing and loot for all, more than enough."

Podarge stood up from her chair and with a sweep of a wing dashed the tableware onto the floor. Her magnificent breasts rose and fell with fury. She glared at him with eyes from which reason had flown. Kickaha could not help shrinking inwardly, though he faced her boldly enough and spoke up.

"Let the Red Beards kill our enemies and die for us," he said. "You claim to love your eagles; you call them your pets. Why not save many of their lives by strengthening ourselves with the Red Beards?"

Podarge screamed at him, and then she began to rave. He knew he had made a serious mistake by not agreeing with her in every particular, but it was too late to undo the harm. Moreover, he felt his own reason slipping away in a suddenly unleashed hatred of her and her arrogant, inhumanly cruel ways.

He shoved away his anger before it could bring him down into the dust from which no man gets up. He said, "I bow to your superior wisdom, not to mention strength and power, O Podarge! Have it your way, as it should be!"

But he was thoughtful afterward and determined to talk to Podarge again when she seemed more reasonable.

The first thing he did after breakfast was to take the craft outside and up fifty thousand feet to the top of the monolith. Then he flew to the top of a mountain peak in a high range near the edge of the monolith. Here he and Anana sat in the craft while they talked loudly of what had happened recently and also slipped in descriptions of the entrance to Podarge's cave. He had turned on the radio so that their conversation was being broadcast. She had set the various detecting apparatus. After several hours had passed, Anana suddenly pretended to notice that the radio was on. She rebuked Kickaha savagely for being so awkward and stupid, and she snapped it off. An indicator was showing the blips of two aircraft approaching from the edge of the monolith, which rose from the center of the Amerind level. Both had come from the palace of the Lord on top of the apical monolith of the planet.

Since the two vessels had undoubtedly located them with their instruments, they would be able to locate the area into which their quarry would disappear. Kickaha took the vessel at top speed back over the edge of the level and on down. He hovered before the cave entrance until the first of the two pursuers shot over the edge. Then he snapped the craft into the cave and through the tunnel without heeding the scraping noises.

After that, they could only wait. The big projectors and hand-beamers were in the claws of the eagles gliding back and forth some distance above the cave. When they saw the two vessels before the cave entrance, they were to drop out of the green of the sky. The Bellers would detect the eagles above them, of course, but they would pay no attention to them. After identifying them, they would concentrate on sending their rays into the cave.

Those in the cave did not have long to wait. An eagle, carrying a beamer in her beak, entered to report. The Bellers, three in each vessel, had been completely surprised. They were fried, and the crafts were floating where they had stopped, undamaged except for some burned seats and slightly melted metal here and there.

Kickaha suggested to Podarge that the two vessels be brought into the cave. There should be at least one craft yet in the Bellers' possession, and they might send that one down to investigate the disappearance of these. Also, there might be more than one, because Nimstowl and Judubra could have had such vessels.

"Twelve Bellers down. Thirty-eight to go," Kickaha said. "And we now have some power and transportation."

He and Anana went out in the half-craft. He transferred into a vessel, brought it into the cave, then came out again to bring in the second. When all three vessels were side by side in the huge cavern, Podarge insisted that the two instruct her and some chosen eagles in the operation of the vessels. Kickaha asked, first, for the return of their handbeamers and the projectors that went with the half-craft. Podarge hesitated so long that Kickaha thought she was going to turn against him then and there. He and Anana were helpless because they had loaned their weapons out to ensure the success of the plan. He did have his knife, which he was determined to throw into the Harpy's solar plexus if she showed any sign of ordering the eagles to seize them. This would not save him and Anana, but he at least would have taken Podarge along with him.

The Harpy, however, finally gave the desired order to her subjects. The beamers were returned; the projectors were put back into the half-craft. Still, he felt uneasy. Podarge was not going to forgive him for being Wolff's friend, no matter what services he rendered her. As soon as his usefulness ended, so would his life. That could be thirty minutes or thirty days from now.

When he had a chance to speak to Anana alone, he told her what to expect.

"It's what I thought would happen," she said. "Even if you weren't Jadawin's friend, you would be in danger because you have been her lover. She must know that, despite her beautiful face and beautiful breasts, she is a hybrid monster and therefore disgusting to the human males she forces to make love to her. She cannot forgive that; she must eliminate the man who secretly despises her. And I am in danger because, one, I have a woman's body, and she must hate all women because she is condemned to her half-bird body. Two, I have her face, and she's not going to let a woman with my body and her face live long to enjoy it. Three, she is insane! She frightens me!"

"You, a Lord, admit you're scared!" he said.

"Even after ten thousand years, I'm scared of some things. Torture is one of them, and I'm sure that she will torture me horribly—if she gets a chance. Moreover, I worry about you."

He was startled. "About me? A *leblabbiy*?"

"You aren't an ordinary human," she said. "Are you sure you're not at least half-Lord? Perhaps Wolff's son?"

"I'm sure I'm not," he said, grinning. "You wouldn't be feeling the emotions of a human woman, would you? Perhaps you're just a little bit fond of me? Maybe a trifle attracted to me? Possibly, perish the thought, you even desire me? Possibly, O most hideous idea, even love me a little? That is, if a Lord is capable of love?"

"You're as mad as the Harpy!" she said, glaring. "Because I admire your abilities and courage doesn't mean that I would possibly consider you as a mate, my equal!"

"Of course not," he said. "If it weren't for me, you'd have been dead a dozen times or would now be screaming in a torture chamber. I'll tell you what. When you're ready to confess you're wrong, I'll save you embarrassment. Just call me lover, that's all. No need for apologies or tears of contrition. Just call me lover. I can't promise I'll be in love with you, but I will consider, just consider, mind you, the prospect of being your lover. You're damnably attractive, physically, anyway. And I wouldn't want to offend Wolff by turning his sister down, although, come to think of it, he didn't speak very fondly of you."

He had expected fury. Instead, she laughed. But he wasn't sure that the laughter wasn't a cover-up.

They had little time to talk thereafter. Podarge kept them busy teaching the eagles about the crafts and weapons. She also questioned both about the layout of Talanac, where she could expect the more resistance, the weak points of the city, etc. She herself was interrupted by the need to give orders and receive information. Hundreds of messengers had been sent out to bring in other eagles for the campaign. The early-arriving recruits, however, were to assemble at the confluence of the Petchotakl river and the small Kwakoyoml river. Here the eagles were to marshal to await the Red Beard fleet. There were many problems for her to solve. The feeding of the army that would gather required logistical reorganization. At one time, the eagles had been an army as thoroughly disciplined and hierarchical as any human organization. But the onslaught on the palace several years before had killed so many of her officers that she had never bothered to reorganize it. Now, she was faced with this immediate, almost overwhelmingly large, problem.

She appointed a certain number of hunters. Since the river areas of the Great Plains were full of large game, they should afford all the food needed for the army. The result, however, was that two eagles out of ten would be absent hunting most of the time.

The fourth morning, Kickaha dared to argue again. He told her that it was not intelligent to waste the weapons on the Red Beards, that she should save them for the place where they were absolutely required—that is, at Talanac, where the Bellers had weapons which could only be put out of commission by similar weapons.

Moreover, she had enough eagles at her command now to launch an attack on the Tishquetmoac. Feeding them was a big enough headache without waiting to add more. Also . . .

He got no farther. The Harpy screamed at him to keep quiet, unless he wanted his eyes torn out. She was tired of his arrogance and presumptuousness. He had lived too long, bragged too much of his trickster ways. Moreover, she could not stand Anana, assuredly a most repulsive creature. Let him trick his way out of the cave now, if he could; let the woman go jump off the cliff into the sea. Let them both try.

Kickaha kept quiet, but she was not pacified. She continued to scream at him for at least half an hour. Suddenly, she stopped. She smiled at him. Cold thrummed a chord deep in him; his skin seemed to fold, as if one ridge were trying to cover itself with another.

There was a time to await developments, and there was a time to anticipate them. He reared up from his chair, heaving up his end of the table, heavy though it was, so that it turned over on Podarge. The Harpy shrieked as she was pressed between chair and table. Her head stuck out from above the edge, and her wings flapped.

He would have burned her head off then, but she was no immediate danger personally. The two attendant eagles were, since they carried beamers in their beaks. But they had to drop these to catch them with one foot, and in the interim, Kickaha shot one. His beamer, on half-power, set the green feathers ablaze.

Anana had pulled out her beamer, and her ray intersected with his on the second eagle.

He yelled at her and ran toward the nearest craft. She was close behind him in his dive into it, and, without a word from him, she seized the big projector. He sat down before the control panel and activated the motors. The craft rose a foot and shot toward the entrance to the tunnel. Three eagles tried to stop it with their bodies. The vessel went thump . . . thump . . . thump, jarring Kickaha each time. Then he was thrown forward and banged his chest on the panel—no time to strap himself in—as the vessel jammed into the narrow bore of stone. He increased the power. Metal squealed against granite as the vessel rammed through like a rod cleaning out a cannon.

For a second, the bright round of the cave exit was partially blocked by a great bird; there was a thump and then a bump and the vessel was out in the bright yellow sun and bright green sky with the blue-white surf-edge sea fifty thousand feet below.

Kickaha restrained his desire to run away. He brought the craft up and back and down, hovering over the top of the entrance. And, as he had expected, a craft slid out. This was the one captured by the eagles; it was followed by the half-craft. Anana split both along the longitudinal axis with the projector on at full-power. Each side of the craft broke away and fell, the sliced eagles with them, and the halves and green bodies were visible for a long time before being swallowed up in the blue of the distance.

Kickaha lowered the craft and shot the nose-projector at full-power into the tunnel. Screams from within told him that he might have killed some eagles and at least panicked them for a long time. He thought then of cutting out rocks above the entrance and blocking it off but decided that it would take too much power. By then the eagle patrols outside the monolith face and the newcomers were swarming through the air. He rammed the craft through their midst, knocking many to one side while Anana burned others. Soon they were through the flock and going at full speed over the mountain range which blocked off the edge of the level from the Great Plains.

15

THEN HE WAS SWOOPING OVER THE PRAIRIE, HEDGEHOPPING because, the closer he stayed to the surface, the less chance there was of being detected by a Beller craft. Kickaha flew just above the grass and the swelling hills and the trees and the great gray mammoths and mastodons and the giant shaggy black buffalo and the wild horses and the gawky, skinny, scared-faced Plains camels; the nine hundred pound tawny Felis Atrox, the atrocious lion, the long-legged, dogfaced cheetah-lions, the saber-toothed smilodons and the shaggy dumb-looking megatherium; a sloth as large as an elephant, the dire wolf, six feet high at the shoulder, and the twenty-one foot high archaic ass-headed baluchitherium; the megaceros, deer with an antler spread of twelve feet, and thousands of species of antelopes including one queer species that had a long forked horn sticking up from its snout; the "terrible hog" which stood six feet at the shoulder, and the dread-making earth-shaking brontotherium, recreated in the biolabs of Wolff and released on the Great Plains, gray, fifteen feet long and eight feet high at the shoulder, with a large flat bone horn at the end of its nose; and the coyote, the fox, an ostrich-like bird, the ducks, geese, swans, herons, storks, pigeons, vultures, buzzards, hawks—many thousands of species of beasts and birds and millions, millions of proliferations of life, all these Kickaha shot over and past, seeing within three hours what he could not have seen in five years of travel on the ground.

He passed near several camps of the Nations of the Plains. The tepees and round lodges of the Wingashutah, the Khaikhowa, the Takotita and once over a cavalcade of Half-Horses, the fierce warriors guarding all sides and the females dragging on poles the tribal property and the young gamboling, frisking like colts.

Kickaha thrilled at these sights. He alone of all Earthmen had been favored with living in this world. He had been very lucky so far and if he were to die at this moment, he could not say that he had wasted his life. On the contrary, he had been granted what very few men had been granted, and he was grateful. Despite this, he intended to keep on living. There was much yet to visit and explore and wonder at and great talk and lovely loving women. And enemies to fight to the death.

This last thought had no sooner passed than he saw a strange band on the prairie. He slowed down and ascended to about fifty feet. They were mounted Drachelanders with a small troop of Tishquetmoac cavalry. And three Bellers. He could see the silver caskets attached to the saddles of their horses.

They reined in, doubtless thinking that the craft contained other Bellers. Kickaha did not give them much time to remain in error. He dropped down and Anana cut all three in half. The others took off in panic. Kickaha picked up the caskets, and later dropped them into the broad Petchotakl river. He could not figure out how the party had gotten so far from Talanac even if they had ridden night and day. Moreover, they were coming from the opposite direction.

It struck him then that they must have been gated through to this area. He remembered a gate hidden in a cave in a group of low but steep-sided hills and rocky hills about fifty miles inland. He took the craft there and found what he had expected. The Bellers had left a heavy guard to make sure that Kickaha did not use it. He took them by surprise, burned them all down, and rammed the craft into the cave. A Beller was a few feet from the large single-unit gate-ring toward which he was running. Kickaha bored a hole through him before he reached the gate.

"Sixteen down. Thirty-four to go," Kickaha said. "And maybe a lot more down in the next few minutes."

"You're not thinking about going through the gate?" she said.

"It must be connected to the temple-gate in Talanac," he said. "But maybe we should save it for later, when we have some reserve force." He did not explain but instead told her to help him get rid of the bodies. "We're going to be gone a while. If any more Bellers gate through here, they won't know what's happened—if anything."

Kickaha's plan had a good chance of being successful, but only if he could talk effectively in its next phase. The two flew up the river until they saw a fleet of many boats, two abreast, being rowed down the river. These reminded him of Viking ships with their carved dragon heads, and the sailors also looked from a distance like Norsemen. They were big and broad-shouldered and wore horned or winged helmets and shaggy breeches and carried double-axes and broadswords and heavy spears and round shields. Most of them had long red-dyed beards, but there were a number clean-shaven.

A glut of arrows greeted him as he dropped down. He persisted in getting close to the lead boat on which a man in the long white and red-collared robes of a priest stood. This boat had used up all its arrows, and the craft stayed just out of axe range. Spears flashed by or even struck the craft, but Kickaha maneuvered the vessel to avoid any coming into the open cockpit. He called to the priest in Lord-speech and presently the king, Brakya, agreed through the priest to talk to Kickaha. He met him on the banks of the river.

There was a good reason for the Red Beards' hostility. Only a week ago, a craft had set fire to several of their towns and had killed a number of young men. All of the marauders had a superficial resemblance to Kickaha. He explained what was happening, although it took him two days to complete this. He was slowed by the necessity of speaking through the *alkhsguma*, as the priest was called in Thyuda. Kickaha gained in the estimation of Brakya when Withrus, the priest, explained that Kickaha was the righthand man of *Allwaldands,* The Almighty.

The progress of the entire fleet down the river was held up for another day while the chiefs and Withrus were taken via air-car to the cave of the gate. Here Kickaha restated his plan. Brakya wanted a practical demonstration of gating, but Kickaha said that this would warn the Bellers in Talanac that the gate was open to invaders.

Several more days went by while Kickaha outlined and then detailed how five thousand warriors could be marched through the gate. It would take exact timing to get so many men into the gate at a time, because mistiming would result in men in the rear being cut in half when the gate activated. But he pointed out that the Bellers and Drachelanders had come out in a large body, so the Thyuda could go in.

Meantime, he was very exasperated and impatient and uneasy, but he dared not show it. Podarge must have taken her huge winged armada to attack Talanac. If she meant to destroy the Red Beards first, she would have descended upon the fleet before this.

Brakya and the chiefs were by this time eager to get going. Kickaha's colorful and enthusiastic descriptions of the Talanac treasures had converted them to zealots.

Kickaha had a mock-up of the big gate in the cave built outside it and he and the chiefs put the men through a training which took three days and a good part of the nights. By the time that the men seemed to be skilled in the necessities, everybody was exhausted and hot-tempered.

Brakya decided they needed a day of rest. Rest meant rolling out great barrels of beer and a flame-threaded liquor from the boats into the camp and drinking these while deer and buffalo and wild horses and bear were roasted. There was much singing, yelling, laughing, boasting, and quite a few fights which ended in severe wounds or deaths.

Kickaha made Anana stay in her tent, mostly because Brakya had made little effort to hide his lust for her. And while he had never offered anything but compliments that bordered on the obscene (perfectly acceptable in Thyuda society, the priest said), he might take action if alcohol uninhibited him. That meant that Kickaha would have to fight him, since everybody had taken it for granted that she was his woman. In fact, they had had to share the same tent to keep up the pretense. Kickaha engaged Brakya that night in a drinking duel, since he would lose face if he refused the king's challenge. Brakya intended, of course, to drink him into unconsciousness and then go to Anana's tent. He weighed perhaps forty pounds more than Kickaha and should have been able to outdrink him. However, Brakya fell asleep about dawn—to the great amusement of those few Red Beards who had not passed out before then.

In the afternoon, Kickaha crawled out of his tent with a head which felt as if he had tried to outbutt a bull bison. Brakya woke up later and almost tore some muscles in his sides laughing at himself. He was not angry at Kickaha and when Anana appeared he greeted her in a subdued manner. Kickaha was glad that was settled, but he did not want to launch the attack that day, as originally planned. The army was in no shape to battle women, let alone the enemies that awaited them in Talanac.

Brakya ordered more barrels rolled out, and the drinking began all over again. At this time, a raven, a bird the size of a bald eagle of Earth, one of Wolff's Eyes, lit on a branch above Kickaha. It spoke in a harsh croaking voice. "Hail, Kickaha! Long have I looked for you! Wolff, the Lord, sent me out to tell you that he has to leave the palace for another universe. Someone has stolen his Chryseis from him, and he is going to find the thief and kill him and then bring his woman back."

The raven Eye proceeded to describe what traps had been left active, what gates were open, and how he could get into and out of the palace safely if he wished. Kickaha informed the Eye that all had changed, and he told him of the Bellers' occupancy of the palace. The raven was not too startled by this. He had just been to Talanac, because he had heard that Kickaha was there. He had seen the Bellers, though he did not know, of course, who they were then. He also had seen the green eagles and Podarge on their way to attack Talanac. They cast a mighty shadow that inked the ground with a signature of doom and the beat of their wings was like the drums of the day of last judgment. Kickaha, questioning him, judged that the armada had fallen upon Talanac the preceding day.

He went after Brakya and told him the news. By then the whole camp was yelling-laughing drunk. Brakya gave the orders; the great horns were blown; the war drums were beaten; the warriors arranged themselves in ragged but recognizable ranks. Brakya and the chiefs were to go first with Kickaha and Anana, who carried a big projector from the craft. Next was a band of the great warriors, two of whom handled the second projector. After them, the clean-shaven youths, who could not grow a beard and dye it red until they had killed a man in battle. Then the rest of the army.

Kickaha, Anana, Brakya, and six chiefs quick-stepped into the circle of gray metal. The chief of the band behind them had started counting to check that the activation time was correct. Abruptly, the group was in a room which was not the vast chamber in the temple which Kickaha had expected. It was a smaller room, though still large by most standards. He recognized it instantly as the gate-chamber near the middle of the city, the one which he had not been able to get to when being pursued by the Bellers. He shoved the Thyuda on out of the circle; they had frozen at the seemingly magical passage.

Thereafter, events happened swiftly, though they consumed many hours and much energy and many lives. The old city seemed to be aflame; fires raged everywhere. These came from torches which the eagles had dropped. There was little material in the jade city burning, but there were thousands of eagles sputtering or smoldering. These had been caught by the Bellers' projectors. The bodies of the big birds, of Tishquetmoac warriors, and Drachelanders lay in the streets and on the housetops. Most of the fighting was now taking place near the top of the city, around the temple and palace.

The defenders and the eagles were so occupied with the struggle they did not notice the Red Beards until there were three thousand gated into Talanac. By then, it was too late to stop the remaining two thousand from coming through. Hundreds of eagles turned from the city-top battle to attack the Thyuda, and from then on, Kickaha remembered only firing the projector and advancing up each bloody, smoky, burning level. The time came when the power packs of the projector had been used up, and from then on the handbeamers were used. Before the summit was gained, these were useless, and it was swords then.

In the temple, he came across a group of charred bodies recognizable as Bellers only because of the silver caskets strapped to their backs. There were six of them, and they had been caught in a cross fire from eagles with handbeamers. This must have been at the very beginning, perhaps the first few moments of the surprise attack. The eagles with the beamers had been killed by projectors, but they had taken a toll catastrophic to the Bellers.

He counted four more dead Bellers before he and Anana and Brakya and other Thyuda burst into the immense room in which the Bellers had installed a large permanent gate. Podarge and her eagles, those left to fight, had cornered a number of Drachelanders, Tishquetmoac and two, no, three, Bellers. There were von Turbat, von Swindebarn, and the emperor of the Tishquetmoac, Quotshaml. They were surrounded by their warriors, who were rapidly dwindling in numbers under the fury of the Harpy and the big birds.

Kickaha, with Anana behind him, and the Red Beards to one side, attacked. He slashed at the eagles from the rear; blood and feathers and flesh flew. He shouted with exultation; the end was near for his enemies.

And then, in the meleee that followed, he saw the three Bellers desert their fellows and run for the big circle of metal, the gate, in one corner. Podarge and some eagles raced after them. Kickaha ran after the eagles.

The Bellers disappeared; Podarge followed them; the eagles close behind her flashed out of existence.

He was so disappointed he wanted to weep, but he did not intend to go after them. No doubt the Bellers had set a trap for any pursuers, and the Harpy and eagles should be in it. He was not going to get caught, no matter how much he wanted to get hold of the Bellers.

He started to turn away but had to defend himself against two of the great birds. He managed to wound them enough to make them uneager to close with him, but they persisted and slowly backed him toward the big gate in the corner of the room. One advanced and chopped at him with her beak; he slashed out to make the beak draw short. The other eagle would then move up a little and feint at him, and he would have to slash at her to be sure that it was only a feint.

He could not call for help, since the others were similarly occupied. Suddenly, he knew he was going to be forced to take the gate. If he did not, he would be struck by one of those huge sharphooked beaks. The two birds were now separating; one was circling to a position behind him, or perhaps they would both attack from his flanks, so, even if he got one, he would go down under the beak of the other.

Despairingly, he glanced about the room, saw that Anana and the Red Beards were still busy, and so he did what he must. He whirled, leaped onto the plate, whirled around to defend himself for the few seconds needed before the gate would activate, and then something—a wing perhaps— struck his head and knocked him half-unconscious.

16

HE OPENED HIS EYES UPON A STRANGE AND WEIRD LANDSCAPE.
He was in a broad and shallow valley. The ground on which he sat and the hills roundabout were covered with a yellow moss-like vegetation.

The sky was not the green on the world he had just left. It was a blue so dark that it trembled on the edge of blackness. He would have thought it was late dusk if the sun were not just past its zenith. To his left, a colossal tower shape hung in the sky. It was predominantly green with dark blue and light blue patched here and there and white woolly masses over large areas. It leaned as the Tower of Pisa leans.

The sight of this brought Kickaha out of his daze. He had been here before, and only the blow on his head had delayed recognition. He was on the moon, the round satellite of the stepped planet of this universe.

Forgetting his previous experiences, he jumped to his feet and soared into the air, sprawling, and landed on his face and then his elbows and knees. The impact was softened by the cushiony ocher moss-stuff, but he was still jarred.

Cautiously, he got to his hands and knees and shook his head. It was then that he saw von Turbat, von Swindebarn, and Quotshaml running with Podarge and the four eagles after them. Running defined the intent, however, not the performance. The three men were going in incredibly long leaps which ended frequently in their feet sliding out from under them when they landed on the vegetation, or a loss of balance while going through the high arcs. Their desperation added to their awkwardness, and under other circumstances, their situation would have been comical to them.

It was comical to Kickaha, who was in no immediate danger. He laughed for a few seconds, then sobered up as he realized that his own situation was likely to be as dangerous. Perhaps more so, because the three seemed to be striving for a goal that might take them away from their pursuers.

He could just see the edge of a thin round stone set in the moss. This, he suddenly knew, must be a gate of some kind. The three had known they would be gated from the temple-room in Talanac to this gate on the moon. They must have deliberately set it up for this purpose, so that they could maroon any pursuers on the moon, while they gated back to Talanac or, more likely, to the Lord's palace.

Undoubtedly, that gate toward which they were racing was a one-time unit. It would receive and transmit the first to step into it. After that, it would be shut off until reactivated. And the means for reactivation, of course, were not at hand.

The trap was one that Kickaha appreciated, since he liked to set such himself and quite often had. But the trapper might become the trapped. Podarge and the eagles were a type of pursuer not reckoned on. Although handicapped also by their unfamiliarity with the low gravity and the shock of finding themselves here, they were using their wings to aid themselves in control and in braking on landing. Moreover, they were covering ground much more swiftly than the men because they were gliding.

Von Turbat and von Swindebarn, jumping simultaneously and holding hands, came down exactly upon the rock. And they disappeared.

Quotshaml was five seconds behind them, and when he landed on the rock, he remained in sight. His cry of desperation sounded in the quiet and lifeless air.

Podarge, wings spread out to check her descent, came down upon his back, and he fell under her weight. Podarge screamed long and loudly, like a great bird in agony instead of triumph, as she tore gobbets of flesh from the man's back. Then the eagles landed and strode forward and circled Podarge and the writhing victim, and they bent down and slashed with their beaks whenever they got a chance.

The casket which Quotshaml had been carrying on his back had been torn off and now lay to one side near the rock.

Twenty-three Bellers to go.

Kickaha rose slowly to his feet. As soon as Podarge and her pets had finished their work, they would look around. And they would see him unless he quickly got out of sight. The prospects for this were not excellent. The ruins of the city of Korad lay a mile away. The great white buildings gleamed in the sun like a distant hope. But even if he did get to it in time, he would find it to be not a hope but a prison. The only gate nearby which he could use was not in the city but hidden in a cave in the hills. Podarge and the eagles were between him and the cave.

Kickaha took advantage of their concentration on their fun to relearn how to run. He had been here many times for some lengthy periods. Thus, the adaptation was almost like swimming after years of desert living. Once learned, the ability does not go away. However, the analogy was only that, an analogy. A man thrown into the water immediately begins to swim.

Kickaha took several minutes to teach himself the proper coordination again.

During this time, he gained a quarter of a mile. Then he heard screams which contained a different emotion than that of bloodletting and revenge gratified. He looked behind him. Podarge and the four birds had seen him and were speeding after him. They were launching themselves upward and covering long stretches in glides, like flying fish. Apparently, they did not trust themselves to try flying yet.

As if they were reading his mind, they quit their hopgliding and took completely to the air. They rose upward far more swiftly than they would have on the planet, and again they screamed. This time, the cries were of frustration. Their flying had actually lost them ground.

Kickaha knew this only because he risked swift glances behind him as he soared through the air. Then he lost ground as his feet slipped on landing and he shot forward and up again and turned over twice. He tried to land on his feet or feet and hands but slammed into the ground hard. His breath was knocked out and he whooshed for air, writhed, and forced himself to get up before he was completely recovered.

During his next leap, he pulled his sword from the sheath. It looked now as if he might need it before he got to the city. Podarge and one eagle were ahead of him, though still very high. They were banking, and then they were coming in toward him in a long flat glide. The other eagles were above him and were now plunging toward him, their wings almost completely folded.

Undoubtedly, the falling birds and the Harpy had automatically computed the ends of their descents to coincide with his forward leap. Kickaha continued forward. A glance upward showed him the bodies of the eagles swelling as they shot toward him. Their yellow claws were spread out, the legs stiff, like great shock absorbers set for the impact of his body. Podarge and friend were coming in now almost parallel to the ground; they had flapped their wings a few times to straighten out the dive. They were about six feet above the moss and expected to clutch him as he rose in the first leg of the arc of a jump.

Podarge was showing almost all her teeth in triumph and anticipation. Her claws dripped blood, and her mouth and teeth were red with blood. Her chin was wet with red.

"Kickaha-a-a-a!" she screamed. "At la-a-a-ast!"

Kickaha wondered if she did not see the sword in his hand or if she was so crazed that she just did not care.

It did not matter. He came down and then went up again in a leap that should have continued on and so brought him into the range of Podarge's claws. But this time he leaped straight upward as hard as he could. It was a prodigious bound, and it carried him up past a very surprised Podarge and eagle. Their screams of fury wailed off like a train whistle.

Then, there were more screams. Panic and fright. Thuds. Wings clapping thunder as the falling eagles tried to check their hurtling.

Kickaha came down and continued his forward movement. On the second bound, he risked a look over his shoulder. Podarge and eagles were on the ground. Green feathers, dislodged by the collision of the Harpy and four mammoth eagle bodies, flew here and there. Podarge was on her back, her legs sticking up. One eagle was unconscious; two were up and staggering around in a daze. The fourth was trying to get onto his talons, but she kept falling over and fluttering and shrieking.

Despite the accident and the new headstart he gained, he still got into the safety of an entrance only a few feet ahead of Podarge. Then he turned and struck her with his sword, and she danced backward, wings flapping, and screamed at him. Her mouth was bloodied and her eyes were pulled wide by insane anger. She was losing blood from a big gash in her side just below her right breast. During the collision or the melee afterward, she had been wounded by a talon.

Kickaha, seeing that only three eagles were following her, and these still at a distance, ran out from the doorway, his sword raised. Podarge was so startled by this that some reason came back to her. She whirled and leaped up and beat her wings. He was close to her and his sword swished out and cut off several long tail feathers. Then he fell to the ground and had to take refuge in the doorway again. The eagles were trying to get to him now.

He wounded two slightly, and they withdrew. Podarge turned to glide back beside them. Kickaha fled through a large hall and across a tremendous room with many ornately carved desks and chairs. He got across the room, down another hall, across a big courtyard and into another building just in time. An eagle came through the doorway of the building he had just left, and the Harpy and another eagle came around the corner of the building. As he had expected, he would have been rushed from the rear if he had stayed in the original doorway.

He came to a room which he knew had only one entrance and hesitated. Should he take a stand here or try for the underground pits? He might get away from them in the dark labyrinths. On the other hand, the eagles would be able to smell him out wherever he hid. And there were things down in the pits that were as deadly as the eagles and far more loathsome. Their existence had been his idea, and Wolff had created them and set them there.

A scream. He jumped through the door and turned to defend it. His mind was made up for him. He had no choice to get to the pits. Now that he had no choice, he wished he had not paused but had kept on going. As long as he was free to move, he felt that he could outwit his pursuers and somehow win out. But now he was trapped, and he could not see, at this moment, how he could win. Not that that meant he had given up. And Podarge was as trapped as he. She had no idea of how to get off the moon and back to the planet, and he did. There could be a trade, if he were forced to deal with her. Meantime, he would see what developed.

The room was large and was of marble. It had a bed of intricately worked silver and gold swinging from a large gold chain which hung down from the center of the ceiling. The walls were decorated with brightly colored paintings of a light-skinned, well-built, and handsomely featured people with graceful robes and many ornaments of metal and gems. The men were beardless, and both sexes had beautiful long yellow or bronze hair. They were playing at various games. Through the windows of some of the painted buildings a painted blue sea was visible.

The murals had been done by Wolff himself, who had talent, perhaps genius. They were inspired, however, by Kickaha, who had, in fact, inspired everything about the moon except the ball of the moon itself.

Shortly after the palace had been retaken, and Wolff had established himself as the Lord, he had mentioned to Kickaha that it had been a long time since he had been on the moon. Kickaha was intrigued, and he had insisted that they visit it. Wolff said that there was nothing to see except grassy plains and a few hills and small mountains. Nevertheless, they had picnicked there, going via one of the gates. Chryseis, the huge-eyed, tiger-haired dryad wife of Wolff, had prepared a basket full of goodies and liquors, just as if she had been a terrestrial American housewife preparing for a jaunt into the park on the edge of town. However, they did take weapons and several taloses, the half-protein robots which looked like knights in armor. Even there, a Lord could not relax absolutely. He must always be on guard against attack from another Lord.

They had a good time. Kickaha pointed out that there was more to see than Wolff had said. There was the glorious, and scary, spectacle of the planet hanging in the sky; this alone was worth making the trip. And then there was the fun of leaping like a grasshopper.

Toward the end of the day, while he was halfdrunk on wine that Earth had never been fortunate enough to know, he got the idea for what he called *Project Barsoom*. He and Wolff had been talking about Earth and some of the books they had loved to read. Kickaha said that when he was young Paul Janus Finnegan and living on a farm outside Terre Haute, Indiana, he had loved the works of Edgar Rice Burroughs. He loved especially Tarzan and David Innes and John Carter and couldn't say that he had favored one over the others. Perhaps he had just a bit more love for John Carter.

It was then he had sat up so suddenly that he had spilled his glass of wine. He had said, "I have it! Barsoom! You said this moon is about the size of Mars, right? And you still have tremendous potentialities for biological 'miracles' in your labs, don't you? What about creating Barsoom?"

He had been so exhilarated he had leaped high up into the air but had been unable to pilot himself accurately and so had come down on the pic-nic lunch. Fortunately, they had eaten most of it. Kickaha was streaked with food and wine, but he was so full of glee he did not notice it.

Wolff listened patiently and smiled often, but his reply sobered Kick-aha.

"I could make a reasonable facsimile of Barsoom," he said. "And I find your desire to be John Carter amusing. But I refuse to play God any more with sentient beings."

Kickaha pleaded with him, though not for very long. Wolff was as strong-minded a man as he had ever known. Kickaha was stubborn, too, but arguing with Wolff when his mind was made up was like trying to erode granite by flicking water off one's finger-ends against the stone.

Wolff did say, however, that he would plant a quick-growing yellow moss-like vegetation on the moon. It would soon kill the green grass and cover the moon from ice-capped north pole to ice-capped south pole.

He would do more, since he did not want to disappoint Kickaha just to be arbitrary. And the project did interest him. He would fashion *thoats, banths,* and other Barsoomian animals in his biolabs. Kickaha must real-ize, however, that this would take a long time and the results might differ from his specifications.

He would even try to create a Tree of Life, and he would build several ruined cities. He would dig canals.

But he would *not* create green *Tharks* or red, black, yellow, and white *Barsoomians.* As Jadawin, he would not have hesitated. As Wolff, he could not.

Aside from his refusal to play God, the scientific and technical prob-lems and the work involved in creating whole peoples and cultures from scratch was staggering. The project would take over a hundred Earth years just to get started.

Did Kickaha realize, for instance, the complexities of the Martian eggs? These were small when laid, of course, probably no bigger than a football at the largest and possibly smaller, since Burroughs had not described the size when they were first ejected by the female. These were supposed to be placed in incubators in the light of the sun. After five years, the egg hatched. But in the meantime they had grown to be about two and a half feet long. At least, the green-Martian eggs were, although these could be supposed to be larger than those of the normal-sized human-type Martians.

Where did the eggs get the energy to grow? If the energy derived from the yolk, the embryo would never develop. The egg was a self-contained system; it did not get food for a long period of time from the mother as an embryo did through the umbilical cord. The implication was that the eggs picked up energy by absorbing the sun's rays. They could do so, theoreti-cally, but the energy gained by this would be very minute, considering the small receptive area of the egg.

Wolff could not, at this moment, imagine what biological mechanisms could bring about this phenomenal rate of growth. There had to be an input of energy from someplace, and since Burroughs did not say what it was, it would be up to Wolff and the giant protein computers in his palace to find out.

"Fortunately," Wolff said, smiling, "I don't have to solve that problem, since there aren't going to be any sentient Martians, green or otherwise. But I might tackle it just to see if it could be solved."

There were other matters which required compromises in the effort to make the moon like Mars. The air was as thick as that on the planet, and though Wolff could make it thinner, he didn't think Kickaha would like to live in it. Presumably, the atmospheric density of Barsoom was equivalent to that found about ten thousand feet above Earth's surface. Moreover, there was the specification of Mars' two moons, Deimos and Phobos. If two bodies of comparable size were set in orbits similar to the two moonlets, they would burn up in a short time. The atmosphere of the moon extended out to the gravitational warp which existed between the moon and planet. Wolff did, however, orbit two energy configurations which shone as brightly as Deimos and Phobos and circled the moon with the same speed and in the same directions.

Later, after sober reflection, Kickaha realized that Wolff was right. Even if it would have been possible to set biolab creations down here and educate them in cultures based on the hints in Burroughs' Martian books, it would not have been a good thing to do. You shouldn't try to play God. Wolff had done that as Jadawin and had caused much misery and suffering.

Or could you do this? After all, Kickaha had thought, the Martians would be given life and they would have as much chance as sentients anywhere else in this world or the next to love, to hope, and so on. It was true that they would suffer and know pain and madness and spiritual agony, but wasn't it better to be given a chance at life than to be sealed in unrealization forever? Just because somebody thought they would be better off if they didn't chance suffering? Wouldn't Wolff himself say that it had been better to have lived, no matter what he had endured and might endure, than never to have existed?

Wolff admitted that this was true. But he said the Kickaha was rationalizing. Kickaha wanted to play John Carter just as he had when he was a kid on a Hoosier farm. Well, Wolff wasn't going to all the labor and pains and time of making a living, breathing, thinking green Martian or red *Zodangan* just so Kickaha could run him through with a sword. Or vice versa.

Kickaha had sighed and then grinned and thanked Wolff for what he had done and gated on up to the moon and had a fine time for a week. He had hunted *banth* and roped a small *thoat* and broken it in and prowled through the ruins of Korad and Thark, as he called the cities which Wolff's taloses had built. Then he became lonely and went back to the planet. Several times he came back for "vacations," once with his Drachelander wife and several Teutoniac knights, and once with a band of Hrowakas. Everybody except him had been uneasy on the moon, close to panic, and the vacations had been failures.

17

IT HAD BEEN THREE YEARS SINCE HE HAD GATED THROUGH TO the moon. Now he was back in circumstances he could never have fantasied. The Harpy and eagles were outside the room and he was trapped inside. Standoff. He could not get out, but they could not attack without serious, maybe total, loss. However, they had an advantage. They could get food and water. If they wanted to put in the time, they could wait until he was too weak from thirst and hunger to resist or until he could no longer fight off sleep. There was no reason why they should not take the time. Nobody was pressing them.

Of course, somebody soon could be. It seemed likely, or at least somewhat probable, the Bellers would be returning through other gates. And this time they would come in force.

If Podarge thought he'd stay in the room until he passed out, she was mistaken. He'd try a few tricks and, if these didn't work, he'd come out fighting. There was a slight chance that he might defeat them or get by them to the pits. It wasn't likely; the beaks and talons were swift and terrible. But then he wasn't to be sneered at, either.

He decided to make it even tougher for them. He rolled the wheel-like door from the space between the walls until only a narrow opening was left. Through this, he shouted at Podarge.

"You may think you have me now! But even if you do, then what? Are you going to spend the rest of your life on this desolate place? There are no mountains worthy of the name here for your aeries! And the topography is depressingly flat! And your food won't be easy to get! All the animals that live in the open are monstrously big and savage fighters!

"As for you, Podarge, you won't be able to queen it over your hundreds of thousands! If your virgin eagles do lay their eggs so your subjects may increase, they'll have a hard time with the little egg-eating animals that abound here! Not to mention the great white apes, which love eggs! And flesh, including eagle flesh, I'm sure!

"Ah, yes, the great white apes! You haven't met up with them yet, have you?"

He waited a while for them to think about his words. Then he said, "You're stuck here until you die! Unless you make a truce with me! I can show you how to get back to the planet! I know where the gates are hidden!"

More silence. Then a subdued conversation among the eagles and the Harpy. Finally, Podarge said, "Your words were very tempting, Trickster! But they don't fool me! All we have to do is wait until you fall asleep or become too thirst-torn to stand it! Then we will take you alive, and we will torture you until you tell us what we need to know. Then we kill you. What do you think of that?"

"Not much," he muttered. He yelled, "I will kill myself first! Podarge, slut-queen of the big bird-brains, what do you think of that?"

Her scream and the flapping of huge wings told him that she thought as little of his words as he of hers.

"I know where the gates are! But you'll never be able to find them without me! Make up your so-called mind fast, Podarge! I'll give you half an hour! Then I act!"

He rolled the door entirely shut and sat down with his back against the red-brown, highly polished hardwood. They could not move it without giving him plenty of time to be up and ready for them. And he could rest for a while. The long hard battle in Talanac, the shock of being hurled onto the moon, and the subsequent chase had exhausted him. And he lusted for water.

He must have nodded off. Up out of black half-oily waters he surged. His mouth was dry, dripping dust. His eyes felt as if hot hard-boiled eggs had just been inserted in his sockets. Since the door was not moving, he did not know what had awakened him. Perhaps it was his sense of vigilance belatedly acting.

He let his head fall back against the door. Faintly, screams and roars vibrated through, and he knew what had cannoned him from sleep. He jumped up and rolled the door halfway back into the inner-wall space. With the thick barrier removed, the sounds of the battle in the corridor struck full force.

Podarge and the three eagles were facing three huge, tawny, catlike beasts with ten legs. Two were maned males; the third was a sleek-necked female. These were *banths*, the Martian lions described by Burroughs and created by Wolff in his biolab and set down on this moon. They preyed on *thoats* and *zitidar* calves and the great white apes and anything else they could catch. Normally, they were night hunters, but hunger must have sent them prowling the daytime city. Or they may have been roused by all the noise and attracted by the blood.

Whatever their reasons, they had cornered the cornerers. They had killed one eagle, probably in the first surprise attack, Kickaha surmised. A green eagle was a fighter formidable enough to run off a tiger or two without losing a feather. So far, though the *banths* had killed one and inflicted enough wounds on the others to cover them with blood, they were bleeding from cuts and gashed all over their bodies and heads.

Now, roaring, they had separated from their intended prey. They paced back and forth in the corridor and then one would hurl himself at an eagle. Sometimes the charges were bluffs and fell just short of the range of beaks as deadly as battle-axes. Other times, they struck one of the two remaining eagles with a huge scythe-clawed paw, and then there would be a flurry of saberish canines, yellow beaks, yellow or scarlet talons, patches of tawny hide flying or mane hairs torn out by the bunch, green feathers whirling through the air, distended eyeballs green or yellow or red, blood spurting, roars, screams. And then the lion would disengage and run back to his companions.

Podarge stayed behind the twin green towers of her eagles.

Kickaha watched and waited. And presently all three lions attacked simultaneously. A male and an eagle rolled into the door with a crash. Kickaha jumped back, then stepped forward and ran his sword forward into the mass. He did not care which he stabbed, lion or eagle, although he rather hoped it would be an eagle. They were more intelligent and capable of greater concentration and devotion to an end—principally his.

But the two rolled away and only the tip of his sword entered flesh. Both were making so much noise that he could not tell which was hurt by the sword.

For just a moment, he had a clear avenue of escape down the center of the corridor. Both eagles were engaged with the lions, Podarge was backed against the wall, her talons keeping the enraged female at bay. The lioness was bleeding from both eyes and her nose, which was half torn off. Blinded by blood, she was hesitant about closing in on the Harpy.

Kickaha dashed down the aisle, then leaped over two bodies as they rolled over to close off his route. His foot came down hard on a tawny muscle-ridged back, and he soared into the air. Unfortunately, he had put so much effort in his leap that he banged his head against the marble ceiling, cutting his temple open on a large diamond set in the marble.

Half stunned, he staggered on. At that moment, he was vulnerable. If eagle or lion had fallen on him, it could have killed him as a wolf kills a sick rabbit. But they were too busy trying to kill each other, and soon he was out of the building. Within a few minutes, he was free of the city and making great leaps toward the hills.

He bounded past the torn body of the eagle crippled from the collision. Another body, ripped up, lay near it. This was a *banth*, which must have attacked the eagle with the expectation of an easy kill. But it had been mistaken and had paid for the mistake.

Then he was soaring over the body of Quotshaml—rather, parts of the body, because they were scattered. The head, legs, arms, entrails, lungs, and pieces thereof.

He leaped up the hill, which was so tall that it could almost be dignified with the name of mountain. Two-thirds of the way up, hidden behind a curving outcrop of quartz-shot granite, was the entrance to the cave. There seemed no reason why he could not make it; only a few minutes ago all luck seemed to have leaked out of him, and now it was trickling back.

A scream told him that good fortune might only have seemed to return. He looked over his shoulder. A quarter of a mile away, Podarge and the two eagles were flapping swiftly toward him. No *banths* were in sight. Evidently, they had not been able to keep Podarge and the eagles in a corner. Perhaps the great cats had been glad to let them escape. That way, the *banths* could keep on living for sure and could enjoy eating the one eagle they had killed.

Whatever had happened, he was in danger of being caught in the open again. His pursuers had learned how to fly effectively in the lesser gravity. As a result, they were traveling a third faster than they would have on the planet—or so it seemed to Kickaha. Actually, the fighting and the loss of blood they had endured had to slow them down.

Podarge and one eagle, at a second look, did seem to be crippled. Their wings had slowed down since the first look, and they were lagging behind the other eagle. This one, though covered with blood over the green feathers, did not seem to be as deeply hurt. She overtook Kickaha and came down like a hawk on a gopher.

The gopher, however, was armed with a sword and had determined what action he would take. Calculating in advance when her onslaught would coincide with his bound, he whirled around in mid-air. He came down facing backwards, and the eagle's outstretched talons were within reach of the blade. She screamed and spread her wings to brake her speed, but he slashed out. His sword did not have the force that his sure footing on the ground would have given it, and the stroke spun him further than he wanted to go and threw him off balance for the landing. Nevertheless, the blade chopped through one foot at the juncture of talons and leg and halfway through the other foot. Then Kickaha struck the earth and fell on his side, and the breath exploded from him.

He was up again sobbing and wheezing like a damaged bagpipe. He managed to pick up his sword where he had dropped it. The eagle was flopping on the ground now like a wounded chicken and did not even see him when he brought the sword down on her neck. The head fell off, and one black, scarlet-encircled eye glared at him and then became dull and cold.

He was still sucking in air when he bounded through the cave entrance twenty yards ahead of Podarge and the last eagle. He landed just inside the hole in the hillside and then leaped toward the end of the cave, a granite wall forty feet away.

He had interrupted a domestic scene: a family of great white apes. Papa, ten feet tall, four-armed, white and hairless except for an immense roach of white hair on top of his breadloaf-shaped skull, gorilla-faced, pink-eyed, was squatting against the wall to the right. He was tearing with his protruding canines and sharp teeth at the ripped-off leg of a small *thoat.* Mama was ripping the flesh of the head of the *thoat* and at the same time was suckling twin babies.

(Wolff and Kickaha had goofed in designing the great white apes. They had forgotten that the only mammals on Burroughs' Mars were a small creature and man. By the time they perceived their mistake, they agreed that it was too late. Several thousand of the apes had been placed on the moon, and it did not seem worthwhile to destroy the first projects of the biolabs and create a new nonmammalian species.)

The colossal simians were as surprised as he, but he had the advantage of being in motion. Still, there was the delaying business of rolling a small key boulder out of a socket of stone and then pushing in on a heavy section of the back wall. This resulted in part of the wall swinging out and part swinging in to reveal a chamber. This was a square about twenty feet across. There were seven crescents set into the granite floor near the back wall. To the right was a number of pegs at eye-level, on which were placed seven of the silvery metallic crescents. Each of these was to be matched to the appropriate crescent on the floor by comparing the similarity of hieroglyphs on the crescents.

When two crescents were joined at their ends to form a circle, they became a gate to a preset place on the planet. Two of the gates were traps. The unwary person who used them would find himself transmitted to an inescapable prison in Wolff's palace.

Kickaha skimmed the hieroglyphs with a haste that he did not like but could not help. The light was dusky in the rear chamber, and he could barely make out the markings. He knew now that he should have stored a light device here when the cave was set up. It was too late even for regret— he had no time for anything but instant unconsidered reaction.

The cavern was as noisy as the inside of a kettledrum. The two adult apes had gotten to their bowed and comparatively short legs and were roaring at him while the two upper arms beat on their chests and the two intermediary arms slapped their stomachs. Before they could advance on him, they were almost knocked over by Podarge and the eagle, who blasted in like a charge from a double-barreled shotgun.

They had hoped to catch a cornered and relatively helpless Kickaha, although their experience with him should have taught them caution. Instead, they had exchanged three wounded and tiring, perhaps reluctant, *banths* for two monstrously large, refreshed, and enraged great white apes.

Kickaha would have liked to watch the battle and cheer the apes, but he did not want to chance wearing his luck through, since it had already given indications of going threadbare. So he threw the two "trap" crescents on the floor and picked the other five up. Four he put under his arm with the intention of taking them with him. If the Harpy did escape the apes and tried to use a crescent, she would end up in the palace prison.

Kickaha lingered when he knew better, delayed his up-and-going too long. Podarge suddenly broke loose—perhaps thrown was a more exact description of her method of departure from the ape—and she shot like a basketball across the cave. She came into the chamber so swiftly that he had to drop the crescents to bring up his sword for defense. She hit him with her talons first, and he was slammed against the wall with a liver-hurting, kidney-paining jolt. He could not bring the sword down because, one, she was too close and, two, he was too hurt at the moment to use the sword.

Then they were rolling over and over with her talons clenched in his thighs. The pain was agonizing, and she was beating him in the face, the head, the neck, and the shoulders with the forward edges of her wings.

Despite the pain and the shock of the wingblows, he managed to hit her in the chin with a fist and then to bang the hilt of the sword against the side of her head.

Her eyes crossed and glazed. Blood flowed from her nose. She fell backward, her wings stretched like outflung arms. Her talons, however, remained sunk in his thighs; he had to pry them loose one by one. Blood ran down his legs and pooled out around his feet. Just as he pulled the last talon loose, the male ape charged on all sixes into the chamber. Kickaha picked up his sword with both hands and brought it down on an outstretched paw. The shock ran up his hand and arm and almost made him lose his grip. But the paw, severed at the wrist, fell on the floor. The stump shot blood all over him, momentarily blinding him. He wiped the blood off in time to see the ape flee shrieking on two feet and three of its paws. It ran headlong into the last eagle, which had just finished disemboweling the female ape with its beak and talons. They locked and went over and over.

At that moment Podarge recovered her senses. She soared from the floor with a shriek and a frantic beating of wings. Kickaga picked up a crescent from the floor, saw that the hieroglyph on its center matched the nearest one in the floor, and set the two end against end. Then he whirled and slashed at Podarge, who was dancing around, trying to frenzy herself enough to attack him. She dodged back and he stepped into the ring formed by the two crescents.

"Goodbye, Podarge!" he cried. "Stay here and rot!"

18

HE HAD GOTTEN NO FURTHER THAN HER NAME WHEN THE GATE
activated. He was out of the cave with no sense of passage—as always—
and was in another place, standing inside another ring of two crescents. The
contact of the two crescents in the cave, plus the entrance of his mass into
the field radiated by the crescents, had activated the gate after a delay of
three seconds. He and the loose crescent had been transferred to the crescent which matched the frequency of the crescent in the cave, at the other
end of the undercontinuum.

He had escaped, although he would bleed to death soon if he did not
find something to staunch the flow.

Then he saw what mistake he had made by acting so quickly because
of pressure from Podarge. He had picked up the wrong crescent after dropping the five when attacked by the Harpy. During the struggle, one of the
trap crescents must have been kicked out of its corner and among the others. And he had picked it up and used it to gate out.

He was in the prison cell of the palace of the Lord.

Once, he had bragged to Wolff that he could escape from the so-called
escape-proof cell if he were ever in it. He did not think that any prison anywhere could hold a man who was clever and determined. The escape might
take a long time, but it could be done.

He groaned now and wished he had not been so big-mouthed. Wolff
had arranged the prison very well. It was set under eighty feet of solid stone
and had no direct physical connection to the outside world. It was an entirely self-enclosed, self-sustaining system except for one thing: food and
water for the prisoner were transmitted from the palace kitchen through
a gate too small to admit anything larger than a tray.

There were gates in the prison through which the prisoner could be
brought up to a prison cell in the palace. But this could be activated only
by someone cognizant in the palace above.

The room was cylindrical and was about forty feet long. Light was
seemingly sourceless and there were no shadows. The walls were painted

by Wolff with scenes from the ancient ancestral planet of the Lords. Wolff had not expected any prisoners other than Lords and so had done these paintings for their benefit. There was some cruelty in the settings of the murals—all depicted the wide and beautiful outdoors and hence could not help reminding the prisoner of his narrow and enclosed space.

The furniture was magnificent and was in the style known among the Lords as Pre-Exodus Middle Thyamarzan. The doors of the great bureaus and cabinets housed many devices for the amusement and education of the prisoner. Originally, these had not been in the cells. But when Wolff had rewon the palace, he had placed these in the prison—he no longer believed in torturing his captives even with boredom. And he provided them with much because he was sometimes gone for long periods and would not be able to release them.

Until now, this room had held no prisoners. It was ironical and sourly amusing that its first prize should be the jailer's best friend and that the jailer knew nothing of it.

The Bellers in the palace would not know of him either, he hoped. Lights would be flashing in three places to indicate that the buried cell now housed someone: a light would be pulsing in Wolff's bedroom; a second, on an instrument panel in the great control room; a third, in the kitchen.

If the Black Bellers were observing any of these, they must be alarmed or, at the least, edgy and uncertain. They would have no way of knowing what the lights meant. The kitchen taloses would know, but even if they were asked, they could not reply. They heard orders but had mouths for tasting and eating only, not for talking.

Kickaha, thinking about this, looked for first aid devices in the cabinets. He soon came across antiseptics, local anesthetics, drugs, bandages, all he needed. After cleaning his wounds, he prepared films of pseudoflesh and applied them to stop the bleeding. They began their healing efforts immediately.

He got a drink of water then and also opened a bottle of cold beer. He took a long shower, dried off, and searched for and found a pill which would dull his overstimulated nerves so he could get a restful sleep. The pill would have to wait, however, until he had eaten and finished exploring this place.

It was true that he should not, perhaps, be thinking of rest. Time was vital. There was no telling what was happening in Talanac with Anana and the Red Beards. They might be under attack this very moment by a Beller flying machine with powerful beamers. And what was von Turbat doing now? After he had escaped Podarge, he and von Swindebarn must have gated back to the palace. Would they be content to hole up in it? Or would they, as seemed more likely to Kickaha, go back to the moon through another gate? They would suppose him to be marooned there and so out of action. But they also must have some doubts. It was probable that they would take at least one craft and a number of men to hunt him down.

He laughed. They would be up there, frantically trying to locate him, and all the time he would be underfoot, so to speak. There was, of course, the possibility that they would find the cave near Korad. In which case, they would test all the crescents left there, and one Beller at least would soon be in this cell. Perhaps he was making a mistake in sleeping. Maybe he ought to keep on going, get out of this cell as soon as possible.

Kickaha decided that he *had* to sleep. If he didn't, he would collapse or be slowed down so much he would be too vulnerable. Light-headed from a bottle of beer and three glasses of wine, he went to a little door in the wall, over which a topaz was flashing a yellow light. He opened the door and took a silver tray from the hollow in the wall. There were ten silver-colored, jewel-encrusted dishes on the tray, each holding excellent foods. He emptied every dish and then returned the tray and contents to the hollow. Nothing happened until he closed the little door. He raised it again a second later. The hollow was empty. The tray had been gated up to the kitchen, where a talos would wash and polish the dishes and the tray. Six hours from now, the talos would place another tray of food in the kitchen gate and so send it to the stone-buried cell.

Kickaha wanted to be up and ready when the tray came through the next time. Unfortunately, there were no clocks in the prison, so he would have to depend on his biological clock. That, in its present condition, was undependable.

He shrugged and told himself what the hell. He could only try. If he didn't make it this time, he would the next. He had to get sleep because he did not know what would be required of him if he ever got out of prison. Actually, this was the best place for him in the universe—if the Bellers did not find the cave of gates on the moon.

First, he had to explore the rest of the prison to make sure that all was right there and also to use anything he might find helpful. He went to a door in one end of the cell and opened it. He stepped into a small bare anteroom. He opened the door on its opposite wall and went into another cylindrical cell about forty feet long. This was luxuriously decorated and furnished in a different style. However, the furniture kept changing shape, and whenever he moved near to a divan, a chair, or table, it slid away from him. When he increased his pace, the piece of furniture increased its speed just enough to keep out of reach. And the other furniture slid out of its way if they veered toward it.

The room had been designed to amuse, puzzle, and perhaps eventually enrage the prisoner. It was supposed to help him keep his mind off his basic predicament.

Kickaha gave up trying to capture a divan and left the room at the door at the opposite end. It closed behind him as the others had done. He knew that the doors could not be opened from this side, but he kept trying, just in case Wolff had made a mistake. It refused to move, too. The door ahead swung open to a small anteroom. The room beyond it was an art studio. The next room was four times as large as the previous and was mainly a swimming pool. It had a steady supply of cool fresh water, gated through from the palace water supply above and also gated out. Inflow was through a barred hole in the center of the pool's floor. Kickaha studied the setup of the pool and then went on to the next room.

This was the size of the first. It contained gymnastic equipment and was in a gravitic field one-half that of the planet's, the field of which was equivalent to Earth's. Much of the equipment was exotic, even to a man who traveled as much as Kickaha. The only things to hold his interest were some ropes, which were strung from ceiling hooks or bars for climbing exercises.

He fashioned a lasso from one rope and coiled several more over his shoulder to take with him. In all, he passed through twenty-four chambers, each different from the others. Eventually, he was back in the original.

Any other prisoner would have supposed that the rooms were connected to form a circular chain. He knew that there was no physical connection between the rooms. Each was separated from the next by forty feet of granite.

Passage from one to the next was effected by gates set inside the doorways of the anterooms. When the door was swung open, the gate was activated and the prisoner was transmitted instantaneously to another anteroom which looked just like the one he thought he was entering.

Kickaha entered the original cell cautiously. He wanted to make sure that no Beller had been gated here from the cave on the moon while he was exploring. The room was empty, but he could not be sure that a Beller had not come here and gone investigating, as he had. He stacked three chairs on top of each other and, carrying them, walked through into the next room, the one with the shape-shifting elusive furniture. He picked out a divan and lassoed a grotesquely decorated projection on top of its back. The projection changed form, but it could metamorphose only within certain limits, and the lasso held snugly. The divan did move away when he walked toward it, but he lay down and then pulled himself along the lasso while the divan fled here and there. The thick rugs kept him from being skinned, although he did get rug-burns. Finally he clutched the divan and hauled himself up onto it. It stopped then, seemed to quiver, solidified, and became as quiescent and permanent as ordinary furniture. However, it would resume its peculiar properties if he left it.

Kickaha tied one end of the lasso to the projection. He then snared the top of a chair which had been innocently standing nearby. The chair did not move until Kickaha pulled it on the rope. Then it tried to get away. He jumped off the divan and went through a series of maneuvers to herd the divan and chair, still connected by the rope, near the entrance. With the other ropes and various objects used as weights, he rigged a Rube Goldberg device. The idea was that anyone coming through the entrance would step inside the noose laid on the floor. The nearby mass of the intruder would then send both divan and chair away in flight, and this would draw the noose tight around the intruder's ankle. One end of the noose was tied to the rope stretched between the divan and chair. Another rope connected the projection on the divan to a chandelier of gold set with emeralds and turquoises. Kickaha, standing on the topmost of the three chairs he'd carried, had performed a balancing act while withdrawing the kingpin that secured the chandelier to the ceiling fixture. He did not entirely remove the kingpin but left just enough to keep the chandelier from falling. When the divan and chair pulled away from the intruder, the strain on the rope tied to the kingpin would yank it the rest of the way out, he hoped. The chandelier would come crashing down onto the floor. And, if his calculations were correct, it would fall on whoever was being dragged along by the noose around his leg.

Actually, he did not expect it to work. He did not think anybody would be imperceptive enough not to see the noose. Still, there was a chance. This world and the next were full of fools and clumsy idiots.

He went to the next room, the art studio. Here he picked up a large ball of plastic. This was extremely malleable and could be fixed to retain a desired shape by shooting a chemical hypodermically into the stuff. He took the ball and needle syringe into the swimming pool room. He dived to the bottom of the pool and jammed the plastic down over the outlet. He molded the plastic into a disc which covered the hole and then fixed it with the hypo. After this, he rose to the surface and drew himself up onto the pool edge. The water level began to rise immediately. It was as he had hoped: there was no regulation or feedback between inflow and outflow, so water continued to pour in even when the outlet was blocked. Wolff had overlooked this. Of course, there was no reason why he should have been concerned about it. If a prisoner wanted to drown himself, he was free to do so.

Kickaha walked into the next room. Here he piled some furniture and statues against the door, dried himself, and lay down to sleep. He was confident that no one would enter the room without having had much difficulty getting there. And no one could enter without making a lot of noise.

He awoke with a jerk and a feeling that bells attached to his nerves were jingling. His heart was drumming like a grouse's wings on takeoff. Something had crashed into his dreams. No, into the room. He jumped up from behind the divan, the sword in his hand. He came up just in time to see a man strike the floor in a wave of water. Then the door automatically shut.

The man was gasping as though he had been holding his breath for a long time.

He was a long-legged, powerfully built fellow with pale skin, large freckles, and dark hair that would be red-blond when it dried. He carried no hand-beamers. His only weapons seemed to be a dagger and a short sword. He was unarmored. He wore a short-sleeved red shirt, a big leather belt, and yellow tights striped along the seams.

Kickaha bounded out from behind the divan and ran up with his sword raised. The man, shocked and seeing that he could not get up in time to defend himself, and that Kickaha was giving him a chance to surrender, took the only course a wise man could. Kickaha spoke to him in Lordspeech. The man looked puzzled and answered in German. Kickaha repeated the order in German, then let him get up so he could sit down in a chair. The man was shivering from the cold water and possibly from the thought of what Kickaha might yet do to him.

The fact that the man spoke German fluently was enough to convince Kickaha that he could not be a Beller. His speech was that of a native of the Einhorner Mountains. Evidently, the Bellers had not wanted to expose themselves to the unknown dangers of the gates and so had sent in expendables.

Pal Do Shuptarp told Kickaha everything he knew. He was a baronet who was in command of the castle garrison of King von Turbat of Eggesheim. He had stayed behind while the invasion of Talanac was taking place. Suddenly, von Turbat and von Swindebarn had reappeared. They came from somewhere inside the castle. They ordered the garrison and a number of other troops to follow them into a "magic" room in the castle. Von Turbat had explained that their archenemy Kickaha was now on the moon and that it was necessary to go by sorcery—white magic, of course—to track him down. Von Turbat did not say anything of what had happened to the soldiers in Talanac.

"They're all dead," Kickaha said. "But how did von Turbat talk to you?"

"Through a priest, as he has done for some time," Do Shuptarp said.

"And you didn't think that was peculiar?"

Do Shuptarp shrugged and said, "So many peculiar things were happening all of a sudden that this was just one more. Besides, von Turbat claimed to have received a divine revelation from the Lord. He said he had been given the gift of being able to speak the holy tongue. And he was forbidden to speak anything else because the Lord wanted everyone to know that von Turbat was favored of the Lord."

"A pretty good rationalization and excuse," Kickaha said.

"A magical flying machine appeared above the castle," Do Shuptarp said. "It landed, and we helped take it apart and carried the pieces into the room where we were to be transported magically to the moon."

It was a terrifying experience to be transported instantaneously to the moon and to see the planet they had been on just a moment before now hanging in the sky, threatening to fall down on the moon and crush them all.

But a man could get used to almost anything.

The cave in the hillside had been discovered by the searchers when they came across the carcass of an eagle minus her feet and head. The cave held two dead adult apes, and another dead eagle. There were five loose crescents on the floor. Kickaha, hearing this, knew that Podarge had escaped via a gate.

Von Turbat had selected ten of his best knights to use the gates, two to a circle. He hoped that some would find and kill Kickaha.

"Two of you?"

"Karl voyn Rothadler came with me," Do Shuptarp said. "He's dead. He did not step into the noose, although he stormed into that room so fast he almost got caught in it. A great one for charging in, swinging a sword, and to hell with finding out first what's going on. He ran in and so that divan and chair moved away swiftly. I don't now how you bewitched them, but you must be a powerful magician. They pulled the kingpin loose and the chandelier fell on his head."

"So the trap worked, though not exactly as planned," Kickaha said. "How did you get through the room filled with water?"

"After Karl was killed, I tried to go back the way I'd come. The door wouldn't open. So I went on. When I came to the door to the water-filled room, I had to push with all my strength to open it. Water sprayed out of the opening. I quit pushing. But I couldn't go back; I had to go ahead. I pushed the door open again. The pressure of the water was very strong. I couldn't get the door open all the way, and the water spurting out almost knocked me down. But I managed to get through—I am very strong. The anteroom was almost full of water by the time I did get through, and the door closed as soon as I was inside the big room.

"The water was clear and the light was bright. Otherwise, I might have drowned before I found the other door. I swam to the ceiling, hoping there would be a space there with air, but there wasn't any. So I swam to the other end of the room. The water pressure had opened the door there and let some water into the next anteroom. But the door had closed itself again. In fact, it must have been doing this for some time. The anteroom was more than half full when I got into it.

"By then, the pressure was also opening the door into this room. I waited once while it closed. Then, when it began to open a little again, I shoved with my feet braced on the floor. And I came out like a marooned sailor cast up by a storm on a desert island, as you saw."

Kickaha did not comment for a minute. He was thinking of the predicament in which he had put himself—and this fellow—by causing the pool to overflow. Eventually, every room of the twenty-four would be flooded.

"Okay," he said. "If I can't figure a way to get out fast, we've had it!"

Do Shuptarp asked what he had said. Kickaha explained. Do Shuptarp got even paler. Kickaha then proceeded to outline much of what was behind the recent events. He went into some detail about the Black Bellers.

Do Shuptarp said, "Now I understand much of what was incomprehensible to me—to all of us—at the time. One day, life was proceeding normally. I was getting ready to lead a dragon-hunting expedition. Then von Turbat and von Swindebarn proclaimed a holy war. They said that the Lord, Herr Gutt, was directing us to attack the city on the level below us. And we were to find and kill the three heretics hiding there.

"Most of us had never heard of Talanac or the Tishquetmoac or of Kickaha. We had heard of the robber baron Horst von Horstmann, of course. Then von Turbat told us that the Lord had given us magical means to go from one level to the next. He explained why he used only the speech of the Lord.

"And now you tell me that the souls of my king and of von Swindebarn and a few others have been eaten up. And that their bodies are possessed by demons."

Kickaha saw that the soldier did not fully understand yet, but he did not try to disabuse him. If he wanted to think in superstitious modes, let him. The important thing was that he knew that the two kings were now terrible perils in disguise.

"Can I trust you?" he said to Do Shuptarp. "Will you help me, now that you know the truth? Are you convinced that it is the truth? Of course, all this doesn't matter unless I can figure out a way to get us up into the palace before we drown."

"I will swear eternal fealty to you!"

Kickaha wasn't convinced, but he didn't want to kill him. And Do Shuptarp might be helpful. He told him to pick up his weapons and to lead the way back to the cell in which they had arrived. On getting back there, Kickaha looked for a recording device and found one. This was one of many machines with which a prisoner could entertain himself. Kickaha, however, had another purpose than amusement in mind. He took the glossy black cube, which was three inches across, pressed the red spot on its underside, and spoke a few words in Lord-speech at it. Then he pressed a white spot on its side, and his words were emitted back to him.

Kickaha waited for what seemed like hours until the topaz above the little door in the wall began flashing. He removed the tray, which contained enough food for two. Two lights were now flashing in the kitchen, and the talos, noting this, had made suitable provisions.

"Eat!" Kickaha said to Do Shuptarp. "Your next meal may be a long way off—if you ever get one!"

Do Shuptarp winced. Kickaha tried to eat slowly, but the sudden slight opening of the door and spurt of water caused him to gobble. The door shut but almost immediately opened a few inches again to spew in more water.

He put the dishes on the tray and set it in the wallchamber. He hoped that the talos would not have something more pressing to do. If they delayed gating the tray back, it might be too late for the prisoners.

Also, the cube he had put on the tray had started replaying his instructions. It was set for sixty times by pressing the white spot three times, but the talos might not take in the tray until after the recordings were finished.

The topaz quit flashing. He lifted the door. The tray was gone. "If the talos does what I tell him to, we're okay," he said to the Teutoniac. "At least, we'll be out of here. If the talos doesn't obey me, then it's glub, glub, glub, and an end to our worries."

He told Do Shuptarp to follow him into the anteroom. There they stood for perhaps sixty seconds. Kickaha said, "If nothing happens soon, we might as well kiss our . . ."

19

THEY WERE STANDING ON A ROUND PLATE OF GRAY METAL IN A large room. The furniture was exotic, Early Rhadamanthean Period. The walls and floor were of rose-red and jet-veined stone. There were no doors or windows, although one wall seemed to be a window which gave a view of the outside.

"There'll be lights to indicate that we're now in this cell," Kickaha said. "Let's hope the Bellers won't figure out what they mean."

With all these unexplained lights on, the Bellers must be in a panic. Undoubtedly, they were prowling the palace to find out what—if anything—was wrong.

Presently, a section of the seemingly solid wall moved and disappeared into the wall itself. Kickaha led the way out. A talos, six and a half feet tall, armored like a knight, waited for them. It handed him the black-cube recorder.

Kickaha said, "Thank you," and then, "Observe us closely. I am your master. This man is my servant. Both of us are to be served by you unless this man, my servant, does something that might harm me. Then you are to stop him from trying to harm me.

"The other beings in this palace are my enemies, and you are to attack and kill any as soon as you see one or more than one. First, though, you will take this cube, after I have spoken a message into it, and you will let the other taloses hear it. It will tell them to attack and kill my enemies. Do you understand fully?"

The talos saluted, indicating that he comprehended. Kickaha spoke into the cube, set it to repeat the message a thousand times, and gave it to the talos. The armored thing saluted again, turned, and marched off.

Kickaha said, "They carry out orders superbly, but the last one to get their ear is their master. Wolff knew this, but he didn't want to change their setup. He said that this characteristic might actually work out to his advantage someday, and it wasn't likely that any invader would know about it."

Kickaha next told Do Shuptarp how to handle a beamer if he should get his hands on one, then they set out for the armory of the palace. To get to it, they had to cross one entire floor of this wing and then descend six stories. Kickaha took the staircases, since the Bellers would be using the elevators.

Do Shuptarp was awed at the grandeur of the palace. The great size of the rooms and their furnishings, each containing treasure enough to have bought all the kingdoms in Dracheland, reduced him to a gasping, slavering, creeping creature. He wanted to stop so he could look and feel and, perhaps, fill his pockets. Then he became cowed, because the absolute quiet and the richness made him feel as if he were in an extremely sacred place.

"We could wander for days and never meet another soul," he said.

Kickaha said, "We could if I didn't know where I was going." He wondered how effective the fellow would be. He was probably a first-rate warrior under normal circumstances. His handling of himself in the water-filled chamber proved that he was courageous and adaptable. But to be in the palace of the Lord was for him as frightening, as numinous an experience, as it would be for a terrestrial Christian to be transported to the City of God—and to discover that devils had taken over.

Near the foot of the staircase, Kickaha smelled melted metal and plastic and burned protoplasm. Cautiously, he stuck his head around the corner. About a hundred feet down the hall, a talos lay sprawled on its front. An armored arm, burned off at the shoulder by a beamer, lay nearby.

Two Black Bellers, or so Kickaha presumed they were from the caskets attached to their backs by harnesses, lay dead. Their necks were twisted almost completely around. Two Bellers, each holding a hand-beamer, were talking excitedly. One held what was left of the black cube in his hand. Kickaha grinned on seeing it. It had been damaged by the beamer and so must have stopped its relay. Thus, the Bellers would not know why the talos had attacked them or what the message was in the cube.

"Twenty-nine down. Twenty-one to go," Kickaha said. He withdrew his head.

"They'll be on their guard now," he muttered. "The armory would've been unguarded, probably, if this hadn't happened. But now that they know something's stalking upwind, they'll guard it for sure. Well, we'll try another way. It could be dangerous, but then what isn't? Let's go back up the stairs."

He led Do Shuptarp to a room on the sixth story. This was about six hundred feet long and three hundred feet wide and contained stuffed animals, and some stuffed sentients, from many universes. They passed a transparent cube in which was embedded, like a dragonfly in amber, a creature that seemed to be half-insect, half-man. It had antennae and huge but quite human eyes, a narrow waist, skinny legs covered with a pinkish fuzz, four skinny arms, a great humped back, and four butterfly-like wings radiating from the hump.

Despite the urgency of action, Do Shuptarp stopped to look at the strangeling. Kickaha said, "That exhibit is ten thousand years old. That *kwiswas,* coleopter-man, is the product of Anana's biolabs, or so I was told, anyway. The Lord of this world made a raid on his sister's world and secured some specimens for his museum. This *kwiswas,* I understand, was Anana's lover at that time, but you can't believe everything you hear, especially if one Lord is telling it about another. And all that, of course, was some time ago."

The monstrously large eyes had been staring through the thick plastic for ten millennia, five thousand years before civilization had set in on Earth. Though Kickaha had seen it before, he still felt an awe, an uneasiness, and insignificance before it. How strongly and cleverly had this creature fought to preserve its life, just as Kickaha was now fighting for his? Perhaps as vigorously and wildly. And then it had died, as he must, too, and it had been stuffed and set up to observe with unseeing eyes the struggles of others. All passed . . .

He shook his head and blinked his eyes. To philosophize was fine, if you did so under appropriate circumstances. These were not appropriate. Besides, so death came to all, even to those who avoided it as ingeniously and powerfully as he! So what? One extra minute of life was worth scrapping for, provided that the minutes that had gone before had been worthy minutes.

"I wonder what this thing's story was?" Do Shuptarp muttered.

"Our story will come to a similar end if we don't get a move on," Kickaha said.

At the end wall of the room, he twisted a projection that looked as fixed as the rest of the decorations. He turned the projection to the right 160 degrees, then to the left 160, and then spun it completely around twice to the right. A section of wall slid back. Kickaha breathed out tension of uncertainty. He had not been sure that he remembered the proper code. The possibility was strong that a wrong manipulation would have resulted in anything from a cloud of poisonous gas or vapor to a beam which would cut him in half.

He pulled in Do Shuptarp after him. The Teutoniac started to protest. Then he began to scream as both fell down a lightless shaft. Kickaha clapped his hand over Do Shuptarp's mouth and said, "Quiet! We won't be hurt!"

The wind of their descent snatched his words away. Do Shuptarp continued to struggle, but he subsided when they began to slow down in their fall. Presently, they seemed to be motionless. The walls suddenly lit up, and they could see that they were falling slowly. The shaft a few feet above them and a few feet below them was dark. The light accompanied them as they descended. Then they were at the bottom of the shaft. There was no dust, although the darkness above the silence felt as if the place had not seen a living creature for hundreds of years.

Angrily, the Teutoniac said, "I may have heart failure yet."

Kickaha said, "I had to do it that way. If you knew how you were going to fall, you'd never have gone through with it on your own. It would have been too much to ask you."

"You jumped," Do Shuptarp said.

"Sure. And I've practiced it a score of times. I didn't have the guts either until I'd seen Wolff—the Lord—do it several times."

He smiled. "Even so, this time, I wasn't sure that the field was on. The Bellers could have turned it off. Wouldn't that have been a good joke on us?"

Do Shuptarp did not seem to think it was funny. Kickaha turned from him to the business of getting out of the shaft. This demanded beating a code with his knuckles on the shaft wall. A section slid out, and they entered a whitewalled room about thirty feet square and well illuminated. It was bare except for a dozen crescents set in the stone floor and a dozen hanging on wall-pegs. The crescents were unmarked.

Kickaha put out a hand to restrain Do Shuptarp. "Not a step more! This room is dangerous unless you go through an undeviating ritual. And I'm not sure I remember it all!"

The Teutoniac was sweating, although the air was cool and moving slightly. "I was going to ask why we didn't come here in the first place," he said, "instead of walking through the corridors. Now, I see."

"Let's hope you continue to see," Kickaha said ambiguously. He advanced three steps forward straight from the entrance. Then he walked sideways until he was even with the extreme right-end crescent on the wall. He turned around once and walked to the crescent, his right arm extended stiffly at right angles to the floor. As soon as his fingertips touched the crescent, he said, "Okay, soldier. You can walk about as you please now—I think."

But he lost his smile as he studied the crescents. He said, "One of these will gate us to inside the armory. But I can't remember which. The second from the right or the third?"

Do Shuptarp asked what would happen if the wrong crescent were chosen.

"One of these—I don't know which—would gate us into the control room," he said. "I'd choose that if I had a beamer or if I thought the Bellers hadn't rigged extra-mass-intrusion alarms in the control room. And if I knew which it was.

"One will gate us right back to the underground prison from which we just came. A third would gate us to the moon. A fifth, to the Atlantean level. I forget exactly what the others will do, except that one would put you into a universe that is, to say the least, undesirable."

Do Shuptarp shivered and said, "I am a brave man. I've proved that on the battlefield. But I feel like a baby lost in a forest full of wolves."

Kickaha didn't answer, although he approved of Do Shuptarp's frankness. He could not make up his mind about the second or third crescent. He had to pick one because there was no getting back up the shaft—like so many routes in the palace, it was one-way.

Finally, he said, "I'm fairly sure it's the third. Wolff's mind favors threes or multiples thereof. But . . ."

He shrugged and said, "What the hell. We can't stand here forever."

He matched the third right-hand crescent with the third from the left on the floor. "I do remember that the loose crescents go with opposing fixed ones," he said. He carefully explained to Do Shuptarp the procedure for using a gate and what they might expect. Then the two stepped into the circle formed by the two crescents. They waited for about three seconds. There was no sensation of movement or flicker of passage before their eyes, but, abruptly, they were in a room about three hundred feet square. Familiar and exotic weapons and armor were in shelves on the walls or in racks and stands on the floor.

"We made it," Kickaha said. He stepped out of the circle and said, "We'll get some hand-beamers and power-packs, some rope, and a spy-missile guider and goggles. Oh, yes, some short-range neutron hand-grenades, too."

He also picked two well-balanced knives for throwing. Do Shuptarp tried out his beamer on a small target at the armory rear. The metal disc, which was six inches thick, melted away within five seconds. Kickaha strapped a metal box to his back in a harness. This contained several spy-missiles, power broadcasting-receiving apparatus for the missiles, and the video-audio goggles.

Kickaha hoped that the Bellers had not come across these yet. If they had guards who were looking around corners or prowling the corridors with the missiles, it was goodbye.

The door had been locked by Wolff, and, as nearly as Kickaha could determine, no one had unlocked it. It had many safeguards to prevent access by unauthorized persons from the outside, but there was nothing to prevent a person on the inside from leaving without hindrance. Kickaha was relieved. The Bellers had not been able to penetrate this, which meant they had no spy-missiles. Unless, that is, they had brought some in from the other universes. But since the crafts had used none, he did not think they had any.

He put on the goggles over his eyes and ears and, holding the control box in his hands, guided a missile out the open doors. The missile was about three inches long and was shaped like a school-boy's folded-paper airplane. It was transparent, and the tiny colored parts could be seen in a strong light at certain angles. Its nose contained an "eye," through which Kickaha could get a peculiar and limited view and an "ear" through which he could hear noises, muted or amplified as he wished.

He turned the missile this way and that, saw that no one was in the hall, and shoved the goggles up on top of his head. When he left the armory, he closed the door, knowing that it would automatically lock and arm itself. He used his eyes to guide the missile on the straightaway, and when he wanted to look around corners, he slipped the goggles down.

Kickaha and Do Shuptarp, with the missile, covered about six miles of horizontal and vertical travel, leaving one wing and crossing another to get to the building containing the control room. The trip took longer than a mere hike because of their caution.

Once, they passed by a colossal window close to the edge of the monolith on which the palace sat. Do Shuptarp almost fainted when he saw the sun. It was *below* him. He had to look downward to see it. Seeing the level of Atlantis spread out flatly for a five hundred mile radius, and then a piece of the level below that, and a shard of still a lower one, made him turn white.

Kickaha pulled him away from the window and tried to explain the tower structure of the planet and the rotation of the tiny sun about it. Since the palace was on top of the highest monolith of the planet, it was actually above the sun, which was at the level of the middle monolith.

The Teutoniac said he understood this. But he had never seen the sun except from his native level. And, of course, from the moon. But both times the sun had seemed high.

"If you think that was a frightening experience," Kickaha said, "you should look over the edge of the world sometime from the bottom level, the Garden level."

They entered the central massif of the building, which housed the control room. Here they proceeded even more slowly. They walked down a Brobdingnagian hall lined with mirrors which gave, not the outer physical reflection, but the inner physical reflection. Rather, as Kickaha explained, each mirror detected the waves of a different area of the brain and then synthesized these with music and colors and subsonics and gave them back as visual images. Some were hideous and some beautiful and some outrageously obscene and some almost numinously threatening.

"They don't mean anything," Kickaha said, "unless the viewer wants to interpret what they mean to him. They have no objective meaning."

Do Shuptarp was glad to get on. Then Kickaha took a staircase broad enough for ten platoons of soldiers almost to march up. This wound up and up and seemed never to end, as if it were the staircase to Heaven itself.

20

FINALLY, THE TEUTONIAC BEGGED FOR A REST; KICKAHA CON-
sented. He sent the spy-missile up for another look. There were no Bellers
on the floor below that on which the control room was. There were the
burned and melted bodies of ten taloses, all on the first six steps of the staircase. Apparently, they had been marching up to attack the Bellers in the
control room, and they had been beamed down. The device which may
have done this was crouching at the top of the stairs. It was a small black
box on wheels with a long thin neck of gray metal. At its end was a tiny bulb.
This bulb could detect and beam a moving mass at a maximum distance of
forty feet.

It moved the long neck back and forth to sweep the staircase. It did not
notice the missile as it sped overhead, which meant that the snake-neck,
as Kickaha termed it, was set to detect only larger masses. Kickaha turned
the missile and sent it down the hall toward the double doors of the control room. These were closed. He did see, through the missile's "eye," that
there were many small discs stuck on the walls all along the corridor—
mass-detectors. Their fields were limited, however. A narrow aisle would
be left down the center of the corridor so that the warned might walk in it
without setting off alarms. And there must be visual devices of some sort
out here, too, since the Bellers would not neglect these. He moved the missile very slowly along the ceiling because he did not want it seen. And then
he spotted devices. They were hidden in the hollowed-out heads of two
busts on tops of pedestals. The hollowing-out had been done by the Bellers.

Kickaha brought the missile back carefully and took off the goggles,
then led Do Shuptarp up the staircase. They had not gone far before they
smelled the burned protoplasm and plastic. When they were on the floor
with the carnage, Kickaha stopped the Teutoniac.

"As near as I can figure out," he said, "they're all holed up now in the
control room. It's up to us to smoke them out or rush them before they get
us. I want you to watch our rear at all times. Keep looking! There are many
gates in the control room which transmit you to other places in the palace.

If the Bellers have figured them out, they'll be using them. So watch it!"

He was just out of range of the vision and beamer of the snake-neck at the top of the steps. He sat down and frayed out the fibers at one end of his thinnest rope and tied these around the missile. Then he put the goggles back on and directed the missile up the steps. It moved slowly because of the weight of the rope. The snake-neck continued to sweep the field before it, but did not send a beam at the missile or rope. Though this meant that it was set to react to greater masses, it did not mean that it wasn't transmitting a picture to the Bellers in the control room. If they saw the missile and the rope, they might come charging out and shoot down over the railing. Kickaha told Do Shuptarp to watch above, too, and shoot if anything moved.

The missile slid by the snake-neck and then around it, drawing the rope with it. It then came back down the steps. Kickaha removed the goggles, untied the rope, seized the ends of the rope, pulled to make sure he had a snug fit, and yanked. The snake-neck came forward and tumbled halfway down the steps. It lay on its side, its neck-and-eye moving back and forth but turned away from the right side of the staircase. Kickaha approached it from the back and turned it off by twisting a dial at its rear.

He carried the machine back up under one arm while he held a beamer ready in his right hand. Near the top, he got down against the steps and slid the machine onto the floor. Here he turned it so it faced the bust at the end of the hall past the control room doors. He set the dials and then watched it roll out of sight. Presently, there was a loud crash. He dropped the goggles down and sent the missile to take a look. As he had hoped, the snake-neck had gone down the hall until the mass of the pedestal and its bust had set it off. Its beamer had burned through the hollow stone pedestal until it fell over. The bust was lying on its side with the transmitter camera looking at the wall. The snake-neck had turned its beam on the fallen bust.

He went back down the staircase and down the hall until he was out of sight of anyone who might come to the top of the steps or look down the side of the well. He replaced the goggles and took the missile to a position above the double doors. The missile, flat against the wall, was standing on its nose and looking straight down.

He waited. Minutes went by. He wanted to take the goggles off so he could make sure that Do Shuptarp was watching everywhere. He restrained the impulse—he had to be ready if the doors opened.

Presently, they did open. A periscopic tube was stuck out and turned in both directions. Then it withdrew and a blond head slowly emerged. The body followed it soon. The Beller ran over to the snake-head and turned it off. Kickaha was disappointed because he had hoped the machine would beam the Beller. However, it scanned and reacted only to objects in front of it.

The bust was completely melted. The Beller looked at it for a while, then picked up the snake-neck and took it into the control room. Kickaha sent the missile in through the upper part of the doorway and up into the high parts of the room, which was large enough to contain an aircraft carrier of 1945 vintage. He shot the missile across the ceiling and down the opposite wall and low to the floor to a place behind a control console. The vision and audio became fuzzy and limited then, which made him think that the doors had been shut. Although the missile could transmit through material objects within a limited range, it lost much of its effectiveness.

Zymathol was telling Arswurd of the strange behavior of the snake-neck. He had replaced it with another, which he hoped would not also malfunction. He had not replaced the camera. The other at the opposite end of the hall could do what was needed. Zymathol regretted that they had been so busy trying to get laser-beam or radio contact with von Turbat on the moon. Otherwise, they might have been watching the monitor screens and seen what had happened.

Kickaha wanted to continue listening, but he had to keep his campaign going. He switched off the missile in the control room and tied the end of the rope to another missile. This he sent up and around the new snake-neck and pulled it down. It tumbled much farther, bringing up short against the pile of talos bodies at the staircase foot. It was pointed up in the air. Kickaha crawled up to it, reached over the bodies, and turned it off. He took it back up the steps and sent it against the pedestal and bust at the other end of the hall. He was down the steps and had his goggles on and another missile on its way before the crash sounded. The crash came to his ears via the missile.

Its eye showed him that the same thing had happened. He turned it to watch the door, but nothing happened for a long time. Finally, he switched to the missile in the control room. Zymathol was arguing that the malfunctioning of the second machine was too coincidental. There was something suspicious happening, something therefore dangerous. He did not want to go outside again to investigate.

Arswurd said that, like it or not, they couldn't stay here and let an invader prowl around. He had to be killed—and the invader was probably Kickaha. Who else could have gotten inside the palace when all the defenses were set up to make it impregnable?

Zymathol said that it couldn't be Kickaha. Would von Turbat and von Swindebarn be up on the moon looking for him if he weren't there?

This puzzled Kickaha. What was von Turbat doing there when he must know that his enemy had escaped via the gate in the cave-chamber? Or was von Turbat so suspicious of his archenemy's wiliness that he thought Kickaha might have gated something through to make it look as if he were no longer on the moon? If so, what could make him think that there was anything on the moon to keep Kickaha there?

He became upset and a trifle frightened then. Could Anana have gated up there after him? Was she being chased by the Bellers? It was a possibility, and it made him anxious.

Zymathol said that only Kickaha could have turned the taloses against them. Arswurd replied that that was all the more reason for getting rid of such a danger. Zymathol asked how.

"Not by cowering in here," Arswurd said.

"Then you go look for him," Zymathol said.

"I will," Arswurd answered.

Kickaha found it interesting that the conversation was so human. The Bellers might be born of metal complexes, but they were not like machines off an assembly line. They had all the differences of personality of humans.

Arswurd started to go to the door, but Zymathol called him back. Zymathol said that their duty demanded they not take unnecessary chances. There were so few of them now that the death of even one greatly lessened their hope of conquest. In fact, instead of aiming for conquest now, they were fighting for survival. Who would have thought that a mere *leblabbiy* could have killed them so ingeniously and relentlessly? Why, Kickaha was not even a Lord—he was only a human being.

Zymathol said they must wait until their two leaders returned. They could not be contacted; something was interfering with attempts to communicate. Kickaha could have told them why their efforts were useless. The structure of the spacetime fabric of this universe made a peculiar deformation which would prevent the undistorted transmission of radio or laser. If an aircraft, for instance, were to try to fly between planet and moon, it would break up in a narrow zone partway between the two bodies. The only way to travel from one to the other was by a gate.

The two Bellers talked nervously of many things. Twenty-nine of the original Bellers were dead. There were two here, two in Nimstowl's universe, two in Anana's, two in Judubra's. Zymathol thought that these ought to be recalled to help. Or, better, that the Bellers in this universe should leave and seal off all gates. There were plenty of other universes; why not cut this one off forever? If Kickaha wanted it, he could have it. Meanwhile, in a safe place, they could make millions of new Bellers. In ten years, they would be ready to sweep out the Lords everywhere.

But von Turbat, whom they called Graumgrass, was extraordinarily stubborn. He would refuse to quit. Both agreed on that.

It became evident to Kickaha that Arswurd, despite his insistence on the necessity of leaving the room to find the invader, really did not want to and, in fact, had no intention of doing so. He did need, however, to sound brave to himself.

The two did not seem the unhuman, cold, strictly logical, utterly emotionless beings described to him by Anana. If certain elements were removed from their conversation, they could have been just two soldiers of any nation or universe talking.

For a moment, he wondered if the Bellers could not be reasoned with, if they could be content to take a place in this world as other sentients did.

That feeling passed quickly. The Bellers preferred to take over bodies of human beings; they would not remain enclosed in their metal bells. The delights and advantages of flesh were too tempting. No, they would not be satisfied to remain in the bells; they would keep on stripping human brains and moving into the dispossessed somas.

The war would have to be to the end, that is, until all Bellers or Kickaha died.

At that moment, he felt as if the entire world were a burden on him alone. If they killed him, they could move ahead as they wished, because only a few knew their identities and purposes, and these few would also die. This was his world, as he had bragged, and he was the luckiest man in two worlds, because he alone of Earthmen had been able to get through the wall between the worlds. This, to him, was a world far superior to Earth and he had made it his in a way that even Wolff, the Lord, had not been able to do.

Now, the delights and rewards were gone, replaced by a responsibility so tremendous that he had not thought about it because he could not endure to do so.

For a man with such responsibility, he had acted recklessly.

That was, however, why he had survived so long. If he had proceeded with great caution because he was so important, he probably would have been caught and killed by now. Or he would have escaped but would be totally ineffective, because he would be afraid to take any action. Reckless or not, he would proceed now as he had in the past. If he misjudged, he became part of the past, and the Bellers took over the present and future. So be it.

He switched back to a third missile and placed it against the wall just above the doors. Then he laid the control box and goggles beside him. He told Do Shuptarp what he meant to do next. The Teutoniac thought it was a crazy idea, but he agreed. He didn't have any ideas of his own. They picked up a talos and dragged the body, which possibly weighed five hundred pounds, up the steps. They pulled it down the hall in the aisle between the detector fields and propped it up in front of the doors. Then they retreated hastily but carefully to the floor below.

After taking a quick look, Kickaha replaced the goggles. He lowered the missile above the door, positioned it to one side of the sitting talos, and hurled the missile against the helmet-head of the talos. The impact ruined the missile so that he could not observe its effect. But he quickly sent another up and stationed this above the doors. The talos had fallen as he had wished. Its head and shoulders were within the detector field. The alarms must be ringing wildly inside the control room.

Nothing happened. The doors did not open. He waited until he could endure the suspense no longer. Though it was essential that he keep the missile posted above the doors, he sent it to the floor and then switched back to the missile inside the control room. He could see nothing except the rear of the control console, and he could hear nothing. There were no alarms whooping, so these must have been turned off. The Bellers were not talking or making a sound of any kind, even though he turned the audio amplification up.

He switched back to the missile outside the doors. The doors were closed, so he returned to the device in the room. There was still no noise.

What was going on?

Were they playing a game of Who's-Got-The-Coolest-Nerves? Did they want him to come charging on in?

He returned to the missile in the room and sent it back along the floor to the wall. It went slowly up the wall, the area just ahead of it clear for a foot and then fuzzy beyond that. He intended to put it against the ceiling and then lower it with the hopes that he would see the Bellers before they saw the missile. The missile could be used to kill as a bullet kills, but his range of vision was so limited that he had to be very close. If a Beller yelled, he would betray his position by sound and Kickaha might be able to send the missile at him before the Beller burned the missile down. It was a long chance which he was willing to take now.

He had brought the device down approximately where the control console it had hidden behind should be. The missile came straight down to the floor without seeing or hearing anything. It then rose and circled the area without detecting the Bellers. He expanded the territory of search. The Bellers, of course, could be aware of the missile and could be retreating beyond its range or hiding. This did not make sense unless they wanted to keep the operator of the missile busy while one or more left the room to search for him. They probably did not know exactly how the missile worked, but they must realize that its transmission was limited and that the operator had to be comparatively close.

Kickaha told Do Shuptarp to be especially alert for the appearance of Bellers at the top of the staircase—and to remember to use the neutron grenades if he got a chance. He had no sooner finished saying this than Do Shuptarp yelled. Kickaha was so startled that he threw his hands up. The control box went flying. So did Kickaha. Yanking off the goggles, he rolled over and over at the same time, to spoil the aim of anybody who might be trying to shoot at him. He had no idea of what had made the Teutoniac shout, nor was he going to sit still while he looked around for the source of the alarm.

A beam scorched the rug as it shot on by him. It came from an unexpected place, the far end of the hall. A head and a hand holding a beamer were projecting from a corner. Luckily, Do Shuptarp had fired as soon as he saw the Beller, so the Beller could only get off a wild beam. Then he dodged back. At this distance, a beamer's effectiveness was considerably reduced. At short range it could melt through twelve inches of steel and cook a man through to the gizzard in a second. At this distance it could only give him a third degree burn on his skin or blind him if it struck the eyes.

Do Shuptarp had retreated to the first few bottom steps of the staircase where he was lodged behind the pile of talos bodies. Kickaha ran down the hall away from the opposite end, wary of what might pop out from the near side. One or both of the Bellers in the control room had gated to another part of the palace and had made a flank attack. Or one or both had gated elsewhere to get help from other Bellers.

Kickaha cursed, wheeled, and ran back toward the abandoned goggles and control box. The Beller at the far end popped his head out close to the floor and fired. Do Shuptarp, at a wider angle to the Beller because he was on the staircase, replied with his beam. Kickaha shot, too. The Beller withdrew before the rays, advancing along the rug, could intersect at the corner. The nonflammable rug melted where the beams had made tracks.

The three grenades were too far away to risk time to go for them. Kickaha scooped up the box and goggles, whirled, and dashed back along the corridor. He expected somebody to appear at the near end, so he was ready to pop into the nearest doorway. When he was two doorways from the end, he saw a head coming around a corner. He triggered off a beam, played it along the molding, and then up the corner. The head, however, jerked back before the ray could hit it. Kickaha crouched against the wall and fired past the corner, hoping that some energy would bounce off and perhaps warm up the person or persons hidden around the corner. A yell told him that he had scared or perhaps scorched someone.

He grinned and went back into the doorway before the Bellers would try the same trick on him. This was no grinning business, but he could not help being savagely amused when he put one over on his enemies.

21

THE ROOM IN WHICH HE HAD RETREATED WAS COMPARATIVELY
small. It was like hundreds of others in the palace, its main purpose being
to store art treasures. These were tastefully arranged, however, as if the
room were lived in or at least much visited.

He looked swiftly around for evidence of gates, since there were so
many hidden in the palace that he could not remember more than a fraction of them. He saw nothing suspicious. This itself meant nothing, but at
this time he had to take things on evidence. Otherwise, he would not be
able to act.

He slipped on the goggles, hating to do so because it left him blind and
deaf to events in the hall. He switched to the missile in the control room.
It was still in the air, circling in obedience to the last order. No Bellers came
within its range. He then transferred to the missile outside the doors and
brought it down the staircase and along the corridor. The closer it came to
him, the stronger its transmission of sight and sound was. And the better
his control.

Do Shuptarp was keeping the Beller at the far end from coming out.
Whoever was at the near end was the immediate danger. He sent the missile close to the ceiling and around the corner. There were three Bellers
there, each with handbeamers. The face of one was slightly reddish, as if
sunburned. At a distance were two coming down the hall and pushing a
gravsled before them. This bore a huge beamer, the equivalent of a cannon. Its ray could be sent past the corner to splash off the wall and keep
Kickaha at a distance while the others fired with the hand-beamers. And
then, under the covering fire, the big projector would be pushed around
the corner and its full effect hurled along the length of the hall. It would
burn or melt anything in its path.

Kickaha did not hesitate. He sent the missile at full speed toward the
right-hand man pushing the sled. His vision was blurred with the sudden
increase of velocity, then the scene went black. The missile had buried itself in the flesh of the Beller or had hit something else so hard it had

wrecked itself. He took another missile from the box, which he had un-harnessed from his back and laid beside him, and he sent it up out of the room and along the ceiling. Abruptly, a Beller, yelling to disconcert anyone who might be in the hall, sprang out from around the corner. He saw the missile and raised his beamer. Kickaha sent it toward him, pressing the full-speed button on the control box. The scene went black. It was deep in the target's flesh, or ruined against the hard floor or wall, or melted by the beamer.

He did not dare to take the time to send another missile out to look. If the Beller had escaped it, he would be looking into the doorways now for the operator of the missile. And he probably had called the others out to help him.

Kickaha snatched off the goggles and, beamer in one hand and goggles in the other, strode to the door. He had left the door open for better control and vision of the missile. In a way, this was a good thing because the Beller would look in the rooms with closed doors first. But, as he neared the doorway, he confronted a Beller. Kickaha was holding his beamer in front of his chest; he squeezed the trigger as the man's shoulder came in sight. The Beller turned black, smoke rose from skin frying and shredding away in layers, the whites of the eyes became a deep brown and then the aqueous humor in the balls shot out boiling, the hair went up in a stinking flame, the white teeth became black, the lips swelled and then disappeared in layers, the ears became ragged and ran together in rolls of gristle. The clothes, fireproof, melted away.

All this took place in four seconds. Kickaha kicked the door shut and pressed the plate to lock it. Then he was across the room and pushing the plate which turned off the energy field across the window. He threw the missile box out so it could not be used by the Bellers. He tied one end of the rope to a post on a bureau and he crawled out the window. Below was a hundred thousand feet of air. This part of the palace projected over the edge of the monolith; if he cared to, he could sweep almost half its area with a turn of his head. At this moment, he did not want to think about the long, long fall. He kept his eyes on the little ledge about six feet below the end of the rope. He slid down the rope until he was near the end, then he swung out a little and let loose as he swung back in. He dropped with both feet firmly on the ledge and both hands braced against the sides of the window. His knees, bent slightly forward, were perilously close to the invisible force field.

Keeping one hand against the side of the window, he removed his shirt, wrapped a hand in it and then took a knife out. Slowly he moved the knife in the shirt-wrapped hand forward. His head was turned away and his eyes were shut. The force field, activated by the knife, would burn it, and the energy would probably lash out and burn the cloth and the hand beneath.

The energy might even hurl the knife away with such violence that it would jerk his arm and him along with it on out the window.

He did have hopes, however, that the field would not be on. This did not seem likely, since Wolff surely would have set all guards and traps before leaving—if he had time. And the Bellers certainly would have done so if Wolff had failed.

A light burned even through his shut eyelids. A flame licked at his face and his bare shoulders and ribs and legs. The knife bucked in his hand, but he kept it within range of the field even when the cloth smoldered and burst into flames and his hand felt as if it had been thrust in an oven.

Then he plunged on through the window and onto the floor. There was a two-second pause between recharge of the field after activation, and he had jumped to coincide with it, he hoped. That he was still alive, though hurt, was proof that he had timed himself correctly. The knife was a twist of red-hot metal on the floor. The shirt was charred off, and his hand was blackened and beginning to blister. At another time, he would have been concerned with this. Now, he had no truck with anything except major crippling injuries. Or with death.

At that moment, the rope fell by the window, its end smoking. The projector had burned through the door and burned off the rope. In a moment, the Bellers would be coming downstairs after him. As for poor Do Shuptarp, he had better look out for himself and fast. The big projector would undoubtedly be used on him first to clear him out of the way. If only he had sense enough to get up the staircase and away, he could cause the Bellers to split their forces.

Kickaha looked out the doorway, saw no one, and fled down the corridor. On coming to the foot of the staircase, he looked upward before crossing in front of it. No Bellers were in sight yet. He ran on down the hall and then down the unusually long staircase and on across the corridor and past the hall of retropsychical mirrors. He had passed several elevators but did not enter them because they might be booby-trapped or at least have monitoring devices. His goal was a room which contained a secret gate he had not wished to use before this. Nor would he use it now unless he was forced to do so. But he wanted to be near it in case he was cornered.

In the room, he disassembled a chair that looked solid and pulled out a crescent from a recess under the seat.

Another crescent came from under the base of a thick pedestal for a statue. Both, though they looked as if each weighed half a ton, were light and easy to move. He stuck the two crescents into the back of his belt and tightened the belt to hold them. They were awkward but were insurance, worth the inconvenience.

There were thousands of such hidden gatehalves all over the palace and other thousands unmarked, in open places. The latter could be used by anybody, but the user would not know what waited for him at the other end of the passage. Even Wolff could not remember where all were hidden or the destinations of all the unconcealed ones. He had them all listed in a code-recorder but the recorder was itself disguised and in the control room.

Kickaha had run fast and gone far but not swiftly enough. A Beller appeared at the far end of the corridor as he stepped out of the room. Another looked around the corner of the corridor at the opposite end. They must have caught sight of him as he ran and had come this way with the hope of catching him. One at least had been intelligent enough to run on past where he was and come down the staircase to intercept him.

Kickaha retreated, deactivated the force field, and looked out the window. There was a ledge about fifty feet below, but he had nothing with which to lower himself. And he did not want to test another field unless he absolutely had to do so. He went back to the door and stuck the beamer out without putting his head out first, and fired in both directions. There were yells, but they were so far away that he was sure he had not hit anyone. The door of the room across from his was closed. He could dash across the hall and into it on the chance that it might offer a better route of escape. But if the door was locked, and it could easily be, then he would be exposed to fire from both sides, and they would have a better chance to catch him during the recrossing.

It was too late for regrets now. If he had not stopped to get the gate, he could have still been ahead of them. Again he was cornered, and though he had a way out, he did not want to use it. Getting back into the palace would be far more difficult a second time. And Do Shuptarp would be left on his own. Kickaha felt as if he were deserting him, but he could not help it.

He put the two crescents together to form a circle. He straightened up just as a grenade struck the inside of the doorway and ricocheted inside the room. It rolled about five feet and stopped, spinning on its axis. It was about thirty feet from him, which meant that he was out of range of the neutrons. But there would be others tossed in, the two he had left behind, and perhaps the Bellers had more. In any event, they would be bringing up the big projector. No use putting off the inevitable until it was too late to do even that.

22

HE STEPPED INTO THE GATE. AND HE WAS IN THE TEMPLE-chamber of Talanac. Anana and the Red Beards and a number of Tish-quetmoac were there. They were standing to one side and talking. They saw him and jumped or yelled or just looked startled. He started to step forward and then they were gone. The sky was starless, but a small glowing object raced across the sky from west to east and a slower one plodded along to the west. The leaning Tower of Pisa mass of the planet hung bright in the heavens. At a distance, the marble buildings of Korad gleamed whitely in the planet-light. A hundred yards away, a platoon of Drachelander soldiers were becoming aware that someone had appeared in the gate. And over a hill a dark object was rising. The Beller aircraft.

Then all was gone. He was in a cave about ten feet across and eight feet high. The sun shone brightly against the entrance. A giant, crazily angled tree with huge azure hexagram-shaped leaves stood in the distance. Beyond it were some scarlet bushes and green vines that rose seemingly without support, like a rope rising into the air at the music of a Hindu sorcerer. Beyond those were a thin blue line and a white thread and a thin black line. The sea, surf, and a black sand beach.

He had been here several times before. This was one of the gates he used to get to the lowest level, the Garden level, on his "vacations."

Though numbed, he knew that he had been caught in a resonant circuit. Somewhere, somebody had set up a device which would trap a person who stepped into any of the gates in the circuit. The caught one could not step out because the activation time was too short. That is, he could but he would be cut in half, one part left behind, the other gated on to the next circle.

The cave disappeared, and he was on top of a high narrow peak set among other peaks. Far to one side, visible through a pass, was what looked like the Great Plains. Certainly, that must be an immense herd of buffalo which covered the brown-green prairie like a black sea. A hawk soared by, screaming at him. It had an emerald-green head and spiraling feathers down its legs. As far as he knew, this hawk was confined to the Amerind level.

Then that was gone, and he was in a cave again. This was larger than the Garden cave and darker. There were wires clipped to the crescents of the gate; these ran across the dirt floor and behind a huge boulder about twenty feet away. Somewhere, an alarm was ringing. There was a cabinet with open doors by the far wall. The shelves contained weapons and devices of various kinds. He recognized this cave and also knew that here must be where the reasonance originated. But the trapper was not in sight, though he soon would be, if he were within earshot of the alarms.

Then that was gone, and he was in a chamber of stone slabs which were leaning in one direction as if they had been pushed by a giant hand, and part of the roof was fallen in. The sky was a bright green. The monolith of which he could see part was thin and black and soaring, so he knew by this that he was in an Atlantean chamber and that the shaft of stone was that which supported the palace of the Lord, a hundred thousand feet up.

Then that was gone, and he was where he had started his hopscotch willy-nilly journey. He was standing in the crescents in the room in the palace. Two Bellers were goggling at him, and then they were raising their beamers. He shot first, because he expected to have to use his weapon, bringing the ray across the chests of both.

Thirty-four down. Sixteen to go.

That was gone. Anana and the Thyuda were standing by the gate now. He shouted to her, "Resonant circuit! Trapped!" and he was back on the moon. The aircraft was a little closer now, coming down the hillside. Probably the occupants had not seen him yet, but they would on the next go-around or the one after that. And all they had to do then was a keep a ray across the gate, and he would be cut down as soon as he appeared.

The Drachelander soldiers were running toward him now; several were standing still but were winding up the wires of their crossbows. Kickaha, not wishing to attract the attention of the Bellers in the craft, refrained from discouraging the soldiers with his beamer.

Followed the Garden cave. And then he was upon the top of the peak in the Amerind level and very startled because the hawk flew into the area of the gate just as he appeared. The hawk was as startled as he. It screamed and landed on his chest and sank its talons in. Kickaha placed one hand before his face to protect it, felt agony as the hawk's beak sank into the hand which was burned, and he shoved outward. The hawk was torn loose by the push, but it took gobbets of flesh of chest and hand with it. It was propelled out of the circle but was not cut in half. The feathers of one wingtip were sheared off, and that was all. Its movement coincided with the border of the field as the gate action commenced. And it passed over the border in the cave on the Dracheland level, and into the chamber itself.

It was unplanned split-second timing.

The enormously fat man who had just entered the cave was holding a dead, half-charred rabbit in one hand and a beamer in the other. He had expected a man or woman to appear though he could not, of course, know just when. But he had not expected a shrieking fury of talons and beak in his face.

Kickaha got a chance to see Judubra drop the rabbit and beamer and throw his hands up in front of his face. Then he was in the ruins of the Atlantean chamber. He squatted down and leaped upward as high and as straight as he could so no part of him would be outside the limits of the circle. He was at the height of his leap, with his legs pulled up, when he appeared in the palace room. His leap, designed to take him above a ray which might be shot across the circle to cut him in half, was unnecessary. The two Bellers lay on the floor, blackened, their clothes burned off. The odor of deeply burned flesh choked the room. He did not know what had happened, but the next time around, there should be Bellers in this room. They would not, he hoped, know any more than he did about what was happening. They would be mystified, but they would have to be stupid not to know that the killer had popped back into the gate and then popped out again. They would be waiting.

He was in the gate of the temple in Talanac. Anana was gone. The priest, Withrus, shouted at him, "She jumped in! She's caught, too, and she . . ."

He was on the moon. The craft was closer but had not increased its speed. And then a beam of light shot out from its nose and centered full on him. The Bellers in the craft had suddenly noticed the excitement of the troops running toward the gate and the crossbowmen aiming at it. They had turned on the light to find out the cause of the uproar.

There was a twang as the crossbowmen released their darts. And he was in the cave on the Garden level. Next stop, the little flat area on top of the peak. He looked down at his chest, which was dripping blood, and at his hand, which was also bloody. He hurt but not as much as he would later. He was still numb to lesser pains; the big pain was his situation and the inevitable end. Either the fat man in the cave would get him or the Bellers would. The fat man, after ridding himself of the hawk, could hide behind the boulder and beam him as he appeared. Of course, there was the hope that the fat man wanted to capture him.

He was in the cave. The hawk and the fat man lay dead, blackened, and the odor of fried feathers and flesh jammed his nostrils. There was only one explanation: Anana, riding ahead of him in the circuit, had beamed both of them. The fat man must still have been struggling with the hawk and so Anana had caught him.

If he had doubted that she loved him, he now had proof that she did— she had been willing to sacrifice her life in an effort to save him. She had done so with almost no thought; there had been very little time for her to see what was happening, but she had done it quickly and even more quickly she had hurled herself into the gate. She must have known that only if she went through exactly after activation would she get through unsevered. And she had no way of telling the exact moment to jump; she had seen him appear and disappear and then taken the chance.

She loved him for sure, he thought.

And if she could get in without being hurt, then he could get out.

The Atlantean ruins materialized like a gigantic pop-up, and he leaped outward. He landed on the floor of the room in the palace, but not untouched. His heel hurt as if a rat had gashed it. A sliver of skin at the edge of the heel had been taken off by the deactivating field.

Then something appeared. Anana. She said, "Objects! Throw them in . . ." and was gone.

He did not have to stop to think what she meant because he had hoped before that she would take these means to stop the resonant circuit. Aside from turning off the activating device, the only way to stop the circuit was to put objects with enough mass into an empty gate. Eventually, when all the gates were occupied, the circuit would stop.

The obvious method of separating the crescents of a gate would not work in this case. A resonant circuit set up a magnetic attraction between the crescents of the gates that could not be broken except by some devices in the palace. And these would be locked up in the armory.

Keeping his eye on the door, and with the beamer ready, he dragged the body of a Beller by one hand to the crescent. He was counting the seconds in an effort to figure the approximate time when she would next appear here. And while he was counting, he saw out of the side of his eye, five objects come into being in the gates and go out of being. There was a barrel, the torso of a Drachelander soldier severed at the belly, half a large silver coffer with jewels spilling out of it, a large statue of jade, and the headless, legless, almost wingless body of a green eagle.

He was in a frenzy of anxiety. The Thyuda in Talanac must be obeying her orders, given just before she leaped into the gate. They were throwing objects into the gate as fast as possible. But the circuit might stop now when she was on the moon, and if it did, she would assuredly be caught or killed.

And then as he was about to topple the body of the Beller into the gate, Anana appeared. And she did not vanish again.

Kickaha was so delighted that he almost forgot to watch the doorway. "Luck's holding out!" he cried and then, realizing that he might be heard outside the room, said softly, "The chances for the circuit stopping while you were here were almost nothing! I . . ."

"It wasn't chance," she said. She stepped out of the gate and put her arms around him and kissed him. He would have been delighted at any other time. Now he said, "Later, Anana. The Bellers!"

She stepped away and said, "Nimstowl will be here in a second. Don't shoot."

The little man was there all of a sudden. He held a beamer in one hand and a beamer in his belt. He also wore a knife and carried a rope coiled around one shoulder. Kickaha had turned his beamer away from the door and held it on Nimstowl. The Lord said, "No need for that. I'm your ally."

"Until . . . ?" Kickaha said.

"All I want to do is to get back to my own world," Nimstowl said. "I've had more than enough of this killing and almost being killed. In the name of Shambarimen, isn't one world enough for one man?"

Kickaha did not believe him, but he decided that Nimstowl could be trusted until the last of the Bellers was dead. He said, "I don't know what's going on out there. I had expected an attack, but it would have been launched before now. They had a large beamer out there; they could have shot it in here by now and cooked us out."

He asked Anana what had happened, though he could guess part of it. She replied that Nimstowl had come into the cave to find his partner dead, caught by the one he had trapped. Nimstowl had decided that he was tired of hiding out in this cave. He wanted a chance to get back to his own world and, of course, as every Lord should, to wipe out the Bellers. He had turned the resonating device off when Anana had appeared again. It had taken only a few seconds after that to set the resonator so it would deliver two people, at safe intervals, into the palace where Anana had seen Kickaha.

He said, "What do you mean? I had to jump out! I got out but lost the skin off my heel."

"Of course, you had no way of knowing," she said. "But if you had not jumped, you could have stepped out quite safely a moment later."

"Anyway, you came after me," he said. "That's what counts."

She was looking at him with concern. He was burned and bleeding, still dripping blood on the floor. But she said nothing. There was nothing to do for him until they found some aid. And that could be close enough, if they could get out of this room.

Somebody had to stick his head out of the room. Nimstowl wasn't going to volunteer and Kickaha did not want Anana to do it. So he looked out. Instead of the beam he expected, he saw a deserted corridor. He motioned for them to come after him and led the way to a room about a quarter of a mile down the corridor. Here he sterilized his wounds and burns, put pseudoflesh over them, and drank potions to unshock him and to accelerate blood replenishment. They also ate and drank while they discussed what to do.

There wasn't much to talk about. The only thing to do was to explore until they found out what was going on.

23

NOT UNTIL THEY CAME TO THE GREAT STAIRCASE WHICH LED UP to the floor of the control room did they find anything. There was a dead Beller, his legs almost entirely burned off. And behind a charred divan lay another Beller. This one was burned on the side, but the degree of burn indicated that the beam's energy had been partially absorbed before striking him. He was still alive.

Kickaha approached him cautiously and, after making sure he wasn't playing possum, Kickaha knelt down by him. He intended to use rough methods to bring him to consciousness so he could question him. But the Beller opened his eyes when his head was raised.

"Luvah!" Anana cried. "It's Luvah! My brother! One of my brothers! But what's he doing here? How . . . ?"

She was holding an object which she must have picked up from behind the divan or some other piece of furniture. It was about two and a half feet long, was of some silvery material, and was curved and shaped much like the horn of an African buffalo. It did flare out widely at the mouth, however, and the tip was fitted with a mouthpiece of some soft golden material. Seven little buttons sat on top of the horn in a row.

He recognized the Horn of Shambarimen. Hope lifted him to his feet with a surge. He said, "Wolff is back!"

"Wolff?" Anana said. "Oh, Jadawin! Yes, perhaps. But what is Luvah doing here?"

Luvah had a face that, under normal circumstances, would have been appealing. He was a Lord, but he could easily have passed for a certain type of Irishman with his snub nose and broad upper lip and freckles and pale blue eyes.

Kickaha said, "You talk to him. Maybe he'll . . ."

She got to her knees by Luvah and spoke to him. He seemed to recognize her, but his expression could have meant anything. She said, "He may not remember me in his condition. Or he may be frightened. He could think I'm going to kill him. I am a Lord, remember."

Kickaha ran down the hall and into a room where he could get water. He brought a pitcher of it back and Luvah drank eagerly. Luvah then whispered his story to Anana. She rose a few minutes later and said, "He was caught in a trap set by Urizen, our father. Or so he thought at the time, though actually it was Vala, our sister. He and Jadawin—Wolff—became friends. Wolff and his woman Chryseis were trapped with others, another brother and some cousins. He says it's too long a story to tell now. But only Luvah and Wolff and Chryseis survived. They returned by using the Horn; it can match the resonance of any gate, you know, unless that gate is set for intermittent resonance at random.

"They were gated back into a secret compartment of the control room. Wolff then took a look into the control room via a monitor. No one was in it. He tapped in on other videos and saw a number of dead men and taloses. Of course, he didn't know that the men were Black Bellers, at first; then he saw the caskets. He still didn't get the connection—after all, it's been, what, ten thousand years? But he gated into the control room with Chryseis. Just to have additional insurance, he gated Luvah into a room on a lower floor. If somebody attacked them in the control room, Luvah could slip up behind them."

"Wolff's cagey," said Kickaha. He had wondered why Wolff didn't see the live Bellers, but remembered that the palace was so huge that Wolff could have spent days looking into every room. He was probably so eager to get some rest after his undoubtedly harrowing adventures and so glad to be home that he had rushed things somewhat. Besides, the control room and the surrounding area were unoccupied.

"Luvah said he came up the staircase and was going to enter the control room to tell Wolff all was clear. At that very moment, two men appeared in an especially big gate that had been set up by the dead men. By the Bellers, of course. There were pieces of a disassembled craft with them and a big projector."

"Von Turbat and von Swindebarn!" Kickaha said.

"It must have been," Anana said. "They knew something was wrong, what with your appearance and disappearance in the gate on the moon and then mine. They gave up their search, and—"

"Tell me the rest while I'm carrying Luvah," he said. "We'll get him to a room where we can treat his burns."

With Nimstowl covering their rear and Anana their front, he lugged the unconscious Lord to the room where he had treated himself a short while ago. Here he applied antishock medicines, blood replenishers, and pseudoflesh to Luvah.

Anana meanwhile finished Luvah's story. The two chief Bellers, it seemed, had expected trouble and were ready. They fired their big projector and forced Wolff and Chryseis to take refuge among the many titanic consoles and machines. Luvah had dived for cover behind a console near the doorway. The two Bellers had kept up a covering fire while a number of troops came through. And with them was a creature that seemed strange to Luvah but Anana recognized the description as that of Podarge. From the glimpse Luvah got of her, she seemed to be unconscious. She was being carried by several soldiers.

"Podarge! But I thought she had used one of the gates in the cave to get off the moon," Kickaha said. "I wonder. . . . Do you suppose?"

Despite the seriousness of the situation, he couldn't help chuckling. One of the gates would have taken her to a cave in a mountain on the Atlantean level. There would have been six or seven gates there, all marked to indicate the level to which they would transport the user. But all lied, and only Kickaha, Wolff, and Chryseis knew the code. So she had used a crescent which would presumably take her to the Amerind level, where she would be comparatively close to her home.

But she found herself back on the moon, in the very same cave.

Why, then, were there only four crescents, when her return should have made the number five?

Podarge was crafty, too. She must have gated out something to leave only four crescents. And since Do Shuptarp had not mentioned finding great white ape cubs in the cave, she must have gated them out. Why didn't she try some of the other crescents? Perhaps because she was suspicious and thought that Kickaha had used the only good one. Who knows what motives that mad birdwoman had? In any event, she had elected to remain on the moon. And the Bellers may have been hunting her in the ruins of Korad when Kickaha saw them while he was in the resonant circuit.

Luvah had been forced out of the control room by the soldiers, some of whom had beamers. This surprised Kickaha. The Bellers must have been very desperate to give the Drachelanders these weapons.

So Luvah had had to retreat, but he had killed a number of his pursuers while doing so. Then he had been badly burned but even so had managed to burn down those left. Six of the killed were wearing caskets on their backs.

"Wolff! Chryseis!" Kickaha said. "We have to get up there right now! They may need us!"

Despite his frenzy, he managed to check himself and to proceed cautiously as they neared the control room. They passed charred bodies along the way, evidences of Luvah's good fight.

Kickaha led the others at a pace faster than caution demanded, but he felt that Wolff might be needing him at the moment. The path to the control room was marked with charred corpses and damage to the furniture and walls. The stink of crisped flesh became stronger the closer they got to their goal. He dreaded to enter the room. It would be tragic indeed, and heart-twisting, if Wolff and Chryseis survived so much only to be killed as they came home.

He steeled himself, but, when he ran crouching into the room, the vast place was as silent as a worm in a corpse. There were dead everywhere, including four more Black Bellers, but neither Wolff nor Chryseis were there.

Kickaha was relieved that they had escaped—but to where? A search revealed where they had taken a last stand. It was in a corner of the back wall and behind a huge bank of video monitors. The screens were shattered from the beamer rays, and the metal of the cabinet was cut or melted. Bodies lay here and there behind consoles—Drachelander troops caught by Wolff's or Chryseis' beams.

Von Turbat (Graumgrass) and von Swindebarn were dead, too. They lay by the big projector, which had continued to radiate until its power pack had run down. The wall it was aimed at had a twelve foot hole in its metal and a still-hot lava puddle at its base. Von Turbat had been cut almost in half; Von Swindebarn was fried from the hips up. Their caskets were still strapped to their backs.

"There's only one Beller unaccounted for," Kickaha said. He returned to the corner where Wolff and Chryseis had fought. A large gray metal disc was attached to the metal floor here. It had to be a new gate which Wolff had placed here since Kickaha's last visit to the palace.

He said, "Anana, maybe we can find out where this gate goes to, if Wolff recorded it in his code book. He must have left a message for me, if he had time. But the Bellers may have destroyed it.

"First, we have to locate that one Beller. If he got out of here, gated back to your universe or Nimstowl's or Judubra's, then we have a real problem."

Anana said, "It's so frightening! Why don't the Lords quit fighting among themselves and unite to get rid of the Beller?"

She edged away. Her anxiety and near-panic at the tolling in her brain, generated by her nearness to the Bellers' caskets, was evident.

"I have to get out of here," she said. "Or at least some distance away."

"I'll look over the corpses again," he said. "You go—hold it! Where's Nimstowl?"

"He was here," she said. "I thought that . . . no, I don't know when he disappeared!"

Kickaha was irked because she had not been keeping her eye on the little Lord. But he did not comment, since nothing was to be gained by expressing anger. Besides, the recent events were enough to sidetrack anyone, and the tolling in her mind had distracted her.

She left the room in a hurry. He went through the room, checking every body, looking everywhere.

"Wolff and Chryseis sure gave a good account of themselves," he muttered. "They really banked their shots to get so many behind the consoles. In fact, they gave too good an account. I don't believe it."

And Podarge?

He went to the doorway, where Anana crouched on sentry duty.

"I can't figure it out," he said. "If Wolff killed all his attackers, a very unlikely thing, why did he and Chryseis have to gate on out? And how the hell did Wolff manage to beam the two Bellers when they should have fried him at the first shot with that projector? And where is Podarge? And the missing Beller?"

"Perhaps she gated out, too, during the fight," Anana said. "Or flew out of the control room."

"Yeah, and where is Nimstowl? Come on. Let's start looking."

Anana groaned. He did not blame her. Both were drained of energy, but they could not stop now. He urged her up and soon they were examining the bodies in the corridors outside the control room on the staircase. He verified that he had killed two Bellers with the spy-missiles. While they were looking at a burned man rayed during the fight with Luvah, they heard a moan.

Beamers ready, they approached an overturned bureau from two directions. They found Nimstowl behind the furniture, sitting with his back against the wall. He was holding his right side while blood dripped through his fingers. Near him lay a man with a casket strapped to his back.

This was the missing Beller. He had a knife up to the hilt in his belly.

Nimstowl said, "He had a beamer, but the charge must have been depleted. He tried to sneak up and kill me with a knife. Me! With a knife!"

Kickaha examined Nimstowl's wound. Though the blood was flowing freely, the wound wasn't deep. He helped the little Lord to his feet, then he made sure that Nimstowl had no weapons concealed on him. He half-carried him to the room where Luvah lay sleeping, put pseudoflesh on Nimstowl's wound and gave him some blood replenishers.

Nimstowl said, "He might have gotten me at that, he jumped at me so quickly. But this"—he held up a hand with a large ring just like Anana's—"warned me in time."

"All the Bellers are dead," Anana said.

"It's hard to believe!" he replied. "At last! And I killed the last one!"

Kickaha smiled at that but did not comment. He said, "All right, Nimstowl, on your feet. And don't try anything. I'm locking you up for a while."

Again, he frisked Nimstowl. The little Lord was indignant. He yelled, "Why are you doing this to me?"

"I don't believe in taking chances. I want to check you out. Come on. There's a room down the hall where I can lock you up until I'm sure about you."

Nimstowl protested all the way. Kickaha, before shutting the door on him, said, "What were you doing so far from the control room? You were supposed to be with us. You weren't running out on us, were you?"

"So what if I was?" Nimstowl said. "The fight was won, or at least I thought it was. I meant to get back to my universe before the bitch Anana tried to kill me, now that she didn't need me. I couldn't trust you to control her. Anyway, it's a good thing I did leave you. If I hadn't, that Beller might have gotten away or managed to ambush you."

"You may be right," Kickaha said. "But you stay here for a while, anyway." He shut the door and locked it by pressing a button on the wall.

24

AFTER THAT, HE AND ANANA CONTINUED THE LONG SEARCH.
They could have cut down the room-to-room legwork if they had been able
to use the video monitors in the control room, since many rooms and corridors could be seen through these. But Wolff had deactivated these when
he left the palace, knowing that Kickaha was able to turn them on if he re-
visited the palace. The Bellers had not been able to locate the source of
control, and they had not had time or enough hands to disassemble the control console and rewire it. Now Kickaha could not use them because the
fight had put them out of commission.

They looked through hundreds of rooms and dozens of corridors and
scores of staircases and yet had covered only a small part of the one building. And they had many wings to go.

They decided they had to get food and sleep. They checked in on
Luvah, who was sleeping comfortably, and they ordered a meal from the
kitchen. There were several taloses there, the only taloses not involved in
the attack on the Bellers. These gated a meal through to the two. After eating, Kickaha decided to go up to the control room to make sure nothing
important had happened. He had some hopes that Wolff might come back,
though this did not seem likely. The chances were high that the gate was
one-way unless the Horn of Shambarimen were used, and Luvah had had
that.

They trudged back up the staircases, Kickaha did not dare use the elevators until he was certain they were not booby-trapped. Just before they
went into the control room, he stopped.

"Did you hear something?"

She shook her head. He gestured to her to cover him and he leaped
through the doorway and rolled onto the floor and up behind a control console. Listening, he lay there for a while. Presently, he heard a low moan.
Silence followed. Then another moan. He snaked across the floor from console to console, following the sounds. He was surprised, though not
shocked, when he found the Harpy, Podarge, slumped against a console.

Her feathers were blackened and stinking; her legs were charred so deeply that some of the toes had fallen off. Her breasts were brown-red meat. A half-melted beamer lay near her, a talon clutched around its butt.

She had come into the room while he and Anana were gone, and somebody had beamed her. Still on his belly, he investigated and within a minute found the responsible person. This was the soldier, Do Shuptarp, whom he had supposed was slain by the Bellers. But, now that he thought back, he had not been able to identify any corpse as his. This was not unexpected, since many were too burned to be recognizable.

Do Shuptarp, then, had escaped the Bellers and probably fled to the upper stories. He had returned to find out what was happening. Podarge had also returned after her flight from the room during the battle between the Bellers and Wolff. And the two, who really had no cause for conflict, had fatally burned each other.

Kickaha spoke to the Teutoniac, who muttered something. Kickaha bent close to him. The words were almost unintelligible, but he caught some of them. They were not in German. They were in Lord-speech!

Kickaha returned to Podarge. Her eyes were open and dulling, as if layer upon layer of thin veils were slowly being laid over them. Kickaha said, "Podarge! What happened?"

The Harpy moaned and then said something, and Kickaha was startled again. She spoke, not in Mycenaean, but in Lord-speech!

And after that she died.

He called Anana in. While she stood guard, he tried to question Do Shuptarp. The Teutoniac was in deep shock and dying swiftly. But he seemed to recognize Kickaha for just a moment. Perhaps the lust to live surged up just enough for him to make a plea which would have saved him—if Kickaha had had mercy.

"My bell . . . over there . . . put it . . . my head . . . I'll be . . ."

His lips twitched; something gurgled in his throat. Kickaha said, "You took over Do Shuptarp, didn't you, instead of killing him? Who were you?"

"Ten thousand years," the Beller murmured. "And then . . . you."

The eyes became as if dust had sifted into the brain. The jaw dropped like a drawbridge to release the soul—if a Beller had a soul. And why not, if anyone did? The Bellers were deadly enemies, peculiarly horrible because of their method of possession. But in actuality they were no more vicious or deadly than any human enemy, and though possession seemed especially horrible, it was not so to the victim, whose mind was dead before the Beller moved into the body.

Kickaha said, "A third Beller usurped Do Shuptarp's brain. He must have taken off for the upper stories then, figuring that if his buddies didn't get me, he would later. He thought I'd accept him as Do Shuptarp.

"Now, there's Podarge. I would have said a Beller had transferred to her on the moon, but that couldn't be. There were only two Bellers, von

Tubat and von Swindebarn, on the moon. And Luvah said he saw them gate into the control room. So the transference must have taken place after Wolff and Chryseis had gotten away. One of those two Bellers took over Podarge, but not until the two had rayed down the Drachelander troops with them to make it look as if everybody had been killed by Wolff and Chryseis.

"Then they switched to Pordarge and one soldier they must have spared for this purpose. And the Beller in that soldier was the one who jumped Nimstowl. So now von Turbat and von Swindebarn are dead, despite their trickery! And the Beller in Podarge's body was to pretend that she had given up the attempt to get me, I'll bet. She was to plead friendship, act as if she'd really repented. And when my guard was down, powie! It's real funny, you know. Neither the Podarge-Beller nor the Do Shuptarp-Beller knew the other was a Beller in disguise. So they killed each other!"

He whooped with laughter. But, suddenly, he became thoughtful.

"Wolff and Chryseis are marooned somewhere. Let's go to his library and look up the code book. If he's logged that gate, then we can know how to operate it and where they are."

They walked toward the door. Kickaha hung back a little because the sight of Podarge saddened him. She had Anana's face, and that alone was enough to make him downcast, because she looked like Anana dead. More-over, the madness of the Harpy, the torment she had endured for 3,200 years, weighed him down. She could have been put into a woman's body again, if she had accepted Wolff's offer. But she was too deep in her mad-ness; she wanted to suffer and also wanted to get a horrible revenge on the man who had placed her in the Harpy's body.

Anana stopped so suddenly that he almost bumped into her.

"That tolling!" she said. "It's started again!"

She screamed and at the same time brought her beamer up. Kickaha had already fired. He directed his ray perilously close to her, at the door-way, even before anyone appeared in it. It was on full-power now, raised from burning effect to cutting effect. It sliced off a piece of Nimstowl's left shoulder.

Then Nimstowl jumped back.

Kickaha ran to the doorway but did not go through.

"He's von Turbat or von Swindebarn!" Kickaha yelled. He was think-ing furiously. One of the two chiefs had possessed Podarge; the other had switched to a soldier. Then they had burned their former bodies and left the control room, each to go his own way with the hopes of killing their en-emies.

The one in the soldier's body had attacked Nimstowl. Perhaps he had actually wounded Nimstowl. He had, however, managed to switch to the Lord.

No, that could not be, since it required two Bellers to make a switch. One had to handle the bell-shape for the transfer of the other.

Then Podarge—rather, the Beller in her body—must have been with the one in the soldier's body. She must have performed the transference and then left. The Beller in Nimstowl's body had put a knife in the belly of the soldier, who must have been knocked out before the switch.

The change to Nimstowl might have worked, if Kickaha had not operated on his usual basis of suspicion. Somehow, the Nimstowl-Beller had gotten out of the locked room. With what? A small low-power beamer hidden in a body cavity?

The Nimstowl-Beller had come back hoping to catch Kickaha and Anana unaware. If he had been successful, he would have been able to fulfill the Beller's plans of conquest. But he had not been able to resist taking his bell with him and so Anana had detected its presence just in time.

Podarge may have been the one to help effect the transference for the soldier-Beller into Nimstowl. But if she were not the one, then there was an extra Beller to be identified, located, and killed.

First, the business of the Nimstowl-Beller.

Kickaha had waited long enough. If the Beller were running away, then he could have gotten far enough so that Kickaha could leave the control room safely. If the Beller were lying out in the corridor bleeding to death—or bled to death—then Kickaha could go into the corridor. If the Beller were not too badly wounded, he might be waiting for Kickaha to come out.

Whatever the situation, Kickaha could not wait any longer.

He motioned to Anana to stand aside. He backed up a few paces, then ran forward and leaped through the doorway. He turned as he soared, his beamer already on, its ray flashing along the wall and digging a two inch deep trough in the marble, striking out blindly but ready to move down or outward to catch the Beller.

The Beller was crumpled against the base of the wall with blood pooling from around his shoulder. His beamer lay at his feet, his head was thrown back, and his jaw sagged. His skin was bluish.

Kickaha landed, shut the beamer off, and slowly approached the Beller. Convinced that he was harmless, Kickaha bent over him. Nimstowl looked at him with eyes in which the life was not yet withdrawn.

"We're a doomed people," the Beller croaked. "We had everything in our favor, and yet we've been defeated by one man."

"Who are you?" Kickaha said. "Graumgrass or the one calling himself von Swindebarn?"

"Graumgrass. The king of the Bellers. I was in von Turbat's body and then that soldier's."

"Who helped you transfer to Nimstowl—to this body?" Kickaha said.

The Beller looked surprised. "You don't know?" he said faintly. "Then there is still hope for us."

Anana unsnapped the casket from the Beller's harness. She opened it and, grimacing, removed the big black bell-shape. She said, "You may think you will die without telling us who that Beller is and what he is going to do. But you won't."

She said, "Kickaha, hold his head! I'm going to put the bell on it!"

Graumgrass tried to struggle but was too weak to do anything except writhe a little. Finally, he said, "What are you going to do?"

"Your mind contents will automatically be transferred to the bell," she said. "As you well know. This body will die, but we'll find you a healthy body. And we'll put your mind in it. And when we do, we'll torture you until you tell us what we wish to know."

Graumgrass said, "No! No!" and he tried again to get away. Kickaha held him easily while Anana placed the bell on his head. After a while, Graumgrass's eyes glazed, and death shook a castenet in his throat. Kickaha looked at the bottom of the bell as Anana held it up for his inspection. The two tiny needles were withdrawn into the case.

"I think his mind was taken in before the body died," he said. "But, Anana, I won't let you strip a man's brain just to put this thing in his body so we can get some information. No matter how important that information is."

"I know it," she said. "And I wouldn't do it, either. I've regained some of my lost humanity because of you. Furthermore, there aren't any living bodies available to use."

She paused. He said, "Don't look at me. I haven't the guts."

"I don't blame you," she said. "And I wouldn't want you to do it, anyway. I will do it."

"But . . . !" He stopped. It had to be done, and he supposed that if she had not volunteered, he would have done so, though very reluctantly. He felt a little shame that he was allowing her to be the subject, but not enough to make him insist that he do this. He had more than one share of courage; he would be the first to say so. But this act required more than he had at this moment or was likely to have, as long as someone else would act. The utter helplessness it would produce made a coward of him. He could not stand that feeling.

He said, "There are drugs here which can get the truth, or what the subject thinks is the truth, anyway. It won't be hard to get the facts out of you—out of the Beller, I mean, but do you really think this is necessary?"

He knew that it was. He just could not accept the idea of her submitting to the bell either.

"You know what a horror I have of the bell," she said. "But I'll put my mind into one and let one of those things into my body if it'll track down the last Beller, the last one, for once and all."

He wanted to protest that nothing was worth this, but he kept his mouth shut. It had to be done. And though he called himself a coward because he could not do it, and his flesh rippled with dread for her, he would allow her to use the bell.

Anana clung to him and kissed him fiercely before she submitted. She said, "I love you. I don't want to do this! It seems as if I'm putting myself in a grave, just when I could look forward to loving you."

"We could just make a search of the palace instead," he said. "We'd be bound to flush out the Beller."

"If he got away, we'd know who to look for," she said. "No. Go ahead! Do it! Quickly! I feel as if I'm dying now!"

She was lying on a divan. She closed her eyes while he fitted the bell over her head. He held her then while it did its work. Her breathing, which had been quick and shallow with anxiety, slowed and deepened after a while. Her eyes fluttered open. They looked as if the light in them had become transfixed in time, frozen in some weird polarity.

After waiting some extra minutes to make sure the bell was finished, he gently lifted it off her head. He placed it in a casket on the floor, after which he tied her hands and feet together and then strapped her down tightly. He set the bell containing the mind of Graumgrass on her head. When twenty minutes had passed, he was sure that the transference was complete. Her face worked; the eyes had become as wild as a trapped hawk's. The voice was the lovely voice of Anana but the inflections were different.

"I can tell that I am in a woman's body," she—it—said.

Kickaha nodded and then shot the drug into her arm. He waited sixty seconds before beginning to dredge the information he needed. It took less time to get the facts than it had for the drug to take effect.

The Lords had been mistaken about the exact number of missing Bellers. There had been fifty-one, not fifty, and the Bellers, of course, had not enlightened their enemies. The "extra" one was Thabuuz. He had been down in the palace biolabs most of the time, where he was engaged in creating new Bellers. When the alarm was raised about Kickaha, he had come up from the labs. He did not get a chance to do much, but he was able to help Graumgrass knock out Nimstowl and then transfer him.

Graumgrass, as the little Lord, was to make one more attempt to kill the two remaining enemies of the Bellers. In case he did not succeed, Thabuuz was to gate to Earth with his bell and his knowledge. There, on Earth, that limbo among the universes, hidden in in the swarms of mankind, he was to make new Bellers for another attempt at conquest.

"What gate did he use?" Kickaha asked.

"The gate that Wolff and Chryseis used," Graumgrass-Anana said. "It leads to Earth."

"And how do you know it does?"

"We found the code book and cracked the code, and so found that the gate was to Earth. Thabuuz had orders to take it if an emergency required that he get out of the palace to a place where he could hide."

Kickaha was shocked, but, on reflection, he was pleased. Now he had two reasons to go to Earth. One, and the most vital, was to find Thabuuz and kill him before he got his project started. Two, he must find Wolff and Chryseis and tell them they could return home. That is, they could if they wished. Undoubtedly, Wolff would want to help him and Anana hunt down the Beller.

He replaced the bell on Anana's head. In fifteen minutes, the withdrawal of Graumgrass' mind into the bell was completed. Then he put the bell containing Anana's mind on her head. In about twenty minutes, she opened her eyes and cried out his name. She wept for a while as she held him. Being in the bell, she said, was as if her brain had been cut out of her head and placed in a dark void. She kept thinking that something might happen to Kickaha and then she would be locked up forever in that bell. She knew she would go mad, and the idea of being insane forever made her even more frenzied.

Kickaha comforted her, and when she seemed to be calmed, he told her what he had learned. Anana said they must go to Earth. But first, they should dispose of Graumgrass.

"That'll be easy," he said. "I'll embed the bell in a plastic cube and put it in the museum. Later, when I have time—that is, when I come back from Earth—I'll gate him to Talanac. He can be discharged into a condemned criminal and then killed. Meantime, let's get ready for Earth."

He checked the code book for information that the Beller had not given him. The gate transmitted to an ancient gate in southern California, the exact area unspecified. Kickaha said, "I've had some twinges of nostalgia for Earth now and then, but I got over them. This is my world, this world of tiers, of green skies and fabled beasts. Earth seems like a big gray nightmare to me when I think about having to live there permanently. But still, I get just a little homesick now and then."

He paused and then said, "We may be there for some time. We'll need money. I wonder if Wolff has some stored somewhere?"

The memory bank of an underground machine told him where to locate a storage room of terrestrial currency. Kickaha returned from the room with a peculiar grin and a bag in his hand. He dumped the contents on the table. "Lots of U.S. dollar bills," he said. "Many hundred dollar bills and a dozen thousand dollar bills. But the latest was issued in 1875!"

He laughed and said, "We'll take it along, anyway. We might be able to sell it to collectors. And we'll take along some jewels, too."

He set the machines to turn out clothes for himself and Anana. They were designed as he remembered the latest American styles circa 1945. "They'll do until we can buy some new."

While they were getting ready, they moved Luvah to a bigger and more comfortable room and assigned the kitchen taloses to look after him. Kickaha left Anana to talk to her brother while he busied himself collecting the necessities for the Earth trip. He got some medicines, drugs, beamers, charges for the beamers, a throwing knife, and a little stiletto for her with poison in the hollow hilt. The Horn of Shambarimen was in a case.

He carried the case into the room where the two were. "I look like a musician," he said. "I ought to get a haircut as soon as I get a chance after we get there. My hair's so long I look like Tarzan—I don't want to attract attention. Oh, yes, you might as well start calling me Paul from now on. Kickaha is out. It's Paul J. Finnegan again."

They made their farewell with Luvah, who said that he would be the palace guardian while they were gone. He would make sure that the taloses put all the bodies in the incinerators, and he would set the defenses of the palace for marauding Lords. He was ecstatic that Anana had been reunited with him, even if only briefly. He was not, it was obvious, the customary Lord.

Despite which, once they were out of his room, Kickaha said, "Did you talk about old times, as I told you?"

"Yes," she said, "and there were many things he just could not remember."

Kickaha stopped and said, "You think. . . ?"

She shook her head and laughed. "No. There were also many things he did remember, things which a Beller could not possibly know. And he reminded me of some things I had forgotten. He is my brother all the way through; he is not a Beller, as you suspected, my suspicious lover."

He grinned and said, "You thought of the idea the same time as myself, remember?"

He kissed her. Just before they stepped onto the gate, which would be activated by a code-sentence, he said, "You speak English?"

"I spent most of my three years on Earth in Paris and London," she answered. "But I've forgotten all my French and English."

"You'll pick it up again. Meanwhile, let me do the talking."

He paused, as if he hated to begin the journey.

"One thing about going to Earth. We have to track down that Beller. But we won't have to worry about running foul of any Lords."

Anana looked surprised.

"Didn't Wolff tell you? Red Orc is the secret Lord of Earth!"